PRAISE FOR
FANTASY AUTHOR JIM MELVIN

The Death Wizard Chronicles (trilogy)

"Melvin shows his literary mastery as he weaves elements of potential and transformation; his tale dances among literal shapeshifters and more subtle powers of mind."
—*Ann Allen, Charlotte Observer*

"Jim Melvin is a fresh voice in fantasy writing with a bold, inventive vision and seasoned literary style that vaults him immediately into the top tier of his genre."
—*Dave Scheiber, nationally renowned journalist and author*

"Action-packed and yet profound, *The DW Chronicles* will take your breath away. This is epic fantasy at its best."
—*Chris Harold Stevenson, award-winning author of everything fantasy and paranormal*

Dark Circles (trilogy)

"*Do You Believe in Magic?* is a delightful beginning to a promising series that's sure to appeal to teen readers who feel like outsiders."
—*Kirkus Reviews*

"*Do You Believe in Magic?* was masterfully written. The fantasy, the premise, the world-building, and character-building are everything I could ever hope for. It is literary gold."
—*Megan Prestenbach, Online Book Club reviewer*

"The fantastical realm that Jim Melvin has created is captivating, and the monsters and magic within it are brought to life with vivid imagination."
—*Pratibha Malav, award-winning author, editor, and reviewer*

Green Bird Publishing
Sunset, SC 29685

For more information, or to book an event, contact:
jimmelvin57@gmail.com
jim-melvin.com
jimmelvin.substack.com

Cover design by miblart.com
Interior art by DepositPhotos

ISBN: 979-8-9924922-2-4
Imprint: Green Bird Publishing

New Edition: April 2025

AUTHOR'S NOTE

In 2012, *The Death Wizard Chronicles* was published by a midsize press where it enjoyed considerable success. However, the rights recently reverted to me, and I'm excited to announce the release of new editions of the acclaimed dark fantasy series. Think of these as the "author's cut."

What you're about to read is an enhanced version of *The DW Chronicles*! I've repackaged the original six-book series into three volumes, with each volume containing two books. If you've already read *DW*, there's enough fresh stuff to make a second go worth your while. And if you're new to this fantastical world, now's the perfect time to join the action-packed journey. This isn't just a tale about dragons, wizards, and warriors. It's about the choices that shape our destinies.

Fair warning: *The DW Chronicles* contains graphic violence and a few scenes of explicit sex. It's intended for audiences 18 and older. If you can handle *Game of Thrones*, this will be a piece of cake.

In addition to *DW*, I recently published an epic fantasy trilogy titled *Dark Circles*, which is a teen adventure appropriate for ages 12 and older. It contains no sex or profanity and only relatively mild scenes of violence.

Other than having the same author, the two series bear no relation to each other.

In early 2025, I published a nonfiction memoir titled *The Adventures of a Florida Boy*, which chronicles my boyhood growing up on the Gulf Coast of the Sunshine State in the 1960s. It's short, sweet, and a ton of fun. And it provides a good-natured look into how my imagination was born and nurtured.

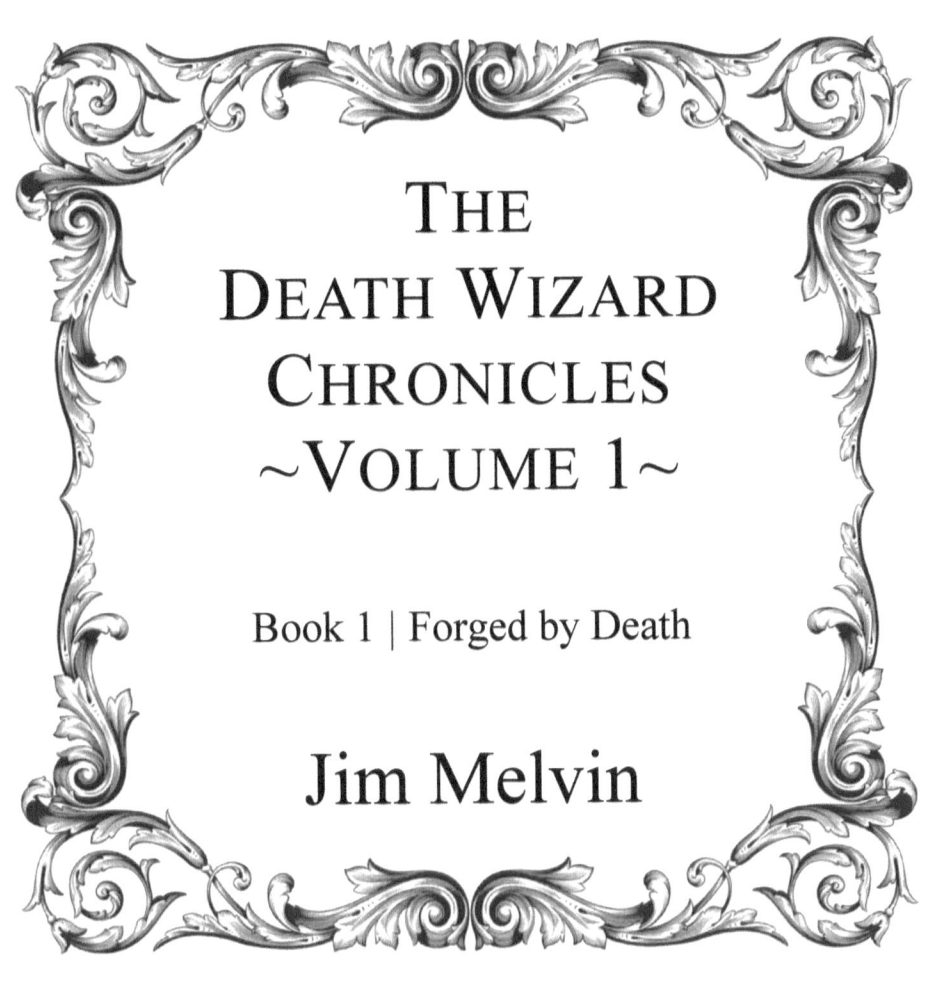

THE DEATH WIZARD CHRONICLES
~VOLUME 1~

Book 1 | Forged by Death

Jim Melvin

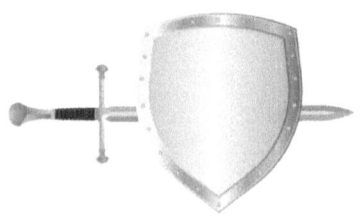

PROLOGUE

Such darkness he had never known. In all the centuries of his long life, the wizard had felt nothing as loathsome as this. Torturous days and weeks lay behind, endless horror ahead. He was helpless in the grip of doom.

For a millennium he had freely roamed the planet Triken, using his prodigious powers to unite the forces of good. But now a sorcerer held him captive in a pit bored into the solid rock of a frozen mountain. Beyond the walls of his prison, a war would soon take place that would dwarf all others. An evil had arisen that threatened not just Triken but the fabric that held together the universe. Only the wizard could stop it. But first he had to survive.

The pit was 200 cubits deep but only three cubits in diameter. The prisoner lay curled at its bottom like a snake in a well. Fetid dankness swirled about him, creeping in and out of his nostrils with every breath. A chill like no other clung to his body, freezing his heart.

All he had left were his memories, which provided his only relief from the relentless blackness. He immersed himself in them, focusing on the past instead of the present. Doing this went against all that he held true. But it kept him sane.

For a fraction of a moment. And another. Another …

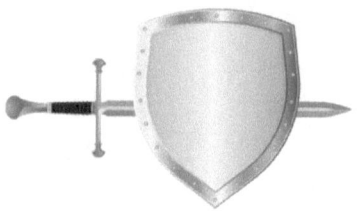

NOBLE ONES

In his mind, the Death-Knower wizard replayed what had led to his hideous imprisonment. His thoughts fled from the pit to a land of fresh air and sunlight where courage and hope still existed. In this place, people knew him as Torg—king of the Tugars—who led his desert warriors against Invictus, a sorcerer determined to ensnare the world in a darkness as terrible as the pit.

More than two months before Torg was trapped in the pit, he and twenty Asēkhas—the Tugars of highest rank—had set out from their encampment on the western edge of the Great Desert. As dawn approached, the desert warriors walked across a dry ravine strewn with crumbled rock, their long strides barely disturbing the loose ground. Torg knew that few living things were aware of their presence. Even a tiny elf owl, hopping from stone to stone in search of beetles, never saw them pass, though its yellow eyes were keen.

Many believed Tugars were magicians capable of invisibility. Others considered them demigods who were matchless in battle. Tugars believed invisibility was a state of mind: silence the mind and the body becomes difficult to see. As for their perceived invincibility, Tugars trained under the intense guidance of Vasi masters for fifty years before attaining the rank of warrior. No better fighters had ever existed.

In the fiery heat of late summer, the small band continued westward for three days, traveling twenty-five leagues across the rocky wastelands called Barranca, which partially encircled Tējo, the Great Desert. At dusk of the third day, Torg and the Asēkhas passed through the wastes into lowland choked with scrub. They scrambled over creosote bushes that stank like skunks and strode past giant sagebrush that stood twenty cubits tall. If the task before them had not been so urgent, Torg would have had them stop and collect parts of both plants, which the Tugars used for medicines and dyes, and to weave hats and bags.

They camped that night in a remote hollow that was another three-day march from their destination: the city called Dibbu-Loka, the realm of the Noble Ones. All was quiet and the Asēkhas slept, except for Torg and one other. The pair stood together on a nearby hillock—two imposing figures dressed in black. Curved swords hung at their hips.

"Lord, is your mind set?'' Chieftain Asēkha-Kusala said. He was the most powerful Tugar in the world besides Torg. "Must you remain with us on this mission? Your people need you more than does our small company."

Torg stood with his back to Kusala and stared at the golden orb in the night sky. For the past several months, the full moon had called to his heart in a confounding manner. He ached when he looked at it, a sensation that was sweet and sour. He didn't understand why he felt this way. It was unlike him. But he recognized this puzzling development as far too powerful and persistent to dismiss as imagination.

"My mind *is* set," Torg said. "I am a Death-Knower. I have lived for a millennium, yet I have died a thousand times. The paradox makes me wise. Do you doubt it?" He glared down at Kusala, who was a shorter but slightly thicker man. "You've been at my side for centuries, chieftain. Do you doubt me?"

The glow of Torg's molten-blue eyes illuminated the darkness. The power blazing behind those eyes was unmistakable. Torg was one of the most formidable beings in Triken's history, renowned as the greatest of all past and present Death-Knowers. Kusala saw him now at the height of his powers, only weeks removed from his latest Death Visit.

"Forgive me, lord," Kusala said, momentarily downcast and obedient. Even the chieftain, revered among the Tugars and throughout Triken, knew better than to antagonize his king. "I meant no disrespect."

But then his countenance changed, as was his custom. Kusala lifted his gaze and his own eyes glowed, bathed in the moon's reflected light. "My love for you inspires my speech and I fear for you!"

Torg smiled. He knew Kusala too well. The chieftain was preparing to give his king a spirited lecture.

"The rise of Invictus threatens Triken and its free people, but we have been slow to respond," Kusala said, his voice rising. "Even the Tugars have stood like statues in this storm. If not for you, we would have already closed the doors of Tējo and vanished from the world and the young sorcerer's grasp. But you've taught us that sloth would merely postpone our demise. Invictus grows strong beyond his merit, and those who would see goodness prevail over evil depend on you more than ever. Who else but a Death-Knower can stand against a Sun God?"

The chieftain stomped his foot on the raspy sand. "And yet his soldiers prepare a trap. An *obvious* one. And you enter it—willingly."

Torg allowed him to finish. Then he calmly said, "There has never been such a dangerous threat in our lifetime. And it comes from someone who—compared to you and me—is relatively young. But this hasn't stopped Invictus from surpassing us."

Torg closed his eyes and breathed in the hot night air. He leaned on his walking staff, which was carved from the ivory of an immense desert elephant found dead of old age at the base of a dry lakebed. He had named the staff Obhasa, which in the ancient tongue meant *container of light*. Obhasa was an impressive weapon, and it crackled with Torg's own magic.

"Invictus' armies, though powerful, are not yet invincible," Torg continued. "But what of the sorcerer himself? Against him, I haven't been tested. Still, as his might spreads throughout the land, my confidence diminishes."

"All the more reason for you *not* to go to Dibbu-Loka," Kusala said. "Let the Asēkhas rescue the Noble Ones. Return to the desert and await us there."

"You're a brilliant chieftain," Torg said. "But your vision can be shortsighted. You underestimate the scope of Invictus' malevolence. The Noble Ones of Dibbu-Loka believe there is only one way to defeat such malice. They say, 'Hatred is never appeased by hatred. Hatred is appeased by love.'"

"They're a gentle and beautiful people," Kusala said. "But they're helpless against such evil."

"Helpless? Is a tree helpless against the wind? The wind blows and fades. The tree bends and remains. Kusala, there are those among the keepers of Dibbu-Loka who are far older than you or I. And they don't waste their long lives on meanderings. Instead, they wisely spend their time learning the true nature of love and hate, good and evil, pleasure and suffering. What you mistake for helplessness is a deep understanding of what is and isn't real."

"You're right, lord. My vision *is* shortsighted. Their 'deep understanding' is beyond my comprehension."

Torg chuckled. "Ah, Kusala. Now it's my turn to say that I meant no disrespect. I don't intend to demean your courage or loyalty. It's just that I've spent much time among the Noble Ones and have grown to cherish them. I couldn't bear to see such an intense and sincere people perish from the world. I would prefer to fail attempting to save them than not make the attempt at all. A trap? Of course. Do I enter it willingly? Yes. But you must trust that I'm not without a plan."

The debate was over.

Torg returned his attention to the moon. When he sighed, a bluish vapor flowed from his mouth, floating seductively in the thick air.

Kusala flared his nostrils and inhaled, then visibly relaxed. Torg knew that his essence had a calming effect not unlike drunkenness, yet it wrought clarity instead of intoxication.

"I love you, lord," Kusala said. "I would cast myself off Mount Asubha if you but said the word."

"Do not speak of Asubha," Torg said. "The prison on the mountaintop is Invictus' most appalling creation. If we're able to defeat the sorcerer, I'll beg the snow giants to cast it down."

Without further speech, Torg and Kusala strode back to the hollow where the others slept. This close to the Great Desert, they had little to fear. But Torg knew that danger lay ahead, and it was worse than anyone else had yet realized.

Three days later, Torg stood with Kusala on the precipice of an escarpment overlooking the temples of Dibbu-Loka. Though it was midday and the air was clear, they were still far enough away to be undetectable to anyone within the holy city, enabling them to remain in the open and take their time studying the surroundings. Thousands of golden flashes burst from the three-cornered conurbation, resembling a wind-ruffled lake sparkling beneath a setting sun.

Two scouts made their way up the side of the cliff. Kusala was so eager to hear their report, he could hardly stand still. But Torg already knew much of what they would say. Invaders occupied the holy city. The flashes were reflections coming off the armor of the Golden Soldiers of Invictus.

Asēkhas Rati and Sōbhana, wearing black silk jackets tucked into their breeches, reached the roof of the escarpment and strode forward. Both were excellent scouts. Sōbhana, especially, was held in high regard. She was a finger-length shy of four cubits, which was short for a Tugarian woman, but she was strong, limber, and could run as fast as a black mountain wolf.

Like many Tugars, Torg's presence intimidated Sōbhana. The Tugar nation considered him to be not just a king, but a king of kings. Her nervousness amused him, and in less troubling times he would have teased her until she grew more comfortable. But there wasn't enough time for that now.

Sōbhana looked at Torg and her face flushed. Then she lowered her gaze.

"Speak!" Kusala said with his customary impatience.

Rati took pity on Sōbhana and stepped forward. "Dibbu-Loka is overrun. At least 2,000 Golden Soldiers control the temples and surrounding walls. The monks and nuns offer no resistance. The soldiers hold daggers to their throats. Even if a thousand Tugars launched a surprise attack, we could save only a few of the prisoners. The soldiers would be easily defeated but not before most of the Noble Ones were slaughtered."

Kusala looked at Torg somberly as if hoping to see resignation that might indicate his king would cancel the mission.

But Torg paid the chieftain no heed, instead focusing on Sōbhana. "What say you?"

Sōbhana looked up, her cheeks still splashed with red. Though she opened her mouth and seemed about to speak, nothing recognizable came out.

"Sōbhana, are you a warrior or a child?" Kusala said. "Report to me if not to your king."

When Sōbhana turned toward the chieftain, her clumsiness vanished. Her cheeks remained flushed, but this time with anger.

"It's even worse than Rati reports," she said. "One of their captains stands boldly on the upper steps of the main temple and calls over and over for The Torgon to come forth. He says they will sacrifice three monks and three nuns every hour that passes, beginning at sundown of this day, unless our king enters the city and surrenders himself."

"The captain claims our king is a traitor to the free people of Triken,'' Rati added, "and that he must stand trial for his crimes before the seat of Invictus. He promises a *just* trial. The Noble Ones roll their eyes. Despite their predicament, they keep their sense of humor and seem to have no fear. They are warriors, as well, it seems."

"We could have killed the fool, we were so close," Sōbhana said, "but it would have done little good. Rati and I suspected our approach was long witnessed, yet they permitted us to enter the city without resistance. It was too easy. Too many heads were turned in the wrong direction. They are poor soldiers, by our standards, but they are well-armed and all too capable of slaying the helpless."

Torg could sense Sōbhana was holding something back. He continued to fix his attention only on her. There was a period of silence. Kusala cleared his throat and touched Torg lightly on the shoulder. "What *is* it, lord?"

Torg twisted around and glowered. The chieftain hastily removed his hand. Torg grunted impatiently, then turned back to Sōbhana. "You fear more than just a fool of a captain or his pathetic soldiers. I can sense it in your bearing. What do you keep from us?"

Sōbhana took a step back, then sighed. Her full lips trembled ever so slightly. "I saw something else. Or think I did."

Kusala ground his leather boot into the dusty earth. "Sōbhana!" He spoke so sharply, all the Asēkhas whipped their heads in his direction. "Tell us everything—*now!*"

Ignoring the chieftain, Sōbhana moved slowly toward Torg and then stood on her toes so that her mouth was just a span below his. Her features softened, and Torg saw her as startlingly beautiful even by Tugarian standards.

This galled Kusala—perhaps perceiving her approach as a burst of arrogance—and he prepared to discipline her.

Torg waved him off. "Sōbhana, speak," he said gently.

"Lord, I saw something ... someone ... in the doorway at the top of the temple stairs. There was a deep shadow near the opening, and the sun's glare prevented a clearer view. But there were glints that didn't resemble the reflections off armor. Two figures loomed within, and one of them was huge—much larger than any of the soldiers, monks, or nuns. I believe it was the terrible monster named Mala. And with him, a Warlish witch."

Though Tējo was his home, Torg had explored much of the world outside the desert. He had visited Dibbu-Loka many times during his long life and knew its history as intimately as most. A greedy king built the city 10,000 years ago to serve as his final resting place. On the day of his passing, King Lobha planned to be buried in the bowels of a majestic pyramid. Its exterior walls were sheathed in contrasting marbles that shimmered in an ever-changing variety of colors depending on the time of day. Erotic paintings of naked men and women slathered the interior walls.

King Lobha originally named the city Piti-Loka, which meant *Rapture World* in the ancient tongue. Lobha was a connoisseur of sexual gratification, especially when forced upon helpless victims. Due to his frequent atrocities, Lobha gained many enemies. But an army of his vicious soldiers kept the king and his city well-defended.

Lobha feared nothing except the demise of his own body, which had somehow retained its sexual prowess despite the feebleness of old age. His hands ruined many lives. One fateful day, the king made the mistake of molesting and murdering a woman his soldiers had captured during a slave-hunting expedition on the border of the Great Desert. She was a member of a mysterious tribe that dwelled within Tējo. Even as Lobha lay in the throes of ecstasy while his chained victim breathed her last, the desert dwellers invaded the city. Though outnumbered ten to one, they routed Lobha's army and slew the evil king.

After that, Piti-Loka was renamed Dibbu-Loka, the ancient words for *Deathless-World*. A remnant of the desert dwellers remained in the city for several years, allowing only peaceful people intent on goodness and charity to enter its walls. Their leader, a wizard of high renown, saw to it that Dibbu-Loka became a holy place. Thirty-three generations later, the trail of that wizard's seed led deep into the desert. A boy emerged during a birth so violent it killed his mother.

This devastated the boy's father, an Asēkha chieftain named Jhana. But the father loved his newborn son and named him Torg, which meant *Blessed Warrior*. His proper name for ceremonial events became The Torgon.

In the current day, Dibbu-Loka remained a magical place. However, it was the monks and nuns who now lived there that made it special. Its desolate location was not the least bit enchanted. Dibbu-Loka rested atop a hill that rose out of dusty land pockmarked with canyons and ravines on ground even more inhospitable than the desert that lay to the east.

The central pyramid of Dibbu-Loka dominated the interior of the city. Bakheng, originally designed to be Lobha's tomb, had been grandly built to match his excessive tastes. The shrine contained three entryways leading to three main chambers. The top chamber was intended to house Lobha's head, the middle his arms and torso, and the bottom his legs. The new rulers gifted the king's corpse to the coyotes and vultures and found more wholesome uses for the pyramid.

A trio of smaller temples surrounded Bakheng, and hundreds of single-story chambers formed a triangular frame around these three. Originally built for Lobha's army, the chambers were now the residences of the 500 monks and nuns who occupied the holy city.

The other interior buildings of Dibbu-Loka lay farther from the pyramid within courtyards linked by a maze-like pattern of paved causeways. The main causeway led from the grand entrance to the central shrine. Smaller roads scattered in confusing directions, often ending abruptly in empty pavilions without doors or windows. Newcomers to Dibbu-Loka frequently became lost if they strayed off the main streets. The Noble Ones, of course, gently set them back on course. Torg also knew the ways.

As the sun fell, Torg strode with the Asēkhas through the grand entrance, his pace solemn and hypnotic. Torg dressed entirely in black. He wore a silk jacket belted tightly at the waist and tucked into his narrow breeches. Cloth gaiters covered his calves. His hair, which hung to his shoulders, matched the color of his clothing. His tanned skin and blue eyes were the only contrast to his monochromatic outfit.

The Asēkhas looked almost identical to Torg. Tugars who had not crossbred with other races always had black hair and blue eyes, and most were between four and four and a half cubits tall, which was considerably taller than almost all Triken's humans. Sōbhana's height was a rare exception.

When Asēkhas wore black, they were in a killing mood. The desert warriors who had defeated King Lobha's army had worn black, but while those warriors had been outnumbered ten to one, Torg and his

Asēkhas were now outnumbered one hundred to one. Even then, Torg wasn't overly concerned.

Their first sighting of Noble Ones was not a pleasant experience. Golden Soldiers had forced more than a dozen monks and nuns to stand along the roadside with daggers held to their throats. The soldiers glared at them behind their plated helms, which glowed crimson in the fading light.

Some of the Noble Ones had trickles of blood on their white robes, but the monks and nuns were unafraid. Torg knew the Noble Ones didn't fear death. In their perception, it was as natural as breathing. Even so, they prized life above all things because it provided them with the opportunity to overcome suffering and achieve enlightenment either in this existence or in one of the countless that followed.

Kusala walked on Torg's right, one pace behind his leader. Tears streaked the chieftain's dusty cheeks, and his eyes were ablaze. If not for Torg's steady presence, he might have already lost control and succumbed to what the Asēkhas called *frenzy*, butchering any soldier within reach. The other Asēkhas also struggled to contain their fury. It wasn't inconceivable the small band of twenty could kill all 2,000 of their enemy if given enough room to maneuver. But the perilous fate of the prisoners—along with Torg's indomitable will—stayed their hand, for now.

"Remember your vows of obeisance," Torg said in a stern voice. "My order is clear. You must not act unless I command it."

The enemy soldiers laughed, moving their daggers even closer to the throats of their prisoners.

"Yes, do not act unless the *King of Death* grants his permission," a soldier said, his voice echoing in the otherwise silent streets. "He, at least, is wise enough to know that if you attacked, you'd be cut down like a helpless woman."

A dagger suddenly buried itself in a wooden pillar next to the soldier's head. The blade hummed and quivered. Torg gave Sōbhana a fiery look.

"I missed on purpose," she said, shrugging her shoulders.

Several Asēkhas chuckled nervously. Even Torg couldn't resist a wry smile. Then he raised his right hand and cried, "*Kantaara Yodha tam*! (A Desert Warrior calls!)" The dagger sprang from the pillar and spun through the air, its handle landing crisply in his palm. Torg noticed a scratch near the tip of the blade before tossing it back to Sōbhana and then continuing onward.

The others followed, probably relieved he'd ignored her insubordination. They marched into the city's depths, but as they neared Bakheng, they heard the captain's dreaded mantra, erasing their brief mirth.

"Come, Torgon ... or the killing will begin. Sundown approaches."

Again.

"Come, Torgon ... or the killing will begin. Sundown approaches."

The chanting didn't cease.

Torg and the Asēkhas continued up the main causeway toward Bakheng. It relieved Torg that the incident with the dagger hadn't created a skirmish. Sōbhana would need to be disciplined, but that could wait for later. By then, he probably wouldn't follow through. Torg treasured her spirit and hoped she would continue her precious bloodline and bear children one day, though he doubted this would happen. More and more, his Tugars failed to proliferate. When needed most, their numbers dwindled. It had become especially troublesome the past hundred years since the birth of Invictus, whose evil had had a deadening effect that reached all the way to Anna, the Tugars' Tent City in the heart of the Great Desert.

More Golden Soldiers appeared along the road, and they too put monks and nuns on display. Without exception, the Noble Ones' faces remained calm. During their many years of meditation, they had studied all things without prejudice. To them, death was an empty threat.

The Noble Ones didn't demand or expect rescue, but Torg couldn't bring himself to accept the sacrilege of such a slaughter. He believed they were an invaluable counterbalance to Invictus, an antivenin to his toxic existence. Without their righteousness, the balance of power would irreversibly favor the sorcerer.

Torg struggled to contain his anger. He ground his teeth so hard they almost smoked. However, he would stick to his plan through success or failure.

Bakheng came into view. A thick formation of Golden Soldiers gathered at the base of the massive pyramid. Several hundred more stood on the steep steps that led to the upper entrance. Their swords were drawn and their shields pressed to their chests. Archers lined the highest platform.

Torg and the Asēkhas marched to the bottom of the stairs. When they looked up, they beheld an abomination. An elaborate wooden bench had been constructed on the balcony at the top of the shrine. Cruelly strapped to it was the High Nun of Dibbu-Loka.

Sister Tathagata, the *Perfect One*, was more than 3,000 years old. But her eyes—ah, her eyes—were as clear as a child's. Torg had spent many long hours with her in discussion and meditation. She liked to call him "young man" before throwing her head back and guffawing. Her laughter was like a waterfall, pleasing more than just the ears. Torg felt insignificant in her presence. For Invictus' minions to threaten her in this way was an insult against anything sane.

They had shoved a pewter funnel into Tathagata's mouth. Even from where he stood, Torg could hear her gagging. The funnel was attached to her jaw with a leather strap. A bronze cauldron was positioned two cubits above her head. A deadly liquid bubbled within.

Torg could sense what the cauldron contained.

Molten gold—super-heated by magic.

This enraged Torg. Swirling specks of blue flame snaked along his fingertips. Tiny sparks spun about his ears and nostrils. He was a volcano about to erupt, but he knew if Tathagata and the other Noble Ones were to survive, he would have to remain calm until he could enact his plan.

The obnoxious captain stood next to Tathagata. He smiled wickedly. Torg smiled back. The captain was unimportant—far outweighed by greater evils. Leering over Tathagata was the Warlish witch, whose face—full of filth and fire—was hideous enough to frighten mortals into flight. But she was not the worst. Not even close. Inside the dark entrance to the shrine stood the witch's true master, an unholy being whose very presence in that sacred place was blasphemy. And it was on that creature that Torg now focused his formidable gaze.

The captain with the loud voice was blind to his peril. He walked to the edge of the balcony and leered down at Torg. Surrounded by archers and armor-clad soldiers, the annoying man must have felt brave and powerful, believing he was the one in control. But he was nothing more than a mouthpiece.

"So, you're finally here," the captain said. "You certainly took your time, *Desert Peasant*. Were you so slow to arrive because your boots were full of sand? Or was it simply because your legs wouldn't stop shaking?"

What happened next didn't surprise Torg, for he had designed it to bewilder his enemies. Even the Warlish witch, who stood guard over Tathagata, was caught unaware. Asēkha-Podhana was suddenly halfway up the stairs standing amid a tight group of Golden Soldiers. The warrior let out a scream that rose in pitch to a maddening intensity, causing dozens of soldiers to tear off their helms and clench their ears. While the attention was focused on Podhana, there was a shuffling sound higher up, away from the diversion. The obnoxious captain cried out, and then his head sprang from his shoulders and tumbled down the stairs— thump, thump … *thump.*

Podhana screamed again. All eyes returned to him. Meanwhile, something dark streaked down the stairs.

Kusala stood next to Torg and flicked blood off the curved blade of his *uttara.*

There was much shouting and confusion. A slew of arrows rained down on the Asēkhas, but none penetrated Tugarian flesh.

Torg reached down, grabbed the captain's head by its long yellow hair, and lifted it high in the air, its face still wearing an expression of disbelief.

"Mala, we could not abide this one," Torg said. "His death wasn't negotiable. I'm sure you understand."

Evoking the name of Mala stunned the gathering into silence. But in place of the monster, the Warlish witch stepped into full view, and a noise far more unpleasant than any scream Podhana could have conjured disrupted the eerie quiet. It began as a low growl like that of a deadly feline sighting prey, though it was interspersed with profanities. The bizarre mixture bred despair as if confirming the worst fears of all living beings: Hell was the only reality and eternal suffering the only true fate. The effect was widespread. Several of the Noble Ones, temporarily freed from the grasp of their captors, bent over and vomited. Sōbhana and the other Asēkhas reflexively drew their swords. Kusala bared his teeth and growled in return, one dangerous beast squaring off with another. But

Torg held up his hand to stay them all.

When he spoke, it broke the spell—at least enough to calm the Asēkhas.

"I didn't come all this way 'with sand in my boots' to deal with the likes of you," Torg said to the witch. "Let your master show himself. He is the only one here worthy of my regard."

Despite Torg's bold words, the witch stood her ground. Mucus squirted from her nostrils and fell to the stone at her feet, smoking and sizzling. She strode to the edge of the balcony and—with a frightening display of strength—kicked the captain's headless corpse off the platform. The lifeless body tumbled halfway down the stairs before crumpling in a bloody heap. Those nearby backed away in disgust.

"Youuu," she purred, pointing a finger at Torg. "I come for youuu."

To Torg, her slurred pronunciations were harmless, even comical. But there was a madness in the way she uttered the words that caused nervousness and trembling among most in attendance. The witch's eye sockets were empty, but they blazed with rancid light. Her scraggly gray hair danced on her head like a tangle of snakes. Worst of all, she stank as if long decayed. Torg could smell her even from where he stood. The soldiers couldn't abide her, and they fled the balcony and scrunched together on the lower stairs. Only the witch remained with Sister Tathagata, who lay beneath her on the wooden bench.

The hideous hag put a gnarled hand on one of the nun's small breasts and squeezed. Tathagata made no sound. If she was afraid, she didn't show it.

"Are you ready?" the witch said to Torg. "It's time for some fuuun."

Though Torg didn't move or blink, the witch laughed. Sōbhana lifted her hand, prepared to throw her dagger again. But the witch was too quick. When she raised her skinny arms, there was a flash followed by a violent boom and a cloud of black smoke. The air cleared slowly. Where a monster once stood, there was now a woman of incalculable beauty. She still wore a ragged dress, but on her it looked like a priceless gown. Intoxicating green eyes filled the once-empty sockets, and waist-length auburn hair replaced the gnarled gray. A perfume as sweet as spring spread outward in waves, enriching the air and making the fear and hopelessness of a few moments ago feel like a foolish misunderstanding. The soldiers, now entranced, raced back to the balcony and bowed low.

Chal-Abhinno, queen of whores, stood before the gathering. Like all her kind, Chal had two forms: one hideous, the other excruciatingly beautiful. The far-more pleasant version now stared down at Torg. When Chal smiled, men and women broke out in a sweat. Her allure even affected the Asēkhas. Sōbhana covered her face. Kusala seemed puzzled and looked at Torg as if seeking guidance.

Torg clenched his left hand into a fist. His right held his walking staff in a death grip. Obhasa's white ivory glowed, causing the air to shimmer.

The next move belonged to Torg. All others waited and wondered.

Even as the witch spread her web of seduction, Torg turned to Kusala and the rest of the Asēkhas.

"I forgive Sōbhana for her digression. If you wish to mistake that for weakness, so be it. But starting now, I will forgive nothing else. Any who disobeys me will suffer at *my* hands. The stakes are high. Do you doubt it?"

Only Sōbhana answered. "It is I who faltered, lord. We ... I ... will not fail you again."

"That remains to be seen. But I say this only once more: Stay where you are until it becomes clear I need you. You may defend yourselves only if attacked. If I'm destroyed, you may kill any you choose. Otherwise do not act, other than to shield innocents from harm."

Not even Kusala protested. Torg's tone had achieved its desired effect. He'd always led with respect, rather than intimidation. This was different—and not open for debate.

Torg turned back to the stairs. "May I come up?" he said to the witch.

Chal smiled again, exposing teeth as white as milk. She spread her arms wide. When dusk arrived, an enchanting breeze arose and caused her now-lovely hair to swirl enticingly about her slim but shapely shoulders.

"Of course, Torg. Youuu and I should get to know each other. Let the others bide their time while we discuss matters that are beyond them. If you're reasonable, all thisss (she waved a hand at Tathagata) will become unnecessary."

"Very well," Torg said.

He then bounded up the steps five at a time and soon stood face to face with Chal. His quickness stunned several guards who rumbled forward to contest him, but the witch ordered them off.

"Back!" Chal said, her voice taking on its former hideousness. Then she regained her composure and became sweetly seductive. "Torg is our guessst. Give him room to stand."

Torg still held Obhasa. The staff vibrated wildly as if struggling to contain a bolt of lightning within its dense fibers. Torg leaned down close to Chal's face. Her physical beauty was the greater, Torg knew, but it was unnatural.

"I find it tedious to repeat myself," Torg said, slowly enunciating each word. "But if I must, I must. I didn't come here to bandy words with a witless whore. Invite your master to show himself."

The smile on Chal's face was replaced by a snarl of such vehemence, even *her* beauty was scarred. Black smoke oozed from the pores of her skin. Her green eyes faded to gray and then white. Her transformation from hideousness to beauty had come with fire and smoke, but this transformation—from beauty back to hideousness—was slow and cruel. Her skin bubbled and popped. Strands of her auburn hair curled and turned gray. The lithe muscles of her tanned arms became lumpy and gruesome. The perfume grew sour, bitter, and then fetid. The Golden Soldiers again fled her presence.

But Torg didn't flee.

Chal growled and swept her right hand—claws bared—at his face. Torg caught her wrist and twisted her arm. The witch yelped and dropped to her knees. Acidic tears sprang from her eyes, hissing on the stone. While continuing to grip her arm, Torg knelt and whispered in her ear.

"You are not my match, but for now you are not my concern. Despite what you've done to Sister Tathagata, I'll give you one chance: Submit to me and live. You and I will cross paths again, I believe."

"Bassstard!"

Torg pressed Obhasa's rounded head against the small of her back. Where it touched her, blue flames arose.

"Submit—or I will end your life. Not even your master can save you."

"I ... will ... not."

Torg lifted her by her arm and flung her into the air. Chal spun off the balcony and appeared headed to her death, but the wizard knew it wouldn't be that easy. Chal landed fifteen steps below the upper platform with the deftness of a cat. There she crouched on all fours—a vile beast full of hate—and glared at Torg. Crimson beams sprang from her eye sockets, scorching the stone at his feet. Red flames spat from her mouth and struck the wooden bench that held Tathagata. Before the flames could take hold, Torg touched the bench with his staff. Blue liquid spilled over the wood, extinguishing the fire.

"Thisss is not over. One day I will kill youuu!" Chal screamed. And then she scrambled down the rest of the steps with the speed of a hunted animal, rushing past the Asēkhas in a torrent of smoke.

Torg knew that Kusala and Sōbhana could have struck her with their swords, but they dared not move, more fearful of his wrath than hers. Chal was a formidable creature, the greatest of all the Warlish witches. But as Torg had said, she was not his match. Chal would have to bide her time.

The Golden Soldiers and the Asēkhas remained still as stones. The brief struggle between the wizard and witch had engrossed all who watched—even the Noble Ones, who had not tried to escape though their captors were temporarily preoccupied. Torg reached down and broke the leather straps that pinned Tathagata to the bench. Then he gently removed the funnel from her mouth. With a mere fraction of effort, he lifted the tiny woman up and away from the precariously balanced cauldron, then set her carefully on her feet. The High Nun staggered briefly before securing her balance.

Tathagata smiled at Torg and started to speak, but then her tongue froze in her mouth and her eyes grew wide. Torg had never seen her react so strongly to anything. He turned around ever so slowly and faced the dark entrance of the shrine's upper chamber. The figure that had long lurked there, watching the proceedings from the shadows, slowly emerged.

Finally, Mala deigned to make an appearance.

On the rooftop of Bakheng, twilight surrendered to darkness. Torches joined the glowing moon and stars. The balcony on which Torg and Tathagata stood shone brightly.

Mala emerged from the murky opening of the upper shrine, squeezing through the entryway and unfolding his enormous body. Though he was more than twice Torg's height and weighed seventy stones, he was still limber and quick. Few but Torg matched his strength.

Before Invictus ruined him with sorcery, Mala was a peaceful snow giant, one of the most wondrous creatures on Triken. Torg even knew his previous name: Yama-Deva. But the only beauty Mala had retained from his previous existence was his silky white mane, which ran down his spine to his waist. Everything else was hideous. His eyes were red and swollen; vile liquids oozed from their sockets. Two blood-stained fangs hung over his lower lip; venom dripped from their pointed tips. His tongue was long and black; it probed and fluttered like a roving snake.

Yet few who dared to look at Mala noticed much about his face. What captivated their attention was something even more sinister. The Chain Man lived up to his name. A single chain wrapped around his shoulders, crisscrossed at his waist and lower back, rode down his hips, and looped around his bulky thighs. The chain had six-inch-thick links forged from gold blended with magical alloys, making it supernaturally strong. It glowed incessantly with a golden fire as hot as magma, burning Mala's thick hide and causing a stink reminiscent of rotten meat cooked over blazing coals. Was the Chain Man's pain constant and hideous? If so, Mala's madness fed off the pain, which only made him angrier and more dangerous.

The monster loomed over Torg like a fully grown man staring down at a 10-year-old boy. Tathagata covered her face and staggered backward, then gagged and collapsed to her knees.

"I'm sorry, Torg," she managed to say. "I've spent so many years harping on your spiritual weaknesses; yet I see now that I'm far weaker than you. I could abide the witch, but in this creature's presence I'm pathetic."

Torg placed himself between the High Nun and the monster.

"Dear one, don't mistake disgust for weakness," he said, still staring at Mala but speaking to Tathagata. "This one is an affront beyond all others, save Invictus himself. I've fought many battles and seen many gruesome things and am more used to such horror, that is all. I would never presume to question your courage."

"My lord, you embolden me. I shall stand and face my doom with as much dignity as I can muster."

Mala watched this exchange with a smirk on his creepy face. The Chain Man didn't doubt his superiority.

"The one who called you 'Desert Peasant' now lacks his head," the monster said. Then he laughed. It felt like poison to Torg's ears. "Yet I dare to call you something worse. The Torgon is a fool and a coward, worth less than the filth on the soles of my feet. Will one of your Asēkha rats come up and try to take *my* head?"

Mala laughed again. With each spasm of his gigantic midsection, gobs of liquid fire blurted from the chain and smote the stone stairs. Several Golden Soldiers were struck and engulfed in flames, vaulting off the pyramid and howling as they died. There was much shouting and confusion. The Noble Ones covered their faces. The Asēkhas stepped out of the way of the scorching liquid that reached the bottom steps but otherwise held their ground, continuing to watch their king's every move.

"Call me what you like," Torg said. "But I name you Yama-Deva; for you were once a snow giant, and it's still possible for you to return to your former glory if you will take me into your heart."

Mala's chain glowed even hotter, black smoke rising from its links.

"Fool ... *fool*!" The booming power of his voice carried far into the deepening night. "Braggart ... *idiot*! You're nothing compared to me. *Nothing*! And yet you *dare* to offer aid to me?"

"I do offer aid," Torg said. "Your anger and hatred are an illusion burned into your mind by your master. But I can see the real you trapped behind the ruin of your eyes."

The Chain Man couldn't bear to be chastised and was beside himself with rage. He sucked in a huge gulp of air and spit a gob of rancid liquid onto Torg's face. Few could have survived this assault. Blindness would be followed by disfigurement and painful death. But the foul acid didn't harm Torg, sizzling and then evaporating soon after it touched his skin. However, a few droplets slipped past the wizard and fell onto Tathagata's cheeks. Torg spun around, faster than the eye could follow, and willed precise beams of blue light to spring from the head of his staff and incinerate the poison before it could do much damage.

The High Nun smiled.

The wizard turned back to Mala. "I'm not one of the Noble Ones. I have neither their patience nor their dignity. I am simply who I am. But for now, that is enough."

Torg took a step toward Mala, pointed Obhasa at the Chain Man's chest, and then swung full circle, pounding the ivory staff against a portion of the chain that wrapped around the giant's torso. A conflagration of flame—Torg's blue and Mala's golden—exploded at the point of impact, and for a moment the two dueling colors blended into a brilliant green. Despite the enormity of the collision, Torg's power proved the greater and blue prevailed. The Chain Man staggered and flailed his arms before falling flat on his back and smiting the balcony with the force of a fallen pillar. The entire pyramid seemed to quiver.

Torg shouted words from the ancient tongue. *"Santharaahi! (Spread!) ... Bandha! (Bind!) ..."*

Thick blue fumes swirled from his staff and billowed into the night sky.

"Niddaayahi! Niddaayahi! (Sleep! Sleep!)"

The smoke spun like a tornado, expanding and encompassing first the balcony, then the temple, and finally what appeared to be all of Dibbu-Loka. The Chain Man rose on his haunches, staring at the broiling sky. The Golden Soldiers raised their swords and prepared to charge but then froze in place as the smoke fell upon them, slithering into their mouths and nostrils. Torg knew that even if some of the more alert soldiers tried to hold their breaths, it wouldn't matter. The fumes would find their way into their lungs. In a show of trust, Tathagata breathed deeply. One by one, the captors and captives sagged, overcome by an inescapable exhaustion. Soon, all but Torg, the Asēkhas, and Mala were sleeping like children kept up past their bedtimes.

The smoke dissipated, whisked away by a frisky breeze. Torg sank to his knees. He had never performed this feat on such a grand scale, and he was weary from the extravagant expenditure of energy. The Asēkhas charged up the steps and encircled him, *uttaras* drawn.

Torg's chin rested on his chest, his breath coming in quick gasps. But his eyes remained alert.

Mala took a long time to stand. His chain glowed with less vehemence, and his anger now seemed more calculated.

"Ahh ... Torg. I have underestimated you. You were outnumbered and overpowered, but you've evened the odds with this cute little trick."

Kusala spoke on Torg's behalf. "Mala, I warn you to stay where you are."

Mala paid no heed to Kusala, glaring at Torg instead. "Do you think these annoying mice can defeat me? And look at you: So weak you can't even stand. You believe you've won, but you're wrong. Do you think I can't crush you?"

With supreme effort, Torg raised his head. "Before you could *crush* me, you would have to deal with the Asēkhas. You might defeat them, but it wouldn't come without cost. By the time you finished, you'd be weaker than I am now."

Mala growled and pounded his boulder-sized fists together. The Asēkhas surrounded the monster, their *uttaras* sparking in response to his chain. Each sword had taken more than a year to craft, and each curved blade was a thousand times finer than the thickness of a human hair. Mala's hide was far denser than ordinary flesh, Torg knew, but it was not impenetrable. The monster seemed to recognize at least some of the truth in Torg's words, and he dropped his massive arms to his sides.

"What do you suggest, Death-Knower?"

Torg coughed and almost fell on his face, but Sōbhana sprang to his side and caught him. Torg smiled weakly at her, then returned his attention to the Chain Man.

"My reason for coming here has always been the same. I don't want the Noble Ones to be harmed, so I'm here to barter—my freedom in exchange for theirs."

Kusala's eyes sprang wide. "No lord, this can't be. We can crush this creature. Leave him to us. When he's vanquished, we'll save the Noble Ones and be on our way."

Torg continued to focus on Mala. "I offer myself to you without further resistance. You and I will leave this place. While your soldiers sleep, the Asēkhas will remove the Noble Ones and take them to a safe place. I give you my word that your soldiers won't be harmed. We both win."

Mala grunted. "Very well, Torg. I'll accept your *word*. But order your rats not to follow."

Torg rose unsteadily to his feet. He turned to Kusala, Sōbhana, and the other Asēkhas and gazed from face to face. Mala loomed behind him like a tower of malice.

The disbelief in the faces of his warriors was easily recognizable, and Torg understood why. They couldn't see inside his mind and know his thoughts. How could they possibly understand what drove him now?

Torg knew more about Invictus than he'd let on to anyone. He could sense the extent of the sorcerer's power. It reminded him of a wildfire obscured by the crest of a tall hill. The others could only see smoke, but Torg could feel the heat.

Despite his relative youth and inexperience, Invictus had become the greatest threat the land had ever known and could not be defeated by ordinary means. Torg believed that to combat Invictus, he would need to perform an act of virtue that would help even the scales between good and evil. A selfless act on a stage of such magnitude would set larger forces in motion. To save the Noble Ones, Torg was willing to sacrifice his own freedom. He did so, however, with an even grander vision: This war would be fought not just on the physical battlefield, but in an arena invisible to all but the wise.

"The soldiers will sleep for at least a day," Torg said to the Asēkhas. "While they are helpless, transport the Noble Ones to our place of safekeeping. I will depart with Mala and permit him to bear me to Invictus."

Kusala interrupted. "Lord, this is impossible. If you—"

Blue light fired from the head of Torg's staff, pounding Kusala in the chest and knocking him off his feet. The other Asēkhas gasped.

"Don't question me!!!" Torg shouted before smashing the butt of Obhasa on the marble beneath his feet so hard it cracked the shiny stone. "Listen carefully ... *all* of you. I will leave with Mala. You must not follow, not *one* of you. Carry the Noble Ones to safety and then return to the defense of Anna. Do not harm any of Mala's soldiers. If you're ambushed after I'm gone, then you're free to kill any and all—and come after me if you still can. Otherwise, stay away from me and alert the Tugars to do the same. If this situation changes, I'll make it known."

"Listen to your master, little cockroaches," Mala teased. "He, at least, has a shred of wisdom. And don't worry. I'll take *good* care of him."

Kusala struggled to breathe, but he regained his feet. "As you command, my king. It will be as you say."

"Yes, it *will* be as I say. If Mala honors his side of the bargain and allows you to remove the Noble Ones without interference, then you must not give chase. Any who follow will die at *my* hands. This, I foretell. As for you, Mala, if your minions attempt some treachery in Dibbu-Loka after you and I have departed, you'll regret it."

"Your threats are empty," the Chain Man said. "But they're also needless. Once you and I are gone, nothing will happen to these pathetic *breath-watchers* unless you break your vow and try to escape. I care less for them than I do for your rats. You, I care for least of all. But Invictus wishes to speak with you face to face. I don't comprehend the reason for this, but I *always* follow orders from my king. So I'll deliver you to him as promised."

Spiky rocks and hidden clefts riddled the arid land that fell steeply beyond the northern wall of Dibbu-Loka. Mala chose this path for himself and Torg. After the ordeal on the balcony of Bakheng, Torg was still exhausted, and his legs felt drained of blood. Even worse, Mala drove him mercilessly forward. Torg's discomfort was the least of the Chain Man's concerns.

"Keep *moving*, you little pig!" Mala commanded, shoving Torg from behind and sending him tumbling partway down the hill. "Do as you're told, or I'll have to carry you. And neither of us will like that."

Torg experienced a surge of anger, but at this point his weakness had not yet dissipated. Also, he no longer wielded Obhasa, having left the staff with Kusala who had cringed when taking it in his hands. Recalling the chieftain's pained expression caused Torg's heart to wither.

I'm sorry, Kusala. I hope one day to regain your trust. But for now, the stakes are too high. I had to make sure that none of the Asēkhas—including you—interfered with my plan.

Mala thrust his foot into Torg's ribs, knocking him farther down the hill.

"Hurry! I want to put several leagues between us and this rathole of a city before I even think of resting."

Torg had never been kicked so hard. Gasping for breath, he forced himself upright and stumbled forward. Realizing that he would have to draw on his warrior's training to survive this ordeal, he cleared thought from his mind and began to move with the instincts of a wild animal, choosing the path of least resistance through the jumbled boulders. Mala soon struggled to keep up.

"Wait, wait! I warned you what would happen to your precious *robe-wearers* if you tried to escape."

"I'm not trying to escape. I'm doing as I'm told. Slow? Fast? Let me know when you make up your mind."

Mala chomped on his lower lip. Blood squirted onto his chin. He reached down, picked up a fair-sized boulder, and heaved it at Torg. It missed by a wide margin. Curses and profanities followed. The Chain Man tromped around like a spoiled child.

Meanwhile, Torg felt his strength returning more quickly than he had expected. He believed he could run off and leave Mala behind. After all, the chain the ruined snow giant bore was a heavy burden. But Torg had given his word and would remain true as long as the Chain Man left the Noble Ones in peace.

"Mala, it doesn't have to be this way. All this kicking and shoving won't speed up either of us."

The monster snarled. But Torg's words had a calming effect. For the rest of the night, Mala allowed him to choose the path and set the pace. They walked until nearly dawn but managed just three leagues as the raven flies, being forced to clamber over jumbled rock and crawl through thorny brush. Several leagues to the east or west, the land was far easier to traverse, but the Chain Man demanded they head north toward the city of Senasana, about thirty leagues from Dibbu-Loka.

"That is where the real fun will begin," Mala said. The monster smiled, and the links of his chain grew red-hot.

As the sun emerged, their pace slowed. Torg found a trickling spring, knelt to sniff the water, and then took a drink. Mala snorted and disdained it.

Torg found some edible berries and offered a few to the Chain Man, whose face contorted in disgust.

"I would eat *your* greasy flesh before I would eat *that*. Meat, blood, and bones make the best breakfast. You're disgusting!"

"Yama-Deva didn't eat meat. He loved all animals. He was a shepherd."

"Say that name again and you'll regret it. You live now only because Invictus commands it."

Torg shrugged and then led Mala to a natural stone shelter. They rested beneath its craggy ceiling for much of the day. The rising sun brought with it a languorous heat. Mala's eyes grew heavy, and he slept. Torg lay nearby pretending to doze, but he watched the Chain Man through the slits of his eyelids.

Mala's long white mane was unchanged, but little else remained of his former glory. Torg pitied the monster. He had not known Yama-Deva before Invictus captured him, but many centuries ago, Torg had climbed high into the peaks of the Okkanti Mountains and visited with several of Deva's kin, including a snow giant named Utu who was Deva's brother.

"I have heard of you, Torg," Yama-Utu said. "Yama-Deva is the only one among us who dares to leave the peaks, and he has brought back word of the desert king who can cheat death. Please, young master … tell us more."

Torg spoke long with the snow giant, his mate, and three of his friends who had magically appeared from behind boulders. Their company and conversation were delightful. Many times they bragged about Yama-Deva, the snow giant with the courage to wander.

More than 700 years later, Torg felt the sting of tears as he studied the ruins of Yama-Deva. He remembered what the Noble Ones said about the impotence of hatred, but he felt hatred toward Invictus growing inside him, anyway. Torg hoped beyond hope there was some way he could help Mala revert to his former self.

Eventually even Torg slept, his dreams drenched in sorrow.

Someone watching from a distance might have mistaken them for friends—rather large friends—traveling together in the wilds. Several times, Torg woke and could have escaped, most of his strength returned. But the wizard believed in the power of karma; if he broke his word, more harm than good would result. His vow at Bakheng would not be fulfilled until he was presented to Invictus.

Torg once asked his Vasi master: "What is the meaning of karma?"

The master answered: "Karma means you get away with nothing."

Torg reflected on those words as he listened to Mala's thunderous snores. When the Chain Man woke, the monster sat up so fast he banged his thick head on the ceiling of the shelter.

"It's a good thing you didn't run off," Mala said, rubbing the sore spot. "I would have returned to Dibbu-Loka and killed every one of the *bald bastards* and *bitches* myself."

"The Noble Ones shave their heads," Torg said, rolling his eyes. "Even the women. They're not bald."

"Whatever."

Torg sighed. "I've told you before—and I mean it. I'll go with you, without resistance, and allow you to imprison me. After that, we shall see what we shall see. As for going back and killing the Noble Ones, that's no longer possible. The Asēkhas have long since removed them from harm. Now, my word is all that binds me to you."

"So full of pride you are. And so bold. It would bring me immense pleasure to strip the flesh off your bones. But my master forbids it, and *his* threats are the only ones I fear. You'll fear them too. If you're lucky, he'll convince you—as he convinced me—to join him on his quest to rid the land of vermin. Otherwise, you'll suffer as he sees fit. And die *when* he sees fit."

Before they set off, Mala allowed Torg to drink from the spring and eat more berries. Quick as a snake, the Chain Man snatched a fat iguana off the side of a boulder and devoured it raw. Although Torg had often eaten salted iguana flesh, he found this sight less than appetizing. However, the fresh meat seemed to improve Mala's mood, and he again permitted Torg to lead.

The unusual pair walked into the evening and throughout the night, rarely resting. In the meantime, the rocky land surrounding Dibbu-Loka succumbed to rolling plains, and the remnants of a road appeared before them. By morning's first light, they had traveled more than ten leagues in one day and were almost halfway to Senasana. During all that time, they had seen only lizards, snakes, birds, and insects. Ravenous flies swarmed around them, but their bites had no effect on Torg's flesh— and undoubtedly none on Mala's, as well. The Chain Man enjoyed snaring the flies with his disgusting tongue and eating them. During these times, Mala resembled a demonic toad.

Once they reached the road, they made much better progress. On the fourth morning since leaving Dibbu-Loka, they came within a league of Senasana and were met by one of Mala's scouts. The Chain Man barked orders, and the scout raced away. As Mala and Torg drew near the city, several dozen Golden Soldiers marched toward them. A captain came forth and stood at the feet of the monster, trembling as he saluted.

"Did you bring it?" Mala said. "*Tell* me you brought it."

"Yes, lord," the captain stammered. "I have it as you commanded."

"It was wise of you not to fail. I haven't yet eaten breakfast."

The captain swayed on his feet as if about to swoon.

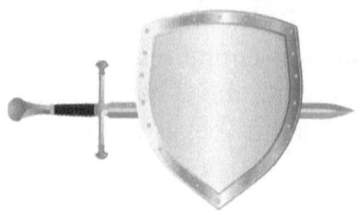

WARRIOR'S SACRIFICE

Sōbhana watched Mala and Torg scramble down the pyramid's stairs and jog along a causeway that led to the northern wall of Dibbu-Loka. The Chain Man shouted orders while shoving Torg from behind. It was unbearable to watch.

Sōbhana was a warrior. Pain and sacrifice were second nature to her, but this was something else. Her lord's commands made little sense. The Golden Soldiers were subdued. Mala stood alone. He was a formidable monster but not invincible.

"Chieftain, this is madness," she said to Kusala. "We must not permit it."

Kusala held Obhasa in his right hand, but his face remained downcast. "He will slay any who follow. I do not doubt it. I've never seen him like this. Madness or no, we won't pursue."

Kusala turned from Sōbhana and swept his arm in a half circle. "All heard the commands of our king. We must take the Noble Ones to the haven we've prepared. Find carts and oxen. I want all 500 of the monks and nuns far from the city by dawn. Don't harm the soldiers unless we're attacked. However, there is one thing—not mentioned by our king—that I will happily endorse: If you feel the need to relieve yourselves, aim for a sleeping face. The color of your urine will match their gaudy armor."

This elicited grim laughter and a few guarantees—even from some of the women—that not a drop would be wasted. Then Sōbhana watched the Asēkhas spring into action. They found thirty long wagons, but only enough oxen to haul half of them. It didn't matter; the Asēkhas were strong enough to tow some of the carts by hand. The Noble Ones, still deeply asleep, were squeezed side by side into the beds. It was a tight fit, but they managed to get them all into the wagons. The evacuation began.

Tugars were not just warriors. They were also determined workers. Twenty Asēkhas could outperform a hundred ordinary men and women. Nineteen Asēkhas could do almost as well.

And nineteen would have to do.

Sleek as a cat, Sōbhana slipped over the northeastern wall. She had not asked Kusala's permission, nor had he demanded it. But it was mutually understood she was on her own.

She watched with rage as Mala jostled and kicked her king. It took every shred of her will to resist pouncing on the wicked monster. But she held herself back. If she attacked now, she believed—as did Kusala—that Torg would kill her. Her own demise didn't concern her, but she would be no good to her lord if she were dead. She had to remain patient and carefully choose the time and place to reveal her presence.

Plus, she knew from firsthand experience that Torg's senses were extraordinary. But she hoped the wizard's focus on Mala would dilute her king's alertness. If she stayed cleverly hidden, she might be able to follow undetected for a considerable distance.

She had no plan other than to be certain that Torg didn't travel this path alone. She loved him, after all—but not only as she would love a king. She yearned to become Torg's wife.

Sōbhana had begun her warrior training at age 16, achieving the rank of warrior at 66 and Asēkha at 78. Both were unprecedented. Torg had not become a warrior until he was 68 and an Asēkha until 80. But he had become a Death-Knower only two years later. Sōbhana knew in her heart she couldn't follow in those footsteps. It wasn't in her to become a Knower of Death. She could, however, fall in love with one.

Sōbhana was brave, loyal, and often told she was beautiful. Why *not* her?

Kusala would have called it infatuation, but she knew better. Sōbhana was in *love* with Torg. It puzzled her that he'd never taken a wife, but at the same time it thrilled her because it gave her a chance to make her dream come true. And if she'd ever seen Torg with another woman, she might have committed murder.

Marriage was relatively rare among Tugars. Most of their men and women preferred sexual freedom—and were promiscuous among their own kind. Unlike the others, Torg was not. He *always* slept alone. Sōbhana once asked Kusala about it, and the chieftain had fidgeted.

"There are rumors, among the elders, that something horrible happened to him when he was young," Kusala whispered. "He won't speak of it. I asked him once, and the look he gave me shriveled my balls. I'll never ask again."

As Sōbhana replayed the chieftain's words, she burrowed beneath a mound of crumbled stone until only her eyes and the crown of her head were exposed. She watched Mala and Torg as they slept under the slanted roof of a rock shelter and saw her beloved open his eyes now and then and look at the Chain Man. Tears coursed down his cheeks. She cried too. If Torg attempted to escape, she would rush to his aid, heedless of her own survival.

She followed them for days, all the way to the outskirts of Senasana. She noted the approach of the scouts, and then the soldiers. As the morning sun climbed in the sky, the small garrison led Torg toward the main gates. People gathered along the wide road that ran through the center of the city. Sōbhana stayed far back, away from prying eyes.

Senasana was an active marketplace. Traders came from as far west as the Kolankold Mountains and as far east as the Barranca wastes. More than 50,000 lived there permanently, and transients doubled its population.

On this day, what Sōbhana saw stunned her. A well-equipped army of 500-score Golden Soldiers occupied the city. In addition to the infantry, there were dangerous monsters: several druids from Dhutanga and a Kojin from Java. Until now, Invictus had not sent this caliber of force this far south. But the sorcerer's boldness seemed to grow by leaps and bounds.

The citizens of Senasana weren't warriors and couldn't forestall an army. Accumulating wealth was their chief talent. Under these circumstances, they were frightened—and cowardly. Accommodating these new guardians was their safest course.

Sōbhana knew that most Senasanans admired Torg, who had been a frequent guest in their city. But this time the wizard was a helpless prisoner. It would be suicide to aid him. And besides, where had the Tugars been when Invictus' soldiers entered the city? Sōbhana sensed that the Senasanans felt abandoned. Perhaps, they were right.

As Torg's captors marched past where she stood, someone on the side of the road hurled a tomato. Its aim was true, striking her king in the face. Mala guffawed. So did the crowd. It was an ugly scene.

This sickened Sōbhana—and further aroused her anger. Still

laughing, the tomato thrower suddenly bent over and coughed up a ball of blood that closely resembled the splattered fruit. He never laughed again. It wasn't wise to offend an Asēkha.

Sōbhana snuck deeper into the crowd. A wagon piled high with women's clothing had been parked on the side of the road by a merchant who had wandered a few paces away to get a closer look at the spectacle. Sōbhana stole a loose-fitting kirtle, a pair of low-cut leather shoes, a cloth purse, and a hat with a linen band that wrapped under the chin. She knelt behind the cart and quickly changed clothing, tucking her *uttara* and dagger into scabbards beneath the dress and stuffing her black Tugarian outfit into the purse. The hat concealed the cut and color of her hair, which would have been suspicious to those with clever eyes. When she emerged, she looked like a typical Senasanan woman, though more attractive in the face than most.

Sōbhana wandered through the mob, which was growing increasingly raucous. Noon approached. There would soon be feasting. The Chain Man and his soldiers would be treated like heroes. But when most of Mala's army followed him back to Avici afterward, few in the merchant city would complain.

The teeming market in the heart of Senasana surrounded a spectacular temple that was larger and more ornate than the pyramid-shaped shrine in Dibbu-Loka. Vinipata was a bulbous dome made of white marble that towered 200 cubits above the floor of the square. Four smaller and less impressive domes served as Vinipata's guardians, and exquisite minarets framed the outer corners. Visitors entered through a red sandstone gate bearing a multitude of ancient inscriptions. The courtyard inside the gate could accommodate many thousands. Sōbhana had been to this place several times, though the other occasions had been far more pleasurable.

Mala escorted Torg into the square. The mob followed. The temple grounds swarmed with soldiers and onlookers. Sōbhana, in her new dress and hat, blended into the throng. She positioned herself as best she could to get a clear view.

Though most areas of the courtyard were packed, an open space remained around Mala and Torg. The Chain Man towered above everyone, and few dared to approach the monster and his prisoner. Several Golden Soldiers stationed themselves a dozen paces away but would go no nearer. The five druids and the Kojin, however, pressed in as close as they could. Mala's presence filled them with bliss.

The druids of Dhutanga stood almost seven cubits tall. They were thin and angular but deceptively strong. Their outer flesh looked more like bark than skin, and they had fiery eyes and enormous mouths, with black holes where there should have been ears and noses.

The Kojin was an enormous ogress with a bloated head and six muscled arms. Only a few of her kind still roamed the world, and those had rarely ventured outside of the forest Java until the emergence of Invictus. Sōbhana recalled her lone confrontation with a Kojin, which had occurred while traveling with two Asēkhas through Java, also called the Dark Forest. A vicious fight ensued—three against one. Despite their most concentrated efforts, the warriors could not seriously injure the beast, and they struggled to avoid its wicked counterattacks. It finally forced them to flee. Sōbhana had never overcome the humiliation. She hadn't thought it possible for a trio of Asēkhas to fare so poorly against a single foe.

The Kojin who stood near Torg was even larger than the one Sōbhana had encountered. It was only a span or two shorter than Mala, dwarfing even the druids in height and, especially, in girth.

Next to these giants, even Torg looked pitifully small.

"How could anyone stand against monsters so hideous?" Sōbhana heard a woman in the crowd say to a man next to her.

He shrugged, looking nervous. "I know I couldn't, is all."

"Where are the Tugars?" another man said. "Where are the Asēkhas? Do they tremble?"

"We all tremble," the first man said.

Mala let out a roar that echoed throughout the courtyard. Flames sprang from his massive chain, flinging gouts of black smoke into the air.

All went silent.

The monster's booming voice was as concussive as thunder.

"Citizens of Senasana … as you know, The Torgon stands accused of treason. He has conspired against King Invictus and his loyal followers. But fear not. We have captured him and will make him kneel before the throne of the king in the Golden City, there to be judged."

Scattered applause and cheers greeted Mala's speech, but also a fair share of grumbling.

Hidden near the gates, Sōbhana shouted, "Liar!"

Soldiers raced over, but by then she was settled in a different place.

"Liar?" Mala said.

His chain glowed like hot coals.

"There is only one liar here, and he kneels before me."

Mala looked down at Torg, who was indeed kneeling, head bowed.

There was a brief silence, broken by a piercing call from a different area of the courtyard. Sōbhana simply could not bear it. "Let him speak!"

Several others, apparently braver than the rest, echoed this request.

"Let him speak!" they also yelled.

Ebony fumes puffed from Mala's mouth and nose. Rancid liquids oozed from his ears. The Kojin, infected by the Chain Man's rage, pounded her fists against her hairy bosom. The druids swayed like reeds in a windstorm, humming in unison.

The event was not proceeding as Mala had envisioned. The monster struggled to control his rage. His instinct must have been to wade into the crowd and bust some heads, but even he was not that crude yet. His king had not waged open war, and a slaughter of civilians might do more harm than good.

"You wish him to speak?" Mala bellowed. "I will honor your requests. Speak, Torg." He lowered his voice and said something to the wizard that Sōbhana couldn't discern.

The Death-Knower lifted his head. Silence again blanketed the courtyard. Even the druids grew quiet. Torg's beauty stunned Sōbhana. In comparison, Mala and the other monsters were utterly repulsive.

"I will appear before Invictus," Torg said, "and be 'judged.'"

The silence broke like shattered glass. Clapping, cheers, and cries of woe intermingled in the courtyard.

Sōbhana shouted, "No!"

But this time her voice was overwhelmed.

"Torg speaks wisely," Mala said. "He trusts the wisdom and mercy of King Invictus. Perhaps, there's hope he can be rehabilitated. But the journey to Avici is long, and I'll take no chances with such a dangerous prisoner. Bind him!"

Several soldiers came forward guiding a four-wheeled wagon hauled by black horses. Others bore a restraining device that had been wickedly conceived. The soldiers laid Torg upon a full-length jacket of thick fabric and guided his arms through holes in the jacket before tying them against his chest with cruel leather straps. They then threaded the jacket from his feet to his chin. After the Death-Knower was secured, Mala wrapped golden ropes, steeped in the sorcerer's magic, around the wizard's prone body. The contraption bound Torg like a caterpillar in a cocoon.

The Kojin lifted the wizard high into the air and used her six arms to strap Torg to a wide board that was attached at an angle to the bed of the wagon.

The Death-Knower was helpless.

And on display.

Sōbhana had never felt so impotent. All she could do was watch and follow.

And so began the lumbering journey from Senasana to Avici, the home of Invictus. By Sōbhana's count, Mala and his army escorted the Death-Knower along the rolling banks of the Ogha River for thirty-eight days. During the slow and dreary march, Torg remained bound, barely able to move anything but his head. Yet Sōbhana didn't once see him squirm or otherwise resist. He lay still as a corpse, eyes closed, accepting occasional sips of water and spoonfuls of gruel without enthusiasm.

Whenever the procession approached a village, the fishermen and farmers who lived near the river bowed their heads. Compared to such a well-equipped militia, they were minuscule. Where was Anna? Nissaya? Jivita? Sōbhana heard them say more than once that Torg had been forsaken.

Sōbhana avoided being seen by any of Mala's soldiers all the way from Senasana to Avici. Twice, she encountered Tugarian scouting parties who were unaware of their king's orders not to follow, having left the Tent City before Torg's capture. She told them what she'd seen and then sent some of them southeast to Anna to give Chieftain Kusala advance notice to ready the Tugars. She sent others west to Nissaya and Jivita to advise their armies to prepare for battle. If Invictus was willing to send forces as far south as Senasana and Dibbu-Loka, then it was clear the young sorcerer wasn't deterred by the threat of reprisal.

Much of Invictus' confidence was based on the impregnable strength of his stronghold: Avici and its sister city, Kilesa. An oblong wall that stood thirty cubits tall with a circumference of almost 200 leagues encompassed both cities. Sōbhana had been told that 20,000 slaves took twenty years to construct the grand bulwark. Invictus even had the gall—and wealth—to have large portions of the stone slathered with gold.

The Golden Wall, as it was aptly named, encircled more than 25,000 hectares. As the Ogha River flowed south on its winding way to Lake Keo, it roared through Avici, cleaving the massive city in half. A pair of majestic bridges—one to the north and the other to the south—spanned the river where it sluiced through gaps in the Golden Wall. Immense iron gates swung beneath the catwalks, protecting Avici from attack at these two otherwise vulnerable locations.

From where she hid, Sōbhana could now see the southern bridge, which towered above the churning currents. When Mala approached the bridge, the main strength of Invictus' army greeted the Chain Man's brigade. Sōbhana guessed that more than 200,000 lined Ogha's steep banks, including some who stood ten-deep on the bridge. Most of the army was comprised of Golden Soldiers, but at least a fifth of it appeared to have been recruited from other places. The druids of Dhutanga, who had spent centuries rebuilding their numbers after a failed war with Jivita, numbered 10,000. The wild men of the Kolankold Mountains had provided 5,000, as had the Pabbajja who lived on the fringes of Java. Added to the horde were 5,000 Mogols from the Mahaggata Mountains.

Many wicked creatures from Mahaggata's interior had also answered Invictus' call, including dracools, Stone-Eaters, and wolves. There were dark places beneath the mountains, and from there Invictus had lured cave trolls and mud ogres and given them potions that enabled them to tolerate sunlight. There were smaller numbers of other zealots: demons, ghouls, and vampires from Arupa-Loka; murderers, rapists, and thieves from Duccarita; Warlish witches and their servant hags from Kamupadana. And a hideous menagerie of misshapen monsters that Sōbhana had never seen: a pair of three-headed giants who dwarfed even Mala; creatures who were part human and part animal or insect; and beasts with mouths full of sharp teeth that hungered for human flesh. The immense scope of the army staggered Sōbhana.

But what she saw next dwarfed her previous dismay. Apparently, the Chain Man wasn't Invictus' only favored pet. As if the sorcerer needed any more weapons in his arsenal, another colossal ally had joined his army. A great dragon perched on the highest framework of the bridge. Even so far away, she could see that the beast was enormous—200 cubits long from head to tail and weighing several thousand stones.

Though she'd never actually seen a great dragon, Sōbhana had heard many tales about them. The eldest was Bhayatupa, who was as powerful as he was ancient. According to legend, Bhayatupa had ruled sprawling kingdoms, fought countless battles, and slaughtered many brave warriors during his millennia-long existence. Could this be that dragon? How could it not? The creature was huge beyond her comprehension.

With the vast gathering watching Mala's every move, the Chain Man strode toward the bridge. The army cheered. Invictus was its king, but Mala was its general. This army had been bequeathed to the Chain Man. When it came time to unleash its power, the ruined snow giant would be at its helm. Sōbhana and the Tugars would be hard-set, to say the least.

Since departing Dibbu-Loka, Sōbhana had barely tolerated watching Torg endure such ruthless torment. But seeing the dragon pained her even worse. Mala was frightening but not invincible. Invictus, whom she had yet to face, felt more like legend than reality. The Golden Soldiers, despite their daunting numbers, were not nearly as well-trained as the Tugars. The other monsters presented difficulties, but they were beatable. The dragon, however, was far more perilous.

From her hiding place in a copse several hundred paces from the bridge, Sōbhana saw the behemoth as the coming of doom. When the Asēkha gazed at the dragon, she felt genuine fear for the first time in her life. This creature was beyond her in all ways.

Finally, she perceived Torg's mind. Her king had recognized—before the rest of them—that the Tugars could not prevail against Invictus by force. The sorcerer would always be capable of conjuring something more wicked than before. The legions of good had enjoyed many years of peace and superiority on Triken, but the Sun God—in a mere century of life—had changed all that. The world approached a dangerous crossroads, and higher forces—karma, truth, love—would play the determining roles in the outcome. Torg had surrendered to Mala to set those forces in motion.

What happened next caused her to tremble again. When the dragon spied Torg, it spread its colossal wings and sprang off the high bridge, landing on the ground in front of the wizard, who was still confined in the wagon by the magical restraining device. The dragon dwarfed all other creatures. Its crimson head alone was twice as long as Torg's entire body, and each of its fearsome eyes was more than two cubits wide. The beast bent down its long neck, tilted its right eye toward Torg, and glided within a few feet of the Death-Knower's face.

All went quiet. Even Mala lowered his arms and froze. There was magic in the air born in a time long past.

Sōbhana was close enough to make out the details of her beloved's face, and she saw that he didn't flinch. His courage made her heart thunder in her chest.

When the dragon spoke, some fell to their knees. Its voice assaulted the senses, reminding Sōbhana of the dust in a hoary crypt.

"*Te tam maranavidum aacikkhanti.* (They call thee a Death-Knower)," the dragon said, speaking in the ancient tongue.

"*Te tam rakkhasam aacikkhanti.* (They call thee a Monster)," Torg responded.

The dragon snorted. Blood-colored flames spewed from its nostrils, bathing Torg's face but doing little visible damage. When the dragon next spoke, it was in the common tongue that most understood.

"I would learn more."

"Tell me why," Torg said.

"*Abhisambodhi.* (Enlightenment)," the dragon said.

"You fear death, as do most," the wizard said. "But what you desire to achieve is beyond you or anyone ignorant enough to join with this mob."

This startled the dragon, and it rose to its full height, towering high above all in attendance. But Mala appeared to have heard enough. He boldly stepped in front of the dragon and slapped Torg across the face.

"Shut up, little fool!" he said to the wizard. "Don't speak again unless my king demands it."

Then he shook his bulky fist at the dragon's titanic presence. "Until we stand before *our* king, all interrogations of the prisoner will be carried out only by me. Do you understand?"

The dragon's head and neck made loud swishing sounds as they swayed through the air. Sōbhana was convinced the beast would bend down and devour Mala whole.

But the dragon surprised her by saying, "I understand ... *Adho Satta.* (Low one.)" But before returning to its perch on the bridge, it said one more thing to Torg: "*Bhayatupa amarattam tanhiiyati.* (Bhayatupa craves eternal existence)."

So it *was* Bhayatupa! This amazed Sōbhana so much she failed to hear Torg's response.

To enter the southern gates of Avici, Sōbhana was forced to kill. When a lone soldier wandered too near her hiding place, she sprang out and drove her Tugarian dagger beneath the back of his helm into the gristle at the base of his neck. With so much excitement surrounding Torg, no one noticed this violent death.

Sōbhana dragged the soldier into thick shrubs and took her time stripping off his golden suit of armor, which was nearly a perfect fit for her height but overlarge for her girth. She kept the arming cap but tossed aside the interior doublet and hose, parts of which had become soaked with the soldier's sweat and blood. Then she meticulously put on the armor, which was difficult but not impossible to do without assistance. First, she slid on the steel-hinged shoes, followed by the greaves, knee-cops, and cuisses. The breast, shoulder, and back plates were cleverly blended into one piece that she could drop over her head, and she attached the brassards and elbow-cops to the shoulder plates with hinge pins. Finally, she donned the single-visor helm, which had narrow eye slits with two dozen breath holes.

The soldier had carried a longsword with a straight blade. Her curved *uttara* wouldn't fit properly into his scabbard, creating a new problem. Up to this moment, she had concealed her sword and dagger beneath the loose-fitting kirtle she'd stolen in Senasana. She wouldn't part with her sword no matter the circumstances, but she believed her weapon was similar enough in appearance to avoid detection if she held it close and obscured the ornamented handle with her gauntleted hand.

Even without the padded undergarments, the metallic armor was more comfortable than Sōbhana had expected. It felt like it had been designed to meld with her flesh. Whoever constructed it must have used magic to enhance its effectiveness. It was stronger than iron yet surprisingly light and pliable. Not even the armor worn by the black knights of Nissaya could match it. This added to her growing sense of hopelessness. Could Invictus do no wrong?

Sōbhana joined the tail end of the brigade as it entered the gates.

Amid the cheering and commotion, she blended in and went unnoticed. Soon, she was inside.

Avici turned out to be everything Anna was not.

Invictus' Golden City swarmed with hundreds of thousands of people. Torg's Tent City in the heart of the Great Desert housed fewer than 20,000 Tugars, including those who had failed to attain the rank of warrior, and about 5,000 others.

Avici was a maze of ponderous stone buildings and temples, interconnected by wide roadways. Its sheer mass astounded her, especially considering it had been little more than a village less than a hundred years before. Anna was a nomadic kingdom, able to pick up and relocate across the sands of Tējo. It contained no structures too large to fold up and transport by hand.

The citizens of Avici were servants of Invictus, subject to his orders and whims. Despite this, some of the community appeared to enjoy enormous wealth.

The inhabitants of Anna were free to come and go as they pleased. They worked hard and lived simply, depending on hidden oases for sustenance.

True to her warrior instincts, Sōbhana memorized each twist and turn of Avici's main causeway. But her efforts lacked conviction. Of what use was resistance? Invictus was too great. With Bhayatupa as its ally, Avici was a power beyond compare. The forces of good were destined for slaughter.

Even so, she continued to follow the horse-driven wagon and the hordes, always staying within sight of her beloved. Sōbhana's spirit was fading, but her love for Torg was not. She would stand by her king until doom took them all, even if the mountainous dragon himself tried to stop her.

They paraded Torg along a paved roadway lined by two-story stone buildings with elaborate facades. Men, women, and children, all wearing white robes, leered from the balconies that leaned over the street, the adults shouting obscenities, the children hurling garbage. This incensed Sōbhana, but she couldn't kill thousands and thousands. She had never seen so many people in one place at one time.

Sōbhana knew through her studies (one of the rare times she had paid attention) that the eastern portion of Avici had been built upon the remnants of a volcano that had raged and fumed before the Ogha River was born. The volcano was now lifeless, its sides long since crumbled and smoothed. A labyrinth of buildings—jammed side by side on the hill—blocked Sōbhana's view of what lay beyond. But when she came to the crest, she beheld the tower of Invictus for the first time.

Uccheda, as the tower was called, dominated the valley on the northeast side of the city. Seeing Uccheda filled Sōbhana with the same dismay she'd felt when she spied the dragon. The evil sorcerer's dwelling place was by far the largest edifice she'd ever seen, dwarfing the temples in Senasana and Dibbu-Loka. Even the central keep of Nissaya, the Black Fortress, didn't match this level of stature and grandeur.

Uccheda was spherical, tapering slightly as it grew—and it was so tall, clouds sometimes gathered about its roof. But the tower's height wasn't its most impressive attribute. What stunned Sōbhana more than anything else was the scope of its decadence. Much of its outer surface was coated with gold. Of all the known bullion in the world, it was rumored that more than a third had been used in the tower's construction. Uccheda blazed beneath the rising sun like a beacon of despair, blinding anyone who looked directly at it.

The main roadway dipped into the valley. Torg was drawn toward the tower. Hundreds of thousands followed. Mala marched ahead of the wagon. Bhayatupa glided in lazy circles above Uccheda's roof. No one paid Sōbhana any attention. She walked freely in her new disguise.

There were no visible apertures at the tower's base, but fifty cubits above the ground, hundreds of doors and windows opened onto a circular balcony. The largest portal, adorned with jewels and inscriptions, faced the roadway. It swung slowly open.

The crowd grew silent—and bowed in eerie unison.

Sōbhana watched Bhayatupa land on the rooftop of Uccheda. Even at such a great height, she could see him clearly on a day as cloudless as this one.

Then her eyes were drawn back to the portal. Invictus wasn't the first to emerge. Ten standard-bearers, adorned in glistening armor studded with diamonds and rubies, led the way onto the balcony, their banners bearing yellow suns outlined in red on backgrounds of white.

Next, a woman of unparalleled beauty appeared, wearing a crimson gown and a bejeweled chaplet. Sōbhana curled her upper lip, recognizing Chal-Abhinno, the Warlish witch who had obviously fled to Avici after Torg humiliated her at Dibbu-Loka.

A pair of dracools, winged beasts that looked like small dragons but waddled on two legs, escorted Chal. Behind the dracools strode an impressive soldier wearing decorated armor. He carried his helm in the crook of his arm, and his long blond hair danced in the breeze.

A stately woman with luxurious blond hair hanging past her waist joined the soldier. Even from a distance, she was tall and magnificent in her white gown. Despite her dignified entrance, she bowed her head as if disturbed.

As soon as the blond woman appeared, Sōbhana saw that Torg resisted the restraints for the first time since the Kojin had strapped him to the wagon. Her king looked up at the woman, who appeared to return his gaze. Suddenly, beams of light—pale as ghosts—leaped from their eyes and collided in midair. Bhayatupa snorted in amusement, and the yellow-haired soldier looked at the woman—and then Torg—with a mixture of surprise and anger.

A thunderous roar from the crowd startled the blond woman and caused her to stagger. The soldier caught her and held her up. Then Invictus came through the door. When Sōbhana had witnessed the woman on the balcony staring at Torg, she had experienced an intense jolt of jealously. But the moment Invictus strode into view, the jealousy was swept away. The young sorcerer commanded her full attention, and his presence rendered her impotent. She watched him walk to the edge of the balcony and raise his arms toward the sun. Invictus bathed in the glory of light.

Physically, the young sorcerer was not as impressive as she had expected. He was smaller and not nearly as muscular as a Tugar, and he was less graceful in his manner than her fellow desert warriors. His yellow hair was shoulder length, his face boyishly handsome, and he wore golden robes that glimmered in the sunlight. In Sōbhana's opinion, he was not as beautiful as Torg or most any Tugar male.

Nonetheless, she sagged to her knees. There was no hope. From where she stood, she could barely tolerate the power that emanated from the Sun God's body. It felt as if she were standing too close to the open door of a blazing furnace. Torg, whom she had long believed to be the most powerful being on Triken, was puny in comparison. The alarming apparition even dwarfed Bhayatupa.

Sōbhana turned to Torg for guidance. Her beloved's face was far away, but she could still interpret his expression. His eyes were closed but he grimaced, apparently feeling the same despair as she. Her king was outmatched. And if Torg was outmatched, so was everyone—and everything—else.

"I will speak to you now," Invictus said to the throng. "Say yes if you hear my words."

"*YES!*"

Of everyone in attendance, only a few, including Torg, didn't respond. Mala leaned over the rail of the wagon and slapped the Death-Knower's face even harder than he had after his encounter with the dragon.

"Did you not hear our king? Respond to him!"

From above, Invictus spoke again. A hidden magic amplified his voice so that it was clearly audible throughout the valley.

"General Mala, Torg doesn't know our customs. Give him some leeway."

The Chain Man stepped aside.

"As you command, my king."

"Yes," Invictus said. "As I command."

"*YES!*" the crowd chanted.

"Now, where was I? Oh ... as I was saying, I have some things to tell all of you. Can you hear me?"

"*YES!*"

Sōbhana unexpectedly shouted along with the obedient crowd. It felt like the word had been torn from her throat, bringing tears to her eyes. Torg remained silent. Mala continued to glare at the wizard but didn't strike him again.

"As you can see, Torg is our prisoner."

"*YES!*"

This time Sōbhana resisted the sorcerer's will.

"He has been brought before me to stand trial."

"*YES!*"

"I will interrogate him now."

"*YES! ... YES!!!*"

"Torg, you have conspired with others to corrupt the free peoples of Triken. I accuse you of treason. What is your plea?"

When Torg responded, it surprised Sōbhana that his voice could also be heard throughout the valley.

"May I tell *you* some things?" the wizard said.

"*YES!*" the crowd shouted.

Mala lunged at Torg with murder in his eyes. But the sorcerer waved his hand, just slightly, and the Chain Man froze.

The Death-Knower's belligerence appeared to amuse Invictus. "Of course, Torg. As my subjects will readily attest, I am fair and just. Say whatever is on your mind."

Torg spoke slowly. "I gave my word to Mala that I would allow him to bring me here to you. As of now, I have honored my vow. And I can sense in my heart that the Noble Ones are safe, which means Mala has honored his."

"Go on," Invictus said. "This is fascinating."

"Henceforth, I consider myself free of any bonds. I will now make every effort to escape. And there's more. I tell you—and all who are present here—that I despise you and your servants. This means, I suppose, that I plead guilty to your charges."

Bhayatupa, still poised on the roof of Uccheda, lifted his head and chortled. It was an eerie sound, deep and rumbling. Mala shook with rage. The Kojin leaped up and down, pounding her many fists. The druids resumed their peculiar rhythmic humming, while in the background the crowd chanted, "*YES! YES! YES!*"

Regardless, the young sorcerer remained unperturbed. He stepped off the balcony, descended slowly to the ground—his golden robes spreading like wings—and landed gently as a fallen leaf. With a quick little hop, he pounced onto the wagon bed and stared into Torg's eyes, shocking the massive gathering into silence.

Sōbhana slithered within striking distance, but she was terrified. If Invictus attacked her beloved, would she have the courage to defend him?

"Ah, such entertainment," the sorcerer said. "You enthrall me, Death-Knower. You're so ... *interesting*. And nowadays, I find so few things interesting. Being a god can be boring. There aren't enough challenges. Everyone does exactly what I say. Do you understand my predicament?"

"I understand that you're a spoiled child," Torg said. "A wicked child, as well, blind to your failings. I can redeem you if you'll allow me into your heart. You won't regret it. But you must somehow find the wisdom to listen."

Somewhere in the clouds, Bhayatupa laughed again. The crowd seemed to stir.

Invictus' composure finally diminished.

"Don't test me too severely. I find you amusing but not so much that you're beyond punishment. I can see you do not fear for yourself, but what of your precious others? Do you truly believe the Noble Ones are safe? Perhaps I could destroy them all with only a thought. Or even worse, I could infect them with an evil that would force them to perform my bidding."

"Not even you are that powerful," Torg said. But Sōbhana heard doubt in his voice.

Mala stood next to the wagon. Though the monster's feet were on the ground, his eyes were level with the wizard and sorcerer's.

"*Pleeease*, my king. I beseech you. Allow me to rip him to pieces."

"Nay. I have prepared a place for him of *my* choosing," Invictus said. "There, he'll endure pain far greater than what you're suggesting. After a time, he'll *beg* to join us—if he manages to stay alive."

Then Invictus raised his arms and his voice again boomed throughout the valley. "You have heard for yourselves."

"*YES!*"

"Torg admits his guilt. I will now pronounce his sentence. We will take Torg to Asubha—and will imprison him there until he repents."

"*YES! ... YES!! ... YES!!!*"

"No," Sōbhana begged. "Please ... no."

They abandoned Torg in the wagon at the base of Uccheda for three days, giving him nothing to drink or eat. Apparently, Invictus wanted to weaken the wizard even further. Twice the skies darkened and rained lightly. Sōbhana watched her beloved catch water on his tongue. Despite his dismal situation, the sprinkles appeared to entrance him as if the scattered drops were things of wondrous beauty. He even smiled a few times.

After Invictus disappeared within the tower, the massive surge of onlookers wandered off and the soldiers returned to their duties, leaving her with fewer places to blend in. Sōbhana didn't dare approach too closely. Even after the others departed, at least fifty Golden Soldiers continued to guard the wagon, and they seemed to know each other well. If she attempted to infiltrate them, they would quickly expose her as an intruder.

Mala, the Kojin, and the druids came often to check on their prisoner. Though Torg was helpless within the magical restraints, they never left him entirely alone. Sōbhana doubted Invictus felt threatened so near his tower, but the king of the Tugars was obviously important to him. You can put a prized jewel in an impregnable chamber and still feel compelled to stand outside and watch the door.

Sōbhana would have sacrificed her own flesh just to speak with her king for a little while. But even if she'd found a way, she remained wary of Torg's vow to kill any Tugar who followed him. She heard him say to Invictus that his pledge was fulfilled. Did that free her too? Could she help him now? Probably, but she wasn't certain.

During the long journey from Dibbu-Loka to Avici, Sōbhana hadn't suffered as much as Torg, but it had been hard on her too. She was hungry, thirsty, and weak. The Asēkha crouched in a damp culvert and shivered in the autumn cold. The stolen armor lay discarded at her side. She could bear it against her skin no longer. Sometime during the third morning, she succumbed to exhaustion.

After an indeterminable stretch of time, Sōbhana jerked awake. As if under a magical spell, she had slept until almost noon. The day had grown unseasonably warm for Avici's northern clime. The sky was cloudless, the air crisp and clear. She crawled to the edge of the culvert and gasped. Torg and the wagon were gone, but swarms of citizens and soldiers were pouring back into the valley. Though it disgusted her, she hurriedly put the golden armor back on and entered the thickening crowd.

Sōbhana searched in all directions, but Torg was nowhere in sight. Tears welled in her eyes, but she fought them back. She was through with self-pity. Whoever had taken her beloved while she slept would pay. She didn't care about her own life. She had failed her king and deserved to die. How could she have slept so deeply? It was like her proximity to the sorcerer had drugged her.

The throng began to chant. "Sampati ... Sampati ... *Sampati!*"

Sōbhana gazed upward. Bhayatupa circled high above the rooftop of Uccheda, a splotch of crimson in the blue sky. But it was not the dragon that occupied the crowd's attention this time. A shimmering black speck appeared in the northern sky, growing larger as it approached. Sōbhana estimated that it was no match for Bhayatupa in sheer size, but it was huge, nonetheless. A Sampati, which meant *crossbreed* in the ancient tongue, flew toward Uccheda, its tremendous wings pumping through the air. Apparently, Torg's transportation to the prison on faraway Mount Asubha was about to arrive.

From where she stood, Sōbhana couldn't see who or what waited on the pinnacle of Uccheda. On this day, there again were no clouds to block her view, but the angle was too severe. Still, she could sense that Torg was on the rooftop. And if he were there, Mala and Invictus would also be present.

Madness overcame Sōbhana. She frantically removed the armor and stood alone in her black outfit among the thousands who wore either gold or white. She held her *uttara* in her right hand and her dagger in her left and entered *frenzy*. Soldiers and citizens collapsed, first just a few and then by the dozens. Wherever she went, there was shouting and confusion. Blood splattered. Heads fell. She murdered all within reach. As the Sampati landed on Uccheda's rooftop, Sōbhana wreaked havoc below. Killing, killing, killing.

As an Asēkha, she could perform feats of strength and prowess superior to all but a few. Not even the magnificent armor worn by the Golden Soldiers could withstand her. Sōbhana cut off a soldier's leg, slicing through his cuisse like it was paper. She spun in a full circle, simultaneously severing the head of a civilian woman with her sword and slashing the jugular of a man with her dagger. The woman's head flipped round and round in the air and tumbled into the arms of a boy, who screamed wildly and tossed it aside.

Although most of the crowd still focused on the approach of the crossbred condor, a few took notice of Sōbhana's mayhem. A dozen druids rushed toward her, humming in their peculiar fashion. She dove into them, slicing and thrusting. Though they were almost twice her size, they were no match. She had trained for fifty years with a Vasi master and was one of the deadliest of her kind. The druids fell in a torrent of green blood. Hacked in half. Beheaded. Stabbed through their foul hearts.

She was, after all, Asēkha-Sōbhana.

One of the most dangerous warriors in the world.

She couldn't kill everyone in the valley.

But she would die trying.

The flat rooftop of Uccheda had no protective wall or other adornments and was the only sizable portion of the tower's exterior not coated in gold. Invictus didn't want the roof to be slippery.

In anticipation of the Sampati's arrival, the rooftop was abuzz with activity. Ten Golden Soldiers faced ten others about fifty cubits apart, holding thick ropes between them. When the huge beast landed, its sharp claws scratched along the surface, tearing up chunks of mortar. The Sampati slid forward, out of control.

"Now!" Mala commanded.

The soldiers heaved on the ropes, which grew taut just as the Sampati rammed into them. The thick strands stretched but didn't break. The hybrid bird slammed to a halt.

A pair of soldiers raced over and attached chains to the beast's legs. A thin but muscular pilot leaped off the condor's neck, strode to Mala, and bowed nimbly before him.

"The Sampati and I are at your service."

The condor, crossbred with a dragon to increase its size and strength, was one of eleven of its kind. Only a few of those remained in captivity. The others had escaped and now flew freely above the peak of Mount Asubha, feeding on prisoners—and prison guards.

The Sampati had a black torso with white splotches at the tips of its wings, which measured forty cubits when extended. Most of its body was covered with feathers, but its head, neck, and feet were laden with crimson dragon scales. A sturdy platform was attached to its back by straps that clung to its torso.

The enormous bird was high strung, struggling against the chains as it flapped its wings. Invictus knew it wasn't wise to keep the creature waiting too long. Its hooked beak could tear and rend. Passengers and supplies—with a combined weight of as much as a ton—were loaded quickly.

"We'll need the Sampati, but not you," Mala said to the pilot. "I'll fly the beast to Asubha myself. This one will carry precious cargo."

The Chain Man nodded toward Torg, who lay on the rooftop, still restrained and under heavy guard.

"As you command," the pilot said before stepping aside.

Mala ordered the guards to secure Torg to the platform, but before they finished, a soldier hustled over and dropped to his knees in front of the Chain Man.

"Pardon my rudeness, Lord Mala. But something is happening in the valley below that might interest you and King Invictus."

Then the soldier turned toward Invictus. "There's an odd commotion, my liege."

With a curious expression, Invictus walked to the edge and looked down at the valley far below, which was bursting with soldiers and citizens. From the rooftop, they looked like a swarm of bugs. Near the base of the tower, some of them had surrounded a single tiny figure.

Mala joined him at the edge of the precipice. "What *is* going on down there?"

Invictus focused his eyes, which upon command could become supernaturally keen. "There's a woman, dressed in black. She fights anyone who comes near. Her swordplay is impressive."

Mala turned to Torg. "An Asēkha! You've broken your promise!"

"It doesn't matter," Invictus said. "What can she do? Defeat us by herself? If she kills a few, who cares? But look at her, Mala. See how she fights. How *interesting* …"

Mala's ghastly face reddened even further. He started toward the wizard, but Invictus stopped him with another wave of his hand.

"Do not cause the Death-Knower further discomfort," Invictus said. "When he arrives at Asubha, I want him to have a little strength left. There'll be no fun in this if he perishes before he's imprisoned."

"Arrrgggh!" was all Mala could manage. He climbed onto the Sampati's back at the base of its neck. Soldiers lifted Torg and strapped him onto the platform, then they released the chains from the creature's legs.

With one massive sweep of its wings, the Sampati was airborne. Mala tugged at its bridle and forced it northward, toward Asubha.

"Fly, you miserable beast … *fly!*"

Mala could still hear Invictus' laughter long after he left the tower.

Several times in his long life, Torg had ridden high over mountaintops on the backs of mountain eagles. Each time he adored it.

Once, while grappling with a pack of dracools, he had been lifted a hundred cubits into the air and then dropped. He didn't much like that.

Riding on the back of the Sampati, trussed in golden ropes and strapped to a wooden platform, resembled the latter. It was miserable.

Torg had been trapped within Invictus' magical restraining device for more than forty days. Even so, he had remained sanitary. Each time he urinated or defecated, he disintegrated his wastes with blue flames.

Until Invictus had greeted him, Torg had honored his word and not resisted his restraints. But once he fulfilled his vow, he fought with all his might to break free. To his despair, he failed. Although the leather and fabric binding him were inconsequential, the golden ropes that encased him from neck to feet were irresistibly strong. Every time Torg twisted or heaved, the ropes grew yellow-hot, squeezing with increased vehemence as if they were living beings directed by a devious mind. The more he struggled, the more helpless he became.

Torg went still. When he did, the ropes loosened their grip enough to allow him to breathe. Escape was impossible. It was all too clear that Invictus was the greater. He lay in the wagon, desperate and depressed. To make matters worse, he couldn't stop from obsessing over his brief encounter with the woman on the balcony. His attraction to her had been immense. Somehow, he knew her—and yet did not. Would he ever see her again? Doubt tore his heart apart.

Then there was the matter of the female warrior that Mala and Invictus had witnessed fighting so fiercely at the base of the tower. Torg guessed it was Sōbhana. Only she would have dared such a thing against his direct order. And now it was probable she was dead.

The Sampati soared at extraordinary heights, higher even than a mountain eagle could fly. Only Bhayatupa could have managed greater altitudes. The cold, thin air seared Torg's lungs; he felt like he was suffocating. But Mala was ecstatic; he chortled, sang, and waved his arms. The hybrid condor struggled against the cumbersome weight on its neck, swaying this way and that in response to the Chain Man's relentless squirming.

"What say you, little sparrow?" Mala yelled at Torg against the roaring sound of the wind. "Do you like the view? Are you comfortable? Is there anything I can get you?"

Then the monster burst into ribald laughter, continuing to bounce on the Sampati's neck. The beast squawked in protest, especially when the chain touched its scales.

"Yes, there *is* something you can get me," Torg said. "Some wax to plug my ears."

Mala found this to be hysterical. His long white mane fluttered in the wind. Huge gobs of spittle flew from his mouth. Droplets showered Torg's face.

"Ahh, Torgon! You have a sense of humor, after all—and you'll need every bit of it. You're going to love the little hideaway Invictus has prepared. It's so *cozy.*"

Mala laughed even harder, and then he succumbed to a spasm of coughing. Grotesque balls of sputum spiraled from his mouth. Torg had already grown to hate the monster, but now he despised him.

"Mala, when you finish your babbling, there's something I wish to tell you," Torg shouted through gritted teeth.

"Yes, dear?"

"I no longer have any desire to rescue you from your torment. I'm going to see to it that you die in a ball of fire."

Mala laughed so hard he almost fell off his perch.

Torg tried to ignore him. The Death-Knower was a creature of the desert. Heat was his natural clime. In temperatures exceeding 130 degrees, he could walk barefoot on burning sands without discomfort. However, he could also endure cold. He had journeyed to Triken's northernmost reaches and lived to tell the tale. But the chill he felt as the Sampati approached the peak of Asubha was like no other. Though winter was still several weeks away, the temperature at this high height was well below freezing, and wet winds intensified the discomfort.

As Torg and Mala neared the prison on top of the mountain, another hybrid condor flew into view. Several ordinary condors also flocked around Mala's mount, sweeping in and snapping at the bridled Sampati. Mala found the intruders annoying, waving his massive hands as if shooing mosquitoes.

"Get back, you filthy buzzards! If you come any nearer, I'll pluck the feathers out of you and eat you raw."

As Mount Asubha came into view, the attackers dispersed. From then on, the Sampati's flight was undisturbed. The prison appeared beneath them, its courtyard several times longer and wider than the rooftop of Uccheda, giving the Sampati more room to land. But Mala was not as good of a pilot as he imagined himself to be, and he forced the beast in too sharply, causing it to smack onto the icy stone and slide precariously before crashing into a lumpy wall. The Chain Man went head over heels. When he came to a stop, he leaped up, cursing and complaining.

"Where's the warden? The little weasel better show up fast!"

One guard, braver than the rest, ran over to face Mala, though even he kept his distance.

"The warden isn't here, Lord Mala," the guard shouted into the wind. "He disappeared several days ago. He said that he needed to feed so that he would be strong when the prisoner arrived."

"Well, he *has* arrived, as you can see," Mala said. "Never mind, never mind. The warden always leaves the important matters to me. Come ... and bring others with you. I want the wizard off the beast before it tries to fly away."

But the Sampati would never fly again. It had broken its massive neck in the crash. Torg sensed the creature's final heartbeat and wished it well in its next existence.

"Remove the wizard from the platform. Bring him to the pit. HURRY!"

The guards started forward but then halted. Most began to retreat, frightened by the look in Torg's eyes. The wizard was determined to make one final attempt to break free. Death Energy sprang from every pore, his body glowing like a blue sun fallen from the sky. The leather and fabric that encased him disintegrated, along with what remained of his black jacket and trousers. Even the golden ropes started to stretch, and for a moment it appeared they might burst asunder.

Mala leaped at Torg and grasped the ropes in his powerful hands, reinforcing their strength. If it had been only Mala's magic against Torg's, the wizard might have prevailed even in his weakened state. But the combined sorcery that coursed through Mala's chains and Invictus' golden ropes was invincible.

Torg's breath was squeezed from his lungs. He felt like a rodent in the murderous grip of a constrictor.

He was lost.

All was lost.

When they removed the magical restraints and lowered him using ordinary ropes to the bottom of the pit, Torg lay as limp as a dead man, barely aware.

A long time later, he woke to a horror far deadlier than any that had come before.

His nightmare in the pit had begun.

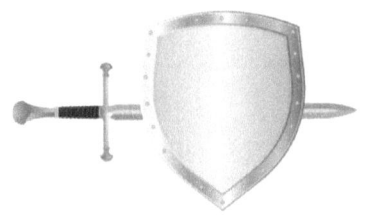

DRAGON'S RUSE

Sōbhana's body was slick with sweat. Her breath tore from her lungs in desperate heaves and her heart was about to burst. More than a hundred of the enemy lay dead, including six druids, several wolves, a huge cave troll, and a disgusting creature that looked like a spider with a human head. Sōbhana had lost the dagger Torg had returned to her at Dibbu-Loka, but she still held her *uttara* along with a dented shield she had plucked from the lifeless arm of a Golden Soldier. Now, tens of thousands surrounded her. She had no chance. She would continue to fight until they slew her. What else could she do?

As the enemy closed around her, a colossal shadow descended from the sky. Something plucked Sōbhana from the ground and lifted her high into the air. The force of the blow knocked her sword and the shield from her grasp. Her beloved *uttara* was lost to her, but she was too shocked to care.

Bhayatupa grasped her in the talons of one of his front feet and lifted her into the clouds as easily as a crow might lift a cricket.

"Quickly, do as I say!" the great dragon growled. "Remove your clothing and drape it on this."

In his other front foot, Bhayatupa held the naked corpse of a young woman similar in size to Sōbhana.

Though horrified, her warrior instincts took over and she managed to tear off her outfit and wrap it haphazardly around the dead woman.

"That's good enough," the dragon said, before deftly slipping Sōbhana's now naked body beneath a massive scale on his crimson breast. All the while, his back was to Uccheda. The dragon flew up into the clouds and momentarily disappeared. When he emerged, he tossed a black bundle into the air and swallowed it whole.

With eyes that had been open to the ways of the world for millennia, Bhayatupa watched Invictus enter a doorway at the top of the tower and disappear. The dragon believed the sorcerer had fallen for his trick. And why not? He had not yet done anything to elicit distrust.

Bhayatupa had lived for 80,000 years, with the specter of his own demise haunting every waking moment. By mortal standards, he would still live an extraordinary span of time—another twenty millennia, at least. But to Bhayatupa, the concept of dying—at any time—was unacceptable. The fear of it consumed him. And though the great dragon wielded formidable magic, death remained an enemy beyond him.

This was the true reason Bhayatupa tolerated Invictus: The sorcerer provided him with the most direct access to the Death-Knower. And not just any Death-Knower. Hundreds had existed during Bhayatupa's tenure, but none like this one. Torg differed from all the rest. Perhaps, the wizard could teach the dragon how to achieve immortality.

Twelve years before he rescued Sōbhana at the base of Uccheda, Bhayatupa had been deep in the throes of dragon-sleep in one of his many hiding places in the remote heights of Mahaggata. Somehow, Invictus had found him in the misty cave. The sorcerer crouched next to Bhayatupa's pointed ear and spoke to him, though it had taken several days for the dragon to fully awaken. But even before Bhayatupa was able to open his eyes, he was aware enough to listen. The extent of Invictus' knowledge stunned him. It was as if the sorcerer could read his mind and regurgitate his thoughts.

Invictus was born of demon blood and knew many things only demons knew. When the sorcerer told Bhayatupa that the great demon Vedana was his grandmother, the pieces of the puzzle came together.

Invictus left the cave on Bhayatupa's back, bragging endlessly about the might of his growing kingdom. As the pair flew over Avici and Kilesa, the dragon saw the sorcerer's massive army firsthand. When they visited the prison on Mount Asubha, Invictus stood proudly next to the pit, acting like a boy unveiling a dark secret. Bhayatupa squeezed his titanic body into the courtyard and managed to bend down his long neck and peer into the hole, which was barely wider than one of his eyes. The dragon jerked upward in pain and disgust, causing Invictus to laugh.

"Be thankful you're too large to fit inside," the sorcerer said. "Not even the demons know the dark magic I used to summon the beings that inhabit the walls of the pit. They are from a place beyond all awareness—save mine."

And now, the Death-Knower was imprisoned in the pit. The best chance at immortality Bhayatupa had ever encountered was in dreadful peril. Unbeknown to Invictus, Bhayatupa had briefly flown alongside Mala and the Sampati just out of eyesight and had considered killing the foul-mouthed *Adho Satta* who clung to the Sampati's neck and then taking Torg to some distant place. He knew, though, that kidnapping the Death-Knower would enrage Invictus and invite open warfare. The dragon wasn't prepared for that. There had been ages in Triken's long history when Bhayatupa had commanded magnificent armies. But now he was alone except for a handful of Mogol slaves. He had to move carefully and choose the perfect moment, so he returned to Avici just in time to rescue the female Asēkha.

Perhaps this warrior could free Torg. It was worth a try—and appeared to be his last chance.

Having such limited options annoyed Bhayatupa, who didn't like being annoyed. If he achieved immortality, he would take revenge on all living beings, including Invictus.

And if immortality were unachievable? Then he would at least force the Death-Knower to teach him how to overcome *Tanhiiyati,* the insatiable craving for eternal existence. If not cured of it soon, he would go mad.

If he hadn't already.

Sōbhana felt drowsy. One of Bhayatupa's crimson scales held her tight against the interior flesh of his breast. The pounding of his massive heart—which she imagined was larger than her entire body—lulled her toward sleep. A fleece as warm and dry as a luxurious blanket grew on the skin beneath the scale.

Her warrior curiosity overcame her weariness, and she squirmed and wriggled until her head poked out from beneath the scale. Thick clouds obscured her vision. Everywhere she looked, the air was white.

Bhayatupa was far larger and more powerful than a Sampati, and his enormous wings stroked steadily through the air. The dragon's neck, which Sōbhana guessed was more than fifty cubits long, stretched straight forward, while his tail, which was even longer, extended straight behind his torso. Despite weighing more than several desert elephants, the great dragon flew faster than a falcon.

Sōbhana realized that Bhayatupa no longer frightened her. Ironically, the closer she got to the dragon, the less she feared him. Was it because she no longer cared if she lived or died? Probably.

There were occasional breaks in the clouds when she could see land far below. To the southeast, Sōbhana recognized Ti-ratana, the largest lake in the known world. To the west was the Gap of Gamana, where Arupa-Loka and its demon inhabitants lay hidden. She'd flown more than once on the backs of eagles, so seeing the land from so high above was not unique to her experience, but it still fascinated her.

The dragon's intentions puzzled Sōbhana. Obviously, he had ingested the corpse that wore her black outfit to fool those who watched from below. But why? And now he flew northwestward toward the mountains. Was he taking her to a secret place to devour her at his leisure?

"Your mind is more closed than most, but I comprehend some of what you're thinking," Bhayatupa said in his indomitable baritone. "You wonder why you're not already dead. Is that not so?"

"I often wonder that," she shouted into the rushing wind.

Bhayatupa laughed. The sound was disconcerting but no longer as eerie as it had first seemed to her.

"You Asēkhas consider yourselves great. But compared to me, you are *Adho Satta*. Do you doubt it?"

This offended Sōbhana. Rising irritation replaced her original fear. "What you consider low is not what I consider low. Compared to you, we're physically puny, that's true. But Asēkhas are loyal and honorable, attributes that are well beyond your level of arrogance."

Bhayatupa sneered. Smoke puffed from his nostrils. Traces of it blew against her face, causing her to sneeze. "Loyalty and honor ... only words. Time is the true master. All else pales before it, but you pale far more than I. Your lifespan is but a single breath compared to mine."

"I've confessed my puniness. What more do you want? Does it please you to denigrate your victims before you eat them? Tell me where you're taking me—and why."

"Such insolence! Your bravery is impressive for one so tiny."

"Tiny? Yes. But not helpless. Even when unarmed, an Asēkha doesn't lack weapons. I'm strong enough to drive my fist through the flesh of your breast and punch a hole in your heart. Do *you* doubt it?"

In reaction to Sōbhana's sudden threat, the dragon panicked, realizing he'd unknowingly left himself vulnerable. He stopped in midair and reared like a horse, his wings beating frenetically. He reached for her with massive talons, hoping to pluck her from his breast before she could attack.

"Whoa!" she said. "Relax ... *relax*!" And then *she* laughed. "If I had wanted to destroy you, I'd have done so without warning you first." And then she sighed. "There's only one desire left to me, dragon. I wish, somehow, to rescue my king."

Bhayatupa warily resumed his flight, but Sōbhana sensed a change in his demeanor. Now there was at least a smidgeon of respect. "I have underestimated you," he admitted. "Mogols, witches, and ghouls have not your substance. That is a good thing. I'm pleased because I have a task for you that will benefit both of us if you're able to succeed."

Bhayatupa landed at the opening of a cave near the peak of a bony mountain. He removed the warrior from beneath his scale and set her down on the stone. A nasty wind blew, causing Sōbhana to shiver in her nakedness.

"Tell me, then, what this task is," she said, staring up at the humongous creature.

"Your desire is my desire. I want to help you rescue the Death-Knower."

Then without saying more, he sprang into the air and flew eastward, faster than the wind.

Sōbhana watched the dragon diminish to a crimson speck. Though exhausted and vulnerable, she had no choice but to enter the cave, which obviously had been Bhayatupa's intent.

The mouth of the cave was five times her height and at least that wide. Just a few strides within its opening, the temperature warmed to above freezing. She followed a long passageway that descended into the bowels of the mountain. Cold water dripped from the ceiling onto her bare back and buttocks. It was unpleasant, to say the least. The stone beneath her feet was smooth and slippery. She pressed her hand against the wall of the tunnel, which was oily and wet as if slick with sweat.

The passageway narrowed slightly, growing so dark she began to stumble. But as she walked farther, the darkness lost its intensity. Eventually, she saw a glowing light in the distance.

The tunnel emptied into a cavern large enough to swallow the entire temple of Bakheng. Hundreds of torches lighted the huge hollow. Sōbhana gasped and pressed her arms against her bosom. Piles of treasure—magnificent to behold—were neatly arranged on the expansive stone floor. Near where she stood was a miniature mountain of gold and silver coins. Another mound contained daggers, swords, and scabbards adorned with jewels. Farther back were belts, buckles, and sandals, all exquisitely designed. Still farther were rings, necklaces, and bracelets. There were five tall trees constructed entirely of black pearls, and ten silver coffins encrusted with fist-sized diamonds. She saw suits of armor made of solid gold, along with axes and clubs, helmets and shields, hauberks and gauntlets. There were plates and goblets, silks and tapestries, crowns and thrones. A vast sea of treasure shimmered in the torchlight. Someone—or something—had kept it dusted and polished.

Walkways wound between the arrangements, and Sōbhana wandered along them, still naked, her jaw slack. She was a warrior, not a princess obsessed with baubles, but it allured even her. The entire room sparkled.

She found clothing in the back of the cavern. Amid a stack of finery, she chose a pair of tight-fitting silk pants and a matching long-sleeved shirt. Both were black, which was to her liking. She picked up a pair of boots made of black leather with wool insoles—and then, a coat of dark fur. The coat was too extravagant for her tastes, but she took it for the warmth it provided.

Off to the side, something caught her eye. A gold crown laden with diamonds, rubies, and pearls seemed to beckon to her. She placed it on her head. It fit perfectly.

She chuckled. If the dragon took her to rescue Torg, she would look good doing it.

There was a sudden movement at the edge of her peripheral vision. She spun, crouched defensively, and then somersaulted forward, grasping a sword from a pile of weapons. Its straight, double-edged blade was longer and heavier than she preferred, but it would do. The crown somehow stayed on her head.

Standing at the entrance to the cavern were a dozen muscular men, their faces colorfully painted. They held long wooden spears and wore deerskin ponchos and furry moccasins. Despite the cold, their hairy arms and legs were bare.

Sōbhana recognized them as Mogols, the brutal enemies of Nissaya who roamed the Mahaggata Mountains. Tugars despised them, hunting them down whenever they could. Though they were formidable warriors, they were no match for an Asēkha. Sōbhana was already planning her mode of attack. Weapons lay all around her, and she knew how to use each one.

But the Mogols didn't strike. Instead, they lowered their spears and knelt before her. A lone woman hurried forward, bearing a tray of dried meat, roasted nuts, and blue grapes. The woman laid it at Sōbhana's feet, then respectfully backed away.

The Mogols spoke a language unlike any Sōbhana could recognize. She tended to avoid such learning—and often had been chastised for this by her Vasi master. Torg could have spoken fluently with them, but her beloved could do many things she could not.

Sōbhana felt something warm and wet in the corners of her mouth and realized it was her own saliva. She'd eaten little for several days, and the fare placed before her was enticing. She bent down—eyes still trained on the Mogols—and grabbed a chunk of meat, swallowing it whole. She stuffed nuts and grapes into her mouth, chewed once or twice, and devoured them too. She wasn't concerned about being poisoned. Tugars were mostly immune to such things. In a rush, Sōbhana ate everything on the tray.

The Mogols remained bowed, except for the woman, who approached the Asēkha and removed the now-empty serving dish.

Sōbhana still held the sword. She rose to her full height and glared at the gathering. "Do any of you speak the common tongue?"

There was a silent pause.

But then, a sinister voice echoed from far back in the tunnel.

"I do. (*I do ... I do ... I do.*)"

The speaker came forward.

It was no Mogol. It was far worse.

A female demon—more dangerous than the most powerful Mogol—entered the torchlight. "How beautiful you are," she said to Sōbhana. "Bhayatupa has chosen a worthy bride."

"What?" was all Sōbhana could manage to say.

The demon sashayed forward and stopped just a few strides away. She had chosen to appear as a mature woman who was not particularly well-preserved. The demon laughed at Sōbhana's bewilderment.

"I speak in jest. Lord Bhayatupa asked me to keep you safe until he returned. I told the Mogols you were their god's bride-to-be. Your choice of that crown completed the effect. His last wife wore the same one 10,000 years ago."

"Wife?" Sōbhana said.

"Child, surely you know that dragons prefer human wives. It's all symbolic, of course. They can't have *sex* with them. *That* would be a little difficult."

Small puffs of gray smoke sprang from the demon's ears as if her insides were burning.

"Come no closer," Sōbhana said, but her arms trembled so much she could barely retain her grip on the heavy sword. "I will slay you! I swear it."

The demon laughed so hard she almost fell.

"Why do you torment me?" Sōbhana said.

"You're so ... innocent. So ... precious. My dear, how can you slay someone who does not live? Do you not know me? Ahh, I see you do not—at least, not fully. Allow me, then, to introduce myself. I am Vedana, mother of all demons, and I am ancient beyond all others. Even Bhayatupa is young compared to me. Your master—the *Desert Peasant*—knows who I am. But alas, he's not here."

At that, Sōbhana's countenance changed. She lowered the sword until its tip pricked the stone at her feet. "Does he live?" she whispered.

Vedana seemed to consider this—and then her eyes widened. "You're in love with him!"

"We all love him," Sōbhana responded too quickly.

"I don't, though he'll still be of use to me. But that isn't what I meant. You *love* him. Ha! Don't you know what would happen to you if he fucked you?"

"Shut your disgusting mouth," Sōbhana said, suddenly enraged. She hoisted the sword above her head. "I will smite you where you stand."

Through all this, the Mogols remained bowed. But their chins were raised, and they watched attentively. Vedana took one step back and waved her arms overhead. There was an explosion, followed by a gout of smoke. When Sōbhana could see clearly, the demon was gone.

Sōbhana scrambled past the Mogols into the passageway. None attempted to thwart her. She left the cave and entered the bitter cold that encased the mountaintop. Now that she was clothed, it didn't affect her so drastically. Vedana was nowhere to be seen. The demon, for reasons of her own, had vanished.

Sōbhana calmed herself by investigating her surroundings. There was a wide stone balcony outside the cave's mouth that provided plenty of room to move about. But beyond the platform, the mountain fell steeply in all directions, its sheer walls coated with an ultra-slippery glaze of ice. It would be near suicide to attempt a descent. The cave was a prison as secure as Asubha. Even the Mogols must have been transported here by the dragon.

Sōbhana turned back toward the cave. The Mogols were there, still bowing. The servant woman gestured to her, enticing her to come out of the icy wind. Sōbhana lowered her head and sighed. She was at Bhayatupa's mercy.

She walked to the edge of the precipice and shouted into the abyss. Her voice echoed for leagues.

"Damn you, dragon! Why did you strand me here? Time is precious. He might already be dead."

The wind rose in response. Within its roar she heard the demon's laughter. Vedana was out there somewhere. But now she wouldn't show herself. Was the demon's bravado overstated? She didn't seem to fear Sōbhana, but did she fear the sword she now wielded?

Sōbhana looked more closely at the weapon. Its double-edged blade gleamed like freshly polished silver, and its hilt was wrapped with a material that resembled blackened leather secured with metal cords. Despite its simplicity, she recognized it as a special weapon.

Sōbhana returned to the cavern and started to make a bed out of a pile of clothing. The servant woman approached her, shook her head, and took Sōbhana's hand, guiding her even deeper into the cave. They arrived at a room the size of an ordinary bedchamber. It was lit by a single torch. A plump mattress on the floor, two low tables, and a simple chair filled the room. Food, wine, wooden utensils, and an ewer of cool water had been placed on one table. On the other lay a basin of steaming water, a cake of soap made from tree bark and oils, a comb carved from balsa, and several wool towels. Before leaving the chamber, the servant drew a heavy curtain across the opening.

Sōbhana was blissfully alone.

When had she last bathed? Other than an occasional dip in the icy waters of the Ogha River, it had been almost two months. Sōbhana's hair was greasy and knotted, and she shuddered to think what her underarms and private parts must smell like. She laid the sword on the mattress, removed her clothes and—despite the cold—took a long time cleaning herself. Then she laboriously combed the knots out of her black hair, which had grown an inch past her shoulders.

Afterward, she spread some nutty-tasting butter onto a slice of crusty bread and ate it along with dried meats and nuts. She drank wine, which was potent and flavorful. This made her wonder how the Mogols had gotten these provisions up to the mountaintop, but drowsiness muddled her thoughts. Her life had become filled with too many questions and too few answers. She lay on the mattress with the sword at her side. Before she slept, she tried to make sense of Vedana's foul words: "Don't you know, child, what would happen ...?"

She thought she knew: It would be paradise. What did the demon perceive that she did not? Vedana had hinted at something. Sōbhana didn't believe it was simply a trick.

Her mind emptied of thought. Overcome by exhaustion, she slept deeply. The sword lay beside her like a cold lover.

Sōbhana spent more than a week in the cave, rarely leaving the small chamber that had become her bedroom. She ate, slept—and waited. Several times a day, the Mogols served her food and wine, and they also provided clean water and towels whenever needed.

On the ninth night of her captivity, she had a wonderful dream. Torg was kissing her on the mouth. How delicately he caressed her lips. How deliciously he entwined his sweet tongue with hers.

In her dream, he was upon her naked body, breathing on her neck, licking her breasts, nibbling her belly. And then his beautiful face pressed against her pubic hair and his tongue went between her legs.

It was glorious.

And all too real.

When she opened her eyes, she recoiled. She was indeed naked, but Vedana was the one between her legs, not her beloved. The demon's tongue was as long as a snake and as black as coal.

Sōbhana kicked in disgust. Vedana tumbled to the floor. Unscathed, the demon bounced up and laughed wickedly.

"Why did you stop me? You were enjoying it so much."

Sōbhana reached for her sword, but it was gone. The demon must have put some kind of spell on her. Otherwise, the weapon could not have been removed from her side.

"You want to fight, my beauty?" Vedana growled. "I want that, too. It makes it so much sweeter."

The demon's glowing flesh was translucent. Sōbhana could see her bones—and her bulbous heart. The warrior felt faint. Vedana was too strong, wielding magic that stole the fire from her limbs, and she rushed toward Sōbhana, intending to defile her.

When all seemed lost, Bhayatupa came to her rescue. A torrential fire blew through the cave, consuming the curtain of her small chamber. The demon withdrew, snarling in frustration.

"You believe you've escaped, that you're safe," she said to Sōbhana. "But I have foreseen your future. You would have much preferred *me* to the suffering that awaits you."

Bhayatupa's deep voice boomed down the passageway. "Vedana! If you've harmed her ..."

The demon stepped back. This time, a circular black hole opened in the wall and Vedana leaped into it. As quickly as it appeared, the hole vanished.

Sōbhana stood naked in the chamber, wiping tears from her eyes. She fell to her knees. Then darkness claimed her and took her to the stronghold of nothingness.

Sōbhana inhaled deeply. A curious aroma entered her nostrils, a wondrous combination of honey, spices, and sweet smoke. Visions flowed into her mind, wave upon wave, endless. Civilizations rose and fell. Brave warriors lived and died. There was glory and shame. Courage and fear. Beginnings, middles, and endings.

When she opened her eyes, she lay at the mouth of the cave. Bhayatupa's head was only a short distance away, and a tendril of smoke oozed from his nostrils to hers. She sat up so fast her face bumped against the dragon's enormous snout. Bhayatupa backed away. "I see you've returned to the living," he said.

The memory of the demon's perverted act flooded Sōbhana's awareness. She spat and then stood, leaning shakily against the stone wall. "I don't understand what's happening."

"Your lack of wisdom doesn't surprise me. You are *Adho Satta*. There are forces at work beyond your comprehension. But Torg knows—and understands."

"What would Vedana have done to me?"

"Who knows? The demon's machinations are beyond my comprehension. But now that I've rescued you, Vedana's schemes are unimportant. As I said before, you and I have a common goal. That makes us allies."

"Why were you away so long? Torg might already be dead."

Bhayatupa's face—which was capable of very human-like expressions—appeared distressed. "I returned to Avici and flew in the skies," the dragon said in his sonorous voice. "I didn't want the sorcerer to become overly suspicious. But he called for me. And questioned me … I was severely tested." Bhayatupa's huge round eyes glazed over. He looked like a wizened king, troubled by the state of his realm. When he spoke again, his voice almost trembled. "Let us say that our situation has grown more urgent. I have underestimated Invictus. For the first time, I felt … *fear*."

Sōbhana saw an opportunity and seized it. "Then why not join our cause? Perhaps you and Torg can defeat Invictus together."

Quicker than an Asēkha, Bhayatupa grasped her in his front talons and rose on his hind legs to his full height. At that point, Sōbhana was higher than the pinnacle of the mountain.

Bhayatupa's eyes reverted from glazed to fiery. "Join your cause? And what *cause* might that be, *Adho Satta*? The cause of insects and worms? You do not comprehend to whom you speak. I am Bhayatupa— the *Mahaasupanna* (mightiest of all dragons)—and I am beyond you. You live only because I have need of your master's wisdom. But my patience has limits. Do not insult me like that again."

He cast her down onto the balcony, and she thudded on the stone.

Cowed by the dragon's outburst, the Mogols threw themselves onto their stomachs and pressed their faces against the cave floor. Sōbhana lay stunned, temporarily unable to move.

"Bring her the sword, and dress her," the dragon said to the servant woman. "Be quick!"

Bhayatupa turned back to Sōbhana. His anger seemed to fade as quickly as it had arisen, and his voice returned to relative normalcy. "If you're sincere in your desire to save your king, then I'm your only hope. Time grows short. You and I must fly to Mount Asubha—now!"

Bhayatupa flew at heights above the mountaintops. The air was so thin, Sōbhana found it difficult to breathe. At least she wasn't cold. The fragrant flesh beneath the dragon's scale kept her comfortable. She peeked her head out.

"Tell me all that you know of Asubha," Sōbhana shouted. "If I'm to succeed, I need to know what I'm up against."

"Indeed, it is time for me to tell you my plan. Your lord's life hangs in the balance."

"Speak, then! I grow weary of you, and I no longer fear you. If Torg were here now, he would order me to forsake this quest and drive the sword into your heart."

"You remain *Adho Satta*, but at least you are now high among the low."

"Thank you *so* much, O Exalted One. May you die soon, for all our sakes."

"How quaint ... and I was under the impression that you enjoyed my company. But enough prattle. You must listen carefully. I have time to say these words only once. Asubha is not far."

"Once is enough."

"It had better be. Now hush and allow me to finish. This is what you will be 'up against.' The prison is not heavily guarded—at least, you wouldn't consider it so—because it's inaccessible to almost anything that can't fly. Invictus doesn't fear attack, so there are only enough sentries to manage the prisoners—fewer than five score. You killed more than that beneath the tower of Uccheda."

"This sounds too easy," Sōbhana said.

"If only it were. But there's more. I believe Mala remains at the prison. That alone makes your task far more difficult. And the warden also presents problems. He is a Stone-Eater. Are you familiar with these creatures?"

"Of course. I'm not a complete fool."

"Then you know of their powers. The warden is not as great as Mala, but he would be a severe test for you. Invictus also keeps several trolls on hand to do the heavy lifting. And I've described only that which lies *within* the prison walls. There are also dangers in the skies. Wild Sampatis hunt from above—and there are dozens of ordinary condors. To me, they are annoying pests. But any of them could be deadly to you. Even if you avoid them, they might cause enough commotion to betray your position. Stealth and secrecy are your best allies."

"I've trained my entire life for this moment."

"As you say. I do not doubt that you're somewhat worthy."

"Why, Bhayatupa … that's the nicest thing you've ever said to me. There's hope for you yet."

"My hope lies trapped in the pit of Asubha. The last hope, perhaps, of my long life."

The dragon flew silently for a brief time before speaking again. "There is one last danger—and it's by far the worst. An ancient evil dwells near Asubha's peak. Her name is Dukkhatu, and she appears as a great horned spider, terrible to behold. Only Vedana and I have survived the passage of more days than she."

"I've never heard of Dukkhatu," Sōbhana said. "But I admit that my learning is not what it should be. I've always focused too much on fighting."

"It's probable that even your lord hasn't heard of Dukkhatu. In recent times, she has shied from the lower lands. Millennia ago, she hunted among the foothills of Mahaggata, feeding on the unwary. Hundreds of brave warriors tried to slay her—and failed. Her hide is tougher than iron and her fangs contain foul poisons. In her old age, she wearied of battle and retired to the highest peaks. Recently, much to her pleasure, she discovered Asubha. Food is her obsession, and the prison provides her with plenty of fresh meat. She waits and watches. You must avoid her."

Sōbhana shivered. "Is the sword I now wield capable of killing her?"

"Child, do you not know? This sword was here before Dukkhatu. Before Bhayatupa. Before Vedana. Before memory. It is called the Silver Sword, and though its name is bland, it is more valuable than any treasure on Triken. The blade contains no special magic, but it will hack or pierce anything it touches. No shield, hide, or demon flesh—not even a dragon's scale—can withstand a direct blow."

"And you left it lying in a pile like it was a trinket," Sōbhana said. "Are you saying it could destroy Invictus?"

"The best hiding places are often the least likely," Bhayatupa said. "As for Invictus, he has grown beyond the bounds of my awareness."

"Maybe one day I'll find out for myself when I put the sword to the sorcerer's throat."

"Perhaps. But in my heart, I do not believe so. That fate lies with someone else."

For a while longer, they didn't speak. Darkness consumed the sky, but there was light all about. The moon was huge and full, and the stars sparkled like white crystals on a black coverlet. The icy air on the warrior's face froze her tears.

"What will become of me?"

"I care naught," the dragon said. "I care only for myself. Have I not said so before?"

Bhayatupa then described Asubha to Sōbhana and told her that he would create a diversion that would distract attention away from her. Bhayatupa circled around and then approached the prison from below. With the grace of a hummingbird, the enormous dragon hovered at the base of the wall and gently placed Sōbhana on the roughly hewn stone. There were many lumps and cracks, making it possible for her to get a firm grip. Then the dragon swerved away.

The thick wall that partially enclosed the peak of the frozen mountain rose fifty cubits above its natural pinnacle. Within the wall, winding hallways led to windowless prison cells, which now contained several dozen Jivitans, Nissayans, and village folk from along the Ogha River judged to be more dangerous than the usual rabble. Several guardhouses were scattered inside a single large courtyard. At the center of the inner ward, the pit held vigilance like a dark eye with a lidless glare.

Without warning to those below, a condor fell from the sky and smote the floor near the pit, flopping about and squawking insanely. One of its wings was broken and blood gushed from its beak, the apparent loser of a fight with another condor, or maybe one of the wild Sampatis.

Before they reached the prison, Bhayatupa had told Sōbhana that he would have to go back to Avici for a brief time to avoid further suspicion. She was on her own until midnight of the following day when the dragon promised to return under cover of darkness and attempt to fly her and Torg to safety. The outcome of the quest rested in her hands. Sōbhana's entire being was consumed with a desire to rush to her beloved's rescue, but she had to remain patient.

Sōbhana had never been afraid of heights, but there was a first time for everything as her Vasi master liked to say. Though it was now deep night, the full moon and abundant starlight made it possible to see long distances. Asubha and its sister mountains glowed like luminaries. Sōbhana looked past her feet and trembled. She could see for several hundred fathoms, but the floor of the abyss was not visible.

She needed to find a place to hide. Too much was going on inside the prison for her to attempt anything this night—and daytime would be impossible. She heard the last shriek of the stricken condor—which Bhayatupa had disabled to distract the sentries on the wall walk—and then the cheering of the men inside the prison. She was further disheartened when she recognized Mala's nauseating voice. Bhayatupa had been right. The Chain Man had remained in Asubha.

"Start a fire, lads. But first serving goes to me. I like my meat *raw*!"

Sōbhana wasn't sure which she disliked more about Mala: his evil deeds or his obnoxious personality. She climbed slowly up the wall. Her luck held, and she found a hollow in the stone deep enough to conceal her. She pulled her dark coat around her body and felt reflexively for the Silver Sword. Its presence somehow comforted her. She allowed herself to sleep.

Sōbhana stirred, then sat up with a gasp, sensing something beneath her, though she could see nothing there. Was it the spider? She dared not sleep again. She was weary beyond measure, but she'd have to stay awake for the rest of the night. Sōbhana slid the sword from its sheath and held it in front of her, awaiting the succor of daylight.

Meanwhile, the men inside the prison shouted and laughed. The smell of roasting bird flesh wafted in the still air. Sōbhana's mouth watered.

When daylight arrived, she allowed herself some scattered moments of sleep. The uneasy feeling of being watched dissipated. Perhaps, the spider preferred to avoid bright sunlight.

It became clear, bright, and unseasonably warm—all unusual events in autumn on the peak of Asubha and likely to be temporary. She ate a light meal from a pack attached to the belt of her scabbard and sipped water from a leather flask. She could hear sentries strolling along the top of the wall. They sounded pleased. The previous night's feast and the pleasant weather must have put them in good spirits—or as good as spirits could be in a place this dismal.

By early afternoon, the weather changed for the worse, which was no surprise. A stiff wind came from the north, running in circles around the mountaintop. Dark clouds followed. Another storm, most likely born in the frozen wastes of Nirodha where few dared to wander, marched toward Asubha. Now, the sentries grumbled.

Though she shivered in her hideaway, Sōbhana was otherwise pleased. If the storm raged into the night, it would provide the concealment she needed to complete Torg's rescue.

When darkness came, the storm fell upon the mountain like a fiend. Sōbhana had never felt such ferocious winds or seen such virulent lightning. She feared she might not make it to the top of the wall, much less reach the pit. And it was wickedly cold. Ice crystals spun in the air like a million miniature daggers, obscuring the moon and stars. Frequent blasts of lightning provided fleeting moments of visibility, during which she studied her surroundings. As Sōbhana peered from her hiding place, hail pelted her. A glaze of ice coated the walls above her. Would she have to wait out the storm before attempting her ascent?

She didn't allow herself to be distracted by the specter of the spider. Could the beast hunt in weather like this? Surely, Dukkhatu was adapted to the cold, so Sōbhana knew she had to be careful. The spider might try to grab her as soon as she started her climb. Still, this didn't daunt Sōbhana. She would rely on her innate ability to sense unseen danger. If she perceived Dukkhatu's presence in time, the sword would take care of the rest.

And if she fell, her role in this gambit would no longer matter.

When she could bear to wait no longer, Sōbhana rose to her knees, faced the wall, and leaned backward just far enough to see beyond the upper lip of her hideaway. From where she knelt, it was thirty cubits to the top of the wall. Under these tumultuous conditions, it might as well have been 300.

Despair overcame her. It could take her until midnight just to get over the wall, much less reach the center of the courtyard, free Torg from the pit, and get him to a place where the dragon could rescue them. To accomplish this feat, killing would be necessary—*quiet* killing. She had assumed that her ascent of the wall would take only a little of the time she had left. Now it was obvious that getting to the top was a much larger challenge than anticipated.

Reason told her to wait, that the storm would pass. If she went now, she might be blown off the wall before she was able to reach the top. But Sōbhana was finished with reason. Madness drove her, born of love.

With her right hand, she grasped a flake of stone. It was not quite as slippery as she'd feared. Her powerful fingers crunched through the ice and pressed against the granular surface of the brick. She raised her left hand higher and inserted her fingers into a thin crack. Now, both her hands had firm holds, and she could stand. She flung her right hand several inches higher, grasping a knoblike protrusion. Then her left hand swung above the right and locked into a jagged tear. Her black boots rose off the floor of her hiding place and dangled in the air. Bit by bit, she climbed.

Bolts of lightning revealed her position, but there was no one to see. Gusty winds punched at her, threatening to knock her into space. Squalls lifted her torso off the wall and nearly yanked her hands and feet free. But she continued upward, not to be denied. At less than an arm's length from the top, her spirits soared. She was going to make it! Once over the wall, she would be more in her element, and her instincts as a trained assassin would take over.

Suddenly, a jolt of intuitive wrongness surged through her body. The inner voice born of her long training warned her to look down. Just then, a blast of lightning careened off the stone, revealing a hideous shape on the rock face below her. The spider was at least twenty cubits wide—if you included her legs—and her gruesome abdomen was twice as thick as an ancient oak.

Quicker than Sōbhana could think, the sword was in her free hand, and she swept it down with superhuman speed. Dukkhatu had defeated many warriors but had apparently fought no one with the prowess and weaponry of this Asēkha. The blade of the Silver Sword hacked off the tip of Dukkhatu's upper right leg, causing black blood to spurt on the stone.

There was another bolt of lightning.

Sōbhana saw the spider leaping sideways along the wall.

Dukkhatu vanished.

Sōbhana's counterattack seemed to anger the storm, and its vehemence increased. She cried out and nearly lost her grip on the sword. If she dropped it, she would be helpless against Mala and the Stone-Eater. Sōbhana replaced the sword in its sheath and took a moment to regain her composure. Then she climbed the remaining distance to the top of the wall and flung herself over the parapet, collapsing onto the narrow wall walk.

She lay there, gasping.

If she'd been discovered then, she might have been easy to capture or kill. But there were no sentries nearby. It appeared none had braved the ferocity of the storm. Sōbhana imagined that they huddled in cold chambers and prayed for death.

The storm maintained its intensity. Sōbhana had never felt so cold, but she ignored her physical anguish. She had no other choice.

The roiling darkness was her friend, though also her enemy. It hid her from prying eyes, but it prevented her from studying her surroundings. Asēkhas were brilliant at assessing situations and taking advantage of their opponents' weaknesses. But that was more difficult to do when you couldn't see much of anything.

Wind, snow, and fist-sized hail pounded Asubha, but the flashes of lightning occurred less frequently. For the time being, Sōbhana couldn't depend on them to provide spurts of visibility. She would have to proceed by feel. At least her foes were in the same predicament.

She worked her way along the wall walk until she came to a spiral stair that corkscrewed steeply downward into blackness. For all she knew, a sentry guarded the lower steps. If so, she would end his miserable life.

Bhayatupa had told her there were several guardhouses scattered around the main courtyard. Within one of those, she should be able to find lengths of rope. If she tied a rope to a plank and laid it across the top of the pit, she could shimmy down to Torg. She hoped that her beloved would have the strength to climb out on his own. If not, she would carry him on her back. She was an Asēkha. All things were possible.

Sōbhana proceeded warily down the stairs. She could see for about ten paces. Beyond that, vague shapes and ghostly blurs haunted her vision. She reached the floor of the courtyard without encountering resistance. Several stubborn torches burned weakly on iron poles driven into the stone, but they provided scant illumination. Sōbhana dropped to her hands and knees and crawled along the ground, peering to-and-fro until she came upon a one-room building with a single window. An oil lamp flickered inside. Though the storm continued to roar, she heard voices. Sōbhana peeked in the window and saw three sentries huddled around a table. They guzzled from large mugs; if they were drunk, all the better.

The door was ajar. She slid inside the lighted room. One sentry was having a good laugh. He slapped his knee. The other two laughed along with him.

With three blurring strokes, Sōbhana decapitated them. Their heads leaped into the air, flipped backward, and fell to the floor, striking the stone in a series of squishy thuds. She waited patiently until the blood finished squirting from their necks, then she repositioned their heads on their shoulders and put the mugs back on the table.

A keg of wine sat next to the wall beneath the window. Sōbhana picked it up and took several long swallows. It tasted awful, but it warmed her insides. She drank quite a bit more before setting it down.

The room had one small closet. She rummaged through it and found plenty of thick rope and a plank that was just the right size. This part of the operation had become easy, which made her wary.

The door swung open. A fourth sentry strode through the entryway. He wore a heavy cloak over his tunic, but he still grumbled about the cold before heading straight for the keg, too stupid to notice Sōbhana's presence. She stepped behind him and slammed the door. He jerked around. With two quick steps, Sōbhana crossed the room and pressed the sword against his throat. She forced him down beneath the window and crouched in front of him.

"I will let you live if you answer all my questions—without pause," she whispered. "Do you understand?"

He nodded fiercely.

"Does the wizard still live?"

"The wizard?"

Her forehead flew forward and butted him between his eyes. Steaming blood oozed from the bridge of his nose. He muttered something that made no sense. "And then I ... I kissed her ..."

Sōbhana slapped him. He started to shout, but she pressed her palm roughly against his lips. "Shhh ... shhh ... if you ever want to kiss her again, then you must answer all my questions. I'm an Asēkha and can silence you whenever I choose. You cannot thwart me. Do you doubt it?"

He shook his head no, then nodded yes, unsure of which way to answer.

"Does the prisoner in the pit still live?" Sōbhana said.

"Yes, warrior. I heard noises coming from that accursed hole just yesterday. I almost soiled my pants."

Sōbhana's cheeks flushed. Her beloved was alive! "What noises?"

"Moans. Shrieks."

Her face turned bright red. "Is Mala nearby?" she said through gritted teeth.

"Yes. He won't leave, though we all wish he would."

She pondered this and then spoke again. "Another question: *Where* is the pit?"

He pointed at the door.

"How far?"

"About one hundred paces."

"Is anything between us and the pit that could get in my way?"

"About fifty strides from here, there's a short wall that encircles the hole. Otherwise, there's nothing."

"Is the pit watched?"

The sentry grimaced. "It's supposed to be. We guard it in pairs. But my friend came here for wine. And I got scared—and followed. The storm ... the cold. We were sure Mala wouldn't bother to check on us. My friend (he pointed to one sentry seated at the table) is over there. Why doesn't he move?"

"He didn't answer my questions—nor did the others. They are no longer."

The sentry shivered. A single tear slid down his rough cheek. "I'll answer your questions, I promise. I truly wish to kiss her again—one day."

Sōbhana felt a twinge of sympathy. "Listen to me *very* carefully."

"Yes. But please don't kill me. I'm not ready to die—not yet."

"I won't slay you unless you force me to. I'm going to tell you a secret, and if you keep it to yourself, I'll let you live. I'm going to free the prisoner. After that, I'll need a place to hide—for a short time—from Mala and the guards. Where might that be?"

"There's no place to hide." The sword pressed against his throat. "Wait ... wait! I meant no *good* place. But if I wanted to hide, I know where I'd go: to the roof of the keep. A narrow stair leads to the top. Few ever use it. No one would think to look for you up there, especially in this storm."

Sōbhana considered his suggestion. "If you're lying ..."

"No, warrior, I speak the truth. But may I say one thing?"

"Quickly!"

"Freeing the wizard is impossible. It hurts just to stand *near* the pit, especially if you're not used to it. If you try to enter it, you won't survive. It's deadlier even than you, mistress. Only the warden has the equipment needed to remove the wizard. It's a special contraption with a large clamp, and it's cleverly made. But it's out of your reach behind barred doors."

"I'll find a way," she said. "And the keep—how far is it from the pit?"

"It's on the northern wall, several hundred paces beyond the pit. You can reach the stairs if you veer around to the left and slip between the walls."

"Very good. You are behaving yourself. One more question: Where does Mala sleep?"

"In a large chamber at the base of the keep. He comes out often— even during the night—to check on the prisoner, but usually not during storms as bad as this one."

"You've been helpful," Sōbhana said. "I'm going to tie you up now. If you struggle, the ropes will strangle you. Do you doubt it?"

"No, warrior. I believe every word you say."

"If you somehow betray me, you'll die in a most painful manner."

When Sōbhana left the guardhouse, the sentry was gagged, bound, and tucked in the closet. Her knots could not be undone without help from others. She left the torch lit and the card players in place. If anyone peered through the window, they would see nothing that appeared unusual, except for frozen splotches on the floor as if they had spilled a lot of wine.

The storm's fury lessened somewhat, but it still blew with considerable force—enough, she hoped, to keep Mala, the Stone-Eater, and the other sentries inside their chambers.

Mala lay awake in his room, his enormous body stretched out on the bare stone floor, his thoughts raging as wildly as the weather. He hated the prison and yearned to return to the tower of Uccheda, but Invictus had ordered him to stay in Asubha for thirty days. If the wizard still lived after that, Mala had been told to remove him from the pit and bring him back to Avici.

The Chain Man doubted Torg could survive much longer. It had been ten days, and Mala could sense that the wizard was near death.

On the first day of the Death-Knower's imprisonment, Mala had peered into the pit. Ferocious pain seared his face, causing him to shout and jerk back, stunned by its vehemence.

Now, as he lay in a heap within his chamber, he grudgingly admitted that he had grown to respect Torg. Anyone—or anything—capable of surviving in the pit for more than a day was extraordinary. Ten days was beyond possibility. And Invictus thought the wizard might live for a month?

Lightning stroked the air, followed by a blast of thunder. Mala sat upright. Maybe he should go out and have a look around. Wind and hail tearing at his flesh would help to clear his mind.

Ten days down. Twenty to go. Would this torture ever end? The things he did for his king.

Carrying the rope and plank on her back, Sōbhana slithered over the low wall that encircled the pit. Occasional bursts of lightning threatened to reveal her position, but she stayed so close to the ground she was all but invisible.

She sensed the pit before she saw it—and recognized it as pure evil. Poison, decay, sickness, despair ... the pit contained them all. Sōbhana experienced the same hopelessness she had felt when she first saw Invictus. She wanted to flee.

But of course she would not. She had come too far and fought too hard. She would rescue her beloved—or die trying. Despite her fear, no other scenario was conceivable.

Buoyed by stubbornness, Sōbhana crept closer. She found it difficult to imagine how the sentries could guard the pit; either they were partially immune to its wickedness, or she was more susceptible. Now just an arm's length from the opening, her eyes watered, her ears rang, and her tongue swelled. Surely, the sentry had lied. Torg must be long dead. Not even one as great as he could have survived inside this monstrosity for a single day, much less ten days.

Then she heard a shriek that almost stopped her heart. Her beloved was down there, enduring horrors beyond her comprehension. But he was alive.

And she was his last hope.

The perfect circle glared at her. It had its own mind, its own voice, and it challenged her to proceed.

Come inside and play with me, little one. You look so sweet and tasty.

Forcing herself to wriggle to the lip of the abyss, Sōbhana peered into the blackness. Instantly, her face was ablaze with pain, causing the muscles in her cheeks to quiver. Mucus gushed from her nostrils, freezing as it fell toward the mouth of the pit but sizzling and bursting into steam as it entered. What kind of hell was this?

"I'm coming, my love," she whispered. "I will not forsake you."

A low moan rose like a reply.

Sōbhana laid the plank across the opening and looped one end of the rope around it, securing it with a sturdy knot. The cord was thick and well made. She hoped it could survive the pit's virulence long enough for her to climb down and bring Torg up. If she fell, all would be lost.

Sōbhana drew the Silver Sword and lowered it partway into the pit, expecting it to melt or wither. But the sword was not affected, and its blade remained cool. Perhaps it would protect her. At least, it would bolster her resolve.

She reluctantly returned it to its sheath, needing both hands for the descent. She lowered the rope into the darkness to estimate the distance. Five cubits. Ten. Fifty. One hundred. Two hundred. Did it touch bottom?

She couldn't quite tell.

She fantasized that Torg would reach for the rope and climb out on his own, relieving her of the burden of entering the pit. But this was a false hope. She had to go down—and she had to do it now.

Sōbhana sat on the plank, which bowed slightly but easily held her weight, and then lowered her feet into the darkness. Even though she wore heavy boots and tight-fitting pants, her feet, ankles, and calves instantly burned like frostbitten flesh submerged in steaming water. The warrior left them there for several seconds, testing her ability to tolerate the pain. It hurt terribly, but at least it seemed to level out. She could not have withstood anything worse.

Sōbhana slid the rest of her body into the hole. To stop from crying out, she bit her lip. Blood dripped down her chin and smoked like burning oil.

She was submerged in agony. But where the sheath of the sword touched her leg, there was no pain. She focused her mind along the length of the blade. It provided comfort. And strength. In some ways, the sword was greater than the pit.

She descended hand by hand. Her stomach soured and she vomited. Now her entire body was sweating profusely, and she believed she might die of dehydration before anything else. How was Torg still alive? She was in awe.

Sōbhana coughed. One of her teeth spit out of her mouth and impaled itself in the side of the pit, where it caught fire and shattered, casting blazing shards that provided a tiny circle of light—just enough for her to see a portion of the wall. Black things wiggled and squirmed like the flesh of a devil.

Down she went, farther and farther. The air was so foul she could barely breathe. The mucus that had gushed from her nostrils was replaced by blood. Warmth oozed from her ears and eyes. Liquids poured from her vagina and anus. If she did somehow rescue Torg and return to the surface, she wouldn't be a pretty sight. But then, she imagined, neither would he.

She had to be getting close. It felt like she'd been descending for days. Just when she was about to give up hope, her foot touched an object beneath her. She reached down with her free hand and grasped something solid. It was his shoulder—his wonderful, muscular shoulder.

Torg moaned again. Sōbhana felt around as best she could and determined that he was curled naked on his side. The warrior hated to do it, but she had to relieve the pressure on her other arm, so she gently placed her boots onto his thick ribs and crouched down onto his body. If only he would wake up, they could escape together. But he seemed incapable of movement. She would have to lift him, and it wouldn't be easy. He was almost twice her weight—and dead weight, at that. *No, don't use that word.*

"I'm here, my beloved," she whispered. "I have come. I will save you. Do not fear."

He groaned but didn't move.

Then to her horror, the rope jiggled. Something was yanking on it from above. She had been discovered. If the rope was severed, they both were doomed.

"I'll be back. I promise you."

Sōbhana climbed with terrific speed, expecting the rope to go slack and dump her into the abyss at any second. It swayed violently, throwing her against the wall and causing her black coat to burst into flame. She cast the coat off, but the skin on her right shoulder bubbled and blistered. Ignoring the pain, she continued to climb.

When she arrived at the top and reached for the plank, something huge and powerful grasped one of her wrists and lifted her from the pit. Sōbhana dangled in front of Mala, less than half his height.

"An Asēkha!" he said, his voice puzzled. "How did you get here? Are you alone?"

With her free hand, Sōbhana drew the sword from its sheath on her left hip and whipped it at his neck. She was fast, but so was he. Mala bent his head back just enough to avoid decapitation. The sword dug into a portion of the chain that was burned into his breast, causing an outburst of blistering flame. This cast the Chain Man backward, and he dropped Sōbhana as he fell. She landed awkwardly on her side next to the mouth of the pit, momentarily stunned.

When she regained her senses, the Chain Man was still dazed. Sōbhana watched his every move. Almost too late she detected a whisper in the air, and she flipped the sword behind her back. Another sword clashed against hers and split. Sōbhana rose to her feet, spun around, and cut her attacker—this one man-sized—cleanly in half with a single swipe.

"What did she do to me?" Mala was saying. "What does she wield?"

More sentries arrived carrying hissing torches. Though Sōbhana had killed the first attacker, she remained dizzy and disoriented, and her shoulder felt like poisoned blades had shredded it. But rage gave her strength. She had been so close! She had *touched* her beloved. And at the worst possible moment, the monster she'd grown to despise had thwarted her.

Her screams of frustration echoed in the night. The sentries retreated. Mala became infuriated.

"Get her, you cowards! Slice her up."

Sōbhana regained her wits. Killing was what she did best, and when she faced superior numbers, she eliminated the most dangerous first. With an anger that had fermented over weeks and weeks, she charged at the Chain Man, intent on making him pay for his cruelty.

Sōbhana's sudden ferocity seemed to awaken Mala. The monster bellowed and golden liquid as hot as dragon fire spurted from his chain. Sōbhana grunted and leaped to the side, barely avoiding the profusion. She fell at the feet of a sentry, rolled to her knees, and swept off both his legs at mid-thigh. Then she stood. Zip! Zip! Zip! Three more of the enemy fell. The sword cut through anything it touched.

The Chain Man picked up a block the size of a boulder and heaved it at her. Sōbhana sidestepped the massive missile and watched it crush a cave troll that had emerged from the darkness. Another block tumbled by, bowling over several approaching sentries.

The storm joined the fight. A blast of lightning blew into the mouth of the pit. A blob of electrical energy spewed upward in response and exploded like fireworks, casting a blanket of dazzling light that illuminated the entire courtyard and revealed the locations of several dozen well-armed men.

Despite the threat of the sword, Mala dared to approach her. Sōbhana believed she could kill him with it, but she had to get close enough to strike, and that wouldn't be easy. His powers were formidable, and she had no magic of her own to counter them.

The Chain Man rushed forward, spewing more liquid fire. The scathing flames were difficult to avoid, forcing her to duck and run while slaying any sentry that strayed within her vision. Most feared her wrath and stayed back. But Mala continued his pursuit, and now he held the advantage. He could destroy her from a distance, but she needed to get within the length of the sword to harm him. She feared she could not prevail.

Sōbhana was corralled away from the pit. More sentries fell beneath her blade but fighting them and avoiding Mala was exhausting. She had already been pushed beyond her limits, and her damaged shoulder felt like it was dissolving. A fist-sized stone—hurled from her blindside—ricocheted off her cheek, filling her mouth with blood. A Golden Soldier could not have thrown the stone with such force. It must have come from a second troll.

Another bolt of lightning struck somewhere in the courtyard. She glanced behind her. She was just a span from the edge of a sheer cliff.

Sōbhana turned back to her attackers, holding the sword in front of her. Then she swung it back and forth, grinning crookedly.

"Come and get me, you bastards. Every one of you will die. I swear it!"

Inspired by Mala, they approached close enough for the torchlight to reveal their grim faces. Sōbhana saw anger, but then fear. They suddenly stopped. Then they gaped at her.

She didn't see—or sense—what rose behind her until it was too late.

Silk threads from the spider's spinnerets wove around her, first pinning her forearms against her torso and then encasing her entire body from her shoulders down. The sword was torn from her grasp and wrapped in a separate cocoon.

Over the side she went.

"No!" she wailed. "Please save me ... my lovvvvvvvvve!"

But there was no response as the spider took her from one hell to another.

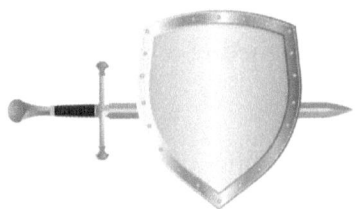

THE PIT

As he had told Kusala that late-summer night on the outskirts of Barranca, Torg had died a thousand times. Each Death Visit enriched him with magical powers—and when he returned to life, he felt paradoxically more alive than most could imagine.

Torg's first Death Visit occurred more than nine centuries ago. Ever since that breakthrough, he had planned the time and place of each "temporary suicide" in precise detail, preferring to wait about a year between visits, though a few times in his life—depending on his needs—he had done so with more frequency.

Now it was mid-autumn and well below freezing in the mountain prison on the peak of Asubha. The air was bitter and useless, failing to nourish Torg's lungs. His breaths came in raspy gasps, and he shivered in a constant state of illness.

Dehydrated and starving, Torg could no longer accurately gauge the passage of time. He was mostly in various states of unconsciousness. When he slept, his nightmares were bizarre and erratic. He dreamed often about Sōbhana as if she were there with him. When awake, every second felt like a week. A small part of him, though, was aware that he'd been trapped at the bottom of the pit for more than three weeks.

Even Torg couldn't bear much more. The insidious magic and acidic poisons imbued in the walls of the pit had ravaged his naked flesh. The hair on his body had dissolved, and his teeth had fallen out. He could feel his strength draining out of him like blood leaking from a wound.

Torg's lone hope, he knew, was a Death Visit—a temporary suicide induced by deep meditation. But something in the pit prevented him from achieving the required level of concentration.

If I cannot die, I will go insane. I must find a way past the barrier Invictus has erected.

And so, he attempted to meditate, again.

Inhale ...

Exhale ...

Even before the completion of the first exhalation, he lost his concentration and his mind wandered aimlessly, still puzzled by the sensual lure of the full moon. His long years of mindfulness training had taught him to recognize these inevitable drifts and gently return to the breath. So he discarded the thought and continued to ...

Inhale ...

Exhale ...

A painful itch tormented the tip of his nose. Torg knew that this, too, could be used as an object of concentration. Without judgment or prejudice, he watched the itch rise and fall of its own accord, studying its beginning, middle, and ending. He observed its effect on his body and mind. When the prickle abated, he returned to ...

Inhale ...

Exhale ...

Inhale ...

Exhale ...

Torg was making progress, but the mysterious barrier continued to thwart his concentration. The walls of the pit made strange sizzling sounds, occasionally spritzing caustic liquid that burned his bare skin. But the pain alone didn't prevent him from emptying his mind or managing his thoughts. There was something else—a madness like no other.

Despite all this, he continued to try.

Inhale ...

Invictus toys with me.

Exhale ...

I will go insane.

Inhale ...

I must find a way.

Exhale ...

I *will* find a way.

Inhale ...

Exhale ...

Watch the breath. Eliminate movement. Watch the breath. Eliminate thought.

Inhale ...
Exhale ...

No movement. No thought. Quiet mind. Peaceful mind. Only the breath.

Inhale ......
Exhale ......

As the torment of the pit further eroded his sanity, Torg struggled one last time to enter the Realm of Death to feed on its power and absorb enough strength to survive a few more days. A successful Death Visit was never easy for Torg, even in the best of circumstances, requiring a magnificently intense form of meditation even greater than that practiced by the Noble Ones of Dibbu-Loka. Torg's mind had to be emptied of all thought—not just for a few breaths, or a series of breaths, but for hundreds of breaths.

A wise Vasi master had taught Torg the art of meditation when he was a young warrior just beginning his training. Concentration creates a state of extreme relaxation. If performed at a deep enough level, meditation can slow the rise and fall of the breath and the beating of the heart to undetectable levels. But it has nothing in common with sleepiness or daydreaming. The meditator is supremely awake. Every thought, emotion, sensation, and occurrence are monitored with ultimate awareness.

Because of their genetics, Tugars possessed a remarkable asset. Their flesh was unusually dense, making it highly resistant to injury. This impregnability continued even after death. An ordinary body began to decay soon after it perished, but Tugar bodies remained relatively unchanged for more than a year, and it took centuries for them to deteriorate into skeletons. Torg was the ultimate Tugar. His physical strength was unrivaled for a creature of his size, but it paled in comparison to his supernatural puissance.

Torg averaged slightly over one Death Visit per year because the act was too dangerous for more frequent attempts. Each episode required that he achieve a state called *Sammaasamaadhi*, the supreme concentration of mind during which Torg's heart rate progressively slowed until his body ceased to live. At that instant, his karmic energy exited his flesh and entered the Realm of Death where it fed on untapped power. But unlike an ordinary death, Torg was able to return to his body before the process became irreversible. His dense tissues—though temporarily deprived of life-giving oxygen—remained receptive to their host.

Now, imprisoned on the rooftop of Mount Asubha, Torg lay in the pit and continued his final attempt toward *Sammaasamaadhi*. If he had been stronger, he would have sat up in a comfortable position to begin his meditation. But he was too weak to twitch a finger.

Invictus' magical barrier continued to wreak havoc within his mind. Torg searched for its source with single-minded determination. Since his first successful Death Visit more than nine centuries before, he had never experienced such difficulty in achieving *Sammaasamaadhi*.

Torg remembered words spoken to him by the Vasi master who was the first to recognize he had the rare potential to become a Death-Knower. At the time, Torg was a juvenile approaching the middle years of his warrior training.

"Live in the present moment," Dēsaka said. "Nothing exists but the present. All else is illusion. To live in the present moment, you must become the master of your mind." The teacher tapped his temple with a long finger. "*Thought is the thinker*. To empty the mind of thought, do not think. It is that easy and that difficult. If you empty your mind of thought, you will become its master."

As a 40-year-old youth who had not yet become a warrior—much less the greatest to ever live—Torg was obsessed with acquiring knowledge, and he had harassed his Vasi master with endless philosophical queries.

"Who holds the sharpest sword?" Torg said.

"A person who speaks out of wrath holds the sharpest sword," Dēsaka said.

"*My* sword is sharpest."

"Your sword is sharp, but your mind is dull. You can see beyond the dunes, but you cannot see what is in front of your eyes. Even worse, you blame your stupidity on others instead of taking responsibility for it."

"But you call me your finest student."

"Enough! Enough!" Dēsaka said. "Now I have a question for *you*. What is the greatest weapon?"

"Wisdom," Torg said without pause.

"Ah, child … you are full of surprises. The only thing that can stop you is yourself. Your father says you're too smart for your own good.

He is correct."

Now, as Torg lay shivering in the pit's darkness, he replayed this tête-à-tête several times before the answer he had long sought arose.

You can see beyond the dunes, but you cannot see what is in front of your eyes.

Torg finally saw what was in front of his eyes. Invictus had never intended to disrupt his concentration; the sorcerer was too confident to consider it a necessity. But Torg's sensitivity to Invictus' unwholesome power had *felt* like a barrier, effectively preventing him from emptying his mind. The magic that created the pit swirled like a filthy tornado. But Torg saw through it, and his sudden clarity gave him a chance, which was better than none.

More of his master's words, spoken in a time long past, entered his awareness:

"Breathe in. Know that you breathe in. Breathe out. Know that you breathe out."

Torg felt chaos drain from his mind ...

Inhale ...

Exhale ...

The wisdom of silence was his greatest weapon.

It also carried a reward: the sweetness of empty mind.

Awareness bloomed like a flower in morning's first light.

Inhale ...

Breathe in and slow the breath.

Exhale ...

Breathe out and slow the breath.

Inhale ...

Breathe in and slow the heartbeat.

Exhale ...

Breathe out and slow the heartbeat.

Inhale ...

Exhale ...

With one final surge of mindful concentration, Torg willed his heart to stop beating. When *Sammaasamaadhi* arrived, his temporary suicide began. What he experienced next occurred to all that ever live—from the simplest bacterium to the most complex animal.

And that is what made Torg so special.

~~

Only a Death-Knower can die.
And live again.

Only a Death-Knower can return from death.
And remember.

Only a Death-Knower can tell us what he has seen.
Not all care to listen.

~~

Torg's lifeless body lay at the bottom of the pit, but his mind exploded out of the hole like a fiery boulder heaved into the night sky. Torg became a swirling sphere of karmic energy, and he leaped vast distances across time and space, drawn by a force far stronger than gravity.

The silence of meditation was nothing compared to this silence. There was no sound at all. There was only sight.

Torg tumbled toward his future. He couldn't see his own sphere, but he could see what surrounded him. Countless others—in a variety of sizes and colors—streaked alongside him like an army of comets. Torg could sense that the spheres were looking at him and at each other with dispassionate interest.

In the far distance, beyond the planets, beyond the stars, Torg knew from firsthand experience that a deep-blue ball awaited their arrival. It was larger than a galaxy, and billions of karmic spheres dove into it from all conceivable directions while just as large a number rocketed outward. The ball was a cosmic headquarters for the natural cycle of life and death, directing and redirecting karma throughout the universe.

In this realm, there was no fear or pain. No pleasure or joy. All emotions were muted. Torg felt only a dry scientific curiosity. It was cold but he didn't shiver. It was bittersweet but he didn't taste. From his experience, the abilities to hear, taste, touch, and smell were reserved for life.

Death was a temporary condition. *Life is short*, the Vasi saying went. But death was far shorter.

The lure of the natural order was seductively strong. Torg's karma yearned to enter the ball and continue to its next existence. His dead body was trillions of miles away on a distant world. His only chance of return was to stop short of the immense ball and hover just above its surface. If he entered, there would be no turning back.

Torg had accomplished this feat a thousand times before, but never while so diminished. A substantial part of him wanted to give in and let the living beings he had left behind fend for themselves. What did it matter, anyway? All of them—except for the demons—would eventually die. All of them would pass through here on their ways to their next existences.

Torg's thoughts strayed to Sister Tathagata, as they often did during his Death Visits. Her wisdom had brought him back from the brink before.

"Use your time wisely, child," the High Nun of Dibbu-Loka had said to him. "Time is precious. What do you gain if you're allotted a million lives but never learn? Don't waste this life hoping that the next one will be superior. Halt your suffering now."

Once again, Tathagata saved him. Torg stopped just outside the surface of the ball. Countless other spheres sped past him, puzzled by his decision. But Torg's mind was made up. He would feed on the boundless energy of death and return to his body in the faraway pit.

Was this a *wise* use of his time? That was yet to be seen.

Like a bird hovering just above the surface of a stormy sea, Torg positioned his essence at the edge of the mottled cloud. All around him, spheres plunged into the broiling blueness, but Torg ignored them. His focus was too intense for distraction.

He inhaled—in a figurative sense—with intense effort. Tendrils of the dark ooze crept slowly up, probing him like cautious fingers. He inhaled again. This time, an enormous draught of the cloud flowed into him.

Torg swallowed hungrily, feasting on death's power. The blue fire engorged his essence with immeasurable pleasure. His sphere bloated to ten times the size of the others, then one hundred. He grew as large as a planet. Fiery blasts of blue light danced around and through him. Incoming and outgoing spheres avoided his presence. If they crashed into him now, they would be obliterated.

"Use your time wisely, child," the mortal from the distant world had said.

In Torg's awareness, the words were quiet and soft, holding little meaning.

But a small part of him tried to listen.

Wanted to listen.

Knew it had to listen.

Opportunities as precious as this should not be wasted.

Torg—aglow with reckless might—reversed his course. He left the cloud behind and roared back to his flesh.

When he returned to life inside the pit on Mount Asubha, his karma tore through his flesh.

And he cried out.

The wizard's scream startled two sentries who stood near the opening of the pit. They yelped and leaped back.

No sound had come from the pit in more than a week. Everyone at the prison believed the wizard was dead—except for Mala, who claimed to sense the Death-Knower's essence, no matter how diminished. With the Chain Man stomping around, they were all on edge, including the lookouts. When the sentries heard Torg's shout, they nearly dropped dead.

Dawn was approaching, but in these lonely heights the air was still as dark as midnight. Enraged winds swept through the gaps between Asubha and its sister mountains. Few places on Triken were as miserable as this peak. Prisoners rarely survived more than a couple of months. Fresh guards, janitors, and cooks constantly replaced the old ones who died—it was claimed—from exposure to the elements. But those forced to serve on Asubha knew better. The place was far too nocuous to abide the living. Depression and fear grew until they became unbearable. Suicide was common. The dead were found frozen at their posts or in their beds with hopeless looks in their eyes.

"I've got to tell the warden that the wizard's still kickin'," one sentry said, regaining some composure. "He'll want to go straight to Mala. Might even have to wake him up."

The other sentry grabbed his partner by the arm.

"You're not leaving me alone," he barked into the wind. "Having to stand guard next to this accursed pit is bad enough, but if that nasty wizard crawls out of it, I'll soil my pants. Let *me* go tell the warden. *You* stay and watch. It was only twelve days ago that the Asēkha almost killed me. I've suffered enough."

"Don't be a fool! You think you're scared now? Think how it'll be if the Chain Man hears you've messed things up again. It'll make soiling your pants feel like a steamy bath."

"Nothing good's going to happen to me up here, I'll grant you that. But I'm not staying alone, no matter what. If you go, I go."

A speckle of starlight that somehow had weaved its way through the swirling clouds reflected off the blade of a dagger. The cowardly sentry grasped his stomach, his hands feeling warmth for the first time since arriving at Asubha. Steaming blood gushed out and bubbled on the gray ground.

"Thank you," the sentry said. "I'm ready to die now." He staggered, slipped on a patch of ice, and fell backward, tumbling into the pit's hungry maw. His corpse clung to the narrow opening, arms and legs draped outside of the perfectly round hole like it was making one last effort to hold on. Then the lifeless body folded and disappeared into the black cavity.

"Thank me in hell," the other sentry yelled. "It can't be any worse than this."

Deep in the depths of the pit, Torg's eyes—full of death's might—suffused the bottom of the pit with blue light. For the first time in many days, he could see something other than blackness. The walls of his prison were horrid, lumpy, and writhing. The sight would have caused a lesser being to scream in hysteria. But Torg had fought too hard to succumb to madness now.

The wizard began the long, cruel trial of sitting up. He had lain in the same position—curled on his side—for what had felt like an eternity. As he tried to move, he groaned like an old man on his deathbed. Then he laughed to himself. *That's exactly what you are.*

Torg was debilitated from weeks in the pit without food or water, but he wasn't dead yet. He had never consumed so much energy in one visit to the Realm of Death, and he felt like a man who had gone a week without sleep and then gulped down a gallon of strong tea. Suddenly, he was bursting with vigor, but he was also stretched thin. What he needed most was water, food, and a week of uninterrupted slumber—and that would be just the barest beginnings of his recovery.

For now, his Death Energy would have to suffice. It always had before.

At least, he no longer felt cold. His body sizzled, but he was as thirsty and hungry as he'd ever been. As a Death-Knower and a Tugar, he could go without sustenance for much longer periods than an ordinary being. But even he required the basics of life.

To his surprise, Torg felt more than heard a commotion above him. Then he sensed that something was falling down the long shaft of the pit straight at him. Just in time, he raised his hands to shield his head. A hard bundle crashed into his side, striking him in the ribs. The force of the blow rocked Torg. A man-sized body had fallen upon him. Torg closed his eyes and lay still for a dozen long breaths, trying to regain his composure.

The body smelled salty and stale. It was obvious the man was dead; the fall alone would have killed him. But there was more. Warm blood dripped onto Torg's naked chest, making it likely that the man had been injured before he fell. But why? What was happening up there? Torg couldn't guess.

The man's arms and legs were propped above his torso and pressed against the narrow sides of the pit. The poison dissolved the exposed skin on the corpse's wrists and ankles. The stench made Torg gag.

The wizard considered his options. Since achieving *Sammaasamaadhi*, he had become dangerous again. He could use his powers to incinerate the body that lay on top of him but expending that much energy wouldn't be wise considering he needed to conserve whatever strength he still had left. Torg knew he was in a grim situation. Just getting out of the pit could prove impossible, much less accomplishing anything once he was free. If he could somehow climb out, dozens of guards—and who knew what else—would likely be waiting for him. Mala still might be up there, and the prison on Asubha was home to other horrors. It was even possible that Invictus would be part of the welcoming committee.

"One thought at a time," Torg said aloud, and the corpse's head flopped down noisily onto its chest.

"I'm glad you agree. You seem like a nice enough fellow. I could use a friend down here."

Torg opened his eyes and willed their bluish glow to illuminate the bottom of the pit again. Then he studied the man's face. His jaw was thick and square, and there was a recently healed wound on his forehead. His dark-brown eyes were wide open, exhibiting an unsettling combination of horror and relief. If you cleaned him up and dressed him in golden robes, he would look like a cousin of Invictus. He even had the long yellow hair, though a lot of it was already disintegrating.

Torg lay still and breathed slowly. To plan an escape, he needed to find out what was happening on the surface. Though the corpse's weight continued to press uncomfortably against his side, Torg managed to delve into his own memories in search of an answer to his quandary. Soon, his mind drifted far away.

Invictus wasn't the only person on Triken who had studied sorcery and magic. There were hundreds of witches, conjurers, necromancers, and demons well versed in spells and potions both good and evil. Torg had spent centuries learning incantations in many parts of the world.

Three times in the early years of his life, Torg had journeyed through the Gap of Gamana—the only passable entrance and exit through the northern range of the Mahaggata Mountains—and entered Arupa-Loka, which meant *Ghost City* in the ancient tongue. The first two times, he'd gone with Asēkhas at his side, and the city's stone buildings had appeared to be deserted. The third time, when he was 300 years old, he went by himself, still curious to see if Arupa-Loka was worthy of its notorious reputation as a haven for demons and other monsters. He was not disappointed. Perhaps sensing that he was more vulnerable when alone, the inhabitants of the Ghost City opened their doors. Lifeless horrors wandered the frozen streets. Though many were powerful, they could perceive Torg's strength—and feared it.

For a long stretch of time during the deep darkness of a moonless night, Torg stood transfixed on the center median of a street in the city's heart. He leaned against his staff and stared at the dwellings that had once housed—in the distant past—living beings. Now, he could see wicked faces peering from windows and doorways. A collective hatred attempted to smother him. Torg wondered what might happen if they all attacked him at once. But he wasn't overly concerned. Even the most powerful of the undead were selfish and cowardly. None in the Ghost City—save the demon Vedana—would dare to stand alone against him. And Torg was certain that Vedana wasn't present. If she were there, he would have sensed her essence.

A ghost-child appeared in front of him. If she had been alive, Torg would have guessed her to be about 10 years old. She smiled at him, her mouth curling upward at its corners. The beauty of her face stunned Torg. She beckoned him to follow her. In the cold of midwinter, they wandered along many winding roads. Some areas were so dark Torg could see nothing but the slight sway of the ghost-child's petite dress, which glowed like phosphorous in a black sea. Obhasa also glowed in response to her power.

She led him to the outskirts of the city where they came upon a modest house of gray stone. The ghost-child stepped inside the front door. Torg had to bend over to clear the entryway. The interior was lit by torchlight—demonic torchlight—and sitting in a decrepit chair facing the door was the long-decomposed corpse of what had once been a tall man. The wizard wondered how long it had been here and why it hadn't already turned to dust. Perhaps, the magical torchlight had played some role in keeping it relatively intact.

"He has a story to tell you," the girl said, her voice as sweet as innocence.

"I'd prefer to hear your story," Torg said.

"They are the same."

Torg looked at the skeleton's face, then turned back to the girl. "I would listen to his story, but he seems incapable of telling it."

The ghost giggled. She walked to Torg and waggled her finger. She wanted to whisper something in his ear. He bent down. "The sirens can make him speak," she said, ever so softly. "I know *where* they hide. I know *when* to listen."

"And what do you hear?" Torg said.

"The word ... the magic word."

"What's the magic word?"

More giggles. The room seemed to wobble. "You have to *hear* it before you can say it."

"I don't understand."

She reached for him. Her tiny hand barely filled his palm, but it burned like ice. Torg psychically sensed her desperation. She had been in Arupa-Loka for a very long time. But it was not of her choosing.

"Come with me," she said.

The torchlight winked out. Torg found himself in utter darkness. For the first time in his long existence, he entered the Realm of Undeath. Never had he seen such unbroken blackness. The souls of the undead were trapped between life and death, and it was horrid and hopeless. He sagged to his knees.

But the girl was there to guide him. "Do you hear them?"

As Torg knew from *Sammaasamaadhi*, the lone sensation of death was the ability to see. But he now discovered that the lone sensation of undeath was the ability to hear.

Female voices were chanting. "*Yakkkkha. Yakkkkha.*"

"I hear them," Torg said. "Tell me what it is you need of me. You know something I do not."

There was a flash and they again stood in the dusty room lit by magical torchlight.

The girl pointed at the skeleton. "His spirit is gone, but his bones remember. Ask him to speak."

"I don't know how."

"Say the magic word."

In a remote corner of his mind, Torg could still hear the chanting. "*Yakkkkha*," he said, though the word sounded like garble in the Realm of Life.

The skeleton moved, its head lolling from side to side.

"I told them we shouldn't attempt the pass," it said.

"Who are you?" Torg said.

"Who am I? I am no longer. I am gone."

"Who *were* you?"

"I was her father."

"Ask him what happened," the little ghost said to Torg.

The skeleton stood, clicking and clacking, and it tilted its skull toward the girl. "Peta? Is that you?"

"Yes, father. And if you still love me, please tell this man what happened. I'm afraid she will make him leave before he can help me."

"I won't leave," Torg said. "There's nothing here that can make me go anywhere."

Torg walked to the skeleton and looked down at its hollow face. "Her name is Peta? And what's your name?"

"I do not remember. I am no longer. I am gone."

"Your daughter needs me. To help her, I need you. What can you tell me?"

"I told them we should go south and avoid the pass," it said.

"His bones remember," Peta interrupted. "Ask him to speak."

Torg nodded. "I'm beginning to understand."

The skeleton's karmic energy was gone, moved on to countless other existences. But its bones *remembered* like a painting that had retained the vision of the artist.

"Did you go south?"

"No."

"Did you attempt the pass?"

"Yes. I told them not to."

"Did you come to Arupa-Loka?"

"I do not remember."

This exasperated Peta. "Please ask him to *speak*."

"Patience," Torg said. "I'm new to this."

The corners of her mouth turned downward, but she grew quiet.

"What happened in the pass?" Torg said.

"They came for her."

"Who?"

"The demons."

"They kidnapped her?" Torg said.

The ghost-child was at his side, nodding vigorously.

"They took Peta. And they took me," the skeleton said. "But they killed her mother and all the rest. It was Peta they wanted. They only took me along to keep her calm."

"Why did they want Peta?"

The little ghost was jumping up and down.

"Because she's special," the skeleton said.

"Special?" Torg said. "How so?"

"She's blind."

Torg sensed he was on the verge of a breakthrough. Peta was at his side, wiggling like a worm.

"Ask him to speak. Ask him to speak!"

Torg couldn't help but smile. He turned back to what remained of her father.

"Why did the demons believe her blindness was special?"

"Yes! Yes!" Peta said, and she bounced around the room.

"Because she could *hear*," the skeleton said.

Torg thought back to his brief visit to the Realm of Undeath. In that dreadful place, he had been blind—just like Peta. But at least he had been able to hear. In life, Peta's blindness must have enhanced her senses, including her hearing. Was it enhanced among the undead, as well?

"Where is Peta's body?" Torg said.

The little girl screamed with delight. "Yes! Yes! *Tell* him!" she said to her dead father.

But the skeleton's response made no sense. "Her body is forgotten."

"I don't understand," Torg said.

"Neither do I," the skeleton said.

Torg turned to Peta. Fluorescent tears now lined her cheeks. "Can you tell me anything? He says your body is forgotten. What does that mean?"

"Ask him to speak."

"You keep repeating that. I *have* asked him to speak, many times. But I have no more questions. Why can't you tell me where your body is? And also tell me why you want me to find it."

"He knows. Ask *him*."

Torg sighed. He walked to the side of the room, leaned against the wall, and slid down on his rump. The skeleton also attempted to sigh. Dust puffed from where its nostrils used to be. Then it stepped back and flopped down in its chair, bones cracking.

Peta wailed. "He knows ... he *knows* ..."

"Peta?" the skeleton said. "Is that you?"

"Oh, shut up!" she said.

"Yes." The skeleton sounded sad.

Torg stood, unsure of what to do next. For reasons he couldn't discern, Peta was unable to tell him what he needed to know, and the skeleton couldn't *remember*. He leaned against the doorway and looked out at the street. They were not alone. Hundreds of the undead stood nearby, still as stones, staring at him but not daring to approach.

Torg shouted at them. "Where is her body? Tell me!"

One by one, they fled from his wrath. Some flew into the night sky.

Others slipped into sewers. The largest and slowest stumbled into nearby buildings. The street was empty again.

"Her body is forgotten," the skeleton said.

Suddenly, Peta's face grew bright. She had thought of something that renewed her hope. "Tell him to *walk*!" she said, her head held proud.

Torg looked at the skeleton. "Stand."

The skeleton regained its feet, but not without a price. Its left arm fell off at the elbow.

"Now, walk to where Peta's body is hidden," Torg said.

"Yes," the skeleton said, and it tottered toward the doorway, bumping hard into the stone frame, crunching several ribs and busting a knee. Undeterred, it staggered into the street and moved awkwardly along the sidewalk. Torg followed. Peta pranced after them, bursting with merriment.

"Tell him to *walk*," she chanted.

The skeleton made poor progress, banging into anything in its path. Large chunks of bone broke off and clattered on the stone roadways. Torg feared that Peta's father would fall apart before they could reach their destination.

"Are we close?" Torg said, his breath smoking in the frozen air.

"I do not remember. I am no longer. I am gone."

But it continued its slow march.

They came at last to a strange tower that stood alone in a cobbled courtyard. Though the tower was just ten cubits in diameter, it was at least fifty cubits tall. An elaborate bas-relief wound upward from its base, and near its pinnacle was a small window where an eerie light shone from inside.

The skeleton had had enough. It collapsed into pieces and said no more.

"Goodbye, father," Peta said without apparent sorrow.

There was a single door at the base of the tower. Torg pushed against it but found it barred. He raised his staff and smote the ancient wood, which splintered and gave way. Torg stepped inside.

The interior of the tower was dark. Torg willed Obhasa to glow, providing enough light for him to see a steep, spiraling stairwell. He started up. Peta didn't follow.

"Will you not come?" Torg said.

Peta bowed her head. Something disturbed her.

As Torg stared at the ghost-child, he saw movement behind her. The undead had returned. Thousands were in the courtyard, watching but not approaching. This time, he disregarded them. Whatever was at the top of the tower now consumed his attention. He strode up the slippery stairs.

At the top was another locked door. It was no more capable of keeping Torg out than the first. He blasted through it and entered a small chamber with a low ceiling that glowed with a sepulchral light.

Peta lay on a stone pallet in the center of the room, her body untouched by the passage of time. If it weren't for the stillness of her chest, Torg would have believed she was sleeping.

She wore the same dress as her ghostly form, and her face was just as beautiful. If she had grown to womanhood, she would have been splendid.

Torg hunched over and approached the pallet, which barely came to his knees. He looked down at Peta. A tiny gold amulet lay on her chest, and it shimmered and purred. Torg could sense it was a talisman of formidable power, perhaps forged by some long-ago demon or sorcerer to preserve flesh. Peta's body was unmarred, but Torg somehow knew that the little girl had lain in the tower for thousands of years.

He took the amulet in his right hand and snapped the thin chain off her neck. Peta sat up and opened her eyes, which were pure white, without iris or pupil. She screamed and her body flailed. For the briefest of moments, she again was alive.

Then her flesh began to curl, hiss, and disintegrate. The little girl writhed in unimaginable agony.

"Kill me," she screamed. "Hurry! ... Pleeeaaassseee ..."

Tears filled Torg's eyes. He couldn't bear to harm her, but neither could he leave her like this. He closed his left hand around her tiny throat and broke her neck with the slightest shift of his thick fingers.

Peta stopped moving. Silently, her flesh withered and even her bones turned to dust. Her body was gone. When Torg left the tower, the ghost-child was gone too. He wept.

Afterward, he departed Arupa-Loka. The undead followed him to the outer boundary of the city and watched as he slipped into the wilderness. Torg sensed they mourned Peta's loss as much as he.

Why had they imprisoned her for so long? What did she mean to them?

For a month, Torg wandered in bitter cold. North of the Gap of Gamana, the Mahaggata Range split into the shape of a Y. Torg headed northwest. In this far realm, the mountains were a jagged jumble of rock and ice. Torg had never felt so lonely. He had spent just a brief time with Peta, but he missed her as he would a daughter.

Torg studied the amulet but could unravel none of its mysteries. It was ancient; that, at least, was obvious. But he didn't know who had made it, or why. The amulet was circular, smooth, and golden, with no visible embellishments. Its simplicity defied him. Torg decided to destroy it so that it would never again perform such a heinous deed. But the amulet's power was too great. He could not even scratch it, so he chose to hide it.

On the peak of Catu, the northernmost mountain on Triken, Torg discovered a hidden cave. He crawled deep inside on hands and knees and covered the amulet with a shaving of granite. It was a relief to leave it behind. After he left the cave, he witnessed a strange occurrence. A shadow crept across the sun, consuming it bit by bit until the day became as dark as night. Torg stood and watched. Two weeks later, as he journeyed back to Anna, the same thing happened to the full moon.

Slowly but surely, Torg's thoughts returned to the present moment. He was back on Mount Asubha, trapped at the bottom of the pit, desperate to find a way out, and eager to rid himself of the corpse that had fallen on top of him. He looked the dead sentry in the eyes. He needed to have a little talk.

During Torg's imprisonment in the pit, his teeth had fallen out, making it difficult to enunciate the syllables he had learned from his visit with Peta to the Realm of Undeath.

But it would take more than that to cause him to falter.

"*Yakkkkha*," he said.

The dead man's eyes sprang open. "You're not leaving me alone. I'll soil my pants."

"You're *not* alone," Torg said, his speech slowly improving as he grew more used to talking without teeth. "And I'm sorry to say that you've already soiled your pants. But I need to ask you some questions."

"Who am I?" it said.

"You are who you were. But that doesn't matter. I need to ask you what you know."

"I am no longer. I am gone. I will never kiss her."

"Kiss her? Who?"

"I don't remember."

"Never mind," Torg said. "Just listen to me and answer my questions."

"Let *me* go to the warden. *You* stay here and watch."

"Why do you want to go to the warden?"

"That nasty wizard is making noises again. He's crawling out of the pit!"

I must have shouted when I returned from death, Torg thought. It was likely that others had already been alerted.

"Was anyone else with you when you heard the 'nasty wizard' make noises?"

"Yes. And the bastard stuck me."

"Where did he go?"

"I didn't see."

"Who else is up there?"

"Up there?"

Torg realized that the man must have been dead before he fell into the pit. The memory that remained in his corpse still thought it was on the surface. But at least he was newly deceased. His recollections would be strong.

"Who else is near the pit?"

"No one. There was just the two of us."

"Is Mala up there somewhere?"

"The Chain Man? Yes! And he's fearsome, I tell you. I soiled my pants around him more than once."

"And Invictus, the sorcerer? Is he nearby?"

"No. I heard the warden talk about him, but I've never seen him. They say even the Chain Man is afraid of Invictus. But I don't believe it. How could Mala be scared of anything?"

"Is there any way to escape the prison?"

"Escape? If there were, don't you think I would have done it?"

"What if you *had* to try? Where would you go?"

"There is nowhere to go. The walls are watched. More than just sentries are on guard. And even though he's small, the warden is almost as dreadful as the Chain Man. It's hopeless. There is nowhere to go."

Torg sighed. The corpse had told him little, other than to warn him it was likely the pit would be guarded if he could somehow climb out.

Torg struggled to his knees and, with great difficulty, he stood. To fit within the pit's cramped confines, he had to lift the dead body up with him. He now stood almost face to face with the corpse, though Torg was more than a span taller. The claustrophobia was intense, but Torg resisted its contagious effects.

"I ask you again: If you had to *try* to escape, where would you go?"

"The only place would be over the cliff," the corpse said. "But if you didn't slip and fall into the abyss, then the birds or the spider would get you. I'd rather fall."

"Where is the cliff? Is it close to the pit?"

"Yes ... too close."

"Thank you. You've been most helpful."

Torg released the dead body. As it collapsed to its knees, its head again flopped against its chest.

"Good luck in your next existence," Torg whispered. "May you be healthy, happy, and peaceful. After what you've been through, you've earned it."

The corpse began to sizzle. The acids and poisons in the walls of the pit had eaten through the uniform and now worked on the flesh. Within a short time, the body dissolved into bloody slush before vaporizing and vanishing. The smell was atrocious. Torg might have vomited, but he hadn't eaten or drunk for almost a month. His stomach was as empty as a dragon's heart.

Torg's tissues were far more durable than the corpse's. Perhaps no living creature could have resisted the pit as long as he. All the same, touching the walls was painful. He ran his hand along his body. His skin, once tanned and flawless, was now mottled and hairless; and his teeth, fingernails, and toenails had fallen out. He could only imagine how hideous he must look. Probably even worse than Mala.

Torg didn't believe there was much chance he could escape the prison. His return from *Sammaasamaadhi* had recharged his body, but he was still a reduced version of his former self. If Mala were waiting for him on the surface, Torg knew he couldn't defeat him. If Invictus were there, Torg would be even more helpless. He clung to one slight hope: If he could climb out of the pit and somehow get over the side of the cliff, he might catch them off guard. Torg had visited the snow giants more than once in his long life, and they had taught him clever ways to climb and descend difficult cliffs without ropes or other devices.

The pinnacle of Mount Asubha towered 12,000 cubits above sea level, the tallest peak of Mahaggata's northeastern range. Asubha and its sister mountains were jagged, sheer, and glazed with ice, their upper heights considered impossible to climb. That had not stopped Invictus from building his mountaintop prison. The sorcerer had invented—or more accurately, bred—a unique form of transportation. Giant condors with wingspans of forty cubits carried men, supplies, and building materials to Asubha's summit. The monstrous birds had been crossbred with a female dragon, dramatically increasing their size and strength. They had flown Torg to the prison on the back of just such a beast.

During the arduous march from Dibbu-Loka to Avici, Torg had lost his desire to convert Mala. Slowly, he had become obsessed with only one thing—revenge. The extent of Torg's hatred would have dismayed Sister Tathagata, but the wizard no longer cared what the High Nun thought. Mala and Invictus would die. Or Torg would die. Too much had happened for it to be otherwise. The pit was a blasphemy. It had not yet driven him insane, but it had put a dreadful stain on his spirit.

Still, Torg knew he had to be patient. First, he must escape the pit; otherwise, revenge would be impossible. The odds were long, but he would fight until there was no fight left.

Torg flattened his bare shoulder blades against the spongy wall. Acids flared. Poisons seeped down his spine and buttocks. The toxins chewed on his skin like a million voracious mouths. He cried out. The pain was abominable, but at least his flesh didn't turn to slush. He pressed one bare foot against the side of the pit. The disturbance caused the nocuous surface to splutter. He jammed his other foot against the wall. Golden flames flared angrily. The effort paid off. His quivering body was now suspended above the floor. For the first time in weeks, he was not at the deepest depth of hell.

Torg pressed his hands against the sides of the pit. His fingers sank into the wall, which had the same texture as a gooey mass of worms. The large muscles of his back, shoulders, and thighs pulsated, and his biceps and forearms shivered. Where the acids and poisons oozed onto his flesh, golden flames erupted. Torg moaned. He had climbed only one cubit.

The pit was 200 cubits deep.

Torg slid his shoulders up another cubit, dragged one foot upward, and then the other. Now he was two cubits above the floor, his knees bent, his buttocks facing downward. The last surviving hair on his body—a single black curl on his left big toe—burst into flame and disappeared in a tiny puff of smoke.

Three cubits. Five. Ten. Frustration caused Torg to shriek. He wriggled like a tortoise flipped onto its back.

Just 190 cubits to go.

Torg sighed. His physical strength would not suffice. He needed his magic. Though his body was drained, he was still internally aflame. Death Energy roared through his sinews. He would call on it now. The power inside Torg obeyed his will like a loving servant. His ability to wield it had been refined over many centuries. He could spray it like a fountain. Or launch it like a bolt of lightning. He could heal with it. Or kill. He could build with it. Or destroy. And now he would use the power within him to save his own life.

Torg enveloped his body in death's broiling might. Blue flames burst from his back, resembling the fiery tail of a comet. He rose, slowly at first but ever quickening—ten more cubits, fifty, one hundred.

Far above, Torg saw a trickle of radiance, and he roared in delight. It didn't matter what happened once he reached the surface. Escaping the pit was his only concern. He would set himself free and hurtle into the frozen air.

Like lava racing up through a fracture in bedrock, Torg surged toward the surface. When his body catapulted from the hideous hole, the peak of Mount Asubha shuddered violently. The pit—as if ashamed of its inability to contain him—boomed like a thunderclap, then exploded in a cataclysm of crumbled stone.

The wizard soared into the air, somersaulted, and fell a long, long way as if in slow motion.

He struck hard stone and lay still.

Torg peered through the snow-choked air and saw that the moon was waning crescent in the sky's midpoint. As a desert dweller, Torg was well-acquainted with the phases of the moon and the movements of the stars. Now he truly understood the extent of his confinement. The moon had not even been full on the day they imprisoned him in the pit, which meant he'd been trapped for more than three weeks.

Torg shook his head and struggled to his knees. Dawn approached and with it a semblance of light. He scanned his surroundings. It felt like he was witnessing the end of the world.

Asubha rumbled. Torg's emergence from the pit had awakened the mountain's inner violence. The stone split and shattered as if crunched by the hand of a god. As the ground beneath him buckled, he was thrown against a low stone wall. He grasped the top of the wall and stood, looking eastward into the first glow of the rising sun.

Though he was half-blinded by a raging storm, Torg could make out the silhouettes of several dozen guards teetering at the edge of a cliff. One fell, but even before he disappeared from Torg's view, a condor swept out of the sky and seized the guard in midair. Then it soared over Torg's head, with the screaming victim in its huge beak.

Torg recalled the words of the dead sentry: "The only place (to escape) would be over the cliff. There is no wall there. But if you didn't slip and fall into the abyss, then the birds or the spider would get you."

Torg had seen one of the birds. Would he also encounter the spider before much longer?

A sonorous voice boomed through the hysteria. Torg recognized it instantly, for he had spent more than six weeks learning to hate it. Mala stood in the center of the prison, waving his arms and bellowing at anyone within range.

"Stay away from the cliff, you stupid donkeys. Come to me!"

Another massive quake shook the prison. Several buildings shuddered and crumbled, tossing Torg to-and-fro. He had used up almost all his remaining strength during his escape from the pit, but he wasn't ready to give up yet. Now, with the mountain threatening to shatter around him, he crawled shakily toward the cliff.

It was his last chance.

The Chain Man had not yet seen Torg, but a much smaller creature—less than a third Mala's height—ran toward him, waving its stubby arms.

"Over here!" it said. "The wizard is free. *OVER HERE*!"

Torg watched the creature approach. He recognized it as an ancient enemy. He had defeated its father's army in a great war many centuries before.

"A Stone-Eater ..." Torg sighed. "And I am already weary."

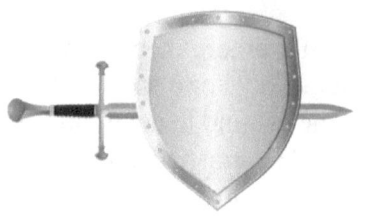

PEAK OF DESPAIR

O ver here!" the Stone-Eater said.
Another immense reverberation jolted the prison, knocking Gulah off his feet. When he stood, he saw Torg squirming toward the edge of the cliff. Somehow, the Death-Knower knew where to go. This puzzled the Stone-Eater but also secretly delighted him. Gulah didn't want the wizard to die just yet.

Despite the mountain's upheavals, the wretched bastard Mala was lumbering toward Torg and making good progress. None of the pathetic sentries could stop the Death-Knower, even in his weakened state, but the Chain Man was more than capable of ruining the warden's plans. Gulah had been a little too rambunctious in his ruse, and now he had to do something fast. Trying not to look overly suspicious, he stepped in front of Mala—and at that moment Asubha lurched again. Gulah seized the opportunity, throwing himself against Mala's stocky legs. Though he was only a third Mala's size, the Stone-Eater was still able to knock the giant sideways. The Chain Man slipped and fell, crashing against the stone floor and cursing wildly. When he tried to stand, Gulah tripped him again.

"You pathetic *ass!*" Mala said. "If you can't help, at least get out of my way."

From the raging darkness, Gulah watched as a wild Sampati swooped down and attempted to grasp the Chain Man in its talons. In an extraordinary feat of strength, Mala grabbed one of its clawed feet and flipped the beast over his back. The creature smote the stone floor and blew apart. Feathers, scales, flesh, and bone splattered everywhere, and a steaming chunk of gore struck Gulah in the face. When the Stone-Eater cleared his eyes, his worst fears were realized. The damnable Chain Man was closing in on the wizard, who was just a stride or two from the edge of the cliff. Would Mala catch him?

Perhaps not. A slab of granite tore itself from the mountaintop, rising between Torg and Mala like the crest of a tsunami. The stone screamed as if in pain, towering above Mala, teetering momentarily, and then falling. The Chain Man scrambled back, barely avoiding the shattering collapse. When the debris cleared, Mala remained standing, waving his arms. But Torg was gone.

The Death-Knower had made it over the cliff!

Gulah smiled, regained his footing, and worked his way through the tempest to a secret exit, leaving Mala—and the doomed prison on the peak of Asubha—behind forever. Gulah knew the ways down through the heart of the mountain better than any other. Even a cave troll could not have kept up with him.

He beamed.

So much had gone right.

If fate allowed, he would encounter the wizard one last time.

And when he did, he would rip Torg's heart from his chest and devour it raw to avenge the long-ago murder of Slag, his beloved father.

The mountain became a symbol of impermanence, tearing itself apart like a man ripping off his own head.

Torg crept to the edge and peered over the side. The icy stone was as slippery as a demon's tongue. Torg couldn't judge the depth of the abyss. The precipice dove downward into a morass of tornadic winds, fist-sized hail, and jagged lightning. In the last breath of darkness before dawn, he could see less than a stone's throw. He believed that if he fell, he wouldn't strike bottom for a long time.

Torg could sense the Stone-Eater behind him, closing fast. He knew the beast well, but it had been many centuries since their last encounter. Besides, Torg had many enemies, and right now it was Mala who was his main concern. If the Chain Man caught him in his current state, Torg would be doomed.

Behind Torg came a whining roar, and the rooftop of the mountain vomited a titanic slab of granite, casting Torg over the edge of the cliff. He would have fallen to his death had he not thrust out his right hand

and caught a tiny lip of stone with his fingertips. He hung there precariously by one hand before grasping hold with his other.

The mountain trembled again. Torg searched for footing with his bare toes, but the cliff wall was too smooth and slippery. He had hoped his rock-climbing skills would get him down, but he now feared he couldn't go much farther without falling, especially with the gusty winds and poor visibility.

The slab of stone above him collapsed, shattering ferociously. A disgusting barrage of screams and curses from Mala soon followed.

With his face pressed against the wall, Torg moved horizontally along the cliff's edge, hand by hand, hoping to find some sort of foothold. As if his predicament weren't bad enough, a wild Sampati emerged from the broiling darkness and hovered behind him, reaching out with its deadly talons and forcing Torg to call on his draining energy reserves to fight the gigantic creature off. The wizard conjured a blue flare that sprang from his eyes and struck the half condor/half dragon on its leg. Squawking in pain, the beast swerved away from the cliff. Half a dozen wild condors—a third of the Sampati's size but still very dangerous—sensed the crossbreed's distress and attacked, tearing at feather and scale.

Mala's obnoxious voice rose above the confusion.

"Help me find the Death-Knower, you slimy worms! Where is Gulah? If the coward has deserted, I'll squash his square little head."

Doing his best to ignore Mala's ranting, Torg continued to creep along the wall. His arms ached and his bare toes couldn't find the slightest indentation. If he lost his grip, he would fall a thousand fathoms.

Dawn continued to push against the darkness, attempting to overthrow the night. But Torg held little hope that the impending daylight would improve his situation much. The storm was too intense.

Before hope faded entirely, Torg discovered a tiny fissure just large enough to contain the big toe of his left foot. The farther he moved to his left, the wider the crack became. Soon, both his feet were rooted in the rock, and he could hold on with only his right hand while he felt along the wall with his left.

At waist level, he discovered a knob of stone and gripped it with his left hand, which freed his right. Then he thrust out his buttocks and squatted. It was a precarious position, but at least it was a start.

The fissure descended. He slid his left foot a few inches along the crack, followed by his right. Then he released the knob with his left hand and grasped it with his right. This enabled him to feel along the wall with his left hand, grab a protruding flake, and use it as leverage to traverse several more inches along the face of the cliff. Now, his head was five cubits below the edge. But his progress was agonizingly slow. And he was so weak. If the mountain shook again, he would probably fall.

"There you are, you ugly rat!" he heard Mala yell. "Where are you *going*?"

Torg saw the Chain Man—on hands and knees—peering over the edge. Mala's eyes glowed red, and not even the surging winds could disperse the stink of his breath.

Lightning crashed nearby, illuminating the two bitter enemies.

"Look at you," Mala said, laughing in the manner Torg had grown to despise. "You're as ugly as a toothless monkey! How did you get down there without falling? *Everyone* falls. Unless the spider gets them."

Torg was five cubits below the edge of the cliff, but Mala's arms were at least six cubits long. The Chain Man dropped to his chest and reached down, trying to grab Torg by the scruff of his neck. With his free hand, Torg swatted Mala's arm and knocked it away. The Chain Man shouted in frustration and lunged for him again.

Torg had little strength left, but he conjured a weak blast of blue fire. It leaped from his eyes and singed Mala's face, but it lacked the potency to do much damage. Still, the Chain Man snarled and drew back.

Something huge and powerful snared Torg's left ankle and pulled his foot away from the fissure. He looked down and saw a dreadful black shape clinging to the sheer wall beneath him. It yanked Torg downward. He scrambled for any kind of hold, but he was torn free of the rock. As he fell, he heard Mala's desperate shrieks: "No ... *NO*! He is not for *you*!"

Whatever grasped Torg's ankle had no problem negotiating the precipice. It descended the wall with an agility that far surpassed the snow giants or any other expert climbers, quickly dragging Torg a long distance. His body slammed again and again against the lumpy stone as he descended. Torg tried desperately to free his ankle, but the black beast drew him into a hole in the cliff's side. His head banged against the cold stone. His consciousness waned.

The rigidity of the stone gave way to spongy silk, softer but more insidious. The silk clung to the surfaces of the tunnel. Torg felt fresh threads fall upon him in gobs, encasing first his arms and then his legs. It trapped him in darkness. He couldn't move.

The immense creature hovered near his feet, but then it squeezed past him toward the opening of the hole. Torg felt the disgusting folds of its thorny hide press against his face. His attacker stopped at the breach and paused there as if guarding a newly won prize.

Torg strained against the silk. The threads were dreadfully strong, and his strength was fading beyond resistance. Death Energy kept him alive, but his ordeal in the pit had weakened him too much. All he could do was lie there, miserable and hopeless. *So, this is how it ends? As breakfast for a spider?* It was absurd enough to make him laugh.

At the opening of its lair, the beast shuffled angrily. Something passed close by—probably one of the wild condors—and the spider took a swipe at it. Torg watched with disinterest. He made one final attempt to break free and failed. Now there was nothing more he could do. He was defeated. Unconsciousness slinked ever closer like a hungry predator. But even as he was fading, Torg sensed movement even deeper in the hole. Then he heard a moaning sound. The intricate assemblage of silk trembled. Torg couldn't see, but he strained to discern what lay nearby.

Someone else was trapped with him—one of Asubha's prisoners or sentries? The poor fool sounded even worse than Torg felt. What hell was this? It wasn't as bad as the pit. But it was close.

The moaning intensified.

And then the spider returned. Ready to eat.

The spider's horrific mouth drew close to Torg's face and neck, the only parts of his body not encased by silk threads. A pair of curved fangs, each as long as one of his arms, snapped upon his upper torso, easily piercing the silk but failing to puncture his flesh. Torg's body remained impenetrable, even in his crippled state.

The spider hissed and chomped on him again with the same result. It crept backward several steps, then dove forward and drove the poisoned fangs against him. Even then, the fangs and their toxins were ineffective.

"Begone, foul beast," Torg muttered. "I am not for the likes of you."

But there was still a lisp in his speech, and his words felt impotent.

And then to his horror, something responded from deeper in the hole.

"My king, have you come to rescue me?"

The spider reacted instantly, bounding over Torg toward the voice. He heard a scream, and then he recognized his fellow prisoner. It was Sōbhana! But how did she come to be here? Confusion and sorrow made him nauseous.

Evidently, the spider was tormenting Sōbhana. She screamed again. Torg couldn't bear it, and he fought with all his might to escape from his silk prison. His panicked anger flooded through him, removing the last remnants of his centuries-old restraint.

Torg's magic became wildly dangerous.

The wizard knew this all too well. He had spent almost his entire existence learning how to bridle the savage might of Death Energy. Mostly he had succeeded, except in one crucial area—sex. When he achieved orgasm, he lost control of his power. Nine centuries before, on the night after he'd successfully returned from his first Death Visit, Torg had made love to a Tugarian woman. During his climax, he had incinerated her and the tent in which they lay, turning the sand beneath them to glass. This devastated Torg, and he hastily arranged an assembly of Vasi masters to confess his crime. But as far as the Tugar elders knew, nothing like this had ever happened to any previous Death-Knower. Because there was no forewarning or ill intention, the masters vindicated Torg. But his guilt continued to haunt him.

Torg was extraordinary, the strength of his magic exceeding any of his predecessors. But that same strength was also a curse, dooming him to a life of celibacy. He craved sex and was highly capable, but he was denied its pleasures. It was a torment and a loneliness he had borne for 900 years.

Torg's reaction to Sōbhana's misery created a similar chaos. His mind and body were drunk with exhaustion, and he no longer controlled his emotions. In an orgasm of anguish, blue flames erupted from every pore. The silk threads caught fire like dry grass, turning the passageway into a conflagration. The spider exited the hole in a panic.

Torg was free of his bonds, but the flames roared on. With every shred of his remaining strength, he willed the blaze to diminish, but it still sizzled in pockets throughout the tunnel. When most of the smoke cleared, enough light remained from the glowing embers to provide visibility.

Sōbhana lay close by, her naked body mutilated. Torg's flames had burned off her hair and scorched her skin, but worse damage had already occurred before his fiery outburst. Large portions of her ears were gone, disintegrated by the spider's persistent attempts to feed, and her right arm and right leg displayed gruesome patches of exposed bone. Worst of all was her right shoulder, which was mangled and diseased. The warrior looked like a flesh-and-blood body slowly transforming into a skeleton. How long had she been here? A day? A week? Longer?

Torg cried out. Anger and sorrow grasped his heart—and squeezed. Tears gushed from his eyes. He crawled to her and cradled her in his arms. He had never experienced such bitterness.

Sōbhana looked at him. Her eyes widened.

"I feared how I might look to you if you ever found me. But you've fared little better, my lord."

She managed a tattered giggle.

This mortified Torg. "Sōbhana. Brave one ... loyal one ... how came you here?"

"I could never forsake my king. You are my life." Then she took a long breath and sighed. "I've never told you—or anyone—but there's no reason to hide my feelings any longer. I love you, Torg. I always have and always will. I would have made you an excellent wife."

Torg's tears drenched her face and dripped into her mouth. Though she was disfigured, he recognized her true beauty for the first time. Then he hugged her so hard she moaned.

Torg heard a noise near the opening of the hole. In his despair, he had forgotten the spider. It stood close by, glaring at them, torn between fear and desire.

"Her name is Dukkhatu," Sōbhana said. "She is almost as ancient as Bhayatupa. The dragon told me so."

"Bhayatupa? What do you mean?"

Sōbhana coughed. Greasy blood spewed from her mouth. She grimaced, struggling to breathe. An ordinary creature would have been long dead. And yet Sōbhana, with the strength of an Asēkha, had endured this torture for ... how long? Torg couldn't bear to even think about it.

"My life is over," she said. "My body will soon perish." More coughing. "We both know what must be done."

"No, Sōbhana. You will not perish! I'll carry you down the side of the mountain. We'll return to Anna together."

"And I will become your wife?" Despite her horrific appearance, her smile was beautiful. In the final moments of her life, Torg fell in love with her. But if they had ever become husband and wife, they would have been forced to live in celibacy, which would have been a greater torment than either could have endured.

There was no need to tell her that now.

"Yes, my love. You will become my wife if you so desire."

She coughed some more, the pain gnawing greedily on the remains of her consciousness. Yet she managed to smile again, and the tenderness in her ravaged expression brought fresh tears to his eyes.

"When Mala took you, I followed despite your orders. You vowed to kill any who pursued; yet I still believed I would somehow rescue you. Now I see how both will occur. We must perform *Sivathika.* Nothing else remains."

Sivathika had existed among the Tugars from the beginnings of their history, though it remained a secret ritual unknown to outsiders. When a desert warrior was mortally wounded in battle, another Tugar would approach and—if granted permission—press his or her mouth against the others. The dying warrior then breathed what remained of his or her *Life Essence* into the survivor's lungs where it was absorbed into the blood like psychic nourishment. The survivor became physically stronger and even possessed a dual personality for a short time afterward. It was a rare and high honor to give or receive *Sivathika.*

"Kiss me, my love," Sōbhana said. "Do not deny me."

The spider crept closer.

"Do it now, before it's too late," she said, her words barely recognizable. "I'll be gone from this body, regardless. It will be my privilege to join your spirit. In that way, I'll become more than a wife; I'll become a part of you."

"No ... *no*! I'm not ready. Your loss will cost too much. I would rather die here alongside you."

"Do not dishonor me with such worthless speech," she rasped, each word growing weaker. "Kiss me, my love—and then avenge me. A weapon is near that can destroy Dukkhatu. When I become a part of you, you'll know where to find it."

Sōbhana reached up and wrapped her left arm around his neck, pressing her mouth against his lips. For a moment, they kissed like lovers. But Torg felt her body fail. At the last instant before her death, she blew her hot essence into his mouth. He inhaled with equal strength.

The Torgon and Asēkha-Sōbhana became one.

As a Death-Knower, Torg believed that nothing in life compared to the wonder of death. All other experiences paled. The fear of death was a waste of energy. Why dread something so magnificent—and so inevitable?

But when Sōbhana's psychic force entered his lungs and flowed into his blood, Torg was as tantalized as he'd been during any Death Visit. A symphony of thoughts, emotions, and memories set his senses ablaze. The sizzling bundle of karmic energy once known as Sōbhana surged into every cell of his being, sharing residence with his mind and body.

When he opened his eyes, Sōbhana's flesh was dead but her karma was very much alive. He gently laid her corpse upon the floor of the spider's lair and then sat up to gather his wits. She was already conversing with him internally, disappointed to discover he had thought so little of her—at least in terms of her potential as a mate. But she understood his dilemma regarding women.

"I'm sorry, my beloved," she said within his mind. "But even without sex, I would have been a good wife. Just sharing ordinary life with you would have been enough."

"I didn't perceive your intentions," he said. "You seemed so young. And I felt so old. But as you now know, I have long admired you for other reasons."

"I know much that I didn't know before. Such wonder! I can only hope to carry some of this wisdom to my next existence. If so, I will perform miracles."

"That, you have already done. I will see to it—if I survive—that the Tugars rank you among the greats."

"Speaking of survival, there's still the matter of the spider. She is tensed and prepared for another attack. Now that we're joined, you know how to kill her—and what to kill her with."

The Silver Sword lay a short distance from where Torg (and Sōbhana) now sat. Apparently, the spider had hidden it instead of discarding it. But Torg's conflagration had uncovered its location.

Torg (and Sōbhana) reached for the sword, causing Dukkhatu to hiss and retreat. They grasped the Silver Sword in his right hand. Instantly, he recognized aspects of it that Sōbhana had not—and now she saw the sword through his perception, and it amazed her. The sword was not forged from silver; or any metal native to Triken. It had been made in a far more ancient time using otherworldly ores. The Silver Sword itself was lifeless; unlike Torg's ivory staff, it harbored no internal magic. But nothing it struck could withstand it. Mala survived Sōbhana's glancing blow only because it had not been a direct hit.

When Torg (and Sōbhana) rose to his knees in the tunnel, his desire for vengeance melded with the Asēkha's. Though still physically drained, Torg was as dangerous as he'd ever been. His sudden burst of strength wouldn't last forever—Sōbhana's essence would fade and Torg's torture-induced exhaustion would return—but for the time being, he (she) and the sword were a lethal combination.

The passageway was tall enough for Torg to stand upright, but it wasn't wide enough for Dukkhatu to fully extend her legs. Inside the hole, she was less mobile than outside on the cliff wall. Her best chance to kill her prey would come in the vertiginous open.

"You are hideous," Torg said to Dukkhatu. "You've destroyed much that is of value. But your reign of terror has come to an end. Prepare to meet your doom."

The last five words were spoken with the woman's voice and facial expressions, which puzzled the spider. The beast froze—paralyzed by uncertainty—as the man moved toward her. Dukkhatu's compulsion to rend and devour was immense, but her dismay continued to expand. First, the prey had unleashed a deadly fire in her lair, and now it wielded the strange weapon. Its eyes held no fear, but they burned with anger. Should she flee? The humiliating thought ate at her evil mind like acid.

The man moved faster than she expected, forcing Dukkhatu to turn and flee but not before she felt the tip of the sword cut through a small portion of her abdomen above her spinnerets. She leaped through the hole and dropped at least fifty cubits before catching hold of the wall. When she looked up, she saw a blurry shape moving at the opening of her lair. The deadly thing was searching for her! She was enraged—and terrified. Her fangs clattered. Her wound dripped black blood. It was little more than a scratch, but it burned.

Never in her long life had Dukkhatu been so ably thwarted. And now it had happened *twice* in just a short time. The other food had resisted her, as well. The meat of the first one was so tough she had had to work on it for days just to drink a few drops. And this second one was even more difficult. She couldn't so much as scratch it.

Dukkhatu desired food, but now revenge had become her greater hunger. The female was dead—as far as Dukkhatu could tell—but the male still lived, and his very presence haunted her. She felt the vibrations in the stone as he began his descent.

But this wasn't over yet. She knew hundreds of places to hide. She would watch, wait, and follow.

If she could attack him unawares, she could wrest away the weapon and have her way with him. Or she could sneak up and knock him off the side of the cliff and watch with glee as he fell to his death.

Maybe after he splattered on the stone, he would be easier to eat.

Torg peered over the edge of the cliff and saw the spider clinging to the wall. A trick of perspective made Dukkhatu look larger from a distance than she had up close. He pounded a fist against the stone. The spider scampered farther downward and disappeared beneath a ledge.

"Dammit! I wasn't fast enough," he said out loud in a nasal voice. "I should've killed Dukkhatu when I had the chance."

"It's my fault, beloved," he said aloud, but this time with Sōbhana's voice and mannerisms. "I distracted you with my silly romantic talk."

"It was both of our faults, then," he thought, attempting an internal laugh. "But now we must find a way to get down. That would be difficult enough, even if the spider weren't out there somewhere."

"We'll find a way," she said within his mind. But already her voice was fading.

The air was calm but wintry. The storm that had wracked Asubha during Torg's escape had relinquished its fury. Snow still fell, but softly. Torg was naked, and he shivered in the morning chill. On top of everything else, he would have to make the descent with little hope of warmth.

Out of curiosity, Torg rolled onto his back on the icy stone and looked up at the peak of the mountain. From this vantage point, he could see only a fraction of the previous night's destruction. He wondered what it might look like from a dragon's perspective. He supposed it would be blown apart. But from where Torg lay, there was little to observe other than several scars along the wall that had been caused by falling boulders.

Torg rolled onto his stomach and searched for signs of Dukkhatu. He couldn't see her, but he knew she was down there somewhere. What were her intentions? Perhaps, he'd injured her sufficiently to scare her off for good.

"You don't believe that and neither do I," he said in Sōbhana's voice. "Dukkhatu won't depart without a fight."

To emphasize this point, Sōbhana replayed her memory of Bhayatupa's description of the spider. Torg became enraged at the dragon for using Sōbhana to get to him, but he didn't blame Sōbhana for not resisting. It was an odd partnership, but they had needed each other. Torg wondered if he would ever meet Bhayatupa again.

"I believe you will," Sōbhana whispered in his thoughts. "But I now understand that the answers he seeks from you will not succor him."

"His cravings have no merit," Torg spoke in his own voice. "His lore is great and his experiences many, but his wisdom has failed to flourish. His ego is so strong, he fails to comprehend that ego doesn't truly exist."

"I know, my lord," Sōbhana said silently. "I'm a part of you now, remember?"

"And I'm treasuring every moment."

"I know that, too."

"Please don't go."

"I won't ... not yet."

Still on his stomach and facing the opening of the tunnel, Torg dropped his legs over the ledge. This forced him to hold the sword in his mouth. The blade burned his toothless gums.

"I must be quite the sight," he mumbled.

"You look atrocious, to be honest," she said. "You have no hair, your skin is covered with sores, and you sound like an old man who has misplaced his wooden teeth. Compared to you, Mala is handsome. But

I love you, anyway."

Torg laughed so hard the sword fell out of his mouth and clattered on the ledge. The laughter was a strange mixture of male and female tones.

Then Sōbhana said, "A wild Sampati comes. I'll keep quiet until we dispose of it."

"How do you know? I don't see it."

"I am fading, beloved. I exist in both worlds and can sense things beyond your awareness. This might prove useful to you, until I am no longer."

Sure enough, the Sampati appeared from around a bend in the mountain. When it saw Torg, it dove toward him like a hawk attacking a pigeon.

Torg, however, was no pigeon. He hauled himself back onto the ledge, picked up the sword, and stood to meet the hybrid monster. As the Sampati made its first pass, Torg hid the sword behind his back, not wanting the beast to sense its supernal power.

The Sampati circled and came for him again, this time intending to strike. Torg waited until the last moment before bounding off the ledge. With the sword again in his mouth, he fell onto the creature. Then he dug his fingers and toes between the feathers and scales and held tight.

The Sampati veered away from the mountain, twisting and shaking like an angry stallion but failing to throw him. When Torg drove the sword into the thick of its back, the Sampati shrieked and tumbled out of control, smiting the mountainside.

Torg was thrown against the stone and knocked unconscious. His limp body slid down the wall and came to rest on a flattened outcrop.

The sword clattered beside him.

Both lay still.

Torg dreamed sweetly of a tender woman. Together they stood holding hands beneath the largest and brightest moon he had ever beheld. Torg assumed he was with Sōbhana, but when he turned to look more closely, he saw someone else. The woman's hair was the first thing to attract his attention. It was blond and hung past her waist—unlike Sōbhana's, which was black and shoulder-length.

The pale stranger was taller than Sōbhana but less muscular and more voluptuous. Her blue-gray eyes contained a sparkling power Torg found both intimidating and enticing. He'd seen her before but couldn't remember when or where.

Was she a Warlish witch? Despite the flawlessness of her beauty, he didn't think so.

Was she a sorceress? That seemed closer to the truth.

Was she good or evil? To Torg, she felt mysterious but unthreatening.

The woman smiled at him, causing his heart to thump. An erection surged inside his trousers, and he backed away. *Don't you know who I am? Don't you know what I do to women who get too close?*

The sorceress didn't seem afraid. On the contrary, she seemed pleased by his presence. And yet she remained silent.

Then Torg heard a faraway voice and spun around to discern its source. In the moonlight, he saw the glowing silhouette of a figure on a distant hill. It was waving, slowly.

"Farewell, my love!" Sōbhana called.

Her words caused so much pain. He dropped to his knees.

"You and I were not meant to be," she said. "A part of me will always love you, but I am no longer. I am gone."

Then she leaped into darkness—but not before shouting an urgent warning: "Wake up, *now*. The spider comes!"

Torg opened his eyes. For a while, his vision was hazy. When he was able to focus, he saw Dukkhatu standing nimbly on the wall just a short distance above him. He sat up. The monstrous spider reacted to his sudden movement, rearing on her back legs, fangs snapping.

Torg looked around for the sword and saw it lying two paces to his left on the flat ledge that had broken his fall. He lunged for it, but in his dazed condition the spider was too fast for him. She swatted the sword with the tip of her damaged front leg, and the weapon tumbled off the ledge and spun downward, sparking as it struck the floor of the talus far below.

Dukkhatu retreated and reared again, her front legs stabbing at the air, hypersensitive to Torg's slightest movement. It surprised him that she didn't attack right then. Perhaps her predator instincts were making her cautious; she hoped to stare down her prey until it panicked and fled, then ambush it from behind. But Dukkhatu had more reason to be afraid than she knew. Exhaustion made Torg vulnerable, but some of Sōbhana's strength still surged in his sinews.

When he stood, the spider retreated a little farther, apparently sensing something in his manner that made her wary. Anger overwhelmed Torg, shoving his spiritual training aside. The High Nun of Dibbu-Loka would have admonished him: *Hate never dispels hate.* Some part of Torg knew Sister Tathagata was correct, but he was beyond caring. He missed Sōbhana too much, despising what had been done to her—and to him. He had grown to hate Invictus and Mala and the wicked creature that now trembled uncertainly above him. Revenge was ugly and ignorant, but it offered sweetness that Torg couldn't resist, especially on this miserable day.

Torg's wrath demanded penance. This time—sword or no sword— he wouldn't fail.

Torg jumped toward the spider. Dukkhatu attempted to skitter backward, but the wizard grabbed a thick segment of her left front leg and held on tight. Her ancient exoskeleton cracked.

Dukkhatu leaned forward and tried to stab her fangs into his face, but he caught one massive tooth in his free hand and snapped it in half. Poison spurted from the break, sizzling on Torg's bare skin, but he ignored the pain. The *frenzy* was upon him. He would settle for nothing less than her death.

Dukkhatu sensed the extent of his malice and tried to shake him. He defied her, scrambling up her leg and onto her back. Torg pounded his great fists against her thorax. There were cracks and crunches and more black blood.

In a final attempt to escape, she curled into a defensive ball and rolled. Torg dug his hands into the grotesque hair that sprang from her bloated abdomen. The spider and the wizard rumbled toward the ledge, struck it hard, and bounced over the side. They fell long and far in an airy silence onto a knot of sharp stones. Torg landed on top of her, his fall cushioned just enough to keep him alive. Then he rolled off her shattered bulk and lost consciousness, again.

This time there were no dreams. When he opened his eyes, the ruins of Dukkhatu sprawled before him. The spider lay on her back, pierced in many places by prickly black rocks. Her hideous legs quivered, and a wet, whistling sound came from her mouth.

The same mouth that had tortured Sōbhana's flesh.

The *frenzy* returned. Torg tore a chunk of obsidian from the ground, climbed onto the spider's exposed belly, and stabbed the stone into her hide, perforating her long, tubular heart. Dukkhatu let out a final, ear-shattering scream—and went still. But Torg didn't stop. He drove the stone into her again and again, punching huge holes in her carcass.

Her body shredded and tore apart.

Her entrails splashed in his face.

Hate and despair drove his madness. When he no longer had the strength to move, Torg collapsed face-first in Dukkhatu's gore.

He didn't remember standing. He wandered—naked and shivering—through and around the crumbled stone. Staggering, falling, crawling. Tears rinsed a little of the filth from his face, but his broken body reeked of the spider's stink.

Heaps of razor-sharp obsidian were scattered among the cluster of smoother stones as if planted there with tiny black seeds. It took all Torg's remaining will not to grasp another shard and drive it into his own heart, ending his pain.

His life had become nothing but pain. Why breathe any longer? His endurance was gone, his hopes destroyed. Who could blame him for giving up? Not even Sister Tathagata could ask any more of him.

What did it matter, anyway? All things were impermanent—he as much as anything else. The time of his ending had come. A future lifetime beckoned.

Perhaps he would live it in a better place than this.

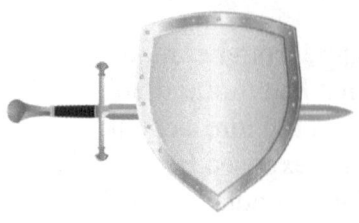

ASTHENOLITH

The Silver Sword came to rest amid a tangle of obsidian, the volcanic glass protruding from the ground like black fangs. Yet the great weapon appeared unharmed. Through his tears, Torg saw it glimmering in the bright noon sun and crawled toward the sword. He wasn't sure why he wanted to retrieve it; he barely had the strength to pick it up. But on this stark and frozen ridge between Asubha and one of its sister mountains, the sword was his last connection to his former self. Though he had held it for only a little while, it felt like his only remaining friend. And it reminded him of Sōbhana, who had also wielded the weapon.

As he struggled forward, Torg laughed and cried like a deranged fool. If a young Tugar had seen him—naked, hairless, toothless—the child would have fled in terror, mistaking him for a sinister monster that had slithered from the dark depths of a cave. But Torg was delirious with grief and had no concern for his appearance. Not even a being of his stature could endure such prolonged torture. He had been placed in the pit while already weak and had spent many long days trapped within its black horror. Finally, he had escaped only to discover that the one person in the world who loved him most had suffered in ways every bit as horrid as his own—and all because she was trying to rescue him. Torg had once thought of Sōbhana as a younger sister, but her genuine connection to him was revealed in her final moments of life. Flashes of her memory and personality still clung to his psyche. Torg mourned her loss like she'd been his longtime lover, as impossible as that would have been.

Hill-sized heaps of stone that had been ripped from Asubha's crown stood in Torg's way, but he clambered over them like a drunken chameleon. He approached the obsidian and climbed onto the razor-sharp rocks.

He reached for the sword and closed his hand on the hilt.

A heavy foot pounded on his fingers. Torg cried out and looked up into a blinding sun.

Something kicked Torg in the face and sent him tumbling into the teeth of the obsidian. When his sight cleared, he saw a stout figure looming over him. Flames flared from its flat nostrils and smoke seeped from its ears. Its hide had the texture of an elephant halfway turned to stone. The creature grabbed the sword from Torg and held it in one hand while waving a spear of obsidian in the other. The beast brought the black volcanic glass to its mouth and chomped on it like it was snacking on an ear of corn. Torg heard loud crunching sounds.

"You murdered my father," it said, spitting out bits of stone as it spoke. "For that, I will enjoy a long-awaited revenge. But first, I have promises to keep."

Several other Stone-Eaters stood nearby.

"Give him a sip of Asava," Gulah said. "We need him alive. But he could still be dangerous. Don't underestimate him despite his pathetic appearance."

One of the Stone-Eaters lifted Torg's head and poured scorching liquid down his throat. He felt like he was swallowing lava. Though his stomach burned, strength surged through his sinews but also a drugged weariness. Sleep strode forward and claimed him. He was incapable of resisting it.

Torg didn't know how long or deeply he slept, but he regained partial consciousness several times. Gulah and his fellow Stone-Eaters had strapped him to a crude litter and were dragging him across the rocks. It was a bumpy ride.

They splashed more of the Asava into his mouth, causing him to gag. But Gulah slapped his hand against Torg's lips and forced him to swallow. Once again, he felt the odd combination of strength and weariness. It was the first nourishment of any kind he'd received in almost a month. But Torg craved water more than anything. If he could take a long drink and pour the rest over his head, he might shake this drowsiness.

Again Torg slept, but his dreams raged out of control. Then a wicked thud shook him awake. He saw that they were approaching the mouth of a broad cave in Asubha's sheer side. Several Stone-Eaters stood guard at the maw of the cavity along with an enormous troll that shied from the bright sunlight. There were also three women, two extremely beautiful and one extremely ugly. Warlish witches ... just what he needed.

The Asava—whatever it contained—had re-energized Torg's vitality. Though he was drugged and barely able to move, he felt his body responding internally to the sizzling sustenance, increasing his desire to resist.

When the Stone-Eaters dragged him into the cave, the ground became smooth and the ride less chaotic. Torg slept in relative comfort and dreamed again. This time, he wandered in absolute darkness. But he could sense objects before bumping into them, which enabled him to move boldly forward, unperturbed by his lack of vision. Torg heard a small figure rise beside him. It grasped his hand. He could not see it, but he knew who it was.

"Peta, I've missed you so much, my dear friend. But how came you here?"

The little girl giggled. Torg remembered the sound of her laughter with fondness.

"You rescued me from the tower. For that, I'm grateful. When you saved me, I foresaw your future and knew you'd need my help. So I stayed to look after you."

"I don't understand. When you died—when I *released* you—your karma should have moved on. Only demons are immune to the natural cycle of life and death. You aren't a demon. This should not be."

"I can't defy my future forever, but a few hundred years is no great matter. In my reckoning, you ended my suffering just a moment ago." Peta then squeezed his massive hand. "But we've already spent far too much time in greeting. I must tell you important things before *she* returns."

"She?"

"The demon ... Vedana."

"Was it the demon who imprisoned you in the tower?"

"Vedana recognized my abilities."

"Your father told me you were blind. But he also said you had powers that the demons found valuable. What did he mean?"

"They ... she ... found my powers valuable enough to imprison me for ten millennia. The amulet you discovered on my chest kept my physical body intact while Vedana's magic controlled my spirit. She used me for terrible things—and eventually for the most terrible thing of all. Without my clairvoyance, she could not have created Invictus."

"You foresaw his birth?"

"I can't deny it. Vedana had spent almost her entire existence breeding with mortals. Her offspring were magical and powerful, but none attained the might she desired. When she discovered me, it renewed her hopes. She knew I could guide her in the ways that mattered. And against my will, I did guide her." Peta paused, deep in thought. Then she said, "But you came along and disrupted her plans, removing me from her sway before she was ready. In most ways, I had already shown her enough. She was able to mate with a man whose bloodlines were interwoven in just the right order, and from his seed she bore Invictus' father, who in turn bore the greatest bane in all of history. However, when Vedana lost my guidance, she also lost the foresight that would have enabled her to control Invictus. And now, no one is his master. The Sun God is like wildfire in a forest long plagued by drought. He threatens more than just our land. If he continues to grow unimpeded, he will endanger *all* things."

"I don't know how to impede him," Torg said.

Peta nodded. "Invictus' rise hasn't gone unnoticed. There are beings beyond all known laws, natural or otherwise, and they are watching the sorcerer with growing interest—and planning his demise."

"How do you know this? Who are you, really?"

Peta giggled again. "I'm just a little blind girl who can see too well for her own good. But allow me to finish before the demon comes to stop me. There's more you must know. Vedana still desires control, but her grandson has become her most lethal enemy. Invictus wields enough power to eliminate the demon and her kind utterly. She and her minions fear that more than all else. For this reason—and others—Vedana schemes to dethrone him. The first step in a long process is for her to become impregnated ... by you."

"Then her plan will fail. I can't impregnate anyone. I can only burn and destroy."

"You're wrong! There are three females on Triken who can abide you. Vedana is one. She is great enough to withstand the fury of your orgasm and retain the wonder of your seed."

Such words, coming from a child, made Torg uncomfortable. But then again, was Peta really a child? "If that is so, then how do I thwart her? I'm a prisoner who lacks the strength to resist."

"I beg you … *do not* thwart her. She must bear your child."

Torg felt pressure on his arms. The skin on his face stung.

"She comes," Peta said. "Farewell!"

Thick hands shook him and tore Torg from sleep. Something slapped his face hard and often. When he opened his eyes, it took a moment for his vision to clear.

There stood Vedana, the mother of all demons.

And she wasn't alone.

"Bastards! Asses!" Vedana was shouting. "I told you to not let him sleep. She has *spoken* to him."

"Who has spoken to him?" Gulah said. "What are you talking about? No one's been near him."

"You don't understand, you idiot," Vedana said. "Who knows what *she* is capable of? She *sees*! How can you be so stupid?"

In a cavern deep inside the mountain, Gulah drew the Silver Sword and waved the point in Vedana's face. "Be careful with your words, demon. I've endured enough abuse in recent days from Mala, and my patience is withered. Because we're allies, I'll allow you to have your way with him. But be quick. I won't tolerate you much longer."

"Put away the sssword, Gulah," a voice purred. Chal-Abhinno's beautiful self strode forward. Then she turned to Vedana. "No ssserious harm has been done, mistress. Who cares what the wizard might have been told. He's our prisoner and far too weak to resssist us. Your plan can't fail."

Ignoring the witch, Vedana continued to glare at Gulah, her eyes blood red, her flesh eerily translucent. "You're too much like your father," the demon said, with a fanged snarl. "*My* patience is also gone."

The tone in Vedana's voice disconcerted the Stone-Eater, but he held his ground. Chal intervened again.

"We're all friends here, Guuulah. We wish to see the Death-Knower punished as much as you do. But Vedana needs him first for one little … *thing*."

This last word caused her to giggle. Chal sounded like a virgin shyly attempting to flirt. Then she turned to Torg and bent over the litter, which had been laid upon a flat stone bed. Her gorgeous, sweet-smelling mouth came close to his lips.

"Ssso, Torg … we meet again. And as youuu predicted at Bakheng, I've been given a second opportunity for revenge. As pathetic as you now look, it hardly ssseems worth the effort. Still, you should have killed me when you had the chance, my darling. A lady doesn't forget these things."

"Lady?" Torg said. "Where?"

Gulah slammed the sword back into its sheath and burst into laughter. The other Stone-Eaters joined him. Even the cave troll grinned and grunted. Torg wasn't sure if they were laughing at what he said or how odd his voice sounded. Either way, Chal became enraged and unwittingly began to transform to her hideous self. But then she reined in her anger and managed to maintain her attractive appearance. The witch stepped back and folded her arms beneath her large, round breasts.

"A *lady* doesn't forget," she said, her voice as cold as a mountain spring. "I'll take great pleasssure in your death, Torg."

"Take pleasure where you will. I don't care."

Gulah laughed again. The cave troll slapped its massive knee. This time the witch couldn't hold back her rage. Her flawless pale skin seemed to catch fire, her long auburn hair wrinkled and turned gray, and her perfect breasts flopped against her suddenly bulbous stomach. Reeking like rotten flesh, Chal reached for Torg with clawed hands.

Gulah stepped in front of the witch and held her back. "As amusing as this is, I've heard enough," he said, shoving Chal out of the way. Though Gulah was shorter than Chal, it was obvious he was far stronger. Stone-Eaters ranked among the most dangerous beings on Triken. "Vedana, I vowed to deliver the Death-Knower to you, and I've kept my promise. Now keep yours. Get on with your business. And then leave him to me."

"On this, we agree. There is no reason to delay any longer," Vedana said. "Too much is at stake. Prepare him for me. Gulah, you can watch if you like. And Chal, I *know* that you like to watch."

"Missstress, you honor me," the ugly witch said with a touch of sarcasm.

"I'll watch," Gulah said. "But only to make sure he doesn't escape."

Vedana laughed. "Come then, my *friends*. Come and watch our *business*."

The cave troll thundered over, grabbed the ends of the litter, and dragged Torg toward another dark tunnel. Gulah, flanked by several Stone-Eaters, led the way. Vedana and Chal walked on either side of Torg. More Stone-Eaters and witches followed behind. The tunnel, lit sporadically by flickering torches, dropped steeply. The farther they descended, the warmer the air became. Torg felt himself beginning to sweat—an unusual sensation after so many days of torturous cold.

As they traveled deep into the bowels of Asubha, Torg could sense the immense weight of the stone. All of them were minuscule when compared to the might of the mountain; even in its broken state, it would exist long beyond their short, bitter lives.

They marched for what seemed like half a day. Blazing light rose beneath them, heating the air like a cauldron. Torg found it difficult to breathe.

The Asava had given Torg vigor, and he tested the straps that bound him to the litter, knowing now that he was strong enough to break them. It would take weeks of rest and healing to return to the fullness of his former strength, but he at least felt like he could put up a fight. However, Peta's words haunted his consciousness: *You must not thwart her.* Torg trusted the little girl. He would do as she said, though disgust rose in his throat like bile.

They entered a cavern of immense proportions. Stalactites hung perilously from the ceiling, and stalagmites as tall and thick as trees littered the floor. In several places the stone growths met, forming thick towers that helped support the high ceiling. There were no torches in this cavern, but it was as bright as the desert under a noon sun—and much hotter.

Torg soon saw why. A circular pool of bubbling magma dominated the center of the cavern floor.

"Welcome, Death-Knower, to the asthenolith," Gulah said, his voice filled with pride.

The asthenolith was at least twenty paces across—and it radiated a skin-searing heat. Torg believed that no ordinary beings could stand near it, but everyone in attendance was extraordinary in some sense. Gulah strode within a few spans of the pool, but even he could go no closer. The magma was hot enough to liquefy metal.

A pair of enormous granite slabs flanked each side of the pool. They appeared ancient, yet still strong. U-shaped grooves had been chiseled into the top of each slab, and a rounded column of stone—about six cubits in diameter—had been placed on top of the slabs, fitting securely into the grooves. The column spanning the pool of magma reminded Torg of an oversized spit. A massive crank was attached to one side.

Only something monstrously strong could turn something that size.

"Give him my potion," Vedana ordered.

With a hand as large as a tortoise shell, the troll grasped Torg's head and held it securely in place. Chal came forward with a steaming stone cup and pinched Torg's nostrils, forcing his mouth open and pouring a nocuous brew down his throat that tasted like a grotesque mixture of honey and acid.

If he'd been at full strength, Torg could have incinerated the potion before it entered his bloodstream. But he had neither the strength nor the desire. He heeded Peta's plea: *Do not thwart her.*

As the potion overtook him, a pleasant drunkenness saturated Torg's awareness, causing him to smile. Suddenly, his situation didn't seem so bad.

"It's working, mistress," he heard Chal say. "Look at him. He's an ass. And ssso ugly! No teeth. No hair. And he stinks! Why, he makes Gulah look almost attractive."

"You're one to talk," Gulah said. "I've seen you both ways."

Still in her ugly state, Chal snorted.

"Quiet, both of you," Vedana said. "I'll be the one to decide if my potion is working. Watch this ..."

The demon took Torg's penis in her hand and stroked it. Chal gasped—and then sighed, wantonly. The five other witches in the cavern put their hands to their mouths. Gulah rolled his eyes. The cave troll grunted and looked between his own legs.

"I'd have to sssay that your potion is working, mistress," Chal said.

Vedana cackled, obviously pleased. "YES! Be quick now. Strap him to the spit."

Two Stone-Eaters released Torg from the litter and carried his naked body up a set of stone stairs on the opposite side of the crank. Though the column was tubular, it was wide enough to walk on without slipping. The Stone-Eaters hauled him to the middle of the pillar where four iron cuffs had been pounded into the granite. Then they laid him on his back and locked his wrists and ankles into the cuffs before returning to the cavern floor.

The witches and Stone-Eaters encircled the pool as close to the magma as they could bear. Chal and her sisters began to sing and chant. Gulah and the other Stone-Eaters stood with arms crossed at their chests. The cave troll walked over to the crank. Torg lay helplessly on the column, his erection resembling the stalagmites that rose from the stone floor.

All was prepared.

Vedana removed her robes. Like the witches, the demon was a shapeshifter, but she was more versatile, able to appear as almost anyone or anything. When Torg turned his head to look at her, he saw Sōbhana's naked body, tanned and erotically muscled. He quivered with passion.

Vedana, in the form of Sōbhana, glided alluringly up the stairs and across the pillar. The demon stood above him, straddling his prone body with her athletic legs. The witches' eerie mantra filled the chamber, increasing in volume, and their bodies changed from beautiful to ugly, ugly to beautiful—over and over. Gray smoke, emanating from their transformations, choked the air.

Slowly, Sōbhana lowered herself onto Torg's rigidity. He succumbed to bliss, moaning as he writhed. Sōbhana moaned too, and the witches sang louder. Even Gulah's Stone-Eaters became entranced, and the troll's drooling tongue lolled from its mouth.

Blood-red tendrils from the asthenolith leaped from its surface and licked the sides of the spit. Miniature bursts of lightning crackled between the tendrils, followed by snapping claps of thunder. The cavern was as hot as an oven.

Sōbhana's well-built warrior body rode Torg deliciously. She growled and screamed, digging her nails into the thick muscles of his chest. Torg also screamed, his head bending back and his eyes clamping shut.

The witches succumbed to frenzy, flinging their heads wildly and transforming back and forth so quickly that no single appearance held sway. They were beautiful and ugly at the same time. Perverted sexual energy blazed within the cavern.

Torg's approaching orgasm surged out of the depths of his frustration. It had been more than 900 years since he had been with a woman, and the abysmal aftermath of that encounter had left a permanent scar on his psyche. His supernaturally vibrant body burned for intimacy, but his centuries-long celibacy had tormented his every waking moment—as well as his dreams.

Torg howled and arched his back, almost casting Vedana into the pool. But with a demon's agility, she held on tight. The pair climaxed simultaneously.

Cathartic energy erupted from every pore of Torg's body, and the cavern filled with blue fire as if a supernova had exploded inside the mountain. Next came a concussive blast of sound, which boomed inside the chamber. Though he was lost in the throes of lust, Torg could still see fissures forming in the surrounding stone, racing this way and that like cracks in a weakening sheet of ice.

First to die was Gulah. His father's death would go unavenged. Gulah's eyes popped from his skull and ruptured. His stony hide burst into flame and incinerated, and his skeleton cracked apart and clattered to the floor. The sword, released from its sheath, bounced on the stone and slipped into the broiling magma.

The other Stone-Eaters suffered similar fates. They were no match for such an expenditure of power. The troll ran toward the tunnel, but his enormous backside caught fire and split in half along his spine. Then his body blew apart, splattering fiery chunks of flesh onto the cavern walls. His bare skull tumbled through the air and landed on top of a stalagmite where it stuck, jaw sprung open, as if pleased to find a less-fragile body.

The conflagration also swept away the witches. Even Chal-Abhinno was consumed, screaming in wild-eyed horror as she recognized, too late, how she'd been betrayed. Her revenge would not be sweet. Nor would Gulah's. Apparently, Vedana had wanted no witnesses. Was this a secret she chose not to share? If so, losing a few underlings would be a small price to pay.

Torg's orgasmic fury sluiced through Vedana's undead flesh like a torrent, but it didn't destroy her. After she was sure of his completion, the demon sprang into the air and leaped over the pool. Then she fled on all fours as fast as a spider, skittering past the carnage into the safety of the passageway. Torg heard her wicked laughter echoing even after she disappeared.

The stone column shattered into a thousand shards. Torg tumbled toward the asthenolith and then sank into its blistering depths. Few living beings could have withstood such fury. But the aftermath of Torg's orgasmic firestorm still clung to his dense flesh, protecting him from the molten stone. He sank deeper and deeper into the viscous magma, tumbling slowly head over heels. The pain was unbearable, and he couldn't breathe. As the blue fire that encompassed his body diminished, the agony of the asthenolith intensified. Yet he continued to live.

The asthenolith's hard walls tapered like a funnel. Torg struck bottom and lay on his side in the super-heated goo. Although his iron cuffs had already melted, he now pressed against something else metallic—and still cold. It was the sword. Its supernal alloys were impervious.

As if guided by an invisible will, a current of magma carried him into a passageway that ran through the surrounding wall. It drew Torg into the tunnel head-first, his broad shoulders barely squeezing through. He couldn't see, but he managed to grab the sword before being swept away. The tunnel ran straight for several paces before bending sharply upward. Torg ascended slowly, lifted by the bubbling surge. At first his body was limp and unresisting, his blue fire nearly gone. The grime and disease in his flesh—accumulated during his imprisonment in the pit—sizzled away. The pain soon reached higher levels of anguish. Torg began to writhe and scream, praying for some form of mercy.

Suddenly, his head was free of the fire. And his hands. And arms. With the last remnants of his strength, he pulled his body and the sword out of the magma and up into a small chamber.

The room was aglow, enabling Torg to see for several paces. He slithered away from the molten rock as far as his strength allowed before collapsing on hot stone.

Torg lay still, fading in and out of consciousness, his body a screaming bundle of misery. Each time he woke, he moaned and then fainted again. This went on for a long while.

When he regained full consciousness, Torg lay face-down and listened to the magma as it bubbled near his feet. It had the sound of hunger as if beckoning him to return to the depths so that it could devour him. He heard another noise—or imagined one—coming from the other direction. It sounded like trickling water, and it drove Torg mad. He had gone without water for almost a month.

He might have lain there and succumbed to the lure of death, but his thirst inspired him to move. Bit by bit, he dragged himself away from the magma, away from the dim light, and into the darkness of the tunnel which soon descended, making it easier for Torg to move forward. But the farther he journeyed the darker it became. The fading blue glow that emanated from his flesh provided little visibility. He clung to the sword like a comrade.

The trickling grew louder. Torg wriggled toward it. The walls of the tunnel became smooth and slippery, and he half-crawled, half-slid, endlessly downward, into the bowels of the mountain.

Into places where there was no light and no life.

His grave, he feared, would be hidden forever. His corpse would decay slowly, and his bones would lie alone—with the sword at their side—lost and forgotten in the great depths of the world.

A drop of water struck his forehead. He reached up with his hands. The roof of the tunnel was moist. Torg screamed—out of joy and relief—and an infinite series of echoes raced through the tunnel. He pressed his face against the stone and licked. Then he scrambled forward several more paces and found the main source, a tiny but steady trickle of water issuing from a prick in the ceiling. The water was lukewarm and metallic in flavor, but to Torg it tasted sweet as nectar. He drank for what seemed like forever until his stomach was too bloated to hold any more.

After that, he slept fitfully. Peta didn't visit his dreams, but Sōbhana was there, naked and alluring. Or was it Vedana?

Torg jerked awake. It was utterly dark. The blue glow of his skin had faded to nothing.

For the first time in weeks, he urinated. It burned his flaccid shaft as it drizzled onto the floor of the tunnel. Now, he was thirsty again, and he drank his fill of the precious water. Hydration slogged its way into his cells. With it came vitality. His body still needed food, but it had needed water more. With his thirst quenched, his mind opened to the possibility of survival.

"*Eso aham idha* (Here I am)," Torg said out loud. His voice echoed. *Eso aham idha ... Eso aham idha ...*

How deep *was* this tunnel? Did it ever end? And would it become too narrow for Torg to navigate? He could barely squeeze through it now.

In a sudden burst of claustrophobia, Torg felt the weight of the mountain all around him. Panic crept into his thoughts, threatening to suffocate his sanity. There was nowhere to escape! If he backtracked, the magma would trap him. If he continued forward, he would descend farther into uncharted territory, ensnared in the fatal grip of a trillion tons of bedrock. He sweated profusely. His heart thundered in his chest. The air was so stale he couldn't catch his breath! His body trembled, making him dizzy and nauseated. He felt an irresistible urge to pound his way free, to smash his fists against the underbelly of the mountain until it collapsed around him.

Torg shrieked in childish terror. It echoed along the never-ending length of his cramped prison, alerting all who might listen to his despair. He scrambled downward in a mad rush, scraping his elbows and knees on the smooth stone, dragging the clattering sword alongside.

Torg's panicked shouts outraced him, piercing the darkness. He went on this way for a long time.

Finally, he fell on his face.

Shivering. Moaning. Whimpering.

The passageway echoed his suffering.

All that he had been taught was a lie.

There was no beginning.

No middle.

No end.

There was only fear—now and forever.

But this time, exhaustion, long his enemy, came to his rescue, and he succumbed to sleep.

Peta remained noticeably absent in his dreams as if Torg had delved too deeply for even her to follow. Instead, nightmares made an unpleasant appearance. The tunnel closed around him, attempting to digest him. Worms chewed on his immobile flesh, devouring his nose, ears, fingers, and toes. His screams sounded like Sōbhana's.

Torg sprang awake, banging his head against the low stone roof. When his brain cleared, he found that his madness had receded. He'd never been claustrophobic before, but his confinement in the pit had given birth to that fear. Now he shut that door with a bang. He would probably die here, but it would not be of fright.

"*Natthi me maranabhayam* (For me there is no fear of death)," he shouted with as much conviction as he could muster.

Natthi me maranabhayam ...

"But I don't want to die," he whispered.

That echoed, too.

Again he crawled forward. He was able to loop his right pinky finger around the sword's crossguard and drag it along with him. He wasn't sure why didn't discard the weapon. It wouldn't do him much good down here in this enclosed space. But out of respect for Sōbhana, he kept it with him.

After blindly feeling his way in the darkness for a long time, Torg came upon a fork where the tunnel split in two directions. He didn't know which opening to choose. Both appeared to continue downward, but the one on the right felt larger and cooler. Torg had no desire to encounter any more magma, so he went that way.

As he descended along the new tunnel, it quickly became very cold, causing Torg to shiver. He hadn't felt this cold since before being captured by Gulah, but he soon became re-accustomed to the discomfort. He certainly had experienced enough of it in the pit.

The tunnel split again. Torg felt around with his hands and discovered at least three different openings. This time, the left tunnel was the largest and coolest, so he went that way.

However, this passageway soon tightened, forcing him to press his shoulders together so that he could squeeze through. He put the sword in front of him and slid it forward, afraid that if he continued to drag it behind him and lost his grip, he wouldn't have the will to back up and retrieve it.

The tunnel split in several more directions. Torg was hopelessly lost, then he laughed aloud. Since this journey began, when had he not been lost? His laughter bounced off countless walls. He was trapped in a maze of passageways that wove in a thousand directions. Even if the tunnels were lighted, he could not hope to escape a labyrinth of such scope.

From then on, whenever there was an option, he chose the middle path. As Sister Tathagata always said, it was this path that led to enlightenment. Luckily, he found more trickling water—cooler and clearer than before. He drank his fill and slept again. What other pleasures were left to him? Quenching his thirst and sleeping had become the extent of his entertainment. And of course, the nightmares. In one, Vedana came toward him holding a squalling baby. When she held it up, Torg saw it had a human head and torso but legs like black worms. Torg recoiled, then reached out with his left hand and broke the baby's neck. The thing turned to dust.

The wizard shrieked and bumped his sore head on the ceiling of the passageway yet again. A cacophony of his own echoing screams taunted his awakening.

When silence returned, he lay still and watched his breath. It was his first attempt at meditation since his escape from the pit. He had no intention of achieving *Sammaasamaadhi*; his broken body was incapable of surviving another Death Visit. But the benefits of meditation were many and varied. At the least, it would calm him. He doubted there was any way he could escape this predicament, but a clear mind was always superior to a clouded one, no matter the precariousness of the situation.

The darkness and quiet aided his concentration. He felt his breath whistling in and out of his nostrils. The skin on the tip of his nose tingled ever so slightly. After several inhalations and exhalations, a thought entered his mind: Where was Vedana now? Was she pregnant with his child? He acknowledged the thought and gently pushed it aside, returning his focus to the skin surrounding his nostrils. Inhale. Exhale. Peaceful mind.

Why had Peta believed it was so important not to resist the demon? Why would a child with Vedana be able to provide him with a weapon to destroy Invictus?

Return to focus. Inhale. Exhale. Peaceful mind. Quiet mind. Clear mind.

Abruptly, an external disturbance interrupted his concentration.

He heard something.

A scraping sound.

A slippery sound.

A slurping sound.

And it was headed his way.

Fast!

Whatever approached came at a speed that was impossible to evade. Even worse, the darkness was disorienting. Torg couldn't tell from which direction the attack would come. All he could do was grasp the sword, brace his body, and prepare for the inevitable.

Something bit down on his left foot and swallowed his leg up to the knee. It chomped with terrific force, attempting to devour him, but it couldn't bite through his dense flesh. Torg spun the sword around and drove it into the monster, piercing something thick and cartilaginous. The tentacle withdrew with a loud hiss.

Although Torg's leg burned, he touched the wound and felt no blood. He attempted to illuminate the tunnel with his magic but was too weak. He would have to wage this fight in total darkness. And the creature he faced must have been born in darkness.

It attacked once more, driving between his legs and snapping at his groin. To protect his genitals, Torg slipped his free hand between his legs. He felt the thing gnaw on his inner thighs, then it reared back and rushed forward again. This time, the creature shoved him twenty body lengths. The passageway narrowed too much to accommodate his girth, wickedly wedging Torg farther into the hole. He managed to retain his grip on the sword, but his arms were locked against his sides.

Torg couldn't move.

The creature sensed his helplessness and renewed its attack. First it bit his right foot. Any normal being would have been dismembered, but Torg's flesh was too great for the toothy mouth to penetrate. Then the creature pulled away and drove forward again, swallowing most of Torg's right leg and crunching on his thigh. Again, it did little damage and was forced to withdraw.

Torg twisted and squirmed but couldn't free himself. He could barely wiggle his fingers. With terrific power, the tentacle struck again, pounding against his feet, ankles, and calves. It bit, hissed, and spat.

It smashed against him repeatedly. The more it failed, the angrier it became. Had it ever encountered a prey so defenseless and yet so invulnerable?

One last time, it crushed its colossal strength against Torg's underside. He felt excruciating pressure build along his torso, pressing his shoulders together until they touched.

Impossibly, his body squirted through the tiny hole into a wider portion of the tunnel.

The tentacle continued to propel him forward at fantastic speed.

Torg exploded from the tunnel into an open expanse and fell a long way, thudding against the hard floor of a magnificent cavern. The sword clattered beside him.

Torg was stunned, but he could see.

There was light, splendid and dappled.

He gazed up in amazement.

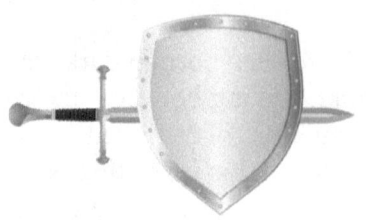

CAVE MONKEYS

The cavern's sheer walls were jammed with flaming torches. A treasure trove of multicolored gems protruded from the stone, reflecting the flickering light. The wall from which Torg had emerged was pockmarked with hundreds of round holes, each less than two cubits in diameter. From each hole a black tentacle extended, flopping frenetically.

A score of furry creatures leaped athletically from tentacle to tentacle. They used sharp stone daggers to hack at a limb before pouncing away just quick enough to avoid being snapped up by snarling teeth. The daggers could not fully sever the writhing tentacles, but they sliced off small chunks of steaming flesh. The raw meat fell to the floor of the cavern where it was scooped it up by other cave monkeys—Torg could think of no other name to describe them—and moved to a safe place away from the wall.

One monkey paused from its frenzied activity and crept within a few paces of Torg, staring at him with obvious curiosity. The creature's expressive face charmed Torg. It appeared capable of humanlike expressions. Was it smiling at him?

The cave monkey had a pointy nose and a mouth full of flat teeth. A pair of bioluminescent eyes three times larger than a Tugar's dominated its small head. Its face and long bushy tail were black, but the top of its head was white and the rest of its body reddish brown. Torg guessed it weighed less than two stones.

Torg felt a tingling sensation inside his skull. The monkey was using telepathy to probe his mind. Was this how they communicated with each other in the darkness?

The tingling increased slightly, but Torg felt no discomfort. The monkey lacked either the power or desire to force itself into his thoughts.

It investigated gently, searching for clues to his intentions. Was the large intruder a friend or foe? Torg sent out a wave of loving kindness, hoping the monkey would recognize his good-naturedness. It seemed to work. This time there was no doubt. The creature did smile.

A sudden squeal interrupted their pleasant encounter. Torg turned to see that a tentacle had seized one monkey and yanked it into a hole. A second monkey chased after it, diving into the darkness. A moment later, the rescuer emerged with the bloodied victim, which was mangled but still alive.

The monkey that stood near Torg scampered off to help. The injured one was carried away from the groping tentacles, which seemed to extend only a short distance from the wall. The monstrous limbs had either come to the end of their reach or were wary of entering too far into the torchlight.

All at once the tentacles withdrew completely, and there was abrupt silence in the cavern. The worm monster—again, Torg could think of no better name—had failed to devour even one of its preys. Perhaps, its frustrating confrontation with Torg had demoralized it.

At least thirty monkeys surrounded him. Each was small but strong, with long flexible fingers and toes. Though Torg was ten times their size, the monkeys worked together and lifted him off the floor. Slowly, they carried him into a dark tunnel.

The last thing Torg remembered was watching one monkey leap along the wall from torch to torch and douse the flames with quick slaps of its little hands. Then all went black as if the lights had been turned off inside his head.

Time passed, but Torg couldn't gauge it. He woke to the most wonderful aroma he'd ever smelled in his life. When he opened his eyes, he saw an ancient woman standing over a stone pot heated by a simmering fire. The woman stirred the pot's bubbling contents with a wooden spoon.

Cave monkeys were everywhere, perching on each of her shoulders and her head. Dozens more scampered about her feet, staring at her with adoring eyes. She appeared to be their master.

Torg lay on a soft bed of sand in a spacious cave. The Silver Sword leaned against the wall nearby. He sat up slowly and looked at the gray-haired woman. He didn't know who she was or how she'd gotten here, but he sensed nothing sinister about her.

"Where am I, dear lady?" he asked. He was pleased to find that his lisp was almost gone.

She turned to him and smiled. Then she answered, in the ancient tongue: "*Tvam saddhim amhaakam bhavasi.* (You are with us.) *Mayam kataññuu homa.* (We are grateful.) *Dharaama bhojanam tam.* (We prepare food for thee)."

One monkey grabbed a clay bowl and held it next to the pot. The old woman filled it with fragrant soup, and the monkey carried the bowl to Torg. Several others followed along excitedly. In the dim firelight, Torg noticed the creatures were similar in size and shape but with a wide variation of coloring. Some were reddish brown, like the monkey that had probed his mind, but with different-shaded faces or tails. Some had gray bodies with black-and-white striped tails. Others were snow white with black-rimmed eyes and ears.

"*Tam bhojessaama* (We will feed thee)," the old lady said. "*Abhiruupam sattam bhojessaama* (We will feed the lovely one)."

She waddled over, knelt beside him, and took the bowl from the monkey. Using the wooden spoon, she fed him. The soup tasted better than it smelled, containing a rich red broth with delicious chunks of tender meat sliced from the worm monster, Torg surmised.

Without his teeth, Torg couldn't chew very well, but the meat was cut into small enough bites to swallow whole. Other than the Stone-Eaters' scorching brew, the soup was the first nutritious thing he'd consumed in more than a month. When the bowl was empty, he begged for another.

"*Bhojanam tam balam karissati.* (Food will make thee strong.) *Kudaa te balam agamissati, amhakam upakarissasi?* (When your strength returns, will thou helpest us?)"

After the meal, they gave Torg several cups of fresh water. He drank deeply and then lay back on the sand bed and took a long nap. But he woke many times to a strange sensation: The monkeys were cleansing every inch of his skin with their smooth tongues. Then they dressed him in gray robes and a pair of straw sandals.

Upon coming fully awake, he was relieved to discover that some of his former strength had returned. His body was responding to the nourishment, rest, and kind treatment.

However, Torg's skin felt itchy. He scratched himself all over, finding nubs of hair already growing back. Plus, his gums were sore. He skimmed along them with his tongue and discovered the rough edges of teeth starting to re-grow. This wasn't unusual for Tugars. When the desert warriors lost adult teeth—which happened occasionally during battles—they routinely grew back, though it usually took several weeks.

The old woman was by his side. Her body shimmered in the gloom. She stroked his head with her tiny hand. Then she leaned over and licked his nose. Her tongue was smooth. When she smiled, her facial expression was familiar.

Torg knew her.

"*Natthi attham imam vesam.* (There is no purpose for this disguise.) *Naaham te santajjaami, vaa te sahaaye.* (I do not threaten you or your friends.)"

The old woman sighed. Then she seemed to fold, fade, and shrink. In her place sat the little monkey who had first approached him in the torch-lit cavern.

"*Eso tvam avoca yam me upakaaram appekhasi* (You said before that you need my help)," Torg said, sitting upright in the powdery sand. "*Te bahukam me katam.* (You have already done so much for me.) *Pamodeyyam bahukam anumatim paccaaharitum.* (It would please me to return the favor.)"

The monkey wriggled her finger, motioning for Torg to follow. He stood and was surprised to find that his legs weren't wobbly. The soup had worked wonders.

I must look disgusting, he thought, *but I feel better than I have in a long time.* It would take a long time to return to his former self, if he ever did, but this was a promising start.

Torg left the sword by his bedside and followed the monkey past the still-bubbling pot of soup and into a smaller chamber where at least twenty of the creatures huddled in a circle. When they saw Torg, they parted to reveal a troubling sight. The monkey that the worm monster had injured lay on the floor. How long had it been since she was bitten? Torg didn't know.

The combined force of their telepathic energy pressed into Torg's mind. A myriad of words swirled within his head. It was confusing, but he understood the general concept.

"*Sakkosi tam tikicchitum*? (Can thou healest her?)"

Torg kneeled and placed his ear on her small chest. Her breath arose in staccato bursts. When he touched her, she grunted. Her external wounds had been tended, but Torg could sense there was life-threatening internal damage. He rued the short time he'd spent in his own recovery, which had delayed helping this creature. But he recognized the necessity of it. Had he been any weaker, he would not have been able to aid her.

At least now, he had the strength to try.

Torg yearned for Obhasa. With the aid of his ivory staff, he could have channeled his blue fire in thin beams, making his magic more effective. He had no doubt he could summon enough power to heal the injured monkey, but he didn't know how much control he could muster. It wasn't as simple as bathing the small creature in flame. Torg had to cauterize individual regions inside her body, one by one.

Without Obhasa, Torg's fingers would have to serve as the conduit. He placed his right hand on the monkey's chest and focused his concentration on the pads of his fingertips, searching beneath her soft fur for hot spots that would guide him to the wounds. There was a bewildering array of damage beneath the creature's small ribs. Torg struggled to pinpoint a specific injury.

The monkeys perceived his hesitation. As a group, they linked their considerable psychic powers to his mind. Their more intimate knowledge of the inner workings of their bodies helped Torg find what he sought.

First, he identified a small tear in her chest that was leaking blood into surrounding tissue. Torg sent a beam of fire into the wound, closing it with precision.

Next, he discovered a broken rib that had punctured one lung. He disintegrated a portion of the rib and sealed the hole.

He observed poisons surrounding bite wounds on the monkey's chest. He super-heated the toxins, turning them into harmless vapors.

Torg's search for injuries continued farther inward. There was a crack in her spine. He healed it. He found a splintered bone in her right leg. He repaired the damage and destroyed the stray splinters. There was mild swelling in her brain due to a skull fracture above the left ear. He sealed the bone and dissolved excess fluid near the swollen area.

Things were going well.

However, Torg found an injury he couldn't heal. One chamber of the monkey's heart had been weakened by the trauma. Mending it would require too much precision, even for his abilities. She would have to lie still for several days—and let her body do the rest. But Torg believed she would survive. As did the cave monkeys. They came to him—now more than seventy in all—and clung to him like bees on a honeycomb.

They appeared to weep with joy. Torg wept too.

The injured female slept peacefully, her breathing slow and steady.

Torg felt drained. He returned to his bed in the adjoining cavern, ate another bowl of soup, relieved himself in the privacy of a back chamber, and then slept for what seemed like an entire night. When he stirred again, he felt groggy but otherwise wonderful. Torg sat up, stretched, and belched.

The sudden noise startled several of the monkeys, who leaped up and almost crashed against the stone ceiling. The others chittered, a sound that resembled laughter. One monkey imitated Torg's belch. Soon they all were laughing, chittering, burping, and coughing. In the dim underground chamber, they made quite a racket. This filled Torg with joy and made him smile.

Several days passed. Torg wandered from cavern to cavern, learning his way around step-by-step. What he saw fascinated him. The monkeys were unendingly clever. They were adept at using fire— always positioning the flames beneath vents in the rock—but that was only one of many things they could do. They cooked, cleaned, and bathed themselves. They used knives, spoons, and pottery. They even had a kind of school. The youngsters watched the elders perform various skills, including the ultra-dangerous method of collecting their main source of food: the slices of tentacle meat.

Their artistic abilities astounded Torg the most. By blending mineral extracts and worm fat, the monkeys created multicolored pigments. Using their fingers as primitive paintbrushes, they adorned the passageways and chambers with images of the other animals that populated their underground world, including many Torg didn't recognize. The worm monster played a dominant role in most of the drawings. On a wall in one of the largest caverns, the monster extended from floor to ceiling, its tentacles roaming hungrily through a myriad of winding tunnels. The illustration portrayed the monkeys as brave warriors, taking on a beast 10,000 times their size. Torg applauded this depiction. The monkeys clapped along with him.

One day, they led him to a well-lit chamber. Its smooth walls were untouched, except for one painting: a life-size image of the wizard— with a huge smile on his face—standing over a pot of soup. Torg got to see what he now looked like. His comical appearance made him laugh until tears sprang from his eyes.

Torg stayed with the monkeys more than a week. They led him through dozens of caves and passageways, some lit by torches, others as black as the Realm of Undeath. Occasionally, they passed an ominous hole—and the creatures taught him how to duck under or scoot around the opening. Several times, a tentacle emerged. The monkeys reacted almost nonchalantly to these appearances.

It took Torg awhile to recognize that the cave monkeys didn't hate the worm monster. For one thing, it single-handedly kept the underground free of vermin, but that was merely a side benefit. The monkeys were utterly dependent on the monster for their survival. If it were destroyed, they would also perish. Without the worm's precious flesh, there wasn't enough food in the lower depths to support their colony. They were unable to bear sunlight and were therefore ill-equipped to hunt close to the surface. They were—and probably always had been—creatures of the underworld.

On the sixth day of Torg's stay, the monkeys took him on a hunt. The monkeys carried their stone daggers, and he brought the Silver Sword. They returned to the cavern where Torg originally had met them. The great wall stood before them, full of empty holes.

Before scampering to preassigned positions, the monkeys lit dozens of torches. Then they rhythmically pounded the handles of their daggers against the wall. Hundreds of tentacles soon emerged from the holes. The monkeys danced from limb to limb, hacking and slicing—and barely avoiding death.

Torg strode forward, holding the sword in both hands. With one lightning-quick stroke, he hacked off the ends of five tentacles—enough food to last the monkeys for weeks. Under these conditions, the worm monster was no match for him. It sensed its peril and withdrew.

Torg held his arms aloft like a hero, the severed tentacles wriggling at his feet. But this didn't please the cave monkeys. He had upset their delicate balance and shamed them. As soon as he understood his mistake, he felt embarrassed and ignorant.

The monkeys forgave him, but they never trusted the sword again. In their minds, it endangered their symbiotic relationship with the worm—and they wanted nothing to do with it. Torg had considered giving the sword to them as a gift. Now he knew better, so he buried it beneath the sand of his bed and left it hidden there.

On the eighth day, the old woman reappeared and spoke to Torg.

"*Abhiruupaa sattaa, puccheyyam ... ciraayissasi ciram?* (Lovely one, I must ask ... how long will thou stayest?)"

Torg paused. Then he sighed.

"*Ye vasanti dure me nissayanti. Eso aham you niyaameti. Nissiiyaami uddham.* (Those far away depend on me. I am one who commands. I am needed above.)"

"*Aham vijaanaami ... mayam vijaanaama.* (I ... we ... understand.)"

The old woman sighed. Tears fell from her eyes. "*Patiyadessami, pana bhavissaama dummanaa.* (We will prepare, but we will be highly sorrowful.)"

"*Me sahaaya piyaa, puna ca me.* (Oh, my wonderful friend, so will I.)"

On the morning of the tenth day, Torg knew it was time to depart. The monkeys gave him a cloth bag containing dried worm meat and raw mushrooms. To find the mushrooms, they probably must have journeyed much closer to the surface than they would have preferred, but providing Torg with food had become an honor. They seemed to love him as much as he loved them.

Torg still wore the gray robes and sandals they had given him. He turned to the leader and asked her where they had gotten the robes and the bag—and where they had found the wood to make torches and cooking utensils. There was no way to weave fabrics in a world of stone, and there was no wood so deep beneath the surface.

She answered, telepathically.

"*Mayam upalabhaama hetthaa kiñci ye no siyum hetthaa. Koci no vatthuu ossajati. Mayam na jaanaama koci va kiñci. Kadaaci, setakesasaaminim passaama.* (We find things down here that shouldn't be here. Something leaves things for us. We don't know who or what. Sometimes, we see a white-haired lady.)"

Torg wondered what else they had discovered. Did they have a stash of hidden treasure? He hoped they did—and that it brought them pleasure. But who was the mysterious being or beings that helped his little friends? Perhaps, he could find out one day.

The reddish-brown monkey who sometimes appeared to him as the old woman came forward and took his hand, leading him toward the middle of the chamber. The colony spread apart, making a path.

The monkey that had been injured stood before him, leaning on a small staff. Tears flooded Torg's eyes. He knelt in front of her and bowed, positioning his face only an inch above the sand floor. When he lifted his head, she came to him, placed her small hands on his cheeks, and licked him on the tip of his nose.

Torg continued to cry. Tears came far too easily these days—especially for one who claimed to be a warrior—but he didn't care. Using his powers to heal a living being, instead of destroying one, pleased him beyond words. He had done far too much killing during his long life. And there was so much more to go.

He rose to his full height, towering above the monkeys. The tallest of them didn't reach his knees. He started to speak, but what he saw stopped him cold. Every member of the colony had imitated him, bowing with their faces close to the surface of the sand.

This astonished Torg. "*Sahaayaa me, titthatha. Tumhe ariyaani sattamaani. Tumhe na koci puujetha.* (My friends, please rise. You are the highest quality. You bow to no one.)"

One by one, they came to him ... and clung to him. Some hugged his legs. Others climbed onto his broad back and shoulders. Each one lifted his robes and licked a portion of his skin. Then they left the chamber, bearing expressions of sorrow.

The sadness Torg felt reawoke his grief over Sōbhana's death. He stood alone for a long time.

His friend—their leader—waited patiently in the entryway. Torg composed himself, picked up the cloth bag and the Silver Sword, and followed her along a familiar tunnel. For his benefit, she carried a torch to light their way. As they walked through the winding passageways, Torg caught occasional glimpses of glowing eyes just out of range of the torchlight. Many of the monkeys were following him. They still weren't ready to say their final goodbyes. The wizard was grateful for their company.

Torg could never have found his way out on his own. The gallery zigzagged many times, opening into countless tunnels and chambers. His guide knew which paths to choose and which to ignore.

The temperatures varied widely. When they came near pockets of magma, the air grew hot. At other times, it was bitterly cold. For much of their journey, Torg was able to walk upright, but several times he hunched over. Sometimes, he crawled.

They traveled more than three leagues, though they probably ascended less than a thousand vertical paces. Boulders and stagnant pools of water hindered their progress. They entered an enormous cavern that was well-lighted—not by magma or torchlight but by sunlight seeping down from above. Torg looked at his friend. She was in pain, her eyes squinting. He understood she could go no farther.

Out loud, Torg said: "*Te ukkanthissaami, piyaa sattaa. Abhitthavaami. Tvam samuddhaasi me jiivitam.* (I will miss you, precious one. Thank you for saving my life.)"

She responded, telepathically: "*Pana te ukkanthissaami, abhiruupaa sattaa. Abhitthavaami. Tvam samuddhaasi jiivitam me bhaginii.* (And I will miss you, lovely one. Thank you for saving my sister's life.)"

The monkey retreated into the semidarkness and then waved her thin arm. Torg could sense her sadness. He felt the same. She gestured toward a small passageway that exited the cavern. Torg nodded. He walked toward the light. But he couldn't resist turning around one last time. At the edge of the darkness, the old woman had reappeared. As always, she was smiling.

Then she vanished.

Torg sat on a flat stone, disconsolate. To take his mind off his sorrow, he ate some of the dried meat and raw mushrooms. The upper edges of his teeth had broken through the surface of his gums, and he could finally chew a little, which made the food taste even more delicious. Near his feet was a clear pool of water. He knelt and drank his fill. Part of him wanted to forsake the surface world and return to his primate friends, but he knew he couldn't find them on his own. Once again, he vowed to return one day—if Invictus were defeated and peace returned to Triken—and try to reconnect with the precious colony.

Until that time, if it ever came, he would mourn their absence.

Torg sighed. It was now or never. He stood, picked up his belongings—a simple bag of food and an ancient sword—and ascended the difficult passageway. It was steep and slippery. He soon found himself gasping for breath. But the higher he climbed, the brighter it became, motivating him.

The quality of the air began to change. During his stay underground, Torg had grown used to mustiness. This air was crisp, dry, and engorged with oxygen. The richness of it overwhelmed his lungs, filling them with sweetness and vitality. Torg was a creature of the surface. And it was to there—after his long suffering—that he would now return.

When he stepped from the mouth of the cave, it was near dusk in the southern foothills of Mount Asubha. Though winter had still not arrived, the temperature was well below freezing, and there were scattered patches of snow on the ground. Most of the trees—except a scattering of hemlocks and pines—had dropped their leaves. The darkening sky was clear and deep blue; almost everything else was white, brown, or gray.

The beauty of it smote Torg's heart.

He held his arms aloft.

Opened his mouth as wide as he could.

And howled.

The sound was deafening.

But he wanted his return made known.

To the Tugars. And to all.

Despair had failed to destroy him.

He was The Torgon.

Still.

And he was … free.

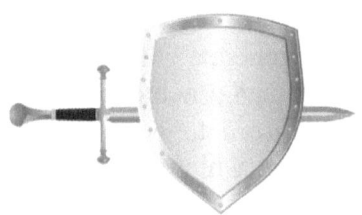

TRAPPERS

Torg stood outside the cave, his breath exploding in white puffs of mist. Other than trees, he saw no living beings. It was late autumn and the ground was bare except for scattered patches of snow. The below-freezing temperature continued to plummet. At least the sky was clear, and there was no immediate threat of a storm.

The thin gray robes the cave monkey had given him provided scant protection. Torg could venture no farther this night. A vast stretch of wilderness stood between him and the nearest civilization. Until he could find warmer clothing, he'd be forced to travel only during the day.

Though he had journeyed to many remote areas of Triken, Torg had never been this far north on the eastern side of the Mahaggata Mountains. Still, he had studied maps and knew the area well enough. He guessed that Kamupadana, home of the Warlish witches and their hag servants, was about ten leagues to the southwest. Avici, the stronghold of Invictus, was about sixty leagues to the southeast. Tējo, the Great Desert, was several hundred leagues away. Torg had some thinking to do, but it was too late to make any decisions tonight. For now, what he needed more than anything was a fire.

Torg wandered into the nearby woods. The oaks, birches, and maples were bare, but hemlocks and pines added touches of green. The trees were widely spaced with little foliage beneath. Portions of the ground were coated with ash from the fallout of the destruction of Mount Asubha. But he found plenty of deadwood and soon had a large-enough pile to burn throughout the night. Most of the logs were damp, so he used the Silver Sword to strip off the moist bark. Then he chose a flat area just outside the cave to build his fire. Using several thick logs, he constructed a teepee-shaped cone over a pile of tinder and kindling.

Torg had exhausted most of his Death Energy. With food and rest, a sizable portion would regenerate, though he believed he wouldn't regain full strength until he again achieved *Sammaasamaadhi*. But to escape the pit, he'd been forced to perform a Death Visit just three months after his previous one, which was too soon. He would have to wait several months before his next attempt. However, he wasn't powerless, even now. He mustered a burst of blue flame from the tips of his fingers, and soon the logs were ablaze. In the night air, the smoke would settle like a fog over the land, and anyone within half a league could smell it. But Torg didn't care. Even in his weakened condition, he was more than capable of defending himself, especially considering he now wielded the Silver Sword.

The fire sparked and crackled. Torg enjoyed the much-needed warmth. He had leaned the sword against a nearby rock, and out of curiosity he picked it up and slid the blade into the hottest flames. Where the sword entered, a pocket of air formed around the supernal metal as if the fire were unable or unwilling to touch it. When he withdrew the sword, he quickly pressed his fingers against the blade and found that it was as cold as if it had been lying in snow.

Torg stared at the weapon for a long time. The sight of it reminded him of his last moments with Sōbhana, causing grief to surge over him. He plopped down on a flat rock, placed the sword at his feet, and buried his face in his hands. When he sobbed, his entire body shook.

The painful bout of tears purged a portion of his lament, and he felt a little better. He opened the bag of food the cave monkeys had given him and investigated its contents. There was enough to last for about three days if he rationed it. But Torg wasn't overly concerned. He needed only enough for a meal now and a good breakfast in the morning. After that he could find more food, even in late autumn. There would be plenty of berries and nuts, and the woods were bursting with deer, possums, squirrels, and rabbits.

Torg ate half of what remained in the bag. The dried worm meat and mushrooms tasted wonderful. Then he scooped up several handfuls of snow. For now, that was enough to quench his thirst. But in the morning, he would need to find running water, which would also not be difficult. It was probable that several active streams were within a thousand paces of where he sat.

Tomorrow, he would go in search of food and clothing. Torg could kill game and tan the hides, but that would take too much time.

Regardless, he believed he could find warmer clothing. The wilderness was vast but not barren, and it was likely that others wandered these woods. In return for a cloak and boots, he would barter his services. And if he ran into any uncooperative sorts, he would convince them that it wasn't wise to make a Death-Knower angry.

In the morning, he would take the first steps on his long journey to vengeance. But he would have to be patient. There were many leagues to travel, many plans to be made. And eventually, many battles to wage. Torg tossed more logs on the fire. Then he sat cross-legged and meditated before allowing himself to sleep.

He dreamed of a time long past when he had seen just eighteen summers. The bulk of his long life lay ahead. Even better, his beloved father, Asēkha-Jhana, still lived. Torg gazed at Jhana, treasuring his presence while omnisciently knowing—as often occurs in dreams—that one day the pair would be tragically separated.

In the fiery heat of *Majjhe Ghamme*, which meant midsummer in the ancient tongue, Torg and Jhana stood on the roof of an escarpment overlooking a dry lakebed. Beyond the mile-wide playa, a series of sand dunes tumbled toward the horizon like stagnant waves. Though it was only an hour past dawn, it was 110 degrees in the heart of the Great Desert, and the crusty surface of the lakebed was a good deal hotter. But this didn't stop the Vasi masters from beginning that day's training session with their Tugar novices.

Fifty masters wore black jackets and breeches; a thousand novices wore white. The teachers ranged in age from 130 to 300 years old. The students were as young as 20 and as old as 75—and a dozen of the eldest disciples were just weeks away from achieving the status of warrior. The following morning, Torg would put on his white outfit and begin the first of more than 18,000 days of training. He was the first Tugar youth in a century to begin before the age of 20.

Jhana admired his son, who already was half a span taller than him.

"Today's lesson is called *Aarakaa Himsaa*," Jhana said. "In the ancient tongue, *Aarakaa Himsaa* means *away from harm*, though the masters prefer to call it 'keeping a safe distance.' The idea is simple: If you stay far enough away from your adversary, he, she, or it can't harm you. This doesn't mean you should run away. It only means you should always remain at least a hair's width from your adversary's longest stroke."

The novices began each day of training with 100 long breaths of mindful meditation and followed that with a carefully orchestrated bow in honor of their masters. The bow contained seven separate movements, each performed with meticulous precision to the rhythm of a thunderous drum.

After the ceremony was completed, the students lined up in fifty parallel columns, with a master at the head of each. The first student in every column was given a *bo*, a wooden stave that was five cubits long. Then the novices were instructed to attack the masters with their *bo*, thrusting and stroking in a series of sporadic movements. With simplistic ease, the masters stayed just out of range, jumping backward, sliding sideways, stepping forward. This fascinated Torg. When the students struck quickly, the masters reacted slowly. When the students slowed their attacks, the masters sped up their defense, constantly changing rhythm but never varying distance.

As far as Torg could tell, not a single instructor was touched.

Jhana laughed. "The masters enjoy *Aarakaa Himsaa*. It gives them yet another chance to show off. But it's clearly valuable. During my training, I spent several thousand hours practicing various forms of these movements. The more you practice, the better you get."

"Fifty years is a long time, father. I don't know if I have the patience. I want to be a warrior *now*!"

"All youngsters feel the same. And many do *not* have the patience—and fail. But a time will come early in your training when your resistance snaps. It becomes easier—and far more pleasurable—after that. Besides, if you train hard enough and long enough, a day will come when you can teach your master a lesson. That is a joyful day!"

"You could defeat a Vasi master? I thought they were invincible."

"I am Asēkha—beyond the masters and all others. One day, you'll become an Asēkha. For me, that will be a *very* joyful day! But I'm already proud of you. You have no idea how much talent you possess. If only your mother were here with us. She was an even better fighter than I."

"You've told me that every day of my life," Torg said. "But I never grow tired of hearing it. I didn't know her, yet I miss her so much."

"Ahh, Torg ... don't despair. She wouldn't allow either of us to mourn. Dying while giving birth to you was her karma, just as growing up without her was yours. But she lives on in you. Your face looks just like her, my beautiful son."

Then Jhana wandered backward.

"Father, where are you going?"

Mist swirled about the Asēkha. He rose into the air and floated toward the blazing sky before a hot desert breeze swept him away.

"Father, wait! Don't go. Not yet."

Torg bolted upright. The first thing he saw was the Silver Sword, pale and lifeless at his side. The sun had risen, but the sky was thick with ugly clouds. The fire he had built the night before still smoldered but emitted little warmth.

Torg sighed.

It had been a dream.

He wasn't 18 years old.

He was more than a thousand.

And his beloved father was long dead, reduced to a memory that grew dimmer with each day.

It had been a dream, no more.

But the two grizzled men and the white-haired woman who approached from the trees were all too real.

One of the men was huge—as tall as Torg and much thicker around the belly—and the dark hair on his head, face, and neck grew together into one grimy tangle. He had small eyes, but his nose was long and oddly shaped. Torg studied him carefully, and soon there was no doubt. This one was a crossbreed—part man, part animal. From the looks of it, the animal portion was a bear. Throughout the land, there were a select few with magic powerful enough to conjure such a creature: Invictus, Vedana, Bhayatupa, the Warlish witches. But whoever had made this one no longer controlled him. He roamed freely, and by the looks of him, was dangerous. In addition to his intimidating height and girth, he carried an ax so heavy few could have lifted the head of it from the ground, much less swung it.

The second man was smaller than the first, though he was large by ordinary standards. He also had long dark hair and a thick beard, but he was better groomed—and startlingly handsome, his wily blue eyes intelligent and alert. This one was not a crossbreed, but that made him no less dangerous. He held a spear in one hand and had a dagger in his belt.

The woman was the smallest of the three. Her hair was white as snow, accentuating her green eyes, and she wielded a fancy wood bow, probably stolen, that already was nocked and drawn with a flint-tipped arrow aimed at Torg's heart.

"Friend, I say to ya, we wish for no trouble," the smaller man said, his eyes fixed on Torg's every movement. "We miserable wretches are tortured enough, as is. Rest assured we'll leave ya in peace once ya meet our slight demand."

"Let me shoot him dead and be done with him," the woman snarled. "Why waste our time with foolish words?"

The leader glared at the woman. Then he turned back to Torg and smiled. "Don't listen to her. If it were my choice, I would stay awhile and make lots of friendly talk. But we've travelled far this morning and our feet are lame. We must be moving along."

The crossbreed tromped forward. "She is right. No more talking is what I want. Give me da sword, Master Ogre, or I'll remove your foul noggin'."

The smaller man shook his head. "Ya heard them," he said as if resigned to an unwelcome fate. "My friends haven't a speck of good humor in their bones. Angry words give me a bellyache, but what am I to do? I dare not try to control da whims of such frightful peoples."

Torg rose to his feet, the Silver Sword at his side. "You've traveled far, but not as far as I," he said in a voice that sounded almost normal to him now that his teeth were growing back. "And I'm exhausted and lack my usual grace. In better times, I might find the three of you amusing. But today I have no patience. Besides, your demand is unacceptable. The sword is precious to me, and I wouldn't abandon it even under threat from an army of enemies. But I have demands of my own, and I counsel you to obey them. I'm in dire need of warm clothing. Take me to your camp and show me what you possess. Be quick, and I'll reward you. Defy me, and I'll strip the clothes off your backs."

Torg's bold words dumbfounded all three of them. The crossbreed's mouth sprang open. The leader clapped his hand against his forehead and chuckled. But the woman reacted without hesitation, letting the arrow fly.

Despite her quickness, she didn't catch Torg unaware. He could have knocked the arrow out of the air with his sword. But he wanted to impress them, so he allowed it to strike his chest. The arrow bounced off.

"He is Demon Spawn!" the woman said. "My arrow would've killed a Buffelo."

"I'm no ogre or demon. I'm far *greater*!" Torg said. Then he willed his eyes to glow with a deep-blue intensity. "If you test my patience too severely, you'll do so at your peril."

Whether frightened or enraged, the crossbreed could stand no more. He rushed at Torg with his ax held high and swung a mighty blow. Torg avoided it easily. Several thousand hours of *Aarakaa Himsaa* were more than a match for such a crude attack.

The smaller man flung his dagger. This time Torg didn't allow himself to be struck. He flicked the Silver Sword, knocking the blade out of the air.

Torg preferred not to kill unless given no other choice, and his instincts told him that these odd companions might be of use to him. They were ruthless but not evil. Still, he needed to disable them, at least temporarily, until he could earn their confidence. They were too feisty to be trusted just yet.

The crossbreed dropped his ax and slung his arms around Torg's torso. This wasn't a prudent move. Torg dropped the sword, placed his palms on the sides of the giant's neck, and compressed the major arteries, temporarily cutting off the flow of blood to the brain. During his warrior training, he'd practiced this move only a few dozen times, but it was simple to learn and always effective. The crossbreed's eyes rolled to the back of his head. He let go of Torg, took a step back, and said "Huh!" before collapsing into unconsciousness.

"Ya have killed Ugga, ya Bastud!"

The smaller man sprinted toward Torg and threw the spear. The wizard ducked as it zipped past and clattered against a boulder. The man continued forward at full speed, but Torg's abilities were superior. In his perception of time, the attacker moved in slow motion. Torg caught the man by his wrists, rotated on his hips, and flung him face-first into the smoldering remains of the fire. His adversary squealed and rolled off the embers, brushing himself frenetically.

"Bard, me dear. I come to save ya!" The white-haired woman

leaped at Torg, snarling like a lioness protecting her cubs. Torg punched her in the solar plexus—lightly, by his standards—and then tossed her aside. She landed awkwardly on the hard stone by the mouth of the cave and lay still.

The one she called Bard stood warily, bits of charred debris still smoking in his beard. Without the dagger and spear, he had no visible weapons, though Torg suspected he had more hidden beneath his cloak.

"Will ya kill us all?" Bard said. "We deserve it, I suppose. But Master Ogre, ya could do me a great favor if ya killed only me and let da others go. I love them and would hate to witness their endings."

"Put your hands down by your side and come to me."

"If I do, ya will skewer me with that blade," said Bard, motioning toward the sword that lay at Torg's feet.

"If you do as I say, I promise not to kill any of you. My word is worth much."

Bard looked down at Ugga, who lay flat on his back, eyes closed, breathing slowly as if taking a nap. The woman lay still as well, though she was moaning.

"And what of Jord?" Bard said, pointing at the woman. "Will ya defile her? I couldn't bear it."

"I'm no defiler," Torg said. "If you could see me as I truly am, you would find my words more believable. Still, you have no choice but to trust me. I say it, again: Put your hands by your side and come to me."

Bard remained unconvinced. "Ya could not best me again, so easy."

Torg sighed. "If you don't come to me, I'll come to you."

Bard reached inside his coat and drew out another dagger, but Torg was too quick. He closed the gap between them and grasped the man's hand with his thumb and forefinger. Then he squeezed wickedly, contorting the wrist. Bard cried out and dropped the weapon.

Torg pulled the man's face close to his. "*Niddaayahi!*" Blue smoke burst from his mouth and swirled into Bard's nostrils. The trapper fell into a deep sleep. The wizard lowered him gently to the ground.

Next, Torg walked over to the woman. Scattered patches of ice clung to the stone floor, and he struggled to keep his footing in his flimsy sandals. Jord gripped her stomach, groaning and coughing. Torg knew he hadn't struck her hard enough to do serious damage, but he leaned down to get a closer look.

Jord was craftier than he'd given her credit. She kicked at his left ankle, knocking his foot off the ground. His other foot slid sideways on the ice, causing Torg to fall on his face. He'd never been bested in such a way before.

The woman ran toward the trees. Torg was up in an instant, kicking off the annoying sandals and chasing after her.

"Wait ... *wait*! I won't harm you any further."

Even barefoot, Torg was quicker. She felt his approach and tried to run even faster, which caused her to stumble and fall. She scrambled to her knees just as he caught up. Torg grabbed one arm, but she spun around and bit him on the wrist. Her teeth were hard and flat, but no match for his flesh. Her eyes flew open like she'd chomped on a piece of wood, and when she felt the strength of his hand, she went limp.

"Don't kill me, Master Ogre! Don't eat my heart or drink my blood. I'll do whatever ya ask. I'll be your Concubeen if I must. But please, don't kill me. I don't want to die so young."

Then she burst into tears and shivered on the ground at his feet. This didn't fool Torg. Her cowardly display was mostly for show, buying her time to think up another way to escape. Torg grasped a handful of her hair and yanked her to her feet. She yelped like a dog kicked in the ribs.

Tugars knew more than fifty pressure points on the human body which, when stimulated, caused debilitating pain. Torg pressed his thick thumb into a spot just below her right elbow. Jord screamed so loud her voice echoed in the trees.

"I'm thinking all three of you are deaf," Torg said. "I'll try to make my intentions clear. If you do as I say, I won't harm you. And I have no desire to make you my *Concubeen*, whatever that might be."

Through the long strands of white hair that had fallen over her eyes, Jord looked up at him with renewed anger.

"Do ya think me ugly?"

Torg couldn't help it. He threw his head back and laughed. "No, you're not ugly. This has nothing to do with how you look, though you're in more need of a bath than I."

She drew her breath in with a hiss.

"Don't take offense," Torg said. "For now, whether you're beautiful or ugly is the least of my concerns. What I need more than anything is warm clothing and a hot meal. I would love some bread. Vegetables. Roasted meat. A mug of beer or a cup of wine. Ahh ... what I wouldn't do for either."

The woman sat on her haunches and brushed the hair from her eyes. She looked at Bard and Ugga. "Are they dead?"

Torg chuckled again. "The big one—Ugga, you call him?—will have a bit of a headache when he wakes up, and Bard might be groggy. But otherwise they'll be fine. I'm glad you care. You'll be more likely to do as I say if you fear for their safety."

"I ran like a coward," Jord said. "I'm ashamed. But ya scared me so!"

"Make it up to them. Do as I say and I won't hurt them. Do you have a camp nearby?"

"We have a house less than a league from here. It's *my* house. We were hunting for our breakfast when we smelled da remains of your fire. We planned to make off with your sword, which has da look of value."

"It does have value. But it's mine and I plan to keep it. Do you have any food at the house?"

"I have flour and yeast for bread, and plenty o' hickory butter. There's a barrel with squashes and wild potatoes. And I have spices, too."

"Take me there. We'll prepare a meal. Before this is over, you and I will be friends."

Jord motioned to Ugga and Bard. "Will ya leave them? Da cold'll kill them before just a short time passes."

"No, I won't leave them."

"But they are too big to carry."

"I can manage it."

Torg offered his hand to Jord. The green-eyed woman allowed him to lift her to her feet. He turned away and walked back to the cave where Ugga and Bard lay unconscious. He reached down, picked up the Silver Sword, and slid it into the belt of his robes.

Jord followed him. Torg imagined she was tempted to pick up a stone and bash his skull, but she'd seen how he had fought and probably didn't dare.

Torg went to Bard and lifted the smaller man with little effort. Then he laid him alongside the giant crossbreed.

Jord got on her hands and knees and put her ear against Bard's chest, and then did the same for Ugga.

"Are ya sure they'll live, Master Ogre? If they die, it'll be da foulest torment to me."

"If they're half as strong as they appear, they won't die. Ugga will wake up first. Bard won't open his eyes until late tonight or early tomorrow, but when he does, he'll feel strong and rested."

"Ya have performed these fantastical deeds before? Where did ya learn such trickery? Ya felled Ugga with a slap of your hands. And ya made Bard sleep with smoke belched from your bosom. I wouldn't have believed it possible. Ugga and Bard have never been bested, at least whilst I was watching. Even da blows of wicked savages don't injure them."

"I've received proper training."

"Ya do not fool me. Ya persist in saying ya not be Demon. But I believe ya not be Man. Ya must be a great Conjurer of Magic, arisen from da bowels of da mountains to haunt this world. What is your name, Master Ogre? Can ya tell me that?"

Torg laughed yet again. "In some ways, you speak the truth. I *did* come from the bowels of the mountains, though not by choice. I'm *not* a man, at least not in the way I take you to mean. And I can conjure magic, though there have been times in my life when I've been more able than now. As for my name, I choose not to reveal it. Don't take offense. I'd make a dangerous ally. Knowing who I am could be perilous."

Jord sighed. "We must call ya something."

"Very well. Call me … Hana. That name is as good as any."

Torg retrieved his bag of food and offered Jord a mushroom. To his surprise, she took it without protest. After tasting it, her eyes opened wide with delight.

"Hah-nah, do ya have great quantities of these mushrooms? They're better than any I've ever tasted. I beg to know from where they came?"

"I have only what you see," Torg said. "As for where they came from, let's just say that the world beneath our feet is not lifeless."

"I hope to never find out," Jord said. Then she reached back into the bag, pulled out another mushroom, and chomped hungrily.

"Wait, Hah-nah! I've changed my mind. I want to go into da cavern and get some more. Will ya show me?"

Torg sighed. He suspected she was exaggerating her pleasure for his benefit. "One day, I'll return to the cave if my karma allows. But for now, my errands are too urgent."

Then he handed the bag to Jord and knelt between the two

unconscious men. The woman gasped when Torg threw Ugga over one shoulder and Bard the other. When he stood, Jord almost swooned.

"Can ya carry Buffelos with your bare hands?"

"I must admit these two are heavier than I thought," Torg said, trying not to grunt too much. "Lead the way, Jord. The quicker we get to your camp, the quicker I can put them down. Their stink is worse than their bulk."

Jord found that quite amusing, bending over and slapping her knee. Then the woman started off through the woods. After a few hundred paces, the land sloped downward into a hollow. The footing was treacherous, especially considering Torg was lugging more than forty stones of dead weight. Plus, he was walking barefoot, and his feet were already numb.

They came upon a clear-running stream. Torg set down his burdens, buried his face in the icy water, and drank deeply despite the cold. Jord joined him, getting down on hands and knees and burying her face in the water, but when Torg lingered too long, she became annoyed.

"Come. It is yet a far ways."

The white-haired woman traveled much lighter than Torg. All she carried was her bow and arrows, Bard's spear, and Torg's small bag of food. She even left behind Ugga's immense ax, which was too heavy for her. But she hid it beneath some leaves before they departed.

Jord sprinted as fast as one of his Tugars. Torg wondered suspiciously how he'd been able to catch her so easily back at the cave. Gasping for breath and sweating profusely, he was forced to halt several times and drop the men on the ground less gently than he should have.

"Must ya wander along so slowly?" Jord said. "We've gone less than da length of a hectare. Almost a league still lies betwixt here and our neighborhood. Would ya like me to carry da sword? Ya keep tripping over it."

"If you had any idea what I've been through in the past few weeks, you'd be impressed that I could walk on my own, much less lug these brutes. And *no*, I don't want you to carry the sword. But if your wildness demands it, go on ahead. I'll follow your footprints."

"An excellent idea, Hah-nah. I'll start da fires. Beyond this hollow, ya will find a splendorous wood where da pines rise to vast bigness. Our house lies beyond da great trees."

"Whatever you say. But in the time it takes me to catch up to you, please try to learn a proper language."

"Hmph! Your speech is da one lacking, Master Ogre."

"You'll lack your head if you're not careful."

She responded with another *hmph!* Then she ran off fast as a filly. Torg watched Jord sprint along the base of the hollow, scramble up the side of a hill, and disappear into the trees. Despite the presence of Ugga and Bard, who lay at his feet like a pair of logs, Torg felt alone. He fantasized about leaving them and jogging after Jord, ridding himself of his annoying burdens. But he knew if he ever did something so selfish, his karma would haunt him. Nothing good ever came from acts of cruelty. For better or worse, Ugga and Bard were in his care. He hoisted the men onto his shoulders, slipped a little on the icy ground, uttered some ancient profanities, and started forward.

"*Must ya wander along so slowly*?" Torg said, mimicking Jord's annoying pattern of speech. "Let's see how fast you could wander with these two Buffelos on *your* back, ya bitch!"

Torg stumbled along the floor of the hollow, which was littered with fallen trees and crumbled boulders. Compared to Jord's joyous trot through the bowl-shaped depression, he moved as slowly as a snail. When he reached the hill that she had ascended so easily, Torg looked up with dread. How could he possibly carry these two barrels of flesh up there and have the strength to go any farther? He was hungrier than he was thirsty, and he remembered—with renewed annoyance—that he hadn't eaten since the night before. To make matters worse, Jord had taken what little food he had left.

Torg's legs were wobbly. His sojourn with the cave monkeys had strengthened him somewhat, but he was not even close to being fully recovered from his ordeal in the pit. A journey this physically stressful was the last thing he needed. But disabling Ugga and Bard had been his choice, so he did his best to quiet his inner whining.

The hill was steep but not tall, only fifty paces to its peak. Still, scaling it turned out to be even more difficult than Torg had feared. About halfway up, he had to put Bard down, hoist Ugga to the top, and return to his smaller companion. By the time all three were out of the hollow, it was almost noon. Torg sprawled on the ground next to the two men, wheezing like a weary old man.

As Torg lay on his back, it surprised him to hear a moaning sound from Ugga. He didn't believe it was possible that the crossbreed could wake up this quickly. Maybe the bear part of him gave him better recuperative powers than an ordinary person's. Torg watched Ugga closely, curious to see what would happen next.

The crossbreed sat up, let out a roar, and struggled to his feet. But he didn't stay upright for long. Instead, he fell forward onto his face and lay still for a few seconds before rising to his knees. Then he made a strange face—and vomited. The stink was dreadful. Torg stood and backed away.

"How did I get here?" Ugga said. "Where are ya, Bard? Where are ya, Bitch? My head hurts terrible. And I've lost my ax!"

"Are you able to walk?" Torg said from behind the crossbreed's back. "I sure hope so. Carrying you has been most unpleasant. You're as heavy as a camel."

Still on his knees, the crossbreed spun around in reaction to the voice. He stood again, lost his balance, and tumbled backward, landing roughly on his rump. Then he sat there with a quizzical expression, staring at Torg with a sort of awe.

"Do ya mean to kill me, Master Ogre? Without my ax, I can't stop ya from ending my days. Have ya murdered Bard and da Bitch? Did ya swallow them while I slept?"

Torg slapped his forehead in frustration. "Let me answer your questions one at a time. Do I mean to kill you? Not if you behave yourself. Have I murdered Bard and da Bitch? Bard is sleeping soundly just a few paces away, and da Bitch, as you call her, is already back at your camp, preparing a meal. Or she'd damn well better be. Have I eaten your companions while you slept? I'm not that hungry yet, but if I don't get some normal food soon, I might eat all three of you ... *raw*!"

Ugga began to cry. It was an unusual sound coming from someone so large and dangerous. "Please, Master Ogre! Don't kill poor, ugly Ugga ... or his two nice friends. Bard and da Bitch have treated me kindly. I *will* behave, I promise." He covered his face with his hands.

"All right! I believe you, Ugga. As I said before, you and the others have nothing to fear from me." Then Torg held out his hand. "Trust me. If I meant to kill you, would I have carried you all the way here on my back and waited for you to wake up? I need food, drink, and clothing— not murder and mayhem. And I'd relish some friendly talk by a warm fire after filling my stomach."

Ugga's small eyes opened wide, apparently stunned by the strength of Torg's grip. He stood and faced him. They were about the same height.

"I trust ya, Master Ogre," Ugga said, bowing his head. "I'll do as ya say." Then the crossbreed looked at his smaller companion, who lay on his back on the frozen ground. "Will Bard ever wake up?"

"Probably not before next morning. But he won't be sick like you were. Still, we need to get him to a warm place soon. Is her house—as Jord calls it—comfortable?"

"Her house is small, but it's very nice. I'll take ya there now, Master Ogre. Would it make ya mad if I carried Bard?"

"Ugga, if you'll carry Bard, I promise to be your friend for as long as we both live. But there's one other thing you *must* do for me, regardless."

"What's that, Master Ogre?"

"Please ... *please* ... call me Hana!"

Torg shivered in his thin robes, and his bare feet were now numb past his ankles. Otherwise, he felt like he was in paradise. He'd forgotten how pleasant it was just to walk on his own without lugging forty stones of odoriferous weight. Ugga now carried Bard, and the muscular crossbreed appeared to be having an easy time of it.

"I smell smoke," Torg said. "Do you think Jord is cooking something? I can't remember ever being this hungry."

"It's not far, Master Ogre ... err ... *Hah-nah*," Ugga said, shifting Bard to his other shoulder. "I smell smoke—and food, I think. Over this hill, we'll come to a line of white pines as tall and broad as any I've seen. Our house is a little ways beyond those trees."

"Jord mentioned nothing about fresh game," Torg said, "but I swear I smell venison."

"Knowing her, she got a deer after she left ya," Ugga said, breathing hard but moving at a steady pace. "There are many in these woods. She can slay a Buffelo from a furlong away. With her help, Bard and I kill lots of beasties and tan da hides—and we sell them to da merchants in Kamupadana for gold coins. But da whores tempt us with their pretty bodies. I like da Brounettos best of all! Bard goes for da Blondies. Da Bitch gets angry if we don't bring back more than a smile."

"Does Jord get jealous?" Torg said. "It seems like she and Bard are a couple."

Suddenly, Ugga dropped Bard to the ground and collapsed like he'd been struck with an arrow. Torg drew his sword and looked quickly around, searching for signs of an ambush.

Ugga's face reddened, his eyes filled with tears, and he appeared to be in severe pain. Baffled, Torg started toward the crossbreed to see what he could do. But then he sighed in relief. Ugga wasn't injured. A titanic fit of laughter had rendered him helpless.

The crossbreed rolled onto his side and held his thick stomach, thrashing his legs and pounding his fists on the ground. Bizarre grunts and squeals came from his mouth. He belched and farted before succumbing to a fit of coughing. A good time later, he composed himself, sitting up and wiping tears from his eyes.

"Master Ogre ... *Hah-nah*, I mean ... if ya don't intend to kill me, ya won't say such a thing again. In all my life, I've heard nothing so funny. Bard and da Bitch, a cup-pull?"

Ugga lost control again. As he laughed, gobs of sputum froze on his beard. It went on for so long, Torg sat cross-legged on the ground and waited for it to stop.

"Sorry ... sorry ... *Hah-nah*," Ugga said. "After we've eaten, we'll tell ya da story of Bard and da Bitch. Then ya will better understand da reasons for my crazy gigglings."

"Don't apologize. It's been a long time since I've heard this kind of laughter. To be honest, it warms my heart. And after you tell me about Bard and Jord, I'd like to hear the story of Ugga."

"Only if ya tell me about *Hah-nah*."

"Fair enough."

Ugga lifted Bard and started up the hill with Torg at his side. When they reached the crest, Torg stopped. The land descended toward a creek and then rose again in a series of lumps and ledges before flattening into a high plain. Where the plain began, a row of pines towered like titans over the lesser trees that stood nearby. Each tree was twice as large as any pine Torg had ever seen, more than 200 cubits tall with trunks eight cubits thick. There were trees in Dhutanga that were greater in size, but Torg had witnessed none so majestic on this side of the mountains.

"What makes them grow so grandly?" Torg said.

"Not even da savages can tell us," Ugga said. "Betwixt here and da mountains, there are none so mighty. Aren't they handsome, Master Hah-nah? I love them. I stand and stare at them until da snow freezes my beard. They love Ugga too. They hide Ugga and his friends from their enemies."

"They're magnificent. But I can't imagine why they're here—and *only* here."

"I don't know. But da Bitch might. When she comes near, da trees sing."

They walked beneath the giant pines. Torg stopped again and counted the wondrous trees. There were exactly thirty in a line so straight it resembled a palisade. He touched the trunk of the nearest tree and felt energy gush through his fingers into his arm.

"Ya are brave," the crossbreed whispered. "I don't dare touch them. They're too strong for me."

Torg approached another tree and pressed his face close to the trunk. He could sense the life energy surging beneath the furrowed bark, and he took a deep breath. Tendrils of green light squeezed from between the fissures and oozed into his nostrils. The Silver Sword glowed in response.

He stood in silence for a short while, feeling peaceful and safe. Then he gazed upward at row upon row of branches that grew in circular patterns along the trunks like stacks of plates. These majestic pines exuded wholesomeness as if tended by a benevolent spirit.

"When she is here, they sing," Ugga repeated. "They don't seem to mind your sword, but they don't like my ax. I hide it when I'm near." Then Ugga lowered his face. "Will someone steal it while I'm away?"

"Don't worry, your ax is hidden well. Besides, who would have the strength to lift it, much less carry it off?"

Ugga's face brightened. "Ya are right! But I miss it so much. I'll go back for it later."

The high plain stretched as far as the eye could see. Beyond the pines, the forest became a traditional mixture of conifers and leafless hardwoods. The smell of smoke and roasting meat intensified. Torg's mouth watered. He had become obsessed with the idea of eating. The cave monkeys had fed him well, but their worm soup—despite its excellent flavor—had grown monotonous. Torg wanted what his Vasi master liked to call a *square meal*: meat, bread, vegetables, fruit.

"How far, Ugga? Will I die of hunger before we get there?"

"A stream meanders down a ways. Do ya hear its bubblies? Beyond da stream, da timber becomes dense. Da Bitch chose that spot long ago. It is *her* house, ya know, but she lets us stay with her. I think she's clever! But da savages are scared of her. When she's around, they act like she isn't even there."

Scared of her? Why that would be? But the puzzlement was driven from Torg's mind by an increasingly intense aroma. Torg was close to madness. He ran recklessly toward the shadowy area where the house was hidden.

The stream was wide and lively, but Torg leaped over it like it was a trickle. He charged into the woods, dead leaves crunching beneath his feet. He jumped over fallen logs and tore through tangled branches before reaching a clearing, within which was a hut. Sweet-smelling smoke poured from a vent in the center of the angled roof, but that was not the main source of the wonderful odor. Jord stood outside tending a blazing fire, and suspended above it on a sturdy spit was the carcass of a skinned and gutted deer. A metal pot containing a fragrant stew hung over another fire. Jord had been busy. It amazed Torg that she had accomplished so much in such little time.

"Da bread is in da oven," Jord said. "Go inside my house and get warm. Ya have earned a bit of rest, me dear."

Torg staggered through the door, and despite his hunger, he collapsed onto a bed of leaves and saw no more. Then he slept for the rest of the afternoon until loud snoring woke him. When he opened his eyes, Bard lay beside him, still overcome by the effects of Torg's spell. But the snoring was a good sign. It meant Bard was sleeping normally and could wake at any time. Apparently, his recuperative powers were almost as strong as Ugga's.

A deerskin cloak had served as Torg's blanket, presumably a gift from Jord. He sat up and saw the Silver Sword leaning against the wall near the door. This relaxed him a bit, and he took the time to examine the interior of the hut. There was a hearth in the center of the round dirt floor. Smoke from a well-tended fire seeped out through a vent in the thatched roof. The walls were made of strips of bark woven between vertical posts and plastered with clay and dried leaves. Near the hearth was a crude table with three stumpy chairs. There were no windows, but the door was ajar. Torg stood and stretched. A pair of boots stuffed with wool socks had been placed near the door.

Torg buttoned up the warm cloak, strapped on the boots, and walked outside, unsure of what to expect.

Jord and Ugga were nowhere in sight. Dusk had not yet arrived, but the sky was gloomy and a breeze blew strong and cold. A storm was in the works, maybe even a blizzard. Torg looked back at the hut with relief. They would need its protection tonight.

The smell of roasting venison drifted in the air. Torg examined the deer carcass with lust in his eyes. Drips of fat sizzled on the fire. Near the spit was an iron pot containing what appeared to be vegetable stew. And nearby on a flat rock were two loaves of bread, recently left there to cool. Jord or Ugga had to be somewhere near, Torg thought, or they wouldn't have left the bread unattended. Raccoons, squirrels, and other wily creatures were numerous in these parts.

Somewhere beyond the clearing, Torg heard a series of loud crashes that sounded like drums or, maybe, the pounding of hooves. He saw flashes of movement, but they were unrecognizable.

"Ya have finished your napping, I see," said a voice from behind.

Torg fell into a defensive crouch. He wasn't used to anyone being able to sneak up on him.

"How'd you do that?"

Jord laughed. "Ya deserved a little fright after all ya have done to me and my friends. Da look on your face was a very funny thing, but ya are still an ugly booger, Master Ogre. Even Ugga is prettier. What manner of beast are ya, anyways, with no hair and such wrinkly skin?"

"My name is Hana," Torg said grumpily, still disturbed she had come upon him unawares.

"Hah-nah ... yes," Jord said. "Sorry! Even Ugga calls ya Hah-nah. Master Hah-nah, he says. He's silly, my big Ugga. But he's quite taken with ya. Ugga says ya liked da trees. If that's so, then I like ya too."

"It's so. Speaking of Ugga, where is he?"

"Where do ya think? He went to get his ax. Couldn't bear to be without it. But he should be back soon. And then we'll eat, before da storm blows in. Da night is going to be nasty, I fear."

"I'm so hungry I could eat a horse."

Jord's eyes blazed. They were the color of pine needles. "We're not Bar-Barians. We don't eat *horses*!"

"Or bears!" came a loud voice from the edge of the clearing. Ugga strode into view, his ax slung over his shoulder. "Hello, Master Hah-nah! Ya have a good rest, I hope?"

"It was grand," Torg said. "Bard's still asleep, but I think he'll be waking up soon."

"Ya think right" came a voice from near the hut. Bard stood just outside the door. "I see that while I slept, ya all have become a happy family. Is there a story to be told, Ugga? Has da Bitch put a spell on da unfriendly ogre and made him a nice guy?"

"I'm impressed," Torg said. "Most would have slept through the night. You're strong."

Bard seemed pleased. "Well, whatever ya did, I feel so very good now. I don't feel good enough to eat a horse or a bear, but I could eat most of that deer."

"Let's do it," Ugga bellowed. He stomped over to the spitted carcass and tore off an upper leg with his bare hand. The shanks had already been removed.

"Ugga!" Jord said. "Where are ya manners?"

"Who cares about manners?" Torg said, ripping off another leg. Bard joined them.

"Men!" Jord said huffily. "Ya are nothing but a bunch of Bar-Barians." She picked up a clay bowl and delicately ladled a modest serving of vegetable stew.

"Have some wine, Master Hah-nah!" Ugga said. He hefted a keg and poured a fragrant red wine into a clay cup. Torg drank it in three big gulps.

"Ahh" was all the wizard could manage.

The men ate and drank like fiends. Torg felt like he'd been invited to the world's finest party, making the suffering of the past three months seem inconsequential. As the evening grew darker, colder, and windier, Torg drank so much wine even he felt its effects. Ugga and Bard became very drunk, and they blubbered like fools. But Jord stood quietly off to the side, watching with sober interest. Her eyes sparkled, but otherwise she remained calm. Torg noticed she ate only one bowl of the stew and drank only a few sips of wine.

Ugga staggered into the hut and brought out another keg. "Here be more, Master Ogre ... er ... Hah-nah!"

"Fill my cup," Torg said. "And bring me more bread!"

"Bread? Bread?" Bard shouted. "Forget da bread! Cut us some more juicy chops with your ax, Ugga!"

Torg lifted the keg over his head. The wine spilled over his face and chest, staining his new cloak. He couldn't remember the last time he'd had so much fun. Ugga and Bard could barely stand. Even so, they demanded he hand over the wine while there was still some left.

"Drink up, ya scoundrels!" Torg bellowed.

The storm came on even faster than expected, its winds armed with ice crystals. Nearby trees shrugged and bent. The outside fires blew out. It became dark as death. Ugga and Bard crawled toward the hut on hands and knees, disappearing inside. Torg followed, but the vicious winds conspired against him. Then something yanked him back.

"Come with me!" Jord shouted through the tumult.

She grasped his thick biceps and led him away from the hut. They ran together into the teeth of the blizzard, through the forest, and over the rushing stream. Jord was supernaturally strong.

Suddenly, they were beneath the giant pines. The power of the storm tantalized the enormous trees. Torg could hear them singing.

"Allow me to do this!" the white-haired woman shouted. "She has left her mark in you. If I don't remove it, her poison will weaken you. I cannot allow this. Do not resist!"

She shoved him roughly onto his back. The snow cushioned his fall. "*Allow* me!"

"What?" Torg muttered. "I don't understand."

Jord tore open his cloak and lifted the thin robes beneath. "*Allow* me. Do not resist! I must remove the poison."

And then she moved her face between his legs. To Torg, it felt like he was being consumed by liquid fire.

"No!" he screamed. "You're in danger. Please ... *stop!*"

Torg tried to push her away, but she was too strong. He couldn't extract himself. "Please ... pleeaaaseeee. I don't want to hurt you!"

But Jord continued to caress him. She wasn't afraid.

"I'll destroy you," Torg stammered. "You don't understand."

She lifted her head and gazed into his eyes. "I'm not what I seem. I won't be harmed."

The storm attacked the forest like an invading army. The magical pines danced. Jord returned to her business, her head bobbing up and down, faster and faster. Torg arched and then howled in ecstasy. The power of his release surpassed the tempest, and his bed of snow melted, bubbled, and boiled. Blue light burst from his body, raced up the trunks of the pines, and erupted into the angry sky. In response, green energy blasted downward and permeated Torg's flesh. Just then, he spit up a crimson ball of pestilence, which hovered magically in the air, searching for a way to escape. But the green fire fell upon the poison and devoured it.

Jord wasn't injured. She finished him lovingly.

Torg lay on his back, still gasping, his body now glowing blue-green. The trees towered over him like guardians. He closed his eyes and listened to the storm. Within the strands of howling wind, he heard drums. Or was it the pounding of hooves?

Then the crossbreed was there, buttoning Torg's cloak and helping him to his feet.

"Da Bitch is gone. Ya must come where it's warm."

"Ugga? Is that you? Where's Jord? Does she live?"

"She's gone. I don't know where." His voice was sad.

Ugga hoisted Torg onto his back.

And carried him to safety.

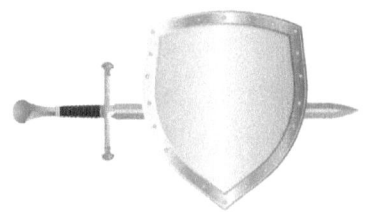

HOUSE OF JORD

The second time Torg woke inside the hut, he was alone. The door was closed and the room dark except for a dwindling fire that lingered in the hearth. At first, he didn't know where he was. The memories of his encounter with Jord consumed his awareness, but they seemed unreal. He lay on the bed of leaves for a long time, trying to decide whether it had been just a dream.

But when he sat up, his body felt strong and his mind clear as if cleansed of putridity.

Was it the height of day or the middle of the night? In the hut's dimness, Torg couldn't tell. And where were Ugga and Bard ... and Jord? Was she standing outside the door, waiting for him to emerge? Though he was more than 1,000 years old, Torg blushed.

He meditated for a short time. When he stood, he felt another surge of vitality. His strength was back, physically and emotionally. The full extent of his powers had also returned. The green energy of the pines had magically restored him. Torg felt as potent as ever.

The sword still leaned against the wall with its tip buried in the dirt. Apparently, his three companions had lost their desire to steal it. Torg swung the door open and stepped outside, entering a world of infinite alabaster. The ground, the trees, even the sky were white. The sun was hidden.

More than two cubits of snow had fallen during the storm. As far as Torg could guess, it was now late morning. The air was desperately cold, but the previous night's winds had fled. All was quiet.

Abruptly, the silence was broken.

"Master Hah-nah!" Ugga screamed. Then the crossbreed charged toward Torg and gave him a powerful hug, lifting him off his feet. "Me and Bard were afraid ya'd never wake up. Ya slept so sound, we feared ya might have passed away."

Bard also approached, bearing his spear along with Jord's bow and arrows. "Good morning, Hah-nah. Glad to see ya aren't a corpse, though ya do kind of look like one."

"Thanks," Torg said. "I suppose."

The crossbreed smiled, his small eyes glistening. "Da storm blowed away all da food and gear we left outside. Me and Bard couldn't even find da pot we use for stew."

"And what of Jord?" Torg said.

"She's gone," Bard said. "I looked everywhere. Ugga, too. But there are no signs."

"I miss her," Ugga said. "Where did she go, Master Hah-nah?"

"How would *he* know, ya dimwit!" Bard said. "Hah-nah was sleeping all night, don't ya remember?"

Ugga ignored Bard's insults. "Will ya help us look for her with your mah-jick-cull powers?" he said to Torg.

Bard stepped between them. "After our party last night, there's not much left in da house to eat. If we want breakfast, we need to hunt."

"I agree," Torg said. "And after we eat, we'll have a long talk and tell each other who we are and why we're here. If Jord hasn't returned by tomorrow morning, we'll search for her then."

Bard asked Ugga and Torg to stay and build a fire, and then he pounded through the snow into the woods. After his companion disappeared, the crossbreed went about collecting deadwood and kindling from beneath the snow. Torg did the same. Neither spoke. Ugga drew a sliver of flint from his cloak and struck it against his ax. The kindling caught fire.

"Are you angry with me over what happened last night?" Torg said.

Ugga's great chest heaved. "I'm just sad, is all. Da Bitch is gone and I don't know why. Will I ever see her again? I love her."

Torg placed his hand on the crossbreed's shoulder. "Who is she? Who *is* Jord?"

"Don't ya know? She is me mumma ... in a way. And Bard's, too."

This surprised Torg. "Your mother?"

Bard trudged out of the woods carrying two hares and a plump possum. Ugga ran to greet him.

"Bard, me love! How'd ya get them so quick? Ya've been gone just da blink of an eye."

"I'd like to say I killed them myself, but that would be lying," Bard said. "A parcel of savages greeted me not a thousand paces from where ya stand. They rushed to me and handed me these fine critters. Their chief said to me, 'Svakara werricauna.' And then he and da savages ran far away."

"Why are the Svakarans afraid?" Torg said.

"Do ya not know?" Bard said. "They are scared of ya. We're not da only folk who call ya an Ogre. They hope to buy your pardon with hares and this fat che-ra. They fear ya have come to murder da men, rape da women, and eat da children."

Torg took a long breath to calm himself. "Why does everyone around here think I'm a monster?"

"Ya look like a monster," Ugga said. "Ya are as strong as a monster. Are ya not a monster, Master Hah-nah?"

Torg wasn't used to being treated like a bogeyman. He took a moment to examine his body, first rubbing his hand along the top of his head. When he had escaped the pit, his scalp had been bare, but now a bristly carpet of hair covered it. He slid his tongue along his teeth. As far as he could tell, they already were about a quarter of the way grown in. But the skin on his arms was still scaly and mottled. The asthenolith had burned off most of the disease, but the healing process wasn't pretty.

Torg guessed it would take several more weeks to look relatively normal and months to grow his hair back to shoulder length.

"Ugga, I'm not a monster," Torg said. "At least, not in the way you mean. It's time to tell you who and what I really am. But first, let's skin these 'critters' and put them over the fire."

"Ya and I are alike," Ugga said. "We're hungry all da time."

While the hares and possum roasted, the crossbreed went into the hut and came out with a keg of wine. "This is da last of da spirits. Water is all we'll be drinkin' for a spell, I fear. But we got some nice skins put away that we can trade for more wine."

"How long does it take to reach Kamupadana?" Torg said.

"In da summertime, we can walk there in one long day," Bard said. "But after yesterday's big snow, I think it will take two days or more."

Torg took the keg from Ugga and drank several gulps of wine.

"The two of you need to go to Kamupadana for fresh supplies. I need to go there for reasons of my own," Torg said. "Here's what I propose: If Jord doesn't return today, we'll spend tomorrow looking for her. The following day, no matter what, we'll begin our journey. Does that sound fair?"

Bard shook his head. "There's no use searching for her. She's where she wants to be. We might as well leave tomorrow morning. I can't go more than three days without spirits. It gives me a bellyache."

Ugga snarled. "Ya would abandon her after all she's done?"

"She's gone 'cause she wants to be. It's not like she hasn't disappeared before. Ya know that as well as I do, ya dimwit!"

Ugga lowered his head. "I love her, Bard. Where does she go? *Why* does she leave?"

"Ask him," Bard said, pointing to Torg. "He knows her better than us. Ya told me so this morning, ya did."

The small portion of Ugga's cheeks that weren't covered with hair turned bright red. "I told ya not to say," the crossbreed muttered.

Torg interrupted. "It's obvious we all have much to say. Let's sit in the hut where it's warm, share what's left of the wine, and tell our secrets. I'll go first."

They went into the hut and huddled around the table. Each drank several more swallows of wine before Torg broke the silence.

"My name is not Hana, as I'm sure you've guessed. My name is Torg—and I am a king."

Bard spat a mouthful of wine onto the table. "Ya are a *king*. And Ugga is a *princess*!"

"Be quiet, ya *katichhei* (rogue)," Ugga said. "Let Master Hah-nah finish his talking. And don't waste da spirits. If ya can't keep it in your mouth, don't drink it!"

"I must not look much like a king," Torg agreed. "Master Ogre is a better description. But my recent travails have been hard on my body—and spirit. Others might not have fared as well. But before I continue my story, I must ask you both a question: Do you know of the sorcerer named Invictus?"

"Surely, ya speak in jest," Bard said. "*Everyone* in these parts has heard of Invictus, even simple wood folk like us."

"Are you for him or against him?" Torg said.

"I'm for Bard and da Bitch," Ugga said. "I don't care about In-vick-tuss as long as he leaves us alone."

"We're too small a bunch for his concern," Bard said. "But I think we'll have to move on one day. Betwixt da Whore City and Avici, it's no longer safe. More and more, his soldiers wander about, causing trub-bulls."

"Good enough," Torg said. "But let this be known: I am Invictus' sworn enemy, which makes me the enemy of any who claim him as friend or ally. I will slay anyone who has joined him as surely as I would slay the sorcerer."

"I believe ya, Master Hah-nah," Ugga said. "Or should I call ya King Torg?"

"Hana is what I prefer," Torg said. "Besides, it will be safer to use that name while we travel. Even in the wilds, the enemy has eyes and ears. I'm hoping Invictus believes I'm dead, and that's the way I want to keep it for as long as possible."

"Da meat is cooked," Bard said.

"Let's eat, then," Torg said. "And while we do, I'll tell you why I like the name Hana."

Torg chomped into the possum's juicy thigh. The fatty meat was as tasty as wild boar. Grease dripped down his chin. He wiped it with the sleeve of his cloak before picking up the keg and taking a long swig. Bard and Ugga sat beside him in the hut. They devoured both the hares and then helped Torg with the remains of the much-larger che-ra.

Afterward, the crossbreed and his handsome friend digested more than just roasted game. For the rest of the morning, they listened as Torg recounted the events of the past several months, including the rescue of the Noble Ones at Dibbu-Loka and his imprisonment in the pit. He told them who and what he was. He even described the death of Sōbhana. But he left out the sexual encounter with Vedana. That was between him and the demon.

Ugga bowed his large head. "I understand why ya want us to call ya Hah-nah. Your Sōb-hah-nah was a great lady. Almost as great as da Bitch."

"In some ways, they were much alike—strong, brave, and beautiful."

"Ya speak like Jord is also dead," Bard said.

"I don't think she's dead. But I have no idea where she is or why she left. Who and what she is befuddles me, as well. Maybe now, you can tell me your tale and help me understand. But do you believe what I told you about me?"

"I believe ya, Master Hah-nah," Ugga said. "Ya are not a liar."

"I believe ya, too," Bard said.

"Good. I've risked a lot telling the two of you about me. But I trust you ... as friends."

"Then friends it is," Bard said. "And friends we'll be."

"Yes," Ugga said. "*Good* friends!"

The crossbreed smacked a hand the size of a bear paw onto the rough wooden table. Torg placed his hand on top of Ugga's. Bard hesitated, then placed his hand on Torg's. Then he leaned over the table and stared at Torg.

"I'm ready to tell da tale of Ugga, Bard, and da Bitch. But first, I have to tell Ugga something." He smiled sheepishly at the crossbreed. "I'm sorry, but I have uttered a white lie. Ya drink so much of da spirits, I sometimes hide some for myself. There is one more keg of wine hidden in da corner where we keep da potatoes."

Ugga smiled broadly. "Some lies are good!"

And so, when Bard began his tale there was plenty of wine to go around.

"What I say now will not be a lie. What I say will be da truth, as I know it. When I first saw Ugga and da Bitch, I was a boy of just ten winters and ..."

The boy lived in a small settlement hewed out of the wilds on the northeastern border of the Dhutanga Forest. The wide mouth of the Gap of Gamana was due east. Duccarita, home to villains and outlaws, was a few leagues north. The Dark Forest lay west and south. And the Mahaggata Mountains—home to Mogols, trolls, and an assortment of bloodthirsty creatures—also loomed nearby. There was danger on all sides.

Many evil beasts dwelled in Dhutanga's interior. The settlers constantly had to watch the trees, never knowing what might emerge. There were fewer than 200 in the colony, and less than half were adults capable of putting up much of a fight. The elders met often about the perils surrounding their homestead. Though they were close to a large stream and plenty of game, they admitted they had chosen a poor location. Their only hope of long-term survival was to abandon the settlement and move south nearer the Green Plains.

Less than a week before their planned exodus, a Mogol war party found them. Dawn of a cool spring day had not yet arrived when fifty warriors swept into the hamlet. They wore only breechcloths, revealing grotesque tattoos that covered their wild faces and muscular bodies. They were armed with clubs, spears, axes, and blowguns. The settlement's lookouts never saw them. In a short time, all the adult men and elderly women were dead, and they captured the younger women and children and roped them together by their ankles.

"We could make no sense of their gibberish," Bard said, "but they beat us and made us watch their savage behaviors. We begged for mercy, but da savages didn't care. They laughed and whipped us."

Bard lowered his head. A single tear fell from each eye, splashing onto the tabletop. Ugga's thick lips quivered.

The Mogols bound their captives by the ankles and forced them to march northward. The boy staggered along next to his mother and heard her whisper to another woman that they were being herded toward Duccarita to be sold as slaves.

"I'm so sorry, me boy," his mumma said. "If ya get a chance to run, ya take it, do ya hear? Don't look back."

The boy cried and told his mother he would never leave her, but then a Mogol warrior came behind him and kicked him between his legs. The boy bent over and gagged, and the warrior kicked him again.

They stumbled along for two days with little food or rest. They beat any stragglers and took the weakest from the main group and clubbed them to death. The boy wished he could die. But he also noticed the knots around his thin ankles coming loose. His mother saw it, too.

"Ya do what I say," she whispered. "If ya get free, I want ya to bolt! It's better one of us escapes than none at all."

The second night after the attack on the settlement, a skirmish broke out among the Mogols. The boy and his mother couldn't tell what was happening, but a rumor passed among the prisoners that a warrior had taken a liking to one of the females and had attempted to carry her off into the woods. The leader of the war party became angry, not wanting to lose any more slaves than necessary. The Duccaritans paid well for women and children.

Mumma gave the boy a look. "I love ya boy, but now's da time. I want ya to run into da woods and hide till we're gone."

"But where will I go after that, mumma? How will I live?' he said to her. She had no answer and turned away.

The boy broke free of his bonds and rushed into the trees. It wasn't until morning that the Mogols noticed he was missing. This enraged the leader. A young male slave was worth even more than a woman. Five warriors tracked him, and it took them less than half a day to find him shivering beside a swollen stream in a tree-choked cove.

The warriors rushed toward him with anger in their eyes. But then a black ball of rage sprang from the trees. The snarling bear leaped upon the nearest warrior and ripped off his head with a single swipe of a huge front paw. But the four remaining warriors, each of whom had killed many a bear, surrounded the beast. They knew the darts from their blowguns couldn't pierce its tough hide, so they attacked it with their spears. There was a violent clash. The boy was too frightened to move. Soon, only one warrior remained alive, but the bear was grievously wounded and lacked the strength to continue. The lone survivor closed in for the kill.

"And that's when she arrived," Bard said, taking several sips of wine as if attempting to drown his pain. "From da woods she appeared, looking just like she does now. Da savage seemed to know her and was scared. He tried to run, but she caught him from behind and broke his neck as easy as you would a dry twig."

The warriors had terrified the boy, but there was something about the woman that didn't seem threatening. He crawled to the dying bear and petted its coarse fur, which was soaked with blood. When he looked up at the white-haired woman, tears streaked his pale cheeks.

"I shall give you a gift," she said to the boy, "and to this fine animal, as well. You both shall stay with me for as long as it takes to heal your wounds—not just the wounds of your bodies but the wounds of your spirits."

"Da bear is dying,' the boy said. "He is cut here and there."

But she only laughed. "For a beast to be reborn as a man, it must perform an act that lifts it beyond its instinctual behaviors. This bear, I believe, will be reborn as a man. So my gift to the bear is human form in this lifetime. And my gift to you will be his friendship."

While the boy watched, the white-haired woman performed her miracle, lifting her arms and speaking strange incantations that caused a blinding green light to spurt from her fingertips. The boy couldn't stand the intensity of it and hid behind a tree, but his curiosity forced him to peer around the trunk. A whirlwind of sparkling energy engulfed the bear, lifting its massive body several cubits off the ground like it weighed less than a feather. The corpses of the warriors also floated in the air, and they spun around the bear—faster and faster—until they blurred.

The woman cried out. There was a radiant eruption, and the boy covered his face. When all went quiet, he looked up and saw ...

"Bard has told me da story many times, but I don't remember the spinning part," Ugga said. "Before I met Bard and da Bitch, all I knew was hunting and running, blood and berries, worms and bugs. And then I remember standing on my hind legs and being amazed by how clear everything looked. I saw da boy, crouched on da ground. And when I looked down, my legs were different, long and pale like most of my fur had fallen off."

After hugging his new friend, the boy begged the white-haired woman to save his mumma. But she refused.

"I could have saved all of you, but I'm not here to rescue the weak or punish the wicked. I'm a watcher—little more and little less. Only on rare occasions am I permitted to interfere."

The boy lay on the ground and wept, and his new friend knelt and comforted him. But the white-haired woman couldn't be swayed. She strode off without another word.

"I picked up Bard and carried him," Ugga said. "She was our only chance. I didn't know any words ... yet. But I knew enough to want to stay with da lady."

The crossbreed and the boy followed the woman for a long time, passing west of Duccarita and journeying north almost to Nirodha. They then turned east, traversing steep mountains and remote valleys that were chilly even in early summer, and eventually settled in the foothills of Mount Asubha. After their arrival, the magical pines began to grow.

"She gave us names from da ancient tongue," Bard said. "My name means *liberated,* Ugga means *mighty,* and she named herself Jord, which meant *guardian.* My old name, before da Bitch saved my life, is lost to my memory. Many winters have passed since those fateful days."

"How many?" Torg said.

"I'm not sure," Bard said, "but I'd guess many thousands."

Torg's jaw dropped.

"Da pines keep us young," Ugga said. "Da Bitch always told us to stay close to them. If Bard and I go too far away for too long a time, we start to feel old and lame."

Torg took one last sip of the wine. Bard and Ugga finished the rest. They then sat in silence for a long time. Bard's tale had taken the entire afternoon, and night's black breath was creeping into the forest. Occasionally, one of them threw a fresh log on the fire. Otherwise, they barely moved. Outside the hut, it was as quiet as death.

Ugga broke the silence. "Do ya know who she is?" he said to Torg. "Can ya tell us, pretty please?"

Ugga's question prompted Torg to silently recall the dream-like conversation he'd had with Peta less than two weeks before when he was the Stone-Eater's prisoner.

"*There are beings beyond all known laws, natural or otherwise, and they are watching the sorcerer with growing interest—and planning his demise,*" the ghost-child had said.

Torg gazed at Ugga and Bard. When he spoke, his voice trembled. "I believe Jord is who and what she claims to be. She is a *watcher*. But don't those who watch usually report to superiors?"

"Who is da Bitch's soo-peer-ee-er?" Ugga said.

"An excellent question," Torg said. "I don't know the answer—and I'm not sure I *want* to."

"I have another question," Bard said, whose tone now contained a hint of anger. "Why does she favor Master Hah-nah?"

Torg again thought back to his conversation with Peta. "*There are three females on Triken who can abide you.*" Vedana was one. He now knew Jord was another. But who was the third?

"I'm not sure *favor* is the proper word," Torg said to Bard. "But I know this: An evil has arisen that threatens us all. The fate of the land lies in the hands of a few. I'm destined to play a role in the outcome. Perhaps the two of you are fated to join me."

Outside the hut, the drums resumed their mysterious beat. Leaning against the far wall, the Silver Sword glowed with incandescence.

Torg, Ugga, and Bard paid little heed. Too much wine. And talk.

The three men—*good* friends, all—succumbed to the lure of drunken sleep.

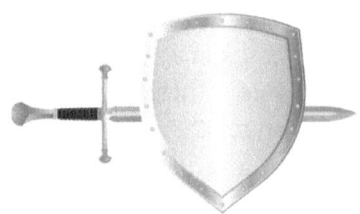

THE OTHER DEATH-KNOWER

Upon awakening, the first thing Torg noticed was the pervasive smell of sweat. Bard was still at the table, but a side of his face was plastered against the splintered wood. Ugga had tumbled out of his chair and lay flat on his back on the dirt floor, his massive chest—and even larger stomach—rising and falling. The fire had burned low, but the interior of the hut remained warm. Torg yawned, stretched, and sat up. At least, he thought proudly, he alone among the three of them had had the sense to crawl over to the bed of leaves, though he had no memory of doing it.

The Silver Sword rested against the wall near the door. Torg walked to it and grasped the black-leather hilt. He noticed for the first time that the asthenolith had damaged the hilt a bit. But for reasons he couldn't understand, the leather was mostly intact. He touched the blade with his left hand, expecting it to be about the same temperature as the room, but instead it was freezing cold. Torg vaguely remembered grasping the blade while in the agony of the asthenolith; even there it had been cool.

Torg put down the sword, opened the door, and stepped outside. More snow had fallen during the night, and the morning sky had remained gloomy. The fire that had roasted the possum and hares was lifeless.

The recent downturn in the weather didn't surprise Torg. As winter approached, storms would be frequent, and there'd be snow on the ground for the better part of four months. Most of the people who dwelled this near to the northern mountains would spend most of their time indoors, wandering out only to replenish water supplies and to hunt for game.

Speaking of game, lying in a split-cane basket near the hut were the carcasses of two wild turkeys and another che-ra. In a second basket were purple berries, hickory nuts, and three bloated skins.

A wooden spear had been thrust into the ground between the baskets. It was two cubits longer than Torg was tall. White and brown feathers attached to the staff hung lifeless in the dead air. Torg had the feeling he was being watched, but when he scanned the surrounding landscape, he saw no movement. Whoever was out there knew these woods as well as he knew the Great Desert.

Torg understood one thing that Bard and Ugga did not. The Svakarans, along with the other native people of the mountains, were not "savages." Some of their actions appeared brutal—especially where the Mogols were concerned—but their ability to live in harmony with their surroundings surpassed most of the "civilized" cultures found on Triken. Only the Tugars, who thrived on the blazing sands of Tējo, were as well-adapted to their environment as the so-called savages of Mahaggata.

Regardless of their reputation, the Svakarans were formidable. If they sensed weakness, they would take advantage. They cared most for their own people and tolerated others only if they feared or respected them. Torg decided to reinforce the fear aspect.

The wizard removed his heavy cloak and laid it on the surface of the snow, then he pulled the spear from the frozen ground and grasped the center of its well-balanced shaft, admiring its sharp tip made of chiseled obsidian. He hoisted it above his shoulder and drew it back. With a hidden surge of magic from the palm of his hand, he engulfed the spear in blue-green flame. Then he let out a howl and heaved the spear with the might and precision of a Tugar warrior. It hurtled through the air before striking the trunk of a thick snag more than one hundred cubits away. There was a booming sound. Shards of wood sprayed outward. The spear pierced the snag, burst out the other side, and buried itself in a living tree several paces farther away.

Ugga and Bard stumbled through the doorway, tripping over each other.

"Here we come, Master Hah-nah," the crossbreed shouted. "Do not fear!"

Ugga brought his ax. Bard carried Jord's bow and arrows. The pair scrambled next to Torg and stood ready, their haggard breaths coming in enormous white bursts. They scanned the edge of the clearing, looking this way and that. A long time passed before Bard spoke.

"What is it, Hah-nah? We see nothing but da trees. Were ya accosted by savages?"

"Someone or something is out there," Torg said. "They left us a gift and then withdrew."

Bard's cheeks turned red with anger. "Are ya trying to end our lives with your wicked shouting? Next time, give Ugga and me some warning before ya go 'round hooting like an animal!"

Ugga, ever the opportunist when it came to food and drink, was already investigating the baskets. "We eat well today!" he said with a smile that exposed his sharp teeth. "I like having ya around, Master Hah-nah. Wherever ya go, food appears like mah-jick!"

Then the crossbreed picked up one of the skins and sniffed its contents. "Beer! *Beeeeeeeer*!"

He danced about absurdly. Torg couldn't help but laugh.

"Ugga, you are a joy."

"Thank ya, Master Hah-nah!"

But then the crossbreed's smile faded. "No sign of da Bitch?"

"I can't sense her presence. For whatever reason, I believe she's far away by her own choice or need. Perhaps, she's been called by her superiors."

As if in response to Torg's words, there was movement in the woods. Bard strung an arrow to the bow and Ugga hoisted his ax. Torg scanned the trees with well-practiced precision.

"Someone hunts us, after all," Bard whispered.

Then a raspy voice came from somewhere outside the clearing. "It *is* you, isn't it? If I didn't know your mannerisms so well, I wouldn't believe it, the way you look now."

"Show yourself," Torg commanded.

"Isn't that just like you," the voice said. "Always showing off and bossing people around. For the sake of Anna, will you never stop?"

Torg couldn't believe it. "Rathburt? Where have you been all these years and how came you here?"

A man emerged from behind a tree. Like Torg, he had black hair and blue eyes, but he was stooped and appeared frail beneath his bear-skin cloak. He leaned against an oaken staff. Ugga took an instant dislike to him.

"Who is da interloper?" the crossbreed said. "His words are nasty."

Bard agreed, aiming an arrow at the man's chest.

"My, my," the man said, slowly approaching the clearing. "Is this how you treat an old friend?"

With one hand, Torg gripped the underside of the arrowhead and pulled it toward the ground. With the other, he grasped the handle of Ugga's ax.

"There's no need for your weapons. He is, indeed, my friend, though I haven't seen him in many years. His name is Rathburt—and he is the only other Death-Knower alive in the world."

Ugga and Bard weren't impressed, but they lowered their weapons. Meanwhile, Rathburt strolled over and stared at Torg's face. Because of his poor posture, he was at least a span shorter than Torg and Ugga. Up close, Rathburt looked much older than Torg remembered. His face was lined and weathered, which was unusual for an ordinary Tugar, much less a Death-Knower. Conversely, Torg must have looked far different to Rathburt.

"Torg, what happened to you? You look terrible."

"Have you not heard? Have you lost touch with our people?"

Rathburt's expression soured. "They're no longer my people, and you know it. Besides, Tugars rarely travel this far north. They prefer to keep their noses buried in the sand where they belong."

"Are ya sure this *occooahawa* (old fool) is your friend?' Bard said. "His words are full of da venom of snakes."

Amusement replaced Rathburt's sour expression. "And what would your name be, sir?"

"My name is my biz-nuss. I only give it to polite peoples."

Rathburt laughed and pounded his staff into the snow. Ugga raised his ax.

"Not even a friend of Master Hah-nah can laugh at Bard that way," the crossbreed said. "Be quiet, rude person, or I'll teach ya some manners."

Torg had heard enough. "*Silence!*"

A sudden gale swept through the clearing, causing the snow to swirl at their feet. Bard and Ugga retreated several steps. Rathburt stayed put but lowered his gaze.

Torg glared at them. "Rathburt is my friend. I didn't say he was *friendly*. Few among our people can tolerate his presence. He's irritating, insulting, and sarcastic. But I've always believed there's more to him than meets the eye. And a Death-Knower should *never* be underestimated, regardless of his or her appearance. This man has left his body—and returned to speak of it. More need not be said."

Bard's cheeks went pale. Tears welled in Ugga's eyes. But Rathburt wasn't so easily cowed. He walked to the crossbreed and wrapped his skinny arm around the giant's massive shoulders. "Don't worry, he's always showing off, demanding this and commanding that. He says our people can't tolerate my presence, but the same goes for him. They act nice to his face but grumble behind his back. He was always the *fastest*, the *strongest*, the *smartest*—and the first to let you know it. For Anna's sake, Torg, will you never change?"

Torg sighed. "I'm too hungry and irritable for such silliness. Much has occurred since you and I last spoke." He pointed toward the baskets. "In the meantime, I thank you for your gifts."

"These gifts aren't really from me," Rathburt said. "They're from my trusty associate. I'd like to introduce him if the three of you don't mind. I believe you'll like him. He works hard and is an excellent cook."

"I'm very hungry," Ugga said, his good humor suddenly returning. "If your ah-soh-see-it can make food taste good, then it's all right with me if he joins us."

"Why, *thank you*," Rathburt said. Then he yelled toward the woods: "Elu, show yourself!"

A small head peeked out from behind the trunk of a yellow poplar.

"There you are," Rathburt called. "Get over here! It's time you earned your keep." Then he turned and whispered to Ugga. "I speak to him harshly, but he's a worthy companion. He loves me like a papa."

Elu sprang through the woods, entering the clearing at a dead run.

"Come to papa!"

Instead of going to Rathburt, Elu ran to Torg and bowed at his feet. "Elu is at your command. Speak, and Elu will obey."

Rathburt looked annoyed. "Showoff," he said.

Torg ignored Rathburt. "Rise," he said to Elu. "That is my command."

Elu was less than half Torg's height, but his face was manly and his body heavily muscled. He dressed in the winter garb of a Svakaran tribesman—a beaver-skin coat threaded with the sinews of a deer. But Svakaran males were relatively tall. This puzzled Torg.

"Who are your people?" he said to Elu.

Rathburt answered for him, his words sounding rehearsed. "He's a

Svakaran. But a Mogol shaman poisoned him when he was a child, stunting his growth. His parents were embarrassed and abandoned him, deeming him a blight to their community. But I was kind enough to take him in." Then Rathburt became more animated. "Despite his demure stature, he's not helpless. He can hunt and cook. And he fights well for someone so small. Why, I daresay he could give even big men like you a tussle. While you're not looking, he'll bite you on the shin."

The crossbreed laughed. "I hope not to fight ya, little guy. Are ya as good a cook as Master Rad-burt claims?"

"Elu cooks very good," he said. "He will cook for the friendly giant. And for the others." He gestured toward Torg. "Elu will do whatever the *great one* says."

"Well, then, get started, you little booger," Rathburt said. "The 'great one' is hungry. And so is the 'poor excuse for a man' standing next to him. Will you lower yourself to cook for him, too?"

"Elu does what he's told."

"Don't worry, little guy," Ugga said. "I'll help ya."

"I'll help, too," Bard said.

"If the friendly giants build a fire, Elu will do the rest. Do you have a pot for a nice stew?" He motioned toward the baskets. "The hickories thicken the broth and the berries add sweetness."

"I found our pot yester-eve," Ugga said. "I'll get it for ya!"

Their friendly repartee diffused the tension. "Rathburt and I have much to discuss," Torg said to the others, and then he grasped the fellow Death-Knower by the arm and dragged him toward the hut. "Call us when dinner is ready. And we'll take one of the skins of beer, as well."

Ugga didn't like that idea so much. "Just one, I hope, Master Hah-nah."

"Why does he call you Master Hana?" Rathburt said.

"It's a long story. Come inside and I'll tell you what has happened to me since you and I last crossed paths. And you'll do the same."

"My tale will be less interesting, I'm sure. But then I've always been less interesting than you."

"Like I said, you haven't changed a bit."

"But you still love me, right?"

Torg held open the door. "I love my people. And I consider you to be one of them. Don't convince me otherwise."

"There you go with your threats."

Inside the hut, the fire had burned out. Torg threw more logs into the hearth and placed his right hand on top of the thickest piece of timber. Blue-green flame surged into the dry wood.

Rathburt claimed one chair next to the table. "It smells like the insides of an Asēkha's boots in here."

"There are worse smells."

"*You* would think so."

"Listen … Rathburt. You commented about my strange appearance. But now you seem to have lost your curiosity."

"I knew you'd tell me without prompting. You've always enjoyed talking about yourself."

Torg sighed, an all-too-frequent occurrence whenever Rathburt was around.

"You seem to blame me for your predicament," Torg said. "But why am I the cause? Your ascension pleased me even more than it did you. I was prepared to welcome you among the greats, and so were the rest of our people."

"I didn't want to be among the greats. My *ascension* was a fluke. I didn't even make it past the first year of warrior training, much less deserve to become a Death-Knower. I'm a freak, and you know it."

Torg protested, but Rathburt waved his bony hands.

"I'm 500 years old. I know that's not as old as *you*, but it's older than any other Tugar, including Kusala. I've been a Death-Knower—if anyone can call me that without snickering—for more than four centuries. And do you know how many times I've achieved *Sammaasamaadhi*?"

"I'm unaware."

"Humor me. Take a guess."

Torg sighed again. "About one hundred times?"

"About one hundred? And how about you, Torg? How many times for you?"

"Around 1,000."

Rathburt chuckled, but there was no humor in it. "Don't you see, Torg? This proves I'm a fraud. You guessed one hundred? I'd be proud of that number. Try … *once*."

Even this didn't shock Torg. "Once is one more time than anyone else in the world besides me. Once is one more time than the Vasi masters who terrorized you. Once is one more time than Kusala, who ranks among the greatest men I've ever known. Once is one more time than all but the rarest of Tugars in our long history. Why do you insist on demeaning your achievement?"

"Because it was a fluke. I never even felt the urge of *Dakkhinā*." Rathburt leaned forward and pounded his fist on the table. "I wasn't destined to become a Death-Knower. I was born to be a gardener. Isn't that the stupidest thing you've ever heard? A gardener who lives in the desert. But it's all I've ever wanted—to tend trees, plants, and flowers, to get to know them, to treasure them, to love them. Which is why I enjoy meditation. To get close to nature, you must *think* like nature. Meditation helped me do that by quieting my mind and raising my awareness. And one night without planning or preparation, my mind cleared, my breath and heartbeat slowed, and my concentration reached a deeper level than ever before. Suddenly, there I was in the Realm of Death where you've been so many times. But unlike you, it wasn't talent, strength, or courage that brought me back to my flesh. Do you know what it was? I missed my garden. It would have struggled without my care, and I wasn't ready to abandon it. So I returned to my body."

Rathburt buried his face in his hands. "I've never made the attempt again. And I never will! I'm a coward, Torg. Our people—*your* people—wanted me to be like you, but I was incapable of it."

Torg placed his hand on Rathburt's shoulder. "You torment yourself needlessly. You're ashamed of your success as a gardener and your failure as a warrior. But what you don't comprehend is that a gardener is the superior being. Nourishing life ranks among the highest states of wisdom, destroying life among the lowest. I've killed many times—with magic, sword, and bare hands—and each time I've fallen further from the attainment of enlightenment. Don't you understand? There's *no* justification for violence. But it appears I'm destined to be a warrior, at least in this lifetime. If you're destined to be a gardener, does that make you a freak? Perhaps, I'm the freak."

"This is just one more thing I hate about you. You're so *nice*. I deserve to be humiliated for my cowardice, not rewarded. And yet you refuse to discipline me. I abandoned Anna and fled into the wilderness, forsaking our people. Why can't you hate me as much as I hate myself?"

"Because you're the only person I've ever known who has seen what I've seen. It's lonely being a Death-Knower. Surely, you understand that as well as I."

"Yes," Rathburt said with a sigh of his own. Then he leaned back in his chair and rested his arms on his bony chest. "At least for today, we can put our loneliness aside and be joined as friends."

"That's the smartest thing I've ever heard you say. But first, come sit with me by the fire. I wish to meditate together."

After Torg and Rathburt stepped inside the hut, the others went about their business. Bard and Ugga built a spit for the turkeys and a tripod to hang the iron pot. Elu dressed the turkeys and then went to work on the possum, scraping off its hair, carving out the musk glands, gutting it, and cutting off its head, tail, and feet. After that, he carried the carcasses to the nearby stream for a quick rinse. On his way back, he searched the frozen woods for herbs and "ground potatoes" to further enrich the flavor of the che-ra stew.

As the turkeys roasted and the stew simmered, the three men sat down and relaxed. Although most of the morning had passed, Torg and Rathburt never emerged from the hut.

"Do ya have more of this tasty beer, little guy?" Ugga said. "I dearly love it."

"Elu and Rathburt live in a longhouse half a day's walk from here," the Svakaran said, pointing westward. "We have lots of beer and can get more from my village, which isn't far from our house. Elu doesn't know how Rathburt will feel, but as far as Elu is concerned, you're welcome to stay with us through the worst of the winter."

"If there is lots of beer, I want to go to your house. Do ya want to go, Bard?"

"I agree with ya, Ugga. I'd rather go there than walk all da way to da Whore City in winter. It's too shivery."

"It's not safe to wander in the woods, anyway," Elu said. "There are bad men in the forest. More than there used to be. They come from the south with deadly weapons. Some among my people believe it's time for our village to move even deeper into the mountains. But Rathburt doesn't want to go. He has a garden near our house that he refuses to leave behind. When spring comes, he will tend it again. Even if Elu were to go with his people, he thinks Rathburt would stay. But Elu would not abandon Rathburt. Elu owes him his life."

"Why do ya say that, little guy?" Ugga said.

"Elu was not always a 'little guy.' Elu was once a big guy—not as big as you but as big as Bard. Rathburt didn't tell the truth about the 'poison.' He made that up to fool you. But Elu trusts Ugga and Bard and wants to tell the real story. Would you like to hear it?"

"I would love to hear your story," Ugga said.

"Me too," Bard said.

"As would I" came a deep voice from behind them. To their surprise, Torg stood outside the hut with a weary-looking Rathburt at his side. "May we join you by the fire?"

"Come sit with us, Master Hah-nah," Ugga said. "Elu is going to tell us a big story about how he got to be so little."

"I've heard this one before, gentlemen," Rathburt said. "I think I'll go back inside and take a nap."

After the stooped Death-Knower closed the door, Elu leaned forward. "Rathburt doesn't like it when people say nice things about him. He wants everyone to believe he's a coward. That way, they'll leave him alone."

"Truer words have never been spoken," Torg said.

This pleased Elu.

"Tell us your story," Ugga prodded. "I want to hear it so bad!"

The Svakaran stood and pranced around the fire. Torg, Ugga, and Bard sat on a fallen log, but even from that position they were taller than Elu. The Svakaran was about the same height as a 10-year-old Tugar.

Elu was an accomplished storyteller, changing facial expressions and tones of voice while gesturing with his stubby arms and legs.

The diminutive Svakaran had once been a proud warrior and renowned hunter, wandering far and wide and never returning empty-handed. During one fateful expedition, Elu and three other warriors set out in search of game. It was early spring and food was plentiful, but the hunting party was in the mood for adventure. The foursome journeyed farther from the village than necessary, traveling along the foothills of the mountains almost to the eastern mouth of the Gap of Gamana.

"The game trails go on for leagues, rising along the sides of mountains before tumbling into hollows and coves," Elu told the three of them. "One night, after we had slain a buck, we set up camp on a flat rock near a stream and built a fire to roast the tenderloins."

"I love da loins!" Ugga said.

Elu nodded at the enormous crossbreed. "While the meat was cooking, we heard scary sounds from the upper heights. We all knew what kind of animal howled like that—black mountain wolves. So we doused the fires and hid, hoping they wouldn't find us. But we weren't so lucky."

Elu and his companions left their gear and jogged northward along the trail, carrying only their bows, arrows, and knives.

"We believed the wolves would find the gutted deer and go no farther. We could hide in the bushes and get our gear the next morning. But the wolves weren't interested in the deer. They ran right past it and followed us."

The trail rose steeply and then flattened along a narrow ridge. The land dropped on both sides into thickets of mountain laurel that were infested with thorny vines.

"The vines were wound all around the mountain laurel. That's where they hide," Rathburt said. They all looked up in surprise. "Sorry … I couldn't sleep."

"Come and listen to Elu's story," Ugga said.

"I've heard this one before," Rathburt repeated.

"Go on, Elu," Torg said.

In the darkness, Elu and the other warriors couldn't see the approaching wolves, but they could hear and smell them. It was impossible to outrun the massive beasts, but if he and his companions stopped and tried to fight, they would be routed.

"Our only chance was to brave the vines," Elu said. "Bears can run underneath them. There's an open area beneath the laurel about this high off the ground." Elu raised his hand to the level of his own shoulder.

"But the black wolves are big as horses," Rathburt said. "It's too difficult for them to hunch down low enough to get through the laurel."

"It's hard for men, too," Elu said. "We can't hunker down like bears."

"Bears can do lots of great things," Ugga said proudly.

"Still, they would have escaped," Rathburt said, apparently unable to resist joining in. "The wolves remained by the edge of the trail, helpless to pursue. But not for the reason Elu and the warriors believed. It wasn't the mountain laurel that caused the wolves to hesitate. It was the vines that wound through the laurel."

Elu lowered his head. "The vines ... eat you."

Rathburt nodded and then took a deep breath. "Mountain laurel is poisonous, so you don't want to eat it. But you can pass through it without too much harm. However, there are places in the mountains where deadly vines grow among the laurel, and they are anything but harmless. They feed not on sunlight and rich dirt, but on flesh—usually the flesh of any animal that enters the laurel. But they will consume humans, too. Elu and his friends escaped the wolves but not the vines."

"I've never heard of these vines," Torg said, "and I've journeyed in the mountains countless times."

"Few have heard of them," Rathburt said. "They're rare—though less rare now than before. Very recently, they've been spreading way too fast. The Mogols call the vines *Badaalataa*, the plant that devours. And that's what it does, gradually and painfully. The animal—or human—doesn't die immediately. The victim becomes a living part of the plant and sometimes survives for as long as a week."

"When Rathburt found us, it was the morning of the fourth day," Elu said, visibly shaken. "We had gotten only twenty paces off the trail when the *Badaalataa* grabbed Elu and his friends. Elu felt like he was being bitten by snakes. The poison paralyzed his body, but it didn't dull the pain."

Suddenly, the Svakaran cast himself onto the ground and sobbed. Ugga knelt and lifted him in his arms, hugging him against his chest.

"Don't cry. I can't stand it," Ugga said, also bursting into tears. "Somebody help him ... *please.*"

"There's little help for such pain of the heart," Torg said. "Not even the passing of time will heal it completely. Let him cry, but don't let him go. Your friendship is what he needs more than anything."

Rathburt also wept. This surprised Torg far more than Elu's outburst. He'd never seen Rathburt react to anything that way.

Elu's sobs faded to whimpers, but Ugga still held him close. Rathburt buried his face in his hands. Bard moved beside him and placed his arm around the Death-Knower's slumped shoulders. As if in response to such tenderness, more of Rathburt's words emerged.

"I was wandering, as I often do. I also heard the wolves and hid in the trees, waiting for them to go away. But they didn't leave, howling nonstop for three days. Something down the trail was enraging them, though I couldn't imagine what. Near the end of the third day, they gave up and loped back to their dark lairs in the upper heights. A pack of fifty passed within a few paces of where I had cowered for so long."

Rathburt looked at Elu, his stoop even more pronounced. "I wanted to be sure the wolves were gone before I investigated what had befuddled them. I was curious, I must admit, but not enough to overcome my fear. So I slept fitfully through another night and didn't leave my hiding place until early the next morning."

Rathburt began to cry again as if shattered by grief too large to bear. Elu squirmed out of Ugga's arms and crawled into Rathburt's lap, calming them both.

"I don't know how much better it would have been had I helped them sooner," Rathburt said. "I suppose I'll never know. But it will always haunt me. The Vasi masters say, 'What's done is done.' I'm not so sure that's true. When morning came, I worked up the courage to start along the trail, and it didn't take me long to find them—or what remained of them. The *Badaalataa* were enjoying their meal. I could see skin, flesh, hair. Lips. Teeth. I remember seeing an ear stuck to the end of a pulsing vine. But what I remember most is their eyes—eight of them, isolated here and there, but still aware. They stared at me, pleading ... not to save them, but to end their misery."

"What did ya do, Master Radburt?" Bard said. "How did ya save Elu from this horrible thing?"

Rathburt looked first at Bard and then at Torg as if begging for permission to stop. But Torg's expression would not permit it.

"You need to understand ... for someone like Torg, magic comes easily. But for me it's difficult—and sporadic. I can't *will* my power to emerge. Sometimes it does, sometimes it doesn't. One day I can heal a dying tree; the next I can't save a blade of grass. I'm not like Torg."

Elu hugged Rathburt even tighter.

"But this time ... *this* time ... the magic roared out of me. I strode into the vines, and they parted like I was their master. Blue fire spurted from my staff and fell upon the *Badaalataa*, withering them. The flow of the magic was addictive. I felt like I could scorch an entire forest. But as suddenly as the bliss arose, the agony followed. The vines were tamed, but Elu and his friends were still there, ripped into hundreds of pieces."

"And?" Torg said.

"And ... that's when it dawned on me." Rathburt grew silent.

"Tell us," Torg said. But there was no command in his voice, only respect.

"Very well. But only this one time, and never again. Because saying the words makes me relive it, which is more than a coward can bear. What I saw frightened me far worse than the vines. I saw the extent of my power and knew I could save them. Or at least, one of them. I could peel the plants off their flesh and mold what remained into a single being. But it would not be pleasant for me—to say the least. The cost to my body would be immense."

Rathburt placed Elu on the ground and stood. Then he strode several paces away, his back to the fire, before whirling to face his audience. "It hurt me to exert the power necessary to mend a broken body. It *hurt* me to save them—to save him. Like being burned. Or frozen. Stabbed. Tortured. Dismembered. It hurt like madness."

These last words stunned Torg and the others into silence. The sweet aroma of roasting fowl wafted throughout the clearing, but they didn't notice it. Elu, Ugga, and Bard fell into a trance. Rathburt stared at the ground, his tears puncturing the snow.

The Svakaran broke the long silence. "The vines were gone, the pain was gone, and Elu was alive. But Rathburt was lying on the ground, and Elu thought he was dead. His face was white like a ghost, and he was wrinkled and weak. To Elu, he looked like a giant—ten cubits tall—but Elu didn't know then how small he had become. Rathburt brought Elu back, but only part of him." Then he flexed one of his arms, displaying a bulging muscle. "Elu had the same strength as before, just in a smaller body, and he dragged Rathburt for many days, giving him food and water when he could. When Elu reached his village, his people didn't recognize him—and they shunned both of us. Elu tried to tell them who he was. They didn't believe ... at first. But when Elu told them the things he knew about each one, then they believed him. So they gave us the longhouse and told us to stay away from the village. Once there, Elu tended Rathburt and brought him back to the world of the living. It wasn't as great as what he did for Elu, but at least it was something."

"It was more than just something," Rathburt said. "Thank you, my friend."

Ugga and Bard cried again. But Torg did not. He stood and held his arms aloft. "I believe the five of us have come together for a purpose," he said in a loud voice as if speaking to more than just his companions.

"The fate of Triken lies in the hands of a few. I stand on the side of good and invite you to join me. What say you?"

There were no dissenters.

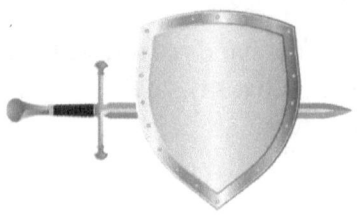

WATERFALL

It took Ugga less than a day to form an adoration for Elu. And if there were any lingering doubts about his feelings, the roasted fowl and che-ra stew seemed to erase them forever. The crossbreed devoured the food with the urgency of an animal, and his contagious smile widened further with every bite. The rest ate with similar passion.

Torg and Rathburt remained silent about whatever it was they'd discussed in the hut, but it was clear it had taken a toll on Rathburt—and the tale of the *Badaalataa* had made matters worse. The gardener, as Bard had begun to call him, looked even older and more haggard than when he'd first arrived.

It was nearly dark when they finished their meal. A new storm was brewing. The wind increased its vehemence, prompting the pines to whisper urgently.

There was still no sign of Jord. If she were anywhere near, she was well hidden. But Torg believed she was far away.

"It's time to go inside," Torg said. "It's going to be an ugly night. In the morning we'll make our final plans. Rathburt suggests it would be wise to wait out the worst of the winter at his longhouse instead of venturing to Kamupadana now. I agree. The longer I remain hidden, the better for all of us."

This pleased Ugga. "Elu says there is lots of beer at da longhouse. I say we stay there all winter—maybe all spring, too."

Rathburt laughed. "Ugga, you're a charmer."

"Thank ya, Master Rad-burt!"

The storm struck not long after they had retired inside the hut, sweeping through the forest like a giant broom. But the house of Jord was up to the challenge. Though winds ferocious enough to topple trees surged all around the small hut, its roof and walls held firm and the hearth fire burned merrily as if unimpressed by what transpired outside. Torg slept side by side with the men, snoring and farting as only men can do, and caring not a whit.

By morning, the storm had dissipated and the sky was as blue as a Tugar's eyes. But it took all Ugga's strength to push open the door. More than two more cubits of snow had fallen, which would make the march to the longhouse even more difficult. Elu predicted it now would take from morning until past dusk to complete the journey. But at least they wouldn't starve. There was still enough roasted turkey left to last through the day, and Elu said there were grapes in the trees that remained edible.

The stockpiles at the longhouse were meant to sustain two men, not five. Once there, they would have to hunt frequently, and fruits and vegetables would be in short supply unless they could convince the nearby Svakaran villagers to part with some of theirs.

"Charming them will be your job," Rathburt said to Torg.

They brought little gear other than their weapons, and they used a litter to haul the impressive stack of skins that had been collected and tanned by Bard, Ugga, and Jord during the fall. Torg carried the Silver Sword, Ugga his ax, and Bard his spear and the bow and quiver of arrows Jord had abandoned. Rathburt bore no weapon except for his oaken staff. Elu had a pair of daggers. They left the Svakaran's tall spear buried in the trunk of the tree, hoping that anyone who found it would take it as a sign that the hut was not to be disturbed.

"Other than our pretty faces, da skins are da only things we'll have to trade in da Whore City's markets," Bard said.

"I have no desire to see Kamupadana," Rathburt said, "but if you want to go, I certainly won't try to stop you."

"I like da Brounettos!" Ugga said.

"Ahh ... I see," Rathburt said. "Beer and Brounettos. What an excellent combination. And what hair color do you favor, Torg?"

Torg reached over and pinched Rathburt on his shoulder near the base of his neck. Rathburt yelped.

"Some jests are beneath even you," Torg said, threateningly.

"Sorry ... *sorry*!" Rathburt said. "Some people have *no* sense of humor."

"I don't understand," Bard said. "Does Master Hah-nah not like Brounettos?"

"Drop it!" Torg said, and he grumpily lifted the arms of the litter and strode into the woods. The others followed.

When they entered a thick grove, Torg stopped and gazed eastward in the opposite direction of the longhouse. The others watched him, puzzled. Finally, Ugga could stand it no longer.

"What is it, Master Hah-nah? Do ya see something? I would dearly like to know."

Torg emerged from his reverie. "Do you not hear their song?"

"Whose song?" Rathburt said.

"The giant pines. Jord's pines. They sing to us."

"I hear nothing," Ugga said. "Do ya hear da pines, Bard?"

"I hear nothing but da crunching of our boots. But if da pines call to Master Hah-nah, I wouldn't be surprised. Maybe it's Jord saying goodbye. If so, I hope it's not forever."

"Me too," Ugga said.

"Elu has seen the pines," the Svakaran said. "His tribesmen believe they're possessed by powerful spirits that protect Bard and Ugga. If not for the pines, our warriors would have raided their hut and stolen their skins."

"We're not helpless to defend ourselves; nor is Jord," Bard said.

"Elu has never seen Jord, only Bard and Ugga, though Elu didn't know your names. Our warriors call you Man and Bear."

Torg raised an eyebrow.

"If ya know of us, ya would have to know of Jord," Ugga said. "She's with us lots of da time. She likes to pretend she's a helpless woman. But when she's angry, she scares even Ugga and Bard."

Elu shrugged.

"Jord played that pretend game with me," Torg said. "But she has revealed herself, and I won't be so easily fooled again. Regardless, the fey mood has passed. Whatever I felt or heard is no longer. I'd like to see the pines again, but my guess is their magic lies dormant. They've chosen to remove themselves from this world, at least for now."

"All your creepy talk is scaring me," Ugga said. "Without Jord around, it feels like we're trespassing."

But Rathburt wasn't quite finished. "When we were in the hut, you mentioned these great trees, but I was too weary to pay much attention. Now you've made me curious. You know how much I adore trees. How far are they from here? Do we have time to see them?"

"We've dallied too long already, thanks to me," Torg said. "We're hardy men and can endure the cold, but I'd prefer to arrive at the longhouse before dark, if possible."

"There are more reasons to arrive before dark than just the cold," Elu said. "Beasts roam the wilds that are new to Elu's land, nameless things that can shrivel the stoutest heart. They come from the south in search of prey and take the unwary back with them."

"How do ya know all this?" Ugga said.

"Elu still has a few friends in the village. The Svakarans know these mountains and foothills better than anyone. Some stray as far as Lake Ti-ratana. When they return, they speak of the sorcerer's slave hunters."

"In that case, I'll visit the trees another time," Rathburt said. "I've no desire to be captured by the sorcerer, especially if he's as powerful as Torg says he is."

"He's more powerful than I am," Torg said. "But enough talk! Let us travel in silence for a spell. Elu, lead the way."

"Yes, *great one*," the Svakaran said. "But Elu must warn you that parts of the trail will be treacherous, especially with all this snow. The litter will make this journey far more difficult than if we were just walking on our own."

Elu took off through the trees. The pines and hemlocks held back a portion of the previous night's snowfall. In some areas, it was only knee-deep to Elu and barely above the ankles of the larger men. The Svakaran expertly avoided the thicker pockets of snow. By noon, they had traveled more than a league, seeing and hearing no humans or animals, not even a rabbit, hawk, or woodpecker. When they stopped near a scree of boulders for a rest and some bites of turkey, Elu scampered into the woods to search for grapes.

"The forest has a strange feel," Rathburt said. "Is it possible that a hidden menace is abroad?"

"I feel it too," Torg said. "Perhaps what we sense is the evil of Invictus. His grasp expands every day."

"I hope to never meet him if his strength is so great that he can change the mood of a forest with his will," Rathburt said.

"I agree with Rad-burt," Ugga said. "I'll leave In-vick-tuss for Master Hah-nah to handle. Or Jord, if she ever returns. Could da Bitch defeat da sore-sir-err, Master Hah-nah?"

"I'm not sure what she can do," Torg said. "She's beyond my

knowledge. But there's one thing I've been meaning to ask you and Bard since we first met. Why do you always call her 'da Bitch'?"

Bard laughed. "Ugga and I have heard da whores call her that when she's not around. They say, 'Ya are grown men and can do what ya want. Don't listen to what da Bitch says. Come in where it's warm and lay beside us.' "

"When we told Jord, she laughed," Ugga said. "She liked it when we called her that."

"Ahh ... now I understand. It appears Jord, whoever she is, has a sense of humor."

Just then, Elu emerged from the trees carrying an armful of frozen grapes.

"There aren't many left. The bears are eating up the last of them. Elu had to climb to find these."

"Bears?" Ugga said. "If ya see one, let me know, little guy. I love bears."

"Elu doesn't like bears. They want to eat Elu. But he will tell Ugga if one comes near."

This pleased the crossbreed.

After a cold meal, they continued their march. To their right loomed the Mahaggata Mountains, which the company skirted along a trail that meandered toward the southwest, rising for hundreds of fathoms along gentle slopes and then tumbling into coves. Hauling the litter became a severe annoyance, and they began to curse it like a hated enemy. But the skins were too valuable to leave behind.

Everyone except Rathburt, who complained of a chronically sore back, took turns hauling the litter. Even Elu managed it for short distances, proving he was far stronger than he looked. Though the temperature was well below freezing, they became sweaty and overheated, and at times two or more of them had to lift the litter over rocks and fallen trees. Other than Rathburt, they were not lacking for physical strength. But the litter was awkward, frustrating, and just plain heavy.

"Are you sure you wouldn't like to try it?" Torg said to Rathburt during one of his turns. "A little exercise might do you some good."

Rathburt rubbed his lower back. "It's an old injury that never fully healed. But you, Bard, and Ugga are so big and strong. It's as if you were born to do this task."

"You've missed your calling," Torg said, his heavy breath casting shafts of white mist into the frozen air. "Instead of a gardener, you should have been a jester. You could make a fortune in the courts of Nissaya."

"Don't forget that Elu is strong too, and he isn't lazy like Rathburt," the Svakaran said.

"Watch yourself!" Rathburt said. "I'll turn you back into a vine."

Elu didn't find that the least bit funny. He pounded his small fists together and then trudged ahead.

"It appears you're a poor judge of talent," Rathburt said to Torg. "I'm not much of a jester, after all."

After Elu disappeared around a bend, Torg counted fifty paces (he could last about a thousand) before the Svakaran returned.

"The worst part of the trail is up ahead," Elu said. "It will soon become steep and narrow, and there are lots of hidden roots. At the top of the path, there is an overlook that is split in two by a stream—and a few paces away is a great waterfall. There is still some trickling, but most of the water is frozen into peculiar shapes. My people believe this is a sacred place, especially in the winter. If you look carefully, you'll see faces in the ice. But don't look too long. Something evil in the water wants you to fall."

"I've been there several times and have never seen any faces," Rathburt sneered. "I've seen carrots, corn, and onions, though. And some lovely wildflowers."

"I don't want to see scary faces in da ice," Ugga said.

"They're not as scary as carrots," Rathburt said.

If anything, Elu understated the severity of the path. Under pristine conditions—and not dragging the son-of-an-ass litter—it would have been difficult to ascend. But with the snow, ice, and gnarled roots, it was close to impossible. It took all Torg's strength to haul the litter to the top, and that was with Ugga shoving from behind, braced by Bard. Elu led the way and disappeared again. Rathburt trailed behind, whining endlessly.

"There are easier ways to go," he mumbled, "even if they add a few leagues to our journey. We must get there *before dark*, after all. Anna forbid we don't get there *after dark*."

When they reached the crest of the path, they passed through a wall of trees and came upon the stream that fed the waterfall. From the overlook, Torg could see for leagues. An endless vista of hills and valleys extended toward the horizon. The men were transfixed. Even in winter, the land was beautiful.

"Elu sees the faces of his brothers," the Svakaran said abruptly, startling Rathburt.

"For Anna's sake, Elu! Give us some warning—"

But the Svakaran, who had crept to the edge without them noticing, appeared hypnotized. "The vines are eating their bodies, but their faces are still beautiful."

"Are ya all right, little guy?" Ugga said. "Aren't ya too close to da edge? I fear ya will fall. Is Elu going to fall, Master Hah-nah?"

"Elu," Torg said. Then louder: "*Elu!*" The second time he said it, a hot gust rustled the Svakaran's hair, awakening him from the trance. Elu slid far enough back for Ugga to grab his shoulder and drag him to safety.

"Don't do that again!" Rathburt shouted. "You scared us half to death."

"The ice spoke to Elu," he said, his voice distant.

"There *is* magic here," Torg announced, "but I sense neither good nor evil. It came from a far distant place, and it cares naught for our world."

"Then why did da mah-jick make da little guy see faces?" Ugga said. "That sounds evil to me."

"Whatever is here is very old," Torg said. "Older than me. Older than you or Bard. Older than any creature on Triken. Can't you feel it? To this level of awareness, a millennium is like a single breath. It has been here since our world was born, existing within the rocks beneath our feet. It loves the water that rushes over its back—so soothing and delicious. But in the winter when the stream freezes, it becomes restless. I don't believe the magic *makes* anyone see faces. I don't believe it even recognizes our presence. But there is something in this ancient power that awakens our karma. Some of us might see what has already occurred. Others might see what is yet to happen. This is an opportunity we should not take lightly."

"What nonsense, Torg!" Rathburt said. "How could you possibly know all this just by standing on these damnable rocks? Have you been chewing on poppies?"

"What are poppies?" Bard said.

"They're little flowers that grow in the northern mountains near Catu," Torg said. "If you eat their seeds, you often have visions. But that's not what's happening here. You ask me how I know this. I am a Death-Knower and comprehend many things others do not. But there's a better reason than that. My encounter with the pines has altered me. Their green magic flows through my sinews. And it's not unlike what lies hidden in these rocks. It speaks to me, inspiring visions as vivid as any the poppies could provide. But it's your choice to believe or disbelieve."

"I believe ya, Master Hah-nah," Ugga said.

"Me too," Bard said.

Elu nodded vigorously.

"You're always trying to make me feel like the bad guy," Rathburt grumbled.

"Look!" Bard said. "Your sword, Master Hah-nah ... it has come to life!"

Torg slid the sword from the belt at his waist. The blade glowed and was hot to the touch.

"The magic of the Silver Sword must be like Jord's trees and these rocks," Torg said. "It comes from an otherworldly place."

"Yes, yes," Rathburt said. "Always the philosopher."

Elu seemed more annoyed by Rathburt's behavior than usual. "You've told Elu many times that the plants talk to you. Why can't the rocks talk to the *great one*?"

"That's different," Rathburt said, but his expression lost its certainty, causing Torg to chuckle.

"Ugga, you go next," Torg said. "Bard, you hold his belt, I'll hold yours, and Elu can hold mine. That way, none of us should fall."

"And I'll hold Elu's belt," Rathburt said with a tone of resignation. "You men can't have all the fun."

"But Ugga is scared! I don't want to see da faces."

"Go ahead," Bard said. "What's da worse that can happen, me dear?"

Ugga's expression suggested that many terrible things could happen, but he acquiesced and walked slowly to the edge on the slippery rocks before peering over the side. He fidgeted but then grew peaceful. Bard held his belt tight. There was no sound to be heard except for trickles of water slipping along the surface of the ice. When Ugga's eyes drooped, Torg became concerned.

"Bring him back."

The crossbreed resisted. "Wait! Not yet."

He stood still a moment longer and then smiled. "All right."

They pulled him from the edge and stood in relative safety a few paces from the drop-off.

"What did ya see?" Bard said impatiently.

"All I saw was ice—pretty, twinkly ice. But then a mist came over my eyes, and when it cleared, I saw da Bitch! It was Jord for sure, and she smiled at me and told me she was doing fine. She said she loved me and was watching out for me. And she said I should do whatever Master Hah-nah tells me. Da Bitch likes Master Hah-nah!"

"What rubbish," Rathburt said.

Torg ignored him. "You're next, Bard."

The handsome trapper walked to the edge. Torg held his belt, followed by Elu, Ugga, and Rathburt. Bard stared down with anticipation. There was another period of eerie quiet, except for the water tinkling like tiny bells.

Without warning, Bard sagged. Torg quickly hauled him from the edge.

"What did ya see, me dear?" Ugga said. "Did ya see da Bitch?"

"I saw da head of a magnificent mare, larger than da greatest stallion. Fire spouted from her mouth and smoke from her ears. What does it mean, I wonder? Do ya know, Hah-nah?"

Torg didn't answer. He only said, "My turn."

"Oh, no, I'm not going *after* you," Rathburt said. "Everyone knows you'll see something grand that will make the rest of us feel insignificant."

"I didn't think you wanted a turn," Torg said. "But my heart tells me that we should not disrupt our order. I'll go next, and then you, if you still desire."

"Always the showoff," Rathburt said. "Always, always."

Torg placed the Silver Sword on the ground well away from the drop-off. Then he reached down, picked up a hefty rock, and handed it to Ugga.

"I want you to hold my belt," Torg said to the crossbreed, "and if I act strangely, take this rock and hit me as hard as you can on the back of my neck—here." Torg pointed to a slightly protruding bone. "It won't injure me. But if you hit me hard enough, it will stun me long enough to allow you to drag me back."

"I'm afraid I'll kill ya," Ugga said.

"No one can kill the great and mighty Torg," Rathburt sneered. "By all means, Ugga, hit him as hard as you can. Give him a really good *whack*!"

"Do ya hate Hah-nah?" Bard said to Rathburt.

"I don't hate him," Rathburt said. "But I find him extremely annoying."

"I think I love him," Ugga said. "Not like I love da Brounettos. More like I love Jord."

"Anna help us," Rathburt grumbled.

Torg smiled. "Thank you for your kind words, Ugga. And the feeling is mutual. But even if you love me, you must do as I say. Hit me with that rock as hard as you can. Or at least hand it to Rathburt and have *him* hit me."

Torg walked to the edge, which was even more slippery than he expected. As he peered down, his inquisitiveness took over. The simple beauty of the frozen falls astonished him. The ice was gnarled like the exposed roots of an old oak, but it was bursting with color. White and blue were predominant, but crimson and gold danced within the cracks and crevices, sparkling like jewels. Torg gasped. *I could stand here all day and just stare at it.*

Then the bright afternoon sun faded. Darkness consumed his awareness. Now, the ice glowed like a full moon in a black sky. The light squirmed and came to life, forming the sweet face of a beautiful woman. She smiled at him, the knowing smile of a lover who is also a friend. Torg reached for her, his hands flailing.

The rock crashed down with precision. Ugga and Bard dragged him away. Torg regained his senses soon after sitting on the bank of the stream. But he didn't speak for a long time. When he looked up, the others were staring at him.

"Ya tried to jump!" Ugga said. "What were ya thinking?"

"I'd like to know, too," Rathburt said angrily. "You frightened us, you moose! What *did* you see?"

Torg rubbed the back of his neck. "I saw ... my future."

"Huh?" Rathburt said. "Your future? What do you mean?"

"I'll say no more."

"No more? *No more*? Isn't that just like you? You get us all so worked up we're about to burst, and then you say, '*I saw my future.*' What an absolute ass you are. *Tell* us what you saw or I'll hit you with the stone even harder than Ugga did!"

"I can't."

"Arrrgggh!"

The rest of them sat silently while Rathburt cursed and waved his arms. Finally, he calmed down.

"How about you?" Torg said to his fellow Death-Knower. "Do you still wish to look at the ice?"

"Believe it or not, I do. For once, I'm *guaranteed* to outshine you."

Torg held Rathburt's belt, followed by Ugga, Bard, and Elu. Rathburt leaned on his walking staff as he peered over the edge. It didn't take him long to complain.

"I see nothing but a bunch of ice. And a long fall. Were all of you playing some kind of joke on me? There's nothing here but ... wait ... *wait* ..."

Rathburt grew placid, and the eerie silence returned. The others watched him, ready to pull him away from the edge as soon as they saw signs of trouble.

Without warning, Rathburt's face contorted. He cried out, lifted his staff, and smote the ice. There was a crackling explosion, followed by hissing bursts of steam, and a massive chunk tore free and tumbled into the abyss, bursting apart on the rocks below. They pulled him from the edge and sat him down in the same spot Torg had been before. Rathburt sobbed hysterically. When he regained control, he looked at the others with horror in his eyes.

"What did you see?" Torg said. "Rathburt, what did you *see*?"

"I saw ... *my* future."

And like Torg before him, he would say no more.

For a long while, Rathburt wouldn't even speak. After his ordeal at the waterfall, he appeared even frailer to Torg than usual, trudging through the snow like a hunched old man. Nothing cheered him up. Even the ebullient Ugga couldn't break through Rathburt's self-imposed silence.

Once they left the waterfall, the trail became easier to traverse. But frequent pockets of snow—several spans deeper than Elu was tall—slowed them considerably. These places forced Torg to use his magic.

The blue-green flames that spouted from his fingertips melted trenches wide enough for the men and the litter. But Torg knew there were creatures on Triken who could sense such displays of power, and many were allies of Invictus.

"I might as well hand out scrolls announcing I'm here," Torg said. "But I suppose it's better than being buried alive."

"I like it better, Master Hah-nah," Ugga said. "And I'm sure da little guy does too."

Elu nodded vigorously. Rathburt said nothing, his chin so low it almost touched his chest.

The arduous journey continued. In the quiet calm of late afternoon, they heard wolves howling in the distance.

Elu went on alert. "Those are black mountain wolves," he said in a panic.

"From the sound of them, there are many," Torg said.

For the first time since the incident at the waterfall, Rathburt spoke, though his voice quivered. "We must find a place to hide!"

"How far is da longhouse?" Bard said.

"We wouldn't reach it before dark," Elu said. "The wolves can run on snow as fast as on grass. If they're aware of us, they'll catch us long before we reach the house."

"Is there any other place to hide?" Ugga said.

"Elu remembers a small cave less than a league from here. We could hide there and hope the wolves pass."

The howling grew louder. "If we're attacked from all sides at once, I fear most for Rathburt and Elu," Torg said. "Rather than hide, we must make a stand."

This offended the Svakaran. "Elu can fight!"

"I meant no offense," Torg said. "If it were just one black wolf against you, I know you would prevail. But if I'm correct, we'll be severely outnumbered. And where there are black wolves, there can be other creatures, some even deadlier. If they diverted my attention, you'd be easy prey. We need your familiarity with this land more than your strength."

"Maybe Rathburt and Elu should hide in the cave while you great men do all the fighting," the Svakaran said angrily.

"For Anna's sake, Elu! None of us doubts your courage," Rathburt snapped. "But for once, Torg is right. Quit complaining and help us find a better place to fight than among these trees."

Elu shook his fist and spat. Then he pointed toward the mountains. "Up there, the land rises sharply. Beyond is a narrow path with great stone walls."

"Good idea, little guy!" Ugga said. "Show us da way."

Then the crossbreed swept Elu onto his shoulders. To quicken their pace, Torg melted a long trench in the snow. Bard took control of the litter and Rathburt, surprisingly, lent a hand, bending over and shoving it from behind.

"If the wolves get too close, we'll have to abandon this," Rathburt said.

"I'll die before I do that," Bard said. "I wouldn't give up da skins to a thousand of them."

"You've been spending too much time around Torg," Rathburt said. "You're picking up his stubbornness."

As the howling intensified, their hopes of escaping undetected diminished, though they could not yet see the wolves. The land rolled and swayed like a stormy sea, restricting their visibility. The wolves could have been just a stone's throw away and still be hidden from view.

"How far, Elu?" Torg said.

"Less than 500 paces."

"We have to give up the skins," Torg said. "They're slowing us down too much."

Bard protested, but Torg cut him off. "It's not what they're after. We'll come back for them after we finish the fight."

They shoved the litter into a dense area of trees and continued their flight. This dismayed Bard—and for a moment it appeared he might stay with the skins instead of following his companions—but Ugga grabbed his arm and yanked him forward.

"Master Hah-nah is right. What good are they to us if we're dead?"

The terrain became treacherous. Even without snow and ice it would have been difficult to traverse, but in the wintry conditions it was tough on all of them. Rathburt slowed them down almost as much as the litter had, frequently tripping and sliding down the slope ten paces or more each time he fell. This forced Torg and Bard to drag him along.

At the same time the narrow path came into view above, the lead wolves appeared below. At first there were just four, and when they caught sight of the men, they rushed toward them at a full run. They were as large and fast as horses, but far more dangerous. Their fangs and claws were as sharp as the point of a Tugarian dagger.

Bard loosed an arrow that caught the lead wolf between the eyes. It tumbled and lay still.

The second wolf leaped over its fallen brother. Torg shifted to his left and whipped the Silver Sword in a high arc over his right shoulder. The blade cut through hide, bone, and sinew. Tar-colored blood splashed onto Torg's face.

The third went for Ugga, but the crossbreed dealt a death blow with his ax.

The fourth got past the three men and lunged for Rathburt, who tried to smite it with his staff but slipped and fell awkwardly on his rump. The wolf went for his throat, but Elu pounced on its back and plunged his dagger between the bones of its spine, killing it with one stab. Then the tiny Svakaran pounded his chest.

"Da little guy is tougher than he looks!" Ugga said.

"Hurry!" Torg said. "The others will soon be here. We must reach the narrow way."

They slogged upward, dragging Rathburt toward the wall of stone, within which was a crevice just wide enough for the largest of them to enter. It was a perfect place for their defense. Rathburt and Elu squeezed through the opening just as the main strength of the wolves rushed forward, growling and slavering, eager for the kill. But something held them back. They approached slowly, side by side, heads down.

"There are too many," Rathburt shouted. "Come with us. We can escape on the other side of the path."

"It would be useless to run," Torg said. "Stay where you are. Elu will protect you."

Bard and Ugga flanked Torg. Both were alert but unafraid.

"The wolves aren't alone," Torg said softly. "Something commands them. I can sense its power. Whatever it is, you must leave it to me."

Just then the line of wolves parted and the woods grew eerily silent. There was a dip at the base of the slope that concealed what approached. But its footsteps boomed.

"A Kojin comes!" Rathburt screamed.

This emboldened the wolves, the hair on their napes bristling. They tore at the ground with their claws, but it was clear the ogress was their master.

"If I fall, you must flee," Torg said, but then added, "I will not fall."

The Kojin crawled up the slope like a sister of the spider Dukkhatu, using her six muscled arms to propel herself. When she reached the wolves, she rose on two legs to her full height, twice as tall as Torg or Ugga and almost three times as heavy.

Torg knew that despite their massive size and strength, the ogresses were also agile. He remembered sitting around a fire one night listening to Sōbhana speak about her encounter with a Kojin while journeying with two other Asēkhas through the Dark Forest. The three warriors could not even injure the beast, much less kill it, and they finally had been forced to run. This had not surprised Torg. Kojins were almost as large as snow giants, and they possessed ancient magic that shielded their flesh. Among the evils of the world, only Vedana, Bhayatupa, and the vampires were older. Eons before, when Java was five times its current size, hundreds of Kojins roamed that forest, terrorizing any who dared enter it. But Java succumbed to the onslaught of a thousand wars and was reduced in scope. Fewer than a dozen ogresses survived.

That didn't make this one any less dangerous. Though it was invisible to the others—except, perhaps, for Rathburt—Torg could see a purplish glow emanating from the beast's scaly hide. An ordinary sword, no matter how skillfully wielded, could not pierce the supernatural buffer. No wonder Sōbhana and the Asēkhas had been so frustrated.

Kojins were incapable of speech, but they weren't stupid. They communicated telepathically, much like the cave monkeys but without the delicacy. As the ogress strode to meet him, Torg felt the beast's will beat upon his brow. The Kojin pounded her fists together, causing the wolves to yip and snarl even more, maddened by her bravado.

The ogress wielded no weapons other than her club-like arms and the poisoned claws on the tips of her fingers and toes. But that was enough to destroy almost any foe.

Torg's magic was also great, and he wielded the Silver Sword. When he confronted the Kojin, the wizard's palpable confidence puzzled the massive creature. It was possible she'd never stood face to face with so bold an opponent.

The wolves sensed the ogress' confusion. As the will that drove them wavered, they rushed forward. But the Kojin let out a high-pitched screech, freezing the beasts in their tracks. Then she regained her composure and returned her focus to the being that approached her.

Torg continued toward the monster, closing within three paces. With long-practiced precision, he grasped the dull portion of the blade near the hilt with his left hand and lowered the sword to his left hip, its point aimed behind him, its pommel facing forward. Then he knelt on his left knee.

The Kojin towered above him, seeming to mistake his movement as an act of submission, and she pounded her hairy bosom and screeched again. The wolves could barely tolerate the intensity, shaking their heads wildly. Bard, Ugga, Rathburt, and Elu made smacking sounds as they clasped their ears.

What happened next took less time than a single long breath. Torg grasped the black-leather grip with his right hand, lunged forward on his right foot, and leaped high into the air, whipping the blade left-to-right across the front of his body. The tip gashed the Kojin's throat. Purple light exploded from the wound.

Torg landed at the Kojin's feet and knelt again. From this position, he again swung the blade across the front of his body, this time right-to-left, and cut off the Kojin's left foot above the ankle.

The ogress cried out and collapsed to her knees.

Once Torg had completed the swing, the sword again pointed straight back on his left side. With barely a pause he leaped upward, raised the blade over his head, and drove the edge into the Kojin's skull. A blinding explosion of purple gore erupted from the wound, scattering the wolves and setting nearby trees aflame.

Torg flicked blood off the blade.

The Kojin collapsed onto its shattered face. It would never again haunt the Dark Forest or any land. It was no longer. Torg stared down at her ruin. The Silver Sword remained lifeless and cold as if disinterested in the carnage. Though the ogress was dead, her body still writhed, and the ancient magic erupting from her skull, neck, and leg scorched whatever it touched. The wolves went wild, attacking anything that moved, including each other. By the time they calmed enough to turn on their intended prey, fully a third of their own were dead or maimed. But that left more than sixty still capable of wreaking havoc, and these fell upon Bard, Ugga, and Torg in a frothy rage. Bard dropped the bow and fought bravely with his spear, skewering two before being driven back against the wall. Ugga killed half a dozen with his great ax but was forced to retreat to help Bard. Without Torg, they would have been lost. The wizard entered *frenzy*, butchering two dozen wolves with a variety of cuts, hacks, and thrusts refined over a thousand years of practice. The surviving wolves—fewer than thirty in all—lost their courage and rushed down the slope with their tails between their legs, yelping as they fled.

Five alpha males remained, still focused on Ugga and Bard. The crossbreed had a deep gash across his forehead that was dripping blood into his eyes. Bard was cut and his spear had been sundered. He held just a pair of daggers. But now Elu joined the fray, and he stood between the men like a boy come of age, waving his own dagger as if daring the wolves to attack.

Still in *frenzy*, Torg pierced the nearest wolf through its heart. The others turned to face him, but they were no match. A second fell, its legs cut out from under. Ugga swung his ax and beheaded a third. Elu stabbed the largest wolf between its ribs, and Torg finished it with a thrust to the throat. The last survivor turned and ran, following the others into the forest.

Bard sagged to his knees. Elu and Ugga knelt near their friend. Torg stood motionless, watching his breath until his rage subsided. Then he motioned for Rathburt to come out of hiding.

"The fight is over, for now. The wolves are routed. Once we regain our strength, we can recover the skins and be on our way."

"Is anyone hurt?" Rathburt said timidly.

As a group, they turned to Bard. But the handsome trapper already was on his feet.

"Nothing that beer won't cure," he said.

The others laughed—except for Rathburt, whose face was red with shame.

"I'm sorry, Torg. I'm too weak to slay a single wolf, much less a Kojin. Once again, I've failed you."

But Torg only smiled. "Sister Tathagata once said something like that to me, and it was foolish coming from her, as well. I inflict death. You do not. Are you inferior? Accept your destiny. And take pride in your accomplishments. They're not as minor as you believe."

Rathburt glared at Torg. "Perhaps there will come a time when I won't fail you."

"You've never failed me."

"Just once ... hate me. Scream at me. Hit me. I can't stomach your love. It makes me feel even more worthless. You ask too much."

"I reserve hatred for a select few. And even then, I'm ashamed of it."

"You don't know the meaning of shame," Rathburt said before stomping off.

"You couldn't be more wrong," Torg whispered.

But none heard him say it.

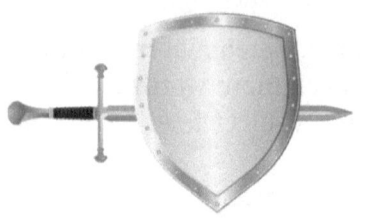

SIGN FROM ABOVE

Before leaving the scene of the battle, Torg tended his companions' wounds. The gash on Ugga's forehead turned out to be the worst of the injuries. Torg cauterized it with a tendril of blue-green flame from the tip of his right index finger, stopping the bleeding and eliminating the chance of infection. The others stared, wide-eyed and silent.

"What should we do with da carcasses?" Ugga said to Torg. "It will take too long to bury them, and burning could attract evil eyes."

"Let them rot. The forest will consume them at its leisure."

"I like that idea," Bard said. "We need to get da skins. If da wolves ruined them, I'll come back here and kill them again."

Elu obviously thought that was funny and wrapped his arms around the trapper's leg.

"When you're finished hugging Bard, can we get back to our business?" Rathburt snapped.

"We should delay no longer," Torg agreed. "The wolves have been routed, but there are other enemies in the forest more dangerous in the dark than in the light."

Elu let go of Bard's leg and inspected the remains of the Kojin. Sparkles of purple light still spun from the creature's wounds. The beast's chest was thicker than the Svakaran was tall. Elu poked at it with his dagger.

"Be careful, little guy," Ugga said.

Torg approached. "Stand back, all of you."

None questioned his order, and they retreated down the slope in a rush.

"*Vanadevataayo!* (Gods of the forest!)" Torg said in the ancient tongue. "*Paapam imam visodetha.* (Purify this evil.)"

Torg lifted the Silver Sword high into the air and whipped the blade down upon the back of the Kojin's neck. The bulbous head fell away, causing a conflagration of purple light to race along the ground. But the remnants of the ogress' power proved impotent.

Torg rejoined the others. "The Kojin is no longer dangerous. Now even the crows can feast on her flesh without fear."

"Always the showoff," Rathburt mumbled, though this time he said it without much conviction.

After retracing their path, it delighted Bard to find the skins unmolested. Torg had been right. The wolves were interested only in their prey. But after they restarted their trek, the litter regained its status as an enormous nuisance. At this pace, they wouldn't reach the longhouse until deep into the evening. Their only consolation was that the sky remained clear.

Torg was now wary of using his powers to clear paths. The litter slid on top of the snow relatively well, but the men's feet dug deep. The whiny Rathburt wondered aloud if they would arrive at all.

"At least we won't freeze," Ugga said. "We have enough of da skins to keep an army warm."

At dusk they stopped briefly near a running stream, drinking their fill of the frigid water and eating what remained of their food. The quarter moon had already reached midpoint in the darkening sky. Stars winked on, one by one. The air became as icy as a demon's breath. But there was no wind, not even the slightest breeze, and the men—clad in thick cloaks and boots—at least weren't shivering.

"How much farther now?" Torg said to Elu, his patience withering along with the rest of them. "It feels like we've been walking for weeks."

"If there were no snow and wolves and skins, Elu could make it to the longhouse in a short time," the Svakaran said. "But as slow as we're going, it will be a while yet. A third of the night will be gone before we arrive. And that's if there's no more trouble."

"I'm surprised we haven't seen someone yet," Rathburt said. "Not that Elu's people make a habit of running around in the middle of the night in the freezing cold, but there usually are a few scouts about, and I'd have guessed they'd be especially vigilant after receiving the news that the Great Ogre (he nodded toward Torg) is in the vicinity."

"We should have met someone by now," Elu agreed. "There are more than a thousand in the village."

"What about da wolves?" Bard said. "Maybe da people are afraid to go outside."

"That could be," Torg said. "Regardless, we have only two choices: Continue; or stop and make camp. But I'm uncertain if we should risk a fire. On a night like this, the smoke will cling to the ground like a fog and attract any number of nuisances."

"Now that we've come this far, we might as well keep walking," Rathburt said. "Once we reach the longhouse, we can build a pleasant fire inside and sleep until noon."

In a rare consensus, everyone agreed with Rathburt. Ugga grabbed the litter while Torg and Bard took the lead and dug a path through the thigh-deep snow. Elu was sent to look for any signs of a fellow Svakaran, but he discovered no other humans out on this night.

They began to hear tormented cries. At first, they mistook them for snow owls, which make haunting sounds that carry long distances on still nights. But the men became convinced that animals weren't making the strange noises. There were words interlaced with the screams.

"Are these woods haunted?" Torg said to Rathburt.

"You believe in ghosts?" the fellow Death-Knower said.

"Of course. I've spoken with them."

"I don't want to speak to no ghosties," Ugga said, his small eyes darting about. "Ya talk to them, Master Hah-nah. I'll stand behind ya."

"Ghosts are nothing to fear. Unlike demons and ghouls, they lack power over the living. But even if they were dangerous, none would dare approach while I'm with you."

"I'm glad ya are here," Bard said. "Da ghosties, demons, and ghoulies give me da shivers."

"Do you fear nothing, Master Showoff?" Rathburt said.

"I fear desire and aversion. Greed and suffering. But I don't fear ghosts. I wish Sister Tathagata were here. She would give you a better answer."

"Who is that?" Ugga said. "I heard ya say her name before."

"A wise woman. Even Jord could learn a thing or two from her."

"Could you learn from her?" Rathburt sneered. "Or are you beyond her teaching?"

Torg didn't respond.

The quarter moon had set by the time they arrived at the longhouse. The men covered the litter with tarps and then went inside, the ghostly cries following them all the way to the door. The weary travelers lit candles and started a fire. They ate jerky and dried apples and then opened the first barrel of beer. But on this rare occasion, they drank little. Overcome by exhaustion, they cast themselves upon furry blankets and slept like dead men. Soon after, ghosts walked among them, caressing their faces with lonely fingers. When Torg moaned in his sleep, the lost souls fled.

In the morning, the men woke amid a cacophony of stretches and groans, their legs and backs sore from the previous day's exertions. All except Torg and Rathburt still had cuts and bruises that Torg had not had time to tend.

The longhouse was divided into three rooms: a main area for cooking and sleeping; a storage area for food and supplies; and a stable housing three goats and nine chickens that had produced several dozen eggs while Elu and Rathburt were away.

The Svakaran built a fire in the hearth, heated slices of salted pork in an iron skillet, and scrambled eggs in the pork fat, tossing in onions and herbs. Then he spread hickory-nut butter onto slices of bread. Even Rathburt got into the act, brewing a pot of black tea.

The men sat on the floor around the fire and spooned the eggs out of wooden bowls. The meal was not large enough to satisfy Ugga, but it worked wonders for the rest of them. Afterward, they went outside to relieve themselves, and when they returned, they drank more tea.

"There's enough food here for two men to survive the winter, but not five, especially the way Ugga eats," Rathburt said. "We'll need to go to the village and barter. Either that or Torg can just scare them into giving us what we need."

"Let's try bartering first," Torg said.

Elu, however, was in no mood for jests. "The village is not far, but it will take until early afternoon to reach it and until dark to return. We should leave as soon as possible."

"What's da hurry?" Bard said. "There's enough food to last awhile. Shouldn't we rest a few days before we go tromping 'round again?"

"Elu is worried," the Svakaran said nervously. "Something is wrong. We should have seen someone by now."

"Your people are hiding from the *great one*," Rathburt said. "Cowering in their huts, afraid to breathe. Maybe they fear he'll stomp into their village and burn it down like an angry dragon."

"I feel it too, Elu," Torg said, ignoring Rathburt's aspersions.

"Did da wolves come this way?" Ugga said.

With that, Elu threw on his deerskin coat and raced out the door. "There are *children,*" he shouted.

The others followed Elu. Each brought their weapons, a bag of jerky, and a single skin over their cloaks to have something to trade if the opportunity arose. They planned on returning to the longhouse by nightfall with more supplies. The weather remained cold and clear, but if a sudden storm arose, they would have to make the best of it.

Without the litter to slow them down, Torg felt like they were flying. Torg, Ugga, and Bard took turns churning trenches through the deepest drifts of snow, and by the time the sun was in the middle of the sky, they were within a league of the village.

That's when they saw the first bodies—or what remained of them. Their small company had stopped to rest, and Rathburt was leaning against a tree when he looked up and yelped. An arm that had been torn off at the shoulder dangled from the crook of a limb. The thumb of its hand was missing, which somehow intensified the gruesomeness. Elu yelped too. The dismembered arm seemed to confirm his worst fears.

They found the head a dozen paces away, resting upright on a bank of snow. It stared at them, mouth agape. No tracks surrounded it and there was little blood except for a trail of red dots that led to even worse butchery. Three corpses lay beneath the trees, disemboweled and shredded. Elu ran to the tattered bodies.

"Are they *all* dead?" Rathburt said. "Did the wolves slaughter the entire village? There were good people here."

"The world has changed," Torg said. "We must proceed, but first— for Elu's sake—we will place these bodies upon a pyre and burn them."

"Shouldn't we rush to the village?" Elu said, so worried he was panting.

"This won't take long," Torg said. "We must counter the evil effects of this blasphemy with a moment of civilized behavior."

Rathburt and Elu hurried to find enough wood to build the pyre. Torg, Ugga, and Bard picked up the bodies, piece by piece. They found six arms and legs but only two heads. The third was missing.

"We now know from whence came the ghosts we heard last night," Torg said. "The violence of their deaths caused their spirits to linger."

Then the five of them encircled the pyre.

"Have you anything to say?" Torg said to Elu.

The Svakaran shook his head.

"Anyone else?"

"You're the only king among us," Rathburt blurted. "*You* say something."

"Very well."

Torg willed his eyes to glow, casting a blue-green light. He raised his hands, extended his palms, and spread his fingers. When he spoke, wisps of vapor seeped from his mouth and nose. "I am a Death-Knower. I have died—and returned. Do not doubt it."

Torg set his hands on the wood. "*Aggi*! (Fire!)"

The pyre burst into flames. "I *know* death. It is nothing to fear. When a person dies, pain, sorrow, and suffering do not follow. All senses are extinguished—save sight. What occurs in the Realm of Death has nothing to do with terror or grief. If you wish to mourn the pain these men suffered ... if you wish to grieve for their loved ones or for yourselves ... then do so. But do not mourn their passing. Death is the least of their worries—or yours."

The flames roared hungrily.

"*Jiivitam maranam anugacchati*!" Torg said in the ancient tongue.

And then repeated, in the common tongue:

"Death follows life."

"*Maranam jivitam anugacchati*!"

"Life follows death."

The fire reduced the wood, bones, and flesh to ash far more quickly than ordinary flames. Torg's magic had accelerated the process. Soon there was just a blackened stain on the ground, but most of the ash was white.

Torg went to each man in the circle and touched his forehead with the palm of his right hand, saying a simple Tugarian blessing: "May you not suffer. May you be healthy. May your mind be clear."

Immediately after, they continued their journey to the village. As they passed out of the trees, Torg saw the missing head. It had been tossed high into the air and was skewered on a branch twenty cubits above the ground. It watched them leave with disinterest. Its karma was elsewhere.

When they reached the village, what they saw stunned even Torg. They stood on a hillock and observed the carnage from above. There had been no fires—they would have noticed the smoke long before they approached—but many of the huts were battered to pieces, and misshapen bodies lay strewn about, some of which were as small as babies. Elu charged down the hill, heedless of the others' cries. Torg, Ugga, and Bard followed, with Rathburt trailing behind.

Most of the victims were disemboweled—the work of black wolves. This became even more evident when they found the carcasses of half a dozen wolves felled by arrows and spears. But the destruction of the huts and other structures made it plain that the Kojin had played a major role in the slaughter. Against such a fiend, even a thousand Svakarans had been helpless.

Elu came to a sudden halt, sat on the ground, and took a corpse in his arms.

Torg knelt beside him. "Who?"

"It's his mother," Rathburt said from behind. "After Elu returned in his new form, she rejected him. But he never stopped loving her."

"I'm sorry, little guy," Ugga said. "But we will take care of ya, won't we Bard?"

"That's very right," Bard said.

Torg slid his hand beneath Elu's cloak, caressing the red-brown skin with glowing fingers. The Svakaran's tensed muscles relaxed, and he gently released his mother's ravaged body.

"All are dead," the Svakaran said. "Should Elu not mourn?"

There was no sarcasm in his voice, only desperation.

Torg stared hard into his eyes. "In this lifetime, their suffering is no longer. But your pain remains. You must find the strength to overcome it."

"And Sōbhana?" Rathburt said sharply. "Did you not mourn for her?"

"I mourned for myself."

Torg turned back to Elu. "We must do for your mother and the rest of your people what we did for the others. A slaughter of this magnitude must be countered. The insanity of such merciless behavior strains the balance of karma. But it will take far too long to burn their bodies in traditional fashion. For this task, I must risk another display of magic. But first let us search for any signs of life."

The men crept through the rubble. In every face, Torg saw remnants of terror. None had been spared. Despite Torg's attempts to calm Elu, the Svakaran's agitation intensified. Torg finally told Rathburt to escort

Elu to the far side of the hill. He, Ugga, and Bard would do the rest.

The trio searched until late afternoon but didn't find a single person alive. If any had survived, they had fled far away. However, plenty of food and supplies were left untouched by the assault. They even found a four-wheeled cart—probably stolen from villagers who dwelled along the Ogha River—and a pair of robust oxen to haul it. The Kojin and the wolves had been intent on murdering people. The animals and supplies had not held their interest.

Torg, Ugga, and Bard loaded the cart with carrots, peas, and beans; dried apples, pears, and figs; venison and pork; cheeses and butter; salt and herbs; and hay for the oxen. And of course, as many kegs of corn beer and apple wine as they could manage. They were not in the mood for it now, but it would be a long winter and their sadness would fade. *Life is for the living*, Vasi masters liked to say.

"Those who desire to watch should do so from the hilltop," Torg said. "Do not stray too near."

"*Torg the Showoff* is about to perform another act of derring-do," Rathburt sneered.

"Why don't ya be *quiet*!" Ugga said. "Master Hah-nah is only doing what's right for those poor peoples."

"Yes, be quiet," Elu said.

"Hmph!" Rathburt said.

While the others climbed to the safety of the hilltop, Torg walked to the center of what remained of the village. He stood there silently, counting fifty inhales and fifty exhales without permitting a single other thought. Then he raised his arms toward the sky. Once again, his eyes glowed blue-green, and tendrils of fire danced along his fingertips, earlobes, and nostrils. When he opened his mouth, a ball of smoke puffed out.

"*Aggi dahanti, te aamantemi*! (The fire that consumes, I summon thee!)"

There came a low rumble as if an earthquake was working up the urge to cause trouble. Torg became engulfed in red fire, but his blue-green power blended with it, turning the flames a tempestuous shade of purple. The fire whirled, slowly at first, but ever faster and more violently, expanding outward and upward, hungry and potent. Bolts of lightning leaped from it, hurtling angrily into the firmament.

The others watched from the hilltop. The fire consumed everything it touched. Buildings, bodies, and bones turned to ash. Without warning, a wave of super-heated air blew across the hilltop, followed by a blast as loud as thunder.

When it was over, the village was gone. The flames receded and the smoke dissipated, leaving nothing but white ash that swirled in the air and coated the ground.

Torg stood in the middle of it all—and he remained there, motionless, for a long time. Then he dusted himself off. His cloak and boots were unharmed, except for the fringes of his sleeves, which were singed. He had protected himself, even his clothing, with a cocoon of magic. The Silver Sword hung from his belt, cold and disinterested. As Torg walked to the top of the hill, flakes of ash still clung to him.

"It's done," he said to the others, all of whom faced him with mouths agape. "I'm tired. We should leave."

It was dark by the time Torg and the others made it back to the longhouse. Even with the help of the oxen, the cart had slowed them down, and they barely had enough strength to unpack the supplies and guide the beasts into the stable. The goats and chickens seemed unhappy with their new companions—especially ones that weighed more than 150 stones apiece—but Torg knelt and whispered to each of them. After that, the animals got along splendidly.

"What next, Torg?" Rathburt said. "Will you part the Salt Sea and stroll among the flopping fishes?"

Torg chuckled weakly. "I've considered it."

The exertion at the Svakaran village had taken its toll. Before casting himself onto a bed of straw in the main room, Torg ate a small meal Bard had hastily prepared. Usually Elu took charge of the food, but the Svakaran had been disconsolate since they had departed what remained of the village, and he went to sleep without eating. While Ugga and Bard built a fire, another storm brewed outside. It had a nasty feel. The storm howled for two full days, piling another three cubits of snow onto an already thick cover. The men drank tea in the mornings, wine in the afternoons, and beer at night. They only left the longhouse for shivering sessions of relief. Rathburt took it upon himself to heat some water and order each man to bathe.

Torg declined. "When the need arises, I can cleanse myself without the use of water."

"There are merchants in Kamupadana who make their living selling soaps and perfumes," Rathburt said. "I'm sure they're pleased there's only one of you, Torg. Otherwise, you would put them out of business."

"I am who I am," Torg said, aggravating Rathburt even more.

When the storm relented, they went outside for a look around. New drifts of snow—some taller than Torg or Ugga—were piled as far as they could see. They were "snowed in," as Bard liked to say, but at least they had plenty of food and drink. Unless they came under attack, there was no need to do anything but pass the time as best they could until winter loosened its grip, which could take as long as three more months this far north.

"The cold is dire," Torg said to his friends. "But our enemies will find it unpleasant as well. I think we're safe, for now. If all goes well, we'll be able to renew our journey at winter's end. I must reach Kamupadana to learn news of the world, but it's wise for me to remain hidden for a while longer."

"And what of your precious Tugars?" Rathburt said. "Don't you want to return to Anna?"

"Avici lies betwixt here and Anna. Besides, I have made Kusala aware that I live, and that is enough. The chieftain is more than capable of preparing the Tent City for whatever dangers might arise. I fear more for Nissaya and Jivita than I do for Anna—and Nissaya, especially. That is where Invictus will strike first. But when? Not before midsummer is my guess. I've seen his army. He has little need for surprise."

"What are your plans after Kamupadana?" Rathburt said.

"My first plan is to remain free. I'll be no good to anyone if I'm recaptured. I must avoid Avici, which means I'll need to travel west before going south. The journey to Jivita—if that is where I choose to go—could take more than a month. Any who wish to join me are welcome."

"I'll come with ya," Ugga said. "But I'm afraid what will happen when Bard and I travel too far from da trees. Will we grow old like Master Rad-burt?"

Rathburt snorted. "You can only hope to look as good as I do at my age."

"Bard and Ugga are not as young as they appear," Torg said. "As for your question, Ugga, I don't know the answer. The trees have played an important role in your longevity. But there's one thing I know for certain: Wherever I go, danger will follow. None of you will be safe as long as you're with me."

"I'll go wherever ya go, trees or no trees," Bard said. "I don't mind a little danger. I get bored sitting around all day."

"Elu will also follow if you'll have him," the Svakaran said. "He might not be the most powerful, but he's the best guide. And he needs to get away from here. This place makes him sad."

"It would honor me," Torg said. "Your heart is large, my friend. And your strength, as well. Still, we're getting ahead of ourselves. What I learn in Kamupadana might change everything. And you never know who we'll meet along the way."

The five men waited out the winter. It was tedious, to say the least. When the days were calm, they allowed the oxen to forage for grasses beneath the snow while the men hunted for game. Squirrels and hares were plentiful, as were possums. Several times they killed deer, and once an elk that was larger than a black wolf. Of course, they avoided bears—Ugga would never allow one to be harmed—and they also didn't harm otters. Torg loved them too much to kill them.

"I was an otter in a previous life. If we can't kill bears because of Ugga, then we can't kill otters because of me."

"The Chaunoc are friendly creatures," the Svakaran agreed. "Elu was an otter once, too."

"And Master Radburt was a carrot," Bard said, which sent them all into laughter, including the butt of the joke, who seemed pleased by the jest.

"Better a carrot than a polecat," Rathburt said, slapping his leg.

Ugga found that even funnier.

Next to bouts of heavy drinking, their meals were the highlights of their days. All of them were adept at cooking, but Elu was the master, especially with sauces and gravies. Once after a big meal, they walked outside for fresh air and found a Tyger the size of a Buffelo standing a few dozen paces away, sniffing the aromas that drifted from the smoke hole in the longhouse's roof. Elu and Rathburt ran back inside. Ugga and Bard stayed close to the door. But Torg strode forward, unafraid, until he stood face-to-face with the beast. Vapors seeped from his mouth and the Tyger became tame, falling on its side in the snow as if wanting to play.

"Bring what's left of the Che-ra," Torg said to Ugga, but the crossbreed wanted no part of the massive feline. Bard worked up the courage, timidly approaching and tossing the roasted remains of the possum a few paces away. The Tyger leaped up and swallowed it whole, then crept to Torg and licked his face with its scratchy tongue.

"Showoff," Rathburt muttered while peeking from behind the door.

Torg and Rathburt meditated several times a day. The others took an interest and joined them. They also passed the time by telling stories. Rathburt enjoyed this as much as any of them, recounting humorous moments involving his failed attempts to become a Tugar warrior. Once, Torg laughed so hard the inside of the longhouse started to super heat, and they had to rush him outside to avoid burning their shelter to the ground.

Elu told many tales of the Svakarans, and the hated Mogols. Bard and Ugga talked at length about Jord and how much they missed her. They also bragged of their sexual exploits—paid for with "da skins"— in Kamupadana.

"I like ya, guys," Ugga said one evening, after his tenth mug of beer. "But I *love* da Brounettos. Will winter never end?"

"It doesn't feel like it ever will," Rathburt agreed.

But winter did end. Oh so gradually, the days lengthened and the banks of snow receded. Like a tired old man losing the will to live, winter released its grip. There was rain instead of sleet, followed by delicious wisps of midday warmth.

Even as patches of snow lingered on the ground, a weeping willow growing near a stream about 300 paces from the longhouse was the first of the deciduous trees to go green. The stream roared again, though chunks of ice tumbled down its long throat.

"When do we leave, Master Hah-nah?" Ugga said to Torg one morning while the men stood together beneath a crystal sky in the late morning. "Now that da snow is melting, Elu says we can reach da Whore City in two days. Our food's low and we're almost out of beer."

"I'm waiting for a sign," Torg said.

"Don't listen to his nonsense," Rathburt said. "He's always saying things like that. *I'm waiting for a sign.* Ooooooo. He won't be satisfied until the sun and moon perform a waltz for his benefit."

Torg was unperturbed. "Something strange is in the air. Do you not feel it?"

"The only thing strange is you," Rathburt said.

But the Svakaran agreed with Torg. "Elu feels it, too. The birds have stopped singing and the chipmunks no longer chitter. Something quiets them."

"Da little guy is right," Bard said. "Where *have* da birds gone, anyways? And there is no breeze."

Torg raised his head, shielded his eyes with his hand, and gazed toward the sun. The others did the same.

"We're about to find out," he proclaimed. "Behold!"

"What are you babbling about?" Rathburt said.

"Be patient. And shield your eyes. Even a Tugar can be blinded if he stares too long at the sun."

"I see something," Ugga said excitedly. "Look, a sliver of darkness."

"I see it too," Bard said.

"You've gone mad," Rathburt said. But then, even he couldn't deny it. "Wait ... I do see something. Torg, how did you know?"

"I am a Death-Knower. I know many things others do not. Besides, I've witnessed this event before and remember how everything felt just before it began. All of us who live long lives will see the moon become enshrouded in shadow many times. But when it happens to the sun, it's far rarer and more spectacular. The Noble Ones say that the sun and the moon circle the skies like birds, and sometimes the moon passes in front of the sun and blocks its light."

"The Svakaran legends say the sun and moon take turns eating each other," Elu said. "And afterward, they're so full they rest for a long time before their next meal."

"Come to think of it, I've seen this too," Rathburt said. "But it was long ago."

They stood silently and watched the eclipse develop. A shadow appeared on the western edge of the sun. Then over the course of 200 long breaths, it widened until the sun was half covered. The sky remained clear, but the blue was less vivid and the light at ground level was noticeably dimmer.

From there, things happened quickly. The western sky darkened like a great storm creeping over the horizon, and the rest of the sky changed from blue to violet. Now, the sun resembled a crescent moon, no longer bright.

"Behold the rising shadow," Torg said, gesturing toward the west.

The shadow widened, resembling the onset of a winter storm from

Nirodha. But there was no snow, lightning, or thunder. Only darkness. The sun shrank to just a sliver. And then, as if in surrender, the delicate crescent sparkled and winked out, becoming a black disk surrounded by a circle of quivering light. Stars were visible in the twilight. The far edge of the horizon glowed like the final moments of sunset. Gusts of cool air stroked their faces. A cluster of bats, believing night had arrived, burst from a nearby cave.

The sun remained dark for twenty-five slow breaths before emerging from the shadow. Not long after, it was blazing as before. The bats returned to their hideout. The brightness of day resumed.

"I have my sign," Torg announced. "We leave for Kamupadana tomorrow morning. Beginning now, my name is Hana—to *all* of you. One slip of the tongue could expose our conspiracy. Thus far, our encounter with the wolves was our only misstep. But wolves can't talk, so their masters will remain confused over who or what defeated them. We must all be like Ugga and Bard: common Woolfolk looking to trade skins for food, drink, coins, and luxuries."

"Brounettos!" Ugga shouted.

Rathburt rolled his eyes, but the others laughed. Elu took Torg's hand.

"Will we be away for a long time, *great one*?"

"If you join me, it will be many months before you return … *if* you return. But as I've often said, I won't force any of you to accompany me."

"I might as well come, anyway," Rathburt said. "Without Elu around, who will do all the chores? And besides, I've stayed in one place for too long. The soil of my garden needs a rest."

"Tonight, we should have a celebration," the Svakaran said. "Elu will prepare roasted goat with mushroom gravy and chicken soup with carrots, onions, and wild potatoes. Even Ugga will have a full stomach."

"What a great idea, little guy," Ugga said. "There's just enough beer and wine left to have one last party. Let's get started!"

After their feast, they went to bed late and got up early, feeling queasy and hung over. Even Torg felt out of sorts. This time, at least, they had the cart and oxen to haul the skins and their supplies. The going would be easier, but still tedious. Though the terrain between the longhouse and the Whore City was traversable on foot, some areas would be difficult. But with Elu, Ugga, and Bard to guide them, it could be done.

As they prepared to leave, the oxen became especially docile as if pleased to have survived the previous night's feast. Torg carried the Silver Sword, but now it was strapped onto his back beneath his cloak. The others laid their weapons in the cart next to the skins. Elu packed cooking gear, bowls, cups, and spoons along with what remained of their herbs and spices. By midmorning, they were ready to depart.

"This was a good home," the Svakaran said, tears in his eyes. "Elu will miss it."

"So will I," Rathburt said. "There are worse places to live."

"There may come a time when you'll return," Torg said.

"I won't be back," Rathburt said.

Torg raised an eyebrow. Then he turned, grabbed one ox by its yoke, and pulled. The beast responded and the cart lurched forward. The others followed on foot, with Elu the last to leave the longhouse behind.

By nightfall they had managed only four leagues. The oxen did their best, but the going was slow. They were forced several times to circle out of their way to avoid deep streams or dense stands of forest. Still, they were pleased. Anything was preferable to hauling the litter by hand.

The first night was chilly. There was just the slightest sliver of moon, and the skies remained clear. They camped inside a cave several times larger than the longhouse, its ceiling towering twenty cubits above a floor covered with crumbled stone.

Ugga became obsessed with bear droppings he discovered deep in its interior, crawling around on his hands and knees and sniffing like an animal. Torg was more interested in drawings he found on the walls, some of which were brightly colored with intricate detail while others were barely visible. In one scene, a hunting party of long-haired men battled a wooly mammoth. The red and yellow ocher used by the artist had faded over the millennia, but large portions of the painting remained intact.

"Mammoths still live in the heart of the frozen wastes of Nirodha," Torg said. "The great dragons have eaten most of them, but the decline of the dragons has enabled a few mammoths to survive. They are mighty beasts, twice as large as desert elephants, though not nearly as intelligent. Shaggy hair covers their hides, and the males have humps on their backs like camels."

"I suppose you've seen them and ridden them, and even taught them the ancient tongue," Rathburt said.

"I wasn't able to teach them the ancient tongue," Torg said blandly.

Elu snorted.

They risked a fire, enjoying a hot meal and some of Rathburt's excellent black tea. After dark, they curled up and went to sleep. Torg saw no need to post a guard. His senses were such that it was nearly impossible to approach him undetected, even while he slept—although Jord had managed it in broad daylight, which still galled him.

"Where are you now, Jord?" Torg whispered to himself. "Are you watching over us, a bird perched high in the trees? Or a bear crouching in the bushes? Ugga would like that. Wherever—and whatever—you are, I thank you for removing Vedana's poison. And I also thank you for filling me with the magic of the great pines. I'll need my strength in the coming months. I hope we'll meet again, one day."

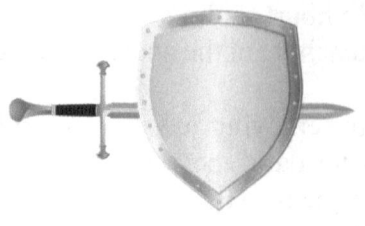

EPILOGUE

Torg meditated for 200 long breaths before closing his eyes and going to sleep. He dreamed he stood on the crest of a fossil dune somewhere deep in the heart of his beloved Tējo. On his right was his father, Asēkha-Jhana. On his left was a beautiful woman with golden hair and flawless skin. It was midnight, and a full moon glowed like the sun. Jhana bent over and scooped a handful of sand.

"I have a lesson for you, my son."

"Tell me, father."

"The Great Desert extends more than a hundred leagues from where we stand. The grains of sand I hold in my hand represent what you've learned thus far in your life. What you still must learn lies in all the sand beyond."

Torg pondered the enormity of such words, and a slew of questions leaped to mind. But before he could ask any of them, Jhana transformed from flesh to black stone. This frightened Torg, and he turned to the woman for support.

"What happened to my father?" he asked her.

She didn't speak, but her smile burned sweet holes in his heart. Torg's fears receded and he lost himself in the glory of her blue-gray eyes. But the pleasant reverie ended when—somewhere in the depths of the darkness—a baby wailed.

This horrified Torg. Who could abandon an infant in such a dangerous place? Surely, only the worst kind of monster would be capable of such cruelty.

He clambered down the side of the dune and charged across the desert, running to and fro in a panic. But the infant was as invisible as a ghost—and try as he might, he could not find her anywhere.

As suddenly as it had begun, the wailing stopped.

And was replaced by wicked laughter.
Torg stood alone in a vast sea of sand.
So much to learn, he thought.
And so little time.
So ... little ... time.

So ends Book 1

Up next:

Book 2 | Chained by Fear

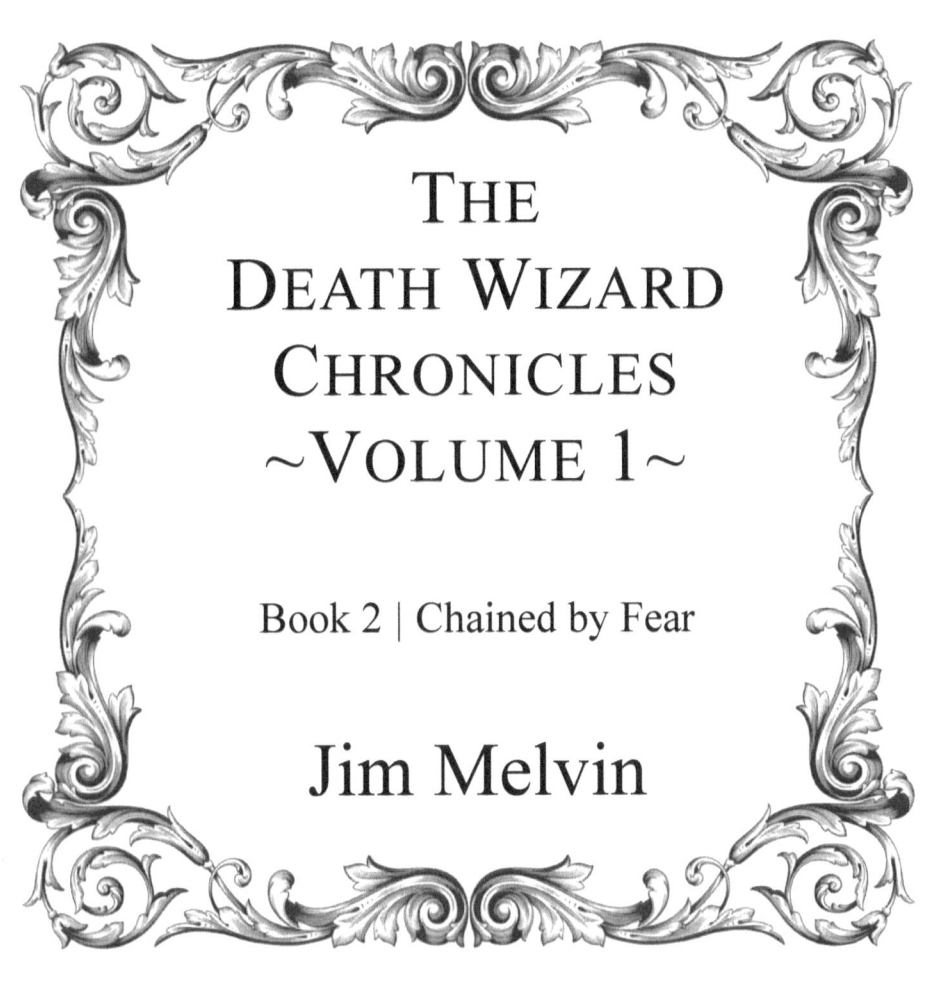

THE
DEATH WIZARD
CHRONICLES
~VOLUME 1~

Book 2 | Chained by Fear

Jim Melvin

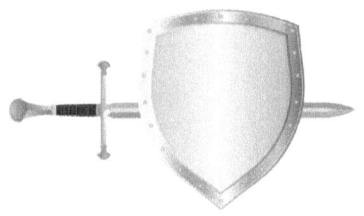

PROLOGUE

(86 years before Torg was imprisoned in the pit)

From his hiding place among the trees, the teenage boy had spied on the little girl for months. Though darkness was not his friend, he had endured it to be near her. How daring she was to leave her house all by herself in the middle of the night, seemingly undeterred by the specter of ghosts and goblins. How foolish of her, too. Laylah would learn one day that monsters existed and that some of them were far deadlier than any her imagination might conjure. She would learn that it was better to stay locked in her room than wander the wilds after dark. She would learn because he would teach her.

Though Laylah was 4 years old, she was already beautiful. He admired her golden hair, which so matched his own. And though her gray-blue eyes were in stark contrast to his deep-brown ones, he permitted her this fallibility. No one was perfect. Well, almost no one.

When they were king and queen, she would birth his heir—a son. Laylah would become his bride whether or not she liked it. He was a god, after all. And who in their right mind would refuse the hand of a god?

Not even the god's sister would do that.

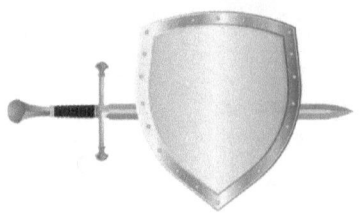

BROTHER

L aylah first met her brother when she was 5 years old. He found her at the rope swing that hung from a sycamore tree on the outskirts of the village known as Avici. With so many children flocking to the swing, Laylah sometimes had to wait forever for a turn. But she knew the best time to go. While her parents slumbered, she snuck out her window and scampered through the darkness. The swing hung there—lifeless but inviting—and she had it all to herself. Shortly before morning arrived, she returned home to sleep.

On an especially beautiful night when the moon was full and the sky clear, Laylah sat on the swing and basked in the reflected light. Luminous streaks emanated from her body as she swept back and forth. When she held up her arm, she could see that her skin glowed magically. She didn't know why but didn't care. To her, it was normal.

The boy who came to her that fateful night wasn't normal. He wore calico robes embroidered with little golden suns, and when he lifted his hood to show his face, Laylah saw something in his expression that felt familiar. He smiled at her, exposing perfect white teeth and disturbingly clear brown eyes. His hair was an even deeper yellow than hers, hanging long and silky about his shoulders. He sat cross-legged in the grass near her feet and rested the palms of his hands on his knees.

"Are you afraid?" he said, whispering huskily.

"No," she said, telling the truth.

He smiled again. "Do you know me?"

"I don't think so."

The smile lessened. "I'm a stranger to you, but you're not a stranger to me. Do you understand?"

"A lot of the old people know my name, but I don't know theirs. Is that what you mean?"

He chuckled, but with a slight hint of irritation. "Not exactly. But it's obvious you're a very smart girl. And so pretty! I like you. Do you like me?"

"How old are you?" she said.

"I'm 15. And you're 5?"

"You *do* know me," she said. "But I don't remember seeing you. Are you new here?"

"Yes … in some ways. I was born here, but I grew up someplace else."

"Have you come back here to live?"

"No … just to visit. With you."

"Why?"

"Because I like you. Do you like me?"

"I guess so."

"Well, that's a good start. I hope you'll like me more when you get to know me. But I must ask you an important question. Can you keep a secret?"

"Yes!" Laylah loved keeping secrets. It made her feel like an old person.

"Good. Well, the secret is … *me*. I don't want you to tell anyone, not even your parents, that you talked to me tonight. If you tell them, do you know what will happen?"

"You'll be mad at me?"

"I won't be mad at you, but your parents will. They'll stop you from going out at night. They'll barricade your door and window. You won't have the swing all to yourself anymore and you won't be able to enjoy the moonlight with no one around to bother you."

Tears welled in Laylah's eyes. Being imprisoned in her room at night would be the worst punishment she could imagine.

"But if you keep *our* secret," the boy continued, "you'll be free to come and go whenever you like. Tomorrow night, the moon will be round again. I'll come to visit. If you're not here, I'll know you broke *our* secret."

"I won't break it, I promise."

"Thank you, Laylah." He smiled so wide she could see his thick red tongue. "And I won't tell anyone, either. See you tomorrow night?"

"Yes."

She went home before dawn and slept until almost noon. Her

parents, Gunther and Stēorra, told her how much it confused them that she slept so much. They put her to bed every night after dark, but she rarely got up on her own before lunch. Yet she was healthy and happy, so they didn't bother her about it too much, enabling her to get away with her nightly wanderings.

Invictus met Laylah at the tree again that night, lavishing her with praise for keeping their secret. He talked to her for a long time and asked many questions: What was her favorite food? He was an excellent cook. Did she have any pets? He had lots of them. Was she satisfied with her clothes? When she grew up, he could buy her some beautiful gowns and shoes. Would she like that?

"Yes."

The third night, he leaned over and kissed her on the cheek.

"Do you love me, Laylah? Because I love you."

The kiss made her feel uncomfortable, and she didn't answer. He became annoyed.

"I won't be around for a while." And he walked away in a huff.

For several weeks, he didn't meet her at the swing. Laylah became used to being alone again. She once tried to tell her mother about the boy, but her tongue dried up and the words wouldn't come out. She hated the feeling of helplessness.

When the moon rose full the following month, he appeared again, strutting out of the darkness with a grin on his face. He gave her a light hug and another kiss on the cheek. Whatever anger he'd displayed when she'd last seen him was gone. He told her how much he'd missed her and how much he loved her. Did she love him? She still didn't answer.

Four days a month around each full moon, he visited her at the swing. He taught her things, such as how to talk to him without speaking; or how to scorch patches of grass with fire from the tips of her fingers. He told her magical words. *Ratana*, repeated three times, turned pebbles into gems. *Khandeti* caused pottery to crack. *Avihethana* healed cuts and bruises. This delighted Laylah.

"Do you love me?" he asked.

"I *like* you, a lot."

"I *love* you, a lot."

One time, he taught her the word *Namuci*, which an ancient demon named Vedana had conjured in a time eons past. When a demon—or a human with demon blood—spoke the word, it gave life to invisible spirits called *efrits*, thousands of which dwelled in the Realm of Undeath. In that eternal darkness, they were harmless. But when summoned to the Realm of Life, they became voracious meat eaters, gorging themselves on the internal organs of any living being unlucky enough to be nearby. The speaker of the word—if she or he had enough demon blood—was safe from harm.

If *Namuci* was whispered, just a few *efrits* responded and only one person died. But if a being of great power screamed it at high volume, thousands of *efrits* emerged, and any human or animal within several hundred paces perished.

When Laylah said it, a sparrow tumbled from the sky and lay dead at her feet. She screamed and cried. He called her a "little baby" and rushed away.

For several months he didn't appear, and Laylah began to think she wouldn't see him again. In most ways, she was relieved. More than once she tried to tell her parents or some of the other old people about her mysterious visitor. But the words wouldn't come. She tried so hard, her eyes filled with tears. When they asked her what was wrong, she couldn't speak. Her tongue felt meaty and swollen.

By the time she was 6 years old, she had learned to spell and write quite a few words, but when she attempted to write something down about the brown-eyed boy, the quill smeared the ink. She even tried to draw his picture, but the same thing happened. It made her sick to her stomach.

He appeared again out of nowhere, smiling like he'd never been gone. She told him she was still mad at him for making her kill the bird. He said he was sorry and wouldn't do it again. Instead, he taught her good words like *Loha-Hema*, which turned copper to gold; and *Tumbî-Tum*, which caused vegetables to grow from seed to full ripeness in just a few days. He showed her how to conjure small spheres of flame that floated in the air, and the two of them tossed them back and forth like toy balls. When an adult villager, perhaps trying to walk off a bout of insomnia, wandered past the swing in the middle of the night, the boy blew smoke from his mouth and said *Niddaayahi.* The man collapsed on the grass, his insomnia apparently cured.

Laylah worried about the old person. He was one of her father's many friends and often had been nice to her. The boy assured her he would take the man back to his house, and he picked up the old person and carried him away like he weighed less than a feather. Laylah never saw the man again, but the boy came back the next night in a better mood than usual.

When she turned 9, the boy handed her an envelope sealed with an insignia of a golden sun and told her to wait until he was gone before reading the letter. He also told her to burn it with her special white finger-fire after she finished it. When he disappeared from her sight, she tore it open.

He had written the letter in gold ink on a single sheet of silky white paper.

My dearest Laylah,

You're so smart and pretty. When we aren't together, I feel sad. I miss you all the time. I love you very much.

Do you love me?

We've known each other for four years, but you've never asked my name. Why is that? Aren't you curious about me? Don't you care?

Remember our secret. Tell no one about me. Our parents will be angry at you if they discover we're friends.

Your brother,
Invictus

Your brother? Our parents? Laylah read the letter several times. She decided not to burn it and instead show it to her parents the next morning. But the moment that thought entered her mind, the paper burst into yellow flame. She cried again.

"You're *not* my brother," she said to him the next night. "I don't have a brother. My mom and dad would have told me."

He stomped around the swing, staring at her with fury in his eyes.

"You dare to call me a liar?" His body, now almost twenty years old and fully grown, glowed like a miniature sun. "Listen to me carefully, little one. I allow you to live because you're my sister, but even *you* need to be careful. Your powers are just a fraction of mine.

Compared to me, you're merely a *reflection*."

Laylah burst into tears, ran all the way home, and didn't return to the swing for months. She trembled in her bed until morning when sleep finally took her, temporarily releasing her from misery. During that dreadful stretch, she never saw Invictus, the boy who claimed to be her brother. But not seeing him had consequences. She became ill.

Her parents were afraid she might die. Shamans studied her but could find nothing wrong. Laylah tried to tell them about the boy and his ghastly powers, but no intelligible words came forth.

One shaman, who was filthy and stank, told Laylah's parents that he needed to be alone with the child to properly diagnose her condition. Out of desperation, they agreed. When they closed the door, the shaman leaned over Laylah and told her that evil spirits possessed her. If she kissed him, the spirits would flee from her mouth into his, where he would devour them. Laylah saw through his guise. Without thinking, she whispered, "*Namuci*!" The shaman fell to the floor, spit out a clump of blood, and died. Her parents rushed back into the room and found her in hysterics. The shaman's death shocked the village, but no one thought to blame her.

For whatever reason, the horror of what she'd done strengthened Laylah's resolve, and in a few weeks her good health returned. This pleased her parents a lot. But it all fell apart for her the morning after her 10th birthday when Invictus crept through her window and entered her room. She tried to cry out but could only manage a few weak grunts. Still wearing his golden robes, he sat next to her on her bed and placed his hand on her stomach. She hated being so close to him, but somehow his presence froze her. A short time later, her parents entered the room and found them together.

"What are you *doing*?" Gunther said. "Get away from my child!"

Her father attempted to pull the young man off Laylah, but Invictus was far too strong, swinging his arm and knocking the older man against the far wall. Her mother lifted a small wooden table and smashed it against Invictus' shoulder, but it didn't seem to faze him. He stood and faced her.

"Mother, don't you recognize me?"

"I recognize you, but I wish I didn't," she said. "Why have you returned to torment us?"

"I love you, mother. Do you love me?"

Then he spit a sizzling ball of spittle at Stēorra's brown eyes. Her mother howled and pressed her hands to her face, staggering backward. When she removed her hands, most of the flesh on her skull was gone, though strands of long yellow hair still clung to the exposed bone.

Her father regained his senses, staggered to his feet, and pounced on Invictus, all the while yelling, "Laylah ... *run!*"

"Father," Invictus said. "I love you. Do you love me?"

Invictus pressed his lips against Gunther's mouth and blew hot breath down his throat. Her father collapsed and went into a wild spasm. Smoke exploded from his ears, nose, and mouth—and his tongue swelled absurdly. When he blew apart, flaming patches of tissue splattered across the room. This terrified Laylah and shook her out of whatever spell Invictus has put on her to keep her still. She sat up and screamed.

Though maimed and blinded, her mother groped for Invictus. But she was no match for him. He grasped her disfigured face and kissed her too. She met the same fate as her husband.

Invictus raised his arms and bellowed. Golden flames erupted from every pore. The house exploded as if dragon fire had struck it from within. Shards flew several hundred paces, casting Laylah into the yard like a piece of broken furniture. When the conflagration cleared, she saw Invictus standing naked amid the smoking debris, his robes consumed but his body unharmed. Her parents were gone.

Laylah stood, unhurt. But her clothes were incinerated and she was also naked. The commotion drew hundreds of villagers, who rushed toward her. But when they saw Invictus, they turned and ran the other way. One man hesitated as if daring to issue a challenge. For him, it was a death sentence. Invictus blasted a bolt of golden flame, ripping off the man's head.

Laylah could stand it no more. But at least she now had full use of her limbs. She ran ... fast and far.

"Laylah! Come back. I love you." Her brother's voice shook the valley. "Laylah, do you LOVE ME?"

She reached the Ogha River. The roar of its swirling waters drowned out her sobs. She felt her brother approaching from behind, but she preferred to die than see him again.

Laylah cast herself into the Ogha. She could swim well for her age, but she was used to the still waters of lakes and ponds, not the nasty swells of the mightiest river in the world. The tumult swept her along, helpless as a leaf. Despite the dangers, she felt peaceful. Death by drowning was a small price to pay to escape such a monster.

But Laylah's life wouldn't end on this day. Something grabbed her and pulled. She glided along the surface of the river on her back and was dragged onto the steep bank on the far side.

She could still hear Invictus' desperate cries.

"Laylah, come back!"

Out of nowhere, powerful arms lifted her and pressed her against wet skin that smelled like a wild animal. She screamed, struggling to free herself. Then a large hand clamped over her mouth and everything went dark.

DEMON

A princess with golden hair stood alone atop a hill overlooking a secluded valley. A warm breeze stroked her face like a loving hand. Just a short time before, her small village had been as steamy as a sweat lodge. But now the last remnants of the sun had disappeared, signaling the start of her favorite time of day. As always, she relished the onset of dusk.

The Ripe Corn Moon would soon rise above the mountains surrounding the valley. She could hardly wait for the full moon to creep over the peaks in the southeastern sky. The sight would fill her with joy.

The princess' name was Magena, which meant *"sacred moon"* in her language. She was an adopted member of the Ropakans, a tribal people who dwelled in the Mahaggata Mountains. Though she knew their ways and traditions, Magena was unlike the other members of her clan. Her skin was the color of cream, while the Ropakans were deeply tanned. Her hair was thin and golden, in contrast to the dense black of her sisters and brothers. Her eyes were blue-gray; theirs, dark brown. Her body was long and voluptuous; theirs, short and stocky.

One difference far surpassed the physical dissimilarities: Unlike the others of her clan, Magena wielded magical powers. But she didn't dare display them openly. Eight years before, her adoptive father had rescued her from the wicked currents of the Ogha River. Since then, he had urged her to hide her gifts to avoid distrust and jealousy among the villagers.

The moon was Magena's friend and ally. She reveled in its reflected light. The sun didn't scorch her, but neither did it nourish; she could wander freely during the day, but she sometimes felt weak and a little queasy. When night came, she burst with vitality. The moon fueled her strength, and when it rose to fullness, her puissance reached maximum potential.

As she stood on the hill that evening, Magena sensed her father's presence before seeing him. His name was Takoda, which meant *friend of all* in the language of the Ropakans. Since the early years of their relationship, Takoda had taken rascally pleasure in sneaking up and startling her, often leaping from behind boulders or trees with a wild look in his eyes. When she shrieked, he would laugh until he cried—and then apologize with the insincere remorse of a trickster. At first, Magena had resented her father's strange sense of humor. But she grew to adore the good nature that anchored it.

Nowadays, he rarely succeeded in spooking her. Magena was 18 years old and in the full bloom of womanhood. She had eyes like an eagle's, ears like a tyger's, and a nose like a bear's. But many of her people made similar claims. What separated her from the others were her supernatural powers, which radiated from her body like heat off a fire. No one could enter her invisible aura without her noticing. At nighttime, especially, it was nearly impossible to approach her undetected.

"Father, will you never tire of this game?" Magena said, her sweet voice barely audible. "I've told you dozens of times you'll never surprise me again. Even asleep, I hear you. You make as much noise as a moose."

Takoda grunted, kicking the grass at his feet.

"I crawled up behind you as slow and silent as a snail," he whined, "and *still* you heard me."

Magena let out an exaggerated sigh. Then she laughed.

"Dear one, if you meant to imitate a snail, you failed. A cave troll is more like it. I heard you *before* you began your climb."

"Bah! You're no fun, anymore."

But then he hugged her. Magena responded lovingly, pressing her cheek against his weathered face. They stood side by side—she a full span taller—and looked down at their village.

"I love you, Magena," Takoda whispered. "You were not born from my seed, but I'm as proud as any father can be. None among the Ropakans can boast of a finer child. Having you as a daughter has been a high honor."

"Dear one, having you as a father has been a far higher honor. You rescued me from a monster and invited me into your family—with arms open wide. I owe you more than my life. Without you, I wouldn't have my soul."

"You owe me nothing that you haven't already repaid a thousand times."

They hugged again and then stood together silently. Below them, their village roared to life. Tonight, the Ropakans would give thanks to the Great Spirit for the year's first crop of corn. Dancing and feasting would last until morning. Venison, bear, and turkey were already roasting. Potatoes, beans, and nuts simmered in clay pots. Peaches, berries, and figs were spread on long tables. Black tea brewed from smoked holly leaves stood alongside apple wine and cornstalk beer. There was more food and drink than twice their number could consume.

"Come, daughter. We must return to the village before your mother's side of the family eats everything."

Just then, the drums rumbled. The ceremony had begun. A smile spread across Magena's beautiful face, and she laughed again.

"Race you there!" she said, sprinting down the hill.

Fewer than 5,000 Ropakans were sprinkled throughout the vastness of the Mahaggata Mountains. Magena's village contained about 500 Ropakans divided into ten clans. Takoda was the village chief and patriarchal head of his clan, whose members were ranked according to the proximity of their kinship to their leader. Highest was his eldest brother, Akando, who would become chief if Takoda were to perish. Next came two younger brothers and three sisters, followed by his father, mother, wife, three sons, four daughters (including Magena), and thirteen grandchildren. But all members of Takoda's clan, regardless of nobility, came to him for advice, guidance, and spiritual blessings.

Magena scampered through an opening in the palisade, a circular fence of pointed logs that surrounded her father's village. She passed huts of various sizes, some housing as few as four, others more than a dozen.

Given her status as daughter of the chief, Magena lived with her family in the largest and most elaborate hut in the village, the lone dwelling in the central plaza. Its roof and walls were water-proofed with sheets of bark from hickory trees. To create more height, the floor was dug several spans below the ground. A hearth used for cooking or heating stood in the center.

Magena joined the rest of the villagers in the plaza and stood beneath the ceremonial pole, which had been hewed from the trunk of a yellow poplar and was fifty cubits tall. She admired the trail of decorations carved on the pole depicting what the Ropakans called the Path of Beauty. To recognize their own inner splendor, Magena's people believed they needed to travel a path that acknowledged the beauty in all living beings. The perfect balance that allowed the pole to stand upright mimicked the balance of nature. All the village's major celebrations and ceremonies occurred in a clearing surrounding the pole.

Several blazing fires lighted the clearing. More than a dozen men carrying deerskin drums already encircled the ceremonial pole. Their faces were painted with red ocher, and they wore feather headdresses adorned with fresh flowers. Jingly bells of varying shapes and sizes hung from their breechcloths, wrists, and ankles.

More scantily clad men and women accompanied the drummers. They shook hollow gourds filled with dried corn. The pounding and rattling produced an infectious rhythm, signaling the official beginning of the celebration. Magena, wearing a mulberry shawl and a short skirt, grabbed a wooden flute and blended into the throng, dancing with her mother, sisters, and dozens of other women around the fires.

The full moon rose over the peaks of the southeastern mountains. Magena left the dancers, walked to the edge of the firelight, and gazed at the golden orb. The sunlight reflecting off its mottled surface filled her with joy, and a blessed strength surged through her body. But something disturbed her. She could sense danger but couldn't identify what it might be. She decided it was just her imagination and rejoined her family by the fires.

Takoda emerged from the darkness. Magena giggled with delight. Her father wore a headdress made from the red-tipped feathers of a war eagle sewn into a deerskin bonnet. Strings of beads and strips of colorful fur dangled over his face, which was painted red with a black circle around one eye and a white circle around the other. He also wore a bear-claw necklace, a brightly dyed breechcloth, and moccasins laden with green gemstones.

When Takoda appeared, it was a signal to begin the communal blessing. In silence, the chief danced slowly within the plaza's interior, pressing his hand against the right breast of each adult male and the right cheek of each adult female. The children received three quick taps on the tops of their heads. Before touching each villager, the chief spoke his or her name and then gazed toward the heavens, the dwelling place of the Great Spirit. When he came to Magena, he smiled more deeply than he had for any other.

The blessing ceremony was long but pleasurable. Afterward, the villagers broke their silence with hoots and screams. The wild dancing resumed, and they consumed large quantities of beer and wine. The intoxicated villagers danced frenetically, stomping their feet and twisting their bodies into impossible postures. Singing, shouting, and chanting grew in intensity until everyone leaped about in a communal hysteria.

Around midnight, the village shaman entered the plaza wearing a fearsome mask. His skin was painted black, and his hair was slathered with bear fat streaked with red ocher. He danced and ranted until he became covered with sweat, the bear fat gushing down the back of his neck. He wailed and fell to the ground, his body squirming. In a bizarre response to his antics, a buzzing swarm of flies swept into the plaza and swirled among the villagers. The children covered their faces and rushed about in a panic.

Suddenly, the shaman's body ceased to quiver, and he lay still as a corpse. The flies flew into the fires, sizzling and popping like kernels of corn. Gouts of black smoke rose from the flames. When all the insects were consumed, a dreadful silence ensued. And the shaman had run off.

The wary villagers whispered among themselves about the meaning of the portent. But Takoda spoke calming words and their good spirits returned along with their hunger. While the Ropakans ate their fill, the two eldest men in the village stood beneath the ceremonial pole and sang a mournful ballad that Magena adored. The somber lyrics described the long history of her people, including the glory of their traditions and the greatness of their ancestors.

As morning approached, unmarried couples separated from the gathering and went to private places. During these special celebrations, there was much lovemaking. Women went from man to man and men from woman to woman, while the married adults and children remained in the plaza.

Magena was the exception. Though unattached, she sat alone at a long table munching on a roasted ear of corn and drinking black tea. She had eaten a great deal, abating her earlier drunkenness. But her head still swam as she watched the others wander into the darkness. Aponi, one of her younger sisters, had gone off with a stout male warrior admired throughout the village. Aponi was 15, old enough to marry if she so desired.

Though three years older, Magena had not yet married. This wasn't unusual. Many chose not to wed, preferring to extend the pleasures of sexual promiscuity. But the white princess, as they called her, wasn't interested in that. Her heart lay elsewhere, though she couldn't say why.

The son of the patriarch of the second highest-ranked clan approached Magena. His name was Kuruk, which meant *"bear"* in her people's tongue. Though he was the same age as Magena, he already was the largest man in the village, as tall as she and heavily muscled. Not even Takoda could match his physical strength.

Kuruk had long desired her, and every time Magena refused him, he grew angrier. When he sat down next to her, she tensed. He was very drunk.

"My pale flower," he said with stinking breath, "now is the time for you and me to join ..."

Magena didn't allow him to finish.

"I've told you I reject your attentions. There are many in the village who desire you, but I'm not among them. I have no interest in you or *anyone*. Please accept this as my final answer."

Kuruk stood awkwardly, knocking the table sideways. Plates of food tumbled onto the ground. This caught the attention of the villagers who had remained in the plaza, including Takoda.

"You filthy *watsquerre* (swine)," Kuruk said to Magena. "If you knew me, you wouldn't speak to me like this. You have no *idea* who I am or what I'm about. I've come to save you. Without me to protect you, they will slaughter you like all the rest."

Takoda became enraged. "What madness is this? Are you *katichhei* (a rogue)? You're no better than the Mogols."

Kuruk spun toward Takoda. The sudden movement caused him to lose his balance, and he almost fell. When he regained his bearings, anger twisted his face. "*Occooahawa* (old fool)! You call me *katichhei*? I call you *tauh-he* (a dog)."

Even as Kuruk uttered his insulting words, a scream erupted from one of the small huts nearest the palisade. The shaman came out of the darkness, holding his throat. Blood spilled between his fingers and seeped down his forearms. He stumbled into the clearing and fell onto the sandy floor of the plaza. The expression on his mask didn't change.

Takoda was the first to realize their peril.

"Mogols have come! Flee ... *everyone!*"

Takoda ran toward his hut to get a weapon, but Kuruk stepped in front of him. The larger man pulled a knife from his breechcloth and swept it at Takoda's stomach, trying to disembowel him. But Kuruk's drunkenness was not feigned and he missed his mark, losing his balance and falling against Takoda, who grasped Kuruk's wrist and then drove his knee into Kuruk's elbow. Magena heard a popping sound. Kuruk collapsed.

Magena picked up the knife and handed it to her father. "What are we to do?" she shouted.

"Take your mother and sisters and escape to the mountains. Stay alive! I will find you."

There was another scream—and then several more. Hundreds of ghostly shapes moved toward the edge of the flickering firelight. It was too late to run.

The adult males who had remained in the plaza—about fifty in all—joined Takoda, encircling the women and children. Most had no weapons, but a few held war clubs and one had a bow and arrow. Meanwhile, the screaming intensified. The invaders were going from hut to hut, butchering anyone they found.

Aponi is out there, Magena thought. *And two of my brothers.* She shuddered. But she also felt rage rising inside her, causing her flesh to glow.

Kuruk regained his feet, but he grimaced as he held his bent elbow. "Come out," he shouted at the dark shapes. "Why do you linger? They're helpless. Kill the chief and the rest will surrender."

"My son, you dishonor me with your treachery," said Kuruk's father, who stood next to Takoda. "I disown you! May your spirit wander forever with the cowards."

Several hundred Mogols entered the clearing. Their faces were adorned with hideous tattoos, and they wore necklaces made from the dried scalps of former victims. They were much larger than the Ropakans—the smallest among them dwarfed even Kuruk—and they carried bows and arrows, war clubs, spears, and long blowguns.

Their leader—the tallest of all—strode to Kuruk and placed his arm around his thick shoulders. But then another person emerged from the darkness, stunning Magena and her father far worse than Kuruk's betrayal.

"How can you do this to our people?" Takoda said to the newcomer, tears spilling from his eyes. "To our *children*?"

Akando, the eldest brother of Takoda, didn't reply with words. He just smiled, which was more disturbing than anything else he could have done.

Magena's heart imploded. She turned to Takoda and saw only misery. Rage boiled inside her, growing stronger and more dangerous with each passing moment.

The Mogol leader was a span taller than Akando. Magena had seen no one so heavily muscled. But something about him didn't look quite human. His skin was too oily and his teeth too sharp.

"Porisāda!" Takoda said.

The word meant man-eater. These Mogols were the most dangerous of their kind. They not only raided other tribes, they also cannibalized them. The Ropakans feared the Porisādas more than any creatures that roamed the Mahaggata Mountains.

"Akando, my brother …" Takoda said, his voice wavering. "Why did you lead these fiends through our gates?"

Akando continued to smile, but his eyes were dull and his arms limp. With a strange feeling of relief, Magena realized her uncle had not committed this treason voluntarily. Another force was at work that was greater than any Mogol.

The Porisāda sneered at Takoda. "Be still, old man," he said in the common tongue. "You lack Akando's wisdom. Your brother's cooperation will be rewarded in this lifetime and the next."

"I will also be rewarded," said Kuruk, still nursing his grotesquely bent elbow.

"Yes, Kuruk will be rewarded," the leader said. To Magena, it felt like he was hungrily eyeing the Ropakan's thick torso. "He'll be the *first* to be rewarded."

But Kuruk didn't recognize his peril. He was too caught up in his own pride. "Akando and I will choose one among you to be our slave," he boasted. "I don't know, or care, who Akando favors, but my choice is clear. Magena is mine!"

A moment later, Kuruk's own knife left Takoda's hand. Five inches of the blade dug into the traitor's chest, piercing his foul heart and ending his life. Immediately after, a single arrow flew from the inner circle, striking one cannibal's thigh. But that was the extent of the Ropakans' resistance. The Porisādas rushed forward, launching poisoned darts with their blowguns and slaughtering men, women, and even children. Magena's mother died before her eyes. Some of her sisters and brothers also fell. Either by luck or design, none of the black-feathered darts struck her. But Takoda was pierced many times. Still, he lurched forward and wrapped his fingers around the leader's throat.

Magena chased after him, but she was too late, watching in horror as the cannibal placed his immense hands on either side of Takoda's head and squeezed. Her peace-loving father was no match for such a monster. His skull cracked.

The sight of Takoda's gruesome death freed Akando from the spell cast upon him. He yanked a dagger from the cannibal's breechcloth and drove it between his enemy's ribs. The Porisāda howled but was not mortally wounded. He swept his arm against Akando's face and knocked the smaller man off his feet. The act of bravery gave Magena just enough time to attack. She leaped over her father's fallen body and pounced upon the leader's chest, pressing her face so close their noses touched.

"*Namuci*," she whispered.

The Porisāda flung Magena away, but his doom was sealed. His head snapped back and he crumpled to the ground, vomiting blood. Soon after, his writhing stopped.

Magena loomed over his corpse, her eyes glowing like the Ripe Corn Moon which was now setting over the northwestern peaks. She raised her head slowly and scanned the plaza. Akando was dazed but otherwise unhurt. The rest of the Porisādas stood still as statues, watching her with a kind of awe. She continued to study her surroundings, trying to determine the scale of the carnage. What she saw wrenched her heart. Most of her people were dead. Several women and children remained standing, but the darts had slain all the men, including her brothers and many other relatives. She remembered Takoda once telling her the cannibals used poison to tenderize the flesh of their victims and prevent the bodies from spoiling.

"I'm sorry, white princess," she heard Akando saying. "The demon Vedana put a spell on me, and I couldn't resist her biddings. I'm weak and shameful. The Great Spirit won't allow me to join our fallen warriors in their place of glory. I'll wander with Kuruk among the cowards."

"Demon?" Magena said, still in a state of shock. "Where?"

"Here … my darling." An elderly woman emerged from the darkness. Her hair was long and gray, and her eyes glowed magically like Magena's. But the similarity between their eyes ended there. The old woman's irises were black instead of blue-gray.

The Porisādas bowed.

"You must say the word, again," Akando said urgently. "Don't be concerned with us. We've already lost. Only you can avenge us."

"But the others …"

"Would you prefer they become slaves—or worse?"

The demon, meanwhile, had approached within five paces, and she listened to their conversation with amusement. "Do you know who I am?" she said to Magena in fluent Ropakan.

"You're a monster and a murderer. But you'll pay for what you've done."

"*You* will make me pay? You would hurt your own grandmother?"

"What?" Magena mumbled.

"Say the word before she puts a spell on you!" Akando said.

Vedana, grandmother of Invictus *and* Magena, glared at Akando. "You're no longer useful." The demon raised her fists in the air and cracked them together. A crimson tendril of lightning leaped from her hands and struck Akando in the chest. His torso burst into flames.

"No!" Magena cried, leaping toward her uncle, but she could do nothing but watch him die.

"Kill them all," the demon said in the common tongue. "Except for the girl."

The cannibals launched more darts, and soon the rest were dead. The screaming ended almost as quickly as it started.

Two Porisādas grabbed Magena's arms, but she barely noticed. Everyone she cared about had perished. Rage consumed her consciousness. "*Namuci!*" she screamed with all the strength she could muster. "*Naaaamuuuuuciiii!*"

"Run, you fools!" Vedana shouted at the Porisādas. "Get out of here now!"

But it was too late. Magena had unleashed an army of *efrits*. The cannibals screamed, fell, and bled. Within a minute, all the Porisādas were dead.

Only two women remained alive.

Vedana and Magena.

The demon and the sorceress.

They stared into each other's eyes, daring the other to make the first move.

"Your powers are impressive, Laylah," the demon said. "But I'll have to insist that you never do that again. My little babies are like bees. Once they sting, they die. And there are only so many remaining in my realm. They're too valuable to be used with such recklessness."

"I don't know what you're talking about," Magena said. "And why do you call me Laylah? That's not my name, foul wench."

"Come now, Laylah," the demon purred, circling her adversary. "Surely you haven't forgotten your *real* name. You were 10 years old when your father—*my* son—was murdered. You were no baby. I'm sure you remember it like it was yesterday."

"You rave. My father was your son? The filth between his toes was sweeter than you. You're despicable. But your time has ended. I will destroy you."

Vedana cackled. "Before you destroy me, wouldn't you like to know who I am and why I've gone to all this trouble?" The demon circled ever closer, her movements hypnotic. "Do you think the tiresome squabbles between Mogols and Ropakans interest me?"

"Monsters need no justification. They take pleasure in torment and suffering. But enough talk. Come no closer!"

Now just a step away, Vedana stopped and faced Magena. She wore robes made of cloth as translucent as her flesh. Magena could see the demon's internal organs wriggling like a ball of snakes.

"Who taught you the word that you used to destroy the Porisādas?" Vedana said.

Magena didn't answer. Her fists clenched and unclenched while her golden hair swirled in the breeze.

"Never mind, you don't have to tell me. Your brother was such a naughty boy. Can you believe I had no idea he was visiting you all those nights? Vedana, mother of all demons, fooled by a child. Vedana, who has existed for a thousand centuries, deceiving kings, seducing warriors, defeating wizards, conjurers, and necromancers. Yet, this *boy* could trick me. He made me sleep without my even knowing it, and he then flew to see you on the back of a dracool. I would have forbidden it. But that wouldn't have stopped him. And to top it off, he had the gall to teach you some of *my* magic."

"Why *are* you here?" Magena said. "Even if I believed your lies, I wouldn't rush to you with open arms. Look at what you've done! These people were my family. My father is dead at my feet."

"Your father has been dead for eight years," Vedana said. "And your people—your *real* people—are now your brother's slaves. But I'm glad to have piqued your curiosity. Perhaps you'll listen to me before you *destroy* me. To answer your question, I'm here because Invictus is as much my enemy as yours." Then Vedana looked around, suddenly paranoid. Her voice fell to almost a whisper. "Do you know he searches for you? That he's obsessed with you? He's close, Laylah. Very close. Do you wish to become his prisoner? Once he captures you, there'll be no escape."

"If any of this is true, why didn't you just come and talk to me about it? Why kill these innocent people?"

"I care naught for people, innocent or otherwise. Their lives are short and pitiful, swallowed by the vastness of time. If 'people' are in my way, I remove them. What does it matter? They will skitter on to their next existences—and the next and the next—always blind, always ignorant. But you're different, Laylah. Demon blood rages through your veins. With me as your teacher, you might one day become strong enough to face your brother and avenge your *real* father's death. There was demon blood in his veins, too. But compared to you and your brother, he was a weakling." Vedana beckoned with her hand. "Will you not come with me? These humans were chattel, doomed to die. Whether today, or a few puny decades from now, what difference is there? Don't waste your energy on sadness or regret. You're the granddaughter of Vedana! You have the potential for *greatness*. I can teach you how to achieve it."

"If achieving greatness means forsaking the ones I love, I'd prefer to die now and be done with it."

"That could be arranged. But not yet."

Suddenly, Vedana was just an arm's length away, her face a mask of rage. Gray smoke gushed from her swollen nostrils. "*Niddaayahi!*" the demon said.

Magena felt darkness press against her consciousness. She lashed out with a blast of power, lifting several bodies into the air, including Takoda's.

But this didn't harm Vedana. Magena struck again and again, but she could not see and could not feel. The foul smoke found its way into her lungs, into her blood, into her heart.

"I'm sorry, father," Magena mumbled. "I've failed you. I've failed everyone."

But whether she actually said it—or just dreamed that she said it—was beyond her awareness. She also wasn't sure to which father she spoke. Perhaps it was both.

When she woke, Magena was no longer.

For better or worse, she was Laylah.

The little girl on the swing.

In love with the night.

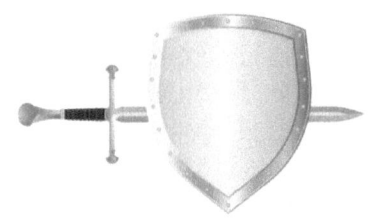

RETURN TO AVICI

In her dream, Laylah was back in the village where she had lived as a child, and she lay on a woolen bed cover in the small but cozy room she had loved so much. She was 10 years old, and her father and mother were alive and happy.

Laylah could smell roasted pork and baked bread. And she could hear her mother chopping vegetables for a salad that would include parsley, borage, and thyme.

A welcomed visitor told a joke, prompting laughter. She recognized Takoda's voice. The chieftain conversed with Gunther and Stēorra in the Ropakan tongue. Her parents replied in the common tongue. But all understood one another like old friends enjoying each other's company. Somewhere in the back of her mind, Laylah knew that Gunther and Stēorra had never met Takoda. But in the dream, it seemed real.

Laylah was in bliss. She would join the three most wonderful people in the world at her parents' sturdy dining table. Before they ate, Takoda would recite a chant to honor the Great Spirit, provider of life. Her parents, whose religious beliefs were like those practiced by the Jivitans, would thank the *One God* for their bountiful meal.

But something was wrong. It gnawed at her, attempting to devour her delight. Her bed used to be so comfortable, but now it felt lumpy.

"Mommy? Are you there? I don't feel very good."

She heard no response. She tried to stand but found she could not. Her thin arms and legs were knotted up in her bed cover. The more she struggled, the more entangled she became. The woolen fibers stank like manure. It was difficult to breathe.

"Time for dinner," she heard Stēorra say. "Laylah … come to the table. We're waaaiting."

But Laylah couldn't escape her bed, which thumped up and down like an angry beast, sickening her stomach.

"Mommy! Daddy! The bed won't let me get up."

She heard her mother giggle. What a silly thing for a child to say. Gunther and Takoda also seemed to think it was funny, but they sounded more like they were growling than laughing.

"Wake up, little one," she heard Stēorra sing. The words made Laylah recoil. Her mother had never called her *little one*. But someone else had, someone she despised.

"Wake up, little one," said the voice that was not her mother's. "We're almost there. Soon, your training will begin."

When Laylah opened her eyes, she found she was strapped to the back of a black mountain wolf, the largest and most dangerous of its kind. Several others were within her range of vision, walking in single file along a path that wound between rock walls leaning inward as if eager to collapse upon her.

The wolf in front of her sensed her awakening and twisted its head back to look at her. She could see its sharp teeth and dog-like face in the dim light of dawn.

"Wake up, little one!" said Vedana, who rode the lead wolf about twenty paces ahead. "After we enter the den, you'll begin your training."

"Never," Laylah muttered.

The wolf she rode growled. Vedana chortled. "We shall see, little one."

Laylah came fully awake. Vedana had tied her arms around the wolf's neck, and a tight stretch of rope ran from ankle to ankle beneath the beast's belly. There was just enough slack for her to turn her head from side to side, though even that was painful.

Laylah wondered how long she'd been unconscious—enough time, at least, for the wolf to carry her out of the valley and onto the slope of a mountain. But Laylah, who had explored all the mountains near her village, didn't recognize this path, which crisscrossed upward toward a towering summit.

"How long have I been asleep?" Laylah said. The wolf growled again, the thick muscles of its neck bulging beneath her breasts.

"Longer than you would like, I'm sure," Vedana said. "You've slept for two full days, mostly on Nagua's back. When I bring on sleep, it lasts longer than any other. We've traveled more than twenty leagues. From the top of this mountain, you can see the Gap of Gamana."

"You lie," said Laylah, who then attempted—and failed—to break her restraints. Nagua twisted his head and snapped at her.

Laylah wasn't afraid. "I'll kill you, wolf. And then I'll kill your master."

"You would find that difficult," Vedana said. "But just in case, I've taken precautions."

"You're full of bluster," Laylah said. "But I don't fear you. What have I to lose? When my strength returns, I'll break these bonds and throttle you with my bare hands."

"Bluster, you say. Was it *bluster* that caused you to sleep for two days? Was it *bluster* that secured the talisman around your throat, rendering you powerless?"

"Talisman?" Laylah suddenly understood why she was having so much trouble breathing. A thin cord was wrapped around her neck. Attached to the cord was a cold sliver of metal that pressed against her skin.

Even as a little girl, Laylah had conjured white flames on her fingertips. The boy—her brother—had helped refine her skills during his frequent visits to the sycamore swing. But when Laylah now tried to summon flames to sunder the ropes that bound her wrists, the talisman flared, causing an eruption of agony. It felt like a hot coal was burning a hole in her flesh.

Laylah cried out.

And coughed.

Up ahead, Vedana laughed heartily. "Keep struggling, little one. The more you struggle, the more pain you'll feel. And the more pain you feel, the more I'll like it!"

Laylah pressed her face against Nagua's coarse fur and sobbed. When she regained some control, she peered down to see if the ropes were charred, but they were unharmed.

"What have you done to me?"

"I've used this talisman against many enemies, all of whom are now dead."

Until this point in her young life, Laylah's strength had never been fully tested. When Invictus murdered her parents, she had fled rather than fight him, making no attempt to rescue Gunther and Stēorra. She spent the next eight years convincing herself there was nothing she could have done, that she was just a child, that Invictus was too strong. Then during her life with the Ropakans, Takoda had urged her to veil her powers, fearing she would become an outcast if she were seen as a sorceress. Her slaughter of the Porisādas had been, by far, her most extravagant display of magic.

But Laylah was finished with cowardice and concealment. While the cannibals writhed in the blood that spewed from their mouths, she had not felt pity. It had been pleasurable to show no mercy to those who tormented her.

Her only desire was to wreak more havoc. Laylah attempted to shout the deadly word Invictus had taught her. She now knew it would have no effect on Vedana, but at least she could kill the wolves. But when she tried to say the word, her tongue became tangled in her mouth in the same frustrating manner she'd endured whenever she'd tried to tell her parents about Invictus visiting her at the swing. The talisman she wore scorched like a fire she could not extinguish. She screamed at Vedana to stop the agony. Then she begged.

The demon only laughed.

"I can make the pain even worse if you don't do what you're told," she heard Vedana saying through the avalanche of suffering. "Eventually, you'll thank me for this."

Unconsciousness took pity on Laylah, closing over her like the lid of a coffin. She returned to the world of dreams. Gunther, Stēorra, and Takoda rejoined her, but now their bodies were bloated and decayed. They reached for her with clawed fingers. Laylah knew, the way you know in dreams, that they blamed her for everything.

When Laylah opened her eyes again, it took her a long time to come to her senses. Now she lay on her back on a bed of stone, iron cuffs securing her arms and ankles. Except for the talisman around her throat, she was naked.

A lone torch provided the only light, revealing a musty cavern somewhere inside the mountain. Water dripped off the stone ceiling. It was a miserable place. She was alone.

Or was she? She heard footsteps. Voices. Unpleasant laughter.

"I believe ssshe's awake," a sultry female voice said. "I've never met sssuch a sleepyhead."

"My talisman has that effect," said a second voice, which Laylah recognized as Vedana.

Laylah lifted her head. Shadows emerged from a passageway and two figures entered the torchlight: Vedana, appearing slightly hunched and elderly, along with the most beautiful woman Laylah had ever seen. She had green eyes and waist-length auburn hair, and she smelled like wildflowers.

"My *my*, she isss attractive," the woman said, admiring Laylah's nakedness. "Vedana, she's the prettiest you've ever made."

"How would *you* know, Chal? I've been making them long before I brought you into the world."

"Oh, mistress ... don't be sssilly. I am Chal-Abhinno, queen of the Warlish witches. I know many things."

"Where am I?" said Laylah, finding the strength to speak. "What are you going to do with me?"

"She livesss" was Chal's response.

The witch and demon walked to separate sides of the stone bed. Chal smiled sweetly, but her eyes roamed, her pupils expanding and contracting eerily.

Laylah blushed.

"Don't be embarrassed," Chal said sweetly. "I don't like girlsss that way ... very often."

"Don't believe her lies," Vedana said. In comparison, the demon's voice sounded uncouth.

"Mistress, why are you being ssso mean today?"

"You know why. Don't play stupid."

"Why do youuu worry so much? If he somehow found us, the Mogols would warn usss before he got here. There are places to hide deep in the mountain that not even he could discover."

"I need *time*, you dimwitted whore. Time to work with her and train her. But it now appears I won't get it." Then she smacked her foot on the hard stone floor. "We're too close to Avici. I should have taken Laylah to the forest instead of here. Invictus' influence doesn't reach *that* far yet."

"What are you going to do with me?" Laylah repeated.

Chal giggled. "And youuu call *me* dimwitted," she said to Vedana.

"Unlike you and me, Laylah has led a sheltered life—except, of course, for the *incident* with her parents and my grandson," Vedana said. "That could not have been pleasant."

"What would Invictus want with me?" Laylah said. "Doesn't he have a wife and family by now?"

Vedana and Chal burst into laughter.

"*Doesn't he have a wife and family by now?*" said Chal, impersonating Laylah with spooky precision. "Does thisss child know *anything?*"

"She's never been properly trained," Vedana said. "First, I would need to break her will. But even then, it would take years to make her truly dangerous. When she was young, Invictus secretly taught her a few words of power and some simple spells. Otherwise, she's a novice."

"What does Invictus want with me?" shouted Laylah, her voice echoing in the chamber. "Do not speak in riddles. *Tell* me!" Laylah fought to break her restraints. Her flesh glowed in the semidarkness, super-heating the iron cuffs. But as soon as her power emanated, the talisman sent blistering jolts of agony into her throat that radiated through her head and chest.

"Are you finished, little one?" Vedana said. "Fighting will do you no good. The talisman is too strong. There are few on Triken with the power to resist it." The demon then turned to Chal. "I can sense my grandson's presence better than anyone. After all, I taught him everything he knows. And what did he do in return? Threatened to destroy me. Not in so many words, but I could see it in his eyes. His growth never slows. Every day, he becomes stronger." Vedana gazed at the passageway. "When he arrives, there'll be no place to hide. Not deep in the mountain. Not anywhere. If we want to survive, our only choice will be to flee and hope that when he finds Laylah, he'll forget about us."

"He believes I'm his friend," Chal said. "I've shown him where to find slavesss. I've lured creatures to Avici to join his army. We're close, Invictus and I. If he had discovered thisss hiding place, I would know it."

"You know only what he wishes you to know," Vedana said. "You're close because he allows you to be. *Fool!* He is beyond you. If he doesn't yet recognize you as a traitor, it's because you're too small in his estimation to be of much concern."

Then the demon glared at the witch distrustfully, with eyes that glowed like fire. "I warn you. Do not betray me! I'm sure it has crossed your mind. But my magic created you. If I perish, so will you—and all your sisters."

Chal backed away, dropped to her knees, and covered her face.

Laylah could see only the top of the woman's head. The witch's auburn hair curled and turned gray, and black smoke oozed from the pores of her skin, saturating the cavern with a sickening stench. When Chal rose to her feet, a devil stood where an angel had been.

Laylah recoiled.

"Oh, don't look so disgusssted," the hideous version of Chal said. "A lady can't always be at her best." Then she turned to Vedana. "I'll never betray you, mistress. You gave me the giftsss of long life and powerful magic. For that, I'll be forever grateful."

Vedana started to respond, but a shuffling sound near the mouth of the passageway stopped her. A second witch—as hideously ugly as Chal had just become—rushed into the cavern.

"Mistress … Invictus approaches!" the witch said to Vedana. "He's alone except for a pair of dracoolsss, but the Mogols and wolves dare not confront him. His body glowsss like the sun. The trees bow before him. Even the stones fear him. What are we to do?"

Vedana hissed. Chal and the other witch backed toward the exit. It wasn't safe to be near the mother of all demons when she was in a foul mood.

Vedana sniffed the air. "Flee! Don't let him see you."

Chal and the second witch scrambled into the passageway. Laylah began to shake uncontrollably. Then she turned to the demon, who seemed amused by Laylah's terror.

"Do *I* make you tremble? Wait until you see what *he* does to you. But there's one last way I can thwart him."

With the agility of a spider, the demon pounced onto the stone bed and crouched near Laylah's feet. Vedana growled, exposing a long black tongue. Then she placed her glowing hand on her granddaughter's stomach and began to knead her flesh.

The mere touch sickened Laylah. She fought against the restraints until her wrists and ankles bled, and she screamed until her throat burned. But the demon would not remove her hand, which scorched her abdomen like a branding iron. The revulsion became too great, and Laylah's mind ran like a coward toward the comfort of unconsciousness.

When she woke, Vedana was gone.

As Vedana pressed her hand on Laylah's abdomen, the demon's dark essence worked its magic. From the Realm of Undeath, she called upon an extra-special *efrit* that was larger and stronger than any other, giving it a silent command that it would follow until the end of its existence: Do nothing to harm Laylah unless Invictus forced his magic on her to impregnate her.

Vedana passed the efrit from her hand into her granddaughter's womb, where it would nestle harmlessly for the rest of Laylah's life if Invictus behaved himself. If he didn't, the *efrit* would awaken and devour Laylah's womb.

A forced pregnancy—even if only a result of magic—would be impossible. Only a seduction Laylah desired would allow her to conceive a child.

Vedana fled the cave. She didn't have the strength to defeat Invictus in open battle, but neither was she helpless. She had accomplished her goal. Laylah would remember little of what happened in the chamber, but Invictus would find out soon enough. Vedana had earned a measure of revenge. And Invictus would be helpless to undo it. If he attempted to remove the *efrit*, it would chew apart Laylah's insides.

Laylah first met Invictus when she was 5 years old. He murdered their parents when she was 10. Eight years after that, she was about to meet him again.

She woke from the demon's spell with a squeal, but when she tried to rise, she found herself still shackled to the stone bed in the dank chamber. Vedana was gone—and the dreadful talisman with her.

Without the evil magic to thwart her, Laylah folded her fingers over the palms of her hands and pressed them against the iron cuffs, bathing the metal with white fire. The cuffs superheated, melted, and disintegrated. Then she sat up and reached for the ones around her ankles. But something in the passageway caused her to pause. She saw a faint yellow glow far back in the tunnel, and she watched with dread as it grew progressively brighter. And hotter. A portion of her mind screamed at her paralysis. *Free yourself! Run! Anywhere.* But a morbid fascination held her in place. Her brother was coming. And she could do nothing.

Laylah's worst fears took hold. Though she'd tried for eight years to erase the memory of that horrid day, it had tormented her mercilessly. Every lurid detail remained embedded in her recollections. She sat on the stone bed and replayed the horror in her mind. When she thought of Invictus, a wicked cramp seized her abdomen. She cried out, held her stomach, and sobbed. How could she bear to look at his face again?

The glow grew painfully bright, turning the oily water on the chamber's ceiling to steam. A spherical blob of energy emerged from the passageway and hovered nearby, resembling a miniature sun. She cowered before it.

Slowly, the radiance dimmed and a human body formed in its place. Yellow hair. Brown eyes. Boyish face.

"Hello, Laylah," Invictus said. "It has been a long time. I've missed you."

"Please, leave me alone," she whimpered.

Invictus smiled. "Do you believe I intend to hurt you?" he said cheerfully. "You're my little sister. I love you."

"You've already hurt me."

Invictus sighed. "What I did wasn't very nice. Is that what you want to hear? But time heals all. Now, both of us are older and wiser. And you've become quite beautiful."

Laylah covered her bare breasts with her arms. His words awoke a long-suppressed rage. When she screamed at him, her voice echoed in the chamber. "You're saying that murdering our parents wasn't *very nice*? I suppose, in your mind, it was their fault!"

Instead of becoming angry, Invictus chuckled. "No, it wasn't their fault. At least, not in the way you mean. But they were expendable. You and I are all that matter. The Sun God and the Moon Goddess, brother and sister, king and queen. Don't you understand? *Anyone* who stands against us—or between us—will perish. We are beyond reprisal."

"You keep saying *us.* But there is no *us.* I despise you!"

Without warning, she rose to her knees and extended her arms. White power spurted from her fingertips, her eyes, her mouth. It blasted him like an inferno. For what felt like a very long time, she bathed him in white flame, howling as she assailed him. Years of accumulated wrath rained down on Invictus' body. The chamber became as hot as an oven. He stood there, neither resisting nor fleeing.

When Laylah expended her strength, she fell forward. Her fire had consumed the cuffs that restrained her ankles and liquefied a portion of the stone at her feet, filling the chamber with smoke. She waited for it to dissipate, expecting to see Invictus' charred bones littering the cavern floor.

But when the smoke cleared, her brother remained standing, unharmed. Even the golden robes he wore weren't damaged. He smiled at her, full of amusement instead of anger.

"Laylah, I'm so *proud* of you. Few beings on Triken could have exerted such force, and you did it all by yourself without the benefit of training or any kind of weapon other than your own body. You're a courageous girl with great potential. I have so much to teach you. One day, you will comprehend me and forgive me."

"Never ... *never!*"

"Darling sister. *Never* is a long time. And starting now, you and I have all the time in the world. We both have the potential to live *very* long lives."

The sorcerer approached her and touched the top of her head with the palm of his right hand. A warm yellow light enveloped her flesh, causing her to collapse into a state of catatonia—but not so deep that she wasn't aware when a pair of dracools entered the room, wrapped her in golden blankets, and carried her from the chamber. And not so deep that she wasn't aware when the dracools leaped off the mountaintop and soared eastward toward Avici with her strapped to one of their backs.

When she came fully awake, what she saw stunned her. The tiny village she so fondly remembered had grown into a bustling city. Where hundreds once lived, thousands now dwelled. Avici mirrored its creator. Like Invictus, it had grown larger and more powerful every day.

Laylah would be forced to watch its continued ascension as helpless to stop it as everyone else.

The first thing Laylah noticed was the pervasive aroma of incense. She opened her eyes and turned her head slowly from side to side, finally realizing she was lying on her back on a wide bed. Her hair had been washed, combed, and strewn delicately on each side of a pillow. A sleeveless samite robe covered her otherwise naked body. Silk sheets caressed her bare arms.

Laylah sat up and gasped. A dozen yellow-haired attendants—all females wearing white tunics embroidered with golden suns—dropped to their knees in reaction to her sudden movement. Then they lowered their faces to the floor. When they finished their bow and looked up, Laylah could see their matching brown eyes.

Laylah studied her surroundings. She was in a large room that was lavishly furnished. Gold and ivory inlays wove through oaken furniture. A polished silver mirror perched enticingly on a dressing table. A marble bath built into the cement floor was well-equipped with soaps, perfumes, and towels. But despite its opulence, the room had only one window and one door. Through the window, Laylah saw a cloudless sky.

As if answering a silent summons, one attendant scampered from the room. After she departed, another woman entered whose appearance was in stark contrast to the others, her hair and eyes black. Laylah could not guess her age.

"Good morning, young princess," the woman said. "My name is Urbana, mistress of the robes, and I am under your command. These others are the ladies of the bedchamber and are under my command. I hope our accommodations meet with your approval. I made certain you were bathed and adorned in a fine robe. Doesn't she look magnificent, everyone?"

"Yes!" the others chanted in unison.

"Where am I?" she said to Urbana.

"You're in the palace of King Invictus, in the Golden City of Avici," the mistress of the robes said.

Palace? King Invictus? *Golden City* of Avici?

Laylah slid off the bed, walked to the window, and peered out the arched window. She was high above the ground in a tower built into a corner of the palace. She recognized the valley that had once contained her quiet village and could even see her precious sycamore tree only a few hundred paces away. The valley was green and untouched. But the dead volcano next to the valley that once held a few scattered huts now bore buildings, temples, and multistoried manses. Where a few had once roamed, thousands now bustled in the streets.

"Isn't it wonderful?" said a deep voice from behind.

"Yes!" the attendants chanted.

"And it's only the beginning," the voice said. "The best is yet to come."

"YES!"

Laylah whirled around. Her brother stood in the center of the room, wearing a gold tunic over a white doublet. A strange heat emanated from his eyes. Laylah felt as if she were standing too close to a fire, but when she tried to back away, she banged into the wall behind her.

"Forgive my intrusion, but your door was ajar," Invictus said. "I see you're enjoying the view. I've accomplished much in the eight years since you and I were last together."

"Yes!" the attendants responded.

Laylah's lips trembled. "You've accomplished *nothing*. You've ruined *everything*!"

Her audacity shocked the attendants, who skittered backward like a swarm of spiders. Urbana hissed. But Laylah seemed incapable of angering Invictus. Instead of lashing out at her, he laughed.

"Little one, can it be you are *still* angry with me? Oh well, it won't last forever. Once you get to know me—*really* get to know me—you will comprehend my motives and behaviors. In the meantime, I give you free rein to explore your new home. If you like, you can even visit the tree. I've left the swing in place, just for you. No one else may use it, under penalty of death." He laughed again. "By the way, don't be late for the banquet. We're preparing a feast in your honor. There are people I'd like you to meet. I have *many* friends."

Then Invictus strode through the doorway and vanished. After he was gone, the temperature in the room seemed to drop several degrees. The attendants resumed their duties. Laylah threw herself onto the bed.

"Don't despair, young princess," Urbana said. "You're safe now. King Invictus will protect you."

"Yes!" the other attendants said.

Laylah glared at Urbana. "Did you say *protect* me? He has destroyed everything—my family, my friends, my people. *Protect* me?"

"Wise kings sometimes make decisions that appear to the lesser among us to be a bit rough around the edges," Urbana said, her black eyes glistening. "When you get to know your brother better, you'll understand what drives him. He knows what is best for all of us."

"Yes!"

"You're the one who doesn't understand. My brother is evil."

"It seems that way now, young princess. But you'll learn otherwise. I can sense you're hungry; it's affecting your mood. Once you've eaten, I'll give you a tour of the palace and valley, and then you can have a bath and a nice nap. Afterward, I'll comb your hair and pick out a gown for this afternoon's festivities. You're an honored guest—sister to the king!"

"Why should I trust anything that comes from your mouth? You say you're under my command. Prove it."

"How so?"

"I command you to answer my questions. Are you in league with my brother willingly or as his slave?"

Urbana shook her head as if amused by such naivety. "I'm neither willing nor enslaved. I'm a disciple—as are all who dwell in Avici. King Invictus is a god, not a man. Compared to him, we are insignificant. But he loves us, anyway. What choice is there but to follow him?"

"You're mad. Leave me alone! Get out of here."

"As you command, young princess."

But before Urbana and the other attendants left the room, one girl placed a tray containing roasted chicken, baked apples, creamed corn, white cheese, crispy wafers, and an ewer of spiced wine on a table near the window. The door closed gently. Laylah was blessedly alone. She immediately ran to the window. She was far too high to attempt a jump, and the walls of the tower were faced with polished ashlars that were probably too slippery to surmount. Frantically, Laylah explored the room, looking for any kind of weapon that might aid in her escape, but she found nothing but a wooden hairbrush.

She went to the door and gently pulled on its handle to test if it was locked. The door swung open, so she peered into the hall. The ladies of the bedchamber knelt on a plush rug on the cement floor. Urbana sat in a padded chair against the far wall.

"Is there anything we can do for you, young princess?" the mistress of the robes said. "Is the food to your liking? What other comforts might we provide?"

Laylah slammed the door, retreated to the center of the room, and buried her face in her hands. For the first time—but certainly not the last—she sobbed.

After what felt like a long time, Laylah stopped crying. Then she lay on the bed, lost in her thoughts. How long had it been since Vedana had approached her in the village? And how much time had passed since Invictus had found her in the cave? She remembered being strapped to the back of a black mountain wolf some time in between. But what stood out most was the dreadful pain of the talisman that had clung to her throat. Laylah could still hear the demon's laughter through the cacophony of her own wails.

Remembering the slaughter of her people reduced her to another fit of sobbing. How could she continue to live after experiencing such horror? Everyone she'd ever loved was dead, and now she was the prisoner of a madman. This time, it took even longer to regain control of her emotions.

Despite the enormity of her sorrow, Laylah found herself drawn to the tray of food. She had no idea how long it had been since she'd eaten. The chicken meat had cooled to room temperature, but it still smelled delicious. As a little girl, she had adored baked apples and creamed corn. And she'd eaten barrels of white cheese. How did Invictus know she favored these foods? Even then, he must have been watching her closely. The thought made her shiver.

Her hunger overcame her despair. A spoon was her only utensil, but the fowl had been cut into bite-sized pieces that she picked up with her fingers, and the apples and corn were wonderful. She ate all the cheese and wafers and drank the entire ewer of wine. After taking her last sip, she heard a tapping at her door.

Laylah stared at the entryway, not saying a word, waiting to see if the visitor would enter uninvited. But no one did. She counted thirty breaths before hearing another series of taps, this time with more force.

Laylah sighed. "Come in! It's not like I can do anything to stop you."

The door opened and Urbana peered into the room.

"You'll be pleased to learn that, starting now, no one may enter your room without your permission," the mistress of the robes said. "This is by order of King Invictus. I'll wait outside your door until you need my services."

"Come in," Laylah said. "I give you *permission*. Besides, I have more questions."

Laylah's submission seemed to please Urbana the way it pleases a nanny when a wayward child finally chooses to behave.

"Certainly. But may I call one of my chambermaids to remove the tray?"

"Too good to do it yourself?"

"It is not my position to clear away the remains of a meal. But if you order it, I will do so."

"Makes no difference to me."

"Thank you, young princess," Urbana said, but there was a chill in her voice.

The mistress of the robes clapped her hands. A girl darted in and removed the tray. In its place, she left a clay bowl containing a steaming towel. Laylah wiped her mouth and hands. As soon as Laylah finished, another maid raced in and removed the bowl.

Laylah was unaccustomed to luxuries or preferential treatment. Her life in Avici had been unadorned, her parents poor but comfortable. Her time with the Ropakans had been even simpler. Peace and joy had brought her pleasure, not fancy clothes or accommodations.

Urbana walked close to Laylah and examined her face. "Your eyes are bloodshot and the rouge I applied to your cheeks is smeared. I have medicine to soothe your eyes and paints for your face and lips. Will you allow me to enhance your beauty?"

"Maybe another time. For now, I have more questions."

"All of which I'll be pleased to answer. Would you care to walk while we converse? We can go outside and enjoy the fresh air, and we can even visit your swing if you like. King Invictus has told me how much you enjoyed it when you were a child."

Laylah's mind raced. Was it possible they would allow her to walk freely outside of her room? Outside of the palace? If so, how closely would she be watched? Perhaps she could find a way to escape. At least she could explore her options. Remaining shut away in the room and feeling sorry for herself would get her nowhere.

"I'll need a veil to protect my face from the sun."

The request seemed to please Urbana. When it came to clothing, the mistress of the robes appeared securely in her element. "Yes, young princess! Your closet is full of veils, hats, and cauls. And gowns designed to fit your lovely figure, little one."

Laylah cringed. "Please don't call me that. *Never* call me that."

"After tonight, I will call you queen," Urbana said. "As will all who dwell in Avici."

"*Queen* would be even worse than *little one*."

"The great cannot deny greatness."

Laylah ignored the comment. "Find me a veil," she said, and then added: "Please."

"Yes, little ... err ... young princess. It will be as you command."

After she was properly attired, Laylah left the room with Urbana at her side. They strode along a torch-lit hallway and started down a winding stair. The ladies of the bedchamber didn't follow, remaining seated on the rug by her door.

Laylah saw no windows or exits until they reached the floor of the tower and came upon two doors: one small and plain; the other much larger and adorned with intricate carvings of the phases of the moon.

"This opens into the interior gardens of the palace," Urbana said, gesturing toward the fancier door. "Many flowers and plants thrive there that don't otherwise grow in this part of the land. King Invictus has developed special ways to keep them alive. Would you care to see the gardens, young princess?"

"Where does the other door lead?"

"To a stone path that extends into the valley. It's well worth the walk. The grass is lush and bursting with blooming flowers. I've never traveled west of the mountains, but emissaries have told me that the valley of Avici is every bit as beautiful as the Green Plains. Would you prefer that door, young princess? Your favorite tree is only a short stroll from here. King Invictus purposely built his palace near the great sycamore, which is much larger, I imagine, than you will remember."

"It has only been eight years. How much could it have grown?"

"Invictus has nourished the tree, just as he has nourished the city. I've been here for only a year, and in that short time, Avici has more than doubled in size."

This didn't impress Laylah. "I'd prefer the valley over the gardens. Is the door locked?"

"It's not locked, nor is the other, but both are guarded—for your protection, of course. King Invictus grows more powerful each day, but he has jealous enemies. Your brother wouldn't want you to be harmed because of his unpopularity in certain circles."

A simple sliding latch held the smaller door in place. Laylah opened it and stepped from the semi-darkness of the stairwell into the blinding light of a late-summer morning. She covered her eyes and winced. As was often the case when she ventured outside on a sunny day, Laylah felt queasy.

But Urbana was pleased. She spread her arms and took a deep breath.

"Isn't it wonderful? Each time I walk in this valley, I feel like it's the first time I've ever walked freely beneath the sun. Come, young princess. Let us follow the path into the clearing."

"You spoke of guards, but I don't see them. Where are they hidden?"

"Do not concern yourself. If there were any trouble, they would make their presence known."

Laylah memorized her surroundings. As she faced outward from the tower, the valley was in front of her and to her right while one of the outer walls of the two-story palace was to her left. The wall was sheathed with cream-gray ashlars interspersed with squares of dark marble, and several arched windows were adorned with molded cornices and monochrome glass. Through one of these windows, Laylah could see the interior garden, where visitors wearing gold and white tunics admired the greenery.

Laylah and Urbana continued along the path. The mistress walked so quickly Laylah struggled to keep up. Thick grass grew right up to the stone, but it was well-groomed and didn't trespass beyond its borders.

They were not alone. Others wandered nearby. But something was amiss. For the most part, the residents of Avici seemed to wear vacant expressions. However, she occasionally passed someone whose countenance was anything but empty. To Laylah, these people looked hungry, and when they sneered, their stained teeth repulsed her.

All seemed to know Urbana and were respectful in her presence, but Laylah recognized no one from her past. Outwardly, this new Avici was a place of peace and prosperity. But Laylah sensed an iniquity that seeped into her bones.

As they approached the sycamore, Laylah's heart sank. The tree was not as she remembered. It had been large when she was a girl, but it was now absurdly huge—at least 100 cubits tall. The rope swing was there, with much longer ropes than it used to have.

"It's not possible," Laylah said, staring upward.

"With King Invictus, all things are possible. The sun is his mother."

"His mother is dead. In fact, he murdered his mother … *my* mother."

Urbana snapped at Laylah with a ferocity that startled her. "Your mother was nothing, *little one*! Just a small piece in a much larger puzzle. Get over it and move on. The great cannot deny greatness."

Laylah stepped back. "Who *are* you? And who are these people?"

As suddenly as her rage appeared, the blissful expression returned to Urbana's face. "I'm the mistress of the robes, of course. Have I not said so before? And 'these people' are the blessed disciples of King Invictus."

"Are they free to come and go?"

The mistress didn't answer.

"And what about me?" Laylah said. "Am *I* free to go?"

"The valley is yours."

"Can I leave the valley?"

"King Invictus would prefer you do not. It took him a long time to find you, and he desires sufficient time to earn back your trust."

"But if I tried to leave, what would happen? That is my question, servant of the *queen*. Answer it!"

Once again, Urbana's face darkened. Her mouth curled, forming a hideous leer that exposed sharp teeth. "There are those among us capable of preventing you."

"Then I'm a prisoner."

"You are god's sister. No other words need be spoken."

As if in response to the woman's pronouncement, a shadow descended from the sky, followed by a loud flapping sound and a blast of air. Several times during her life with the Ropakans, Laylah had seen dragons, though they had been just specks flying high above. But once, she'd seen a dragon up close. She and Takoda were following a blind mountain path lined on one side with a rock wall, and when they came around an exposed bend, a massive female dragon was sunning herself on a ledge. The beast was deeply asleep and didn't hear their approach, but she and Takoda were paralyzed with fear, unable to move. The dragon's golden scales glittered in the sunlight and her massive torso expanded and contracted ever so slowly as she breathed. Laylah and her father retreated, not wanting to face the beast's wrath if awoken.

In some ways, the creature that landed near Laylah looked like the dragon she'd seen that day with Takoda. But in others, it was far different. The real dragon was 100 cubits long. This creature was much smaller, about twice the height and weight of an ordinary man. And unlike a full-sized dragon, it walked on its hind legs. But it still looked dangerous, its heavy muscles covered with scales and its enormous snout filled with fangs. Laylah had heard of dracools before but had never seen one in real life.

Laylah backed away not sure what to expect, but then an even greater horror emerged from behind the dracool. Invictus climbed off its back and strolled toward her, a grin on his face. The dracool remained where it stood in obeisance to the sorcerer's will.

"Are you pleased, my sister? I preserved the tree just for you. I knew one day you would return."

"You haven't preserved it. You've changed it into a monster as gruesome as yourself."

Urbana gasped. The dracool reared up on its clawed toes and spread its leathery wings. Invictus' eyes narrowed, but he didn't lose his temper. When the dracool tromped forward, the sorcerer waved his hand and caused the creature to halt.

"After the banquet, your attitude will change. Things will be different between you and me. You have much to learn that only I can teach you. But I believe in you. And I love you. One day you will love me, too."

"I'll *never* love you. I'll *always* hate you. How many times do I have to say it?"

Invictus climbed onto the dracool's back, ignoring her comments. But just before the beast flew off, he said one last thing. "I get what I want. Not even hatred can prevent it."

Then the dracool leaped up and spiraled into the sky. Laylah watched it soar toward the palace and land on the flat roof. With Invictus gone, she felt like she could breathe again. But she knew it was temporary. She had to find a way to escape. And she needed to learn more about the layout of her prison before making the attempt.

Laylah returned to her room without resistance. To her surprise, she took a nap as Urbana had suggested, not waking until midafternoon. The breeze pouring through her window retained the unwavering warmth of late summer.

Not long after she opened her eyes, someone tapped at her door. Laylah wondered if she was being watched through a hidden hole in the wall or ceiling. The suspicion made her even more desperate. She remembered how happy she'd felt while standing on the hill with Takoda. Now that seemed like an impossibly distant memory. As long as she remained her brother's prisoner, her suffering would never cease. She would prefer to die attempting to escape than remain his captive. But if she freed herself, what then? Where would she go? Her only hope was to return to the mountains and attempt to find another Ropakan village. But she recognized—with a jolt of despair—that she would endanger the lives of anyone she joined. Would this force her to spend the rest of her life wandering alone in the wilderness, a recluse without family or friends? Even that would be preferable to her current situation.

She heard a second bout of tapping, this time with more insistence. Laylah stared at the door with dread, but she knew she couldn't continue to hide in her bedchamber feeling sorry for herself. To escape, she would need a plan. If she ran heedlessly, she wouldn't get far. Even if she could destroy those who hunted her, she would be helpless when her brother appeared. She had tested herself against him and had failed. She would have to be far from Avici before he became aware of her disappearance. It wouldn't be easy.

"Come in," Laylah said.

Urbana entered. The mistress of the robes was already dressed for the night's festivities, adorned in a full tunic with surcoat and cloak, all black. Her eyelids and lips were darkened with kohl, but her skin was as pale as white chalk. The severe contrast was disturbing, causing Laylah to shrink away.

Which made Urbana smile.

"Your brother passed me in the garden a short while ago and told me how beautiful I looked. It's obvious you agree. But enough small talk. We have barely the time to prepare you, properly, for the banquet. This is the most important night of your life, young princess. You must look the part. The guests are eager to meet you. King Invictus has bragged shamelessly about you."

"I'll gladly trade places with you."

"You see, you're regaining your sense of humor," Urbana said. "Soon, Avici will feel like home again."

"Forgive me if I disagree."

"It's futile to resist the king."

"That might be true. But there's one thing I comprehend better than anyone—the depths of his evil."

"Gods are beyond judgment. They do as they please, when they please. I've found it's best to join rather than fight. There are benefits to being a disciple of Invictus. One day, I'll tell you the wonderful things he has done for me. What your brother can accomplish when he sets his mind to it will astonish you."

Laylah changed the subject. "Let's get this over with. What am I to wear?"

Urbana's face lit up. She led Laylah to her magnificent closet on the far side of the room. Inside was an array of gowns, cloaks, undergarments, headdresses, hose, and shoes. Laylah had never seen such a fabulous wardrobe made from such exquisite fabrics and materials.

"Anything you desire will be yours. As well as growing powerful, King Invictus has become rich."

The mistress of the robes strolled to the back of the closet and brought out a silk gown with a fur-trimmed collar, cuffs, and hem. The gown looked white at first glance, but it changed colors depending on the light, transforming from white to gold to crimson.

Urbana clapped her hands, prompting an attendant to dart into the room. She was another one of her brother's bizarre look-alikes, with yellow hair and brown eyes, and she performed whatever duties Urbana commanded with the nervous rush of one who has been frequently punished for the slightest misbehavior.

"Why is she so skittish? Do you beat her if she pops a button?"

"The ladies of the chamber are my servants. And I am your servant. You need not concern yourself with their behavior."

Urbana then slapped the girl in the face. "Leave us! You've offended the young princess. Send in someone who is less clumsy."

A trickle of blood oozed from the corner of the girl's mouth. She bowed and ran from the room. Another quickly took her place.

Laylah glared into Urbana's black eyes. "*Never* do that in my presence. If you do that again, I'll slap *you*."

Urbana snarled, exposing her swollen red tongue. "My allegiance is to King Invictus. And he has commanded that I obey your orders. For that reason only, I'll do as you say. But even a queen needs to know her place."

"Our situations are more similar than you might think. Invictus protects me from you. But he also protects you from me."

The mistress of the robes smiled wickedly. "Perhaps I have underestimated you. Very well. I'll be more *respectful* to the servants while in your presence." Then she smiled in a more pleasant fashion. "But now we must hurry. King Invictus prefers to conclude his affairs before nightfall. Your coronation rapidly approaches. It will be grand, I assure you."

Laylah permitted herself to be dressed and perfumed. They braided diamonds and rubies into her lush hair, strung a pearl necklace tight to her throat, and placed a golden ring on each finger. Her youthful skin needed little adornment, but Urbana painted her lips red, put crimson rouge on her cheeks, and rubbed blue chalk beneath her eyes. When Laylah looked at herself in the silver mirror, what she saw amazed her.

"You look lovely, young miss," the new servant girl said, and then lowered her gaze as if expecting punishment for daring to speak.

But if Urbana was angry, she didn't show it.

"Doesn't she, though?" the mistress of the robes said. "This will please King Invictus."

Someone pounded on the door. The servant girl opened it and then fell to her knees with her face pressed against the floor. A dracool stood in the opening. The tall creature had to bend way down to peer into the room.

"King Invictus requests your presence immediately," the dracool said, its tongue flicking the air. "The guests grow impatient."

"We're ready," Urbana said. "Will you be so kind as to be our escort, Dracool-Izumo?"

"With pleasure."

Izumo bowed and then stomped toward the stairs, his heavy tail swaying back and forth. Laylah took a deep breath and followed the dracool, with Urbana and the young attendant at her side. Laylah was so tense she could barely breathe.

They reached the bottom of the stairs and then entered the garden. To Laylah's left was a series of open doors, revealing a green lawn that stretched for several furlongs before bending upward toward a hill smothered with wildflowers. The interior garden smelled like a mixture of perfume, fresh leaves, and rich soil. Stone trails wove through the flowers and shrubs. On the far side of the garden, a bronze door towered fifteen cubits high. A pair of columns framed the door and supported an arch partially obscured by a twining vine sprouting hundreds of yellow flowers. In front of the door, a cord dangled from the high ceiling.

"Are you ready, young princess?" Izumo said, his tongue flicking rapidly.

"If I said no, would it matter?"

"King Invictus awaits," the dracool said.

"Don't worry," Urbana said. "Izumo doesn't bite. Nor do your other guests; at least, not today. They're eager to meet you. There will be fabulous foods and exquisite wines. For as long as you live, you'll never forget this day. Your brother is a generous host."

Izumo tugged on the cord. Bells chimed in response. Laylah took a long breath, and a single tear ran down her cheek. The young attendant dabbed it with a scented cloth.

"Be of light heart, little one," the attendant said. Then she whispered, "Not all at this place are allies of the king."

She bowed and backed away.

The massive door swung open, revealing the ballroom. Izumo gestured for Laylah to make her entrance. She stepped inside and looked around. The grandeur stunned her.

Invictus emerged from a crowd of faces wearing a high-collared gown draped over his shoulders. Colorful folly-bells hung from his girdle. The young sorcerer took her hand.

"Behold, Princess Laylah!" he said, his voice echoing throughout the room. "Beyond hope, my sister has returned from her wanderings. Welcome her with great joy!"

Cries, shouts, and applause greeted her.

"Yes! YES!"

A servitor came forward and offered Invictus and Laylah crystal goblets of sparkling wine. Then the sorcerer guided her into the room. She didn't protest. A golden flow of energy surged from the palm of his hand into hers, deadening her resistance as effectively as if she'd been drugged. Her mind observed the movements of her body, but she was helpless to control them. She felt like a puppet.

Invictus took her to a spectacular fountain in the center of the ballroom. Twelve silver dryads spurted water from their mouths, the jets crisscrossing in the air before spilling into a foamy pool.

"What do you think of my palace?" Invictus said. "It's only a temporary residence until we complete the tower, but it's still beautiful, don't you think?"

Laylah didn't respond, but Invictus compelled her to tilt her head toward the high ceiling, which was laced with golden vaults supported by marble columns. Chandeliers sparkled in the soft light that entered the room through windows set into lavish indentations along the upper walls.

Without her permission, her eyes were forced downward along colored mosaics on the walls. Arched windows studded the lower portion of the room. Through these, Laylah could see portions of the impressive green lawn.

A receiving line formed. Invictus continued to grip her hand. She stood still as stone. First to greet her was the most beautiful woman Laylah had ever beheld. She seemed vaguely familiar, but Laylah couldn't imagine where she might have seen her before. The woman took Laylah's hand.

"My sister," Invictus said. "Allow me to present Chal-Abhinno, queen of the Warlish witches."

"The pleasure isss mine, Princess Laylah," Chal said, her green eyes darting to-and-fro as if afraid to look directly at Laylah.

"Thank her for her courtesy," Invictus said to Laylah.

"Thank you …"

The witch nodded and then walked away looking relieved.

Next up was a handsome soldier wearing golden armor that matched his long yellow hair. He cradled his helm in the crook of his arm.

"My sister," Invictus said. "Allow me to present General Lucius Annaeus, the *legatus* of my army."

"A hearty welcome, Princess Laylah," General Lucius said. "I'm at your command, as are all of the king's subjects."

"Thank you …"

After Lucius came a druid. Laylah had never seen one of these creatures, but Takoda had ventured into Dhutanga Forest several times and had seen druids there. This one was more than seven cubits tall, and its fiery eyes glared down at her as if enraged. But it took her hand in its long bony fingers and bowed awkwardly.

"My sister," Invictus said. "Allow me to present Druggen-Boggle, a druid representative from Dhutanga."

Boggle didn't speak. Instead, he hummed with great force, causing Laylah's teeth to chatter.

"Tha-a-nk you …"

The druid clattered off. Next came a grotesque beast with the head and torso of a woman but with bat-like wings in place of arms. Laylah would have fled at the sight of it, but Invictus' grip held her in place. The creature's flesh was bizarrely translucent, reminding her of Vedana's.

"My sister," Invictus said. "Allow me to present Pisaaca, a demon representative from Arupa-Loka."

"Your blood is my blood," Pisaaca said.

"Thank you ..."

After the demon came Izumo.

"My sister," Invictus said. "Allow me to present Dracool-Izumo, from the cliffs of Mahaggata."

"We have already met, my liege," Izumo said to Invictus. Then he turned to Laylah. "May our lives continue to entwine."

"Thank you ..."

Izumo tromped off. A relatively tiny figure, almost two spans shorter than she, came next. But despite its small size, it looked more dangerous than the dracool. Tendrils of flame flared from its flat nostrils and wisps of smoke seeped from its pointy ears.

"My sister," Invictus said. "Allow me to present Gulah, a Stone-Eater from the bowels of Mount Asubha."

"The honor is mine," Gulah said.

"Thank you ..."

Next up was a sinister-looking woman dressed in red robes. Her hair and eyes were black, but her skin was white. When she smiled, her teeth were jagged.

"My sister," Invictus said. "Allow me to present Broosha, a vampire from Arupa-Loka."

The vampire repeated the same disturbing words the demon had spoken: "My blood is your blood."

"Thank you ..."

The next creature was the strangest yet, smaller than the Stone-Eater and covered from head to foot with tangled hair. Its eyes protruded almost finger-length from their sockets.

"My sister," Invictus said. "Allow me to present Gruugash, a representative of the Pabbajja, the homeless people from the borders of Java."

"My people will not forsake you," Gruugash said with surprising tenderness.

"Thank you ..."

She met a slew of others—a grotesquely tattooed Mogol who gripped her hand so hard it hurt; a gigantic, six-armed Kojin who was more than twice her height; a cave troll who drooled on her shoes; a feisty ogre who leered at her breasts; and a one-armed ghoul who unwittingly dropped flakes of his own stinking flesh on the marble floor.

The procession went on for most of what remained of the afternoon. Laylah said *thank you* over and over, but she never meant it. The power that flowed from Invictus rendered her impotent. Her mind screamed, but her body showed no signs of discomfort. Invictus' hideous friends frightened her, but no one in attendance could have recognized it by her demeanor.

While the procession took place, servitors erected a long dining table with fifty chairs arranged on one side and ten oversized sofas on the other. Two chairs were at the head of the table and two more were at its foot.

A trumpeter announced the meal. Servants rushed in with washbowls for the human-sized guests to cleanse their hands. Invictus released his grip for the first time since she entered the ballroom. When the flow of golden energy was cut off, Laylah regained a portion of her senses.

"Bathe your hands, sister," she heard him say. She placed her hands in the lukewarm water, but this time her own will directed the movement.

When Invictus led Laylah to the head of the table, he placed his hand on her shoulder and zapped her again. She was the first to be seated, and then he joined her. Chal and Lucius sat at the foot of the table. The couches were reserved for the largest in attendance: the Kojin, the cave troll, Izumo and two other dracools, and Boggle and four other druids.

The table settings included cups made from the eggs of flightless birds that lived in the Gray Plains near Barranca. She saw silver spoons, pewter bowls, and wooden trenchers. Servitors stood ready to wipe mouths and fingers. They poured more sparkling wine. Invictus stood and surveyed the eclectic gathering.

"Today is a special day for the citizens and allies of Avici."

"Yes!"

"Today, my sister will become queen."

"Yes!"

Laylah tried to protest, but Invictus placed his hand on her shoulder and quieted her.

"Long live Queen Laylah!" he said.

"And long live King Invictus!" Chal-Abhinno said from the other end of the table, her voice as sweet as nectar.

"Yes! YES!"

"Thank you, Queen Chal," Invictus said. "And now, let us enjoy our meal. I'm sure you're all famished."

The servitors came forward with the first course, but Invictus waved his hand, freezing them in place.

"I apologize, but I forgot one small matter. Regarding my sister, I will not tolerate rude behavior."

There was a swell of murmuring. Invictus walked slowly down one side of the table, stopping behind the ogre who had leered at Laylah's breasts.

"Olog," Invictus said. "Do you find my sister attractive?"

Olog remained silent as if he didn't realize he was the one being addressed. But Invictus grabbed the ogre's chair and slid it backward. The room became deathly quiet.

"I asked you a question."

The ogre laughed, hoping to diffuse the tension. But it didn't amuse Invictus. Olog squirmed in the chair.

"I don't understand your question, my liege. Do I find your sister attractive? Of course, as do we all. She's a lovely young girl."

Invictus lowered his face within an inch of the ogre's gnarled nose.

"I *saw* the way you looked at her. Do you think me a fool?"

Apparently not knowing what else to do, Olog tried to appear offended. "My liege, are you accusing me of misbehavior? If so, I wholeheartedly protest ..."

But Invictus reached down and grasped the ogre's throat, cutting off the rest of the sentence. With one arm, the sorcerer lifted the beast out of his chair. Male ogres were much smaller than their female counterparts and nowhere near the size of Kojins, but they were only slightly smaller than men. Yet Invictus effortlessly suspended Olog high above the floor. The ogre grabbed the sorcerer's wrists but could not tear free, kicking at Invictus with clawed feet. As the ogre fought to escape, Invictus' arm glowed. Suddenly, yellow fire surged into Olog, blowing him apart. Chunks of flesh spewed outward, but before any of the gore could shower the guests, the yellow fire consumed it. All that remained were delicate flakes of ash, fluttering to the floor like a handful of feathers.

"*No*," Laylah screamed. "Don't kill because of me! I want no *part* of it."

"You're under my protection," Invictus said, returning to her side. "I'll do *anything* for you." And then he took her hand, quieting her again.

The other guests quickly returned to normal conversation. If what occurred had upset anyone, none dared show it. Olog hadn't been the most powerful among them, but the ease with which Invictus dispatched him was unsettling.

Despite the grotesque spectacle, the guests ate heartily—at least the ones who most resembled humans. A first course of spiced vegetable soup and white bread was served. Poached eggs, roasted duck, salted pork, and baked fish followed. Cooked apples, plums, pears, and peaches came next. Stuffed pastries, cakes, and cookies were offered for dessert, along with tea made from parched holly leaves. And of course, a never-ending supply of wine.

Whenever Laylah became agitated, Invictus calmed her with his power. She ate and drank obediently but without pleasure, the food and wine filling her stomach but not warming her heart.

After the meal, the guests milled about in the ballroom. Final goodbyes were said near the fountain. As sunlight dwindled toward dusk, the visitors departed. Only Invictus, Laylah, Urbana, the young chambermaid, and the other servants remained.

Invictus took Laylah's hand, forcing her to stand helplessly beside him. Urbana had drunk a great deal of wine. The young chambermaid appeared wary but not frightened.

"Darkness approaches," Invictus said to Laylah. "It's time, my sister. Tonight, you shall become my queen. Are you ready?"

"Thank you ..." Laylah said.

Urbana's red tongue slid seductively along her jagged teeth. "Let us retire to her chamber," the mistress of the robes said. "Why delay any longer?"

Invictus laughed. "Your impatience is legendary, Urbana. But this time, I agree. I don't want my sister's coronation to occur in total darkness. Come along—and bring the girl. I want her to watch so that she can spread the tale of my benevolence."

With Urbana in the lead, the four of them left the banquet room, passed through the garden, and entered the stairwell that led to Laylah's bedchamber at the top of the tower. Invictus continued to grasp his sister's hand, and though Laylah's mind raced and her heart pounded, she couldn't convince her body to do anything but follow.

The small company ascended the stairs and approached her door. Urbana started to enter, but Invictus held her back.

"Mistress of the robes," he said formally, "have you forgotten my command?"

Urbana looked puzzled. Then she smiled.

"I apologize, my liege. Where *are* my manners?"

She turned to Laylah, who remained ensconced in her magic-induced trance.

"May we have your permission to enter?" Urbana said in a voice sweeter than honey.

"Thank you ..." Laylah said.

"I take that as a yes," the mistress said, and then walked into the room.

"Chambermaid," Invictus said to the girl, "watch closely. After tonight, it will be your duty to spread this story far and wide. As you are about to see, I am a man of honor."

"Yes, my liege," she said obediently.

Invictus led Laylah toward the bed. "Place my sister on her back on the bed," he said to Urbana, "and loosen the front of her garments."

The mistress of the robes fiddled with the cloth straps that secured Laylah's undergarment, but Invictus growled and shoved her aside. He grasped the chemise and tore it off. Laylah lay naked, still as a statue, but her eyes were wide with fear. Darkness crept into the sky outside the window.

"Do not fear me in *that way*," Invictus snarled. "You're not my type. As I've told you, I only desire an heir, and you're the only woman whose body can provide me with one."

Then the sorcerer placed his hand upon Laylah's abdomen, much as Vedana had done back in the cave. A great glow erupted from his wrist and burned Laylah's stomach. Her head lolled to the side, and a portion of her remaining consciousness seized on the chambermaid, who stood with thin arms crossed beneath small breasts. In her cloudy awareness,

Laylah became fascinated by the girl's eyes, whose pupils flared and receded with hypnotic rapidity.

"You idiot!" the chambermaid suddenly shouted, but no sound came from her mouth. Instead, the words careened inside Laylah's mind. "He's attempting to use his magic to impregnate you. Don't waste my precious gift. Resist with your thoughts if you can't with your body."

Laylah's drugged awareness slowly grasped the concept, and a pain far worse than she had ever experienced exploded in her abdomen, dwarfing even the torture of the talisman. Although she was near catatonia, she grasped the sides of her stomach with her hands and let out an eerie cry that caused Urbana to yelp. This even startled Invictus. He yanked away his hand and glared at Laylah.

"What's this?" he said. "What's happening?"

Then he looked at Laylah's stomach and saw the flesh beneath her navel writhing. At that same moment, a torrent of black smoke arose from the chambermaid's pale flesh, unveiling Vedana's gray-haired incarnation. The demon's translucent body shimmered in the dimming light.

"Complete your magical spell if you like, grandson," the demon said while backing toward the open window. "But if you do, her womanhood will be consumed and you'll never have an heir."

"Grandmother, what have you done?" Invictus said, still puzzled.

Then he again placed his hand on Laylah's abdomen and finally understood. "No!" he screamed.

But Vedana had already taken the shape of a raven and flown out of the tower. Invictus raced toward the window too late.

"I'll destroy you," he shouted. "Do you doubt it?"

Too late. Vedana was gone.

Laylah remained on the bed, the pain in her abdomen slowly receding. Urbana knelt beside the bed, sobbing.

"I'm sorry, my king," the vampire moaned. "I didn't know."

Invictus looked at Urbana and sagged against the wall. But then a smile came to his face. "Grandmother, you're full of surprises."

Invictus strode across the room and grabbed Urbana's hair, dragging her away from the bed and slamming the door behind them.

Boom!

Laylah was alone. She had survived her first day in Avici. Would tomorrow be this bad? She would find out in the morning.

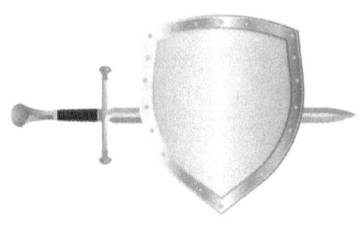

SERVANT

In the middle of the night, Laylah woke from a dreamless slumber with a burning distress in her stomach. Near the bed was a basin of water with fresh towels. She rinsed her mouth and cleansed her body. She then slid a chair next to her arched window and gazed at the night sky.

The moon was waning gibbous, and its glow strengthened her heart. It amazed her that only a few days had passed since she'd stood beneath the full moon with Takoda and looked over their valley. Now her adoptive father was dead, along with his people, and the most dangerous madman ever had imprisoned her.

Laylah's recollection of the previous evening was mercifully hazy. She remembered a ripping agony within her abdomen and Invictus being angry, but she didn't know why the pain occurred other than a misty memory in the dark recesses of her mind. Was it some sort of demonic spell that not even the sorcerer could overcome? It appeared, in this instance, that the demon Vedana had been her ally.

Laylah gazed at the moon. The reflected light felt warm and fecund. The longer she stared the more her fear diminished, finally reaching a level of tolerability she wouldn't have thought possible after such recent trauma. Laylah's survival instincts swelled within her. Taking her own life remained an option, but not on this night. She decided to give herself one chance to escape before she revisited that loathsome possibility.

As dawn approached, the sister of the king returned to her bed and fell into a deep sleep. When she opened her eyes, it surprised her to find that her room was bright and warm.

Then came a familiar tapping at her door.

"Young princess, are you awake?" Urbana said. "We have prepared your dinner. After last night, you must be hungry."

"If you enter the room, I'll kill you."

"We hold grudges, do we? You have no idea how much I'd relish the opportunity to confront you. But I remain forbidden, though after last night I'm not sure why. Your value has diminished, it would seem."

"Take a swim in the Salt Sea. It'll do your complexion a world of good."

"I couldn't care less if you eat or not. I'll leave your dinner outside the door. Come and get it. Or do not. If you need anything else, your chambermaids can serve you. And don't worry. I went to great pains while you slept to make sure none of the rest of them are demons in disguise. I'll never forgive Vedana for making me look so clumsy."

A long silence followed. Laylah went to the door and placed her ear against the polished wood. She heard nothing other than the grumbling of her own stomach. She was ravenously hungry, and if she were to attempt an escape, possibly as soon as tonight, she would need her strength. If weak and wobbly, she would stand little chance.

Laylah's innate magical powers made her dangerous, but she was untested and inexperienced. Could she destroy a creature as malicious as Urbana? Could she withstand an attack from a dracool? And what about the other monsters she had met at the banquet? Was she an equal to any of them? The death word Invictus had taught her as a child might destroy some of them. Or her white fire might incinerate them. But she didn't know. And not knowing was as great a weakness as anything else. She needed the time and patience to learn more about herself and her predicament. She appeared to have plenty of time, but she had little patience.

Would he come to her room later this afternoon and place his hand on her again? Maybe this time, whatever was inside her wouldn't awaken. How long could she bear such assaults before insanity rose up and overtook her? She didn't know, and the less she knew the more vulnerable she became. Against monsters like Invictus, knowledge was power. And you also needed help from unexpected places. Vedana's surprise appearance had taught her that.

If she were to believe what Vedana told her, the demon blood that flowed through Invictus' veins also flowed through hers. Demons—she had heard shamans say—were capable of intricate deceptions. Well, Laylah was part demon. Of what was she capable?

She pushed her door ajar and peeked through the crack. A tray of food sat on the floor, containing white fish with a crust of fried almonds, pureed vegetables thickened with breadcrumbs, and several varieties of fruit. There was also a loaf of bread and an ewer of goat's milk. Whatever horrors Invictus intended to inflict upon her, starvation didn't appear to be among them.

On the large rug in the center of the hall, ten chambermaids sat on their haunches and stared at her with a blend of apprehension and curiosity. With their matched golden tunics and long yellow hair, they looked like an arrangement of jasmine—and they appeared prepared to obey any command. Laylah gestured to the one closest to the door.

"What's your name?"

"Bhacca," she said timidly.

"Bring my dinner. The rest of you, stay where you are."

"Yes, young princess," Bhacca said, expertly lifting the tray. When she entered the room, Laylah shut the door. The chambermaid carried the tray to the table near the window and poured some of the milk into a pewter cup. She then retreated a few steps and kneeled on the marble floor, waiting silently for further commands.

The fish was excellent, the bread freshly baked, and the vegetable puree heavily spiced. Laylah ate everything without speaking. Bhacca watched but didn't move.

When Laylah finished, the servant girl started to rise. But Laylah motioned for her to remain on the floor. She had questions. Maybe this girl could answer them more effectively than Urbana had the day before.

"How old are you?" Laylah said, trying to relax the girl.

"This is my third summer, young princess."

"What do you mean?"

Bhacca shrugged. "I don't understand your question, young princess."

"I would guess you're as old as I, but you said this is your third summer."

"I'm not like you, young princess."

"In what way?"

"I was spawned in Kilesa."

"I don't know what you're talking about."

"Do you not know of Kilesa, young princess?"

"When I was a child, I sometimes heard my parents talking about a village to the east called Kilesa."

"I've never heard Kilesa described as a village. Countless thousands live there, and many more are spawned there. The king needs soldiers and servants, and he doesn't have time to recruit them all … so he *spawns* them. I was spawned in Kilesa three summers ago. After I grew to maturity, I was brought to Avici."

"You grew to maturity in three years?" Laylah said, clasping her hand to her mouth.

"King Invictus has great powers, young princess. Hundreds of newborns arrive every day. The king has given us the gifts of life, health, and beauty. We even *look* like our king. What a wonderful privilege! All that he asks in return is that we serve him and the citizens of Avici. And it's our most sincere pleasure to do so. I consider King Invictus to be my father. Which, if I may be so bold, makes you my aunt."

Bhacca giggled, but Laylah remained quiet. The girl's face grew pale. "I meant no offense. Would you like me to leave? I'll report to the mistress of the robes and receive my punishment for displeasing you."

"No, don't do that!"

"As you say, young princess."

Laylah sat in stunned silence, studying the girl's innocent face. Could she even call her a girl? Was she human? How could she have grown to maturity in less than three summers? Was there no end to the extent of Invictus' perversion? What he did the previous evening was bad enough, but at least she was just one person who meant little to the world. But to twist life itself? Maybe her brother *was* a god.

If only Takoda was here. He would say just the right things. And he would help her plan her escape. They would flee into the mountains and this time find a better place to hide.

"Young princess," Bhacca said, interrupting her reverie. "May I prepare your bath? Afterward, I'll show you the gardens, if the mistress of the robes allows it."

"The mistress of the robes does what she's told, just like you," Laylah said. "There's only one voice in Avici, and it belongs to my brother."

"Should not the most powerful have the most say? That's what I've been taught."

"I've been taught to respect my family and my people. To treasure nature. That the greatest force in the world is love."

"Your words are strange to me. But I'm just a lowly servant, while you are wise and magnificent."

Laylah smiled at the humble chambermaid. Whoever or whatever Bhacca was, Laylah enjoyed her company. But just when she was beginning to believe her second day in Avici might be less horrible than her first, a flash of light boomed in her hallway, causing Bhacca to throw herself face down on the marble floor.

"Good day, my sister," Invictus said from the doorway, honoring his word not to enter her room without an invitation. "I trust you slept well and your dinner was to your liking?"

Tears sprouted from Laylah's eyes and crept down her soft cheeks. "Stay ... away ... from ... me."

"Come now," Invictus said, sounding more amused than annoyed. "Aren't you overreacting just a bit? It's not like I tried to kill you—or even hurt you. I just wanted to claim what is rightfully mine. It was your grandmother's little trick that created all the confusion."

"Why are you torturing me?"

Invictus pounded his fists against the doorframe. It felt like the entire tower was shaking. "My sister, you're being melodramatic. All I did was touch your belly with my hand. Do you call that torture? If so, you don't know the meaning of the word. I'm capable of far worse things."

For a moment, he looked like a dangerous predator, but then his expression softened. "Of course, I would *never* torture my dear sister. I admit last night was overly bold—and I apologize. I'm not used to waiting for what I want. From my point of view, if I used my magic to impregnate you quickly it would be like yanking a splinter out of a child's finger; the pain would be over before you knew it. Now I understand you have a say in this matter. I've developed a desire for an heir—someone I can train and trust to rule my growing kingdom when the time comes that I grow weary of it. And you're the only vessel I know of with the capacity to make my dream a reality."

"Even if you're using magic, what you propose is unholy. It makes me want to vomit. I will *not* carry your child! I will *die* first."

"Unholy? What is and isn't holy is not for you to say." Then he frowned. "I'm not easily denied, lovely Laylah. But despite my superiority, I'm willing to negotiate. I desire an heir; you desire freedom. Can we achieve both?"

"I don't trust you."

Invictus ran his fingers through his hair. "Sister, sister. You're so *suspicious*. I suppose you have legitimate cause, but there are aspects of your situation that you fail to comprehend. First, if I chose to enter your room, no one in the world could stop me. So by asking your permission, I honor your privacy. Second, I've admitted that my behavior last night was a little uncouth. In this way, I honor your dignity. You consider me a monster, but you know so little about me. Shouldn't you learn more before you make such harsh judgments?"

"Forcing your magic on someone isn't *uncouth*. Murdering someone's parents isn't *impolite*. You can't simply apologize and expect me to act like it never happened."

This didn't deter Invictus. "You're beautiful, of that there is no doubt, and I believe you're somewhat intelligent. But you're not yet wise. I do what I need to do to advance my position in the world. The further I advance, the better off the world will be. You haven't yet seen all the wonders of Avici, and you don't yet know my vision of its future. I am beyond right or wrong. I am *Akanittha*, servant only to the sun."

"If you're so great, show some mercy and kill me quickly."

This caused Invictus to finally lose his patience. "Stubborn *bitch*! You test me at your peril."

A second explosion of light filled the doorway, causing the floor to shiver. Laylah was temporarily blinded. When she was able to see clearly again, her brother was gone.

Beneath her, Bhacca trembled.

Laylah walked to the door and inspected the hallway. The other chambermaids remained on the rug, tears in their eyes.

Laylah slammed the door shut. Then she went to Bhacca and knelt beside her. For a long time, both were silent.

"I'm as frightened as you," Laylah said. "Will you be my friend?"

"I would be honored."

"Good. Let's start with my bath. Afterward, I'd like to walk in the gardens. Will you join me?"

"Yes, young princess."

"While we walk, I'll tell you stories of my life. Will you do the same for me?"

"There's little to tell," the young chambermaid said.

As evening approached, Laylah and Bhacca strolled through the interior garden on a walkway of white marble squares. Ingrained in the marble were traceries of gold spun into the outlines of suns. The room was only fifty cubits long and thirty wide, but the ceiling was tall and the plants cleverly arranged, including several dozen species of flowers and shrubs. But all had one thing in common: either the bloom or foliage was yellow.

Laylah recognized many of the plants, some of which had grown in the Mahaggata valley she adored. She now stood next to one of Takoda's favorites. He had called it a butterfly bush, and it was aptly named. Hundreds of butterflies and bees flocked to the honey-scented nectar in summer and fall. She and Takoda used to sit near the bushes at sunset and watch the delightful conglomeration of insects swarming around the yellow flowers.

Laylah also recognized a shrub she remembered her parents calling golden bell. But in her memory, it only bloomed in early spring. In this garden, it remained in full bloom in late summer.

Something else puzzled her. Most of the flowers and shrubs in the garden required a lot of sun. The room had many open windows, but not enough to provide the amount of light these plants needed to thrive. They should not have grown well indoors; yet they were perfectly healthy.

As if in response to her bemusement, the gold traceries in the marble began to glow, and Laylah felt a surge of warmth rise beneath her dress. Without warning, the room became as bright as the noon-day sun, forcing Laylah and Bhacca to squint.

"It does this about five times a day," the chambermaid said. "If you visit here often enough, your skin will darken."

"It is great magic, is it not?" came a baritone voice from behind them. Laylah jerked around, expecting to see Invictus. Instead, she saw the soldier she'd met at the banquet the previous night, although he had discarded his armor in favor of a gold doublet with a bejeweled belt. His cape and hose were matching crimson. Like Invictus, he was clean shaven with long blond hair and brown eyes. His jaw was square, his teeth flawless.

"Pardon the interruption, my lady," the soldier said. "I wander the garden every day, yet this is only a small taste of the beauty of this valley. There's a vast field of wildflowers a short walk from here. And beyond the wildflowers stretch the Gray Plains. Would you care to take a stroll? The sky is clear and the moon will be beautiful when it makes its appearance. The chambermaid is welcome to join us if that would make you feel more at ease."

Bhacca bowed. "It would honor me to be in your presence, sir."

This didn't impress Laylah. "You would dare walk with me? Aren't you afraid my brother will have another fit of jealousy? You saw what happened at the banquet."

"I witnessed what happened, yes, but perhaps I understood it better than you. King Invictus can see far. Some say he can even see *into* a person's mind. The ogre was more than just a lecher; he was a traitor to our cause. Most of the others in the room were already aware of this and were not at all surprised by your brother's actions. Invictus regretted that you were offended. He told me so just a while ago."

"Good for him and good for you. As for walking with you, I'd rather not. Anyone who is a friend of my brother is no friend of mine."

A man and woman strolling in the garden scampered off as if afraid to be in the presence of such heresy. Laylah laughed.

"Apparently, they're as in love with him as you are, General Lucius. Is that your name? I'm having a hard time remembering what happened last night."

"General Lucius is indeed my name. As for last night, I'm truly sorry for whatever discomfort you experienced. I'm not your brother's keeper. Like any powerful king, he does what he pleases when he pleases. I'm just an officer who follows orders."

Lucius was probably play-acting, but something in his tone rang true to Laylah, lessening her resistance. If she were to study the grounds outside the palace, this was an opportunity she shouldn't dismiss.

"Bhacca can come with us?"

"Of course. It would be my pleasure to escort both of you."

The general clapped his hands, and a servitor raced forward with two cups of wine.

"Bring a third," Lucius said, tilting his head toward the chambermaid.

The servitor raised an eyebrow.

"Now! And *hurry*."

When they entered the yard behind the palace, all three held silver cups filled with luscious red wine. Dusk had dissolved into darkness and a warm breeze caressed their brows. Lucius walked between Laylah and Bhacca. To Laylah, the chambermaid looked like the general's younger sister. But it was clear there was a division in rank. Bhacca skittered alongside Lucius like an adoring puppy, hardly daring to look him in the eye.

The general didn't speak to the chambermaid again. His entire focus was on Laylah.

"Does the wine please you?"

"A prisoner doesn't take much pleasure in food or drink."

"I'm sorry you feel that way."

"You mean I'm not a prisoner? I can leave?"

"Your brother would prefer you do not. He fears for your safety. Like any great king, he has enemies—and some might already be aware of your arrival. If you were to wander too far from the protection of Avici, you could be in danger."

"I'm sure my brother's good intentions are the only reason I'm being held here. How *noble* of him."

If this shocked Lucius, he hid it well. "As I said, I'm not your brother's keeper."

Laylah started to like the general a little. And perhaps she could make use of him. She didn't have other options.

"Show me the wildflowers, and what lies beyond. My memories of Avici are dim. So much has changed."

"With pleasure."

The servitor trotted out and refilled their glasses. Bhacca was already acting a little tipsy. Laylah could tell she was enjoying being so prominently displayed with such important people.

The wildflowers were fragrant. Once again, yellow was the predominant color. Laylah took off her sandals and walked barefoot through the field. The breeze stroked the petals like a gentle hand sweeping along the blooms.

"I can tell you the names of all these flowers," Lucius said with something resembling pride.

"Go on."

He knelt, picked one, and handed it to Laylah.

"This is a dogtooth violet. The vines that grow along the border trestles are yellow jessamine. There are trillium, star-grass, and milkwort, all in bloom. Invictus' magic is magnificent. Plants that normally bloom only in spring remain in flower through the summer and fall. And those that usually wait until fall bloom here in the spring along with the others."

"I feel sorry for the plants. What Invictus is doing to them is obscene."

"Whatever you say, my lady. I only report what I see. How you perceive it is up to you."

Laylah tossed the violet into the air. It tumbled in the breeze. "And beyond the flowers lie the Gray Plains?"

"There is a nearby hill from which you can see a great distance."

"I used to go there as a child, though I spent most of my playtime at my favorite tree."

"We can visit the sycamore if you like. It's your brother's favorite, though I'm sure that brings you no pleasure."

"You're beginning to comprehend me. Yes, I'd like to go there. The night is so pleasant. Under this sparkling sky, I can pretend for a little while that I'm free."

"You can be free if you allow yourself to be."

"Not as long as my brother is alive."

"He has tormented you, but he will do so no longer. He wants you to be happy."

"You're a liar. But a *smooth* liar."

Lucius sighed and then started through the flowers toward the hill. Bhacca came up beside Laylah and whispered in her ear. "Young princess, how do you dare say such things? Except for the king, General Lucius is the most powerful man in Avici. Even the dracools follow his commands."

Laylah only laughed. "What have I to lose?"

Lucius walked about twenty paces before stopping and waiting for Laylah to catch up. She came up beside him. Bhacca trailed behind. They went to the top of the hill and looked out at the Gray Plains. Though it was now well into evening, the light from the newly risen moon illuminated the countryside, revealing a wide expanse of flat, gray land extending for countless leagues—northeast to the Ice Ocean, east to the Salt Sea, and southeast to the Great Desert.

Though she had been young, Laylah still remembered a scarcity of rainfall on this side of the mountains, especially in late spring and summer. The arid conditions stunted the prairie grass and gave it a gray-green hue. From her viewpoint on the hill, Laylah could see a paved road plunging eastward that glistened in the moonlight.

"Where does that lead?"

"Isn't it impressive? We began construction only a few years ago, yet it stretches more than fifty leagues, attaching our city to Kilesa where we nurture the newborns. Large portions of the road are paved with a special metal that shines like gold but has the feel of granite."

"Who are the newborns?" Laylah said, pretending she knew nothing.

"We're the children of Invictus. Born to look like him, act like him, and serve him. Bhacca is a newborn, torn from her pink sac just three years ago. We are birthed into the world and grow quickly from precious drops of our king's own blood. I'm the first of the newborns, born six years ago."

"How can that be? You're a fully grown man. And a general. I would have guessed you to be closer to 50 years old."

"They bred me to look this way. Invictus says I'll live several hundred years, with little change in my appearance. As for being a general, I was schooled in Kilesa on the subtleties of the martial arts. I'm a formidable tactician, and though never tested in battle, my time will come. One day I will lead an army."

Laylah stared at Lucius' face. His eyes were lined and there were streaks of gray above his ears, exactly what a boy playing in his room would imagine a general to look like. The thought made Laylah shiver. Did that describe Invictus? A boy playing with toys—but capable of bringing his toys to life?

Lucius misread her dismay. "I'm not a monster but a man of flesh and blood. I can be injured and killed. My life has been short, but my future has grand possibilities. You can understand, at least, why I don't hate him."

"One day, I was running free through the wilderness. The next, my people were dead and I was imprisoned. You can understand, at least, why I *do* hate him."

Lucius gave her a strange look. Then he attempted to change the subject. "More wine is in order. It lightens the heart. It's too late to show you the rest of Avici, but we can enjoy the great sycamore before we say goodnight."

Tears ran down Laylah's cheeks. Suddenly, she found herself confiding in the stranger.

"I sound angry, but it's only to cover my fear. Will he come for me again? Tonight, after you're gone? Tomorrow? The next day? If he does, will you protect me, General Lucius?"

As if experiencing a swell of sympathy, he stroked her cheek. But then he backed away. "I can't make such a promise. But I can promise that I will never hurt you."

Laylah sobbed. Bhacca came over and hugged her from the side. Lucius stood still as a statue, but a single tear slid down his cheek.

Though Laylah was unaware, Invictus watched her from his tower with trembling anticipation.

"Very good, General Lucius," he whispered to himself. "You've made excellent progress in just your first meeting. We'll build on this, you and I, until my sister puts aside her anger and trusts us both. I shall have my heir."

Invictus left his room and followed the secret ways that led to the catacombs deep beneath the palace where he could lie on a bed of stone amid a million candles while the horrid night ran its course and gave way to the blessedness of morning.

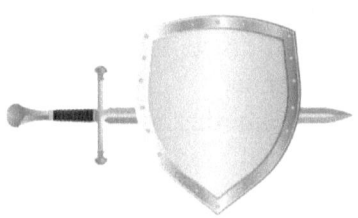

LIFE IN PRISON

Seventy years is a long time, even for those with the thaumaturgic capacity to live many times longer. And when each moment feels like a day, seventy years becomes an eternity. It would have been impossible to describe every time Laylah sighed, sobbed, or stared silently at the moon yearning for freedom. More than a dozen times during her captivity, the full moon acted strangely as if sharing her depression, becoming partially and sometimes fully enshrouded in shadow. During these episodes, Laylah felt even worse than she did in full daylight, often collapsing into troubled sleeps. But the following night, the moon returned to normal and the illness dissipated.

How often did she try to escape? As often as she failed. The first attempt was only five days after her arrival in Avici. She made it beyond the wildflowers as far as the hillock before dracools surrounded her. First, she tried the death word, but the baby dragons were unaffected. In the desperate battle that followed, she injured two with her white flames before they threw a magical net over her that pinned her to the ground, its thin gold fibers negating her powers. Urbana joined them, laughing wickedly. Lucius appeared just in time to save her. If not for the general, they might have killed her. In most ways, that would have been a blessing. But something inside her fought to survive, regardless of her despair.

The next day, Lucius came to her room. She thanked him for rescuing her, and he vowed to discipline the beasts and the vampire for their rough treatment. He seemed sincere enough.

Days, weeks, and months passed without harassment from Invictus. She saw him a few times but rarely face to face. Sometimes he waved. Other days he simply ignored her. Laylah traveled the grounds more freely, though a menagerie of dracools, vampires, Mogols, wolves, and newborn soldiers guarded her.

Whenever she attempted another escape, she never got far. She once made it to a densely populated area of Avici and lost them for half a night, running through alleys and crouching in doorways. But Urbana and her fiends found her, and the vampire got close enough to throw a sparkly powder in her face. When Laylah woke the next morning, she was back in her room covered with scratches and bite marks. Lucius saw the wounds and became enraged, summoning Urbana and screaming at her for what seemed like forever. The vampire stood silently during the tongue lashing and slinked away like a whipped dog. Lucius' authority impressed Laylah.

Months stretched into years while Avici grew ever larger before her eyes, bloating like a gourmand's stomach. Thousands of newborns came from the east, traveling in huge caravans on the Golden Road. Rumors of wealth and opportunity lured townsfolk into the city from up and down the length of the Ogha River. And a seedier crew also arrived: pirates from Duccarita, Warlish witches from Kamupadana, Pabbajja from the fringes of Java, and wild men from Kolankold. The worst, in Laylah's eyes, were the wolves and Mogols from Mahaggata, long the dreaded enemies of the Ropakans.

Laylah watched the army increase from less than 20,000 to more than 200,000 while the civilian population swelled to half a million. A new manse, temple, or tavern appeared every day, and the city sprawled in all directions, even spilling over to the west side of the Ogha River where there was plenty of open land for further expansion. But the valley—*her* valley, as Invictus liked to call it—was off-limits to development.

Her brother left her alone for ten years. The memory of her parents' murders faded ever so slowly, and she eventually blamed Vedana more than Invictus for the slaughter of the Ropakans, who felt less like her people and more like a dream. Even the memory of his attempt to use his magic to impregnate her lost its acuity. Each day that Invictus stayed away, her belief strengthened that he intended no further harm.

Some parts of her life were not unpleasant. She was fed, clothed, and bathed in luxurious fashion. Even better, she and Bhacca became loyal friends. The newborn felt like a little sister and often accompanied her on her middle-of-the-night wanderings in the valley. Laylah also conversed frequently with Lucius, who bragged incessantly about the growing might of his army.

Near the end of her first decade of captivity, it stunned Laylah to learn that Invictus had chosen a queen. Her name was Asamāna, a young countess from a wealthy Senasanan family. Laylah attended a banquet during which Invictus put on a touching show of adoration for his bride-to-be. Could it be that his obsession with her was over? The sorcerer spoke to Laylah several times during the banquet—in a respectful, brotherly tone. Asamāna smiled and bowed but said little. Laylah found the vacant look in her eyes disquietingly familiar.

More than 10,000 attended the royal wedding, which was held on the grounds of the palace. The wealthiest of Avici were invited, along with a score of Senasanans. When it was time to present the ring, a golden dragon appeared in the sky and landed near the wedding party. The wondrous female bent down her long neck and dropped the ring from her mouth into Asamāna's trembling hand. Shouting and applause followed. This impressed even Laylah.

Invictus' first wedding present to his new bride was an announcement that construction would soon begin on a tower that would dwarf any structure on Triken. Uccheda—as it would be called—would reach to the clouds and be as magnificent as the new queen.

Lucius raved to Laylah about Asamāna. "You and she will become wonderful friends."

Just a week after the wedding, Asamāna tapped on her door. Laylah invited the new queen into her bedchamber. The woman was almost as beautiful as a Warlish witch, but she seemed to lack confidence, stuttering frequently when she spoke.

"I would like to discuss some important matters with you. My king has great p-plans for Avici, but there is something he needs from you that he can't get from m-me."

"What could he possibly need from me? The two of you seem so happy."

"We *are* happy. B-but ... B-but ..."

Asamāna burst into tears. Laylah put an arm around her slim shoulders.

"How old are you, child?" Laylah said.

"Eighteen."

"You're ten years younger than me," Laylah said, trying to calm her with mundane conversation.

Asamāna's lips quivered, but she seemed determined to say what she'd come to say. "He wants a *son*! But I can't give him one. Both the child and I would d-die. Only you can do it! He doesn't care about you as a wife. He only cares about having a son. If you'll just let him do it, just let him t-touch you with his hand for a couple of minutes, that's all, then he won't be m-mad. After you give birth, he'll leave us both alone. He won't hurt us ... h-hurt *me*."

"Is that the reason you've come here?" Laylah said, suddenly angry. "To beg me to bear your husband's child? Tell the perverted bastard I'd rather *die*. And tell General Lucius that I've seen through his facade."

Asamāna grimaced. "Then you *will* die! All of us will die. Y-you don't understand what he *is*! Y-y-you don't understand what he *does*!"

The next day, Laylah heard tragic news. The queen had fallen down the stairs leading to her bedchamber and had broken her neck. A few hundred attended a private funeral where there was a conspicuous lack of a body.

When Lucius came to her room, Laylah charged at him and pounded on his chest. "How *dare* you! This sham marriage was just another ploy to trick me into trusting my brother, and you were part of it, pretending to be my friend. I was starting to like you. Now I *hate* you!"

Thus, the waiting game began again. In the months that followed, Laylah attempted several more escapes, each forcibly thwarted. During one battle, she managed to injure Urbana, torching the vampire's face. This put Laylah in a pleasant mood for several days.

Though she had rejected Lucius, Laylah didn't lose faith in Bhacca. They remained friends and continued to spend time together. One evening, Bhacca came to her red-faced and animated, announcing she had been promoted from chambermaid to mistress of the robes, replacing Urbana, who had been assigned other duties.

Once again, a tedious string of years blunted Laylah's outrage. They permitted her to wander as far as a league from the palace, though dracools still circled in the skies and vampires and Mogols kept track of her from the ground. Meanwhile, Invictus ignored her completely, not even acknowledging her presence. And whenever she saw Lucius, the general bowed his head in shame. Laylah started to feel sorry for him. Though he had betrayed her, she respected him for not trying to deny it. And in her heart, she didn't believe he was evil. Lucius was her brother's pawn, just like everyone else who dwelled in Avici. Even the most powerful among them were subservient.

Despite Asamāna's death, the construction of Uccheda began on schedule. Laylah watched it rise from her window in the palace, disquieting in its magnitude. Invictus brought in scientists, architects, masons, carpenters, and quarrymen. Tens of thousands of slaves worked under the whip. Even then, it took twenty years to complete the tower, which ended up being more than 600 cubits tall. But more impressive than its height was its decadence. Invictus demanded that they coat its exterior with a thin layer of magically enhanced gold. While Uccheda was under construction, the slaves also built the Golden Wall, a formidable bulwark that encircled Avici and its sister city Kilesa. Her brother's grand ambitions became an indomitable reality.

Laylah was 50 years old when they moved her from the palace to Uccheda. The tower—now the largest edifice in the world—became one more negative in her life. In comparison, the much-smaller palace seemed charming and comfortable. Her new bedchamber was near the top of the tower, 500 cubits above the floor of the valley, and though metal transport cages inside the tower rode up and down on cables, it still took her an uncomfortably long time to get from her room to the ground. She found herself spending more and more time sleeping during the day and sitting by her window at night, gazing at the moon and stars. Except for Bhacca's frequent visits, the comforting glow of the moon was the only thing that kept her sane. Otherwise, she became lazy and listless. She even lost the desire to escape.

One night, approximately forty years into her captivity, Laylah worked up the energy to leave the tower and walk the grounds. Urbana, her damaged face long since healed by sorcery, joined the inevitable collection of tag-along guards. Before exiting the tower through the soundless doors that magically appeared out of the wall, Laylah caught sight of her reflection in a silver mirror. Though she now was almost sixty years old, her physical appearance had changed little since she had first arrived, other than a slight hint of maturity. Her demon blood kept her perpetually young, but Laylah took little pleasure in it.

On this night, the moon was swollen, which probably explained her vivacity. She wandered to the top of the hillock and lay down amid fragrant flowers. The full moon seemed oh so close. She felt like she could reach out and touch its mottled surface with her fingertips.

Blaring horns and beating drums startled Laylah. A brigade of Avician soldiers marched toward the city along the Golden Road, with dracools circling overhead. One of the baby dragons broke from formation and hurtled toward the tower, landing on its roof and disappearing from her view. It soon reappeared and flew back to meet the soldiers. Laylah recognized that the dracool carried Invictus, who was making a rare appearance in the darkness. Whatever was happening had to be important.

She rolled onto her stomach and propped her chin in her hands, watching the proceedings with cautious curiosity. As the caravan grew closer, she focused her attention on a dozen oxen hauling a wagon. An enormous creature, chained at the neck, wrist and ankles, stood in the bed. Even from a distance, she could make out the color of its eyes.

Laylah experienced a surge of pity for the beast, and she raced down the hill and crouched behind some bushes near the road. Urbana and the guards approached within fifty paces of her, suspicious of her intentions. But when they saw Laylah stop, they stopped too.

The brigade came to a halt. Feeling bold, she stood and strode to the edge of the road. Laylah wanted to see this creature up close. Warily, she watched her brother approach the wagon.

"What do you think you're doing?" a voice hissed from behind her. "You've no business here."

"Oh, shut up, Urbana, or I'll burn your face again. I'm trying to see what's happening. Do you *mind*?"

"You little bitch. If it weren't for your brother, I'd bite a chunk out of your throat."

Laylah barely heard the threat. She focused on the giant, which appeared to be at least ten cubits tall, even larger than a Kojin. But while the ogresses were hideous, this creature was beautiful. A white mane extended from the top of his head down the center of his broad back, and his face exuded gentleness despite an imposing pair of fangs that protruded over his lower lip. The giant saw her—and Laylah was convinced he smiled. But the smile was poignant as if recognizing that she too was a prisoner.

"What's your name?" she heard Invictus say to the creature.

"I am Yama-Deva. I would also know your name, but the more important question is: Why do you chain me?"

A soldier climbed onto the cart and struck the creature's thighs with a flail.

"Do not speak to the king with such insolence," the soldier said.

Yama-Deva didn't flinch, but Invictus snarled and then raised his hand. Golden light leaped from his palm and incinerated the soldier, armor and all. The killing had little effect on Laylah. Nothing her brother did surprised her anymore. The sorcerer turned back to the creature and smiled.

"Yama-Deva, I apologize for any rudeness on the part of my associates and assure you it won't happen again. Allow me to answer your questions. My name is Invictus, and I am king of Avici. And your chains? A simple misunderstanding. You're an honored guest, not a prisoner."

"False words cannot fool a snow giant. But my perception extends beyond the ability to perceive deception. It's plain to me that you're strong … too strong even for me."

Laylah interrupted. "Let him go."

The sorcerer twisted around, startled. At first he appeared angry, but then a smile spread across his face.

"And if I set him free, will you do something for me?"

Everyone stared at Laylah—except for the snow giant, who lowered his gaze and sighed.

"No," Laylah said. "I will not. Cannot."

Invictus' expression became that of a frustrated child. "Then this beast will pay the price for your insolence! I will subject him to torture that will ruin his mind. Is that what you want? With but a word from you, I will return him to his home and never trouble him or his kind again."

The snow giant raised his head and met her eyes. He spoke words she barely understood.

"*Naham te dhuram, kumarakaa. Ma bhayi. Me niyati saniyati.* (I'm not your responsibility, child. Do not fear for me. My fate is my own.)"

Invictus snarled.

Urbana cackled.

Laylah ran.

Another night ruined.

A decade after Invictus imprisoned the snow giant, Laylah still obsessed over the creature's dismal fate. Then his name had been Yama-Deva, but ten years of torture had transformed him into a hideous monster. Now he was Mala, the latest and greatest horror in her brother's expanding menagerie. It sickened Laylah that such a beautiful creature could be so thoroughly ruined, especially when she felt partially to blame. But the Chain Man was so repulsive it became impossible to pity him. Laylah grew to hate him as much as she did Invictus, Vedana, and Urbana.

The day after her brief encounter with Yama-Deva on the Golden Road, Laylah endured a new form of psychological torture. Just after sunset, Invictus appeared in the hallway outside her bedchamber. As he had vowed more than forty years before, he didn't enter her room without her permission. But for the short period between dusk and full darkness, he tapped on the door and begged her to reconsider.

"I want a son, Laylah … that is all. Give me an heir and I swear I'll set you free. Why won't you believe me?"

"Please go away," she said.

And he did.

But the next night …

"I have potions that will make you sleep. You won't even know I'm there. Give me a son and I'll set you free. You may go wherever you desire. I swear it. Why won't you believe me?"

"Please go away."

The next night, and the next, and the next, more of the same. He begged, pleaded, cajoled. Some nights his voice was indignant. Others, it was like honey.

"Give me a son and I'll set you free."

"Please … go … away."

When blessed darkness arrived, Invictus would depart. But Laylah's suffering didn't end there. She would shake and sob, knowing all too well that he would come again the next evening. How long could she bear it? She questioned her own resolve. Maybe he was right. Just let him impregnate her with his magic and get it over with. Still, she resisted.

The visits continued without fail for ten more years. To keep her sanity, she occasionally spoke to Lucius but cautiously and without warmth. The general remained as kind and forthcoming as ever, and he apologized profusely whenever she gave him the opportunity. His attraction to her was obvious.

When the idea first arose in her mind, Laylah was lying in bed in the late afternoon. She scolded herself for taking so long to think of it. How could she have remained blind to something so obvious? Just as her brother was slowly and steadily attempting to seduce her, she could play the same game. With Lucius.

It made sense in so many ways. The emergence of Mala as a new force in Avici had effectively shoved the general aside. The Chain Man now commanded the army that had once belonged solely to Lucius. Invictus clearly had a new favorite pet.

Laylah had watched Mala interact with Lucius. The ruined snow giant showed the firstborn little respect, ordering him around as cruelly as any subordinate. Wouldn't this make Lucius less loyal to Invictus and more susceptible to her charms?

What if she could seduce him? Not into bed, but into obsession. Eventually, he would do whatever pleased her, even if it meant risking his position—and his life—by betraying his king. Lucius was not as powerful as he used to be, but he was still formidable. If anyone had the means to help her escape, the firstborn did.

For the rest of the afternoon, Laylah couldn't sleep. She sat at her desk and wrote a brief note:

Dear Lucius,

Would you meet me by the swing at midnight? This time of year, the nights are so lovely. And the moon will be full. You know how much I love the Ripe Corn Moon.

There are some things I wish to say to you. I will bring Bhacca to avoid any appearance of impropriety.

Warmly,
Laylah

She folded the note, sealed it with a crescent moon insignia, and summoned Bhacca to her bedchamber. But Laylah's request discomforted the mistress of the robes.

"The Chain Man watches everyone. If a person so much as belches, Mala reports it to the king. If he or one of his spies were to see me pass a note to Lucius, we'd all be in trouble."

"That's why you'll be extra careful," Laylah said. "Besides, there's nothing *bad* in the note. I'm only asking him to meet me tonight so that we can converse. I even told him that you'll be with me. You and I often stroll the grounds late at night. General Lucius does, as well."

"What if the general shows this to the king?"

"He won't. Given my circumstances, I have little experience with men, I admit. But I think I have enough to know he won't betray us in that way. At the least, he'll want to hear what I have to say first. Wouldn't you?"

"Well, yes. But ..."

"Trust me, then, as I trust you. Nothing will be spoken tonight that will cause any harm. After all these long years, I just want to clear the air with a former friend."

Bhacca acquiesced. "Very well, my queen. You've always treated me with respect, so I'll do as you ask. If not for you, I wouldn't be mistress of the robes."

That night, Laylah sensed Lucius' approach long before he arrived at the sycamore. She sat on the swing, her silky hair dangling past her waist. She wore a crimson dress that was slit to expose her muscular calves, thin ankles, and bare feet. Lucius' cheeks became flushed and sweat beaded on his brow, but he tried to act nonchalant.

"My queen," he said, nodding to Laylah. "And mistress." Another nod, to Bhacca. "It's my pleasure to join you on such a fine summer eve. You wish to speak with me?"

"I do. Are others about? What I have to say is intended for your ears only."

Lucius' eyes narrowed. Then his head swiveled but so slowly as to be imperceptible. "No one is nearby," he whispered. "But I don't have the stomach for such intrigue."

Laylah laughed. "I'm just joking, Lucius. My brother and Mala could stand among us and no harm would occur."

Lucius looked relieved. "Well then, please speak your mind."

"Many years have passed since my *anger* damaged our friendship. Too many years, to be honest. I miss our strolls—and our long conversations. I wish to learn more about Avici. It has grown so huge. And there's so much else I would know. Has the Golden Wall been completed? And what about …"

This time it was Lucius' turn to laugh. "Laylah … *Laylah*! One question at a time. Renewing our friendship would be my fondest dream. I only hope that I can keep it this time."

"So do I!" Bhacca said. "The queen is in much better spirits when you're around."

They all laughed.

The following evening, Invictus didn't appear at her doorway. In some ways, this amused Laylah. It was obvious Lucius had reported their meeting to Invictus, prompting her brother to lie low to see what might develop. This lasted for several blessed months as Laylah and Lucius strolled each evening—with Bhacca in attendance. A miniature army of Invictus' minions watched them from a distance. The dracools flew especially high, and on dark nights they were impossible to detect. But when the moon was aglow, Laylah could see black specks circling above. Sometimes, soldiers were nearby. Or white-robed spies posing as civilians. She and the general kept their distance, physically, and their conversations purposefully bland.

However, when Laylah felt the moment was right, she would give Lucius the kind of look that caused his cheeks to redden again.

"You're a nice man," she said on a rare night when Bhacca had not joined them.

His expression grew anxious—almost paranoid.

But she added quickly: "My brother is so fortunate to have you as his friend."

He relaxed, somewhat. "And I'm fortunate to serve such a great king," he said louder than necessary.

"What makes you happy makes me happy," she whispered to him.

He didn't respond, but the muscles in his face crumbled. The next words he spoke came as soft as a wisp of breeze. "We can trust Izumo."

And then he turned and started back toward the tower.

"It grows late, my queen," he said.

"Feel free to depart," Laylah said. "I'll remain here and enjoy this lovely night from the hilltop. The moon is so close. Maybe tonight I'll finally be able to touch it. Until we meet again …"

"Indeed."

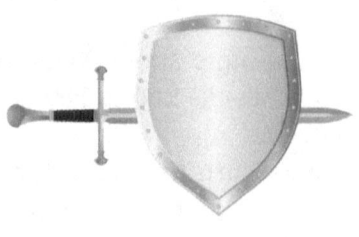

CONSPIRACY

It's one thing to love your creator, another to respect him. After all that had occurred, General Lucius still loved Invictus for giving him the gift of life. But he no longer respected him. Lucius had seen too much.

Laylah's hatred of her brother had been born above the surface. But the sorcerer's worst deeds, as far as Lucius was concerned, occurred in the labyrinth of dark tunnels beneath Uccheda.

As general of Invictus' growing army, Lucius had spent many hours in the hidden chambers the sorcerer had bored out of solid rock using his magic. Invictus' powers appeared limitless. Where it might take a thousand slaves more than a year to tunnel through a wall of granite, Invictus could do it in the time it took to dig a single grave.

Not that the sorcerer lacked slaves, some of whom were better treated than others. For the most part, the newborns from Kilesa were respected in Avici. Almost all the males became soldiers while the females filled the most prestigious servile needs. But the slaves brought from outside the Golden Wall were not so lucky. Invictus took great delight in the art of torture, both viewing and performing. And most of it occurred in the underground.

Sadistic sexual orgies were a major part of what the general found so distasteful. But what else would you expect from a collection of monsters? They hungered for suffering as much as blood. The more fear and anguish they inspired, the more they relished it.

Invictus often summoned Lucius to watch the proceedings. They sat on stone benches in a cathedral-sized chamber. When you received a direct invitation from the sorcerer, you agreed enthusiastically without protest. But the libidinous gatherings secretly sickened Lucius. Most times, he could barely fend off vomiting.

As repulsive as the orgies were, they were not what caused Lucius to betray his king. Instead, it was the ruin of the snow giant. The general had paid little attention to the creature, considering him just one prisoner of many. But an unplanned encounter disturbed him profoundly. Lucius was making his rounds through the lower chambers, which served as a dungeon for the most volatile and valuable prisoners, when he came upon the cell that held Yama-Deva.

"You are like him and yet are not," the snow giant said. Golden chains imbued with the sorcerer's magic pinned him against a wall of granite. He'd been whipped, beaten, and starved. But his voice still sounded kind. "What I mean is, you *look* like him. But you don't *behave* like him."

"Haven't you learned by now to keep your mouth shut?" Lucius said. "If someone hears you, you'll be castigated. Why do you risk further abuse?"

"Do you see?" the giant said, laughing softly. "You are not like him. You care about the innocent."

"I do what I'm told. My personal feelings mean nothing."

"I can see your future," the giant said. "You will perform remarkable deeds before your life takes its final unexpected turn. A great many will rally around you and call you a king." Then Deva lowered his head and sighed. "I can see my future, as well. It won't be as heroic as yours."

"What do you mean?"

"I will become the thing I most despise. But that's not the worst of it."

"What could be worse?"

"I won't be able to remember who I am. My name is Yama-Deva. My people call me *The Wanderer*. But I won't remember. It will be as if I'm dead, but my body will live on without me. Could you do me one favor?"

"I make no promises," Lucius said, stepping back.

"Fair enough. But at least I can ask. If you're ever given the opportunity, would you tell whoever might listen that I'm sorry for the harm I will cause? Yama-Deva doesn't intend to hurt anyone. But what I'll become will take pleasure in inflicting pain. My only hope is I will redeem myself in the end."

"How can you know this?"

"*Eso aham himamahaakaayo* (I am a snow giant)," he said, as if that explained it all.

The next time Lucius saw Yama-Deva, the snow giant no longer existed. Mala, a.k.a. the Chain Man, stood in his place. Lucius soon recognized that his days as the king's right hand were over. In some ways, he no longer cared. In others, he was appalled. Yama-Deva had been such a wondrous creature, and now he was the epitome of evil. It was an affront to anything sane. This pleased Invictus, of course. In his twisted mind, ten years of torture and humiliation had paid off handsomely.

Lucius still loved Invictus. How could he not love the being who gave him life? But he also despised him. How could he not despise the being who introduced him to evil?

As the seeds of traitorous thought took root in Lucius' mind, he soon discovered that Izumo was also turning against the sorcerer—and for a similar reason. As he later described to Lucius in intimate detail, Izumo had adored Yama-Deva from the first moment he saw him foraging for roots in the foothills of Okkanti. When the slave-hunting expedition encircled him, Yama-Deva barely put up a fight. But Izumo could sense it had nothing to do with cowardice. The creature had failed to resist out of concern for the welfare of his assailants. This had impressed the dracool. Only a being of extreme intelligence could be so selfless.

Lucius knew that dracools were called baby dragons because of their similarity to actual dragons except for their much smaller size. Indeed, dracools and dragons shared common traits—a lizard-shaped snout, heavily scaled flesh, flexible necks and tails, and powerful wings—but their commonality did not breed respect. They hated each other intensely. Dragons enjoyed eating dracools, for one thing, and they considered themselves superior not just in size but in intelligence. Dracools, on the other hand, claimed to be the most learned beings alive, and they classified dragons as crude bullies. Great dragons were more than twenty times larger, but dracools were more numerous. Gatherings of dracools sometimes killed great dragons in battle.

Since they were long-lived, dracools had witnessed the rise and fall of many kingdoms. Like mercenaries, they allied themselves with whoever appeared most powerful, making Invictus an irresistible lure. But there was more. The sorcerer was the first being in an eon that possessed knowledge beyond their awareness. To the dracools, meeting the Sun God was like discovering a library filled with unread books.

Dracools didn't give much credence to the concepts of good and evil. In their minds, erudition and strength were good, obliviousness and weakness were evil. An intelligent devil was superior to an ignorant saint. Invictus' sadism and perversion meant little in terms of how they judged him. But wasteful behavior was another matter, and dracools viewed it with disdain, regardless of the circumstances. When Izumo watched Invictus destroy Yama-Deva, he lost respect for the king. Orgies and bloodbaths with meaningless slaves were one thing; mutilating a creature with so much to offer was another. The dracool told Lucius that he had been looking forward to spending long years with the snow giant, whose wisdom was impressive. Yama-Deva was also like a library, but instead of magic, potions, and spells, the snow giant burst with placidity. After the sorcerer ruined him, Deva had become a loud-mouthed buffoon.

And the dracool became Invictus' secret enemy.

Lucius and Izumo discovered the similarity of their feelings by accident. While the two of them were overseeing military exercises ten leagues east of Avici, Mala had approached and lambasted them for not following one of his inane dictates regarding troop deployment.

"What part of my order did you not understand?" Mala said to Lucius, towering over him like he was a child.

Lucius removed his helm. "The cohorts on the right flank were loosely assembled," the firstborn said. "Jivitan horsemen could penetrate this too easily. I ordered a tighter formation to mimic the left flank. Am I deemed incapable of modifying a command when I see fit?"

The Chain Man's swollen eyes sprang wide open. He turned his rage on Izumo.

"You delivered Lucius' *modification* to the commander on the field," Mala said. "Did *you* not understand my command?"

"I've followed General Lucius' orders since I arrived in Avici," Izumo said.

This enraged Mala. Molten profusions gushed from his chain. To avoid being scorched, Lucius dove sideways and Izumo sprang backward, barely dodging the acidic fusillade. Before Lucius could stand, the Chain Man leaped upon him, grabbed his armor at the shoulders, and lifted him five cubits off the ground. Izumo took to the air, hovering just out of Mala's reach.

"Listen to me," the Chain Man said to Lucius, easily loud enough for Izumo to hear. "I know things neither of you know. There are reasons for what I do. I want the soldiers to march until they're exhausted ... and nothing more! Do you understand? If you ever *modify* my commands again, I'll shove my fist up your bony ass, grab your tongue, and yank it back between your cheeks. And the same goes for you, dracool. I don't know how to make it any clearer. I am General Lucius' superior in all ways. I am the superior of every member of this army and of every being who dwells in Avici and Kilesa. I am *superior* to all, save Invictus himself."

Mala then tossed Lucius onto the grass. "Now, if you wish to challenge my superiority, here's your chance. It's two against one. No others are near enough to aid me. Fight me if you dare."

Izumo continued to hover but didn't come closer. Lucius stood, brushing blades of grass off his armor, but he too remained in place. The Chain Man stared at them both—and then laughed.

"As I thought ... a pair of worthless weaklings." Then he pointed at Lucius. "I knew you didn't have the courage to change. But I don't want anyone saying I'm not fair. If either of you wishes to pursue this further, feel free to go to Invictus and complain in person. Otherwise, heed my warning. If you disobey me again, I will end your lives."

Mala stomped away, leaving Lucius and Izumo to mull over their cowardice together.

The dracool landed next to the firstborn.

"Your face is red and swollen," he said to Lucius. "Are you injured?"

"Only my pride," Lucius said, though he did feel peculiar, almost feverish. "Without Invictus' backing, I'm no match for Mala. And he knows full well that Invictus loves him more than me."

"The other members of my flock still support the sorcerer, but I can no longer tolerate his behavior," Izumo said. "My time in Avici is nearing its end."

"Mine too. But when I leave, I plan on bringing someone with me."

"Who might that be?"

"Laylah."

"The queen? Invictus watches her every move. *You* might escape. But Laylah? Never."

"I don't have much of a plan," Lucius admitted. "In fact, I just now thought this up. But Laylah wants to go, and I'll do my best to aid her."

"Are you in love with her?"

Lucius sighed. "I am."

"Well then, consider me your ally."

This amazed Lucius, but he was in no mood to turn down such a valiant offer. "We dare not move quickly. Invictus can read minds—and mine the easiest of all, for I was born from his blood. We must not speak of this again for a long time. Exactly one year from now, let's meet at this same spot at midnight and talk briefly. Otherwise, we'll do as we're told."

"One year from now," Izumo said before springing into the sky.

Afterward, Lucius stood alone, viewing the proceedings from a lonely and dangerous place.

Laylah's wine tasted especially bitter, but that wasn't unusual. In her life, all things had become bitter: the dreadful and relentless lack of freedom; the constant fear and anxiety. How much longer could she bear it? How many more years? Months? Weeks? Days? Breaths?

She now had been a prisoner in Avici for sixty years. She knew this not because she had kept count but because her "return," as Invictus liked to call it, was marked on the Avician calendar, which recognized Day 1, Year 1 as her brother's first birthday. It now was Day 1, Year 88, her brother's 88th birthday. To celebrate this grand occasion, he had held a midday feast in the main banquet room of Uccheda. One thousand soldiers, dignitaries, high-ranking civilians, and the usual menagerie of monsters filled a great circular table. Laylah sat on Invictus' left, while Mala squatted on the floor at his right, stink wafting off his tortured flesh.

The main course was garlic beef ribs crusted with breadcrumbs and served with salted potatoes, roasted corn, and white muffins. Servitors presented the meal on silver platters and poured the wine into glass goblets imbedded with diamond chips. Mala ate mounds of ribs, eschewing the vegetables and bread.

"I want my next serving rare," he bellowed. "How many times do I have to say it?"

"If it were any rarer," Laylah said, "it would be *raw*."

"Exactly!"

Invictus laughed. Her brother was in an excellent mood—and on this day he was treating her with respect, which made Laylah distrust him even more.

"Mala doesn't have your sensibilities, my dear sister. Concentrate your attentions on General Lucius. He has impeccable manners."

Lucius sat on Laylah's left, but during the meal he had stared straight ahead and said only a few words. That was part of their plan ever since he'd involved her in it. They now communicated blandly, and then only late at night when Invictus was underground and when Mala had gone to Kilesa or was traveling the wilds with the slave hunters.

If Invictus suspected Lucius was a traitor, he would execute the general, ruining any hopes of her escaping. But their best chance of success had come not from Lucius but from a strange occurrence Izumo had hastily described. The dracool had been on a nightly patrol above Avici, flying in circles over the city, when a tasty bird flapped close by. Izumo lunged for it, but the bird easily evaded him and then flew alongside him, unafraid. Izumo recognized this was no ordinary creature.

"What business have you with me?"

"How nice of you to notice me, Dracool-Izumo," the bird said.

"Do I know you?"

"The dracools know me well. I am Vedana, mother of all demons."

This frightened Izumo, but he tried not to show it. "It's safe to assume you haven't come to kill me. If so, the deed would have already occurred. But why would one as great as you wish to speak to me? Might it have something to do with your grandson?"

The bird's black beak moved like soft clay in the darkness. "He's a troublesome boy," Vedana said. "*Too big for his britches*. Spoiled, too. In the ancient tongue, he'd be called *nikkaruna*."

"I speak the ancient tongue as well as any," Izumo said. "*Nikkaruna* translates rather loosely as heartless."

"Heartless, he is," Vedana said. "The only problem is—as I'm sure you've discovered—he's also disturbingly strong. Even I've been forced to cower in the shadows, which doesn't suit me."

"And you need *my* help? What could a *baby dragon* possibly offer the most vaunted of demons?"

"It's not what you offer me. It's what I offer you. Invictus is not yet aware of your … how should we say? … conspiracy."

"Why do you rave? It doesn't become you."

"Don't be dismayed. You and I are on the same side. My grandson has angered me, and I don't handle anger well. It makes me petty and vengeful. I've been watching carefully from my little hidey-hole. You and Lucius have provided me with an amusing opportunity to further injure him."

"I'm listening."

"Invictus is *Akanittha*. Being such an expert in the ancient tongue, you know the meaning of that word. With each sunrise, his strength increases. However, he has one weakness that even he hasn't considered. There's a date you and your fellow conspirators need to circle on my grandson's annoying Avician calendar. Day 75, Year 100. Easy enough for an intelligent fellow like you to remember."

"And what will occur on that fine day?"

"Something very special … you'll find out. In the meantime, I recommend you don't try to escape with Laylah before then."

"And you tell me this only to hurt Invictus? You've nothing else to gain?"

But Vedana didn't answer. A black hole appeared in the sky and the bird dove into it, vanishing from sight.

While sitting at the banquet table, Laylah puzzled over Izumo's tale. But Invictus suddenly rose to his feet and shattered her thoughts.

"My friends, I have a birthday announcement. My court has a new member. And I would like to introduce him now."

This caused a hush, puzzling even Mala. Invictus swept his hand toward the wall of the tower where an aperture appeared, humming as it enlarged until it spread thirty cubits tall and twenty wide. A feisty breeze swept into the room, flinging napkins into the air and blowing crumbs off platters.

"Behold, Bhayatupa!" Invictus said. "The greatest of all dragons."

Bhayatupa's head, larger than Mala's entire body, slid through the window into the banquet room. Screams and shouts ensued, and many of the guests fled, including all the dracools except Izumo.

"*Bhayatupa aviddeso* (Bhayatupa is without enmity)," the dragon said in a booming voice that caused several goblets to shatter.

The words were meant as a concession. It appeared Bhayatupa

didn't plan to incinerate them. Invictus laughed, pleased by the hysteria.

"This has been my best birthday ever!"

Later that day, Laylah sipped more wine in her bedchamber. She normally slept during the day, but the strange banquet—punctuated by Bhayatupa's arrival—kept replaying in her mind. The more wine she drank, the less bitter it tasted. Her body felt like it was shimmering. Waves of pleasure swept through her. Not since she'd run wild in the mountains had she felt such joy.

A tapping at her door interrupted her reverie. Was it her dear friend Bhacca? Or General Lucius? Oh, she hoped it was him. They could have a pleasant talk.

More tapping.

"Who is it?"

"It's Lucius. May I come in?"

"Of course!" Laylah said. "Please do."

Laylah's vision was blurry. She could see Lucius' golden armor, but the visor of his helm was closed and fastened with a locking hook.

The firstborn guided a pewter goblet toward her mouth.

"More wine, my queen?"

She didn't want or need more wine, but Lucius pressed the goblet against her lips. Her dizziness intensified until she fell backward on the soft mattress, digging her fingers into the silken sheets.

She heard noises beside her, the creaking and clanking of metal armor being removed and dropped to the floor. Lucius was making himself comfortable. And why not? Must she spend the rest of her life in celibacy? She didn't love him, but the firstborn was better than anyone else in this rotten place.

While wearing no armor except for his helm, he placed his hand on her stomach and pressed gently. Would he proceed further than that? Why stop him? Was it so wrong to have some fun? Since arriving back in Avici, she'd had so little fun.

In her drugged state, her awareness fled to a distant place where she lay alone on a bed of white sand in a dry cave. But wait? She wasn't alone. Someone approached—an enormous man with black hair and blue eyes. The sight of him caused her heart to pound. This was the man that she wanted to give herself to.

She screamed with joy.

But Lucius still stood above her, his hand on her stomach glowing like the sun.

"No," she whispered. Then, "No ... *no!*"

Agony flared inside her abdomen, and she arched upward with a surge of panicked strength. Lucius removed his helm and heaved it to the floor. Invictus stood in the general's place. The extravagant potion he had magically blended into her wine had so nearly achieved its purpose.

The sorcerer stormed toward her, lifted her from the bed, and flung her across the room. She crashed onto the top of her dressing table, knocked over the silver mirror, and slid off the edge. When she struck the marble floor, she banged her head. Her brother loomed over her and kicked at her stomach. She enveloped her flesh in white magic just in time to absorb the worst of the blow, but it still knocked the breath out of her and intensified the pain she already felt.

"How much longer do you expect me to wait? How *dare* you deny me a son? No one can deny me. I am *Akanittha!*"

Then he left, slamming the door so hard it splintered. She remained on the floor, hugging her stomach, teetering on the edge of sanity. But a part of her rejoiced. She had thwarted him again.

Aloud, she whispered: "Day 75, Year 100."

There were only twelve years to go. They didn't pass quickly, but they did pass. In the early morning of Day 330, Year 99, someone pounded on Laylah's door. As usual, she had stayed awake through the night and was just nodding off to sleep. Laylah sat upright with a yelp. Was it Invictus? He never came to her room this early in the day. After the second aborted attempt at magically impregnating her, he had given her a few months of peace but had then resumed his habit of begging at her door at dusk.

This morning, though, the voice she heard came from Urbana's foul mouth.

"Queen Laylah! The king will entertain an important guest today, and he demands your presence."

"Tell him I'm not feeling well."

"I couldn't care less how you're feeling and neither could he," the vampire said. "This is an *order*, not a request. I'm sending Bhacca in now to prepare you. You must hurry!"

The door swung open and Bhacca skittered in. Several chambermaids followed. They offered her breakfast, but Laylah wasn't hungry. They dressed her in a white samite gown laced with silver, combed her hair, applied cosmetics to her face and lips, and dabbed frankincense perfume on her neck, arms, and inner thighs. Throughout the entire process, Urbana waited in the hallway, her foot tapping impatiently. For reasons Laylah didn't understand, the vampire continued to honor Invictus' original command never to enter her room without an invitation.

Izumo appeared outside her door. Whenever Laylah saw the dracool, her heart skipped a beat. He had become a friend, but she tried to conceal her pleasure. The dracool did, as well.

"It's time," Izumo said in his raspy voice. "Are you ready?"

"Yes ... *hurry!*" Urbana said. "Bhacca, are your fingers made of clay? Finish those laces! Time is short."

They followed Izumo down the hallway to one of the metal transport cages. The dracool was almost too large to fit into the cage, so he motioned for Laylah and Bhacca to go first. Urbana tried to squeeze in with them, but Izumo held her back.

"You don't want to wrinkle her dress," the dracool said.

Urbana snarled. "I'd love to spit blood on it."

Izumo latched the door and pulled on a cord that set the cage in motion. It dropped more than 400 cubits, slamming to a halt so abruptly that Laylah nearly lost her footing.

"I'll never get used to that," she said to Bhacca.

"I don't like it either, but the tower is so tall it takes forever to walk up and down the stairs. I wish I was like Izumo and could leap out a window and fly down."

When they stepped out of the cage, General Lucius and several Golden Soldiers greeted them. Lucius wore his finest armor and carried his helm in the crook of his arm, his long yellow hair skimming his shoulders.

Once again, Laylah's heart skipped a beat.

"Good morning, my queen," Lucius said. "I apologize if you've been inconvenienced. Please follow me. The guest has arrived amid much fanfare."

"Is he a guest or a prisoner?"

"That is not for me to say. But he has come with Mala, if that answers your question."

One soldier chuckled, then looked nervously around to see if he were being watched. Laylah didn't laugh. "I pity him, whoever he may be," she said.

Lucius led them down a corridor lined with marble sculptures of Invictus in a variety of regal poses. The lifeless eyes seemed to follow her. She stopped to catch her breath.

"Is something wrong?" Lucius said. "You don't look well."

"When is the last time I was well?"

After a brief rest, they continued through the corridor before entering a crowded room ablaze with sunlight pouring in through immense windows. She saw Invictus, adorned in golden robes that hung to the floor, conversing with Chal-Abhinno, the Warlish witch. Chal was resplendent in a crimson gown and bejeweled chaplet. Ten standard-bearers wearing golden armor studded with diamonds and rubies stood near the windows. Their banners bore yellow suns outlined in red on backgrounds of white. Two dracools, both of whom had helped to recapture her several times during her frequent attempts at escape, stood nearby. She looked around for Izumo, but he had gone off somewhere and was nowhere to be seen.

A horn sounded and then a portal swung slowly open. The standard-bearers marched onto a circular balcony. An immense roar greeted them. It became apparent to Laylah that most of Avici had gathered at the base of the tower. How important was this prisoner?

Chal-Abhinno sauntered out next, escorted by the dracools. There was another roar.

"Follow me," Lucius said. "It's our turn."

Laylah walked behind Lucius. When she stepped onto the balcony, the blazing heat of the sun smacked her in the face. She bowed her head and focused on Lucius' hinged sollerets, following him to the edge of the balcony.

A wagon was positioned at the base of the tower. Invictus' *guest* was strapped to an angled board attached to its bed. Laylah felt compelled to gaze down at the poor man. He seemed to look back at her, which surprised her.

What happened next almost caused her to swoon. A blue glimmer leaped from his eyes. In response, white light sprang from hers. The beams, pale as ghosts, collided in midair.

In her peripheral vision, Laylah felt Lucius glare at her disapprovingly. But she didn't care. The man in the wagon consumed her attention. Though he was more than one hundred cubits away, she could make out his features like he was an arm's length from where she stood.

His face ... his mouth ... his eyes ...

Another roar startled her. Invictus strode onto the balcony. The hundreds of thousands gathered beneath the tower howled in unison. Laylah collapsed into Lucius' arms.

Invictus spoke first to his people and then to the man in the wagon, his voice magically amplified.

Laylah could hear Mala bellowing below, the dragon chortling above, Lucius whispering in her ear.

Those sounds were meaningless.

All she could think about was the man in the wagon.

For the briefest of moments, she had loved him like no other.

Less than a month later, she overheard Mala say the man was dead.

On Day 74, Year 100, more than 600,000 hours since Invictus had first imprisoned her, Laylah paced her room in Uccheda. She would attempt the escape tomorrow, regardless of the outcome.

Izumo seemed confident Vedana wouldn't betray them, but their reliance on the demon discomforted Lucius, who feared a trap. Despite her hatred of her grandmother, Laylah agreed with the dracool. Besides, it wasn't like they had other options.

Laylah had spoken to Lucius about their conspiracy less than a dozen times over the past twelve years, and those were brief encounters late at night. Because of their extreme need for secrecy, Laylah had spoken to Izumo about their plans even less frequently, but Lucius assured her the dracool remained an ally.

"What will become of Bhacca?" Laylah whispered to Lucius one summer evening as they stood on the wildflower hillock overlooking the valley. "She'll be lost without me."

"A dracool can carry only two people ... and that, not easily," Lucius said. "I weigh more than fifteen stones and you at least nine. I've already told Izumo that if we're pursued too closely, I'll jump off to lighten the load. But bringing Bhacca along would be impossible unless

I didn't come. You'll have to choose between us."

"I choose you, of course. I'm worried about her, that's all. And don't you dare jump. I'd never forgive you."

"If sacrificing myself meant saving you, I'd do it without hesitation."

Laylah knew he meant it, though she still didn't love him the way he loved her. But she didn't have the energy to worry about that now. The future would decide the fate of their relationship.

Their last contact regarding their conspiracy had occurred more than two years ago. Any more talk would have been too dangerous. Invictus interrogated Lucius daily, wanting to know everything Laylah said and did. In some ways. Laylah believed these interrogations were as difficult on Lucius as Invictus' visits were on Laylah. Lucius was destined to be a traitor, but somehow Invictus couldn't detect it. Was it because the sorcerer was incapable of believing his firstborn could betray him? Or was it simply because the firstborn's behavior had aroused so little suspicion? To further cement his position as a person of trust, Lucius had become subservient to Mala, doing whatever the Chain Man told him without the slightest resistance. The ruined snow giant bossed him around like he was a boy, but the general bore it with borderline enthusiasm.

And now, the eve of the fateful day had arrived. Over the past seventy-two years, Laylah had attempted to escape many times. But she had never come close to succeeding. Like a fly with broken wings trying to climb out of an anthill, she was too weak and her enemies too strong and too many.

Would tomorrow be any different? It wasn't as though they could simply clamber onto Izumo's back and fly merrily away. The other dracools, unburdened by passengers, would catch them with ease. To succeed, they would need an extraordinary diversion. Vedana had hinted at just such an occurrence. But what could it be? They would have to wait and see. And hope.

Laylah knew one thing: If she failed this time, that would be that. She would escape or die trying. Freedom cried out like a long, lost friend. Without it, she could survive no longer. She had already borne her imprisonment for an impossibly long time.

When dusk settled on Day 74, she heard the notorious tapping on her door. As always, her tortured psyche reeled. As always, the ceiling, walls, and floor of her room glowed with golden flames that crept along the surface of the stone, wood, and metal. The flames even danced on her skin.

"Sister … may I come in?"

"*Please* go away."

"You've denied me for such a long time. Won't you change your mind? If you do, I promise on the blood of our parents that I will set you free. Once you give me a son, you can go wherever you choose—even to Nissaya or Jivita. You can become their queen and lead their armies against me. I don't care."

"The blood of our parents is dry."

"I can see you're not in a forgiving mood tonight, sister. Very well. I have learned the art of patience. Our lifespans have no foreseeable end. So why rush? One day—whether tomorrow or a thousand years from now—you will bear me a son."

And then he was gone, along with the eerie flames.

Laylah flung herself onto her bed. Sweet Bhacca soon came to comfort her. The mistress of the robes brought poached eggs, thick slices of sizzling pork, white cakes, and a goblet of apple cider. Laylah ate without hunger, but with determination. She would choke down another meal in the morning. After that, she would wait, watch, and remain alert.

Uncharacteristically, she slept several hours in the middle of the night, during which she had a disturbing dream.

She stood on the crest of a mountain of sand beneath the most glorious moon she'd ever seen. When she looked to her right, the man in the wagon was there, but now he was free—and very much alive. He wore a dark jacket and matching breeches, and the enormous muscles of his chest, back, and thighs caused the fabric to swell. A breeze rustled his long black hair. Laylah felt as though she might swoon. It was all she could do just to smile. The man spoke to someone on his right. She couldn't hear their words. Then he turned to her, his face confused. She so desperately wanted to talk to him. But when she tried to speak, her lips were locked in a stupid smile. And that is when she heard Vedana cackling in the darkness—and another sound that resembled a squalling baby. The man raced down the side of the mountain, sprinting across the soft sands with ridiculous ease. She tried to follow, but it felt like she was running through knee-deep snow.

When Laylah woke, her heart was pounding. She rose from her bed and walked to the window. Dawn approached—for her, usually a cause of sadness. But not this day. For the first time in as long as she could remember, she had hope.

Through a psychic connection they had developed over the decades, Laylah summoned Bhacca. Soon, the door opened and the mistress of the robes entered bearing another tray of food. This time, it was roasted chicken, sweet potatoes, and slices of red melon. Laylah ate everything, sopping up the butter and garlic with the potato skins, and she rinsed her mouth with several cups of apple wine. Then she bathed and dressed in a dark-blue undertunic with a purple surcoat—rugged but not overly restrictive—and bleached leather boots.

She sat by her window in a padded chair. Bhacca remained with her but seemed confused.

"After your morning meal, you always lay down to sleep. Is something wrong, Laylah?"

"I wasn't feeling well during the night, and I slept then. Now I'm refreshed. I'd like to sit in my chair and admire the grounds in daylight."

This pleased Bhacca. "A wonderful idea. The valley is beautiful when the sun first rises. Spring is almost here. The sky is clear, the air warm. It should be a glorious day."

"I certainly hope so," Laylah said.

"My queen?" Bhacca said, sensing queerness in Laylah's tone.

"If I'm to stay up past my bedtime, then I hope you're right about the weather," Laylah said, attempting to deflect suspicion. "Leave me now. I'm sure you have plenty to do."

"As you command," Bhacca said, though she still seemed wary.

Laylah's only window faced northwest. She couldn't see the sunrise from her bedchamber, but she watched the last remnants of darkness creep away like a shrinking ghost. Morning took full hold and illuminated her surroundings. Though spring was still a couple of days away, the grass in the valley was already greening up. At the height of spring and summer, it was the finest sod east of the mountains, more like the Green Plains than the Gray. From 500 cubits above the ground, the valley looked lush and perfect as if painted by the hands of a god. But nothing that Invictus touched could ever be admired. Laylah hated the tower, the valley, and the stone city that sprawled to the west.

Someone knocked on her door. Laylah gasped as it swung open and Bhacca charged inside, slamming it behind her.

"You're going to leave me behind? Don't you know what will happen to me after you're gone? I thought you were my *friend*!"

"Bhacca ... I don't know what you're talking about."

"Don't *lie* to me, Laylah! After you acted so strangely this morning, I confronted General Lucius. He denied everything. I told him I would go to Mala with my suspicions if he didn't tell me the truth. But he just said that if I cared about you, I wouldn't pursue this."

"I would have told you, but—"

"Then you *are* planning an escape! And you were going to leave me here? Do you think they'll believe I didn't know? They'll feed me to the monsters."

Laylah mumbled and stuttered, trying to think of something to calm Bhacca down. She didn't see the raven flutter through the open window. Then a streak of black flashed in her peripheral vision and the large bird perched on Bhacca's shoulder. Its beak moved like soft clay as it whispered in the newborn's ear.

"*Namuci.*"

"No!" Laylah said.

But it was too late. Bhacca's face contorted. Blood trickled from her nostrils and the corners of her mouth. She reached for Laylah, her hands flailing. Then she grasped her stomach and groaned. The newborn was dead before she struck the floor.

Laylah dropped to her knees. The raven hopped onto the windowsill.

"Today's the day, *little one*. It's now or never. I couldn't allow one of Invictus' freaks to ruin our plans. The newborns are born from a drop of demon blood, but it's not enough to protect them from my babies. Be a brave girl and hide the body in your closet. And clean up any mess before you go."

"I will destroy you, Vedana," Laylah said between sobs.

"That's an unkind thing to say to someone who's gone out of her way to help you," the raven said with a touch of petulance.

"Bhacca and I were friends for more than seventy years."

"Seventy years? I've lived a thousand times longer—and then some. Seventy *years*? Are you trying to impress me?"

Laylah held Bhacca in her arms. The newborn's eyes remained

open, still expressing horror.

"My dear Bhacca ..."

"Oh, *grow up!*" the raven snapped. "She's not even real. She has no karma, no soul. She's an abomination! Focus on your desire for freedom. Focus on your hatred of me, if that helps. You won't be able to avenge Bhacca's death if you die here today."

"It's not true," Laylah said to Bhacca's corpse. "You have a soul."

"You're such a romantic," the raven said. "But are you a survivor? If so, you'll do what's necessary. At noon, leave the tower and go to the sycamore tree. You'll be watched, per usual, but it won't matter. What will happen next will be obvious, even to you. Stay put! Izumo and Lucius will find you when the critical moment arrives."

And then the raven vanished.

Laylah sat on the floor for most of the morning, cradling Bhacca's head in her lap. But the time came when she heeded Vedana's advice. Laylah *was* a survivor. How else could she have endured an imprisonment that had lasted for decades?

Laylah lifted Bhacca's slim body and carried it into the farthest corner of the closet. The newborn felt as light as a roll of parchment.

Laylah covered the corpse with the gown she'd worn at the original banquet in the old palace. Then she wiped a few drops of blood off the floor with a towel and hid the towel beneath the gown.

When she left her room, Izumo was pacing in the hallway.

"There's no need for concern, Dracool-Izumo," Laylah said calmly. "Everything in my room is in order. I wish to visit the sycamore on this fine day. Is it cold outside? Should I bring a cloak?"

"For a woman of your delicacy, a cloak might be appropriate, at least until the chill of the morning dissipates," Izumo said, playing along. "May I escort you, my lady?"

"That would please me."

Though it wasn't easy, the dracool squeezed into the cage with her. He rode to the base of the tower and then left her at the swing. It was indeed a pleasant day, but the brightness of the sun made her dizzy.

The horror in Bhacca's face consumed Laylah's mind, and she fought back tears as best she could. Laylah didn't want to attract too much attention. But now, even the possibility of escape felt trivial. She had betrayed her longtime friend. Of what worth were her own needs?

Tens of thousands stampeded into the valley and gathered near the base of the tower. The only other time she had seen so many was when the man in the wagon was brought to Avici. Something significant was about to occur, but Laylah had no idea what it might be.

While she puzzled over this new development, the raven appeared again and perched on a branch close to where she sat. Then it cocked an eye toward her. When it spoke, it made no audible sound. But Laylah heard the words within her mind.

"*Little one*, you're about to witness a spectacle never seen in the history of Triken: the humbling of a great dragon," the silent voice proclaimed. "But Invictus chose the wrong day to make an example of an ancient titan."

Then the raven took flight. A blaring of horns sundered the air, prompting a profusion of cheers. Laylah leaped off the swing and tried to blend into the masses, but Golden Soldiers, druids, and vampires—all of whom appeared out of nowhere—encircled her. In addition, at least 100 dracools flew in the skies. Laylah searched frantically for Lucius or Izumo, but too many people surrounded her, making it difficult to identify individual faces.

"Don't attempt to flee," Urbana snarled from behind her. "After all these years, we know your tricks, you horrid bitch."

"All the commotion has kept me awake," Laylah said. "Is anything wrong with that?"

"And where is the mistress of the robes?" the vampire said. "Doesn't your bitch-twin Bhacca usually join you on your walks?"

Laylah's heart skipped a beat, but she tried to appear calm. "Unlike you, she has important tasks to perform."

The horns sounded again, this time much nearer. The reverberations drew Laylah's attention. From the broadest causeway of Avici came the immense army of Invictus, the breastplates of the Golden Soldiers gleaming beneath the blazing sun. Mala strode at the front, his golden chain glowing brightest of all. The army included druids, Stone-Eaters, witches, ghouls, vampires, wolves, Mogols, Pabbajja, wild men, dracools, and several Kojins. There were other monsters too, some of which she'd never seen before. One beast stood almost thirty cubits tall, thrice Mala's height, and it had three bulbous heads. But all of this paled in comparison to what she witnessed next.

Fifty cave trolls, each almost as large as a Kojin and magically altered to endure sunlight, pushed and pulled a massive stone platform that rolled on iron wheels. Bhayatupa lay imprisoned on its flat surface, dozens of magical chains pinning his head, neck, torso, and tail to the stone. The dragon's wings, which when extended were 150 cubits from tip to tip, were lashed against his sides. His nostrils were stuffed with large golden spheres. The beast seemed barely able to breathe, hissing through the tiny gaps between his fangs.

Without warning, a voice exploded from above. All eyes turned toward the looming malice of Uccheda. Invictus stood on the balcony, his robes swirling in the early afternoon breeze. When he spoke, everyone could hear.

"There are traitors among us," he said.

"Yes!" the throng shouted in unison.

Bhayatupa growled.

"The dragon has conspired against my realm."

"Yes!"

"He attempted to free one of my prisoners from Mount Asubha. But of course, he failed."

"Yes!"

"I say to you, my loyal subjects, any who stand with me will thrive! And any who stand against me will perish!"

"YES!"

"Behold, Bhayatupa! All have trembled before him. Until now."

With every shred of his ancient might, Bhayatupa fought against his restraints. But the power of Invictus was too great even for the dragon.

Mala laughed. "Our king has spoken," the Chain Man said in a voice that also boomed throughout the valley. "Bhayatupa is a traitor. Of that, there is no doubt. But there is more."

All went silent.

Invictus chuckled. "Yes, General Mala ... there is more."

Guards dragged two chained figures—mere specks compared to the dragon—to the front of the platform. They struggled mightily, but their efforts were futile. Lucius and Izumo were put on display next to the dragon. Laylah collapsed, but Urbana caught her with steely arms.

"You won't want to miss this," the vampire said.

Bhayatupa heaved against the chains like a mountain trying to tear itself from the ground. But the more the dragon struggled, the tighter the restraints became. Laylah became convinced she was doomed. Vedana had been lying the entire time. Nothing could free her from this nightmare. But just then, the most peculiar thing occurred. Invictus—always in command, always in control—let out a yelp, and his magically amplified voice surged across the valley, suddenly high-pitched and petrified.

"What is it?" Invictus screeched. "What is happening to the sun? Someone … help. IT HURTS!"

All eyes looked skyward. A shadow had emerged over the western edge of the round yellow orb. Few would have noticed this unusual event—at least at this early stage—if the sorcerer hadn't reacted so intensely. To Laylah's surprise, her brother turned and fled through a doorway into the tower, trailing fire and smoke.

The momentary silence that followed was as profound as death—then came hysteria as if acid were raining from the skies. From above the tumult thundered an even greater sound, an enraged growl that swept over the valley like a tidal wave.

Snap. *Snap*! SNAP! One by one, the chains that held Bhayatupa fell away.

In the end, it was the corpse that betrayed him. He was sure of it. As Bhayatupa licked his wounds deep within his smoldering cavern, his treasure glimmering all about him, the most fearsome dragon to ever live pondered his options. Now that Invictus had turned against him, those options were fewer than before.

On one of the last days of winter, the sorcerer had asked the dragon to carry him to Mount Asubha. Bhayatupa had agreed, knowing the windy slopes would be navigable if they arrived between storms. Secretly, he was confident there was nothing on the mountaintop that could reveal his betrayal. Even Dukkhatu was dead. He had discovered and then eaten the spider's shredded carcass, enjoying the gooey flesh. Except for Mala, anyone or anything else that once occupied the prison was also dead. The explosions that tore the summit asunder left nothing but a rooftop of jagged rock.

When they arrived at Asubha in the early morning, Bhayatupa perched on a pillar of gneiss. The sorcerer pounced off his back and scrambled deftly among the debris. It astonished Bhayatupa to watch

Invictus leap from boulder to boulder, unafraid of falling. Bhayatupa doubted Invictus would be harmed if he plunged a thousand cubits onto solid granite. He'd never been in the presence of anyone or anything like the Sun God, and that was saying a lot, considering the dragon had lived more than 80,000 years.

The sorcerer climbed far enough down the side of the mountain to reach the former lair of Dukkhatu. Then he disappeared inside the dark hole and didn't emerge for quite some time. Invictus finally came out of the cave, but with a change in his expression. When Bhayatupa asked him what he'd found, Invictus replied, "Nothing but bones."

However, to someone like Invictus, bones were valuable. The sorcerer was bursting with demon blood and was a master of their spells. So it only made sense that he knew the spell that woke the remains of the dead. Ironically. it was Sōbhana—who hated Invictus as much as anyone—who had betrayed Bhayatupa. Her remains had told the truth.

As they flew back to Avici, Invictus played coy, but Bhayatupa became suspicious when the sorcerer asked him to land in the valley instead of on the rooftop of Uccheda.

"There is someone I wish to see before I retire," the sorcerer said.

"As you say," Bhayatupa responded.

But when Invictus dismounted, he revealed his anger.

"Do you believe you're greater than I?" he said, facing Bhayatupa. A disturbing yellow light smoldered in his eyes. "You dared to defy me! Surely you must know the price of treason."

Bhayatupa's eyes also smoldered. He was unused to other *dragons* challenging him, much less a creature smaller than one of his talons.

"Defy you? Since you woke me from my long sleep, I've been your constant ally."

"Liar! You conspired to free the Death-Knower, knowing full well the consequences of such a traitorous act."

Bhayatupa's anger, seasoned over the millennia, rose to the surface. "I needed the Death-Knower for reasons of my own. It had nothing to do with betraying you. Besides, Bhayatupa does not ask permission."

"Fool! Any who stands against me will perish. I am *Akanittha*, highest of the high. I am GOD!"

With that, Invictus raised his hands and spewed golden energy from his fingertips. Bhayatupa attempted to escape, but a glowing whirlwind of liquid sunlight encircled his wings and squeezed them against his ribs, causing him to crash to the ground. During his long life, Bhayatupa had been responsible for dispensing more pain, perhaps, than any living creature. But rarely had he *felt* pain—and never like this. The golden fire ravaged him from head to tail, including the tender flesh beneath his scales.

For the first time in his existence, Bhayatupa lost consciousness for a reason other than sleep. When he woke, he discovered that he was strapped to a massive stone platform by a dozen glowing chains. He could barely breathe, and the more he struggled, the tighter the chains wound about him.

The humiliation was worse than the pain. He had ruled a hundred kingdoms, terrorized entire cities, slaughtered countless foes. No one could stand against him, not even Vedana. And yet here he was being paraded through the streets of Avici like a freak. An *Adho Satta* threw a tomato—a *tomato!*—and struck him in the eye. For that insult alone, he would have incinerated every living being within leagues if not for the suffocating power that bound him.

A contingent of cave trolls—delicious food for the dragon in ordinary times—rolled the platform toward the base of Uccheda. Without warning, a voice exploded from above. Invictus stood on the circular balcony of the tower, his golden robes swirling in the early afternoon breeze.

"There are traitors among us," he said.

Traitors, plural.

Bhayatupa didn't focus on much of what Invictus said next. A voice out of nowhere whispered in his ear. Vedana, the troublesome demon, had come to pay a visit.

"You've gotten yourself into quite a quandary, *Mahaasupanna*," Vedana teased. "You need to choose your friends more wisely."

Bhayatupa didn't believe it was possible to experience such anger. He tore at his restraints frenetically, but the power of Invictus was too strong even for him. Off to the side, the despicable Mala was laughing.

"Are you going to just lie there and let them treat you this way?" Vedana said. "I've seen starved dogs with more fight in them."

They dragged two others in front of the platform where Bhayatupa lay: a human and a dracool. The dragon paid them little heed. He heaved against the glowing chains with all his magnificent strength. But the restraints drew ever tighter, threatening to strangle him. Bhayatupa's rage gave way to doubt.

"Do not fear, *Mahaasupanna*," Vedana taunted. "The tide is about to turn. Just remember who was nice to you when things were going poorly. You and I might need each other before all is said and done." And then she chanted, in a singsong manner, "*I know something you don't know. I know something you don't know.*"

"Someone … help. IT HURTS!" Invictus screeched.

The chains binding Bhayatupa weakened. The will that engorged them was fading. Now they were mere metal, no longer imbued with the supernatural might of a Sun God.

Snap. *Snap*! SNAP! The chains fell away.

Bhayatupa rose to his full height on his hind legs, his wings spread wide. Golden spheres—their magic also removed—blasted from his nostrils and punched holes in Uccheda's side with several times the force of boulders cast by trebuchets.

"*Adho Satta*! Who will protect you now? You *dare* to chain me? To drag me through the streets like a dog? I am Bhayatupa, you *fools*! Prepare to die."

Bhayatupa was 200 cubits long and weighed several thousand stones. The liquid fire that gushed from his throat was hotter than magma. In Invictus, the dragon had met his match. But with Invictus no longer in control, Bhayatupa was again the master.

As the shadow of the moon consumed the sun, Bhayatupa pounced on Mala with stunning speed, lifting the Chain Man in his jaws and casting him through the air. Mala fell upon a horde of screaming civilians, crushing them. Then he lay still, crumpled in a heap.

The dracools, mortal enemies of the dragon for countless millennia, swept down from the sky. Some snapped at Bhayatupa's eyes while others attempted to land on his back where they could pry open a crimson scale and claw at the vulnerable flesh beneath. These tactics had worked before against other dragons, but never against Bhayatupa. He had devoured thousands of dracools in his lifetime. These were no match for him. Red fire poured from his mouth, consuming half a dozen baby dragons, and his huge tail whipped back and forth, snapping dracools out of the air and sending them tumbling to their deaths. The surviving dracools fled.

But not all of Invictus' army was afraid. The three-headed giant stomped forward wielding an ax the size of a small tree. Several Kojins pounded their chests. The cave trolls, too stupid to be fearful, tore up chunks of the stone causeway and hurled them at their foe. Even the witches, wolves, druids, and Stone-Eaters joined the attack.

However, except for the dracools, none of Bhayatupa's enemies could fly. With one stupendous sweep of his wings, the great dragon rose upward and then landed on the shoulders of the giant, which he dwarfed like an eagle perched on a toddler. Bhayatupa chewed off the middle head. Black blood spurted like a geyser. The two remaining heads howled in agony.

A boulder the size of a wagon smote Bhayatupa in the ribs, causing him to lurch sideways and fall. Instantly, the witches, druids, and Stone-Eaters swarmed over him. Red flames spurted from the witches' eyes and corrosive acid from the druids' mouths, but the crimson scales were barely harmed. The Stone-Eaters vomited a scorching liquid almost as hot as Bhayatupa's own fire, but this also did little damage. Bhayatupa raised his head and spat again. Several druids, witches, and a Stone-Eater were incinerated.

By the time the moon's shadow had halfway obscured the sun, Invictus' army had suffered heavy casualties. Besides the dracools killed in the initial attack, several dozen druids, witches, Stone-Eaters, trolls, and wolves were destroyed. It would have been even worse, but Mala regained consciousness in time to coordinate a counterattack. A thousand of the bravest Golden Soldiers loosed arrows at Bhayatupa's eyes.

The trolls continued to hurl rocks and other debris. Whenever Bhayatupa landed, the wolves snapped at his talons. This weakened Bhayatupa and diminished his rage. None among the creatures—Mala included—dared to stand against him alone, but not even *Mahaasupanna* could defeat an army of this caliber himself. He was forced to retreat.

As the peculiar darkness deepened, Bhayatupa soared westward as fast as the wind. Dracools pursued him, but this time an army on the ground didn't back them up. Bhayatupa was not yet so weak that he couldn't deal with baby dragons, no matter how many dared accost him. After he had flown safely away from Avici, he suddenly turned and attacked. He was faster, stronger, and far deadlier. The dracools fought bravely, but when the thirtieth fell, the others recognized the futility of their efforts and gave up the chase. Bhayatupa snarled one last time and then sped away, a crimson comet in the blue-again sky.

Bhayatupa returned to his lair in the remote mountaintop. Lying with his treasure calmed him, but he had wounds throughout his body and his ribs were especially sore where boulders had struck him. Blood seeped from beneath several scales, one of his fangs was chipped, and a talon on his rear left foot was snapped almost in half. He had never suffered such severe injuries, and they would take months to fully heal. He had to admit that the might of Invictus' army impressed him. If Bhayatupa the Great had to flee from it, all others would do the same.

Bhayatupa wasn't sure where to go from here. This lair was far from where the sorcerer originally had found him, and it remained undiscovered. But Invictus would re-focus his attention on Bhayatupa's whereabouts and surely find him. What a predicament—the greatest of all dragons running scared. To make matters worse, his best chance at eternal existence had perished when The Torgon died on Mount Asubha. Now, all he could do was hope that another Death-Knower as accomplished as Torg would rise before Bhayatupa's long life faded away.

Bhayatupa closed his eyes and tried to rest. But Vedana's singsong words echoed within the chambers of his enormous brain.

"I know something you don't know. I know something you don't know."

Mala stood in the king's bedchamber, trembling despite his best efforts to appear calm. To say that Invictus was angry was a gross understatement. Before the sorcerer regained control, he could destroy anyone too near, just out of spite.

"The dragon has *betrayed* me. For that, he shall lose his life. But even worse: The Death-Knower may still live!"

Mala took a step back. "I don't understand. How can you know these things?"

"Do not question me! Just *listen*. The dragon has been restrained and will be brought before the tower. I will destroy Bhayatupa in full view of my people. Find Lucius and order him to bring Laylah to the balcony. I want her to witness the demise of the dragon along with the rest of us."

"It will be as you command, my king."

"Yes, it will."

Mala fled the bedchamber, ran through the catacombs, and thundered up the wide stairs. He came upon several members of Lucius' personal guard, squeamish little men whom Mala could barely stand. When they saw him coming, they attempted to retreat down a hallway, but he screamed at them to stop.

"Where is Lucius, you worthless rats?"

They looked at each other with panicked faces, but none dared speak. Mala towered over them, each of his arms as large as their entire bodies. One guard stepped forward.

"The last I s-saw him, he was leaving the tower of Uccheda as if on an urgent mission. He didn't speak to me or any other."

"What good are any of you worms? I should tear out your guts and feed them to one of the Kojins. Arrrgggh! If you see Lucius, tell him to report to me immediately."

Mala was too large to ride in the tower's metal cages, forcing him to run up the spiral stairway that led to the rooftop, several thousand steps in all. But Mala wasn't headed all the way to the roof. He decided to go to Laylah's room and escort her down to the balcony himself. Afterward, he would find Lucius and drag the former general somewhere private. There, he would end his pathetic life. He was finished with the little man, firstborn or no. He didn't think Invictus would mind.

For such a large creature, Mala was quick. He charged up the stairs ten at a time. The ceiling of the stairwell was twelve cubits high, just tall enough for him to run without having to duck his head. Though he was supernaturally strong, he still had to rest several times on the way up. The heavy chain wrapped around his body weighed him down like an anchor. When he reached the fiftieth floor, it took him longer than he liked to catch his breath. Then he pounded down the empty hallway to Laylah's room. No chambermaids were about, which struck him as odd. Either they had hidden when they heard him coming or they were already aware of the spectacle in the valley and had left their posts to claim prime viewing spots.

Laylah's door was closed.

"Queen Laylah, the king summons you," Mala said, still panting.

"Open the door and come with me … now!"

There was no answer, which enraged Mala even more. He bashed his fist against her door, expecting it to be latched, but it swung open and crashed against the wall. He lowered his head and peered inside. The bedchamber appeared empty, but something didn't feel right.

"Queen Laylah, are you here?"

Silence.

Mala entered the room. *To hell with permission. Why did Invictus stick to that stupid promise, anyway?* The ceiling was tall enough for him to stand upright except for several annoying chandeliers. Nothing seemed out of place, but he could smell something that took him a while to identify—a faint but undeniable residue of demon magic that reminded him of Invictus, but not quite. It wasn't Laylah's smell either. This was someone else. And then it came to him. Vedana had been here—recently!

Mala started to rush out to tell Invictus but then decided to search the rest of the room first in case there were other details to report. Mala stooped and passed through the doorway into Laylah's wide closet. He saw nothing unusual, but this didn't fool his superb sense of smell. He crawled to the corner where a gown lay neatly on the floor. He flung it aside, revealing the corpse.

Though Mala had seen the newborn with Laylah countless times, he couldn't remember her name. She lay on her back, fully clothed, her eyes closed and lips slightly parted. A splotch of blood stained her face. Mala dabbed it off with a thick finger and licked it clean. Then he leaned over her and smelled her mouth and armpits before rolling her onto her stomach and sniffing her anus. He could sense internal ruin. This was Vedana's work, all right.

Mala had to force himself not to take a bite out of her. Even dead, she looked so tasty. But his king might want to examine the newborn while her body was in one piece. A pity.

A short while later, Invictus stood in the closet and spoke to the corpse. It was the first time Mala had witnessed such a thing, and he found it quite amusing. And what Bhacca's dead body said to the sorcerer filled the ruined snow giant with even more pleasure. It revealed Lucius as a traitor. And Bhacca's corpse also mentioned the dracool named Izumo, who was especially friendly with Lucius. It would be sweet to see them both suffer.

Instead of relying on the clumsiness of newborn soldiers, Mala sent wolves, witches, and Mogols in search of Lucius and Izumo, and he dispatched Urbana and a crew of vampires to find Laylah. The queen's punishment would be ongoing imprisonment. But the firstborn and dracool would suffer far worse fates. If Mala was really lucky, Invictus would allow him to eat them. Lucius was scrawny, but the dracool would be delicious. Baby dragons truly did taste like chicken, and Mala could hardly wait.

Later that day, Mala stood on the floor of the valley and gazed up at the dragon. Watching Invictus obliterate the big bastard would be the highlight of his life. Of all the creatures he'd ever faced, only Invictus, Bhayatupa, and the damnable Death-Knower had ever intimidated him.

"There are traitors among us," Invictus said, his voice booming throughout the valley.

"Yes!" the throng shouted back.

The dragon fought against his restraints, but Mala could see it was useless. In his own tortured past, he had learned the penalty for resisting Invictus. Better to join him, heart and soul. A death as painful as eternity was the only other option.

"Our king has spoken," Mala said. "Bhayatupa is a traitor. Of that, there is no doubt. But there is more."

All went silent. Invictus chuckled. "Yes, General Mala ... there is more."

Guards dragged Lucius and Izumo out of the tower. They were bound with magical chains. Mala saw Laylah collapse and Urbana catch her before she struck the ground. *Now there's something I wouldn't want to eat*, Mala thought about the vampire. *But the queen would taste sweetest of all.*

Bhayatupa continued to struggle, to no avail. Invictus was so powerful, everything paled in comparison. But then, just as Mala was preparing to enjoy the dragon's demise, something strange occurred.

"What is it?" Invictus screeched. "What is happening to the sun? Someone ... help. IT HURTS!"

The king turned and ran.

This shocked Mala as much as anyone. For the first time since the conflagration had changed him into a monster, the chain that encased his torso and thighs went cool. The relief from the constant pain was unnerving. Mala barely noticed the deathly silence, but he did notice the chaos that followed as if the doors of hell had burst asunder.

Bhayatupa broke his bonds. The golden spheres—stuffed into his nostrils to prevent the dragon from incinerating the cave trolls—blasted out and smote the tower.

Mala couldn't seem to shake his disorientation. The sudden elimination of pain confused him. He considered tearing the chain off his flesh. The thought was strangely tempting. But then the dragon was upon him, his great jaws clamping onto his torso. The chain, though lifeless, was still physically strong—and it saved his life. Without its presence, the dragon would have bitten him in half. Mala was flung high into the air. He fell a long way and lost consciousness.

A surge of agony awakened Mala, reminding him of the torture he'd endured for most of his first decade in Avici. Red-hot power again blared through the chain, and he sat up and screamed. But the sounds of battle drowned out his cries. His chain cooled again, then flared, cooled, flared. Through his bursts of anguish and moments of intense relief, Mala could sense Invictus somewhere deep in the bowels of Uccheda, writhing in his own form of agony.

The three-headed—now two-headed—giant was running crazily around the valley. A Kojin lifted a massive boulder and flung it at the dragon, striking him in the side. The witches, druids, and Stone-Eaters fought bravely, but they lacked discipline. Mala joined the fray, shouting out orders to any who would listen. The dragon was great, but he could be beaten. No one—except for Invictus—could stand against Mala's army of monsters.

The dragon retreated. Mala watched the dracools chase after him. His chain continued its erratic behavior, but he forced himself to ignore it. Blood oozed from a wound near his right temple and from his mouth and nostrils. He wasn't sure if the fall had caused the injuries or Invictus' unpredictable ravings. Probably a combination of the two.

Mala sent trolls and a Kojin after the maddened giant, hoping they could put it out of its misery before it did too much damage. For a short while, the day became dark as night, and then the brightness of the sun returned with a vengeance. Mala did his best to restore order. Amid this, the hideous vampire assigned to watch Laylah came over to pester him.

"She is *gone*!"

"Who is gone? Speak up!"

"Queen Laylah is gone. The bitch has escaped."

Mala looked toward the platform and saw that Lucius and Izumo were also missing. The day had gone from good to bad in a hurry.

Mala left orders with the leaders of the witches and Stone-Eaters to calm things down and clean up the mess. After that, he rushed into Uccheda and descended the passageways in the bedrock that led to Invictus' chamber. When he opened the door, it frightened him to see that the room's furniture had been reduced to cinders. Invictus lay on the stone floor in a fetal position. Mala closed the door and went to his master, sitting down and taking the Sun God in his arms. Invictus sweated and trembled.

"Don't let them hurt me," the king whispered. Then he arched his back and screamed. Yellow energy surged through the chain. Mala screamed too.

"Please don't let them hurt me."

"I'll protect you, my king."

"Do you love me?"

"Yes."

"Good. Because I love you."

Invictus was vulnerable enough to be killed. And if the sorcerer were destroyed, Mala would return to being Yama-Deva. But the part of him that yearned to do so also stayed his hand. Murdering a helpless being was not part of a snow giant's makeup. Furthermore, the far-more dominant part of him had no desire to kill the king. If Invictus continued to live, Mala's life would be filled with every conceivable pleasure, not the least of which would be leading the greatest army in history to victory over the infidels that dared oppose him. Soon, all would be under the rule of Invictus. Once Nissaya, Jivita, and Anna fell, most other resistance would collapse. After that, there would be plenty of opportunities elsewhere to provide entertainment, including the unexplored lands east of Tējo and south of Dibbu-Loka. The fun was in the slaughter, not the ensuing peace.

Instead of killing Invictus, Mala tended him the rest of that day and night and through the following day. The sorcerer slept most of that time, though he was wracked by violent nightmares. Interspersed with gibberish, he alternately shouted and whispered words from the ancient tongue. It went on for what seemed like forever.

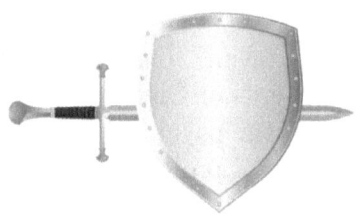

GREAT ESCAPE

The mother of all demons was not as adept a soothsayer as the ghost-child Peta, but her ability to foretell the future was superior to most. The Realm of Undeath existed on a different plane than the living. Time passed more slowly and with fewer distractions. Huddled in the absolute darkness, Vedana watched the Realm of Life flash past in a blur of activity, and she often foresaw important events before they occurred even without Peta's help. From her hidden throne in the dark chambers of nothingness, Vedana schemed to overthrow Invictus and crown a new Sun God. But the next being strong enough to break the bonds that bound her to the demon world would be her pawn, not her master. She had spent one hundred millennia in her quest to create Invictus, but the Death-Knower wizard had stymied her efforts when he unexpectedly freed Peta from her imprisonment. Without the ghost-child to guide her, Vedana had made a lone mistake, giving birth to Invictus' father one day too soon, which created just enough karmic turbulence to rob her of control. Since then, the misstep had threatened her existence. While her grandson lived and breathed, she and her kind were in danger. But his obsession with Laylah had distracted him from most other matters, allowing Vedana to take risks she might otherwise not have dared.

Almost a decade before it occurred, Vedana foresaw the solar eclipse that would be visible only from a relatively narrow stretch of land that passed over Mount Asubha on its way to Avici. But more importantly, she recognized the effect it would have on Invictus. The demon knew it wouldn't destroy him, but she guessed correctly that it would sicken him many times worse than the more common lunar eclipses which he slept through while barely aware of their presence. Vedana also believed that Invictus would be weak long enough afterward for her to put the next stage of her plan into motion.

In the incarnation of a raven, Vedana perched on the rooftop of Uccheda and watched the events of Day 75, Year 100 unfold far below. Before the bloodbath began, she psychically entered Bhayatupa's mind and teased him, intensifying his humiliation. This amused her to no end. The stodgy old dragon had been rude to her for as long as she could remember, and it felt good to cause him some discomfort in return.

Though it had been three centuries since a solar eclipse had last swept over Avici, Vedana knew the exact moment the shadow would begin to devour the sun. Her grandson had never felt much physical pain before, and she guessed he wouldn't tolerate it well. He was a spoiled brat at heart, selfish and immature. And sure enough, like a child who puts his finger in a fire, Invictus had screamed like a baby and fled.

When the sorcerer's immense power was removed from the magical restraints that held Bhayatupa in place, the great dragon broke free and sought revenge. Vedana watched with fascination as a supernatural battle between Bhayatupa and the other monsters unfolded. But before the entertaining spectacle became really interesting, she was forced to leave her perch. Her granddaughter and the two conspirators were standing there like mindless zombies, wasting the most golden of opportunities. Must she do *everything*?

The raven flew down—barely avoiding blasts of dragon fire and hurtled chunks of debris—and circled around Izumo and Lucius' heads.

"Now, you imbeciles!" the raven said. "Follow me!"

Even with their magic removed, the chains that held the conspirators were still strong enough to constrain Lucius, but Izumo tore both of them free. As the bizarre darkness deepened, the firstborn climbed onto the back of the dracool, who then took flight and followed the raven as it swerved through the chaos toward Laylah. Once Laylah was also aboard, the overloaded dracool limped into the air and struggled northward. The raven flapped alongside, shouting encouragement.

"Follow me. I'll lead you to safety."

"Leave us, demon," Lucius screamed back. "You've done enough foul work for one lifetime."

"Hmph!" the raven said before swerving away and vanishing.

When Invictus howled in pain, something also happened to Laylah. Her mind lost focus and the ground felt like it was swaying. Exposure to broad daylight was unpleasant enough, but this was far worse. Though she was a creature of the night, the solar eclipse sickened her as well.

"What is it?" Invictus screeched. "What is happening to the sun? Someone ... help. IT HURTS!"

The dragon bellowed.

Mass panic ensued.

Laylah was swept along in a current of chaos. *This is how I'll die*, she thought, *trampled by cowards*.

When Lucius reached down and lifted her onto Izumo's back, everything went black. She barely heard the dracool's labored breath as he struggled to stay aloft. She caught a glimpse of the raven flying next to them and then departing. She had scant memories of them stopping to rest near a cluster of boulders alongside the banks of the Ogha. And she was barely aware when they took flight again and landed, under cover of darkness, on a small boat in the middle of Lake Ti-ratana.

When she came fully awake, it was past midnight. Her bed of straw was swaying much like the ground had before, only more subtly. Above her, a thatched roof blocked her view of the sky. She sat up too quickly and grew dizzy, tumbling backward. Strong hands caught her before she hit her head.

"Laylah, are you all right?"

It was the steady voice of General Lucius. He held her in his arms, his face partly hidden in shadow. He looked much older than before, his eyes bloodshot, his cheeks covered with stubble, his hair greasy and tangled—all unusual for the general, who took pride in his grooming.

"What happened?" she said, hoarsely. "Where am I?"

Laylah sat up again. This time she was less dizzy. Lucius looked relieved. She saw the love in his eyes, and it made her sad. She could never return it, but she wouldn't tell him that now.

"We're among the boat dwellers of Lake Ti-ratana," Lucius said, sitting next to her in a narrow dugout hull. "We're many leagues from shore, floating within a community of boats called kabangs, maybe fifty in all. Do you know anything about the boat dwellers?"

"My father ... Takoda ... used to talk about them," Laylah said. "He crossed the lake several times on kabangs."

The boat that carried her and Lucius was twenty cubits long but only four cubits wide. Beneath its thatched roof were two straw beds and a small, metal stove. When Laylah looked over the side of the hull, she saw other boats floating lazily beneath a moonless sky, but no other passengers.

"Where's Izumo?"

"He and I waited on the eastern bank until darkness and then flew just above the surface of the lake all the way here. After that, he disappeared. I suppose he was exhausted and needed to feed. And like dragons, dracools are not fond of open water. But he said he'll return at midnight and check on us. Your illness concerned him greatly. Were you injured somehow during the battle? I could find no bruises or scratches."

Laylah wondered how thoroughly Lucius had examined her while she was unconscious.

"I don't know what happened to me. When Invictus screamed and ran, a sudden weakness overcame me. I still feel shaky. But enough about my problems. Were we followed? Are we safe? This is the first time in seventy-two years that I've been this far from Avici. I'm scared they'll hunt us down."

"As far as I can tell, we weren't followed. But before our flight, something occurred that nearly ruined us. Invictus somehow discovered that Izumo and I were scheming to help you escape. I'm not sure what happened, but the dracool believes your brother found Bhacca's body and gleaned information from it using dark sorcery."

As if Bhacca's death weren't bad enough, even her corpse had been befouled. This shamed Laylah.

Lucius grew quiet, gazing at her face. His expression softened. "Are you hungry?"

"Not very. My body still feels … hollow. Maybe I *should* try to eat something, though, to get back some strength."

"We have dried fish, bread, and hickory butter. Also, some wine. We won't starve. Ti-ratana is well-stocked with fish and clams."

Lucius arranged her meal in a scraped-out turtle shell and poured wine into a clay mug. Although she wasn't hungry, Laylah forced herself to eat. She felt somewhat better and tried to take her mind off her discomfort with conversation.

"I suppose we should be celebrating," Laylah said. "But it doesn't feel right, just yet. Now that we're away from Avici, you must tell me everything."

"Yes, my queen. What would you have me say?"

"Many things. How is it we came to be here? I knew you'd arrange something, but I assumed we'd flee to the mountains."

"Which is one of the places Invictus would expect us to go. We might end up in Mahaggata—or farther south in Kolankold—but there's nowhere in the mountains you can go where one of his Mogols won't find you. During the tedious years before our escape, I thought long about where we should go after we fled. And Ti-ratana began to make more sense than anywhere else."

Lucius took a swig of wine and refilled Laylah's cup. His brown eyes glistened in the starlight that reflected off the surface of the lake.

"The boat dwellers are an unusual breed," the firstborn said. "They love only their own kind and have no allegiance to Invictus or anyone else. They go months at a time without ever stepping on dry land, and then only to trade for supplies they can't acquire on their own. They dive for pearls, which the drylanders prize, and trade them for salt and spices. I've seen them travel as far inland as Kamupadana, but mostly they don't go more than a league from shore."

Lucius patted the kabang. "In planning our escape, I knew we'd need a place to hide that Invictus wouldn't expect. His bond with you might enable him to sense your whereabouts, and I feared he would find us no matter where we ran. But open bodies of water have a deadening effect on sorcery, and I gambled that the immensity of Ti-ratana would thwart Invictus' abilities enough to throw him off our trail. I also believed it wouldn't enter his mind that we might choose to go here."

"That all makes sense, except for one thing. If the boat dwellers love only themselves, as you say, why did they risk their lives to protect us? It sounds like we have nothing to offer as payment."

Lucius drank more wine. "The boat dwellers don't desire wealth. At least, not what drylanders consider wealth. But I didn't say they're without need."

"I don't understand."

Lucius sighed. He looked old again. "My queen, you must realize I did things for you that I wouldn't otherwise have considered."

"What are you talking about? Lucius, you're frightening me."

"The boat dwellers are few. This sometimes creates problems."

"What problems? Speak plainly!"

"Too much inbreeding becomes unhealthy. Their children are sometimes born with deformities. Because of this, the boat dwellers desire—for lack of better words—new blood. But they're not warriors and can't take it by force, so they barter for it. Pearls are what they normally offer. But to me, they offered a place to hide."

"What did you give them in return?"

Lucius rubbed his exhausted eyes. "Every day, slaves are brought to Avici—men, women, *and* children. The boat dwellers prefer infants, and it was relatively easy for me to provide them. I was limited as to where I could go and what I could do. But Izumo could travel more freely. Over a period of several years, he gave the boat dwellers six infants—three boys and three girls. In return, they provided this kabang and their pledge of secrecy."

Laylah's blue-gray eyes filled with tears. "Losing Bhacca was bad enough. But this is even worse. You used innocent babies to pay for *my* freedom? It's too large a price. What joy can my life hold when burdened by such guilt?"

Lucius grew stern. "Before you judge my actions too harshly, you must consider the ramifications. The boat dwellers may appear peculiar, but they're not cruel. They'll love these children and raise them as their own. Can the same be said of Invictus? When it comes to satisfying *his* pleasures, infants have special value. Don't ask me to explain further. Suffice it to say that the babies Izumo delivered to the boat dwellers are far better off now than if I hadn't made this arrangement."

Lucius' words contained a desperate truth. The rise of Invictus was changing the rules of civilization.

Laylah tried to stand, but the boat rocked so much she feared she might capsize it. Somewhere among the kabangs that floated nearby, a baby was crying.

"I've seen things, disgusting things," Lucius said, still trying to justify his behavior. "However horribly Invictus treated you, he never forced you to witness what happened *beneath* Uccheda. But I was there, many times. If he catches us, I'm not sure what he'll do to you but I'm quite certain what he'll do to me. We both needed a safe place to hide, and this was the best I could arrange. Forgive me if it doesn't suffice."

Then the firstborn eased himself onto one of the straw beds and instantly fell into a deep sleep. Laylah watched him for a while, the man who had sacrificed everything to save her.

Lucius loved her. A woman—even a woman like her—knew these things. But she didn't love him in return. Why? Was it because he was one of Invictus' newborns? She didn't believe that was the reason. In her eyes, he was as much a man as any other. Why then could she not bring herself to love him? Had all her years of suffering and torture rendered her incapable? Still pondering the question, Laylah wrapped herself in her cloak and fell asleep. As the night wore on, she dreamed again of the man in the wagon with the long black hair and fierce blue eyes.

It was still dark when she woke, but she could sense the coming of dawn. The eastern horizon was a shade lighter than the rest of the sky.

A pleasant breeze caressed her face. The surface of the water rippled. Lucius snored softly. Laylah rose to her knees, stretched out her stiff upper body, and studied her surroundings. She could see little in the darkness, but she heard splashing—accompanied, strangely, by tinkling laughter.

The more she stared at the water, the more convinced she became that she saw movement other than waves. Dark shapes broke the surface and quickly descended. She heard puffs of air, intermingled with ghostly whispers and chittering that were charming and unthreatening.

Laylah lowered her right hand and dipped her fingers into the liquid darkness. It was icy cold.

Something grasped her fingers and squeezed. She jerked her hand away with a gasp and found that she held a small, wiggly fish. Startled, she tossed it back. It pierced the surface of the lake like a spear. Lucius stirred but didn't wake up.

Laylah put her fingers back in the water. Something hard and round was placed in her hand, and she lifted a white shell from the lake. This made her giggle, which was greeted by high-pitched laughter all around her. This time Lucius did wake up, and he banged his head on a rib of wood that supported the thatched roof. The laughter intensified. Even Lucius chuckled.

"Our hosts have come for a visit," the general said in a raspy voice. "But I'm not sure why we call them boat dwellers. They spend more time *in* the water than on it. Izumo claims they can swim as well as ocean porpoises. And he says they can stay underwater far longer than ordinary people. No one knows how deep Ti-ratana is, but the boat dwellers can swim all the way to the bottom in search of food. I'm sure that's where the clam you're holding came from."

Lucius took it from her and separated the shell with the tip of a dagger. Then he scooped out the flesh and dropped it into her palm.

"The boat dwellers call them quahogs. They are a delicacy and are best eaten raw. Try it. They're watching to see if you'll accept their gift."

Laylah dropped the quahog into her mouth. It was excellent. She put her hand back in the water and felt another one placed there. More laughter followed.

"They like you. But why shouldn't they? You're the most amazing woman to ever live."

Laylah blushed. The firstborn was quick to notice.

"I'm sorry if I embarrassed you," Lucius said. "It's just that I've never been able to express how I feel about you without the fear of being overheard."

Laylah's heartbeat quickened. She had dreaded this moment for years. Lucius deserved more than she could give. "You didn't embarrass me. It's just that … I need time. So much has happened to me. To *us*. I'm still frightened by what might yet happen."

To her relief, her response seemed to satisfy Lucius. "Of course, my queen. We must focus on safety and survival. Our future need not be rushed. For now, just being in your presence is enough."

"Thank you, general. I feel the same."

Lucius smiled. "Speaking of how we feel, how do *you* feel? You seem so much better than yesterday."

"I'm better, for now. The true test will come when the sun rises."

"I predict you'll be fantastic, even then. And when Izumo returns at midnight, he'll be pleased to find that you're fully healed."

The firstborn reached into the water and splashed his face. Just then, a pair of small brown hands grasped the bow, and in one fluid motion a tiny man—about the height of a 5-year-old boy—lifted himself into the boat and stood in front of them, dripping wet but apparently not the slightest bit cold. Now there was just enough light in the east to provide visibility. The man was dark-skinned, muscular, and not embarrassed by his nakedness.

"Hello" was all Laylah could think to say.

This delighted the little man, who ran to her, wrapped his stubby arms around her neck, and hugged her tight. Then he turned, leaped high into the air, and dove into the water, splashing her cloak. Laylah laughed again.

"Can they speak?" she asked Lucius.

"A few of them know words in the common tongue and can converse well enough, though they sound like children to us. But only their own people can understand their true dialect. It baffled even Izumo who is fluent in many languages, including the ancient tongue where magic was born."

"But they're so small. What of the babies you provided? They'll become giants in comparison."

"Izumo says the babies raised by boat dwellers don't grow to what we consider normal size. I don't know why. Is it because of something they eat or drink? Perhaps the dracool can tell us when he returns. He is wise in the ways of the world."

As Lucius spoke, Laylah felt a flare of discomfort in her right temple. She turned to the east and saw the first sliver of the sun creeping above the horizon.

"My queen, what's wrong? Are you in pain?"

Laylah leaned over the side of the boat and vomited.

As Lucius knelt beside her, the little man pulled himself back onboard.

"She sick?" he said in a high-pitched voice.

"I don't know. Laylah, what's wrong?"

As the sun climbed, her pain intensified. Waves of dizziness and nausea wracked Laylah, causing her to shiver.

"The sun is … *ill*."

Despite the coming of a clear, bright day, darkness overcame Laylah and she knew little more.

From then on, she lay on the kabang wracked with fever. She vomited constantly, becoming dangerously dehydrated. Dozens of boat dwellers came to visit, popping in and out of the craft like flying fish. They brought her potions intended to rouse her from her torpor. But nothing had much effect. During the late afternoon, Lucius told her that he was worried she might not survive her fever, and he allowed six of the tiny boat dwellers to lift her over the side of the kabang into the chilly water. They held her there, submerged to her chin, while she spluttered and shivered. When they returned her to the boat, her body temperature had lowered enough for her to sleep.

Laylah woke after sunset, her fever broken. Lucius forced her to sip some water. The boat dwellers brought her raw fish eggs. Though they went down cold and slimy, her stomach welcomed their arrival. By mid-evening, she could sit up.

"What happened to me?" she asked shakily.

"As soon as the sun showed its face this morning, your fever returned," Lucius said. "You muttered something about the sun being 'ill.' Your condition worsened as the day grew brighter, and it was all we could do to keep you alive. Whatever happened to Invictus at Avici also seems to have affected you. I'm hoping Izumo will know more when he returns at midnight."

Laylah asked for more water. The later it became, the better she felt. Several of the boat dwellers peered at her over the side of the kabang. They smiled and giggled, pleased by her improved condition.

"I don't know what's happening to me," she said to Lucius. "The sun has always sickened me, but never to this extent. But when the sun rose this morning, I felt like I was being poisoned. Now that it's dark, I feel a little better. In another day, the first crescent moon will appear in the western sky. Perhaps by then I'll be healed."

Later that evening, Laylah ate a fish stew the boat dwellers had prepared. The man who appeared to be their leader, introduced as Moken, served her. He could speak the common tongue well enough to be understood.

"Eat … pale lady," Moken said, presenting her with a turtle shell of bubbling stew. A clam shell served as a spoon. "This make you strong."

"Thank you, Moken," Laylah said. "It smells delicious. But my stomach is queasy."

"Eat!" he insisted. "You feel better."

He dove over the side and disappeared.

Laylah took a few bites. "I'm sorry, Lucius. That's all I can manage. Maybe you should eat the rest. It will do us no good if I recover and you become ill."

Lucius reluctantly agreed but then devoured the rest of the stew with ravenous delight. He offered her wine, but she declined. They sat together and waited for Izumo to arrive.

Shortly after midnight, the dracool appeared and landed roughly on the bow. His cumbrous weight—almost thirty stones—unbalanced the small craft, causing it to rock and shudder. Izumo was clearly uncomfortable. His wings, made of scale, flesh and sinew, did not respond well to saturation. If dracools fell into deep water, they sank like boulders.

"Good evening, Laylah," Izumo said. "I'm pleased to see you're well."

Before Laylah could respond, Lucius interjected. "She appears well now, but she was horribly ill throughout the day. So much so that I feared we might lose her. The sun sickens her far worse than usual. Do you have any idea why?"

"I don't understand any of this," Izumo said. "But the event at Avici was not as unusual as you mortals might believe. The sun darkens many times each millennium, though it's only visible each time in certain areas of the world. Still, I've never seen it harm anyone."

"I don't expect you to solve my problems," Laylah said to the dracool. "Thank you for everything you've done for me. There's no way I'll ever be able to repay you."

"Your appreciation isn't necessary. I never would have aided you if I didn't believe I was helping my flock. Your brother is a blight. If allowed to flourish, he will destroy the glories of the world. If helping you somehow thwarts his ambitions, then I have chosen properly even if my brothers and sisters don't agree."

"What news have you of Invictus?" Lucius said.

"I dared not approach too near to Avici, so I flew west to the foothills and hid in a cave. Most of the dracools in Invictus' service— more than one hundred in all—followed Bhayatupa toward the mountains, but I don't know what happened afterward. Lord Bhayatupa is beyond all. Perhaps no creature, save Invictus himself, could stand against *Mahaasupanna* (mightiest of all dragons)."

"You saw nothing unusual?" Lucius said.

"West of the lake, the skies were empty. No ravens, eagles, dracools, or dragons, though the latter is not a surprise. Besides Bhayatupa, there are only nine great dragons still active of which the dracools are aware, and none can abide the *Mahaasupanna*. Once he was resurrected, all fled to the southern regions of Kolankold, including a golden female that at one time served Invictus."

"Even where you hid, there should have been winged spies in the sky," Lucius said. "It surprises me how slowly Invictus is reacting."

"Could it be that my brother remains disabled?' Laylah said. "Does chaos reign over Avici?"

"We dare not depend on it," Lucius said.

"Tonight, I'll fly to the east and see what I can see. But I'll have to return to my hiding place before dawn. Expect me again at midnight tomorrow. By then, I should know more."

"Take care," Lucius said. "Laylah and I need you more than ever."

"Yes, take care," Laylah said.

"I'll do my best. You should be safe here if Laylah doesn't become ill again. Guard her well, Lucius."

The dracool vanished into the dark sky. The rest of the night was uneventful. But when dawn arrived, Laylah's sickness returned. Lucius could do nothing but cool her brow and force her to sip water. To make matters worse, a storm approached from the east at midday, blasting their boat with stinging rain, hail, and strong winds. For a short while, it became almost as dark as during the eclipse two days before. The fleet of kabangs proved surprisingly seaworthy, riding the waves with the ease of much larger crafts. But it was rough on Laylah, whose condition worsened. And Lucius—who had little experience with boats—also became nauseous.

Just when it appeared it would never weaken, the storm passed. Lucius felt better, but Laylah continued to struggle. For her, the bright sun was worse than the storm. *How ironic*, she thought, during a rare moment of clarity, *that I could die out here as a free woman while staying alive for so long in Avici as a prisoner*.

With the arrival of dusk, Laylah's illness dissipated. As the crescent moon set in the west, she was able to drink water and eat fish stew, replenishing a portion of her strength. A long time later, the dracool appeared again.

"Avici is no longer in paralysis," Izumo said shakily. "I found a hiding place within a league of the city and was able to watch some of what occurred. Sixty of my flock flew in a continuous circle in the skies above Uccheda. Only sixty. It appears Bhayatupa killed more than three dozen of my brothers and sisters. And I wasn't there to fight alongside them."

"It's not your fault," Lucius said. "Invictus is to blame. He lured the dragon from his long sleep."

"My legacy will be that of traitor and coward," Izumo said.

"If Invictus is defeated, your name will be cleared," Lucius said.

"I won't live to see that day. Already, my flock conspires against me. The minds of dracools are interwoven. They can't determine my exact whereabouts, but given enough time they can delve into my mind and end my life from afar. Still, I knew this and accepted the risk. Do not mourn."

"What good could come of your death?" Laylah said.

"It is beyond the comprehension of mortals to understand the ways of the dracools," Izumo said.

Laylah sighed. "Regardless of what happens, Lucius and I will remain your dearest friends. We have nothing but respect for you. You're beyond our comprehension, as you say. But that doesn't stop us from loving you."

"What's done is done," Izumo said. "I must depart. I'll be back at the usual time tomorrow night."

As dawn approached, Laylah sensed the return of her fever. She wasn't sure if she could survive another day of such horrific illness. While Lucius slept in the stern of the kabang, the boat dwellers laughed and splashed in the dark water. But suddenly they grew silent. Something frightened them and they fled. Laylah turned her head slowly and gasped. A raven perched on the side of the hull, studying her with glowing eyes.

"You're not nearly as strong as your brother, and even he required Mala's aid to recover from the effects of the eclipse," the raven said. "There's only one way for you to survive. You must find the healer."

"Why should I believe what you say? You've destroyed all that I hold dear: my father, my people, even Bhacca. If I weren't so weak, I'd break your scrawny neck."

The raven sounded offended. "Grudges are a sign of immaturity. You know why I'm trustable. If not for me, you never would have escaped Avici. If I wished you dead, you would be dead. Even now, I have the strength to capsize this craft and laugh as you drown. But I do *not* wish you dead. For once in your pathetic life, show some smarts and listen to me. *You must find the healer.*"

"Who is this healer and how do I find her? You speak in riddles."

"Find *him*, not *her*! When the dracool returns, I'll reappear. In the meantime, convince the others to listen to my words. For your sake."

Then the raven fluttered away.

As the sun rose bright and cheerful over Lake Ti-ratana, Laylah succumbed to the sickness again. She remembered little of the day, other than a constant series of hot flashes, chills, nausea, and muscle cramps. She had little memory of a dismal moment during the late afternoon when Lucius thought she'd died, causing him to sob. But when darkness arrived, her illness released its grip, leaving her weak but alive.

When she opened her eyes, Laylah saw Lucius lying next to her, dozing fitfully. The firstborn looked ragged and filthy. Though the boat dwellers had submerged her in the lake several times each day during the worst of her fevers, Lucius never entered the water. He didn't know how to swim and feared the depths almost as much as Izumo. But Laylah didn't care how bad he looked or smelled. How could she complain when he'd done so much for her? By all rights, she *should* love him. No matter how hard she tried, though, the feeling wouldn't surface. Her thoughts returned to the stranger in the wagon, which made her angry and frustrated. She was obsessed with someone she'd seen only once in her life.

When Moken entered the kabang with another helping of fish stew, his movements caused Lucius to stir. The general tried to feed her, but Laylah pushed his hands away and told him she could fend for herself. Moken returned with more stew for Lucius before diving back into the water and disappearing for the rest of the night.

When she felt strong enough to speak, Laylah looked at the general with desperation. "Just before dawn, you fell asleep. And soon after, the raven paid us another visit."

Lucius sat up so fast, he shook the small craft. "Why didn't you wake me? Did she threaten you?"

"She didn't do much of anything, much less try to hurt me. But she left a message: She said that I will die unless I'm taken to a healer. But not just any healer. She said she'll explain more when she returns tonight."

Lucius covered his face with his hands. "Just what we didn't need. If the demon knows where we are, how soon will it be before Invictus finds us? When Izumo returns, we should leave this place. Maybe we can hide for a while in the cave he found near the mountains."

"Vedana would find us there too. She seems able to travel long distances in an instant and appear in whatever form she desires."

"Then what are we to do?" Lucius said. "I'm no match for the demon, and neither is Izumo. Can you defeat Vedana?"

"Right now, I doubt I could slay an ordinary raven, much less a demon in disguise. But even at full strength, I'm not her match. At least, not yet. Other than Invictus and Bhayatupa, she seems to fear no one."

"Then what are we to do? We can't flee. We can't fight. Should we just lie here and pray for death?"

"Our only choice is to trust her, at least for a while longer."

"I'd sooner trust a pirate from Duccarita."

Laylah placed her hand on the general's thick forearm. "We've no other options. In one regard, the demon speaks the truth: If I don't find some sort of healing, I will die."

"My queen—"

"Shhhhh. Let's not argue. I hate the demon more than anyone. But I believe some of what she says. She could have betrayed us already. And it's within her power to harm us now. For whatever reasons, she wants to help. Not because she cares for us, of course. She cares only for herself. But regardless of her motivation, we should take advantage of her aid."

"What if this is just another of her tricks?" Izumo said after arriving at the kabang later in the evening and hearing the news of Vedana's visit. "It's even possible she's the one making you feel so ill."

"For what gain?" Laylah said.

"To give you no choice but to visit the healer," the dracool said. "Maybe she's in league with him."

"I certainly am not," the raven said, startling the three conspirators. "Laylah, I thought I told you to convince them to listen to me. I go to all this trouble to help you—and when I return, I find the three of you bickering like children."

"We're at your mercy," Laylah said. "If this is some sort of trick, then get it over with and kill us now."

"Oh, relax! I want nothing but the best for all three of you. I don't deny I have my own agenda. But for now, it coincides with yours." The raven then cocked its head at Izumo. "Dracool, are you strong enough for one more long flight? I need you to carry Laylah and Lucius to Kamupadana. Once there, I'll lead Laylah to the only person in the world who can save her. Not even Invictus or I can do what this man can do."

"You're insane if you think we'd willingly follow you to Kamupadana," said Lucius, his cheeks so swollen with anger that his head seemed to enlarge. "The Whore City is swarming with witches. Other than Avici, I could think of no worse place to go."

"Normally, I'd punish you for being so rude," the raven said. "But we don't have time to squabble. The dracool hides his discomfort from you, but soon he won't be able to disguise it."

"What does she mean?" Laylah said to Izumo.

The dracool took a long breath. "I am under assault. My flock has discovered me."

"Discovered you?" Lucius said. "They know where you are?"

"Don't be so stupid!" the raven said. "Don't you ever listen? The dracools are intertwined."

"It's a difficult concept for mortals, but for lack of better words they are seizing control of the primitive portion of my mind," Izumo said. "They'll soon have the power to quiet my heart and stop my ability to breathe. I can resist a while longer. But my life will end before this day is done."

"No!" Laylah said. She turned to the raven. "Can't you stop them from killing him?"

"I do not desire it," the dracool said.

"You *wish* to die?" Lucius said.

The dracool sighed. "You can't comprehend me—any more than a toddler can comprehend an elderly man. The longer you live, the more important is your legacy. What good is long life if you don't leave behind something worth remembering?"

"What does that have to do with being murdered?" Laylah said.

"At the moment of his death, they will comprehend the full extent of his motives," the raven said.

Izumo nodded.

"So we're supposed to sit here and watch you die?" Lucius said.

"If you must know, I couldn't save the dracool without exerting enough power to alert Invictus, anyway," the raven said. "Thanks to that damnable Mala, my grandson is nearly recovered. When Invictus' full strength returns, he'll be more dangerous than ever. The specter of his own demise has never occurred to him. I doubt he liked the taste of it." Then the raven cocked its head this way and that, as if seized with paranoia. Then she whispered, "The wheels have been set in motion. I'm your only chance." And then louder: "Follow me, *now*—or sit in this silly boat and await your doom. What's your decision? Be quick!"

"If Izumo will carry us, we'll follow," Laylah said. "At least, I will."

"Where you go, I will go," Lucius said.

"I will carry you," the dracool said. "But as the demon warns, we must hurry. If we plunge into Lake Ti-ratana because of my weakness, all will be for naught."

Laylah waved goodbye to the boat dwellers, doubting she would ever see them again. Then she and Lucius climbed onto Izumo's back. At first the dracool struggled to remain aloft, brushing the surface of the lake. But steadily they rose into the sky and followed the raven. When they reached the northern shore of the giant lake, Izumo was forced to rest.

"Come on, come on!" the raven said. "Less than forty leagues remain. If we fly like the wind, we can be there before dawn. Why do you tarry?"

"Leave him alone," Laylah said. "Can't you see he's suffering?"

"Suffering, smuffering!" the raven said. "Mogols and other niceties are everywhere. You're not playing a child's game, granddaughter. Only the strongest will survive."

"Let us continue. I have the strength for one last effort," Izumo said. "After that, I will leave you. I wish to perish in a place of my own choosing. Where and how you die is more important than when you die."

They continued their journey, skimming the tops of hills and the canopies of trees. The raven was tireless, but Izumo was not. He stopped again and lay down on the gray grass, wrapping his wings around his muscled torso like a blanket.

"We can't ask him to carry us any longer," Laylah said. "How far is the city? Could we walk the rest of the way?"

"You couldn't make it before daylight," the raven said. "Walking is not an option."

Izumo stood and stretched. "I can do it."

"And where will we go when we arrive?" Lucius said. "We can't just fly over the walls. We'll be seen, even in the dark. The Sāykan warriors who guard Kamupadana are everywhere—and the witches also watch."

"I have a plan, general," the raven said. "Trust me."

Lucius sighed. "As you say, we have no choice," he whispered to Laylah.

During the last leg of the journey, the dracool struggled just to remain in the air. One time Laylah pressed her palms against his back and bathed him with white energy, but the raven flew over and pecked at her.

"Stop, you little fool! It's too soon for you to be using your powers. You might as well hand Invictus a map."

They could see the Whore City in the distance, its ramparts aglow. Outside of the city's boundaries was a dark area dotted with small campfires. The raven headed that way. Izumo followed. They landed near a copse of trees and quickly hid within the shadows. The dracool collapsed. Laylah knelt next to him.

"What can I do for you, Izumo? I feel so helpless."

"Stay alive," the dracool said. "Resist your brother. That's all I ask."

"It's time to go," said a voice off to the side. Near where the raven had perched, a grandmotherly woman wearing tattered robes now stood. With a gnarled finger, she pointed toward the fires. "Dawn will soon arrive. Laylah must be hidden before then. I have prepared a place. Hurry!"

"We can't leave him," Laylah said, gesturing toward Izumo.

The old woman rolled her eyes. "Idiot! The dracool is beyond your meager aid. He craves privacy, not someone cloying over him."

"The demon speaks the truth," Izumo whispered hoarsely. "My end is near, and I choose to die alone. Take care, Laylah. And Lucius. In the deep sleep of death, I will dream of you."

Then Izumo stood and sprang into the air, sputtering northward toward the mountains. Laylah never saw him again.

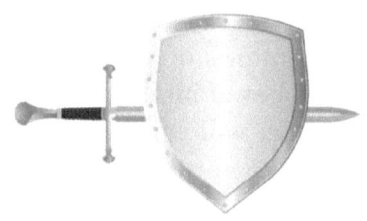

HEALER

Soon after Izumo's departure, dawn announced its arrival as if in a hurry to betray them. Laylah's dreaded sickness returned, forcing her to lean against Lucius for support. The two of them stumbled behind the old woman, who set a surprisingly brisk pace. When they entered the refugee camp, the filth and suffering stunned Lucius, but Laylah was too ill to pay much attention.

Vedana appeared pleased to be there. She seemed right at home in the sordid maze of shacks and tents. The demon led them past stinking piles of garbage, moaning cripples, and squalling babies. They entered an alley and squeezed through a curtained doorway into a shack pieced together with scraps of metal and broken boards. A man slept in the small room on a bed of dirty blankets. Vedana kicked him in the buttocks. He bolted upright and drew a rusty sword. But when he saw the look in the old woman's eyes, he yelped, dropped his weapon, and scrambled out the door.

"Trespassers!" Vedana said. "You can't leave your house unlocked these days like you could a hundred thousand years ago." She threw her head back and guffawed, causing Laylah to grimace.

"What do we do now?" Lucius said to the demon, carefully placing Laylah on the bed of blankets. "We left the boat so quickly I didn't have time to pack food or water. And our clothes are even filthier than these blankets."

"The dracool couldn't have carried more weight, anyway," Vedana said. "But please forgive my *thoughtlessness*. I forget that those made of flesh and blood need sustenance. When you're around your own kind long enough … but enough prattle. Don't worry; I won't let the two of you starve."

The demon handed Lucius the sword the trespasser had dropped.

"Don't leave the blessed comforts of this marvelous abode. If anyone other than me tries to enter, skewer him. I'll return with food, water, and clean clothes. Not that Laylah will care. She's going to be sicker than ever. But it's too late to find the healer today. We'll have to wait until tomorrow morning and hope her demon blood provides enough strength for her to survive until then."

After Vedana twirled and vanished through the entryway, Laylah became almost comatose. Lucius sighed so deeply it hurt his throat. He wasn't sure *he* could survive another day of this.

Guilt and shame washed over him as he kissed her lips, but that didn't stop him. He couldn't believe some of the things he'd considered the past days. During her periods of unconsciousness, he'd been tempted to lay upon her and enter her, but he was too afraid she would wake up later with soreness and despise him. No ... he couldn't do that, no matter how much he lusted for her. But he allowed himself a peek at her breasts, admiring their fullness and gazing overly long at her nipples. When she coughed, he was so startled he had to fight back a yelp. He covered her up, turned away, and buried his face in his hands. What would he do if it turned out she didn't love him? In so many ways, he was a fraud created by an evil god out of bubbling goo. What rights did he have to such a wonderful woman? And yet, who else deserved her as much as he? Could she put aside what he was and love him for who he was? If not, could he bear to live another day?

Just then, Vedana burst through the opening. She carried a woven basket. Lucius smelled roasted fowl and baked bread.

"I went to the market and bought you a new tunic and breeches and Laylah a plain brown dress so that she won't attract attention. You can pay me back later." There was a pause. "Okay, I didn't buy it. I just took it—and fuck anyone who can't take a joke. Anyway, there's chicken, bread, and apple wine. I don't go for this stuff myself. Raw flesh is my favorite food—and blood is my beverage of choice. Oh ... don't look at me like that. You're not so perfect. Have a wonderful time changing her clothes." Then she winked and slipped out the door again.

"Foul beast!" he shouted after her, his face red with anger—and shame. But in his heart, he knew she spoke the truth. He *wasn't* perfect. How could he be? In most ways, he wasn't even real.

The day passed so slowly he felt like eternity had crept up and cradled him in its arms. He ate most of the bread and chicken, stunned by how good it tasted, but he saved enough for Laylah to have a snack in case she woke with any kind of appetite.

Despite the demon's taunting, he enjoyed removing Laylah's clothes. He left her naked on the blankets far longer than was necessary, studying the entire length of her perfect body while she slept. The delicate place between her legs almost stopped his heart. He could no longer resist, and he touched it with his fingers and then licked it with his tongue. Her abdomen clenched and bulged, which startled him again. After that, he didn't dare touch her anymore.

When eternity became bored and left him alone, dusk arrived and then darkness. It rained briefly, then a rush of cool air followed. Laylah slowly woke from her stupor, shivering as she rubbed her eyes.

"Where are we?"

"We're in some kind of hellhole outside the city's walls. But the demon brought us clean clothes. I dressed you while you slept."

Laylah blushed. "Do we have water?"

"No, but we have wine … and I saved you some chicken and bread."

"I'm not hungry. But I'll have a sip of wine. Did Vedana say anything more about the healer?"

"She said we wouldn't be able to find him until morning. I don't know what makes him so special. I'll believe it when I see it."

Laylah sat up. "I hope Vedana is right about the healer. I have little strength left."

Lucius peered out the door into the alleyway. "I can't believe how cold it's become. It feels more like early winter than nearly spring."

"It will be cold tonight, but warm tomorrow," she said. "Don't ask me how I know. I just do. What do you see?"

"Darkness and shadows, though I hear all kinds of strange sounds. This is a dreadful place."

"All we can do is wait for Vedana to return. I feel weak, but at least I don't feel so sick."

Lucius stared at her, his face stern. "Laylah, there's something I need to say. I've tried to keep it to myself until now because it was never safe for us to talk in Avici."

"Lucius—"

"Just listen! When we first met, Invictus assigned me to befriend you and to report back everything you said and did. In that regard, I betrayed you. But as you know, I turned against your brother. And along the way, I developed feelings for you that went beyond friendship."

"Lucius ... as I said on the kabang, I'm still too frightened to talk about this. What do you expect from me?"

"I'm frightened, too. Yet my fear doesn't diminish my feelings for you. It *strengthens* them. What do I expect from you? I want to hear you say that you love me as much as I love you."

Laylah closed her eyes. This was the last thing she needed right now. But he deserved the truth.

"Lucius, I'll try to be as honest as I can. I've spent most of my life as my brother's prisoner. He humiliated and tortured me. But of all the bad things that happened to me, there were two wonderful things: Bhacca and you. Bhacca became the dearest friend I've ever known. And you kept me sane. Without you, I wouldn't be alive today. So I owe you more than I'll ever be able to repay."

Lucius started to respond, but Laylah stayed him with her hand. "You ask me if I love you. My answer is ... I don't know. Not because of any failure in you but because of failures in me. I'm not an ordinary person and I haven't lived an ordinary life. Does that mean I'm incapable of love? Maybe it does. But I can tell you one thing for certain: I'm terrified of being forced back into that nightmare to the point that it has stunted my other emotions. I can't tell you whether I love you, at least not in the way you mean. I love you as a friend. But until I'm in a place where I feel completely safe, I don't know if I'll ever be able to tell you that I love you the way you want me to."

She had managed not to lie to him. But she had left out one crucial element: her obsession with the man in the wagon. How much of a role was that playing in her lack of feelings for Lucius? She wasn't sure. Then another thought occurred to her. Maybe her obsession was just a symptom of the abuse she'd endured for so long. After all, the man she couldn't seem to forget was probably dead. It was absurd to pine for him. But before she could explore that idea further, Lucius interrupted her thoughts.

"Laylah, I'm so sorry. What you say makes perfect sense. It's selfish of me to pressure you. I'll try not to bring it up again until we *both* agree the time is right."

Then he lay down and turned away from her. He had a soldier's ability to take advantage of brief opportunities for sleep and was snoring in an instant. But he still held the hilt of the rusty sword in his hand.

Laylah didn't believe it would be easy to surprise him. This reminded her of the game she used to play with Takoda. Her adopted father would become so frustrated every time he failed to sneak up on her. Even now, more than seventy years later, Laylah missed him so much. And she missed her first father and mother. And Bhacca. The tears came then, mindful of the past.

Inside the filthy shack, Lucius slept most of the night. Laylah was grateful for his snoring, which drowned out most of the sounds from outside. Several times, she heard footsteps in the alleyway, but no one tried to enter. Had Vedana cast a protective spell? She wasn't sure and didn't care. Nothing could happen now that would be any worse than what she'd already endured.

When least expected, Vedana appeared. "Hurry ... *hurry*! I've found the healer."

Lucius woke, grabbed Laylah's hand, and followed the demon through the opening. Outside, it was warm and still. Most of the fires had burned out, and even the hardiest refugees were asleep. But dawn was near, and Laylah felt like she was getting sick yet again.

"We must pass through the gates," Vedana said. "It's half a league just to the ninth wall—and more than a mile after that to where we need to go. Carry her if you must, Lucius. Time is precious."

"We're going as fast as we can," Lucius barked. "What's the big hurry? So we can meet the marvelous, stupendous *healer*? I couldn't care less."

"You had better care if you want your sweetie to live another day," the demon snarled. "Put aside your jealousies and stop acting like such a boy."

Vedana led them onto a roadway. Though it was still dark, several hundred joined them who were also headed to the markets. Most appeared to be traders on their way to their booths within the ninth wall. They walked alongside ox-drawn carts stocked with fresh meats, fruits, vegetables, clothing, perfumes, and even jewels. Female soldiers patrolled the road, questioning anyone who looked suspicious, but they gave Vedana and her two companions a wide berth. It wasn't apparent to Laylah whether they were aware of the demon or just discomforted by her aura. But it made their going easier, and when they passed within the ninth wall, no one accosted or detained them.

They walked without incident within the eighth wall, wandering past a line of inns and taverns. Though the sun had not yet risen, the morning was growing bright—and with the new light came a blast of illness that caused Laylah to gasp. By now, Lucius was almost carrying her, but no one seemed to pay them any attention. Others stumbled along the road, returning drunk from the previous night's gallivanting. The firstborn and Laylah blended right in.

They stopped in front of a tall inn with a single turret on its roof. An armed guard watched them suspiciously from above.

"Wait here," the demon said. Her robes and flesh became translucent, and then she spun and vanished. Soon after, a stout iron gate opened and an extremely obese but cheerful-looking woman thundered out to greet them.

"Come in. Come in," she said, taking Lucius by the arm. "I've been waiting for you. Let me show you to your chambers."

Lucius and Laylah followed woodenly, staggering up the stairs like a couple of drunken dotards. The fat woman led them to a vacant room and sat them down on the side of a bed facing a window. They could hear snoring in the adjacent room through a small door left ajar.

"Do not wander," the innkeeper said. Then she departed.

Laylah sagged against Lucius, her breath coming in ragged bursts. The long walk had nearly done her in. The firstborn looked around the room and found a pitcher of water, but when he offered some to Laylah, she refused. She was too ill even to swallow.

So they sat, waited, and wondered.

In most ways, Laylah felt at peace. Dying would be far preferable to how she had spent most of her life. And dying would free her of the sickness. She leaned against Lucius, engulfed in the sweat and grime of his flesh beneath his clean clothing. But it was not unpleasant. The odors reminded her of death. She was ready.

Laylah barely heard the creaking floorboards or the door opening slowly behind her. But suddenly she felt a blast of heat on her back.

Now she was awake, and she saw Lucius leap to his feet. Then she fell backward onto the bed.

"I was told you could help her," Lucius snapped at someone. "She's dying. You must save her."

"I don't know who she is or who you are," came a powerful male voice. "Why do you say she's dying? Is she injured or ill?"

Lucius sat next to her and took her protectively in his arms. "Never mind who she is. If you're a healer, then surely you can recognize that she's sick. Will you help her or not? If not, then tell me quickly so that I can leave this stink hole and try to find someone who can. I've wasted enough time listening to the snoring. I was tempted to cut some throats to shut them up."

Weak but curious, Laylah peered through the slits of her eyelids at the man who stood before her. He was huge, at least a span taller than Lucius, but he wore peculiar clothing: a pink tunic and a pair of worn-out sandals. Still, beneath the comical outfit was a body that emanated strength. Laylah felt an instant attraction.

"I *am* a healer, and you'll find none better. Whoever brought you here was right to do so. But before I help her, you must tell me who led you to me."

Laylah could feel Lucius' body tensing. "Who are you to give me orders? I don't answer to oversized jesters! Why are you dressed so strangely, anyway?"

"It's a long story," the healer said.

Lucius grunted. "Either help her or don't. But be quick. I'll strike down anyone who hinders us."

"Very well, I'll try to help," the healer said. "But you must move away and give me some room. I can't heal her with you clinging to her like she's some kind of doll."

Lucius stood slowly and backed away from the bed, but Laylah paid the firstborn little heed. Her full attention was on the healer, and the closer the man got to her, the more intense were her feelings of attraction. When he sat down on the bed next to her, she nearly swooned. When his leg pressed against hers, it was like a dam had burst within her heart, and she unwittingly emitted a surge of white energy.

"Why must you sit so close?" she heard Lucius saying in the background of her euphoria.

"Be quiet and let me concentrate," the healer said. "Do you always whine so much?"

Lately ... yes, he does, Laylah thought.

And then, gloriously, the healer was lifting her in his arms. His strength was shocking. Now her eyes were clamped shut, but she could smell his skin.

"Yes, she's pretty," she heard Lucius saying. "But are you going to help her or just stare at her? She could die at any moment. *Hurry!*"

The healer placed his large hand on her abdomen. A surge of blissful energy plunged into her. It felt like her lifeblood was being restored. Without warning, her body went into a spasm.

"What are you doing to her?" Lucius shouted.

But all she wanted to say was "don't stop. Please don't stop."

"I won't harm her," the healer said. "But I must *concentrate*. Stop annoying me."

Yes, Lucius ... shut up!

"Get on with it, then!" the firstborn retorted.

Laylah heard the healer sigh, and she sighed along with him. What he did next created the single most pleasurable feeling she had ever experienced. He pressed his mouth against hers, forced her lips apart with his tongue, and blew his hot breath down her throat, engorging her lungs with scorching energy. Her eyes sprang open and she convulsed. Without thinking of how Lucius might react, Laylah flung her arms around the man's broad back and clawed at him. The healer wrapped his arms around her and squeezed. A blue-green shimmer flowed from his flesh, prompting her white energy to rise and greet it. This swept away her illness and filled her with relief. But she was also alert enough to sense Lucius' distress. Reluctantly, she let go of the healer and slid a couple of feet away.

The man in the wagon, she thought, her mind full of wonder as she gazed at his handsome face. *Beyond hope, he's alive.*

The fat innkeeper was suddenly at the door, and she was shouting at two bearded men who were holding Lucius' arms. The general struggled, but they obviously were too strong for him. One man spoke to the healer with an unusual accent.

"What should we do with him, Master Hah-nah? We found ya with da whore, and this man was trying to beat ya up or rob ya or something. Would ya like Ugga to crack his head open?"

"*No!*" Laylah shouted. Then she regained her composure. "Don't harm him. He's my friend and is only trying to protect me."

"I don't care if he's the *One God* come to cleanse our souls," the fat innkeeper said. "If you don't quiet him down, my boys will."

"Please, Lucius. Don't fight them—if not for your own sake, then for mine."

In reaction to her voice, Lucius calmed down. The bearded men released him, and he hurried to Laylah's side.

"Are you ... healed?"

Laylah sighed. "I believe I am."

Lucius held out his hand to her. "Good. We must be on our way. Quickly, come with me."

"Did ya bed this man's wifey?" the larger of the two bearded men said to the healer, obviously confused.

Laylah suppressed a giggle.

"I met her only a moment ago," the healer said. "She was ill and came to me seeking aid."

Then he turned to her, his face kind and beautiful. "But you're not healed ... entirely. For reasons I don't understand, your life force was drained beyond anything I've ever encountered. If you go now, the sickness could return."

"He's just saying that to frighten you," Lucius said. "We don't know who these people are or what they're about. Let us flee the city while we still can."

"If you wish to flee," the healer said, "then you would be wise to join us. We're also leaving the city. You can come with us until you're far from the walls and safe from harm—and then go freely wherever you choose."

After a heated discussion, it was determined that she and Lucius would accompany them. They ate a quick meal that even Laylah enjoyed, then left the inn. The street swarmed with people. Their group joined a raucous gathering of men and women. True to her previous night's prediction, the day had become unseasonably warm. The air was thick with dust.

Lucius clung to her like a jealous lover. She found it annoying, but she could do nothing about it. She was still a little weak, and it helped to lean against him. But what she really wanted to do was lean against the healer, who had changed his clothing and was now adorned in black, which suited him far better. He looked strong enough to carry her for leagues. And she would allow him to do so, blissfully. She felt hope for the first time since that horrific night in her village when Vedana and the Mogols butchered her people and took her prisoner.

Now, anything was possible. Escaping Invictus could be done.

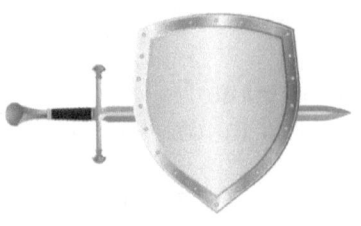

KAMUPADANA

Two days before Torg first saw the man and woman sitting on the bed in the inn, the wizard and his companions camped about a mile from a massive gathering of refugees in a wide field just north and east of Kamupadana. At least 10,000 fugitives from the Gray Plains, the shores of Lake Ti-ratana, and the foothills of Mahaggata had constructed crude shelters on the tromped-down grass, raiding the garbage heaps of the Whore City for wood, metal, and discarded fabrics. Within the camp, there was little room and less food. Mayhem and murder walked hand in hand with disease and death. The fugitives had fled to this foul place for a variety of reasons. Rumors of the horrors of Avici were spreading, and many lived in terror that one of Invictus' slave-hunting expeditions might capture them. Poverty and filth were preferable to torture and dismemberment. And there were other reasons to run. The Mogols had grown bolder and were taking their own slaves, destroying entire communities and feasting on the flesh of their victims. As if that wasn't bad enough, the black mountain wolves were on the rise, venturing farther from the heights than ever before. Anyone who lived near Avici was in peril.

As darkness fell, Torg stood on a hill overlooking the camp. Trails of smoke rose from a speckling of bonfires. Beyond the camp, he could see the first and largest of Kamupadana's nine walls. And in the distance, inside the walls, Torg recognized the upper portion of the mammoth ziggurat in the center of it all. Except for the tower of Uccheda and the main keep inside Nissaya, the ziggurat was the largest edifice on Triken. And it was ancient. Some said the ziggurat had stood for fifty millennia. The Warlish witches had become its masters fewer than ten millennia ago.

Torg had entered Kamupadana several times in his life, but never since the birth of Invictus. The last time had been at least two centuries ago, but Torg still remembered it well. After he agreed to tolerate an escort, a cadre of witches and hag servants had taken him on a tour of the ziggurat. At the time, the witches feared the might of Anna and were relatively well-behaved, at least in their public dealings. But now the recent rise of Invictus had emboldened them. Some roamed freely, wreaking havoc throughout the land—including at Dibbu-Loka, as Torg had recently discovered firsthand when Chal-Abhinno made her blasphemous appearance on the balcony of Bakheng.

Bard walked next to Torg. The trapper had entered the city hundreds of times but had never passed within the sixth wall. The markets were within the ninth wall, the inns within the eighth, and the brothels within the seventh. After that, Bard and Ugga said that they knew no more, nor did they care.

"When Ugga and I were last here, there were not so many of them," Bard said, referring to the refugees. "It's getting worse."

"There is death in the air," Torg said. "And so much pain."

"Ugga and Elu found a place to conceal da cart and skins. Dare we light a fire tonight, Hah-nah?"

"If you wish. There are fires everywhere. Another won't draw attention."

"Should we retire, then?" Bard said. "In the early morning, we can enter da city. There will be a tremendous crush of peoples. It's easy to blend into da crowds."

Torg continued to gaze at the camp. The crescent moon was already setting in the cloudless sky. "I'm not ready to retire. I can't resist the urge to explore."

"It's not safe, Hah-nah. I can see from here that this is a dangerous place."

Torg wouldn't relent. "Tell the others I'll return by morning. If for some reason I don't, go on without me."

Bard protested again but then recognized no further argument would be tolerated, so he left Torg alone on the hill. Torg pulled his hood over his head to conceal his face. The Silver Sword was strapped to his back, hidden by his cloak. He started toward the camp, feeling the need to witness the suffering firsthand to harden his resolve.

When Torg reached the base of the hill, the stink assaulted his sanity and made him feel dizzy, reminding him of the claustrophobia he'd experienced in the labyrinth of tunnels beneath Mount Asubha. But the wizard was not one to give in easily. He entered a narrow alleyway that wound through a maze of poorly constructed shacks and tents. As Torg progressed deeper into the camp, the odors grew more wretched. All about him was a cacophony of despair—moaning, sobbing, and occasional screams. He passed through the ramshackle structures and came upon a group of refugees gathered around a bonfire and drinking from wooden cups. Torg approached them.

Before he reached the fire, an old man staggered into his path. He was bent and broken, forced to use an old sword as a cane.

"Can you help me find my daughter?" the man said, peering at Torg through watery eyes. "She is lost."

"There are so many places she could be," Torg said. "But I think I can help."

Torg placed his hand on the old man's lower back. There was a cracking sound like the breaking of a dry stick. Then the man was able to stand upright.

"Maybe I can find her now," he said before walking away without use of the makeshift cane.

Torg approached the fire. Six men stood around it, their breath reeking of spoiled wine. One man coughed and spewed blood from his mouth. It sizzled in the flames. He then grasped his stomach and collapsed.

"He told me to cut his throat when the sickness got too bad," one man said. "Is now the time?"

"Yes," another said.

The first man reached into his belt. A dagger sparkled in the starlight. He walked behind the coughing man, yanked back his head, and ran the blade against his neck, ending the sick man's life.

"They are burning bodies over there," another said. "You can put him there. The fire is big and hot."

"How far?"

"A hundred paces. No more."

"Too far."

"I'll carry him," Torg offered.

The others wandered off in relief. Torg lifted the bloody corpse in his arms. Though the man had been tall, Torg guessed he weighed less than ten stones, his body wasted away.

Torg found the pyre. More than two dozen corpses already were burning. He tossed the body into the fire. One of its arms flopped in a wide arc as it fell.

Torg continued his journey and came upon a sobbing woman holding a silent baby. He touched the infant's forehead with the tip of his right index finger, but he was too late. The fever had already consumed the little girl. He took the baby from the woman's arms and placed her in another fire. When he turned to speak words of comfort, the woman was gone.

Torg walked some more. A girl with a grimy face and yellow teeth came to him and offered her services.

"I have no money," he said. "How would I pay you?"

"After you're finished, great lord, stay the night with me and hold me in your arms. That would be enough."

Torg pressed his lips against hers and exhaled blue-green vapor into her mouth. She stepped back, startled, and then smiled. Her teeth were now white. She trotted off.

Near the center of the camp was a single tree, stunted and bare. Torg touched its bark and sensed remnants of life still flowing in the surface of the wood. A man in orange robes sat beneath the tree, his back pressed against the trunk, his face peaceful and radiant. Torg sat beside him and closed his eyes, counting 500 long breaths in silent awareness. Now it was the middle of the night. The man remained in the same position. Torg couldn't guess his age.

"May I ask your name, sir?" Torg said.

The man opened his eyes, slowly registering his presence.

"Why do you hide your face?" he said to Torg.

"Will you not answer my question first?"

Without warning, the man pounced upon Torg, knocking him backward with a surprising burst of strength. Then he pressed his face close. Torg could see portions of his skull beneath his translucent flesh.

"Your daughter is lost in the blackness! Why won't you help her?" he whispered urgently. But then his body slackened, collapsing onto Torg as if pierced through the heart.

The wizard rolled him off and then placed his ear against the man's chest. He heard no heartbeat.

Torg carried him to the fire.

One more death. One more mystery. *My daughter*?

Torg walked deeper into the darkness. Everywhere he went, he encountered suffering.

A gang of would-be rapists chased a woman. Torg struck one pursuer in the temple with the base of his palm, killing him instantly. The others ran, but the woman also fled as if Torg were as much an enemy as the rapists.

Torg came upon a boy spitting blood on the gray grass. Torg held him in his arms and hugged him. When he placed him back on the ground, the boy's body was healed. But not his mind. Angry shadows swallowed him as he wandered away.

Next, Torg saw a fat bully threatening a skinny man, demanding the services of the smaller man's wife in return for another day of life. Torg punched the bully in the back of his neck, ending his existence. But the skinny man offered no thanks.

Sister Tathagata would have lectured him. *Live in joy, not in anger. Forgiveness is more powerful than revenge. If you love yourself, your hatred will fade.*

On this night, Torg felt no love—for himself or any other. His hatred blazed like a pyre, fueled by suffering and death. Someone had to confront Invictus. It was his destiny to try.

When he returned to his friends, it was nearly dawn. They were already stirring. An obviously annoyed Rathburt tromped over to give him a lecture.

"For Anna's sake, Torg! Where have you been and what have you been doing? We were worried half to death and hardly slept."

"Where I go and what I do are my affair," Torg said dangerously. *"Don't ask again."*

Rathburt was speechless.

The next morning dawned bright and clear. And there was warmth in the air—even so early in the day—that he hadn't felt since being imprisoned in the pit. But Torg's moment of comfort ended abruptly. Ten poorly armed but nasty-looking brutes approached their cart. The leader was a heavy man who had probably seen better days, at least in terms of his physique. He wore a waist-length coat of mail but no helm, and his two-handed sword was notched.

"Hallo, friends!" the leader said. "We were passing through and couldn't help but notice the contents of your cart. We've come to offer you a better price than you'll receive in the markets."

Still concealing his face within the folds of his hood, Torg walked over to the leader. Torg was a span taller and thicker in the chest and shoulders, though not nearly so large in the waist.

"We'll keep what's ours," Torg said. "If you and your friends wish to live to see another day, you'll run as fast and far from this place as your legs can manage. But all of you must empty your pockets first."

The heavy man seemed bewildered and for a moment could think of no response. But when he regained his wits, his voice sounded threatening.

"There are ten of us and five of you," he said, and then looked at Elu. "Make that four and a half." Then he guffawed.

"Were there a hundred of you, you would not be our match," Torg said.

Elu brandished a dagger, causing the thug to laugh even louder. But this didn't amuse Torg. "I'm in no mood for debate. I'll give you one more chance. Empty your pockets—and flee. If you do this, I'll allow you to live."

Bard and Ugga joined Torg and Elu. Rathburt remained by the cart, looking uneasy.

"Let Elu kill the nasty fat man!" the Svakaran said, his face flushed.

Howls of laughter ensued but were cut short when Elu lunged and buried his dagger in the leader's lumpy thigh. As the bandit howled, Torg struck him between the eyebrows. The man's skull shattered, killing him instantly.

A wiry man, the most courageous of those who remained, leaped at Torg. But Ugga was quicker, striking him with his ax. The man's head flipped in the air and landed near Rathburt's feet. In quick succession, Bard struck three more of the men in their chests with arrows loosed from Jord's bow. The others screamed and fled toward the woods, with Elu in hot pursuit. The Svakaran caught up to one, jumped on his back, and cut his throat. The pair tumbled head over heels, but Elu scrambled to his feet, unharmed. The four remaining thugs escaped into the nearby forest, but not before discarding their purses and weapons. Elu returned with their purses while Bard and Ugga searched the dead men nearby. Rathburt walked over to Torg, his slump more pronounced than ever.

"Was that really necessary? Wouldn't a 'no thank you' have sufficed?"

Torg gestured toward the refugee camp. "Anyone despicable

enough to take advantage of such pitiful people must be a friend of the sorcerer—and therefore, my enemy."

Elu emptied the purses and held out his small hand to Torg. "Just a dozen pence."

"Da fat guy had one gold coin and a few pence," Ugga said. "That's all we can find."

"What should we do with da bodies?" Bard said.

"Throw them in a gully," Torg said. "I doubt any of the soldiers from Kamupadana will come this way."

After that dirty business was done, they started down the hill toward the ninth wall, skirting the edge of the refugee camp to avoid as much of the stink as possible. A deluge of people now flowed along the paved processional that led to the massive exterior wall. Oxen and mules toted carts filled with food, fabrics, spirits, and a variety of narcotics. They saw merchants, noblemen, village folk, and whores of both sexes. Most were headed for the congested markets within the ninth wall where an astonishing variety of goods could be purchased, sold, or traded.

Though Torg and his companions had seen the ninth wall before, it still amazed them. It was the tallest and broadest of the nine, standing one hundred cubits high and forty wide. A series of merlons and embrasures protected the soldiers on the walk, and more than twenty watchtowers rose another thirty cubits above the crenellation. An army of sorcerers had built the perfectly square wall fifty millennia ago, or so it was believed, molding it out of a cream-colored stone that resembled obsidian in feel and granite in strength. All told, it was ten miles long, two and a half miles per side. No army could scale it, no war machines assault it. It had no equal, except for the three concentric bulwarks that enclosed the fortress of Nissaya.

On this morning, more than 70,000 made their way toward the gateway. The lone visible entrance was guarded by a single slab of stone, which was raised and lowered like a titanic portcullis. When closed, it was as impenetrable as any other part of the wall. But with the strength of Avici protecting its back, the keepers of Kamupadana lived without fear, leaving the door open day and night to admit and release the inundation of vendors and visitors. Despite the width of the entryway, a funneling effect occurred that created a dangerous crush of flesh, wood, and metal. Torg knew that the soldiers of Kamupadana, all of whom were female, watched the influx from the ground and from above.

Occasionally, a visitor who looked especially filthy, diseased, or troublesome was dragged away, never to be seen again in this world.

Once inside the gate, the mob split left and right, heading toward whatever vendor held the most promise for their needs. A staggering array of markets—some huge, some managed by single merchants—was arranged side by side within the ninth wall. Just 300 paces separated it from the eighth wall. The most prosperous markets were near the entryway, while the least prestigious booths were miles from the gate, making for a wearisome walk.

Ugga and Bard veered to the right and moved down a narrow dirt road choked with hordes of people. The crossbreed didn't hesitate to shove anyone aside who blocked them. Few protested once they got a look at him. Torg and Rathburt guided the oxen while Elu rode in the cart to avoid being trampled. It took the rest of the morning for them to reach the first corner of the giant square. At least the crowds had thinned enough to permit steady progress.

"How much farther?" Torg said to Ugga.

"Less than a mile," the crossbreed said. "But we don't have to go hungry till then. There's a vendor just a little ways ahead who sells skewered meat and roasted corn. Bard and I know her well. Our gold coin will buy us hefty meals and goblets of da best wine around."

"Lead on," Torg said. "We're all hungry as bears."

"Elu has had the skewered meat too," the Svakaran said. "People from my village used to come here a lot. But now ..."

He bowed his head.

"Don't cry, little guy," Ugga said. "Ya won't enjoy your wine if ya get all weepy."

The gold coin was good for ten skewers of beef, twenty ears of corn, five loaves of bread, and a large keg of wine—and they even received two silvers as change. The vendor, a woman not much taller than Elu, allowed them to sit beneath a tarp out of the sun. She seemed to like Ugga, but she especially adored the handsome Bard.

"If you get sick of the Blondies, come and see me before you go," she said. "I'll treat you better than any of them, and it won't cost you a single pence."

Rathburt laughed at every word she said, slapping Bard on the back several times.

"Why would you want a Blondie when you could have such a

diminutive beauty?" Rathburt said.

"If ya keep saying that I'll knock off your head and have her skewer that too," Bard whispered harshly. "Quit giving her ideas, Master Slump! It's hard enough for me to get away from her with my breeches still on, as is."

"Master Slump!" Ugga said. "That's a good one. *Master Slump*!"

Now it was Bard's turn to laugh, while Rathburt seethed.

After yet another tedious walk, they found the merchant who paid the most for quality hides. He was a grouchy old man used to standing up to people more dangerous than him. Ugga and Bard argued with him until midafternoon before agreeing on a price. After the skins and coins passed hands, they seemed to become great friends, hugging and laughing. Torg, Rathburt, and Elu sat in the shade with their backs against the eighth wall, watching the proceedings.

When Bard and Ugga strolled back to their three friends, they bore rascally smiles.

"*Well*?" Rathburt said.

Bard snatched Elu's cooking utensils off the cart and rushed away.

"Wait!" Rathburt said. "Where are you going?"

But Bard and Ugga trotted several hundred paces before feeling comfortable enough to tell the others what happened.

"We robbed him," the crossbreed said in a low voice. "He paid us more than ever before. He even bought da cart and oxies!"

"We're rich," Bard said. "Thanks be to our dear Jord, wherever she might be."

"What exactly is your definition of rich?" Rathburt said.

"Ten golds for da skins," Bard said, "and twenty silvers and a hundred pence for da cart and oxies."

Rathburt let out an exaggerated gasp. "Oh my, we're rich," he said, rolling his eyes. He then turned to Torg. "For Anna's sake, you or I could have gotten three times that much in any market in Senasana."

Bard scrunched his face. "Ya are a mean old man, Master Slump. Ya are always saying bad things about me and Ugga."

Torg stepped between them. "The coins you received are more than enough to meet our needs. I don't plan to stay here long—probably not longer than a single night. And it's good you sold the cart. When we leave here, we'll be carrying our provisions on our backs. That is, whoever still wishes to go with me. Anyone who would prefer to stay here and spend the rest of our newly acquired riches on Blondies and Brounettos is welcome to do so. Where I'm going, coins won't have much value."

"Ya know we're all going with ya," Ugga said. "But can't we have a couple days of fun before we head back into da wilderness? Bard and Ugga know where to find a comfy inn with soft beds, good food, and great beer. It even has copper tubs with lots of sweetsy soap. And fine robes to wear while they're washing our clothes. Later, we can go to da brothels. One silver will buy a Brounetto for da whole night."

"Lead us to the inn," Torg said. "I need a bath less than any, but that doesn't mean I won't enjoy one. Just remember our plan. Call me Hana. And stay out of trouble. The Saykan soldiers are quick to anger."

"They'll be good boys, I'm sure," Rathburt said. "But let's stop all this chatting. A hot bath in a copper tub sounds more attractive than an *army* of Brounettos."

The ninth wall had only one visible gate. But the eighth wall, which was miniature in comparison, contained hundreds of doors leading to the inns and taverns, all of which employed their own warders. The brothels within the seventh wall were also self-policed, while soldiers frequented the public baths within the sixth wall.

During the height of day, more than 100,000 occupied the Whore City, and 10,000 female soldiers, whose quarters were within the fifth wall, patrolled the city inside and out. The royal personnel who served the Warlish witches lived within the fourth wall. A dozen temples were within the third. Four castles housing noblewomen and their slaves stood within the second. And the ziggurat, home of the Warlish witches and their hags, dominated the heart of the city within the first.

Once rid of the cart and its skins, the men felt as free as parents who had arranged a nanny for a brood of squalling brats. As a cool breeze swirled, Ugga and Bard led them through a small bronze gate in the eighth wall.

"Winter isn't finished yet," Rathburt said. "It appears this beautiful day will end on a sour note. How far is the inn?"

"Not far, Master Slump," Ugga said.

"We hold grudges, do we?"

"Hmph!"

A thousand paces separated the eighth and seventh walls, creating a much roomier feel than the cramped space that contained the markets.

Inns and taverns stood side by side as far as the eye could see. But few had vacancies. Kamupadana was a gathering place for almost everyone and everything that traveled the wilds of the north on the east side of the mountains. Humans were the most numerous visitors, but it wasn't unusual to see monsters of various shapes and sizes wandering the streets. Some who visited the Whore City were mortal enemies outside the walls, making murder and mayhem a common theme within. But crimes almost always occurred in dark rooms or back alleys. The soldiers treated harshly anyone who disrupted order in plain sight. And if the occasional monster was too difficult for the soldiers to handle, the Warlish witches were more than equal to the task. A single witch was dangerous enough, but when witches fought in groups, they ranked among the deadliest beings on Triken.

How many witches lived in Kamupadana? Only the Warlish knew the exact number, but Torg had heard there were more than a hundred. Plus, each witch traveled with as many as a dozen hags as personal servants. The hags were failed witches, born either hideously ugly or wondrously beautiful, but without the ability to change appearances. They lacked the magical powers of a full witch but were physically strong and adored their mistresses, fighting to the death in their defense.

Ugga and Bard's favorite inn was sturdily made of smooth stone blocks. A turret stood ten cubits above the inn's flat roof, with an archer serving as lookout. A grated gate protected the front entryway. Ugga rang a bell.

After a short wait, Rathburt impatiently reached for the string, but Bard stepped in front of him.

"She gets mad if ya ring it twice."

Ever cautious, Rathburt backed away.

A heavy wooden door inside the gate swung open and an obese woman eased her way into the foyer.

The crossbreed approached her, his arms spread wide. "Surely, ya remember your good friends, Ugga and Bard! Do ya have any rooms to spare? There be five of us needing a turn in your tubs in da worst way."

The woman tugged on a thick chain. The grated gate rattled inward. At first, she glared at Ugga as if infuriated. But then she surrendered her ruse and laughed good-naturedly.

"It's so wonderful to see you," she bellowed. "Do I have rooms to spare? As a matter of fact, I've a pair on the third level that will hold all five of you. As for your needing baths, I wholeheartedly agree. Each one of you, except for your hooded companion, smells like a wild beast."

"Even I crave a hot bath, good lady," Torg said softly.

"Ahh! A man with manners. Will wonders never cease? The comforts of my inn are yours to enjoy—for one gold coin per night."

Rathburt eyed her suspiciously. "Is that one for all of us? Or apiece?"

"One for all, of course. Do you take me for a thief?"

"My pardon, madam. That's certainly a fair price for such a fine establishment. We've dealt with unwholesome characters lately, and I've become distrustful."

The woman wrapped a flabby arm around Rathburt's shoulder. "Well, it would be one apiece if *you* weren't so handsome."

"Madam, you honor me. And the feeling is mutual. What's your name, if you don't mind my asking?"

She frowned. "Around here, people don't reveal their names. Madam, good lady, missus, or even fatso will suffice." Then her expression brightened again. "Come in, gentlemen. It's been a gorgeous day, but I do believe it's about to rain. Allow me to show you to your rooms. And it just so happens I have five copper tubs sitting vacant. I'll prepare your baths while my assistant beats the dust out of your cloaks and washes your underclothes. Will you be dining out or in your rooms? This late in the day, I can only provide a cold meal with some beer. But if you prefer something hot, the tavern next door serves supper till past midnight."

"We'd like to eat in our rooms," Torg said. "But we'll go to the tavern later in the evening."

Compared to what they had become used to over the past several months, the accommodations were luxurious. They lathered up with the "sweetsy soap," smelling even better than the Blondies and Brounettos. Then they neatened their hair and beards with metal scissors and wooden combs. Torg examined his face in a polished mirror. Over the winter, his hair had grown past his ears and his teeth to full size. Even his skin had healed, though he was pale by desert standards.

"If you admire yourself too long, you'll miss dinner," Rathburt said.

Torg laughed. "Even a Death-Knower is allowed a moment of vanity. Especially after what I've been through. I'm not used to being mistaken for an ogre."

"Don't worry ... you're as handsome as ever, you bastard."

When the men returned to their rooms, the sun was setting over the mammoth ninth wall. It had rained a bit while they bathed, but the storm had passed quickly, leaving much cooler air in its wake. The nameless innkeeper supplied them with bathrobes, and they wore only those—legs spread unabashedly—as they sat in wooden chairs around a sturdy table eating cold beef sprinkled with salt and garlic, and dark bread slathered with chestnut butter. For dessert, they had ripe cheese and dried berries. The beer, as Ugga had promised, was excellent. By the time darkness arrived, they had eaten all the food and drunk an entire keg. Except for Torg, their spirits were high. Ugga and Bard seemed ready for a party, and even Rathburt and Elu were laughing. The Svakaran, however, was the first to notice Torg's melancholy mood, and he climbed out of his chair and placed a small hand on Torg's knee.

"What troubles you, *great one*?"

As if in a trance, Torg took a moment to answer. "It's the moon," he said. "It affects me in odd ways."

"The moon is barely a sliver," Rathburt said. "What does it have to do with anything?"

"It's always in my dreams."

"Do da dreams have anything to do with a Brounetto?" Ugga said.

Torg chuckled. "Am I that obvious? To be honest, she's a Blondie. At least, I think she is." He turned to Bard. "If we ever encounter her, you had better leave her to me."

They all laughed.

"I have seen da way ya fight," Bard said. "I'm not about to argue with ya over da first pick of da women."

"Fair enough," Torg said. Then he smiled. "Thank you, my friends. You lighten my heart." The wizard stood and stretched out his long frame. "Now that night has arrived, it's time to wander over to the tavern for more beer. The stories we hear might be enlightening."

The innkeeper's assistant, a scrawny man with a pointed nose, entered the room, tossing their cloaks and underclothes onto one bed. He left the room without saying a word but quickly returned with a small rolling cart.

"I did the best I could," he said, huffing and puffing, "but everything was so *filthy* I had to throw some of your clothes away. I hope you're not offended. I offer you these fine garments at a fair price."

They were not at all offended, gratefully examining the clothing. For another gold coin, they bought loose-fitting breeches with stirrup bottoms; tunics with dagged edges; tall boots made of black leather; and fur-lined cloaks with drawstring hoods. The assistant included undergarments at no extra charge. An outfit designed for a boy fit Elu perfectly. Torg also purchased a black scabbard that fit the Silver Sword surprisingly well.

"We look like a bevy of dandies," Rathburt proclaimed.

When they stepped outside, the briskness in the air surprised them, especially considering how warm it had been earlier in the day. Torg strapped the Silver Sword to his back, covered it with his cloak, and then pulled his hood over his face. The others carried only daggers. The streets swarmed with people, all of them shouting, laughing, or arguing. Torg strode hurriedly to the tavern.

A forest troll guarded the smoky doorway. The beast wasn't as big as a cave troll, but it was taller than Torg and Ugga and far thicker in the belly and legs than even the crossbreed. It stared at the newcomers suspiciously, but its partner—a squint-eyed man with sunken cheeks—waved them in as if the whole affair bored him.

They entered the common room, which already bustled with activity. The long tables and benches were almost filled, and most of the sofas along the walls were also occupied. A log fire provided the only light, which pleased Torg. They found empty seats at the end of a table in the darkest part of the room. So far, so good.

A server greeted them. She had pretty eyes and an impressive cleavage. But her greasy hair and malodorous underarms overpowered her other assets, at least in Torg's opinion.

"What you be having tonight?" she shouted above the din.

"Double pints of your best dark," Ugga shouted back.

The server returned with a tray of pewter mugs weighing half a stone apiece. It surprised Torg that the girl could carry them all at once. No wonder she was sweaty. She thrust them down on the table and rushed off to other patrons, snatching several silver coins from Bard before she left. Rathburt, already inebriated from the beer he'd drunk at the inn, lifted his mug and offered a toast.

"To my friends—Elu, Ugga, Bard and *Tor*- … err, Hana. May the Blondies and Brounettos spread their legs wide and scream in delight when you present yourselves for their perusal."

Ugga guffawed and drained the contents of his mug in only a few gulps. Elu stood on the bench and peered into the empty mug, amazed.

"I've seen Ugga drink twenty of these in one night and still perform his duties with da Brounettos," Bard said.

"More!" the crossbreed shouted when the girl passed his way.

Torg paid little attention to his companions. Instead, he scanned the murky room and studied the other patrons. He saw village folk from the Gray Plains, fishermen from the Ogha River, a pair of boat dwellers smaller than Elu from Lake Ti-ratana, and white-robed noblemen from Avici. He also saw a sleazy bunch who appeared to be pirates from Duccarita in poor disguise, and even a flirty, pasty-skinned woman whom Torg recognized as a vampire. Who would be her victim tonight?

A fancy gentleman with a thin mustache sat alone on one sofa and delicately sipped spiced wine from a pewter cup. Torg had seen his sort before—a wealthy merchant, probably from Senasana, who would risk the journey to Kamupadana only if it involved lucrative dealings. This man would have news from the south, but he would be tight-lipped.

"I need to speak to someone," Torg said to his friends, but they were on their second mugs of beer (Ugga his third) and didn't pay him much attention. Torg slipped across the room, blending with the surroundings as he moved. He sat next to the merchant and waited to be noticed. When the man turned and saw him, he spilled some of his wine.

"This seat is taken," the merchant said, regaining his composure.

"Yes, it is," Torg said.

"Is there something I can do for you?"

"I've wandered long in the north and would learn what's happening in the rest of the world."

"I'm unaccustomed to conversing with strangers who hide their faces and poke about in the darkness. Leave now, or I'll call for protection."

"You'd be dead before it arrived."

The merchant's eyes sprang open, but it was obvious he believed Torg wasn't bluffing. "What is it you want?"

"News is all. I'm not a murderer or thief, only a lonely traveler who desires friendly conversation. I mean you no harm."

The merchant relaxed, but only slightly. Torg placed his hand on the man's knee. An imperceptible glow flowed from his fingertips through the fabric of the merchant's houppelande into his flesh.

"How goes it in Senasana?" Torg said.

The man's body went limp, and he answered in a monotone whisper. "Since the Golden Soldiers departed last summer, all appears as before. But fewer outsiders come to our city and business is not what it used to be. The Tugars have returned and wander about in plain sight, but they are angry with us for not helping the Death-Knower. They treat us like enemies."

"Are you not enemies?"

"We're not warriors. We obey whoever doesn't kill us."

Torg nodded. "How goes it in Jivita?"

"I've heard naught from the White City and care little for what occurs west of the mountains."

"I see. And Nissaya?"

The merchant fidgeted. Torg increased the energy flow to compensate.

"I haven't been to the fortress in several summers, but it's said Nissaya prepares for war, storing food and supplies and beseeching aid from allies. The black knights fear Avici, it seems."

"Have you been to Avici?"

The merchant squirmed and tried to stand. The strength of his will impressed Torg, who commanded more energy to flow from his fingertips into the man's flesh. The merchant sagged.

"I've been there," he said.

"And?"

"I saw a great city. And a great army. Too great. Not even the Tugars can defeat it. They are too many and the Tugars too few."

"Will Nissaya be attacked?"

"I'm only a merchant. How could I know such a thing?"

Torg nodded again. Then he said, "Why are you in Kamupadana, merchant?"

The man quivered and pressed his hands to his chest. "Please, don't force me to answer."

Torg doubled the flow of energy. The man could not survive much more.

"Your secrets are safe. I won't betray you. Tell me."

The merchant paused ... and then: "It's the witches. They brew a special potion—barrels and barrels of it—and they've offered to pay me to bring it back in my caravan to Senasana and dump it into the river about a league north of the city."

"What kind of potion?"

"I don't know … but I'm worried. Tens of thousands in Senasana depend on the river for their drinking water. And thousands more live along Ogha's banks as it bends toward Lake Keo."

"Why you? Why don't they take it there themselves?"

"I'm known in those parts and wouldn't look suspicious to prowling eyes." Then the man whimpered. "They offer chests of golds. With that much wealth, I can follow the ancient road, disappear into the southern infernos, and live like a king. It's that choice—or death."

"Death is better than betraying innocents."

The merchant's voice, though still under Torg's hypnotic spell, became defensive. "*Am* I betraying them? I don't know what the potion is supposed to do. Maybe it's a good thing."

"You don't believe that any more than I do. Speak truth to me."

"The truth is I'm a coward."

"You're one of many, so don't hate yourself too much."

"What should I do?"

"For your own sake, you must not perform this deed. An act of bravery performed now will enhance your future—if not here, then elsewhere."

"An act of bravery? I don't understand. What can a simple man hope to accomplish against such evil?"

"Bravery comes in many forms."

"I know none of them."

Torg chuckled. "Have you seen the barrels?"

"No. But I believe they're somewhere in the ziggurat where the witches perform their wicked magic. I'm to receive them two mornings from now."

Torg nodded. "You've said enough. I'll release you now, but I want you to return to your room, wherever it might be, and stay there until all this is over."

"Yes."

"There's one more thing. You bear a weapon. I can sense it."

"How did you know?" The man looked like he might cry. "I carry a Tugarian dagger purchased at considerable expense from a Golden Soldier who claimed to have slain an Asēkha at the base of Uccheda. The blade is scratched but still gleams so bright it hurts my eyes."

"The soldier was a liar as I'm sure you've already guessed. Give the dagger to me. It belonged to a person I once knew."

"Yes."

The man gently placed Sōbhana's dagger in Torg's hand. Then he stood and wandered from the room. A hag spy, by far the most beautiful woman in the tavern, stood and followed. She had been watching Torg and the merchant with intense interest. But Torg had noticed her, too. As she walked toward the door in pursuit of the merchant, the dagger struck her in the back. It took a considerable amount of time for anyone to even notice she was dead. A large man stumbled over her, laughing.

"Get up, you drunken bitch!" he said, nudging her ribs with the toes of his boot. When she didn't move, he called a server. There was a yelp. Someone screamed, "Blood!" And then the troll and the squint-eyed man were leaning over her.

Torg returned to his friends, who hadn't even noticed he was gone.

"What's going on over there?" Bard said to Ugga.

"I don't care," Ugga said. "I want more of da beer!"

Torg leaned down and whispered in Elu's ear. "I have a gift for you."

He slid Sōbhana's dagger into straps on the side of Elu's boot. "This dagger is quite valuable. I'm counting on you to keep it safe for me."

Despite his drunkenness, the Svakaran smiled. "As you say, *great one*. I will guard it with my life."

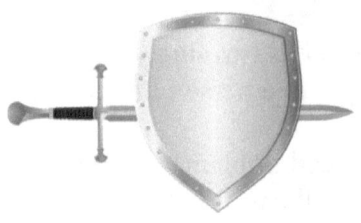

ZIGGURAT

When midnight arrived, the tavern was bursting with drunken fools, including Ugga, Bard, Elu, and Rathburt. The four of them stood in front of the log fire, their arms draped around each other at various heights, singing like loons. In a short while, they would most likely head for the brothels within the seventh wall.

By this time, Torg was gone. He sat alone in his room at the inn, attempting to meditate. But he couldn't clear his mind, continually replaying his conversation with the merchant. Whatever the barrels contained, it couldn't be good. But why would the witches want or need to poison an entire city, especially one as prosperous and militarily neutral as Senasana? Torg was missing something, but he couldn't determine what.

The more he thought about it, the more convinced he became he needed to find out what was in the barrels. And the only way to do that was to open them himself. He cursed the starlight, which provided too much illumination on such a clear night. But he was a Death-Knower, Asēkha, and Tugar wrapped into one. His abilities would suffice.

Torg had earlier chosen a belted black tunic and breeches from the batch of new clothes. His hooded cloak also was black, but it was too cumbersome for his intended mission. He went to the latrine where there was a pewter basin filled with clean water. Then he dumped the water down a small drain and stuffed the now-empty basin with towels. With a burst of flame from his fingertips, he reduced the towels to ash. It happened so quickly, there was little smoke. Torg ground the ash in his hands and rubbed it on his face.

With the Silver Sword strapped to his back in its new scabbard, Torg exited the room through the window. His stealth was such that the warder in the turret noticed nothing unusual.

The gaps between the stone blocks provided adequate grips. Torg wound his way around the back of the building and dropped into a narrow alley between the inn and the seventh wall. He knelt there and examined his surroundings. A hundred paces to his left, a door swung open. Someone stepped out and emptied a bucket of garbage onto the pavement. Torg saw a dozen fist-sized shapes converge on it, tearing into the discarded scraps.

Torg slipped along the base of the seventh wall, examining its texture with his fingertips. It was made of the same slippery stone as the ninth wall but otherwise was far less grand, smaller even than the eighth. He crouched on his haunches and leaped upward, landing like a cat on the top of the wall. From this vantage point, he could see the brothels, which swarmed with late-night business. Behind dark windows, men, women, and even monsters engaged in every conceivable form of sexual activity and depravity. Few paid any attention to what was going on in the streets. Torg passed by unseen.

The sixth wall was also small and undefended. He sprang over it and dropped onto a walkway of tiny white pebbles. The crunch of his landing was the first discernible sound he'd made since climbing out the window of the inn.

Torg slinked around the side of a white building that was raised off the ground on squat pillars. He knelt and peered into the crawl space where he saw a sunken area containing a wood furnace stoked by male attendants. Heat rose through hollowed spaces in the walls. Torg stood, slid the toe of his boot into a crevice, and clambered up to a small window. He looked into a well-lighted chamber that contained a pool of heated water. A dozen naked women lounged around the steamy bath, while several more were submerged past their shoulders. The ones he could see were tall, muscular, and small-breasted, with short-cropped hair. Torg recognized them as Sāykans, the famed female soldiers of Kamupadana. The Warlish witches had been masters of the Whore City for 10,000 years, but a never-ending line of Sāykans had served as the city's guardians for millennia beyond count. With the rise of Avici removing any serious threat of attack, the Sāykans were now used primarily as a police force. But they remained capable of holding the walls against great armies. In the bath's corner, Torg could see their weapons arranged in open cabinets. Several female attendants stood nearby.

The Sāykans' taut bodies were extremely pleasant to observe. They reminded Torg of Sōbhana, and he lingered by the window longer than was wise. The Sāykans were not as skilled as Tugars, but they were well-trained and clever. One soldier noticed his shadow.

"We are watched!" she said.

They went on alert, racing toward their weapons and shouting orders to the attendants to sound an alarm. Torg cursed himself for his lapse of concentration and fled down a narrow space between the concrete buildings. He needed to get as far from the commotion as possible before attempting to scale the fifth wall, which he knew was the most heavily guarded of all save for the ninth.

The alley opened into a manicured courtyard. A small group of Sāykans, wearing studded leather tunics and leggings, stood near a bubbling fountain. These soldiers still seemed unaware of any disturbance.

A building next to the bathhouse had a low balcony facing the courtyard. Torg pulled himself onto the balcony and crept along the flat stone on his stomach like a centipede. He soon heard a scourge of shouting from a dozen half-dressed soldiers who poured out of the bathhouse and called to their sisters by the fountain. In response, several Sāykans raced into the alley to investigate. Torg waited until they returned so that he could hear their report. They had found nothing and had given up the chase. He waited until they dispersed.

Torg dropped off the balcony and slipped along the borders of the courtyard. He passed a second bathhouse, slithered through a narrow alley, and raced along a lonely street for half a mile without encountering anyone. When he passed between another pair of buildings, he saw the fifth wall. It wasn't as enormous as the ninth, but it was easily the second largest of all, almost fifty cubits tall and surmounted by walks with machicolated parapets. A deep moat—swarming with small but deadly eels capable of stripping the flesh off a person in moments—protected its base. He remembered from his previous visit centuries ago that a lone drawbridge spanned the moat, but it wasn't visible from where Torg now stood. In the starlight, he could see dozens of soldiers patrolling the walks. Even late at night and with little threat of direct attack, they remained on alert. Torg wondered if the mysterious barrels in the ziggurat were the reason for heightened security.

Torg crouched in the dirt and gauged his situation. The fifth wall was 400 paces from where he stood. On the far side of the moat at the base of the wall was a narrow expanse of hard-pressed clay with scattered patches of gnarled grass. This provided plenty of visibility for the archers on top of the wall. Torg wondered if it might be impossible—even for him—to advance much farther without being seen.

However, the water was dark enough to provide concealment at least until he reached the other side of the moat. Torg wasn't in the mood to wander around naked the rest of the night, so he stripped off his clothes to protect them from the eels, wound them around the leather scabbard, and stepped into the water, holding the scabbard above his head so that his black outfit wouldn't be chewed to shreds.

The eels attacked his exposed skin. While most other beings would have been bloodily devoured, Torg wasn't harmed. He walked into the chilly water up to his chin and then swam one-handed until he could stand again. The eels continued to gnaw at him, unsuccessfully. He veered to his right and waded in the direction of where he believed the drawbridge to be, which was his best—and perhaps only—chance of continuing this mission. He couldn't conceive of any way he could scale the wall without being discovered.

The crescent moon had long since set in the west, but the night was only half over. Torg would need every bit of what darkness remained. He hoped to be back at the inn by dawn.

Torg shuffled through the water for a long time before the drawbridge came into view. Blessedly, the wooden bridge was lowered. But it was heavily guarded. He counted twenty Sāykans in plain sight.

He saw a dry area beneath the bridge on the far bank. Torg lay there on his side and dressed while the eels flopped and snapped in the shallow water just beyond.

The soldiers on the bridge talked among themselves, sensing no need for discretion. Torches lit the twin towers that framed the gateway. To enter undetected, he needed a diversion.

The iron bands underneath the drawbridge that secured the wooden planks provided handholds. Torg slid beneath the bridge over the deepest area of the moat—and waited. Boots thumped above him. He heard laughter, one soldier teasing another. Quick as a snake, Torg reached around the edge of the bridge, grasped an ankle, and yanked a woman over the side. The soldier screamed as she fell. The dark water broiled. The others raced to the edge of the bridge but were too late to save her. Meanwhile, a silent black shape passed through the gateway unseen.

The gap between the fifth and fourth walls was the narrowest of all, containing rows of wooden barracks that had been built and rebuilt thousands of times over millennia while the nine stone walls had magically resisted disintegration, requiring little maintenance.

Most of the Sāykans were asleep, but hundreds still wandered the pathways between the barracks. The cramped conditions worked to Torg's advantage. He slipped from shadow to shadow, approaching the fourth wall in just a few quick steps. This one was only ten cubits tall and unguarded. Torg vaulted over it.

Within the fourth wall stood the quarters of all nonmilitary personnel who lived in the city—grooms, maids, cooks, kitchen helpers, servitors, heralds, minstrels, stewards, and other laborers. Of these, most were women, while men, the inferior species, occupied only the lowliest positions. Any male living within the fourth wall was either a eunuch—and not by personal choice—or a man used as a breeder.

Torg moved through this area easily. Almost everyone was asleep. He saw few soldiers on the streets. The third wall was the same height as the fourth and contained many gates left untended to allow residents to enter the temple complex.

Strangely, thousands of multicolored candles lined the top of the third wall. He had never seen or heard of this before. Tendrils of wax coated the stone. Torg slipped inside an open door. The temples were dark. He noticed a lone woman in white robes standing on a ladder, replacing sagging candles with new ones.

Torg stood still and watched her for twenty long breaths. She appeared to be the only person in the immediate area. He came up from behind, kicked the ladder out from under her and caught her as she fell, suppressing her yelp with the palm of his hand. When she struggled, he compressed a pressure point behind her right ear. The girl went limp.

Torg carried her into a nearby thicket and held the Silver Sword against her throat. Her face was pale with fear, but when he removed his hand from her mouth, she didn't scream or struggle.

"If you do as I say, I won't harm you," Torg whispered. "But if you cry out or try to run, I'll kill you. Do you doubt it?"

She nodded, almost coolly.

"Good. Answer my questions quietly, and I give you my word

you'll live to see the morning."

She nodded again, this time more vigorously.

"Why the candles?"

In a steady voice, she whispered, "There's a special ceremony inside the ziggurat. The candles have been placed here to stop spirits from approaching the grand temple. They cannot pass beyond the holy light. At least, that's what the witches tell us."

"What spirits?"

"The Warlish do not say. But whenever the witches perform their magic, the spirits are aroused." And then she whispered, even more quietly: "And I've overheard the royal priestesses speak of *undines*."

This stunned Torg. *Undines* were creatures that normally dwelled in the demon realm. When summoned into the world of the living, they entered human flesh and multiplied until the host body swarmed with them. The result was a grotesque ruination of the mind and body that created a cannibalistic fiend capable of infecting others with their bites. Torg knew that summoning *undines* from the Realm of Undeath was difficult and time-consuming. Only powerful and learned beings were capable of the undertaking, which took more than a full day of undisturbed incantation. If a single step in the process was interrupted, the transference would fail. In the Realm of Life, *undines* appeared as black specks resembling tiny tadpoles, and—outside of living flesh— could survive only in cool, clear water. If a person or animal drank the water, they became infected. If enough *undines* were released into the Ogha River near Senasana, the entire city could be in danger.

Torg now understood *what* was happening, but he didn't understand *why*. Turning Senasana into a city of fiends made little sense—*unless* someone planned to unleash the newly created monsters on nearby Nissaya? Or perhaps even his beloved Anna?

Torg needed more information, but the girl in the white robes— probably a lowly apprentice—wouldn't have the answers. He pressed his face against hers and breathed blue-green vapor into her mouth.

"*Niddaayahi,*" he whispered. The girl went limp. Torg laid her near a hedge and covered her with fallen leaves, leaving just the tip of her nose exposed. While under the effects of the magic sleep, she wouldn't wake until morning.

Torg left her and proceeded toward the second wall.

After the wizard was gone, the girl sat up and smirked. Then her pale body twisted, shrank, and blackened. In its place, a raven appeared—and it fluttered into the sky, following Torg's progress from above. It stunned Vedana how easily she had fooled the father of her latest child. However, it disappointed her to discover that the poison she had magically spewed into his flesh during their lone sexual encounter in the bowels of Mount Asubha had somehow been removed. She could have controlled him more easily if the poison were still in his body. But even this wasn't the end of the world. Her plan was proceeding well enough, regardless.

To achieve ultimate success, she needed to keep the Death-Knower alive—at least for now. His crazy wanderings inside Kamupadana were threatening her plans, so she would have to lend a hand—or wing, if necessary—to make sure he didn't stumble into something that was too big for his britches.

This batch of *undines* wasn't her idea, anyway—though what Invictus planned to do with her wicked little creatures was beyond her comprehension. Of course, the spoiled Sun God hadn't asked for her permission, had he? Why was everyone always stepping on her turf? If they would just move aside and let her run things, then the world would be a better place. With Vedana as queen, life would be one big party. Why was she the only one who got it?

As Torg headed for the second wall, he fretted over how much time remained before daylight. Was it enough? He wasn't sure.

At thirty cubits, the second wall was the city's third tallest and third most heavily guarded. Royal priestesses, ancient rulers of Kamupadana but now eager servants of the Warlish witches, occupied four castles within this wall. The priestesses were lore masters. Their magic came from spells and incantations, not from innate ability. Stripped of books, talismans, wands, and weapons, they became quite ordinary. But the extent of their knowledge was not. The priestesses had the lore—and the witches the power—to summon the *undines*. Together, they were a formidable pairing.

Three iron portcullises, suspended by chains and lowered into deep grooves, defended the gateway tunnel in the second wall. Torg lay in the shadows and explored his options, admitting he had few. Scaling the wall would be difficult if not impossible; it was too smooth and sheer. And if he tried to force his way through the gateway, he would attract far too much attention. A pair of guards stood outside the first portcullis, and he was certain many more were within.

A paved road extended a thousand paces from the third wall to where Torg now lurked. From his hiding place, Torg watched the approach of a group of soldiers, each bearing a silver pentagram on her breastplate. The soldiers escorted a covered litter carried on long poles by eunuchs, whose heads were shaven and who wore brown cloaks and straw sandals. A Sāykan captain blew three blasts on an ivory horn. In response, the first of the three portcullises creaked upward. Several soldiers emerged to greet the captain. Torg was close enough to hear their discussion.

"You must permit us to enter," the captain said. "We bear evidence of a conspiracy."

"Ur-Nammu has ordered that none shall pass within the second wall tonight," one guard said. "Something big is going on in the ziggurat, but it's all hush-hush. What's your conspiracy?"

"See for yourself," the captain said.

The guard lifted the curtain and peered into the litter. Then she stepped back.

"Pass through. We'll lead you to the front steps of the temple."

Just then, a guard on the wall walk above the gateway let out a shout. A large black bird had streaked from the sky and taken a chunk out of her ear. Torg heard more shouts as the raven attacked again, prompting laughter. The guard drew her dagger and slashed at it, cursing. The eunuchs didn't seem to notice when the weight of the litter increased by twenty stones. They too seemed to enjoy the unexpected entertainment, though they dared not laugh.

Archers took aim at the bird, but its movements were so frenetic they couldn't even loose an arrow. As if losing interest in its quarry, the raven veered away, flew down along the wall and zoomed past the litter, cawing loudly before soaring back into the sky.

More laughter followed. Then the eunuchs were ordered to carry the litter through the gateway. Torg clung to its underside. His view was limited, but he could see the lowest steps of one of the castles about a hundred paces to his right. Soon they would pass within the first wall and approach the most ancient edifice in the known world.

The ziggurat towered 300 cubits above the ground and was shaped like a pyramid with receding tiers built upon a square platform. When Torg had first seen it centuries before, he had remarked that it resembled a gigantic layer cake. The witches had not been amused.

From the outside, the ziggurat had only one visible opening—a massive set of double doors on the ninth story. A wide stairway led up to that entryway. Further enhancing its exotic appearance, the ziggurat had no windows. In their place, thousands of fist-sized holes punctured the walls. When the witches bolted the double doors, the building was impervious to attack from anything other than an army of snakes. Even so, it was not designed to be a fortress. Whoever built it had intended it as a place of worship to gods long forgotten even by the Sāykans.

Torg's grip on the underside of the litter had been precarious from the start. But if he let go, hundreds of soldiers would discover him. Just when he thought he could hold on no longer, the party passed within the first wall, rejuvenating his resolve. The base of the ziggurat loomed just a few dozen paces away. When they started up the stairway, Torg let out a silent sigh of relief.

Finally, they reached the ninth story just as the iron doors creaked open.

"We must see Ur-Nammu," he heard the Sāykan captain demand.

"No one may enter," a female voice answered.

"We wouldn't be so rude if the urgency of our mission didn't require immediate attention," the captain said. "If we can't see Ur-Nammu, then allow us to present our evidence to Jākita-Abhinno."

Whoever greeted them turned and spoke to someone inside the edifice. After a heated exchange, she allowed the caravan to enter a chamber containing hundreds of lighted candles.

Just before the doors clanged shut, a burst of wind swirled through the opening, though the night was otherwise calm. The candles were extinguished, causing the room to go dark except for dim pricks of starlight peeking through the fist-sized holes. The eunuchs dropped the litter to the floor with a thud. By the time some of the candles were relighted, swords were tensely drawn.

"Hold ... *hold*!" the captain said. "We're not enemies!"

"What happened?" the woman who had greeted them shouted. "What devilry have you brought with youuu?"

"None of which I am aware," the captain said. "But even without devilry, my tidings are not good. Look within the curtains and see for yourself."

Torg recognized the voice. It belonged to Jākita-dEsa, one of the hag servants of Jākita-Abhinno, who was the most powerful Warlish witch in the world now that Chal-Abhinno was dead. All Warlish witches used the surname Abhinno, which meant *witch* in the ancient tongue. Their hags used the same first name as their assigned master along with the surname dEsa, which meant *servant*.

This Jākita-dEsa was the strongest of Jākita-Abhinno's brood. She was also the most attractive, locked forever in a state of beauty—which is why, Torg had to admit, he remembered her so clearly. To those outside the coven, this would have been considered a stroke of luck. But to the hags, neither eternal beauty nor ugliness was superior. Beauty had the advantage of seduction, but ugliness inspired fear. Both were powerful weapons.

Jākita-dEsa peered into the litter, but Torg wasn't in a position to see what lay within.

"How did they die?" Jākita-dEsa said.

"The merchant appears to have ended his own life," the Sāykan captain said. "But a dagger struck the hag's back. The force and accuracy of the throw has the feel of a Tugar."

The merchant? So you were brave, after all.

"Isss it possible a Tugar is in the city without our knowing it?" Jākita-dEsa said.

"Our contacts believe the desert warriors haven't ventured north of Senasana," the captain said. "But a single Tugar—perhaps an Asēkha— might be spying on us. If that's true, they might know more about what's going on tonight than the witches or priestesses believe. Do you still desire to thwart us?"

"Thwarting the Sāykans has never been my desire," the beautiful hag said. "What youuu don't seem to understand is that the witches and the priestesses are—how shall I sssay it?—*indisposed*. I couldn't interrupt even if I wanted to."

"Very well, sister," the captain said with an air of concession.

"Nonetheless, I will triple the guard within the first gate. The ill wind disturbed me. This would not be an opportune time for the ziggurat to be breached."

"Agreed," Jākita-dEsa said. "Let us russsh to our duties."

During their banter, Torg moved quickly downward and soon had descended to the sixth floor, though he'd been forced to kill a pair of hags and four soldiers to avoid further detection. They lay dead on the smooth stone steps of a winding interior stairway leading to the bottom of the edifice. To Torg's dismay, he had found no place to hide the bodies.

Where the winding stair intersected each floor, he stopped and listened. The deeper he descended, the more convinced he became that the barrels lay at the base of the temple, either on the first floor or below the surface. During his only visit to the ziggurat two centuries before, they had invited Torg to descend only as far as the fourth floor, so he already was approaching uncharted territory.

A bog-like mist choked the air in the deeper portions of the temple, making the stone steps slippery. The lower he went, the darker it became. He moved in a silent crouch, his weapon drawn. But the Silver Sword remained cold. Whatever magic existed within the ziggurat didn't affect the supernal blade.

Or so Torg thought. At one point, a pair of guards came up the stairs, forcing him to kneel behind a marble statue until they passed. After they were gone, the point of the sword accidentally touched the wall. At that instant, the blade glowed like it was on fire, illuminating the darkness. As soon as Torg removed it from the stone, it winked out. Apparently, the otherworldly stone of the ziggurat was akin to the metal used to forge the sword.

When he reached the second level, Torg sensed an effusion of magic somewhere beneath him. He detected movement at the base of the stairs and could hear female voices chanting phrases from the ancient tongue, though the words were too faint to make out. He snuck toward them a step at a time.

The first floor was comprised of a single broad chamber with a tall ceiling. In the center was a wide but shallow pool. Standing in knee-deep water were Ur-Nammu, the high priestess of Kamupadana, and Jākita-Abhinno, newly crowned queen of the Warlish witches.

"*Mara-maccha, pariyuttha* (Devil fish, arise)," the high priestess chanted. "*Pavisatha udakam parisuddham* (Enter the holy water)."

Jākita-Abhinno writhed in the clear waters of the pool, transforming from beautiful to ugly and back again amid explosions of crimson light and putrid smoke. One hundred other witches mimicked her movements. Meanwhile, dozens of hags scooped water from the pool with silver goblets and poured it into nearby barrels. The summoned *undines* were being stored for future use.

Torg heard cries from above. Someone must have discovered the dead bodies. But the participants in the bizarre ceremony beneath him—more than 200 women if he included hags and other priestesses—appeared too enraptured to notice the disturbance. He stepped into the chamber and walked nonchalantly toward the barrels. They didn't even see him at first, but the women finally emerged from their trances and turned toward him. Torg approached the oak barrels, raised the Silver Sword, and hacked at them. The wood split apart, spilling the liquid contents onto the stone floor.

One of the witches—in her hideous state—was the first to draw a dagger from the folds of her gown. It thumped against his back, piercing his tunic but failing to pierce his flesh. Another witch leaped onto his shoulders and bit his neck. Torg reached back, grasped her head, and flung her across the room. More witches rushed forward, red fire spitting from their eyes, nostrils, and mouths. Much to his chagrin, Torg's clothing was incinerated. But his body wasn't harmed. He ignored their attacks and continued to destroy the barrels until he was finally forced to confront them.

"*Paapaa-itthiyo* (Wicked women), return to the darkness from which you came and cower there until I depart. Any who attempt to thwart me will perish. You are not my match."

"I know youuu," Jākita-Abhinno said, eyeing Torg's nakedness with a mixture of rage and lust. "We've met before, many centuries ago. You're no friend of the coven. Youuu did great harm to our queen at Dibbu-Loka, and we recently sensed her demise. How dare you disrupt our sacred sssummoning!"

"I do as I please."

Ur-Nammu, the high priestess of Kamupadana and second in rank only to Jākita-Abhinno, stepped out of the pool and approached Torg. The priestess wielded an oaken staff with a silver pentacle embedded in its head. Apparently in no mood for further debate, she smote the floor at his feet. Acidic tendrils scurried along the surface of the stone and wound around him like a crimson web. The priestess wielded no physical magic, but her staff was bloated with supernatural might.

Against Torg's blue-green power, though, her magic proved ineffective. The cocoon that encased him shattered like glass.

"Don't say I didn't warn you," he said.

Ur-Nammu lunged with surprising speed, attempting to smash the staff against his head, but Torg blocked the downward blow with his sword, and the staff was cleaved. Its pentacle, still attached to a splintered portion of oak, somersaulted through the air and exploded. But Torg wasn't through. In less time than it took for a single inhalation, he whipped the sword in front of his body and thrust straight ahead, stabbing Ur-Nammu between her breasts.

The high priestess remained standing—as if nothing unusual had occurred—but then her eyes rolled back and she collapsed. She was no longer.

A dozen more hags and at least that many soldiers—including Jākita-dEsa and the Sāykan captain—entered the chamber from the stairs. The hags attacked like a pack of rabid wolves, their poisoned claws tearing hungrily at his face. Torg beheaded three, cut two in half at the waist, and hacked the legs out from under four more with a series of lightning-quick strokes. After that, he scanned the room for Jākita-Abhinno. If he could kill her, it would reduce his enemy's ability to summon more *undines*. But between Torg and the queen of the witches stood Jākita-dEsa, her perpetually beautiful face made ugly by rage. A glittering metallic ball about the size of an apple sparkled in the hag's hand, and she hurled it at his feet. When the ball struck the hard floor, it detonated and cast shards of glowing metal. He heard a boom—and then the room filled with black smoke. Torg could now only see an arm's length in any direction, but he heard the witches cackling within the nocuous cloud. Obviously, this was a tactic they had employed before with success. But against a Death-Knower, it was another mistake. During his fifty years of warrior training, Torg had spent thousands of hours practicing in deep darkness, which enabled him to sense the whereabouts of his enemy.

Torg pointed his sword straight forward and turned the double-edged blade on its side. He lifted his left foot off the floor and pressed its sole against the inside of his right knee. Then he rose on the toes of his right foot and began to spin, slowly at first, but then faster and faster until his body became a tornadic blur. When the first women attacked, he cut them to shreds. Instead of retreating, the others waded in, their desire to rend even greater than their fear. By the time the smoke dissipated, fifty were dead or dying, and Torg still was on the attack. Panic overcame their anger. Most clambered up the stairs, but a few disappeared through hidden doors into dark catacombs beneath the edifice.

Torg knew that his best chance of escape lay below. It would be nearly impossible to depart the way he'd come. He was powerful, but not even he could defeat an entire army by himself. And the magical spells he'd used at Dibbu-Loka and the Svakaran village couldn't subdue an enemy of this scope. The only way out was underground. But to navigate the catacombs, Torg needed a guide. He searched among the bodies for Jākita-Abhinno but found no evidence of her remains, which meant he had failed to remove the threat of more *undines* being summoned after he was gone. At least he had destroyed all the barrels, but the pool still swarmed with squirmy black specks. Torg kicked the short retaining wall but couldn't damage it. Then he struck it with the sword. This time the wall cracked, and he continued to hack at the stone until a portion crumbled, flooding the floor. Like fish out of water, the wriggling *undines* perished at his feet.

Though Jākita-Abhinno had escaped, Torg found the severed head of her favorite servant. Jākita-dEsa would have to do. He picked up the head by its hair and stared into the hag's eyes. He could hear noises building in the stairway. Reinforcements had arrived and were working up the courage to attack. He had little time.

"*Yakkkkha*," Torg said.

The head sprang to life. "If you attack my master, I will kill you!" it snarled.

"You're already dead."

"I am no longer," the head agreed. "I am gone."

"I wish to depart the chamber and get from here to the seventh wall without being seen. Are there tunnels beneath the ziggurat that lead that far?"

"Yes" what remained of Jākita dEsa said.

"Tell me where to go."

"You're blocking my vision."

Despite his precarious situation, this made Torg chuckle. Then he lifted the head and faced its eyes outward, slowly showing it the room.

"Many others are no longer," the head observed.

"These deaths are not your concern. Time runs short. Tell me where to go."

"Dozens of doors open to tunnels that lead from the first wall to the seventh and beyond—some far beyond."

As angry shouts grew louder in the stairway, Torg sprinted to the opposite wall.

"Show me a door."

"Each has its own command."

"Speak quickly!"

"*Phalati*," the head chanted.

A portal swung open, revealing a cramped tunnel. Torg scanned the chamber one last time. None of the enemy had dared to enter from the stairway behind him, and it was possible no one would know which passageway he now chose. He dove inside and slammed the door. Now it was utterly dark.

"How do you see in these tunnels?" Torg said.

"We bring torches."

Torg kicked himself. Then he stumbled forward. Before long, he walked straight into a wall. The tunnel had taken an abrupt turn. To go farther, he needed light. Then an idea came to him. He brushed the blade of the Silver Sword against the wall. The sword glowed, providing enough illumination to see for several paces. He continued to scrape the tip of the blade along the wall as he moved forward. It made an eerie screeching sound that made his skin crawl, but what else could he do? If he used his own magic, they would discover him too quickly.

The tunnel descended steeply. Torg guessed he was more than one hundred fathoms below the surface before it leveled out. Once again, he found himself deep beneath the ground in a mysterious labyrinth, and once again he wasn't enjoying the experience.

Several times, he encountered crisscrossing passageways that led to more darkness, but the head directed him forward. Torg saw no witches, hags, priestesses, or soldiers. Somehow, he had evaded them. Or were they afraid to follow?

"Are these tunnels always this empty?"

"Most shy from the darkness."

After remaining level for more than a mile, the passageway ascended. Torg came to another small door. This one led to his escape.

"One last question before I release you," Torg said. "What were the witches going to do with the *undines*?"

"The hags were not told," the head said. "We weren't worthy."

Torg growled in frustration. He feared he hadn't seen the last of the *undines*.

"One final favor, then. Tell me the magic word for this door."

"*Dakhīla*," the head chanted obediently.

The door swung open, revealing the bright sunshine of a cool morning. This blinded Torg, but after his eyes adjusted to the light, he put the head down on the floor and stepped out of the darkness into a remote area of the market. Just then, a tall but effeminate man wandered by wearing a pink doublet that hung past his knees. Torg rendered him unconscious with a blow to the temple and dragged his limp body a few paces back into the tunnel. Before stripping the man of his odd clothes, Torg cleansed his own flesh, incinerating large patches of dried blood with a flow of blue-green energy. The doublet was too small for a man of Torg's stature, but he managed to squeeze into it without tearing apart most of the seams. Straw sandals and a felt hat completed his bizarre new outfit.

Before re-entering the market, Torg picked up the hag's severed head and tucked it into the stranger's arms. As he was shutting the door, what remained of Jākita-dEsa continued to speak. "I am gone. I am no longer," it told its new master, who undoubtedly would get the fright of his life when he woke up.

Torg worked his way through the market, which was slowly becoming crowded. Small groups of soldiers ran to-and-fro, but Torg believed it would take the Sāykans at least half the day to organize a full-scale response, and he hoped to be away from Kamupadana by then.

Soon he passed through an open door within the eighth wall and found the inn. When he rang the bell, the fat innkeeper let him in.

"Your friends came home last night without you, and it appears they fared better than you. I have to say that you look rather silly. Did the whores steal your clothes?"

"That's not entirely inaccurate," Torg said.

"Would you like another bath? I'd be happy to provide personal service."

"Trust me when I say you'd be better off if you did not. But I need another black tunic with breeches and boots. Do my friends have any coins left, I wonder?"

"For you, there'll be no charge," the woman said. "I suggest, however, that you leave the city before too long. Don't misunderstand … I enjoy your company. But something has aroused the Sāykans, and that's never a good thing around here. Will you be needing supplies?"

"Anything you can provide will be a blessing," Torg said, and he gave her an appreciative hug.

"Ah, will wonders never cease? In all my years, I've never been held by a handsome man so poorly dressed." But then she grew serious. "Early this morning, I allowed two people to join your party. One was a man with yellow hair and the other a woman who appeared to have had too much to drink and could barely walk. They are waiting for you while the others sleep off the night's adventures."

"I'll see for myself," Torg said. In truth, he had no idea who these two might be.

When the wizard was gone, the innkeeper's eyes changed from light blue to black.

"So easy to deceive. And to think I once feared him."

The innkeeper flopped down onto a couch. Vedana had no more use for her body.

On the first floor of the ziggurat, the beautiful version of Jākita-Abhinno stood near the now-empty pool, surveying the recent carnage. The dead numbered fifty-two: six eunuchs; eight Sāykan soldiers; sixteen priestesses, including high priestess Ur-Nammu; eighteen hags, including her favorite Jākita-dEsa; and four precious witches. The Sāykan captain who had brought the bodies to the ziggurat was one of the survivors, though there was a tear on the right side of her leather tunic, exposing her bloodied ribcage. The captain stood next to the new queen of the Warlish witches and awaited her orders.

"I've seen no one fight like that," the captain said. "Did we face a god?"

"He isss no god," Jākita-Abhinno said. "But he's almost as dangerousss as one."

"Unless he can fly as well as he fights, I believe he's still somewhere within our walls," the captain said. "My soldiers can find him before nightfall. Shall I order a full search of the city?"

"No," the queen said.

"Master, we must avenge this blasphemy!"

"We'll do no such thing. I answer to a higher power—she who gave birth to my kind. And she has ordered me not to pursssue."

The captain sighed. "I don't understand, but the Sāykans will do as you command." Then she bowed and left the chamber.

Jākita-Abhinno watched the captain depart. Then she stared forlornly at the blood and gore, the shattered barrels, and the lifeless black specks on the cream-colored floor. The dead *undines* looked like seeds that would never sprout.

"I don't understand, either, but my orders are clear," the witch whispered to herself. Then she bowed before the dead. "I will avenge you, my sssisters. Some day. Somehow. The Death-Knower will perish at *my* handsss."

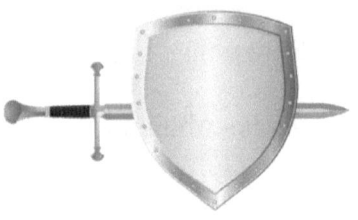

DREAM COME TRUE

The door to one of their rooms on the third floor was ajar. Torg tried to be silent, but the old wood beneath his feet refused to cooperate. It creaked so loud he might as well have alarmed an army of chipmunks. At least, it felt that way to him. But several styles of snoring—from Ugga's bear-like growl to Rathburt's sniveling whimpers—concealed his approach.

Torg crept into the entryway and peeked around the door. He saw Bard sprawled on a couch, drool dripping into his thick beard, and Elu on a rug on the floor, wrapped in his cloak. Torg stepped inside. Near the window were two sturdy beds with wool-stuffed mattresses: Ugga had claimed one, Rathburt the other.

The strangers had to be in the adjacent room.

A small door connected one room to the next, and it was also ajar. Torg began to push it open, but apprehension stayed his hand. Whoever was on the other side of the door wielded enormous power. Rather than feeling threatening, though, the aura appealed to him like exotic perfume. His breath quickened and his heart raced. To his surprise, Torg experienced a wave of dizziness. He wondered if he could find the courage to look inside.

Torg considered waking up Rathburt and asking him what he knew of their visitors, but he remembered the innkeeper saying she had let the strangers in after his friends had returned from their gallivanting. It was possible—even probable—that they were unaware anyone else was with them. Torg couldn't depend on Rathburt or the others for support.

Ever so gently, he pressed against the door—and as he stepped inside, the aura nearly overwhelmed him, causing a single tear to slide down his cheek. His reason for existence was only a few paces away. She was the woman in his dreams—the moon, incarnate. The other half of his soul.

She sat on a bed, facing away from him. A cascade of blond hair reached all the way to the mattress. A strange man pressed against her, with his arm around her shoulders. Torg felt an intense surge of jealousy, and it took all his will to resist yanking the man off the bed and breaking his neck.

But he would not. Not yet, at least.

Besides, he could sense the man meant her no harm. The way he held her made it obvious that he loved her.

Torg approached the bed, silent as air. But the noisy floor gave him away, causing the man to bolt to his feet and spin around. The woman sagged backward onto the mattress.

Torg's eyes widened. The man looked like a slightly older version of Invictus. He was larger but had the same yellow hair, brown eyes, and square jaw.

"I was told you could help her," he snapped. "She's dying. You must save her!"

"I don't know who she is or who you are," Torg said, trying to appear calm. "Why do you say she's dying? Is she injured or ill?"

When Torg looked at her again, his heart performed a crazy dance in his chest. He wanted to hold her—and never let go. The yellow-haired man sensed something in Torg's demeanor that he didn't find to his liking, and his face became red and puffy. Then he sat back down and took the woman in his arms like she was his possession. Torg again had to stifle a desire to throttle the Invictus look-alike.

"Never mind who she is," the man said. "If you're a healer, then surely you can recognize that she's sick. Will you help her or not? If not, then tell me quickly so that I can leave this stink hole and try to find someone who can. I've wasted enough time listening to their snoring. I was tempted to cut their throats to shut them up."

Torg felt a sudden urge to slap him. He took a step forward, but the woman on the bed moaned, causing him to freeze. It broke his heart to hear such a desperate sound pass through her lips. Torg regained his composure. "I *am* a healer and you'll find none better. Whoever brought you here was right to do so. But before I help her, you must tell me who led you to me."

"Who are you to give me orders? I don't answer to oversized jesters! Why are you dressed so strangely, anyway?"

"It's a long story," Torg said.

The man grunted. "I'll tell you nothing beyond what I choose. Either help her or don't. But be quick. I'll strike down anyone who hinders us."

As he spoke, the man hugged her even tighter. She moaned again. Torg's face flushed. "Very well. But you must move away and give me some room. I can't heal her while you're clinging to her like she's a doll."

The man grunted, then reluctantly stood and backed over to the window. Torg sat on the bed and looked at the woman. She wore a plain brown dress, clean but threadbare. When his left thigh pressed against her leg, a jolt of energy blew into his flesh, causing him to gasp. He already loved her so much it was suffocating. And they were yet to speak a single word to one another.

"Why must you sit so close?" the man said suspiciously.

"Be quiet and let me concentrate. Do you always whine so much?"

The man grunted again but otherwise held his tongue.

As gently as he could manage, Torg lifted her into his arms. Her eyes were clamped shut and her cheeks smudged with soot, but her beauty was still evident. In Torg's dreams—and in the ice at the waterfall—he had seen her face before.

"Yes, she's pretty," the man said. "But are you going to help her or just stare at her? She could die at any moment. *Hurry*!"

"Hush!"

Still gazing at the woman's face, he placed his right hand on her abdomen. Energy sparkled at his fingertips and crept along the wool of her dress. She jerked spasmodically and then yelped. The man charged over.

"What are you doing to her?"

Torg glared. "I won't harm her. But I must *concentrate*. Stop annoying me."

"Get on with it, then!"

Torg sighed and returned his focus to the woman. *So very lovely.*

Then he lifted her face within a finger-length of his and pressed his mouth against hers, spreading apart her lips with his tongue—and exhaling.

"Stop that!" the man said, but Torg could barely hear. His life force blew into the woman's lungs, filling her with healing energy. As her body convulsed, her eyes sprang open, and she flung her arms around his back. A blue-green shimmer emanated from Torg's flesh. From hers came a white glow. The two sheaths of energy intermingled, slowly at first—as if exploring each other—and then eagerly.

They had found each other, at long last.

Somewhere in the far reaches of his awareness, Torg could sense the yellow-haired man tugging on his arms, but it meant little. An infant couldn't have done less harm.

She let go of him and slid a few inches away on the bed. When their bodies no longer touched, their intertwined energies winked out, but she continued to stare at him with blue-gray eyes. Her face looked so familiar. He knew her not just from dreams and visions, but also from somewhere else. *How many lifetimes have we spent together?*

Torg heard noises behind him. Kicking and stomping. On the old wooden floor, it sounded like drumbeats.

"Here! Here!" came a loud voice. "There'll be no fighting in my inn. I'll call my boys and have you all thrown out if you don't get control of yourselves."

Torg turned and saw the innkeeper standing in the doorway, her cheeks ablaze and her mouth coated with spittle. Nearby, Ugga and Bard were holding the yellowed-haired man's arms. He was kicking and flailing and his face was as red as a dragon scale, but the woodsmen were too strong.

"What should we do with him?" Bard said to Torg. "We found ya with da whore, and this man was trying to beat ya up or rob ya or something. Would ya like Ugga to crack open his head?"

"*No!*" said the woman on the bed, startling them all. "Don't harm him. He's my friend and is only trying to protect me."

"I don't care if he's the *One God* come to cleanse our souls," the innkeeper said. "If you don't quiet him down, my boys will."

"Please, Lucius!" she said. "Don't fight them—if not for your own sake, then for mine."

At the sound of her voice, Lucius calmed down, though his face remained swollen. Ugga and Bard released him. The man rushed toward the bed.

"Are you … healed?"

The woman sighed and gazed at Torg. "I believe I am."

"Good," Lucius said, ignoring Torg. "We must be on our way.

Quickly, come with me." He held out his hand to her.

This confused Ugga. "Did ya bed da man's wifey?" he said to Torg.

"I met her only a few moments ago," Torg said. "She was ill and came to me seeking aid."

Torg turned to the innkeeper. "My dear lady, do you have the clothes you offered me earlier? It's time for us to go."

"What do you mean?" the innkeeper said. "I offered nothing. I haven't spoken to any of you since last night."

Torg eyed her suspiciously.

"What happened to your clothes?" Rathburt said to Torg, peering over the fat woman's shoulder. "You look like a jester, all dressed in pink."

"*I'm in no mood for jokes*!" Torg snapped with enough force to split the wooden door, causing the innkeeper to squeal.

"I'll give you whatever you want," she said breathlessly. "All you had to do was ask!"

"I thought I already had. Bring me a black tunic, breeches, and boots … *please*. And arrange food and supplies."

Then he turned to Ugga and Bard. "I don't suppose you have any coins left to pay her for her kindness."

Ugga smiled and pounded his chest. "I won lots of money at da card tables. We're rich! We spent many coins on da Blondies and Brounettos, but there's still plenty left." He handed the innkeeper two gold pieces. "Will that be enough?"

The fat woman's expression changed from frightened to pleased. "More than enough. And in exchange for your generosity, let me give you some advice from one who knows the ways of Kamupadana. Take only the supplies you can conceal beneath your cloaks. Just before I came upstairs, I was told the Sāykan soldiers are stopping people and asking questions. This day has a strange feel."

Torg agreed they needed to be cautious. "If we try to rush out now, it will look suspicious. Let's take the time to eat a meal in our rooms before we go. If we're forced to fight, we'll need our strength."

Then he gestured to the innkeeper. "Will you serve us here?"

"With pleasure," she said.

Elu walked to Bard and tapped him on the leg. "Can we trust the big lady?"

Bard looked down. "I think so. What do ya think, Ugga?"

"She has never done us wrong before," the crossbreed said.

"I don't trust *her* or any of you," Lucius said, and then he wagged his finger at Torg. "Least of all, you!" The yellow-haired man reached for the woman's hand again. "Will you heed my advice and come with me?"

"I want you by my side," she said, "but I need this man … these men … as well. They have promised their protection. We should accept it." She turned to Torg. "But we have nothing to offer in payment for your service. Will you have us as traveling companions even so?"

Torg's heart leaped with joy, but he was careful to appear calm. "We would be honored."

"Wait a minute," Rathburt whined. "This woman is sick and weak and will slow us down. What have we to gain from taking her with us? We don't even know who she is."

"If I say she comes, she comes," Torg said. "Does anyone else object?"

"I like da lady," Ugga said. "But da man with her is mean."

"Where I go, Lucius goes," she said to the crossbreed and the others. "If you don't want him to join us, then we should part ways now."

"He may come, if that's his choice," Torg said. "But if he betrays us, he will do so at his peril."

"The same goes for you," Lucius said to Torg.

"You don't know to whom you speak, so I'll forgive your brash words for now," Torg said.

The innkeeper entered the room with her scrawny assistant, both of whom carried trays of food laden with trenchers of stale bread topped with sizzling chunks of venison. The trays also contained peas, beans, and onions; cheese spiced with salt, pepper, and garlic; waffles with apple jelly; and dandelion wine. They ate and drank like animals, including the woman, who attacked her food as though she hadn't eaten in days. Ugga was so hungry he even devoured most of his trencher.

While they ate, Torg did his best not to stare at the gorgeous woman. The yellow-haired man sat next to her at the table and watched Torg's every move. The woman, for her part, glanced at Torg often, but turned away quickly each time.

After their meal, the innkeeper presented Torg with new clothes, and he dressed in an anteroom behind a dark curtain. When he emerged wearing a black tunic with loose-fitting breeches, the woman put her hand to her mouth. The man named Lucius saw that—and scowled.

Elu walked over to the woman and tugged on her skirt. "What's your name, nice lady? Mine's Elu."

Lucius scowled again. "Her name's not your concern."

"Don't worry," the woman said to Lucius. Then she looked down at Elu and smiled. "I promise to tell you later, Elu … once we're safely away from the city. All right?"

"Sure. Until then, Elu will call you Nice Lady."

"That sounds wonderful."

When they went downstairs, it was almost noon. The innkeeper and her assistant had packed dried meats, fruits, and vegetables into leather pouches small enough to tuck inside their cloaks. They carried only a little water, but water was plentiful in the mountain wilderness.

Ugga and Bard gave the innkeeper a goodbye hug. Elu trotted over and wrapped his arms around one of her massive thighs.

"One day, we hope to be back," Bard said. "If not, it's been a pleasure doing business with ya."

"You'll be back," the innkeeper said. "I'm not worried. There's no place better."

"Thank you for your courtesy," the woman said. "You trusted a pair of strangers. Few would do that in these times."

"I don't know what you mean," the innkeeper said. "How did you get inside, anyway?"

The woman looked puzzled, but Torg took her arm and led her toward the door. "It's time to go. Thank you for your hospitality. If the moment ever comes when I can return the favor, I most certainly will."

The innkeeper smiled and nodded; then her face turned serious. "The streets are dangerous. Blend in as best you can. If you can make it to the markets without being stopped, you'll have a chance. May the *One God* see you clear of the walls."

They stepped outside onto a street swarming with people, some headed outward to the markets, some inward to the brothels and baths, some just wandering from tavern to tavern. Despite the previous night's chill, the day had become unseasonably warm. Torg hid his sword beneath his cloak, but Ugga carried his ax openly, and Bard his bow and arrows. This wasn't unusual. Visitors were permitted to carry weapons outside the fifth wall.

Even with his unusual size, Torg had ways of remaining unseen. He was trained in the art of evanescence. Among this many people, he could flit from place to place; especially if he were alone or with other Tugars. But his companions hindered him. Elu was the cleverest of the bunch, but even the Svakaran slowed him down, preventing Torg from taking full advantage of his instincts.

Armored Sāykans patrolled in small groups. Torg studied their behavior and found it curious. Their efforts to catch him—if they were trying at all—appeared half-hearted. Rather than accost and detain, they were simply watching. Or pretending to watch. Was it possible they believed he had already fled the city? Torg was dubious. They should have been doing more. The Sāykans were capable soldiers, but they were behaving like they were under orders to fail. And if so, whose orders? And why?

Disturbing Torg even more was Lucius' behavior. The yellow-haired man hovered over the woman like she was his child. It was obvious she was still weak, but to fawn over her so lavishly might draw attention. And that was the least of it. Torg could barely tolerate Lucius touching her. His jealousy eroded his concentration, and he couldn't afford to make a mistake now. If they were discovered, they would have to fight their way free—and she might be harmed. That was not an option. He would have to overcome his annoyance until they escaped.

Among the sea of faces flowing past them, Torg unexpectedly saw someone he'd known for many years, and a warmth flowed through him that smote his heart. This man wore the robes of a wealthy merchant, but Torg knew better. The others revealed their presence, each in a different disguise.

Beyond hope, the Asēkhas had found him. Torg recognized nineteen faces, one of them newly promoted to replace Sōbhana. The twentieth would still be in Anna, left there to lead the Tugars. But the greatest of them all was here in Kamupadana.

Torg and Kusala briefly clasped each other's forearms. Then the chieftain handed Torg a tall staff—Obhasa stained brown by pomegranate and sulfur to avoid unwanted attention. None of Torg's companions seemed to notice this encounter.

When his faithful warriors surrounded him, Torg could not have been more pleased.

Now ... anything was possible.

Escaping Kamupadana could be done.

The Asēkhas encircled their king and his six companions, none of whom seemed aware of the warriors' presence. Even Rathburt, who should have been able to recognize fellow Tugars, was oblivious.

Kusala walked three paces to his king's right dressed as a well-to-do merchant. Three paces to his left, Podhana shuffled along pretending to be crippled. Three paces in front walked Rati appearing as a warder from one of the inns. Three paces behind was Tāseti, the most powerful female Tugar in the world and first in line to succeed Kusala as chieftain; she wore a narrow cloak with silken cords, mimicking a noblewoman strolling among commoners. The male Asēkha next to her was also fancily dressed, playing the role of her husband. Fourteen others completed the circle, each indistinguishable from the swarms of people around them despite being a span taller than most others in the crowd. They hid their *uttaras,* daggers, and slings, the latter of which the warriors used as effectively as bows and arrows, casting metal beads with wicked force and accuracy.

Although Torg was in the center of the circle, it was he who led their procession. The Asēkhas were sensitive to his every movement: a twitch of a finger, tilt of the head, shift of the shoulder. They veered to the right and passed through one of the widest gates in the eighth wall, flowing into the crowded market area. Though they appeared to be strolling from booth to booth, Torg and the Asēkhas were on high alert, watching the movements of the Sāykan soldiers with a mixture of interest and bafflement. Torg was convinced some of the soldiers were aware of his presence, but they feigned disinterest. He could think of no explanation for their behavior, which made him distrust it even more. Were they waiting until he reached open ground before attempting an ambush? That was possible, he supposed, but would they risk giving him that much of an opportunity for flight? Torg couldn't help but think they were under orders to avoid him. If so, whose orders? Only a Warlish witch or a high priestess would have the authority to command such an act, and why would they want to help him, especially after the damage he had inflicted inside the ziggurat? The only other being who could direct the Sāykans was Vedana—and again, why would the demon want him to escape?

Your daughter is lost in the blackness!

Kusala looked at him with puzzlement. Torg's mind had wandered, and it had shown in his expression. This was no time for carelessness.

Too much was at stake. The wizard took back control of his concentration. His musings would have to wait.

Torg gestured to his traveling companions, and the Asēkhas took note. For whatever reason, their lord wanted these six to accompany them. The warriors wouldn't question his command, but they were confused. The strangers would slow them down. Of what value could they possibly be? Regardless, the warriors would defend each of them with their lives.

Now it was well past noon. The sky was perfectly blue and the sun ablaze as if too impatient to wait for spring before spewing its fire. As many people were leaving the city as entering, with most of the early morning crowd returning to a heavily populated area along the Ogha River about a half-day's journey to the east.

Torg, however, had no plans to go that way. East and south would bring him ever closer to Avici. He decided to head southwest toward the Gap of Gamana and then turn west and skirt the northern edge of the gap using the foothills and forests as cover. If he could journey past the city of Duccarita, he would come to the portion of the Dhutanga forest that reached almost all the way to the mountains, avoiding a dangerous north-to-south crossing of the gap.

But that was weeks into the future. Assuming they could escape Kamupadana, they still faced three leagues of open plains before reaching the foothills. In that regard, Rathburt had been right: The woman *would* slow them down. Considering how ill she'd been just a short time ago, she was moving along quite well now. But would she be capable of outrunning pursuers?

As they approached the grand gateway of the ninth wall, Torg's suspicions expanded. Their departure was progressing far too conveniently. If the Sāykans were determined to prevent his escape, they at least would have lowered the massive stone slab and sealed the entrance. Yet the gateway was open and lightly guarded. The Warlish witches had chosen to let him go. The more he pondered this the more Vedana entered his thoughts. Somehow the demon had become his ally—at least temporarily.

Dozens of soldiers paced the wall walk above them. For every visible soldier, ten more crouched behind crenellated parapets and peered through loopholes. But if any of them saw him, they didn't react. Torg, the Asēkhas, and his six companions walked out of the city as easily as everyone else. In a short time, they were more than a mile from the wall—and still there was no pursuit.

When they veered toward the southwest, they separated from the crowds. For the first time, Torg's companions recognized the presence of the Asēkhas.

"Do not fear." Torg gestured toward the warriors. "They are with me."

This didn't impress Lucius. "I don't know them," he said angrily to Torg. "What other surprises do you have in store?"

In two strides, Kusala reached Lucius and knocked him to the ground. Then the chieftain placed the cutting edge of his *uttara* against the man's throat.

"Speak to my king like that again and I will spill your blood."

"Do not harm him … *please*," the woman pleaded. "If not for him, I'd be dead."

"Kusala, desist," Torg said regretfully.

"As you command," the chieftain said, backing away. Lucius stood and brushed himself off, his face filled with rage.

Torg walked over to Kusala and placed his hand on his shoulder. "He doesn't know me. But now is not the time or place for introductions. I have much to say to you. But we must reach the foot of the mountains before exchanging pleasantries. Consider these six as my guests and treat them accordingly."

Then Torg nodded at Rathburt, who was watching with mouth agape.

"Kusala, it has been long since you've last seen him, but Rathburt has returned. Another Death-Knower walks among us."

The Asēkhas bowed.

"See, Bard?" Ugga said. "I told ya Master Slump isn't such a meanie."

The Asēkhas laughed heartily at the crossbreed's words, which surprised Ugga, but after their mirth subsided, the warriors urged the others to proceed as quickly as possible. Lucius remained red-faced and angry, glaring at Kusala whenever the chieftain appeared not to be watching. But the Invictus look-alike continued to assist the woman, who obviously wasn't in the best condition for such a brutal march.

The ground was thick with the iron-colored grass of the Gray Plains, and though the land was relatively flat, sneaky swells sucked the energy out of unwary travelers. The Asēkhas, who never seemed to tire, brought forth tubular skins and passed them to the others.

"Ahh, the nectar of Tējo," Rathburt said after a long swig. "There's not much I miss about Anna, but this wine is unsurpassed."

"And it makes ya feel good all over," Ugga bellowed, wiping his mouth with his sleeve. "Master Hah-nah, please thank your brave buddies for me. It's dee-*licious*!"

The wine cheered up everyone except Lucius. Torg offered to help with the woman, but the yellow-haired man growled at him. Kusala nudged Lucius aside and lifted her in his arms.

"The foothills are still two leagues distant," the chieftain said. "Unless we quicken our pace, it will be dark before we reach them. This woman isn't well. We should take turns carrying her."

"If you harm her—" Lucius said.

"You will do what? Cut off my head with the back of your hand?" Kusala said. "It's unwise to make empty threats."

"If we wished to harm either of you, it would have already happened," Torg said. "But our intention is only to help. Our enemy has not pursued us yet. The reasons for this are unclear. But we're not free from danger."

Kusala nodded briskly. Though he walked and carried the woman at the same time, his voice remained steady. "Indeed, there is much evil about—north, south, and east. Wolves, Mogols, and monsters roam the land in search of someone—or something. When we arrived at Kamupadana this morning, a sizeable force was only half a day from the city."

"Avici has come alive because of me," the woman said.

"Do not say more!" Lucius snapped.

"Of what use is secrecy? These men and women are not allies of Invictus."

"Allies, we're not," Torg said. "Invictus has no greater enemies. These 'men and women' are the Asēkhas of Tējo, and you can't hope to match them. Do not doubt it, for I am their king."

Torg sent four Asēkhas out as scouts, one in each direction. They sprinted through the grass and vanished, leaving no evidence of trampling in their wake. The remaining warriors took turns carrying the woman. By midafternoon, the foothills were within sight and there still was no sign of pursuit. One after another, the scouts returned. The last to appear was the only one with anything substantial to report. Churikā, who had replaced Sōbhana as the newest Asēkha, had witnessed wolves, Porisādas, and monsters within a league of Kamupadana.

"But that's not the worst of it," Churikā said. "Mala was among them—and with him, a Kojin."

"Let them come," Bard growled. His memories of the cannibalistic Mogols were fresh in his mind, despite the many centuries that had passed since his traumatic boyhood.

"There are too many for us to face openly," Torg said. "Flight is our only recourse." Then he turned to Churikā. "Are we being followed?"

"Not yet. It's like we remain invisible."

"But it won't take the wolves long to pick up our scent," Elu said worriedly. "And they run faster than horses."

"Your friend is correct," Kusala said. "The wolves and their riders travel long distances quickly. We can't outrun them over a long stretch."

"It doesn't matter how much danger we're in," Rathburt said. "Some of us are not Asēkhas. We must rest."

"As you say, my lord," Kusala said.

The chieftain's reverence for Rathburt impressed Ugga. "Is Master Slump a king, too?"

"In some circles," Torg replied.

Rati and Podhana were sent ahead to search for a hiding place. By the time they returned, the rest of the party had reached the foothills. Majestic mountains loomed on their right.

"My lord, we found a shelter hidden by boulders on the side of a slope," Rati said. "An angry stream blocks our way, but there's a shoal on which to cross. I believe we'll be safe at the shelter, at least for now."

"Lead us, then," Torg said.

Once they reached the foothills, the woman demanded to be allowed to walk, and they granted her wish. They then entered a dense forest. The oaks had not yet flowered, but a few of the other hardwoods had begun to bloom, filling the woods with sweet perfumes. After traveling another league, dusk approached like a blanket as broad as the sky. They encountered the stream and passed along a series of rapids and eddies before finding the shoal. The woman started to cross on her own, but Tāseti came behind her and lifted her as easily as Kusala had earlier.

"If you weren't ill, I'm sure you would be more than capable, my lady," the Asēkha said. "But your body is not as bold as your spirit."

Though the water came up only to the knees of the warriors, the current was powerful and the rocks slippery. Elu considered it but then wisely leaped onto Ugga's shoulders. Even Rathburt succumbed, allowing Kusala to carry him. Lucius struggled but made it on his own. The others crossed easily, except for five Asēkhas, who Torg sent back to disguise whatever tracks they might have left.

They marched another mile—much of it a difficult uphill climb—before reaching the rock shelter. Try as she might, the woman couldn't manage it, so the Asēkhas took turns carrying her again. But Torg avoided her, believing Lucius would rage out of control if he touched her.

Torg considered eliminating Lucius in a way that would look like an accident. But he pushed that thought aside. Even that kind of death would upset the woman too much, which was the last thing he wanted. Her well-being was his prime concern, even if it meant swallowing his frustration.

The shelter was tucked into the side of an abrupt incline. Giant oaks clung precariously to the steep slope, their roots resembling twisted fingers. The entrance was about five cubits wide and only three tall, but it opened into a chamber tall enough for even the Asēkhas to stand upright with room to spare.

Inside the cave it was too dark to see, so they dared a single torch in the far back. The Asēkhas, who carried their supplies in cloth packs wrapped around their waists, dealt out dried meat and fruit, including small squares of a green cactus called *Cirāya* that, when chewed, flooded the mouth with a tangy but refreshing juice. When Tugars were on the move, especially in the heat of the desert, they chewed the flesh of *Cirāya* for long stretches. Just a small amount kept a warrior going for a full day with no other food or liquid. The more the body relied on only the cactus juice, the more beneficial its effects became.

Bard and Ugga broke out their own supplies, but Torg stopped them.

"Save that for later."

After their quick meal, the Asēkhas fanned out along the hillside.

"Now would be a good time to sleep, if you can," Torg said to the woman. A lingering glance passed between them. Then he left the cave with Kusala and climbed up the slope. He and the chieftain reached a ledge of banded gneiss and sat. Then they clasped forearms and stared silently at each other for fifty short breaths in deference to the number of years it took to become a warrior.

Finally, Torg spoke. "Kusala, I apologize for my behavior at Dibbu-Loka. I struck you with Obhasa and humiliated you. Can you forgive me?"

"There's nothing to forgive, my lord. Your word is law." Then the chieftain's eyes glowed. "There was a time when our connection to you was severed and we believed you were lost to us forever. Even the Vasi masters lost hope. But then you re-emerged in our consciousness. Every Tugar heard your call. The Asēkhas and I left Anna the next morning, but it still took us months to find you. Early on, scouts who had encountered Sōbhana along the river brought reports. But later, there was no word of you anywhere. We sent hawks and owls, but even their keen eyes couldn't locate you. It was like you were in disguise. My lord, how could you be gone and yet not gone?"

"Every time I achieve *Sammaasamaadhi*, I am gone and yet not gone. But I don't mean to bandy with words. Let me try to explain."

Torg then described his long journey with Mala; his encounters with Bhayatupa and Invictus at Avici; his imprisonment in the pit; and Sōbhana's death.

"I was lost to you and the Tugars as soon as they lowered me into the pit. As for being 'in disguise,' let's just say that the poisons and evil magic changed my appearance. Only recently have I returned to my former self. So it's possible your spies saw and yet didn't recognize me. More likely, they flew the other way in a panic."

Kusala laughed briefly, but then his sober side took over. "Sōbhana was a formidable warrior. Churikā sensed her death and ascended, but we knew nothing more about Sōbhana's fate until now. She will be sorely missed."

"I won't ever forget her," Torg said. "Her place among the greats is beyond question."

Kusala nodded. "I wish now that I hadn't been so hard on her."

"We both have regrets," Torg agreed.

They paused for a moment and said nothing. It didn't surprise Torg that Kusala was the first to speak again.

"It's a long journey from Anna to Kamupadana," the chieftain said. "We rode camels to Dibbu-Loka and then marched from there to Nissaya. The black knights knew nothing of your whereabouts, but they didn't take the threat of Invictus lightly. I've never seen the fortress so well-prepared. At least 50,000 knights walk the walls. And they have nearly one hundred conjurers, as well."

"That is welcome news, though I've heard some of it already. What do you know of Jivita?"

"We've heard that the White City is also strong, boasting more than 40,000 horsemen and thousands more infantry."

"Yet the army of Invictus is greater still," Torg said. "I've seen it with my own eyes. Jivita, Nissaya, and Anna combined are outnumbered two-to-one—and that, just against his main strength, which includes many terrible creatures. Countless more will join the Sun God when summoned, including the druids, whose numbers are unknown. Alas, if only the Tugars were as prolific as their enemies. We have only 10,000 warriors. I fear we are too few."

"The Tugars are never to be underestimated," Kusala said fiercely. "But there are many reasons for concern. Not all news from the fortress was good. Nissaya and Jivita are on poor terms. Neither seems willing to aid the other, both desiring to remain within their borders. In some ways, I can't blame them."

"Intelligent decisions are one thing, disharmony another. If ever there was a need to band together against a common foe, it's now. Even unified, we will be hard-pressed. Divided, we will be easy prey." Torg grew silent. When he looked up, his eyes glowed blue-green in the darkness. "How are the Tugars dispersed?"

"I didn't wish to leave the citizens of Anna entirely unguarded, so I ordered Asēkha-Dvipa to remain in the Tent City with 1,000 warriors. I then sent 2,000 each to Nissaya and Jivita. The remaining 5,000 are camped on the northern shore of Lake Hadaya ready to march east or west, wherever the need is greatest."

"You've done well," Torg said with relief in his voice. "But there's more I must tell you before I speak with the woman."

"I've seen the way you look at her. Is there a special attraction?"

"We shall see what we shall see."

"As you say, my lord. What are your wishes?"

"Invictus has powers that are beyond anything we've faced before. If he has devised a means to threaten the Tent City, then you must be there to counter him. My command is for you to return to Anna at dawn."

"But lord, who will protect *you*?"

"The Asēkhas will stay with me—except for four of your choosing. You are to return the way you came along the eastern foothills of the Mahaggatas. I want you to send one of your party to Nissaya, the second to join our force at Lake Hadaya, the third to proceed to Jivita, and the fourth to patrol the banks of the Ogha River just north of Senasana."

Torg briefly described his ordeal in the ziggurat, including the threat of the *undines*.

"I will do as you command," Kusala said. "But where will you and the remaining Asēkhas go?"

"We can't travel the same path as you," Torg said. "Invictus is too strong east of the mountains, and I have no desire to make it easy for him to hunt me down. My plan is to stay just north of the Gap of Gamana until I reach the northern border of Dhutanga. From there, I'll travel south to Jivita."

"My heart is lighter knowing that some of the Asēkhas will journey with you, though my instincts tell me that my fate doesn't lie in Anna."

"If you're wasted at Anna, then *my* heart will be lighter. Tell me one other thing before we part. How go Sister Tathagata and the Noble Ones?"

"They rest comfortably in the haven."

"Good! When you return, bring them with you to Anna. And tell the *Perfect One* that I miss her. She'll scoff. But do it anyway."

"As you say, my lord."

"And thank you for taking such good care of Obhasa for me. I didn't feel whole without my staff."

When Torg returned to the rock shelter, the crescent moon had already set and the night had become as black as the shivery depths of Lake Ti-ratana. While Kusala collected reports from the Asēkhas, Torg slipped into the chamber. Some of his companions were asleep and snoring, but the warriors had smeared a paste of mint on the offending nostrils, reducing the intensity. Despite the sputtering torch, it was even darker inside the chamber than out, but the Asēkhas moved about effortlessly, using senses other than sight to navigate their surroundings.

Torg willed Obhasa to glow just enough to illuminate a portion of the chamber. Bard, Ugga, Rathburt, and Elu slept soundly. Lucius lay next to the woman, asleep but restless. Torg knelt next to him and lowered his mouth close to his face.

"*Niddaayahi*," he whispered.

Blue vapor slipped into Lucius' nostrils, and he grew still.

But the woman was awake, staring at him with wide eyes. Torg held out his broad hand.

"Will you come with me?" he said in a tender voice.

She did not resist.

Though she tried to sleep, Laylah could barely relax enough to close her eyes. The four strange men she'd met in Kamupadana were already snoring, and so was Lucius. In the darkness of the shelter, they lay on blankets the healer's friends had provided. The Asēkhas moved about silently, performing various chores. They had shed their disguises—at least, that is what Laylah presumed them to be—for black jackets and matching breeches. Their gracefulness awed her. No effort was wasted, no movement unplanned. Watching them caused her blood to boil. When it became too dark to see, she lay soundlessly and listened. All she could hear was the snoring. The Asēkhas were as silent as air.

A soft blue glow illuminated a portion of the shelter. Laylah's heart skipped a beat. The healer approached, causing Lucius to stir.

Stay asleep, Lucius. I don't know if I'll be able to stand any more of your complaining.

And then the healer leaned down and spoke a word from the ancient tongue. A tendril of blue vapor slipped into Lucius' nostrils, and he went as still as a well-fed baby.

The healer turned to her. "This will make him sleep deeply for a little while." Then he said softly, "Will you come with me?"

Once they were outside the shelter, he took her hand. It felt like they were being shocked, causing them both to jerk away. But then he grasped her hand again and held on tight. The sensation subsided, replaced by tingling warmth.

He led her up the side of a steep slope to a ledge of banded stone. The night was overcast, but just enough light remained for her to make out his features. His eyes were blue as sapphire, his hair black as coal, and there was a kindness to the set of his mouth. She imagined what it would be like to make love with him and was surprised to feel no painful response in her abdomen. This man's presence didn't appear to threaten whatever guarded the flesh of her womb.

"My name is Torg. I'm also called The Torgon." The powerful sounds of his voice almost made her swoon. But she sensed an undercurrent of nervousness. She was affecting him, too.

"I am a king and a wizard. They call me a Death-Knower. I'd tell you more if we had time. It's my desire to sit with you and talk long into the night, but I fear we don't yet have that luxury. Will you tell me your name?"

"I'm Laylah. Some call me sorceress and some call me queen. I'm the sister of Invictus."

If this shocked Torg, he didn't show it.

"But I despise him," Laylah continued. "I've been his prisoner for the past seventy years. But I never gave up hope that one day I would be free. And now … here I am. I saw you once. Mala had imprisoned you in the wagon. The memory burns in my mind. Do you remember me?"

"Oh, yes. You have consumed my thoughts ever since—and even before."

She smiled warmly. "I thought you were dead. Mala returned to Avici and said so himself. And yet somehow you live. For me, meeting you is a dream come true."

"For me, as well," Torg said, lifting his hand to caress her lovely cheek. "I've dreamed of you *so many times*. When the moon was full, I felt your presence. There's so much I would know about you. How were you able to escape? And who led you to me? But I assume it's a long story, and our time for now is short. You need to rest. Tomorrow, we'll travel far."

"Life is cruel. Most of mine has been miserable, but now that I've found reason for joy, I'm not permitted to savor it."

"To hear you say those words fills me with more happiness than you can imagine. I've lived a long life, more than a thousand years, but before meeting you, it was incomplete. I can wait a while longer if I know you feel the same."

"I do. And more. I've lived fewer than 100 years, but they've felt like a thousand."

Then she leaned forward, wrapped her arms around his neck, and pressed her mouth against his, white energy bursting from her lips. He nudged her away as if afraid.

"Have I offended you?" Laylah said.

"Quite the opposite. But there's more you must know about me before we proceed further. Being with me can be dangerous."

She sighed. "I think I understand. And there's more you must know about me, too. Will you take me back to the shelter? You've done much to heal me, but I'm still weak."

"Of course. But there's one thing I must know before you retire: Who is the man with you? It's obvious you care about him."

Laylah couldn't help but giggle. "Are you jealous?"

"If I denied it, I'd be a liar."

She giggled again, but then her face grew serious. "His name is Lucius. Before the rise of Mala, he was Invictus' greatest general. But he became disillusioned with my brother and switched his loyalty to me. Without his help, I would have never escaped from Avici. I owe him my freedom and my life. But I love him only as a friend."

Torg looked relieved.

"One problem remains," she continued. "Lucius loves *me* as more than a friend, and he has openly professed it. I hesitate to tell him how I feel about him. I don't know how he'll react, but it wouldn't surprise me if he became violent."

This time, it was Torg's turn to laugh. "The man you call Lucius lacks the strength to harm me. But I understand how much you owe him—and, in turn, how much *I* owe him. So, what do you propose? Do we pretend not to care for each other?"

"For a while … until I can find a way to tell him the truth once and for all. But know this: You are my one and only."

"I'll do as you ask, for as long as you ask. But regardless of what games we must play, I won't tolerate being separated from you. I plan to travel west and then south and seek shelter in a city called Jivita. Next to Anna and Nissaya, there will be no safer place in the world once Invictus unleashes his army. Will you come with me? It will be a long journey."

"If you'll have me."

Then she kissed him again. This time, he held still and relished it.

When she returned to the shelter, she collapsed into the deepest sleep of her life.

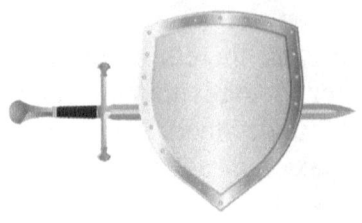

ON THE RUN

The morning after the eclipse, Invictus came to his senses. He sat up and demanded boiled eggs and salted pork, which he ate ravenously. He then ordered Mala to escort him to the main balcony.

"Ahh, the sun loves me again," Invictus said, basking in the bright light. "I owe you a great deal, General Mala. You won't regret your loyalty. Tell me everything that happened while I was incapacitated. I remember so little. Bhayatupa has escaped, I presume. What else?"

"I have shocking news, my liege. The dragon was not the only one to escape. When Bhayatupa attacked, he knocked me unconscious. When I woke, Izumo and Lucius had fled along with the queen."

Mala didn't know what to expect. It wouldn't have surprised him if Invictus had burned him to a crisp, but the sorcerer reacted calmly.

"I should have listened to you more closely, Mala. You never trusted the firstborn, but I had a tender place for him in my heart and wanted to believe he was loyal. I suppose, until recently, he was. And I assume there's no word of my sister's whereabouts?"

"We've begun the search, but the land is wide and there are many places to hide," Mala said. "I've sent auxiliaries north, south, and west; and our people in Kilesa protect the east. Some dracools are patrolling the skies along the foothills of Mahaggata, but most have stayed in Avici and are attempting to locate Izumo from here, though I don't understand how they are claiming to do it. Laylah and the traitors were far away before anyone noticed them missing. Where were they headed? Nissaya seems most obvious. Or the mountains. Do you sense anything, my liege?" Invictus didn't answer so Mala continued his ramble. "A force of wolves and Mogols is ready to march under my command, along with a Kojin and some cave trolls and druids. But I didn't want to leave your side until I was certain of your recovery."

Invictus faced the sun, holding his arms aloft. Mala waited, not daring to say more. The sorcerer didn't speak again until the fiery orb was directly overhead.

"Laylah remains alive, of that I'm certain, though I believe she will continue to be sick much longer than I was—for I am far greater, and your strength quickened my recovery even more than you might realize. Without similar aid, my dear sister will have a far more difficult time. Still, my ability to determine her whereabouts is diminished, and I'm assuming this is due to Vedana. Why else would my grandmother have murdered the newborn servant? Perhaps she thwarts my perception in some way that I can't detect. Because of this, the dracools might be our best chance. They can meld their minds and kill from afar, and if they can eliminate Izumo, Laylah's ability to travel will be curtailed. We must wait to see what the dracools perceive. In the meantime I will delve further. Once we discover Laylah's location, we must act quickly. I *will* have her back."

Later that day, a dracool came to Mala and reported that Izumo had been detected somewhere east of the mountains near the Gap of Gamana. When Mala told the king, Invictus digested this information slowly, though it was obvious it puzzled him.

"Why would they still be east of the mountains? Has Izumo weakened so much that he can no longer carry them? There are many places to hide in Mahaggata. What are they waiting for? What scheme has Lucius devised?"

"Perhaps I should march toward the gap now," Mala said. "You can send dracools to alert me when you learn more."

"Wait until morning," Invictus said. "I'll make my decision then."

But the following morning, they still knew no more. It was like Laylah and Lucius had vanished from the world. The dracools continued to report that Izumo was somewhere near the southeastern tip of the gap, though now he was moving about. Invictus finally ordered Mala to proceed, but it was midmorning by the time the Chain Man began his march.

The mouth of Gamana was a rushed two-day journey from Avici. A thousand wolves, 500 Mogols, 100 druids, several cave trolls, and a Kojin accompanied him. The dracools were able to spare ten from what remained of the flock in Avici, and they flew ahead as scouts. Ravens joined them.

Mala marched northward along the left bank of the Ogha until late afternoon before veering westward. By nightfall, he had reached the shore of Lake Ti-ratana where he rested until midnight while waiting to hear from his airborne spies and messengers. When none came, he continued his march. By morning, he had reached the northernmost point of Ti-ratana and there was still no word from Invictus. This perplexed Mala, so he chose to wait until further orders came from his king.

Just before noon, a lone dracool approached from the southeast. Mala stomped about impatiently until the *baby dragon* landed a few paces away. The dracool, a female, had been flying hard and was out of breath.

"Speak quickly," said Mala, towering over the dracool as he did most other beings. "What have you to report?"

"Izumo has gone to the Whore City," she said, hissing through the round holes in her snout.

"Kamupadana ... what the hell?" Mala said, his chain glowing ominously. "And where are Laylah and Lucius?"

The dracool shrugged. "We know naught. But the king wants you to go to Kamupadana, meet with Jākita-Abhinno, and hear her report."

Mala thought that was a stupid idea, but at least he had a clear destination. His army moved again.

Although Kamupadana was twenty leagues away, most of that distance was across a grassy plain that was easy to traverse. To avoid outrunning their masters, the wolves slowed their pace, but the army still covered ground abnormally fast. By late afternoon of the following day, Mala came within sight of the ninth wall.

Fifty Sāykan soldiers raced out to meet them and then escorted Mala, the Kojin, one dracool, and one Porisāda inside the walls. At dusk, the hideous version of Jākita-Abhinno greeted them inside the ziggurat and led them to the scene of the carnage.

"Lord Mala, your arrival pleases us," the new queen of the Warlish witches said. "As you can sssee, a terrible thing occurred here this very morning. We were outmatched—and the marvelous *undines* were destroyed."

"This is the work of the Death-Knower," Mala growled as he tromped around the bloodied chamber. "The bastard has as many lives as a Tyger. So where is he now, you witless whore? How did he escape when thousands of Sāykans had him surrounded? Are you harlots that incompetent?"

Jākita was aghast. "I won't be spoken to this way!"

Mala swept out his hand and sent her flying against the wall. She crouched on all fours and hissed. Sāykan guards rose to defend her, but they retreated when the Kojin pounded her chest.

"I will speak to you however I choose," Mala said. "Do you dare oppose the might of Invictus? Answer my questions like *he* was asking them—for I am his eyes and ears, and I speak for him in all ways. Compared to me, you are *nothing*."

As if accepting the truth in his words, the witch crawled over to him, whining and submissive. After an explosion of fire and smoke, the beautiful version of the queen rose and stood before him, her voice as intoxicating as the milk of the poppy.

"My lord, I meant no offense. It's just that I'm still upset over this morning's incident. My city and sssoldiers are at your command. As for the Death-Knower, he escaped through a passageway that runs beneath the walls. We sssearched for him everywhere, but he hasn't been found."

"I'm not surprised. Women can't do anything right."

Jākita's anger rose again. A single strand of her auburn hair curled and turned gray. But she regained control before another transformation took place.

"As you sssay, my lord. What will youuu do now?"

"The Death-Knower is not the reason I'm here. He can be dealt with later. I search for others: Queen Laylah and General Lucius. Where are they?"

"There are tensss of thousands within the walls. Until now, the assassin has been our only concern."

"It's believed a dracool accompanied the woman and the firstborn."

"There are no dracoolsss in the city, other than the one that accompanies youuu." She turned to a Sāykan captain who stood nearby, nervously eyeing the Kojin. "Have there been any reports of baby dragons?"

"None that I am aware, my queen," the captain said nervously. "Though it's not unusual to see them in the skies."

"You twats are worthless!" Mala said. "*Nothing* ever gets done unless I do it myself."

"As you sssay, my lord," Jākita sneered, her green eyes glistening.

"Out of my way, you smelly slut. I have work to do."

When Mala and his companions passed through the ninth gate and rejoined his small army, it was deep into the evening. But one of the Porisādas was waiting for him with news.

"Master, the wolves have picked up the queen's scent," said the cannibal, who bore skull tattoos on both sides of his face. "And Lucius' too. They have headed southwest toward the foothills—and the gap."

Mala stomped around angrily, spitting globs of mucus that sizzled in the gray grass. "How long ago? How far ahead? Was it just the two of them?"

"We believe their lead is less than a day," the cannibal said. "But there is more you should know, master. They are not alone. We count others."

"How many?"

"There are strange signs and scents. Is it possible there are Tugars among them? Maybe even Asēkhas? The desert warriors leave no marks when they walk, but the wolves can sometimes sense their presence. Our mounts are acting strangely, growling and snapping at each other."

A loud screech startled Mala and the others. The Kojin had walked into the field and was on her knees, sniffing the ground. Then she stood and pointed all six of her index fingers toward the southwest.

"That's all I need to know," Mala said. "Let's move! Take fifty Porisādas and ride ahead on wolfback. And spread out the dracools. The woman must be taken alive, but feel free to kill the rest, whoever they might be, including Lucius and Izumo."

Another dracool waddled forward. "Izumo is no longer," she said. "I have sensed his demise. His life is ended."

"Good riddance," Mala said. "One down, two to go. Make that three. I want the Death-Knower's head, too. If he and his ratty Asēkhas have joined the queen, I can get rid of all of them at once."

Torg let them sleep until midnight. He and several Asēkhas meditated for fifty long breaths before rousing the others. It was cool, overcast, and extremely dark outside the cavern. Before departing, they ate squares of *Cirāya* and drank desert wine. They had no time for anything else. Torg was too anxious.

"We have a head start, but it's not enough. Mala won't rest."

Ugga belched and then stretched. "I was having da best dream. Too bad we must go in such a hurry. I haven't felt this good in a long time."

"Me neither," Bard said. "Da wine has filled me with vigor. How are ya doing, Elu? I'll bet ya have growed an inch already."

"Elu feels wonderful," the Svakaran said. "But he doesn't like wolves chasing him."

"Who are these wolves after, anyway?" Rathburt said, gesturing toward Laylah and Lucius. "Us or them?"

"You know full well who they're after," Lucius said. "But there's no need to worry. The two of us will be on our way and trouble you no longer."

"Don't be foolish," Torg said. "You'd stand no chance without us. You're obviously no woodsman, and Laylah isn't fully recovered."

"Laylah? Is it *Laylah*, now? How did you come by that name?"

Kusala stepped forward. "My lord, must you abide his insolence? His king has tortured you enough. Why should you have to suffer further insults from such an ass? I say we take out his tongue and put an end to his foul words."

"You would attack an unarmed man?" Lucius said.

"I would gladly arm you, but it would make no difference."

Once again, Laylah came to Lucius' defense. "Please don't harm him. He has endured more than you know, and if he speaks harshly, it's out of concern for my welfare." Then she walked over to Lucius and stared into his face. "I can't protect you forever. If for no other reason, will you try to get along with these men to please me?"

"Very *well*," Lucius said, but he refused to leave Laylah's side.

As they left the shelter and strode into the darkness, Elu came alongside Laylah and tugged on the sleeve of her dress.

"You are called Laylah? That's a nice name. May Elu call you Laylah now?"

She smiled. "It would be my pleasure."

"Yeah, why don't you?" Lucius snarled. "In fact, why don't you scream it all over the woods?"

"Lucius is right," Torg said, trying to sound conciliatory. "Let's use names as little as possible, and then only in whispers."

Then he patted Lucius on the shoulder. "It's time we all try to get along. We have a common enemy. I'm willing to call a truce if you are."

Lucius grunted but his expression softened. Laylah looked at Torg and mouthed the words *thank you.*

They continued southwest as the night deepened, skirting the feet of several mountains that towered above them on their right. The uneven ground would have been treacherous even in daylight for anyone not used to such terrain, but Torg and the Asēkhas never stumbled, and Ugga, Bard, Elu, and even Rathburt were at home in the woods. For Laylah, it had been more than seventy years since she'd run wild and free in Mahaggata, but she quickly regained her confidence and walked as effortlessly as the rest. However, Lucius cursed under his breath every time he lost his footing or bumped his head. Despite the yellow-haired man's struggles, the others dared not light a torch or make use of Torg's staff. Wolves had excellent night vision and could detect the scent of smoke or magic for leagues. And dracools could see almost as well as dragons.

Tāseti rushed forward and bowed to Kusala. "Chieftain, we've seen a dracool in the sky. We don't believe it has found us, but it soon might. What should we do?"

Kusala turned to Torg. "Lord?"

"Is it within reach of a sling?" Torg said.

"It can be done," Tāseti said.

Torg nodded, and Kusala's heir raced into the darkness.

"A dracool aided us," Laylah said to Torg. "He told us that their kind is interconnected through their minds. Will the ones with Mala be able to sense if one of their own has fallen?"

Just hearing her voice made Torg dizzy, but he tried not to show it. "I'm not sure. But I still believe it will be best to eliminate any spies that come near. With the Asēkhas leading us, we hope to go a long way before we're discovered. However, the wolves will eventually find us. And then I'll have decisions to make."

"Whatever decisions ya make, don't leave Ugga out of them," the crossbreed said. "Bard and me want to stay with ya, Master Hah-nah. Will ya keep us by your side?"

"I'd have it no other way," Torg said. "For better or worse—and probably worse—you're stuck with me."

"Don't forget Elu," the Svakaran said. "He wants to stay too."

"Elu will stay. And even Rathburt," Torg said.

"Lucky me," Rathburt responded gloomily.

Just then a loud crash erupted in the nearby brush. Soon after, Tāseti came into view.

"A clean kill, my lord. It fell without a cry."

"It's a pity that such an ancient creature had to perish," Torg said. "Given the proper direction, dracools might prove worthy of our friendship. But they seem more attracted to evil than good."

"Izumo wasn't that way," Lucius said. "Without him, Laylah and I wouldn't be alive."

"I wish I had met Izumo," Torg said. "The dracools remember much that most others have forgotten. But they've never been fond of speaking about it to me."

"You would have liked Izumo," Laylah said. "In some ways, you remind me of him."

Rathburt laughed too loudly. "I've always said he looks like a dracool—without the wings."

Kusala gave him an angry stare. Rathburt shut his mouth and faded into the darkness.

"Master Slump is always like that," Ugga explained to Laylah. "But he's not such a meanie when ya get to know him."

Kusala scolded them for making too much noise, so they continued in silence. The Asēkhas led them along game trails that followed the instincts of wild animals which unerringly chose the path of least resistance. This enabled the party to sidle around the slopes and conserve valuable energy. The trails wound through stands of hemlocks, chestnut oaks, and yellow poplar, though the trees themselves were just another part of the darkness, and only an up-close view of their bark could differentiate them. At one point, the group came across a rock outcropping that hung precariously above them. Cold water from a nearby springhead trickled off the ledge. They stopped, bent back their heads, and drank. It was delicious. Torg watched Laylah take her turn. It was too dark to see much, but he could make out the tendons in her neck as she leaned back. The urge to kiss her—there or anywhere— almost drove him mad.

Torg remembered the words of Peta: *There are three females on Triken who can abide you.* Vedana was one, Jord another; he knew those two from recent experience. And the third? Could it be? Laylah was the sister of Invictus, which meant she was a creature of magic.

Peta, is she the one? Please tell me it's true.

An owl hooted in response.

After drinking their fill, they continued their journey. The only sounds they made were the occasional curses from Lucius. Torg could sense the Asēkhas' distrust of the man and their growing admiration of the others. Elu moved almost as quietly as a Tugar, and even Ugga—as tall as Torg and a good deal heavier—had his own form of grace. Laylah seemed at home in the darkness, walking with the suppleness of a Tyger. Every glimpse made Torg desire her even more.

Peta, if she's not the one, I don't think I can bear it.

But in his heart, he knew she was. He could sense her internal power, had already tasted it—and it had blended seductively with his own inner flame.

Damn this Lucius. Why should I worry about his feelings?

But he knew the answer.

Because Laylah asked you to. Be patient, Torg. Patience is the path to bliss.

By the time dawn arrived, they had traveled four leagues from the rock shelter. The sky had cleared overnight and was now crystal blue. They entered a cove pervaded with magnolias, basswood, and giant poplars. Silver bells blanketed the forest floor, their blooms eagerly greeting the rising sun and the welcome warmth of spring. Golden butterflies fluttered among them. Crimson cardinals flew from tree to tree, males tussling with males and chasing after the less-colorful females. If the specter of pursuit had not harassed them so much, the group would have stopped and stared, soaking in the beauty and enjoying the sweet-smelling air.

Even Laylah seemed stronger.

"It's time, my friend," Torg said to Kusala. "Which four will you take with you?"

The chieftain started to speak but was interrupted by Rati, who rushed down the side of a nearby slope and ran to Torg.

"Lord, a pack of wolves is on the prowl—fifty, exactly! And Porisāda warriors ride them. I witnessed their approach from the ridge above. They'll be upon us before the sun is overhead. And their howling has alerted the dracools. Mala will soon know our location. The main strength of his army was not within my vision, but we must prepare for an attack from these foul beasts and their riders."

"I can't leave now," Kusala said. "You still need my help. Surely one more day away from Anna can't hurt."

Torg agreed. "We'll need all the Asēkhas. Things are going to happen in a hurry. We must be prepared to run as fast as the wolves. Have your weapons ready."

"What about me?" Lucius said. "I can wield a sword or bow. Will you leave me defenseless?"

"When the fighting begins, I'll make sure you're armed," Torg said. He then turned to Laylah. "Both of you will be armed."

Except for their midnight snack of cactus squares, they hadn't eaten since dusk of the previous night. Although time was precious, they gobbled a light meal to keep up their strength. Then they drank deeply from a nearby stream before continuing their flight. Now that morning had arrived, visibility was plentiful despite the dense canopy. The cove ran east to west. To the north, the land rose like a stormy sea toward a range of vast mountains, while to the south it smoothed considerably. But the forest—an eclectic mixture of hardwoods and conifers—became even denser. Some of the hardwoods, the oaks especially, had not begun to leaf out, and their bare branches reached toward the sky like the gnarled limbs of skeletons. But hundreds of dogwoods were in bloom, their spectacular white flowers gleaming like leftover patches of snow. Torg loved to walk these trails in the late winter and early spring, but he had no time now to enjoy their splendor.

As Rati had predicted, they heard the howls of the wolves around noon.

"How many did you say there were?" Rathburt said, panting and wheezing.

"Fifty … with Porisādas on their backs."

Rathburt looked at Torg. "You, Ugga, Bard, and Elu whipped a larger pack than that led by a Kojin. With the Asēkhas at our side, it shouldn't be a problem."

"The wolves we defeated didn't carry Porisādas," Torg said. "Even so, if we faced just this small band I wouldn't be concerned. It's Mala and the rest of his army that endanger us. Once these wolves and their masters recognize us for what we are, they won't attack directly. But the cannibals are excellent bowmen and can shoot while they ride. I believe they'll attempt to encircle us and hinder our progress, giving the monster and his minions more time to catch up."

Lucius joined the discussion. "I know the Chain Man better than any of you. He's confident to the point of recklessness. Once the dracools report our number and location, he will send orders to harass us and slow us down, as you said. And then, when his army is within striking distance, he'll attack all at once with every bit of his strength. If that happens, one hundred Asēkhas won't suffice."

"One hundred Asēkhas *would* suffice," Torg said, "but, alas, we do not have one hundred and therefore cannot defeat Mala's army by force. Flight is our best option, but even that will be difficult. We might outrun Mala, but we can't outrun the wolves."

"If we can't fight and we can't run, then what *can* we do?" Rathburt said. "It's like you're saying we're doomed."

"*You're* not doomed," Laylah said despondently. "Only Lucius and me. This doesn't have to be your fight. Maybe Lucius has been right all along about the two of us separating from you. Mala will come for us and allow the rest of you to escape."

"Don't say such words again!" Torg snapped at Laylah. "We're in this together until the end." He turned to Lucius. "All of us."

The howling intensified. The wolves were less than a league away.

"We must reach higher ground," Torg announced. "I want to stay above the enemy. Mogol arrows can't harm the Asēkhas, so they will guard our flanks. Don't be without hope. I have a plan. If I'm right about what lies ahead, then we might yet have an advantage. But we have little time to waste. Elu, you know these lands better than any in our company. Lead us up the mountain!"

The Svakaran turned northward and scrambled up the side of a knoll. The trees were less dense here, but tangled masses of shrubbery and brambles now blocked their way. The Asēkhas wielded their *uttaras* like scythes, hacking openings through the brush. Torg held Obhasa in front of him and burned wide avenues with sizzling bursts of blue-green flame. But when he incinerated what hindered them, he also cleared the way for the enemy.

Kusala unveiled his sling and let fly a silver bead. Another dracool smote the slope. The chieftain and the others reached the crest of the knoll and made for a steep-sided ridge that was attached to a range of towering mountains still crowned with snow. The ridge was as sharp as the spine of a giant dune in the heart of the desert Tējo.

They started across just as the lead wolves and their riders came into view behind them. The Porisādas launched a flurry of arrows, but none found a mark. Several Asēkhas broke off from the company and met the attackers head-on. The horse-sized beasts tried to trample them, but the Asēkhas stepped aside and hacked at their front legs with blurring strokes from their *uttaras*. The wolves tumbled forward, throwing their Porisāda riders, who were then stabbed through their hearts before they could stand. Soon, ten wolves and nine riders lay dead, the lone survivor having leaped off his mount and retreated into the trees.

A dracool attempted to take advantage of the commotion, streaking toward Laylah like a diving hawk, its front talons spread wide. But a single blast of blue-green fire from Obhāsa blew the *baby dragon* apart. A strip of charred flesh splashed against Torg's lips.

Now they were alone on the ridge. The rest of the wolves and Porisādas hung back under the cover of the trees. Torg and his company had barely enough room to walk in single file. One misstep could lead to a deadly fall.

The rest of Mala's dracools, eight in all, circled out of range of the Asēkhas' slings. But Bard loosed an arrow from the bow of Jord and another *baby dragon* fell. After that, the remaining dracools flew so high they looked like black specks.

Elu led them to the far side of the ridge. Torg left two Asēkhas behind to hold the narrow way. The others crossed over onto the steep back of a massive mountain. Their company was still several thousand cubits from the summit, so the trees and foliage remained dense.

They came upon a stream littered with odd-shaped boulders. Foamy bursts of water coursed between gaps in the stone. Hemlocks and shrubs lined its banks, and massive layers of gray-green rock anchored its bed, spurring a series of small waterfalls and swirling pools.

They followed a game trail upstream along the right bank. The path was strewn with gnarled oak roots, making it difficult even for Torg and the remaining Asēkhas not to stumble. And where there were no roots, swaths of gooey mud took their place. At one point, the immense Ugga sank almost to his knees, and it took two Asēkhas to yank him free.

The roar of the stream blocked out most other sound. They couldn't hear if the Asēkhas they had left behind were engaged in battle or if pursuit came from somewhere other than the ridge. The path and stream wound in tandem like a pair of snakes slithering side by side. At some points, they could see only several hundred paces, making them feel entrapped and claustrophobic. But they rushed along the rolling bank as fast as they could, higher and higher.

The first sign of the enemy came when a Mogol arrow buried itself in a tree next to Lucius' head. Several Asēkhas peeled off into the brush, and a short time later the rest of the company heard shouts. Elu led the rest of them tirelessly along the path, which suddenly veered left, crossing over the stream on a smooth stone floor made slick by a sheet of rushing water. Then the path rose abruptly up a steep bank and drew away from the stream until the watercourse was no longer visible, though they still could hear its roar.

The Asēkhas returned—without blood on their swords.

"The wolves and Mogols are too fast for us," one warrior said. "They leap through the brush and brambles as easily as air. They must have found another way to approach. Many more have arrived and follow us on both sides just out of sight. Even if we come upon an open place to meet them, we will be hard-pressed. The wolves are larger and more dangerous than any we've ever seen."

Just then, a gigantic male wolf bearing a shrieking Porisāda warrior crashed through the trees and leaped at Lucius. Kusala shoved Lucius aside but caught the full brunt of the wolf's charge and was knocked backward into the brush. An instant later, a slew of *uttaras* pierced the wolf and the cannibal. The chieftain stood, more embarrassed than hurt.

"I thank you for saving my life," Lucius said. Then he turned to Torg. "I think it's time you armed Laylah and me, as promised."

Torg agreed. A warrior gave Lucius a *uttara*, a more precious gift than the firstborn probably realized, and Torg presented Laylah with his ivory staff.

"I'm afraid this is just a loan," Torg said, a wiry smile on his lips. "Obhasa is dear to me and I'll have need of it in days to come, but for now I pray it keeps you safe. Use it like a stave. No matter what it strikes, it will not sunder. There is power in it that—combined with your own— will be difficult to withstand."

"If I take your staff, what weapon will you wield?"

Torg drew the Silver Sword from the sheath beneath his cloak. "I won't be defenseless."

More arrows fell upon them. The Asēkhas hacked most of them to pieces in midair, but one found a mark, striking Rathburt squarely in the back. His Tugarian flesh—though long untested in battle—resisted penetration, and the arrow snapped and tumbled to the ground. Rathburt whined anyway, looping his long arms behind him to rub the sore spot.

Most of the Asēkhas re-entered the forest, attempting to chase off the closest pursuers. The rest of the company continued along the path, which veered to the right and approached the stream again. They crossed over on another slippery rock floor, and then the path veered upward. Several varieties of trees clung to the side of the bank, hanging so precariously they appeared ready to fall at any moment.

Roots stuck out of the path like hungry hands. Bard twisted his ankle and was limping. Rathburt had a complaint for every step. Lucius hunched over, gasping for breath. Laylah was also exhausted, but Torg could tell she was doing her best not to show it. Elu, the smallest, and Ugga, the largest, appeared as tireless as the Asēkhas.

The bank continued to rise steeply above the stream, which now was fifty cubits below the path on their left. One slip could send any of them tumbling onto the rocks below. Just when Torg felt they might have to stop and rest, the path suddenly smoothed out and became easier to traverse. They veered north away from the stream. In a short time the air became noticeably warmer, and the trees thinned out. Now it was sunny enough to see a long way. The Asēkhas returned, this time with stained swords.

"We have killed many but not enough," Podhana said. "They've retreated, but it's only a matter of time before they regroup and swarm upon us."

"My lord, you told us you have a plan," Kusala said. "We're in need of one. I hope you'll inform us soon."

"I will, when the time is right," Torg said. "But know this: The Asēkhas—all of them—will be needed elsewhere more than here. I've already lost Sōbhana; I don't wish to lose any others. You must *not* die while defending us. When it becomes obvious that you're outmatched, I want all of you to flee this place and regroup in Nissaya. And you, Kusala, will honor my original intentions."

"Lately, I rarely comprehend your mind," the chieftain said. "But I will never again argue with you. It will be as you say."

They raced along the trail, but their strength was fading. Through gaps in the surrounding foliage, they saw a series of snow-crowned mountains. The land ascended on their right and descended on their left, while the trail rose and fell wherever it desired. Purple crocuses grew out of piles of dead leaves. Brown moths clung to bare branches. They could no longer hear the roar of the stream. All was silent, except for their footsteps, their breaths, and the sound of the wind rushing through the trees.

All at once, the trail plunged into a thicket of mountain laurel entangled with vines that had nasty thorns. Elu, who until that point had been leading the way, came to a halt and trembled, his dark skin growing pale.

"It's just mountain laurel, little guy," Bard said. "Harmless enough."

"Yes, but that's not what Elu fears," Rathburt said. "Something lurks within the laurel—the vines that nearly killed him before."

"*Badaalataa*," the Svakaran said, like he had seen a ghost.

The howling began anew, but this time it was far louder. The vanguard of Mala's army had arrived. The Chain Man, the Kojin, and his other monsters wouldn't be far behind. Soon, escape would be impossible. Even in these narrow quarters, they would have to fight.

"Kusala, deter Mala for as long as you can," Torg said. "But *do not die*. When you're overmatched … *flee!*"

The chieftain nodded, and he and the other Asēkhas raced down the path, retracing their steps.

Now only seven remained: Torg, Laylah, Lucius, Rathburt, Ugga, Bard, and Elu.

"What do we do?" Rathburt said, his slump more pronounced than ever. "*Now* will you tell us your plan?"

"What do *you* think we should do?" Torg said to the only other living Death-Knower in the world.

"Why ask me? You're the hero!"

Just beyond their vision, they could hear the first sounds of fighting. The Asēkhas had met the enemy. Torg ignored it. "These vines," he said to Rathburt. "How dangerous are they?"

"How should I know? We need to *run!*"

"Rathburt, listen to me. Our survival depends on it. How dangerous *are* they? Can they kill an Asēkha? Can they kill you? Can they kill *me*?"

"Who cares? What does it matter? Can they kill one of your precious Asēkhas? *Yes!* Can they kill me? Yes. Can they kill you? Maybe. I don't know. *I don't know!*"

"Rathburt, *listen* to me. If the vines can kill us, then they can also kill the monsters who hunt us."

"So what? We're the ones who are trapped."

"I see what Master Hah-nah is saying," Ugga said. "Master Rad-burt has da power to control da vines. He did it before, when he saved little Elu. He can do it again. He can open da way."

"Huh?" Rathburt said. "You've got to be joking. I could never—"

"If ya don't, we'll all die," Bard said.

"Don't be stupid," Rathburt wailed. He turned to Laylah. "Give Torg back that staff, woman! He can burn a hole through the vines as wide as a processional."

"I'm not sure I can," Torg said, "but if I do …"

"… it will enable Mala's army to follow," Lucius finished.

"Forget it!" Rathburt said. "I've already been through this once. And once is enough. It's *difficult,* you know. It *hurts*!"

The sounds of the battle grew ever closer. Torg could tell, just by listening, that the Asēkhas were struggling. An arrow whizzed by Rathburt's head.

"Rathburt, LISTEN TO ME!" Torg pleaded. "You can *do* this. We will follow. Save us, my friend. *Please* …"

Tears sprang from Rathburt's eyes, but he turned to face the vines and held his oaken staff aloft. At first nothing happened—and Torg wondered if his faith in the Death-Knower had been misplaced. But then the staff glowed. Blue fire crawled along the shaft and spurted from its head, fanning outward over the laurel like water from a fountain. The vines responded, snapping like whips and tearing at each other in frustration. When Rathburt stepped off the path and into the thicket, the vines shied from him. He was their master.

"I believe the *Badaalataa* will stay back as long as my strength holds," Rathburt said through clenched teeth. "But the ordinary laurel couldn't care less. You'll have to clear a path with your blades but stay as close to me as you can. I can sense the *Badaalataa's* fear—but also their hatred. And they're ravenous."

Torg and Ugga led the way, slashing and hacking with sword and ax. Elu was the last to leave the path, but his love for his companions gave him the courage to follow. By the time they were twenty paces off the trail, the vines had closed behind them, forcing them to proceed in a tight circle just large enough to contain all seven. Where Rathburt's blue fire formed a dome over their heads, the vines dared not protrude.

Torg heard a piercing cry, so high-pitched that only his ears could detect it. A signal from Kusala. The Asēkhas were withdrawing.

A moment later, a dozen Porisādas and several druids burst down the path. A cave troll wielding an iron hammer as large as a man came next. The troll saw them first and stormed off the path in pursuit, but it made it only ten paces before the vines—enraged by their inability to consume the first set of intruders—closed around the huge beast. The troll howled in agony and fought with a sudden madness, but even its tremendous strength was insufficient. The vines wrapped it up like a caterpillar in a cocoon and carried it away.

"*Badaalataa! Badaalataa!*" the Porisādas chanted. They knew the danger of the vines better than any living creature, and they dared not stray from the path. The druids also stayed back. Like Rathburt, they were masters of trees and plants, but Dhutanga—far to the west—was their stronghold. They held no power over this threat.

Meanwhile, Torg and Ugga continued to clear a way through the ordinary vegetation. They progressed slowly and were only 500 paces from the path when Mala and the Kojin appeared. For the first time since Dukkhatu had dragged him from the summit of Asubha, Torg heard the Chain Man's disgusting voice.

"After them, you filthy cowards. *After them*! Must I do everything?"

Other voices responded. Torg couldn't discern what they were saying. But it was obvious the Chain Man didn't like what he was being told.

"You're afraid? Stand aside, you squirmy worms. I'll hunt them down and kill them myself."

Mala plunged into the laurel, inspiring the Kojin to join him. When they were a few steps off the trail, the *Badaalataa* attacked, engulfing the Kojin and tearing her off her feet. The vines then hauled her away almost as easily as they had the troll. Even her protective shield of magical energy was no match for the accumulated weight of the vines. But Mala was another matter. When the vines wrapped around his mammoth legs and drove their hungry thorns into his flesh, his chain responded with supernatural fury, spewing thick globules of molten fire. The vines withdrew—but only a few paces—and then danced around him, looking for any sign of weakness. This enraged Mala, but not to the point of stupidity. He backed out of the laurel and watched helplessly as his prey escaped.

"Arrrgggh!" was the last thing Torg heard him say.

The second floor of the ziggurat was dank and dark. In its farthest corner, a glass basin filled with a silver liquid sat on a pedestal. Vedana leaned over the basin, the tips of her scraggly gray hair disrupting the smooth surface. She was long practiced in the art of scrying, and when she waved her hands, the liquid came colorfully to life.

"*Look* at them. My *Badaalataa* are so hungry! I might have to call them off."

"Why would you want to, mother?" said Jākita-Abhinno, currently in her hideous form. "Let the vinesss have them. Good riddance to the Death-Knower, especially."

"There are two Death-Knowers among them," the mother of all demons said. "Don't take that too lightly, though I admit the one you despise is the more powerful. He reminds me of Invictus, but they both underestimate my *connections*. Besides, do you think I'd allow the father of my youngest child to perish? All kids need a daddy."

Jākita snarled and a drop of gray mucus slid out of one of her bulbous nostrils and plopped into the basin, sizzling like water in hot oil.

"I hate him, mother," she said in a raspy voice. "I ssso wish to end his life."

"You'll do no such thing without my permission. As I created the *Badaalataa* and enabled them to exist in the Realm of Life, so did I create you and your kind. Do you think I cannot destroy you and the other witches whenever I choose? Chal became too big for her tight britches and look where it got her."

Jākita sniveled and then curled into a ball on the floor at the demon's feet. Several explosive flashes and gouts of black smoke later, she had become her beautiful self.

"I'll obey your commands, mother. All I asssk is that you leave him to me in the end."

"I'll do as I please, whore."

Vedana returned her gaze to the magical basin, watching Torg, Laylah, and the others move slowly through the laurel, entrapped by thousands of hectares of *Badaalataa*. Her perspective was like that of an eagle—or more accurately, a dracool. Speaking of dracools, several of them still hounded the seven companions from above. If they weren't eliminated, the damnable Mala would know where to find the wizard and sorceress once they emerged from the vines. That wouldn't do. For Vedana's plan to succeed, Torg and Laylah had to remain alive and free, at least for the foreseeable future.

"I've created so many things," Vedana mused. "The witches, vampires, trolls, ghouls … even the dragons. Did you know about the dragons, Jākita? Bhayatupa would scoff—talk about someone who's too big for his britches—but it's true. And after all these millennia, I have no intention of casting my efforts aside. Invictus will fall. And I will be free. Do you doubt it?"

"No, mother … I do not. And I desire your freedom as much as youuu. If released from the darknesss, you'll become queen of the world and the Warlish witches will thrive as your favorite servants. Tell me what to do and I'll do it. But youuu must protect us from Invictus. If he discovers we conspire against him, he'll destroy Kamupadana and all who live within its wallsss."

"Don't worry too much about my grandson. His eyes are elsewhere. Invictus is obsessed with his precious sister and pays scant attention to the rest of us. You should worry more about me! Your orders are to stay in the ziggurat and await my commands. I might need you again—and I might not. Either way, you'll do as you're told. If you don't, I'll blink you out of existence."

"Yesss, mother."

Vedana grunted and then turned back to the basin. "Look at them run. Will they escape? The vines are so *hungr*y. Should I intervene? Those troublesome dracools are always sticking their snouts where they don't belong." Then she sighed. "I guess I'd better do something."

When Vedana appeared among the dracools as a raven, they hardly noticed. But when the bird spoke to them, their stomachs turned to fire and they fell from the sky.

The vines feasted on their flesh.

The slumped man was struggling. As dusk closed in, Laylah and the others had advanced less than a league beyond the path. The swirling vines remained a palpable force, tormenting them with strange sounds—a blend of snapping fingers, creaking doors, and howling winds. This dismayed her. If Rathburt succumbed, all of them would die.

"I don't know how much longer I can last," she heard him say to Torg. "They can sense I'm weakening—and there's still a long way to go. The entire side of this mountain crawls with them. They extend for at least as far as we've already come."

"We must move faster," Laylah said to Rathburt. "Can you hold them off at the same time that you run?"

"Maybe ... but the ordinary laurel is too thick to run through," Rathburt said. "Torg and Ugga can only clear it so fast."

"You didn't want to use Obhasa because we'd also be clearing a path for Mala and his army," Laylah said to Torg. "But that's no longer a concern. They're closed off from us. Can't you use your staff now?"

She started to hand Obhasa back to the wizard, but his response surprised her.

"You do it."

"I don't have your strength."

"That remains to be seen."

"Somebody better do something," Bard said. "Master Slump doesn't look too good, if ya ask me. And those vines are getting braver. I saw one take a stab at Elu's leg just a minute ago."

"You can do it," Lucius said, staring at Laylah with adoring eyes. "I believe in you, my queen."

"We all believe in you," Torg said. "If you will it, Obhasa will respond."

"Hurry!" Rathburt said.

Arguing was useless. For whatever reason, Torg wanted her to save them. If he was testing her, she didn't quite like it. But she didn't think that was the case. He simply trusted her.

The moon appeared in the darkening sky, and it made her feel uncomfortable, a sensation she had never experienced in its presence. But she passed it off as imagination. She couldn't allow her mind to play tricks on her. Burning the laurel was her idea, and they were depending on her to execute it.

Laylah held the staff in both hands and aimed its head at the laurel. When she had first seen Obhasa, it was stained brown. But when Torg had used it during their flight from the wolves, the brown had burned away, revealing a milky white exterior. Now the staff thrummed in her hands. Obhasa's power was frightening and alluring—exactly the way she felt about Torg. A part of his magic coursed through the ancient ivory. And it responded hungrily to her innate power. Blue fire, laced with sparkling white strands, spurted from the head and blew a deep path through the laurel.

"Run!" she heard Torg say.

Again and again, she used the might of the staff—combined with her own magic—to blast a trail through the shrubs. Such a grand use of power was intoxicating—and exhausting. But thus far, she was succeeding. They ran as a group through the charred avenues, staying as close together as possible without tripping each other. Meanwhile, the vines became frenetic, snapping and creaking. The darkness seemed to embolden them, but the blue fire from Rathburt's staff and the blue-white fire from Obhasa thwarted their rage.

Just when it appeared Laylah's plan would succeed, Rathburt suddenly collapsed. In response, a vine leaped out of the darkness and wrapped around Ugga's throat. Torg hacked it in two with a swipe of his sword, but other vines danced among them, closing in fast.

Torg sheathed the sword and placed both hands on Rathburt's oaken staff. There was a thunderous blast, followed by a renewed shower of blue flame. The vines retreated. Then the wizard lifted Rathburt in his arms with surprising ease.

"Hold the staff," he said to Rathburt. "I'll join my strength to yours. Elu, guide us. Laylah, clear the way. We're so close!"

Wherever Elu pointed, Laylah used the blue-white fire to incinerate the laurel. With Torg's strength buffeting Rathburt, the vines stayed back. A short time later the group burst out of the shrubbery and stumbled into a quiet cove as ordinary as it was beautiful.

Now there were no deadly vines—just ordinary trees, bushes, and wildflowers.

They were free.

All seven collapsed onto a blanket of fallen leaves. Somehow, they had escaped Mala's army and the *Badaalataa*. But none of them had any idea how far they were from the Chain Man and his minions. The monster wouldn't give up the chase this easily. He had been sidetracked, but for how long?

Torg was the first to speak. "We've gained valuable time. Even the dracools seem to have lost us. To pick up our trail, Mala will have to go far out of his way. By then, we'll be a long way from here." The wizard sighed deeply. "We've earned a brief rest. Let's eat some of the food the innkeeper gave us. And I can hear the gurgles of a stream. Lead us, Elu. There we can drink, eat, and sleep for a bit before continuing our march. I plan to veer northward, away from the gap. The land will be even more treacherous, but this will help to cover our tracks."

What happened next caused Laylah to cringe.

"Why is it *you* give all the orders?" said Lucius, his conciliatory mood vanished. "If we head north, we'll be going *away* from Jivita."

"I suppose ya would rather be da one to tell us what to do," Ugga said. His thick neck was purplish and swollen where the vine had grabbed him. "Mayhap we should march right to where this Mala guy is waiting. Is that what ya be wanting?"

Lucius stood his ground, holding the Tugarian *uttara* at his side. Laylah could sense the rising anger of the others. She wasn't sure how long she could continue to shield the firstborn. Even she was growing weary of his contentiousness.

"It makes little sense to surrender our gains," Lucius said. "We should turn south immediately and cross the gap while we still have a lead. There are as many places to hide south of Gamana as north."

"At its narrowest, the gap is ten leagues wide," Torg said. "And as you well know, many unfriendly eyes watch it. I don't believe we could cross without confrontation. The longer but wiser course is to stay north of the gap and pass above Arupa-Loka and Duccarita. From there we can skirt Dhutanga's eastern border until we reach the Green Plains. Or make for Cariya and find a boat that can take us downriver to Jivita. Either way gives us a better chance than crossing the gap where you suggest."

Lucius turned to Laylah. "We could go alone, you and I," he said, his voice pathetically hopeful. "I know Gamana well. There are more places to hide than the *healer* lets on. And even if we're found, there are some among Invictus' forces that remain loyal to me. If we follow the path he suggests, it might add weeks to the journey. As for Jivita, I'm not so sure that's the best place for us, anyway. Within the year, Invictus will crush the White City, and we'll have to flee again."

"Lucius—" Laylah started to say, but the firstborn interrupted her.

"The *healer* said we would be free to go once we were safe in the mountains. Well, here we are, looking safe to me. What do you say, *healer*? Does your word still stand?"

"The *healer* is a king," Rathburt said. "Can you say the same? If you wish to stay alive, you'd be wise to follow him. If not, then go. None of us will stop you."

Ugga walked over and patted Rathburt on the back. "Master Slump, I'm proud of ya!"

"Don't get too used to it, any of you," Rathburt said.

Torg chuckled. "I'll try not to." Then he looked down at Lucius.

"My word always stands. You're free to go. Both of you. But it's as much Laylah's choice as yours."

Torg went to Laylah and loomed over her. Despite being tall for a woman, the top of her head didn't reach the base of his neck.

"What say you, Laylah?"

"If I come with you, is Lucius still welcome?"

There were four quick noes from the others, but Torg said yes.

"Then I choose to follow you. Will you stay with us, Lucius? I'll beg if I must."

The firstborn bore a look of betrayal, but it had long since become obvious that where Laylah went, he would go.

"I'll follow you till the end, my queen," he said softly, his head downcast. "But I believe you're making a terrible mistake."

After that, they quit talking for a while. In his usual competent fashion, Elu quickly found the stream. It was barely a stride in width, but its waters ran swift and pure. They drank as much as their stomachs could hold and then opened the leather pouches the innkeeper had provided, finding dried meats and fish, mincemeat pastries, apples and pears, and chunks of sour cheese. It was only enough to last a few days, but in early spring finding more food wouldn't be a problem. The time it took to prepare meals in the wild would be their more immediate concern.

They slept until almost midnight before heading off again. The air was relatively warm and the sky clear and full of stars. After Laylah woke, she lay on her back and stared at the quarter moon, which now was setting in the west. Instead of feeling strength and comfort, she saw the moon as an unwelcome presence. Some of the nausea and sickness she had suffered during the days following the eclipse haunted her at night for the first time. She sat up and rubbed the sleep from her eyes. Torg and Ugga already were awake, and the wizard was tending the giant's wounds. A thin tendril of flame from Obhasa poured over the damaged flesh on Ugga's neck. After Torg finished, he crawled over to her. It impressed her that someone so large could move so soundlessly.

"You were moaning in your sleep," he whispered to her. "How are you feeling?"

"To be honest, I don't feel well," she said. "Before, the sickness was worse in the daytime. But that's to be expected. I've never been comfortable in daylight, even as a child. The night has always been my favorite time. I am not *Akanittha* like my brother. Whatever powers I possess come from the moon, not the sun. But now the moon has a queer feel."

"Could it be that you're exhausted from all this running? It has been less than two days since I healed you. It's amazing you've done as well as you have. You're a strong woman, especially considering everything you've been through."

And then to her most pleasant surprise, he leaned toward her and gave her a quick kiss on the mouth. He would have lingered longer, but as soon as their lips touched, Lucius coughed and sat up.

"It's time we go," Torg said hastily. "We must cover many leagues during what remains of the night. Leave nothing behind that could attract unwanted attention."

"We aren't children. Or fools," Lucius said, too loudly.

"Some of us aren't," Bard said.

Laylah sighed. Lucius' relationship with the others was getting worse again. Had he seen Torg kiss her? Or was he just in a foul mood over her choice to stay with the wizard? She stood and stretched, feeling mildly dizzy. Torg handed her Obhasa.

"Take it. It will give you strength."

A surge of power from the ivory staff rode up her arm, and she immediately felt better.

Elu led them through a pass between a pair of young mountains. The snow-covered summits towered thousands of cubits above them. More mountains loomed ahead, strung together as far as the eye could see, shimmering eerily in the starlight. If the members of the company could have sprouted wings and flown to the northwest, they could have reached Nirodha, the icy wasteland where the mammoths roamed. But they were still fifty leagues south of there.

They descended into a peculiar valley choked with leafless trees. While living with the Ropakans, Laylah had become used to green valleys.

"This is a strange place," she said. "It looks like a forest of tangled sticks."

"Many things are strange in the north," Torg said. "I've wandered as far as Catu, many leagues from where we stand, but the valley we're now entering made a greater impression on me than did that frozen mountain."

"You've been here before?" Rathburt said.

"One time, a few centuries ago. I had visited Kamupadana—during a time when the witches were not so openly hostile—and then traveled west in search of Arupa-Loka."

"What do you remember of this valley?" Laylah said.

"When I passed through, it was late in spring, but even then these trees weren't lush. There was not a single leaf, yet the trees thrived."

"I don't understand," Rathburt said. "Are you saying these trees don't bloom until summer?"

"I don't believe they ever bloom—or sprout leaves anymore," Torg said. "They're nothing but root, trunk, and branch."

"That's impossible," Rathburt said.

"They're called *Pacchanna* in the ancient tongue, Hornbeam in the common tongue," Lucius said in a matter-of-fact way that surprised Laylah. "They're devoid of leaves, but their roots grow deep and their wood is as hard as iron. I doubt even Ugga's ax could damage them."

As they all gaped at the firstborn, he explained further. "I spent a lot of time in the libraries of Avici where I once read about the Hornbeam. But much of what I learned didn't make sense. For instance, according to Mogol legends, if you walk among the Hornbeam at night, you'll go mad."

"Ridiculous," Rathburt said. "These are just trees. I sense no malice in them."

"The Hornbeam, as Lucius names them, *are* dangerous," Torg said. "In some ways, they're as deadly as the *Badaalataa*. But I am greater than the trees. If you stay by my side, you'll be safe."

"There he goes again," Rathburt said. "You know, Lucius, I take it back. Torg is even more annoying than you."

Lucius chuckled. Laylah silently thanked him for it.

"The Svakarans know of this place," Elu said, "but none dare approach it at night. They say it's haunted."

"All I know is, I don't like these trees," Ugga said. "They remind me of da ghosties in da woods. I'm glad Master Hah-nah is with us."

I have no idea why they call you Master Hana, Laylah thought. *But, oh yes, I'm glad you're with us, too.*

Then they entered the valley.

Into the heart of the Hornbeam.

The madness engulfed them.

BATTLE OF TITANS

As Bhayatupa lay in half-sleep, his titanic mind replayed all that had occurred since Invictus had woken him from dragon-sleep twelve years before: his conversations with the sorcerer, which had become more and more disturbing; his brief interaction with the Death-Knower, which confused but enticed him; his traitorous partnership with the female Asēkha, which resulted in monumental failure; and the fateful moment Invictus turned against him, which nearly ended his long life.

As he examined these thoughts in minute detail, he knew he was missing something. He was there the day Asubha blew itself apart—just a speck in the sky flying in air so thin even he could barely breathe. After watching the destruction from above, he had believed the Death-Knower was dead; and the next day Mala confirmed it, bragging like he had killed Torg with his bare hands. *Adho Satta* were such disgusting creatures. But without them to use and abuse, life would be far less amusing.

Nothing amused Bhayatupa right now. He had several lacerations beneath his scales that wouldn't stop bleeding, the broken talon on his hind foot was aching, and his ribs remained sore. The Mogol servants he kept imprisoned on the mountaintop attended to his every need, rubbing salve on his wounds and sliding chunks of ice beneath the scales that protected his ribs. But it wasn't the physical injuries that kept him in such a foul mood. It was mental anguish that tormented him. *Tanhiiyati,* the insatiable craving for eternal existence, ate at his sanity like a cancer. He obsessed over it every waking moment—and wallowed in it even in his dreams.

Bhayatupa didn't fear pain. Or darkness. Or even retribution from some higher power. He simply couldn't bear to die. His existence was too precious. He wanted to extend his life until the world fell to ruin— and beyond. A million millennia weren't enough. He wouldn't settle for anything less than eternity. And the Death-Knower who had perished on the peak of Asubha was the one being capable of teaching him how to achieve endless life.

How strange it was, however, that Bhayatupa had not sensed the wizard's demise. In certain ways, all the great beings of Triken were magically linked. If Vedana, Invictus, or even another dragon perished, Bhayatupa would know it. So why hadn't he felt the death of The Torgon? Why did it still seem unreal?

He was missing something.

Then he remembered the shattered carcass of Dukkhatu. He had sniffed it, studied it, and then eaten it. The spider had been much smaller than a great dragon, but she was similar in mass to the mammoths he devoured when he felt the urge to fly to Nirodha. Dukkhatu had been a powerful beast, almost invincible when compared to mortals. He could have easily killed her, of course—but who else was capable of such a feat? When he first discovered her remains, he assumed that the ruin of Asubha had caused her to fall. But why had she been unable to save herself? She could climb as well as he could fly. Besides, her lair had remained relatively intact. Why hadn't she waited there until the eruptions ran their course?

Bhayatupa raised his head and opened his eyes. The Mogols gasped and fell on their faces.

What if the Death-Knower had found Sōbhana—and with her, the Silver Sword?

I know something you don't know. I know something you don't know.

What if?

Of all the living beings on Triken, only a select few—the Warlish witches, the great dragons, and now Invictus—could see Vedana as she existed in the Realm of Undeath. When she entered the Realm of Life, she assumed many forms, both human and animal. But in her own realm, she had a singular essence. Now, as she entered Bhayatupa's lair, she chose to appear as her true self. In the past, this sometimes had unnerved the dragon, making him more pliable to her machinations. And she needed his cooperation now.

Though it was the middle of the day, the passageway that led to the inner chamber of the lair was dark. The dragon had ordered his Mogol slaves to extinguish all torches. Bhayatupa's eyes were profoundly sensitive, sometimes making it difficult for him to sleep even in dim light.

As Vedana undulated toward the dragon, the blackness of her coming made the natural darkness appear gray in comparison. Her gooey, tubular essence slithered toward Bhayatupa like a magical snake, slow but dance-like in its movements. The Mogols who stood guard at the inner mouth of the passageway couldn't see or hear her approach, but chills ran up their spines.

The dragon, however, saw her. Heard her. And felt her.

Bhayatupa raised his head. His mouth opened wide, exposing an angry set of glowing fangs.

"Vedana, this had better be good. I'm not in the mood for your nonsense. The past few days have been difficult."

Her black essence came forward and caressed the dragon's snout, slipping in one nostril and out the other. Bhayatupa snorted in disgust.

"You were always my favorite creation," Vedana purred.

"I was born from the seed of the old gods and am far beyond the likes of you."

"That's not so. It was my vision that gave birth to all the dragons, including you, *Mahaasupanna.*"

"Then why do you fear me?"

"It's possible to fear your own handiwork. Not pleasant, but possible. I fear Invictus. Do you doubt I created him?"

He snorted again. "What do you want? As you can see, I'm trying to sleep. I don't feel particularly well, thanks to your *handiwork.*"

"Don't be so gruff. I want what you want. Control over everyone and everything. Short of that, I've come here to ask you to perform an errand. If you do, I'll reward you with some valuable information."

"What could you possibly offer that would provide any interest to me?"

"There's the little matter of your craving."

Anger flared in the dragon's huge eyes. Spurts of crimson flame leaped from his nostrils, illuminating the chamber. His treasures sparkled like the surface of the sea at sunset.

"Do not toy with me, demon. You're not immune to harm. Speak quickly! Or leave my presence."

"Allow me to confirm, then, what you already suspect: Your precious Death-Knower lives."

"How do you know this?"

"I've seen him. I've … how would you say it? … *been* with him. But more importantly, I've aided him."

"I don't believe a word. Why would you want to help the Death-Knower? He is honest and moral, qualities you despise."

"Ha ha! As my witches would say, you are ssso funny. Why would I want to help the Death-Knower? There's a perfectly good explanation."

"You speak gibberish."

"Do I? You and I are both having *difficulties*, wouldn't you say? Invictus has outgrown himself, but that only makes him more dangerous. If he appeared in this chamber right now, he could destroy both of us—and you know it."

The dragon sighed. "I'm listening."

"It took you long enough. Well then, hear my plan—and see for yourself if it serves us both. And when I'm finished, there's an obnoxious monster that needs to be dealt with. I'll even tell you where to find him. A dracool girlfriend of mine has been most helpful."

Then Vedana whispered in the dragon's ear, telling him how she intended to defeat Invictus. The more she spoke, the more interested Bhayatupa became. The dragon was pleased, and he eagerly agreed to carry out Vedana's errand.

"You need not have offered a reward. I would have rewarded *you* for the opportunity to destroy this despicable *Adho Satta*."

"Don't underestimate Mala," she said. "He won't be easy to kill. The Chain Man has an odd sort of luck. There are no guarantees."

"I care naught for luck. I care only for myself. Have I not said so before?"

"More times than I can count," Vedana said, and then she vanished. These days, her schemes required a lot of moving around—in ways of which only she and her kind were capable.

Good thing she finally had some help.

When the vines encircled his bulging calves, Mala instantly knew what was attacking him. Most believed him to be an ignorant bully, though none dared say it to his face. Was he a bully? Yes. Ignorant? No. Mala loved to learn. It was one of the few traits of his former self that remained intact. The only difference was that while Yama-Deva had studied out of a simple love of life, Mala did it to gain advantages over his enemies.

The *Badaalataa*, according to Invictus' historians, were demonic creatures Vedana had incarnated into the world of the living, though the books called the demon "Invictus' grandmother" as if that were her only claim to fame. Once introduced to the land, the vines had spread like weeds, but only where large swaths of mountain laurel were present. The reason for this was obvious: Laurel provided the *Badaalataa* with excellent concealment.

When the vines entrapped him, Mala became enraged. The queen, the traitor, and the Death-Knower were so close he could taste it. If not for the *Badaalataa*, he would have had them. But somehow his enemies could move through the laurel without being harmed. Was it some conjuration of the wizard? Or maybe even Laylah's doing? This puzzled him. At the same time, he realized that if he didn't retreat, the vines might get him. Anything that could take down a Kojin that easily was extremely dangerous, even to him.

With the *Badaalataa* snapping at his heels, Mala returned to the safety of the trail and then backtracked to where the bulk of his army cowered. Except for the cave troll, only the Kojin had dared to venture into the laurel. Mala mourned her passing. He could count on the ogresses for loyalty and adoration, and so few of them were left.

Mala stormed over to a Porisāda chieftain, pounding his boulder-sized fists together to gain his full attention.

"They are escaping, you red-skinned moron. We must follow!"

"Lord Mala, the *Badaalataa* are everywhere," the chieftain said. "We *cannot* follow. We must approach from another direction."

"If we do that, they'll be lost to us. And I don't plan on allowing that to happen."

A dracool waddled up, her leathery wings spread wide for balance.

"Lord Mala, may I have a word?"

"Why should I listen to you? You're not large enough to carry *me* where I need to go. All of you are worthless. *All* of you!"

"But lord, there is something you must know," the dracool rasped. "The others of my kind who flew with your army are dead. A mysterious illness befell them and they plunged into the vines. I only survived because I was returning with news of the enemy's whereabouts."

"What does this have to do with anything?"

"I've seen the extent of the laurel and the direction the enemy was headed. If they survive the vines, they'll be many leagues from where we now stand. Given a day and night, a black wolf at full run could not overtake them, even if our quarry were to sit and await its arrival. If you wish to catch up quickly, you'll have to fly."

"Do you expect me to magically sprout wings?"

"No, lord. But if you command it, I will fly to Avici and return with a Sampati and more dracools. We can be back by midmorning."

"Go then!" Mala said.

As the *baby dragon* disappeared, Mala ordered the Porisādas and the rest of the Mogols to ride on wolves along the edge of the laurel forest and attempt to pick up the enemy's trail on the other side. When the Sampati arrived, Mala and the dracools would join the search from above. Meanwhile, he told the druids and remaining monsters to march into the gap and watch for any attempts at a crossing. If the fools turned south, they would be easy prey. But Mala believed they would continue north and west. Lucius and Laylah were too stupid to think clearly, but the Death-Knower was a sly one. With him as their guide, they would be difficult to track. Maybe impossible.

While he waited for the dracool's return, Mala got hungry. He eyed the remains of a dead troll the Asēkhas had slain, but it already was burning within a massive pyre, and therefore not raw enough for his tastes. A single Mogol had remained to service Mala, and the Chain Man ordered him to go into the forest and bring back fresh food. A short time later, the Mogol returned with the carcass of a small black bear. Mala tore off one of its hind legs and tossed it to the Mogol and then devoured the rest of the beast fur, bones, and all. After that, he slept through the night. While roasting his portion of the bear, the Mogol was told to stand guard over his leader, though Mala knew it was a needless act. Who or what would dare ambush a fanged monster that stood ten cubits tall and weighed seventy stones?

When Mala woke, the eastern sky was brightening. The Mogol presented his master with three wiggly rabbits (their hind legs broken), which Mala greedily chewed up and swallowed. The juicy flesh and crunchy bones put him in a good mood. He even joked around with his companion and smacked him on the back—a little too hard. The Mogol quivered, spit blood, and stopped moving. "Oops!" Mala said, looking around guiltily. Then he picked up the warrior and cast him into the laurel, laughing hysterically when the *Badaalataa* fell upon the corpse. If it was a corpse. Mala wasn't certain if the Mogol had been dead. But who cared? He commanded thousands of them. Plenty more would die before the wars were over. Gods, he thought, this is going to be fun.

Halfway through the morning, the dracool returned along with a Sampati. Nineteen other baby dragons and a flock of ravens joined them. The Sampati's rider climbed off and bowed to Mala, who shoved him aside and clambered onto the hybrid condor's scaly neck. As soon as they launched into the sky, Mala could see the full extent of the laurel forest. The breadth of it amazed him. Thousands of hectares dominated the slope of the mountain. The *Badaalataa* lay hidden within, quiet but hungry. It would be an amusing place to bring prisoners later.

Mala was no dragon, but his eyes were keen. To the southwest, he saw his wolves and Mogols marching along the border of the laurel. But they were far away. Of more interest were the wide scorch marks running through the middle of the laurel. To Mala, they resembled a giant arrow aimed at his prey. He grinned.

Mala motioned to one of the dracools, which peeled off and dove toward the wolves to report what he saw from the air. Mala believed he could handle the enemy himself, but the memory of his painful encounter with the Death-Knower at Dibbu-Loka still haunted him. It never hurt to have some backup, even if it took a while for the backup to catch up.

Out of nowhere, something huge streaked down and crashed into the dracool, tearing it to pieces in midair.

"Huh?" Mala said as a great dragon swept around and flew directly at the Sampati.

Squawking loudly, the crossbred condor swerved, forcing Mala to hold on for dear life. Somehow, Bhayatupa had found him, and the great dragon was angry.

The ravens flew at the dragon's face, pecking at the ear holes beneath his horns. But blasts of crimson fire incinerated most of them. The dracools attacked next, barely slowing Bhayatupa's approach. But they purchased, with their lives, enough time for Mala to force the Sampati toward the blackened trail that led to the end of the laurel. As fast as a diving hawk, the massive beast shot downward.

Mala was confident in his own abilities, but he knew he was no match for Bhayatupa without Invictus to protect him—especially a thousand cubits above the ground. Either the dragon would kill him in the air, or he would perish when he fell into the vines. He had to reach the forest beyond the laurel and find a place to hide.

A torrent of super-heated flame engulfed him and his mount. Mala cried out. The Sampati lurched forward, most of its wing and tail feathers incinerated, exposing bare scales. As the creature tumbled out of control, Mala fell off.

He and the Sampati were now only a few cubits above the slope. Mala fell into the trees just beyond the border of the laurel, crashing to the ground in a painful series of thuds and grunts. The Sampati smote the side of the slope just a few paces beyond and lay still.

Though he was injured in many places, Mala knew he couldn't lie there and feel sorry for himself. The dragon would be upon him before he knew it, so he scrambled on hands and knees into the thickest stand of trees, attempting to conceal his massive frame. But he might as well have tried to hide a mammoth in a bale of hay.

Still, the trees provided some protection. Bhayatupa could see him but couldn't approach. He was twenty times as long as Mala and many times his weight. Though he was as flexible as a worm, the dragon still didn't have room to squeeze between the sturdy trunks.

"*Adho Satta*, why do you cower?" the dragon said in a growling voice that made Mala shudder. "You so love to give orders. Why not come out from your hiding place and order me around?"

"When Invictus hears of this, you'll not speak so boldly," Mala said, but his voice quivered.

"Ahh … so that is how it is. When the sorcerer is near, you're big and brave. But when you're alone, you're a coward, low among the low. How pathetic you are. How obscene. I was hoping you would at least put up a fight. But alas, when it comes to facing me, few have the courage to raise a sword. Most just relieve themselves in their breeches and force me to endure the taste of their scat when I devour them."

Mala knew the dragon was hoping to anger him enough to lure him into the open. And it was working. Smoke puffed out of his mouth, nostrils, and ears, and his chain glowed hot enough to catch nearby trees on fire. But without Invictus or an army of monsters to back him, he was not Bhayatupa's match. Of all the beings on Triken, only Invictus could humble the dragon on his own.

"*I* will be the one to devour *you*," Mala said, trying to sound brave. "But I'll be sure to wash you nice and clean first."

"Tsk. Tsk," the dragon said, and then slowly reared back. What happened next was not slow. Bhayatupa brought his head forward with such force it caused his neck to crack like a whip. When he opened his jaws, Mala could see down his cavernous throat—from which came a blast of crimson fire that blew Mala back against the trunk of a thick oak. The tree shivered so hard its upper half split and fell.

Blood flowed from a gash on the side of his head, but he stood and cleared his vision. Now the forest was burning, and amid the flames the dragon approached, knocking down trees with wicked sweeps of his neck and tail. In self-defense, Mala commanded a gout of molten gold to spray from his chain, showering Bhayatupa's face and front talons. The dragon screeched and pulled back, fanning his snout with his wings.

You can be injured, Mala thought with exhilaration. *Here's some more*!

The bubbling liquid that burst from the chain was born of the magic of Invictus and was even more destructive than dragon fire. More of it stung the great lizard. Bhayatupa swiped at the viscous fluid with his wings, feet, and tail attempting to brush it off, but it clung to his scales like hot wax. Finally, the dragon used his own fire to incinerate the poisons and then turned to face Mala again, his rage tenfold.

But Mala had not been idle. He knew he couldn't defeat the dragon in open combat, but his counterattack had distracted Bhayatupa long enough for him to run. Now he thundered down the slope like a maddened elephant, weaving through the trees as best he could. His feet struck stone, and before he could slow his descent, he tumbled over the lip of a rock overhang and fell a hundred cubits into a gorge cleaved by a roaring river. Mala let out a long cry. It felt like he fell forever.

The Chain Man landed in deep water. His dense body sank quickly to the bottom where the swirling currents momentarily pinned him. Then he was blown downstream. Mala struggled to the foamy surface and took a gulp of air, only to squeal as the dragon's front talons closed around his shoulders, lifting him from the river like a squirming fish. As the talons ripped into his thick hide, the chain erupted. Bhayatupa howled and dropped him back into the river just a few paces from the edge of a titanic waterfall. The powerful rapids spilled Mala over the side, and he fell fifty fathoms toward a pile of boulders. But halfway down, Mala reached out one of his huge hands and caught hold of an outcrop, slowing his momentum. He lost his grip and fell a few more cubits onto a ledge where he lay stunned behind a rumbling buffet of water. When Mala lifted his head, Bhayatupa was just a few cubits away, hovering like a hummingbird the size of a mountain.

A lethal blast of dragon fire flared all around him, but the wall of water between Mala and the dragon saved him. He rolled away, not sure what to do next, but fate—or luck—provided him with a chance to escape. Behind the ledge was an opening in the rock. The dragon snapped at him, but the power of the falling water thwarted his attempts. Mala squirmed inside the cave, deeper and deeper, until he could go no farther. Then he collapsed on the dripping stone, bleeding and exhausted.

For a long time after, he heard Bhayatupa cursing him and saw blasts of dragon fire lighting up the mouth of the cavern. But he was safely beyond reach. The hole was too small for the dragon to enter.

Mala lay in semi-consciousness. He barely noticed when dusk approached and Bhayatupa gave up the chase, flying off in a rage. The Chain Man lay there all through the night, shivering and incoherent. By morning, he was near death.

But he wouldn't die on this day.

A band of Mogol warriors found Mala and began his rescue. Blood as foul as poison oozed from a gash on the side of the Chain Man's head and from a dozen other places on his huge frame. His chain glowed sporadically, spitting molten liquid that killed several Mogols trying to help him. But the rest of the warriors kept up their efforts. Invictus had given them orders, and they knew he could be watching them even now.

They finally managed to drag Mala through a tunnel that led out the back of the cave. They then built a great litter. It took ten warriors to hoist him onto it. Moving Mala was slow work, even with a team of wolves dragging the litter. All the rest of that day and night, they managed only two leagues. At that rate, Mala would be long dead before they reached the Golden City.

Bhayatupa had slaughtered the dracools and the Sampati that had been summoned to aid Mala during his search for Torg and Laylah, but a few of the ravens survived the battle and returned to Avici to alert Invictus of his general's dire situation. The next day around noon, a Sampati and a dracool landed nearby. Invictus climbed off the dracool. A thin, muscular pilot leaped off the crossbred condor and quickly roped one of its massive legs to the stump of a tree.

As Invictus approached, the Mogols fell to the ground and buried their faces in the grass, not daring to move. A happy band of crickets stopped chirping, a bubbling spring slowed to a crawl, and a frisky breeze lost its way, no longer rustling the leaves. It was as if Invictus' mere presence turned off nature's sound effects.

With surprising tenderness, Invictus climbed onto the litter and placed his hand on Mala's boulder-sized forehead. "My dear, loyal pet. I'm sorry you've been through so much, and that it took me so long to come to you. But do not doubt that I will avenge you. Bhayatupa will become my puppet before all is said and done."

The Chain Man moaned but didn't open his eyes.

Invictus turned to the Mogols. "You've done well and will be rewarded. But you're no longer needed here. Return to Avici and await further orders."

As if in relief, the wolves and Mogols fled. Only the dracool, the Sampati, and the pilot remained. The man came forward, his wiry limbs trembling.

"Do you wish *me* to leave?"

"I have need of you," Invictus said. "Come here now."

"My liege?"

"I have need of you," the sorcerer responded.

The pilot hesitated. "I should stay near the Sampati, my liege. It has a wild temperament."

"Do you disobey me?"

"No, my liege. I would never dare such a thing. It's just that—"

"Come here."

"Yes, my liege."

The pilot stumbled forward, clambered onto the litter, and stared into Invictus' brown eyes.

"Give me your hand," Invictus said.

"Yes, my liege."

The pilot held out his right arm.

"You must have misunderstood my command," Invictus said. "Must I repeat it?"

"My liege?"

Invictus sighed. Then he grabbed the pilot's forearm and spat a ball of yellow mucus onto his wrist. The flesh and bone sizzled and the hand fell onto Mala's chest, its fingers still wiggling.

While the pilot howled in agony, Invictus calmly said, "If you wish to live, give me your hand."

"Yes ..." the pilot mumbled. He reached down with his remaining hand, picked up the severed one, and gave it to Invictus.

"Very good," Invictus said. "You're free to go."

The pilot scrambled off the litter and ran, disappearing into the woods. Invictus could hear him emptying the contents of his stomach somewhere behind the trees. The sorcerer then returned his attention to his prized servant.

"Everything's going to be all right, my general. You saved my life. Now I'll save yours."

Invictus' body glowed. In a slow and controlled fashion, the severed hand began to melt, dripping droplets of flesh, blood, and bone. Invictus picked it up and waved it over Mala, allowing the steamy goo to ooze into the Chain Man's wounds.

"My most loyal servant deserves nothing but the best," Invictus whispered tenderly.

Mala groaned and his eyelids fluttered. Suddenly, the ruined snow giant tore away the restraints that bound him to the litter and sat upright. Even in a seated position, he towered over Invictus.

"Where am I? What's happening?"

"You're with me. I'm healing you."

Tears sprang from Mala's eyes.

"Tears of joy, my general?" Invictus said. "Now that you're healed, you and I have much to celebrate."

The Chain Man smiled broadly, his fangs glistening in the sunlight. "My king. You have not forsaken me. I feared you'd be angry over my failure."

"Angry? Never. I love you. You did your best, my pet. Rejoice! Your dreams will come true, I promise you."

Mala stood shakily. Invictus reached up and clasped one of the Chain Man's fingers. Like a tiny father with a colossus for a son, they walked through the field toward their mounts. The Chain Man climbed aboard the Sampati, Invictus the dracool, and side by side they flew back to Avici.

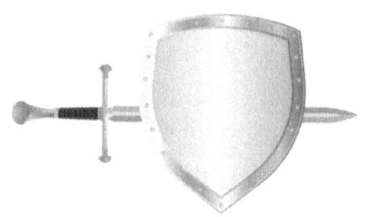

DARK SIDE

Torg didn't fear the Hornbeam, even in the darkness. He sensed the despair in the heart of the forest, but it held no power over him. The trees couldn't harm him. But they wanted to … oh, so much. Would they settle for harming his companions?

Some believed the Hornbeam were the oldest living creatures on the surface of Triken. The trees reminded Torg of Bhayatupa. They feared death so much, they refused to die. Even when they had lost the ability to bloom, grow leaves, and feed off sunlight, their roots had dug deeper and deeper into the earth and their wood had hardened like iron. And still they lived. They were old when Vedana was born. Ancient when the great dragons emerged. In their regard, Torg was just a wisp of wind. But he knew things they did not. He knew death. All he had to do was show them what it was, and their indomitable will would splinter.

Don't test me, Torg said in his mind. *Allow us to pass.*

The Hornbeam listened, but they weren't so easily cowed.

That was when Rathburt lost control. Now he could hear the trees too, and he lacked the strength to resist their desperation. "It's terrible," he said, his voice frenetic. "They live and yet do not. And they hate us so much. They despise the blood that flows in our veins and the water that soddens our flesh. They scream. Can you not hear?"

"I don't hear nothing," Bard said. "But I don't feel very good, either. I want to lie down and go to sleep."

"Me too," Ugga said. "What's da use? We're all going to die, anyway. Who cares whether it's now or later?"

Lucius sat and leaned against the trunk of one of the Hornbeam, tears streaking his cheeks. But Laylah stood tall, holding Obhasa in front of her. The ivory staff glowed.

"The Hornbeam are sad," she said to Torg. "They fight so hard to live, but without the wisdom to do it properly."

Torg smiled, proud of her. "All things are impermanent. There is a beginning, middle, and an end to everything. That is the law—and it is irrefutable. One day, I hope to introduce you to one of my favorite people, a wise woman named Tathagata. She once said to me: 'Living one day with truth is superior to living a thousand years without it.' The Hornbeam live without truth. I could provide it to them, but it will be better if they discover it themselves. Either way, they'll eventually perish. And when they do, they'll go where all living things go when they die—except for the enlightened, who go to another place."

"I was born of the madness of Invictus," Lucius said, startling Torg and Laylah. "Will I also go where all living things go when they die?"

Torg knew enough about the newborns to understand what Lucius meant. For the first time since meeting the golden-haired man, Torg felt empathy. How tortured he must be.

Torg knelt beside the firstborn and placed a hand on one of his upraised knees. "Life is driven by karma. Living beings carry it from place to place as surely as their own shadows. I believe the same applies to you, Lucius. Your karma is young. But it exists. When you die, you *will* go to the place I and all others will go. And once there, you won't fear it. I promise you."

Lucius grasped Torg's hand and then burst into tears. His sobs were so loud they echoed among the trees. Suddenly, Rathburt was crying, along with Bard, Ugga, and Elu. But it was less about empathy for Lucius and more about the sadness the trees exuded. Laylah sat next to Lucius and took him in her arms, cradling him. In this one instance, Torg felt no jealousy. Their tears finally gave way to chuckles and then laughter. And the power in that sound forced the menace of the Hornbeam to withdraw.

"In Invictus, we have a common enemy," Torg said after the mirth subsided. "From here on, let us behave with that in mind. We must trust each other if we're to survive the coming days."

Before venturing farther into the valley, they sat among the trees and ate a small meal. They were also thirsty and—for the first time since reaching the foothills of Mahaggata—no source of water appeared to be nearby.

"How vast are the Hornbeam?" Elu asked Torg.

"If my memory is correct, the forest extends about two more leagues.

There are no rivers or streams within the valley, but if we walk without rest, we might pass beyond their stronghold before dawn. After that, water will be plentiful again. But it will be a long night for parched throats."

The others followed Torg deeper into the valley. Now the Hornbeam were all around them, their bark smooth and gray. They looked less like trees and more like the skeletons of trees, and the tips of their branches were as sharp as swords. The companions saw no other life in the valley: no animals, ordinary trees, or even shrubs and grasses. The floor of the forest was as gray as the Hornbeam, and it kicked up an eerie dust that coated their boots and the legs of their breeches. Beneath the gray powder, the ground was spongy and devoid of visible roots, so they could walk quickly. But when they reached the heart of the valley, the insidious will of the Hornbeam made one last attempt to infect them. Their expressions bore fear, sadness, and regret—all except for Torg.

To take their minds off the torment, the wizard told them a story about Sister Tathagata, the eldest of the Noble Ones. Once every year, Tathagata would make the long journey from Dibbu-Loka to this northern clime with her disciples.

"On bright afternoons in early spring, Tathagata sometimes took young nuns and monks deep into this valley. Once there, she would begin long sessions of meditation that would extend into the night. She instructed the novices to label each breath as rising and falling, rising and falling. They were told to resist all drifts of the mind other than those that seized on emotion. When that occurred, Tathagata counseled them to observe the emotion—whether it was fear, anger, joy, lust, or any other—with utmost attention."

As Torg spoke, he and his companions continued their trek through the forest, but his story was serving its purpose, distracting them from the madness of the Hornbeam.

"While the sun was still bright, the novices had no problem with their meditation. As they sat silently together beneath the trees, their minds went through the usual slew of wanderings. And each time an emotion emerged, they studied it dutifully."

"It's easy to guess where this is going," Rathburt said. "When night came, the novices got the fright of their lives."

"In a manner of speaking," Torg said. "You see, the power of the Hornbeam comes from their despair. When living beings pass through this forest, the trees bombard them with what the Noble Ones call *Death Fear*. All mortals are aware—on a surface level—that they will one day die. But only a few times in their lives will they confront this awareness on the deepest levels. The Hornbeam are consumed by *Death Fear*, and they exude this obsession onto others."

"Why is the forest only dangerous at night?" Lucius said.

"A good question," Torg said, "and I'm not sure I know the answer. But most of our fears are worse in the darkness, don't you think? The Hornbeam know this. Perhaps they save their strength for when it will be most effective."

"What happened to da nah-veeces?" Ugga said, his small eyes glistening.

Torg chuckled. The crossbreed's gentle curiosity never failed to lighten his heart. "Keep in mind, Ugga, that the novices were unaware of any danger from without. They knew nothing of the Hornbeam, other than that the trees looked strange. When darkness came, the trees bent their will upon them. The novices attempted to study what each one believed to be the emotion we call fear. However, most of them were incapable of facing it on such an intense level, and they broke down. Senior nuns and monks, who had remained hidden nearby, led them away. Only a few of the novices had the strength to last through the night, and they received quick promotions."

"It sounds cruel," Laylah said. "The novices didn't deserve to suffer that way."

"Deserve has nothing to do with it," Torg said. "Sister Tathagata could sit alone among the Hornbeam for a month and feel not the slightest discomfort. The despair of the trees holds no sway over her. She knows better. After their night in this forest, the novices knew better too. In a short time they learned a vital lesson: *Death Fear* is an illusion we experience through ignorance of the truth."

"Then I must be *very* ignorant of the truth," Rathburt said, "because I'm afraid of *everything*."

They all laughed, Lucius loudest of all.

When Lucius laughed at Rathburt's jest, Laylah felt a surge of joy.

Ever since the firstborn broke down at the base of the Hornbeam, his attitude had changed. Now when he looked at Torg, the distrust and dislike seemed muted, replaced by a grudging respect. The wizard behaved similarly. It was obvious Torg and his friends were a kind-hearted bunch willing to give even someone as troublesome as Lucius another chance to win their hearts. Laylah especially liked the giant and the dwarf, so dissimilar in size but so similar in personality. She wanted to hug them all for their roles in keeping her free. But Torg was another matter. Hugging was the least of what she wanted to do to him.

Still, all was not well. When she held Obhasa, the magical staff kept the fever and nausea at bay. But if she set the staff aside, the illness crept back. It felt like her previous sickness in some ways, different in others. The intensity was less, but the insidiousness stronger. Ironically, when dawn arrived she felt better. For the first time in her life, morning brought relief instead of discomfort. When they emerged from the last of the Hornbeam, the bright sunlight stroked her face like a friend.

Elu led them to a stream. Laylah laid Obhasa aside to wet her parched throat. Shortly after, she realized she felt fine even without the staff in her grasp. This confused her, but she wasn't about to complain.

They came to a sparkling pond, its surface as blue as the sky. Colorful waterfowl frolicked in the water. The birds scattered as they approached, settling on the far bank. Bard reached for his bow, but Torg waved him off.

"Soon enough we'll be forced to kill to eat, but not here, not now," the wizard said. "I can't bear to harm such wondrous creatures. We carry enough food to last for a while. Let us come in peace and bathe in these still waters as friends of nature."

The kindness in his voice warmed Laylah's heart. She leaned against Obhasa and felt the staff thrum. When Lucius placed his hand on her shoulder, she nearly screamed.

"Isn't it wonderful?" he said, not seeming to notice he had startled her. "To look upon such beauty as a free man and woman. I can't describe the feeling. Invictus poisoned everything he touched, including me. But there's hope now for both of us."

Ugga, Bard, and Elu discarded their clothes and plunged naked into the crystal water. Rathburt did the same—but more timidly, off to the side. With a wild look in his eyes, Lucius let out a howl and followed them. Laylah couldn't help but laugh. When Torg came up beside her,

her smile widened.

"Thank you," she said.

"For what?"

"For saving my life, for one thing. But also for being so patient with him."

"If it brings you pleasure, it brings me pleasure."

She smiled again. "Speaking of pleasure, I could use a bath as much as anyone. But I don't think it would be ladylike to join them."

"Nor would I want you to. I wish for no man to see you but me."

"I feel the same about you … no *woman*."

"Allow me to bathe with the men, and then I'll see that you have privacy. But know that it will pain me not to look at you."

"If you do, I won't be offended."

This time, it was his turn to blush. "There'll come a day when I'll do more than that." And then he sprinted toward the water, casting off his cloak and other clothing as he ran. She watched longer than she should have—and was not disappointed, to say the least.

When it was her turn to bathe, the others respected her privacy. The water was cold, pure, and sweet. She had no soaps or perfumes, but she scooped handfuls of sand from the bottom of the pond and rubbed them into her hair and onto her skin. When she emerged, she felt as clean as she ever had in her life. She soaked her dress and then put it back on still dripping wet.

Laylah found the men leaning against a boulder and eating from their packs. She joined them. Her newfound freedom from illness increased her appetite, and she had to force herself to save something for the next day.

"When should we continue our march?" Lucius said to Torg without a hint of derision in his voice.

"Our successful passage through the vines and Hornbeam bought us considerable time," Torg said. "I believe we can rest here until late afternoon as long as we then march all through the night."

"Where are we now?" Laylah said.

Torg started to answer, but without warning he bolted upright and stared toward the pass from which they had come.

"What is it, Torg?" Rathburt said. "Have the wolves found us again?"

"Do you not see?" Torg said.

"See what? The mountains? What's so special about them?"

"Bursts of light. And wisps of smoke."

"I see nothing," Ugga said, "but my eyes don't work so great. I smell better than I see."

"That's a matter of opinion," Rathburt said.

Laylah's eyesight was also magnified by her magic. She saw a crimson flash—and then smoke drifting high in the air and whisking away.

"What is it?" she said to Torg.

"It appears to be a battle between two angry enemies," the wizard said. "I would guess Mala to be one of them. But the other? In my knowledge there is only one being besides Invictus capable of creating such explosions—the dragon Bhayatupa."

Now there was no doubt. All could see a thick column of smoke rising between the mountains and bending westward in the swift currents of air. Something was on fire.

"It's not the laurel that burns," Lucius said. "The vines can suppress fire, or at least the books say so. It appears Bhayatupa has remained active despite his battle in Avici."

And then Lucius told them everything about his and Laylah's escape from the Golden City and eventual meetup with Torg in Kamupadana, including Izumo's role, Invictus' collapse, and Vedana's constant meddling. Laylah's memories were not as clear, but she contributed when she could, especially concerning the demon. Torg seemed fascinated, listening intently to their description of the sorcerer's bizarre reaction to the eclipse and asking many questions about Vedana.

"Once Invictus fled, Bhayatupa broke free of the chains," Lucius said. "There was intense confusion, but then Vedana came in the guise of a raven and led us to Laylah, who had fallen and was about to be trampled. I know this sounds ridiculous, but the demon saved Laylah's life. And mine."

"Vedana is as much my enemy as Invictus is," Laylah said, "but what Lucius says is true. Apparently, my grandmother hates her grandson even more than the rest of us."

"Your grandmother?" Rathburt said. "Torg, did you know this?"

"I have known for a time that Vedana was Invictus' grandmother, so I assumed it was also true of Laylah," Torg said. "But don't be so amazed, Rathburt. Many people have demon blood in their veins, though most aren't aware. Most of the magic in the world—both good and evil—began with the demons."

"Was da Bitch a demon?" Bard said.

"Da Bitch?" Laylah said.

"Now it's time for *our* story," Torg said, "but we must tell it quickly and then get some rest. If Mala and Bhayatupa are fighting each other on the other side of those mountains, we might be in even better shape than I'd hoped. But we still must be prepared to continue our march in the late afternoon. We have many leagues to travel, and there are enemies everywhere, not just those your brother employs."

And so, Laylah and Lucius heard the tales of Bard and Ugga, Rathburt and Elu, and Torg. The wizard gave few details about what happened with Vedana in the cavern and Jord beneath the trees, but Laylah discerned more than she should have, curling her lip and grunting. Lucius saw her jealousy and grunted, as well—and for a short time afterward, he returned to his former surliness. Then they all lay down and slept, keeping no watch.

Just before dusk, the wizard woke them. They drank from the pond and ate most of what remained of their food, leaving just enough for a light breakfast the following morning. After breaking camp, Elu found a patch of blackberry bushes, the wild fruit sour but edible. They gorged themselves and put more in their packs. As they walked, the Svakaran occasionally veered into the trees and returned with edible nuts, roots, and even bark and leaves.

When full darkness arrived, the quarter moon was well past the midpoint in the sky. Laylah felt the sickness return, even worse than the previous night. Torg gave her his cloak and Obhasa. When she grasped the ivory staff, the queasiness lessened.

"I'm worried," Torg said. "I can't comprehend the origin of this illness."

"I'm not sure what's happening," Laylah said. "But when I hold Obhasa, the discomfort is tolerable."

"What could it be?" Lucius said. "If her illness returns, it could kill her."

"I'm as confused as both of you," Torg said.

They continued their march. The valley extended beyond the range of the Hornbeam, but it gave way to a rapid series of dips and rises, finally forcing them to trudge up the side of yet another titanic mountain.

"We are northeast of Arupa-Loka," Torg said, "but the *Ghost City* is still ten leagues from where we stand."

"Not that we'd want to go there," Rathburt said. "You're the only one who wanders into places like that for the fun of it."

"I wouldn't call it fun, but it was interesting."

"I've never been to Arupa-Loka, but I've been to Duccarita several times," Lucius said. "The pirates are not overly fond of visitors, but Invictus intimidated them, so they behaved in our presence. Besides, the sorcerer paid well for slaves: silver for young men and women; gold for children. He was popular among the riffraff."

"In-vick-tuss is not a nice guy," Ugga said.

"He certainly is not," Lucius agreed.

"Duccarita is about forty leagues due west," Torg said. "North of the city, the terrain is treacherous but barren, while south it's easier to traverse but filled with 'riffraff,' as you say. We must choose north or south, but it will take us two weeks to reach the City of Thieves on foot, so we have some time before we're forced to decide."

"What is Duccarita?" Laylah said, relishing a chance to stop and catch her breath. "Invictus sometimes spoke of it, but I never paid him much attention."

"Lucius might be able to answer that question better than I," Torg said.

The firstborn grimaced. "My queen, Duccarita is not a pleasant place. All manner of vermin lives there—slave traders, pirates, thieves, murderers, rapists—more than 50,000, all told. They raid and pillage along the borders of Dhutanga, the western foothills of Mahaggata, and the coast of the Akasa Ocean. The pirates even bring thousands and thousands of slaves from across the sea, strange-looking creatures with pink skin, purple eyes, and hairless bodies. The Porisādas covet these slaves, for they are pudgy and tender. Your brother also prizes them—for they make obscene noises when tortured. Their language was beyond my understanding. To me, it sounded like squawking and squeals. But Invictus knew it well. Few things surpass him."

"The inhabitants of Duccarita are only part of the problem," Torg said. "Riffraff is easily defeated. But Duccarita still stands despite the many horrors it has inflicted on the free people of Triken. Why is that? One reason is that Duccarita is far from the forces capable of opposing it. But there is another more recent reason that Duccarita has flourished.

A sinister power now resides in the city. I've been within the walls—in disguise—several times, but I couldn't locate the source of the evil. Do you know anything about it, Lucius?"

"I didn't sense any evil powers," the firstborn said. "But it's true something exists there that even Invictus respects. Mala urged the king to demand the allegiance of Duccarita, giving Avici control of its wealth. But the sorcerer was hesitant for reasons I never understood. Could it be that something stronger than Invictus lurks in the depths of the City of Thieves?"

"Stronger than Invictus? Highly doubtful," Torg said. "But stronger than me? That remains to be seen."

Torg and his companions journeyed west through the mountains for almost a week, never coming within ten leagues of the northern border of the Gap of Gamana. With Elu's considerable help, Torg led them up, down, and around a dozen mountains of varying heights and girths. They traveled mostly at night and were never seriously threatened. They saw no signs of pursuit from Mala or any of Invictus' minions, though they occasionally hid from wandering tribesmen and snuck past small villages.

They began killing game and daring to build fires. Their cooking implements consisted of one pan, a metal spoon, and their daggers. Roasted meat sliced from the bone made up most of their diet. But they also found berries, rhubarb, roots, and roughage. Fresh water remained plentiful. They never went hungry or thirsty.

One night they came upon a small hunting party of Mogols camped within a cavernous rock shelter. The warriors had built a fire and were roasting a boar. They were also making a lot of noise and seemed to have no fear of intrusion.

When Torg stepped into the firelight, the Mogols quailed like children. Wielding the Silver Sword, he slew five before they stood. Bard, Ugga, and Lucius dispatched the others and dragged the bodies deep into the woods, covering them with deadwood and leaves before returning to the fire for a tasty meal.

Inside the shelter they garnered valuable supplies, including a pouch packed with a delicious paste of blackberries, dried apples, deer meat, and bear fat. Ugga wouldn't touch it, but the others loved it—and it never spoiled.

Elu uncovered another pouch stuffed with dried herbs such as bugloss, thyme, basil, and rosemary.

Laylah found two mulberry shawls, one for her upper body and one to wrap around her waist, allowing her to discard the old brown dress she had grown to dislike.

Lucius picked up a war club carved from ironwood and decorated with potent symbols. Including the *uttara*, he now carried two dangerous weapons.

Bard discovered a quiver of arrows with sharp flint points.

And Rathburt found a stone pipe and a pouch of fresh tobacco.

When Torg and Ugga emerged with deerskin blankets and two kegs of apple wine, their haul was complete. That was a fun night.

But their concern over Laylah's deteriorating physical condition outweighed the pleasurable moments of their journey. She continued to be fine during the day, but when the moon glowed in the sky, her illness invariably returned—and each night, it worsened. Without Obhasa, she wouldn't have been able to walk more than a few paces, much less march for leagues along rugged—and often treacherous—mountain trails. Torg wasn't sure who worried about her more: he or Lucius.

On the morning of the sixth day since departing the valley of the Hornbeam, Lucius pulled Torg aside while Laylah slept.

"What's happening to her? Why is she ill again? I thought you healed her. I *saw* you do it. Can you help her? Why won't you try?"

"You didn't like it much the first time."

"Don't mock me. Things have changed. I love Laylah, and you know it, but her life is more important than my feelings."

"Is it? Are you sure?"

"Yes, I'm *sure*. But you still haven't answered my questions. Why is she sick again? Can you heal her a second time?"

"I don't know why she's ill," Torg said. "It's obvious it has something to do with the moon, which—as she says—is normally her source of power. I'm especially worried about what might happen tonight. The moon will be full in a clear sky. You and I will have to keep a close watch. As for your second question, Obhasa is doing as much for her now as I can. The staff sustains her. In her weakened state, I'm not sure how much more of my energy her body could ingest without causing more harm than good. In the long run, it's up to her to recover from this malady."

They passed the rest of that day in a sheltered hollow. The sky became overcast, it began to rain, and the temperature dropped to near freezing. They shivered beneath their blankets. Torg covered Laylah with his cloak, but she trembled in her sleep. He feared the worst. The full moon would rise at sunset. What would happen then?

In the late afternoon, the skies cleared. As darkness approached, the air grew slightly warmer. Elu prepared a possum stew in a clay pot he'd taken from the Mogol camp. He added wild potatoes, herbs, and ground hickory nuts to thicken the gravy. They ate out of Sassafras bowls and guzzled the rest of the wine. Laylah devoured her meal, picking up the clay pot before it even cooled and licking it clean. Her hunger seemed to have no end, which Lucius took as a good sign. But Torg became even more worried. Her mania was disconcerting.

When darkness descended on the forest, the night was as clear as any Torg had seen. The stars emerged, one at a time, and sparkled in the sky. When the moon rose above the canopy of trees, it appeared twice as large as normal, like a hole was opening in the firmament large enough to swallow them all.

Laylah fainted. Lucius caught her before she struck the ground and laid her on a blanket. The others rushed over and encircled her. Torg knelt and felt her forehead. Her fever was back. When he tried to place Obhasa in her hands, her body went into a spasm.

"What is it?" Lucius screamed. "The moon is killing her! What are we going to do? *Help* her."

"We must find a cave," Torg said. "The deeper and darker, the better. Search in all directions."

The others raced into the woods, leaving Torg and the sorceress alone. Torg sat on the blanket and lifted her into his arms, kissing her cheeks and then her lips. "Laylah, my love … how can I help you? What am I missing?"

She opened her eyes briefly. They glowed like cinders, projecting a hot white light that burned Torg's face, forcing him to look away. When he turned back, her eyes were closed but she trembled and moaned, sweat beading on her face, neck, and upper chest. Then her legs went into a series of quivers and her flesh shimmered.

Torg wracked his brain. Something nagged at him. He replayed every thought and conversation he had ever had regarding eclipses, including his conversation with his companions before they left Elu and Rathburt's longhouse.

"I am a Death-Knower. I know many things others do not. Besides, I've witnessed this event before, and I remember how it felt just before it began. All of us who live long lives will see the moon become enshrouded in shadow many times. But when it happens to the sun, it is a far rarer and more powerful occurrence. The Noble Ones call it a solar eclipse. They say that the sun and the moon circle the skies like birds, and sometimes the moon passes in front of the sun and blocks its light."

Torg thought back to the other times he had witnessed a full solar eclipse. The first was at Mount Catu after he'd hidden the mysterious amulet that preserved the flesh of Peta the ghost-child. The second was in the skies of Anna, casting the Tent City into darkness. The third was from the banks of Lake Keo. All three occurred long before Invictus was born, and centuries separated them. Torg's memories were hazy, but he sat—with Laylah in his arms—and watched his breath, clearing the silt from the waters of his mind.

Ugga and Elu returned first. The giant crossbreed had come across a rock shelter, but it was too small and open. The Svakaran, however, had found just what Torg wanted—a narrow but deep cave that extended more than thirty paces into the side of a rock slope. Torg told Ugga to wait in the hollow for the others, then he wrapped Laylah in the blanket, picked her up, and followed Elu into the darkness.

The cave was less than half a mile away. Its opening was so small he had to back in and drag Laylah behind him along the smooth stone floor. At the end of the passageway, he found a chamber just large enough for Torg, Laylah, and one other person to fit comfortably. Torg placed the sorceress on the blanket, laid Obhasa next to her, and told Elu to bring the rest of their companions back to the mouth of the cave.

"When you return, send Lucius in first," Torg ordered.

After Elu sprinted away, Laylah's condition deteriorated. Seizures wracked her body, froth oozed from the corners of her mouth, and mucus drained from her nostrils. Her flesh was so hot Torg could barely touch it. Before long, she emitted wretched bursts of white energy. Torg feared she might incinerate their only clothing, so he removed his tunic and breeches and Laylah's shawls and crawled to the opening of the cave, tossing them into the clearing outside. Then he returned to the sorceress and lay down beside her, pressing their naked bodies together. In any other circumstance, passion would have consumed him. Her body was beautiful. But though he craved her beyond reckoning, his growing fear that she might die extinguished his sexual urges.

As he held her, he recalled the first time he had witnessed a solar eclipse, at Catu. The bizarre darkness had stunned him as if it were a sign that even the sun mourned the ghost-child's passing. Afterward, another unexpected event had interrupted his lonely trek back to Anna. Two weeks after the solar eclipse, a full eclipse of the moon had occurred. This second episode lasted far longer than the first. Torg had sat in a meditative pose and observed the phenomenon in silence.

Torg's mind returned to the present moment. Finally, he recognized what was wrong. He left Laylah on the blanket, crawled through the passageway, and peered out at the full moon. As he expected, a shadow consumed its bottom left portion.

In Torg's recollection, the eclipse would last halfway till dawn. He sighed. Would his love survive? He crawled back to her side, his heart full of trepidation.

It was going to be a long night.

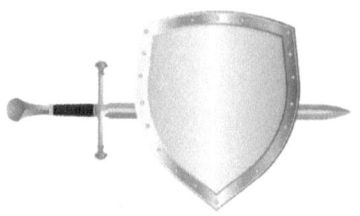

EPILOGUE

When Lucius and the others arrived, they weren't able to enter the cave. A conflagration of white light—mingled with blue and green—blared from the narrow opening, followed by crackling explosions. Lucius tried as best he could to crawl inside, but the heat seared his swollen face and crisped his yellow hair. The powers within were beyond him—and he realized Laylah would never be his, could never be his.

It was not meant to be.

He collapsed on the ground outside the cave and wept. He had learned in only one oh-so-short lifetime how cruel life could be. He pitied those who had endured thousands upon thousands.

So much pain.

So much suffering.

And all of it … inevitable.

The others wept too.

For Laylah. Torg. Lucius.

And themselves.

We have all wept this way at some point in our lives.

Have we not?

The moon continued to darken.

So ends Book 2

Up next:

Volume 2 of
The Death Wizard Chronicles

Get to know Jim Melvin

Jim is a novelist who lives in the foothills of the Southern Appalachians. He is the author of *The Death Wizard Chronicles*, a dark fantasy series for readers 18 and older.

Once upon a time, Jim's youngest daughter asked him to write a series more appropriate for her age group. Hence, *Dark Circles* was born. The teen fantasy adventure trilogy is for ages 12 and older.

Jim has been a professional writer for most of his life. Besides being a novelist, he was an award-winning journalist at several national newspapers and a communications director at a large university. He has written more than a thousand articles for newspapers and magazines.

Website: jim-melvin.com
Free newsletter: jimmelvin.substack.com
Email: jimmelvin57@gmail.com

Please leave a review

If you've gotten this far, I'm assuming you've read Volume 1 of *The Death Wizard Chronicles*. If so, I hope you enjoyed it!

Please take a minute to post a review.

Thank you!

–Jim Melvin, April 2025

Subscribe to Jim's newsletter

Realms of Fantasy at jim-melvin.com. Be

sure to click on the NEWSLETTER tab at the

top of the author's home page.

The newsletter is free and has a lot of

interesting content.

Novels by Jim Melvin

The Death Wizard Chronicles **trilogy** (18 and older)
Volume 1: Forged by Death | Chained by Fear (April 2025)
Volume 2: Shadowed by Demons | Torn by War (July 2025)
Volume 3: Blinded by Power | Healed by Hope (October 2025)

Dark Circles **trilogy** (12 and older)
Book 1: *Do You Believe in Magic?* (May 2023)
Book 2: *Do You Believe in Monsters?* (October 2023)
Book 3: *Do You Believe in Miracles?* (April 2024)

Non-fiction books
- *Eclipse Over Clemson: The day Tigertown will never forget*
- *The Adventures of a Florida Boy: In the 1960s, kids ran as far and wild as their imaginations would take them*

GLOSSARY

Aarakaa Himsaa (ah-RUH-kah HIM-sah): Defensive strategy used by Tugars that involves always staying at least a hair's width away from your opponent's longest strike.

Abhisambodhi (ab-HEE-sahm-BOH-dee): Highest enlightenment.

Adho Satta (AH-doh-SAH-tah): Anything or anyone who is neither a dragon nor a powerful supernatural being. Translates to *low one* in ancient tongue.

Akando (ah-KAHN-doh): Eldest brother of Takoda.

Akanittha (AHK-ah-NEE-thah): A being able to feed off the light of the sun. Means *Highest Power* in the ancient tongue.

Akasa Ocean (ah-KAH-sah): Largest ocean on Triken. Lies west of Dhutanga, Jivita, and Kincara.

Ancient tongue: Ancient language now spoken by only Triken's most learned beings.

Anna: Tent City of Tējo. Home to the Tugars.

Arupa-Loka (ah-ROO-pah-LOH-kah): Home of ghosts, demons, and ghouls. Lies near northern border of the Gap of Gamana. Also called Ghost City.

Asamāna (ah-sah-MAY-nah): Senasanan bride of Invictus.

Asava (ah-SAH-vah): Potent drink brewed by Stone-Eaters.

Asēkha (ah-SEEK-ah): Tugars of highest rank. There always are twenty, not including Death-Knowers. Also known as *Viisati* (The Twenty).

Asthenolith (ah-STHEN-no-lith): Pool of magma in a large cavern beneath Mount Asubha.

Avici (ah-VEE-chee): Largest city on Triken. Home to Invictus.

Badaalataa (BAD-ah-LAH-tuh): Carnivorous vines from the demon world.

Bakheng (bak-HENG): Central shrine of Dibbu-Loka.

Bard: Partner of Ugga and Jord, trappers who live in the forest near the foothills of Mount Asubha.

Barranca (bah-RAHN-kuh): Rocky wasteland that partially encircles the Great Desert.

Bell: Measurement of time approximating three hours.

Bhacca (BAH-cuh): Chambermaid assigned to Laylah.

Bhayatupa (by-yah-TOO-pah): Most ancient and powerful of dragons. His scales are the color of deep crimson.

Black mountain wolves: Largest and most dangerous of all wolves. Allies of demons, witches, and Mogols.

Cariya River (cah-REE-yah): Largest river west of Mahaggata Mountains.

Catu (cah-TOO): Northernmost mountain on Triken.

Cave monkeys: Small primates that live in the underworld beneath Asubha.

Chain Man: Another name for Mala.

Chal-Abhinno (Chahl-ahb-HEE-no): Queen of the Warlish witches.

Che-ra (CHEE-ruh): Svakaran name for a possum.

Churikā (chuh-REE-kah): Female Asēkha.

Cirāya (ser-AYE-yah): Green cactus that, when chewed, provides liquid and nourishment.

Cubit: Length of the arm from elbow to fingertip, which measures approximately eighteen inches, though among Tugars a cubit is considered twenty-one inches.

Dakkhinā (dah-KEE-nay): Sensation that inspires the urge to attempt *Sammaasamaadhi*. Means *holy gift* in the ancient tongue.

Death-Knower: Any Tugar who has successfully achieved *Sammaasamaadhi*. In the ancient tongue, a Death-Knower is called *Maranavidu*.

Death Visit: The temporary suicide of a Death-Knower wizard.

Dēsaka (day-SAH-kuh): Famous Vasi master who trained The Torgon.

Dhutanga (doo-TAHNG-uh): Largest forest on Triken. Lies west of the Mahaggata Mountains. Also known as the Great Forest.

Dibbu-Loka (DEE-boo-LOW-kah): Home of the Noble Ones. Means *Deathless World* in the ancient tongue. Originally called Piti-Loka.

Dracools (drah-KOOLS): Winged beasts that walk on hind legs but look like miniature dragons. Almost twice the height of a man. Also called baby dragons.

Druids (DREW-eds): Seven-cubit-tall beings that dwell in Dhutanga. Ancient enemies of Jivita.

Dukkhatu (doo-KAH-too): Great and ancient spider that spent the last years of its life near the peak of Asubha.

Elu (EE-loo): Miniature Svakaran who is an associate of Rathburt.

Eunuch (YOO-nuk): Castrated male slave who resides within the fifth wall of Kamupadana.

Fathom: Approximately 16.5 feet.

Gap of Gamana: Northernmost gap of the Mahaggata Mountains.

Gap of Gati: Southern gap that separates the Mahaggata Range from the Kolankold Range.

Golden Road: Road paved with a special golden metal that connects Avici and Kilesa.

Golden Soldiers: Soldiers of Invictus, mass-bred in his image.

Golden Wall: Oblong wall coated with a special golden metal that surrounds Avici and Kilesa.

Gray Plains: Arid plains that dominate much of the land east of the Ogha River.

Green Plains: Lush plains that surround Jivita.

Gulah (GOO-lah): Stone-Eater who became warden of Asubha.

Gunther: Son of Vedana, father of Invictus and Laylah.

Hornbeam: Ancient trees whose twisted lust for life causes madness. Called *Pacchanna* in the ancient tongue.

Ice Ocean: Ocean that lies northeast of Okkanti Mountains.

Iddhi-Pada (EED-hee-PAH-duh): Series of four roads that leads from

Jivita to Avici, passing west-to-east through Lake Hadaya, the Gap of Gati, Nissaya, and Java. Also called the Great Road.

Invictus (in-VICK-tuss): Evil sorcerer who threatens all of Triken and beyond. Also known as *Suriya* (the Sun God).

Izumo (ee-ZOO-mow): Dracool from Mahaggata.

Jhana (JAH-nah): Father of Torg.

Jivita (jih-VEE-tuh): Wondrous city that is home to the white horsemen. Located west of the Gap of Gati in the Green Plains. Also called the White City. Known as *Jutimantataa* (City of Splendor) in the ancient tongue.

Jord: Mysterious partner of Ugga and Bard, trappers who lived in the forest near the foothills of Mount Asubha.

Kamupadana (kuh-MOO-puh-DAH-nah): Home of Warlish witches and their lesser female servants. Also called the Whore City.

Kilesa (kee-LAY-suh): Sister City of Anna.

Kincara Forest (KIN-cah-ruh): Forest that lies south of the Green Plains.

King Lobha (LOW-bah): Sadistic king who built Piti-Loka.

Kojin (KOH-jin): Enormous ogress with six arms and a bloated female head. Almost as large as a snow giant.

Kolankold Mountains (KOH-lun-kold): Bottom stem of the Mahaggata Mountains, located south of the Gap of Gati.

Kuruk (KERR-uck): Traitorous Ropakan who desired Magena.

Kusala (KOO-suh-luh): Second most powerful Tugar in the world next to Torg. Also known as Asēkha-Kusala and Chieftain Kusala.

Lake Hadaya (huh-DIE-yuh): Large freshwater lake that lies west of the Gap of Gati.

Lake Keo (KEY-oh): Large freshwater lake that lies between the Kolankold Mountains and Dibbu-Loka.

Lake Ti-ratana (tee-RAH-tah-nah): Large freshwater lake that lies west of Avici.

Laylah (LAY-lah): Younger sister of Invictus.

Long breath: Fifteen seconds. Also called slow breath.

Lucius (LOO-see-us): General of Invictus' legions before the creation of Mala.

Magena (mah-JEN-nah): Name given to Laylah by the Ropakans.

Mahaggata Mountains (MAH-hah-GAH-tah): Largest mountain range on Triken. Shaped like a capital Y.

Mala (MAH-lah): Former snow giant who was ruined by Invictus and turned into the sorcerer's most dangerous servant. Formerly called Yama-Deva.

Majjhe Ghamme (Mah-JEE GAH-mee): Means midsummer in the ancient tongue.

Mogols (MAH-gulls): Warrior race that dwells in Mahaggata Mountains. Longtime worshippers of the dragon Bhayatupa. Ancient enemies of Nissaya.

Moken (MOH-kin): A chosen leader of the boat people.

Mount Asubha (ah-SUE-buh): Dreaded mountain in the cold north that housed the prison of Invictus.

Namuci (nah-MOO-chee): Magic word that summons *efrits* from the Realm of Undeath.

Nirodha (nee-ROW-dah): Icy wastelands that lie north of the Mahaggata Mountains.

Nissaya (nee-SIGH-yah): Impenetrable fortress on the east end of the Gap of Gati. Also called the Black Fortress, which is the home of the black knights.

Noble Ones: Monks and nuns who inhabit Dibbu-Loka. Also called deathless people.

Obhasa (oh-BHAH-sah): Torg's magical staff, carved from the ivory of a desert elephant found dead. Means *container of light* in the ancient tongue.

Ogha River: (OH-guh): Largest river on Triken. Begins in the northern range of Mahaggata and ends in Lake Keo.

Okkanti Mountains (oh-KAHN-tee): Small range with tall, jagged peaks located northeast of Kilesa.

Pabbajja (pah-BAH-jah): Homeless people who live in the plains surrounding Java. Little is known of their habits.

Pace: Approximately 30 inches, though among Tugars a pace is considered 36 inches.

Peta (PAY-tuh): Ghost girl of Arupa-Loka. In life, she was blind.

Piti-Loka (PEE-tee-LOW-kuh): Original name of Dibbu-Loka. Built by King Lobha 10,000 years ago as his burial shrine. Means *Rapture World* in the ancient tongue.

Podhana (POH-dah-nuh): Asēkha warrior.

Porisāda (por-ee-SAH-dah): Most dangerous of all Mogols. Are known to eat the flesh of their victims.

Rathburt (RATH-burt): Only other living Death-Knower. Known as a gardener, not a warrior.

Realm of Death: Temporary portal between life and rebirth.

Realm of Life: Home of living beings.

Realm of Undeath: Home of the demons.

Rebirth: The process of being reborn into a new incarnation.

Ropaka (row-PAH-kah): One of the large tribes of the Mahaggata Mountains.

Salt Sea: Dead inland sea south of the Okkanti Mountains.

Sammaasamaadhi (sam-mah-sah-MAH-dee): Supreme concentration of mind. Temporary suicide.

Sampati (sahm-PAH-tee): Giant condors crossbred with dragons by Invictus. Used to transport people and supplies to the prison on Mount Asubha.

Sāykans (SAY-kuns): Female soldiers who defend Kamupadana.

Senasana (SEN-uh-SAHN-ah): Thriving market city that lies north of Dibbu-Loka.

Short breath: Three seconds. Also called quick breath.

Silah (SEE-luh): Female Tugar warrior.

Silver Sword: Ancient sword forged by a long-forgotten master from otherworldly metals.

Simōōn (suh-MOON): Magical dust storm that protects Anna from outsiders.

Sister Tathagata (tuh-THAH-guh-tuh): High nun of Dibbu-Loka. More than 3,000 years old. Also known as *Perfect One*.

Sivathika (SEE-vah-TEE-kuh): Ancient Tugar ritual. Dying warrior breathes what remains of his or her *Life Energy* into a survivor's lungs, where it is absorbed into the blood.

Snow giants: Magnificent beings reaching heights of 10 cubits or more that dwell in the Okkanti Mountains.

Sōbhana (SOH-bah-nah): Female Asēkha warrior.

Span: Distance from the end of the thumb to the end of the little finger of a hand spread to full width. Approximately nine inches, though among Tugars a span is considered 12 inches.

Stēorra (STEE-oh-rah): Wife of Gunther, mother of Invictus and Laylah.

Stone: Equal to fourteen pounds.

Stone-Eater: Magical being that gains power by devouring lava rocks.

Svakara (svuh-KAR-uh): One of the large tribes of the Mahaggata Mountains.

Takoda (tuh-KOH-duh): Adoptive father of Magena.

Tanhiiyati (tawn-hee-YAH-tee): Insatiable craving for eternal existence.

Tāseti (tah-SAY-tee): Most powerful female Asēkha in the world.

Tējo (TAY-hoh): Great Desert. Home of the Tugars.

Tent City: Largest city in Tējo. Home to the Tugars. Also known as Anna.

The Torgon (TOR-gahn): Torg's ceremonial name. Also Lord Torgon.

Torg: Thousand-year-old Death-Knower wizard. King of the Tugars. Means *Blessed Warrior* in the ancient tongue.

Triken (TRY-ken): Name of the world. Also name of the land east and west of the Mahaggata Mountains.

Tugars (TOO-gars): Desert warriors of Tējo. Called *Kantaara Yodhas* in the ancient tongue.

Uccheda (oo-CHAY-duh): Tower of Invictus in Avici. Means *annihilation* in the ancient tongue.

Ugga (OOO-gah): Human-bear crossbreed who was a partner of Bard and Jord, trappers who lived in the forest near the foothills of Mount Asubha.

Undines (oon-DEENS): Creatures of the demon world who—when summoned—can infect living bodies and turn them into zombies.

Urbana (urr-BAH-nah): Mistress of robes assigned by Invictus to attend Laylah. A vampire.

Ur-Nammu (ur-NAH-moo): High priestess of Kamupadana.

Uttara (oo-TAR-uh): Specially made sword wielded by Tugar warriors and Asēkhas. Single-edged, slightly curved.

Vasi master (VAH-see): Martial arts master who trains Tugar novices to become warriors.

Vedana (VAY-duh-nuh): One-hundred-thousand-year-old demon. Grandmother of Invictus and Laylah. Mother of King Lobha.

Vinipata (VEE-nee-PAH-tuh): Central shrine of Senasana.

Warlish witch (WOR-lish): Female witch who can change her appearance between extreme beauty and hideousness.

Wild men: Short, hairy men who thrive in the foothills of Kolankold.

Worm monster: Nameless beast with more than a thousand tentacles that lives beneath Asubha. Largest living creature on Triken.

Yakkkkha (YAH-kuh): Magic word from the Realm of Undeath that brings corpses and skeletons temporarily back to life.

Yama-Deva (YAH-muh-DAY-vuh): Ruined snow giant that became Mala.

Yama-Utu (YAH-muh-OO-too): Snow giant. Brother of Yama-Deva. Husband of Yama-Bhari.

Ziggurat (ZIG-guh-raht): Nine-story temple located within the first wall of Kamupadana.

ACKNOWLEGEMENTS

Any descriptions of meditation in this volume were based on the Buddha's teachings in the *Mahasatipatthana Sutta*.

Dennis Chastain enriched the beauty of the land by answering endless questions.

Margo McLoughlin was the true master of the ancient tongue. Any inconsistencies in the translations are my fault, not hers.

Finally, my wife Jeanne Malmgren and friend Cory Dodgens applied the finishing touches.